CHRONICLES
OF THE
LENSMEN,
VOLUME 2

Books by E.E. "Doc" Smith

The Skylark Series

The Skylark of Space
Skylark of Valeron
Skylark Three
Skylark Duquesne

The Lensmen Series

Triplanetary
First Lensmen
Galactic Patrol
Gray Lensman
Second Stage Lensmen
Children of the Lens

An associational Lensman novel

Vortex Blaster

The Subspace Series

Subspace Explorers
Subspace Encounter

The Galaxy Primes
Master of Space (with E. Everett Evans)
The Best of E.E. "Doc" Smith

Chronicles of the Lensmen, *Volume 2*

Gray Lensman
Second Stage Lensman
Children of the Lens

E.E. "DOC" SMITH

First SFBC Science Fiction Printing: May 1999

Published by arrangement with:
Old Earth Books
Post Office Box 19951
Baltimore, MD 21211

Visit us online at *http://www.sfbc.com*

ISBN 0-7394-0262-5

PRINTED IN THE UNITED STATES OF AMERICA.

CONTENTS

FOREWORD

by
John Clute

So here we are. The story has started, and it does not stop. After the pleasures and miseries of *Triplanetary* and *First Lensman*, after two tumultuous volumes of prelude and back story and dark hint and deck clearance, we are ready to begin at the beginning. We open the first page, and we plunge headfirst into the heartwood and arterial surge of the vast edifice of the *Lensmen* sequence as E.E. Smith first conceived it, in the 1920s, long before he began parcelling his tale out in serial form over a 12-year period (1937–1949) through the increasingly dignified pages of *Astounding Science Fiction*.

The first of them, *Galactic Patrol*, appeared in 1937–1938, before John W. Campbell, Jr. became editor of *ASF* and—fully conscious that he was attempting to do so—created the first and best Golden Age of Science Fiction, which lasted from 1939 until World War Two took most of his writers away (they never came back, not really, not in their hearts, but that is another story). *Galactic Patrol* was soon followed by *Gray Lensman* (1939–1940) and by *Second Stage Lensmen* (1941–1942) and, several years later, by the final volume, *Children of the Lens* (1947–1948). The gap between the first three volumes and that last installment may be variously explained: Doc Smith was involved in non-combatant war work, which may have kept him from concentrating fully on his History of Civilization; the series reaches a penultimate climax with *Second Stage Lensmen*, 20 years of internal chronology now having to pass before the Kinnison children—the Children of the Lens themselves—are old enough to take their places at the very tiptop of the great hierarchical ladder of Civilization; and John W. Campbell himself may have had some practical reservations about the nature of the future promulgated by Smith (and by *ASF*'s other great wartime writer, A.E. Van Vogt).

These reservations—if he indeed felt or expressed them—were entirely justified, of course. Campbell's Golden Age of Science Fiction heralded not only a maturation in the style and subject matter of American pulp sf, conveyed primarily through the explosive irruption into the field of writers such as Isaac Asimov, L. Sprague de Camp, Robert A. Heinlein, Theodore Sturgeon, but also a *domestication* not simply of the future as such but, more importantly, of the profound oddness of the futures typically envisaged by pulp writers of the preceding generation, such as E.E. Smith. (One of the reasons Van Vogt is best understood as a pulp writer—a pulp writer who photosynthesizes cut helium for breakfast—is the profound weirdness of his future worlds.) This oddness of American pulp sf cannot be conceptually soothed away by references to (or fondish memories of) the stylistic crudeness of so much of what appeared in the magazines between 1925 and approximately 1940, nor is it enough to say that a Technic Age writer such as E.E. Smith is a kind of Grandma Moses, an Outsider Artist from the earliest days of pulp, an author of cartoon edisonades we can enjoy for their rural innocence, of space operas that perfectly (though crudely) limn the American Dream *circa* 1930, the way Heinlein and Asimov clearly limn something like the American Dream a few significant years later.

All of that may be true, or sort of. But it's not enough.

Because there's a secret here.

This is the secret. Doc Smith and his peers—and A.E. Van Vogt, who walked alone—may all have loved the task of conceiving futures, but, at the same time, each one of these sf writers manifestly displayed a very deep distrust and fear of anything that hinted at any of the unfolding "real" futures that have refilled the water holes of our infancy with mutagens. The *Lensmen* series is escapist, as much good fiction is, and we love it for that, but it does not escape 1930: it escapes the future.

Certainly both writers invoke superscience and super Technics, in terms only marginally more magical than those used by Golden Age writers, but they do so to transport us out of reach of anything that might actually happen. If it can be said that, in 1998, sf is best defined as an historical body of story concerning the real nature of the 20th century, then it must be said that neither E.E. Smith nor A.E. Van Vogt could remotely be described as contributing to that body of story. Hence the extraordinary cultural fixity of our home planet in Doc Smith's vision of Tellus: it is a world in which nothing dangerous (i.e., nothing that might resemble 1998 or, for that matter, 1938) has been allowed to happen. Women are gals, nuclear families are tender-trap monads, "culture" is a froth of vaguely indecent curds and whey, there is no democracy to take away the toys of the game, because the World Government (which seems to have been run for hundreds of years by successive Kinnisons) has solved every political problem in the entire world. There are no computers (not even in the last-written volumes of the series), no punk, no genetic engineering, no Marlon Brando, no perestroika, no Bob Dylan, no cities, no Hillary Clinton Wife Spoof, no Unabomber, no ghettos, no suburbs, no planetary crises of any sort (atomic, ecological, ethnic, whatever), nothing. This may sound as though Smith is trying to describe Paradise, but, of course, he's not, because Eden is not best described by what it is not. Tellus in the *Lensmen* is a spinster's bedroom, a mantra of denials limned through a sleight-of-hand of side-of-the-mouth descriptive passages designed precisely *not* to describe the penis swamp of the world to come.

Hence—finally—we see the basic structure of Civilization as it is defended by the Arisians. For once the world and human nature have been stripped from a definition of Civilization, it is no hard task to describe it. Civilization consists in not being tempted by the world or by human nature—two regions of discourse occupied solely by Boskone. Civilization is everything the 20th century is not, except maybe Nancy Reagan. Civilization is Just Say No. Civilization is pesticide. Civilization is easy.

Lensmen Civilization is, of course, instant death for you and me.

So how can we love E.E. Smith so deeply? (I myself am a Boskonian bug any Kinnison would spray, but I reread the *Lensmen* as often as I reread Tolkien or Freddy the Pig.) I can think of two reasons. First, it is a deep relief to escape from the live world, to pretend for a nonce that the real world is a spinster's bedroom with a secret portal starward. Second, the *Lensmen* is one of the greatest stories ever told. That may be all we need. (I think it may be all I need.)

And so here we are. The story has started, and it does not stop. It is a tale that expands remorselessly in space and time. We begin with the graduation of Kim Kinnison at the top of his class from the top of the (surely unconsciously) phallic Wentworth Hall, a 90-story prong "dominating twice a hundred square miles of campus, parade-ground, airport, and spaceport." He then gets his Lens, the Arisian device that authenticates his physical and moral right to act, to own the world of action to come. Licensed by this opening sequence as a paladin, as an arrowhead of the self-ruling chivalry of Lensmen, Kinnison is immediately plunged into the galaxy-wide war between Arisia and Eddore, goes through a maelstrom of adventures in *Galactic Patrol*, by virtue of which he meets new races, discovers new weapons, infiltrates Boskone, defeats vast space armadas, and, in a superbly violent final cataclysm, personally defeats Helmuth, who speaks for Boskone:

> First Kinnison; the bullets whining, shrieking off the armor of his personal battleship and crashing through or smashing ringingly against whatever happened to be in the ever-changing line of ricochet. Then Helmuth; and as the fierce-driven metal slugs tore in their multitudes through his armor and through and through his body, riddling his every vital organ, that was THE END.

It is, of course, not the end. The first paragraph of *Gray Lensman* makes that clear:

> Among the world-girdling fortifications of a planet distant indeed from star cluster AC 257-4736 there squatted sullenly a fortress quite similar to Helmuth's own. Indeed, in some respects it was even superior to the base of him who spoke for Boskone. It was larger and stronger. Instead of one dome, it had many. It was dark and cold withal, for its occupants had practically nothing in common with humanity save the possession of high intelligence.

For readers of *ASF* in 1939, this first paragraph must have had an astonishing impact, one we can never quite replicate in our own imaginations. But it's worth saying a couple of things. First, in 1939, sequels were still uncommon in the sf world, and nothing would have prepared readers for the explosive vista of this opening, which swallows its predecessor whole. Second, readers in 1939 did not quite share Kinnison's limited knowledge of the unfolding situation, as this first paragraph creates a powerful dramatic irony—and hence, in the context of space opera, a powerful sense of wonder—that will deeply "tease" readers' understanding of the story. But neither they, nor anyone else in 1939, could know that there would be two more volumes—Smith would not retrofit the back story of the History of Civilization into the full series for another 15 years—and that each succeeding volume would also eat its predecessor whole. So, the readers of 1939 plunged wide eyed into wonder.

This is what they found, as the years passed.

Each volume of the *Lensmen* main sequence ends in a defeat of Boskone, and each new volume (except, of course, the last) begins with the discovery that the Boskone so resoundingly eliminated is nothing but a young and subordinate version of what must surely be the true and final Boskone, that the "true" Boskone is older, more malevolent, more powerful, and more insidious than could have been dreamed. But E.E. Smith's genius does not lie in the notion of an hierarchy of evil (and few contemporary readers are likely to pay much attention to the phobic response to this century that underlies Smith's description of Boskonian evil); his genius lies in his construction of a story that, like peeling an onion outward, narrates hierarchy.

It is absolutely brilliant, and it works each time. No wonder we come back, again and again, to the heart of the onion that is the heart of Story and await there, eyes peeled, for the peeling to begin.

Gray
Lensman

To
Lloyd

CONTENTS

FOREWORD

Two thousand million or so years ago, at the time of the Coalescence, when the First and Second Galaxies were passing through each other and when myriads of planets were coming into existence where only a handful had existed before, two races of beings were already old; so old that each had behind it many millions of years of recorded history. Both were so old that each had perforce become independent of the chance formation of planets upon which to live. Each had, in its own way, gained a measure of control over its environment; the Arisians by power of mind alone, the Eddorians by employing both mind and mechanism.

The Arisians were indigenous to this, our normal space-time continuum; they had lived in it since the unthinkably remote time of their origin; and the original Arisia was very Earth-like in mass, composition, size, atmosphere, and climate. Thus all normal space was permeated by Arisian life-spores, and thus upon all Earth-like or Tellurian planets there came into being races of creatures more or less resembling Arisians in the days of their racial youth. None except Tellurians are Homo Sapiens, of course; few can actually be placed in Genus Homo; but many millions of planets are peopled by races distantly recognizable or belonging to the great class of MAN.

The Eddorians, on the other hand, were interlopers—intruders. They were not native to our normal space-time system, but came to it from some other, some alien and horribly different other, plenum. For eons, in fact, they had been exploring the macrocosmic All; moving their planets from continuum to continuum; seeking that which at last they found—a space and a time in which there were enough planets, soon to be inhabited by intelligent life, to sate even the Eddorian lust for dominance. Here, in our own space-time, they would stay; and here supreme they would rule.

The Elders of Arisia, however, the ablest thinkers of the race, had known and had studied the Eddorians for many cycles of time. Their integrated Visualization of the Cosmic All showed what was to happen. No more than the Arisians themselves could the Eddorians be slain by any physical means, however applied; nor could the Arisians, unaided, kill all of the invaders by mental force. Eddore's All-Highest and his Innermost Circle, in their ultra-shielded citadel, could be destroyed only by a mental bolt of such nature and magnitude that its generator, which was to become known throughout two galaxies as the Galactic Patrol, would require several long Arisian lifetimes for its building.

Nor would that building be easy. The Eddorians must be kept in ignorance, both of Arisia and of the proposed generator, until too late to take effective counter-measures. Also, no entity below the third level of intelligence, even—or especially?—of the Patrol, could ever learn the truth; for that knowledge would set up an inferiority complex and thus rob the generator of all ability to do the work for which it was designed.

Nevertheless the Arisians began building. On the four most promising planets of the First Galaxy—our Earth or Sol Three, Velantia, Rigel Four, and Palain Seven—breeding programs, aiming toward the highest mentality of which each race was capable, were begun as soon as intelligent life developed.

On our Earth there were only two blood lines, since humanity has only two sexes. One was a straight male line of descent, and was always named Kinnison or its equivalent. Civilizations rose and fell; Arisia surreptitiously and unobtrusively lifting them up, Eddore callously knocking them down as soon as it became evident that they were not what Eddore wanted. Pestilences raged, and wars, and famines, and holocausts and disasters that decimated entire populations again and again, but the direct male line of descent of the Kinnisons was never broken.

The other line, sometimes male and sometimes female, which was to culminate in the female penultimate of the Arisian program, was equally persistent and was characterized throughout its prodigious length by a peculiarly spectacular shade of red-bronze-auburn hair and equally striking gold-flecked, tawny eyes. Atlantis fell, but the red-headed, yellow-eyed child of Captain Phryges had been sent to North Maya, and lived. Patroclus, the red-headed gladiator, begot a red-headed daughter before he was cut down. And so it went.

World Wars One, Two, and Three, occupying as they did only a few moments of Arisian-Eddorian time, formed merely one incident in the eons-long game. That incident was important, however, because immediately after it Gharlane of Eddore made what proved to be an error. Knowing nothing of the Arisians, or of what they had done to raise the level of intelligence of mankind, he assumed that the then completely ruined Earth would not require his personal attention again for many hundreds of Tellurian years, and went elsewhere: to Rigel Four, to Palain Seven, and to Velantia Two, or Delgon, where he found that his creatures, the Overlords, were not progressing satisfactorily. He spent quite a little time there; time during which the men of Earth, aided almost openly by the Arisians, made a phenomenally rapid recovery from the ravages of atomic warfare and fantastically rapid advances in both sociology and technology.

Virgil Samms, the auburn-haired, tawny-eyed Crusader who was to become the first wearer of Arisia's Lens, took advantage of the general demoralization to institute a really effective planetary police force. Then, with the advent of inter-planetary flight, he was instrumental in forming the Interplanetary League. As head of the Triplanetary Service, he took a leading part in the brief war with the Nevians, a race of highly intelligent amphibians who used allotropic iron as a source of atomic power.*

Gharlane of Eddore came back to the Solarian System as Gray Roger, the enigmatic and practically immortal scourge of space, only to find his every move blocked—blocked so savagely and so completely that he could not even kill two ordinary human beings, Conway Costigan and Clio Marsden. Nor were these two, in spite of some belief to the contrary, anything but what they seemed. Neither of them ever knew that they were being protected; but Gharlane's blocker was in fact an Arisian fusion—the four-ply mentality which was to become known to every Lensman of the Galactic Patrol as Mentor of Arisia.

The inertialess drive, which made an interstellar trip a matter of minutes instead of lifetimes, brought with it such an increase in crime, and made detection of criminals so difficult, that law enforcement broke down almost completely. As Samms himself expressed it:

---

* For a complete treatment of matters up to this point, including the discovery of the inertialess—"free"—space-drive, the Nevian War, and the mind-to-mind meeting of Mentor of Arisia and Gharlane of Eddore, see *Triplanetary*, Fantasy Press, Reading, Pa.

"How can legal processes work efficiently—work at all, for that matter—when a man can commit a murder or a pirate can loot a space-ship and be a hundred parsecs away before the crime is even discovered? How can a Tellurian John Law find a criminal on a strange world that knows nothing whatever of our Patrol, with a completely alien language—maybe no language at all—when it takes months even to find out who and where—if any—the native police officers are?"

Also, there was the apparently insuperable difficulty of the identification of authorized personnel. Triplanetary's best scientists had done their best in the way of a noncounterfeitable badge—the historic Golden Meteor, which upon touch impressed upon the toucher's consciousness an unpronounceable, unspellable symbol—but that best was not enough. What physical science could devise and synthesize, physical science could analyze and duplicate; and that analysis and duplication had caused trouble indeed.

Triplanetary needed something vastly better than its meteor. In fact, without a better, its expansion into an intersystemic organization would be impossible. It needed something to identify a Patrolman, anytime and anywhere. It must be impossible of duplication or imitation. In fact, it should kill, painfully, any entity attempting imposture. It should operate as a telepath, or endow its wearer with telepathic power—how else could a Tellurian converse with peoples such as the Rigellians, who could not talk, see, or hear?

Both Solarian Councillor Virgil Samms and his friend of old, Commissioner of Public Safety Roderick Kinnison, knew these things; but they also knew how utterly preposterous their thoughts were; how utterly and self-evidently impossible such a device was.

But Arisia again came to the rescue. The scientist who had been assigned the meteor problem, one Dr. Nels Bergenholm—who, all unknown to even his closest associates, was a form of flesh energized at various times by various Arisians—reported to Samms and Kinnison that:

1) Physical science could not then produce what was needed, and probably never could do so. 2) Although it could not be explained in any symbology or language known to man, there was—there *must* be—a science of the mind; a science whose tangible products physical science could neither analyze nor imitate. 3) Virgil Samms, by going in person to Arisia, could obtain *exactly* what was needed.

"Arisia! Of all the hells in space, why Arisia?" Kinnison demanded. "How? Don't you know that nobody can get anywhere near that damn planet?"

"I *know* that the Arisians are very well versed in that science. I *know* that if Councillor Samms goes to Arisia he will obtain the symbol he needs. I *know* that he will never obtain it otherwise. As to *how* I know these things—I can't—I just—I *know* them. I tell you!"

And, since Bergenholm was already as well known for uncannily accurate "hunches" as for a height of genius bordering perilously closely on insanity, the two leaders of Civilization did not press him further, but went immediately to the hitherto forbidden planet. They were—apparently—received hospitably enough, and were given Lenses by Mentor of Arisia. Lenses which, it developed, were all that Bergenholm had indicated, and more.

The Lens is a lenticular structure of hundreds of thousands of tiny crystalloids, built and tuned to match the individual life force—the ego, the personality—of one individual entity. While not, strictly speaking, alive, it is endowed with a sort of pseudo-life by virtue of which it gives off a strong, characteristically-changing, polychromatic light as long as it is in circuit with the living mentality with which it is in synchronization. Conversely, when worn by anyone except its owner, it not only remains dark but it kills—so strongly does its pseudo-life interfere with any life to which it is not attuned. It is also a telepathic communicator of astounding power and range—and other things.

Back on Earth, Samms set out to find people of Lensman caliber to send to Arisia. Kinnison's son Jack, and his friend Mason Northrop, Conway Costigan, and Samm's daughter Virgilia—who had inherited her father's hair and eyes, and who was the most accomplished muscle-reader of her time—went first. The boys got Lenses, but Jill did not. Mentor, who was to her senses a woman seven feet tall, told her that she did not then and never would need a Lens—and it should be mentioned here in passing that no two entities who ever saw Mentor ever saw the same thing.

Frederick Rodebush, Lyman Cleveland, young Bergenholm, and a couple of commodores of the Patrol—Clayton of North America and Schweikert of Europe—just about exhausted Earth's resources. Nor were the other Solarian planets very helpful, yielding only three Lensmen—Knobos of Mars, DalNalten of Venus, and Rularion of Jove. Lensman material was extremely scarce stuff.

Knowing that his proposed Galactic Council would have to be made up exclusively of Lensmen, and that it should represent as many solar systems as possible, Samms visited the various systems which had been colonized by humanity, then went on: to Rigel Four, where he found Dronvire the Explorer, who was of Lensman grade; and next to Pluto, where he found Pilinixi the Dexitroboper, who very definitely was not; and finally to Palain Seven, an ultra-frigid world where he found Tallick, who might—or might not—go to Arisia some day. And Virgil Samms, being physically tough and mentally a real Crusader, survived these various ordeals.

For some time the existence of the newly-formed Galactic Patrol was precarious indeed. Archibald Isaacson, head of Interstellar Spaceways, wanting a monopoly of interstellar trade, first tried bribery; then, joining forces with the machine of Senator Morgan and Boss Towne, assassination. The other Lensmen and Jill Samms saved her father's life, after which Kinnison took Samms to the safest place on Earth—deep underground beneath The Hill: the tremendously fortified, superlatively armed fortress which had been built to be the headquarters of the Triplanetary Service.

But even there the First Lensman was attacked, this time by a fleet of space-ships in full battle array. By that time, however, the Galactic Patrol had a fleet of its own, and again the Lensmen won.

Knowing that the final and decisive struggle would of necessity be a political one, the Patrol took over the Cosmocrat party and set out to gather detailed and documented evidence of corrupt and criminal activities of the Nationalists, the party then in power. Roderick ("Rod the Rock") Kinnison ran for President of North America against the incumbent Witherspoon; and, after a knock-down-and-drag-out political battle with Senator Morgan, the voice of the Morgan-Towne-Isaacson machine, he was elected.

And Morgan was murdered—supposedly by disgruntled gangsters; actually by his Kalonian boss, who was in turn a minion of the Eddorians—simply and merely because he had failed.*

North America was the most powerful continent of Earth; Earth was the Mother Planet, the Leader, the Boss. Hence, under the sponsorship of the Cosmocratic Government of North America, the Galactic Council and its arm, the Galactic Patrol, came into their own. At the end of R. K. Kinnison's term of office, at which time he resumed his interrupted duties as Port Admiral of the Patrol, there were a hundred planets adherent to Civilization. In ten years there were a thousand; in a hundred years a million: and it is sufficient characterization of the light but effective rule of the Galactic Council to say that in all the long history of Civilization no planet whose peoples have ever voted to adhere to Civilization has ever withdrawn from it.

Time went on; the prodigiously long blood-lines, so carefully manipulated by Mentor of Arisia, neared culmination. Lensman Kimball Kinnison was graduated Number One of his class—as a matter of fact,

---

* *First Lensman,* Fantasy Press, Reading, Pa.

although he did not know it, he was Number One of his time. And his female counterpart and complement, Clarrissa MacDougall of the red-bronze-auburn hair and the gold-flecked tawny eyes, was a nurse in the Patrol's immense hospital at Prime Base.

Shortly after graduation Kinnison was called to Prime Base by Port Admiral Haynes. Space piracy had become an organized force; and, under the leadership of someone or something known as "Boskone," had risen to such heights of power as to threaten seriously the Galactic Patrol itself. In one respect Boskonia was ahead of the Patrol, its scientists having developed a source of power vastly greater than any known to Galactic Civilization. It had fighting ships of a new and extraordinary type, from which even convoyed shipping was no longer safe. Being faster than the Patrol's fastest cruisers and yet more heavily armed than its heaviest battleships, they had been doing practically as they pleased throughout space.

For one particular purpose, the engineers of the Patrol had designed and built one ship—the *Britannia*. She was the fastest thing in space, but for offensive armament she had only one weapon, the "Q-gun." Kinnison was put in command of this vessel, with orders to: 1) Capture a Boskonian war-vessel of late model; 2) Learn her secrets of power; and 3) Transmit the information to Prime Base.

He found and took such a warship. Sergeant Peter vanBuskirk led the storming party of Valerians—men of human ancestry, but of extraordinary size, strength, and agility because of the enormous gravitation of the planet Valeria—in wiping out those of the pirate crew not killed in the battle between the two vessels.

The *Britannia*'s scientists secured the desired data. It could not be transmitted to Prime Base, however, as the pirates were blanketing all channels of communication. Boskonian warships were gathering for the kill, and the crippled Patrol ship could neither run nor fight. Therefore each man was given a spool of tape bearing a complete record of everything that had occurred; and, after setting up a director-by-chance to make the empty ship pursue an unpredictable course in space, and after rigging bombs to destroy her at the first touch of a ray, the Patrolmen paired off by lot and took to the lifeboats.

The erratic course of the cruiser brought her near the lifeboat manned by Kinnison and vanBuskirk, and there the pirates tried to stop her. The ensuing explosion was so violent that flying wreckage disabled practically the entire personnel of one of the attacking ships, which did not have time to go free before the crash. The two Patrolmen boarded the pirate vessel and drove her toward Earth, reaching the solar system of Velantia before the Boskonians headed them off. Again taking to their lifeboat, they landed upon the planet Delgon, where they were rescued from a horde of Catlats by one Worsel—later to become Lensman Worsel of Velantia—a highly intelligent winged reptile.

By means of improvements upon Velantian thought-screens the three destroyed a group of the Overlords of Delgon, a sadistic race of monsters who had been preying upon the other peoples of the system by sheer power of mind. Worsel then accompanied the two Patrolmen to Velantia, where all the resources of the planet were devoted to the preparation of defenses against the expected attack of the Boskonians. Several other lifeboats reached Velantia, guided by Worsel's mind working through Kinnison's ego and Lens.

Kinnison intercepted a message from Helmuth, who "spoke for Boskone," and traced his communicator beam, thus getting his first line upon Boskone's Grand Base. The pirates attacked Velantia, and six of their warships were captured. In these six ships, manned by Velantian crews, the Patrolmen again set out for Earth and Prime Base.

Then Kinnison's Bergenholm, the generator of the force which makes inertialess flight possible, broke down, so that he had to land upon Trenco for repairs. Trenco, the tempestuous, billiard-ball-smooth planet where it rains forty-seven feet and five inches every night and where the wind blows at eight hundred miles an hour—Trenco, the source of thionite, the deadliest of all deadly drugs—Trenco, whose weirdly-charged ether and atmosphere so distort beams and vision that it can be policed only by such beings as the Rigellians, who possess the sense of perception instead of those of sight and hearing!

Lensman Tregonsee, of Rigel Four, then in command of the Patrol's wandering base upon Trenco, supplied Kinnison with a new Bergenholm and he again set out for Tellus.

Meanwhile Helmuth had deduced that some one particular Lensman was the cause of all his set-backs; and that the Lens, a complete enigma to all Boskonians, was in some way connected with Arisia. That planet had always been dreaded and shunned by all spacemen. No Boskonian who had ever approached that planet could be compelled, even by the certainty of death, to go near it again.

Thinking himself secure by virtue of thought-screens given him by a being from a higher-echelon planet named Ploor, Helmuth went alone to Arisia, determined to learn all about the Lens. There he was punished to the verge of insanity, but was permitted to return to his Grand Base alive and sane: "Not for your own good, but for the good of that struggling young Civilization which you oppose."

Kinnison reached Prime Base with the all-important data. By building super-powerful battleships, called "maulers," the Patrol gained a temporary advantage over Boskonia, but a stalemate soon ensued. Kinnison developed a plan of action whereby he hoped to locate Helmuth's Grand Base; and asked Port Admiral Haynes for permission to follow it. In lieu of that, however, Haynes told him that he had been given his Release; that he was an Unattached Lensman—a "Gray" Lensman, popularly so called, from the color of the plain leather uniforms they wear. Thus he earned the highest honor which the Patrol can give, for the Gray Lensman works under no supervision or direction whatever. He is as absolutely a free agent as it is possible to be. He is responsible to no one; to nothing save his own conscience. He is no longer of Tellus, nor of the Solarian System, but of Civilization as a whole. He is no longer a cog in the immense machine of the Patrol: wherever he may go he *is* the Patrol!

In quest of a second line upon Grand Base, Kinnison scouted a pirate stronghold upon Aldebaran I. Its personnel, however, were not even near-human, but were wheelmen, possessed of the sense of perception; hence Kinnison was discovered before he could accomplish anything and was very seriously wounded. He managed to get back to his speedster and to send a thought to Port Admiral Haynes, who rushed ships to his aid. In Base Hospital Surgeon-Marshal Lacy put him back together; and, during a long and quarrelsome convalescence, Nurse Clarrissa MacDougall held him together. And Lacy and Haynes connived to promote a romance between nurse and Lensman.

As soon as he could leave the hospital he went to Arisia in the hope that he might be given advanced training—a theretofore unthought-of idea. Much to his surprise he learned that he had been expected to return for exactly such training. Getting it almost killed him, but he emerged from the ordeal infinitely stronger of mind than any man had ever been before; and possessed of a new sense as well—the sense of perception, a sense somewhat analogous to sight, but of vastly greater power, depth, and scope, and not dependent upon light.

After trying out his new mental equipment by solving a murder mystery upon Radelix, he succeeded in entering an enemy base upon Boyssia II. There he took over the mind of a communications officer and waited for the opportunity of getting the second, all-important line to Boskonia's Grand Base. An enemy ship captured a hospital ship of the Patrol and brought it in to Boyssia Base. Nurse MacDougall, head nurse of the captured vessel, working under Kinnison's instructions, stirred up trouble which soon became mutiny. Helmuth, from Grand Base, took a hand; thus enabling Kinnison to get his second line.

The hospital ship, undetectable by virtue of the Lensman's nullifier, escaped from Boyssia II and headed for Earth at full blast. Kinnison, convinced that Helmuth was really Boskone himself, found that the intersection of his two lines—and therefore the pirates' Grand Base—lay in star cluster AC 257-4736, well outside the galaxy. Pausing only long enough to destroy the Wheelmen of Aldebaran I, the project in which his first attempt had failed so dismally, he set out to investigate Helmuth's headquarters. He found a stronghold impregnable to any massed attack the Patrol could throw against it, manned by beings each wearing a thought-screen. His sense of perception was suddenly cut off—the pirates had thrown a thought-screen around the entire planet. He then returned to Prime Base, deciding en route that boring from within was the only possible way in which that stupendous fortress could be taken.

In consultation with Port Admiral Haynes, the zero hour was set, at which time the massed Grand Fleet of the Patrol was to attack Helmuth's base with every projector that could be brought to bear.

Pursuant to his plan, Kinnison again visited Trenco, where the Patrol forces extracted for him fifty kilograms of thionite, the noxious drug which, in microgram inhalations, makes the addict experience all the sensations of doing whatever it is that he wishes most ardently to do. The larger the dose, the more intense the sensations; the slightest overdose resulting in an ecstatic death. Thence to Helmuth's planet; where, working through the unshielded brain of a dog, he let himself into the central dome. Here, just before the zero minute, he released his thionite into the air-stream, thus wiping out all the pirate personnel except Helmuth, who, in his inner sanctum, could not be affected.

The Grand Fleet of the Patrol attacked, but Helmuth would not leave his retreat, even to try to save his Base. Therefore Kinnison had to go in after him. Poised in the air of Helmuth's inner sphere there was an enigmatic, sparkling ball of force which the Lensman could not understand, and of which he was in consequence extremely suspicious.

But the storming of that quadruply-defended inner stronghold was precisely the task for which Kinnison's new and ultra-cumbersome armor had been designed; and in the Gray Lensman went.*

---

* *Galactic Patrol,* Fantasy Press, Reading, Pa.

1

PRIMARY BEAMS

Among the world-girdling fortifications of a planet distant indeed from star cluster AC 257-4736 there squatted sullenly a fortress quite similar to Helmuth's own. Indeed, in some respects it was even superior to the base of him who spoke for Boskone. It was larger and stronger. Instead of one dome, it had many. It was dark and cold withal, for its occupants had practically nothing in common with humanity save the possession of high intelligence.

In the central sphere of one of the domes there sparkled several of the peculiarly radiant globes whose counterpart had given Kinnison so seriously to think, and near them there crouched or huddled or lay at ease a many-tentacled creature indescribable to man. It was not like an octopus. Though spiny, it did not resemble at all closely a sea-cucumber. Nor, although it was scaly and toothy and wingy, was it, save in the vaguest possible way, similar to a lizard, a sea-serpent, or a vulture. Such a description by negatives is, of course, pitifully inadequate; but, unfortunately, it is the best that can be done.

The entire attention of this being was focused within one of the globes, the obscure mechanism of which was relaying to his sense of perception from Helmuth's globe and mind a clear picture of everything which was happening within Grand Base. The corpse-littered dome was clear to his sight; he knew that the Patrol was attacking from without;

knew that that ubiquitous Lensman, who had already unmanned the citadel, was about to attack from within.

"You have erred seriously," the entity was thinking coldly, emotionlessly, into the globe, "in not deducing until after it was too late to save
your base that the Lensman had perfected a nullifier of sub-ethereal
detection. Your contention that I am equally culpable is, I think, untenable. It was your problem, not mine; I had, and still have, other things
to concern me. Your base is, of course, lost; whether or not you yourself
survive will depend entirely upon the adequacy of your protective devices."

"But, Eichlan, you yourself pronounced them adequate!"

"Pardon me—I said that they *seemed* adequate."

"If I survive—or, rather, after I have destroyed this Lensman—what
are your orders?"

"Go to the nearest communicator and concentrate our forces; half
of them to engage this Patrol fleet, the remainder to wipe out all the life
of Sol III. I have not tried to give those orders direct, since all the beams
are keyed to your board and, even if I could reach them, no commander
in that galaxy knows that I speak for Boskone. After you have done that,
report to me here."

"Instructions received and understood. Helmuth, ending message."

"Set your controls as instructed. I will observe and record. Prepare
yourself, the Lensman comes. Eichlan, speaking for Boskone, ending
message."

The Lensman rushed. Even before he crashed the pirate's screens
his own defensive zones flamed white in the beam of semi-portable
projectors and through that blaze came tearing the metallic slugs of a
high-caliber machine rifle. But the Lensman's screens were almost those
of a battleship, his armor relatively as strong; he had at his command
projectors scarcely inferior to those opposing his advance. Therefore,
with every faculty of his newly-enlarged mind concentrated upon that
thought-screened, armored head behind the bellowing gun and the flaring projectors, Kinnison held his line and forged ahead.

Attentive as he was to Helmuth's thought-screen, the Patrolman was
ready when it weakened slightly and a thought began to seep through,
directed at that peculiar ball of force. He blanketed it savagely, before
it could even begin to take form, and attacked the screen so viciously
that the Boskonian had either to restore full coverage instantly or else
die there and then.

Kinnison feared that force-ball no longer. He still did not know what
it was; but he had learned that, whatever its nature might be, it was

operated or controlled by thought. Therefore it was and would remain harmless; for if the pirate chief softened his screen enough to emit a thought he would never think again.

Doggedly the Lensman drove in, closer and closer. Magnetic clamps locked and held. Two steel-clad, warring figures rolled into the line of fire of the ravening automatic rifle. Kinnison's armor, designed and tested to withstand even heavier stuff, held; wherefore he came through that storm of metal unscathed. Helmuth's, however, even though stronger far than the ordinary personal armor of space, failed; and thus the Boskonian died.

Blasting himself upright, the Patrolman shot across the inner dome to the control panel and paused, momentarily baffled. He could not throw the switches controlling the defensive screens of the gigantic outer dome! His armor, designed for the ultimate of defensive strength, could not and did not bear any of the small and delicate external mechanisms so characteristic of the ordinary space-suit. To leave his personal tank at that time and in that environment was unthinkable; yet he was fast running out of time. A scant fifteen seconds was all that remained before zero, the moment at which the hellish output of every watt generable by the massed fleet of the Galactic Patrol would be hurled against those screens in their furiously, ragingly destructive might. To release the screens after that zero moment would mean his own death, instantaneous and inevitable.

Nevertheless he could open those circuits—the conservation of Boskonian property meant nothing to him. He flipped on his own projector and flashed its beam briefly across the banked panels in front of him. Insulation burst into flame, fairly exploding in its haste to disintegrate; copper and silver ran in brilliant streams or puffed away in clouds of sparkling vapor: high-tension arcs ripped, crashed, and crackled among the writhing, dripping, flaring bus-bars. The shorts burned themselves clear or blew their fuses, every circuit opened, every Boskonian defense came down; and then, and only then, could Kinnison get into communication with his friends.

"Haynes!" he thought crisply into his Lens. "Kinnison calling!"

"Haynes acknowledging!" a thought instantly snapped back. "Congrat . . ."

"Hold it! We're not done yet! Have every ship in the Fleet go free at once. Have them all, except yours, put out full-coverage screens, so that they can't look at this base—that's to keep 'em from thinking into it."

A moment passed. "Done!"

"Don't come in any closer—I'm on my way out to you. Now as to you personally—I don't like to seem to be giving orders to the Port Admiral, but it may be quite essential that you concentrate on me, and think of nothing else, for the next few minutes."

"Right! I don't mind taking orders from *you.*"

"QX—now we can take things a bit easier." Kinnison had so arranged matters that no one except himself could think into that stronghold, and he himself would not. He would not think into that tantalizing enigma, nor toward it, nor even *of* it, until he was completely ready to do so. And how many persons, I wonder, really realize just how much of a feat that was? Realize the sort of mental training required for its successful performance?

"How many gamma-zeta tracers can you put out, chief?" Kinnison asked then, more conversationally.

A brief consultation, then "Ten in regular use. By tuning in all our spares we can put out sixty."

"At two diameters' distance forty-eight fields will surround this planet at one hundred percent overlap. Please have that many set that way. Of the other twelve, set three to go well outside the first sphere—say at four diameters out—covering the line from this planet to Lundmark's Nebula. Set the last nine to be thrown out about half a detet—as far as you can read them accurately to one decimal—centering on the same line. Not much overlap is necessary on these backing fields—just contact. Release nothing, of course, until I get there. And while the boys are setting things up, you might go inert—it's safe enough now—so I can match your intrinsic velocity and come aboard."

There followed the maneuvering necessary for one inert body to approach another in space, then Kinnison's incredible housing of steel was hauled into the airlock by means of space-lines attached to magnetic clamps. The outer door of the lock closed behind him, the inner one opened, and the Lensman entered the flagship.

First to the armory, where he clambered stiffly out of his small battleship and gave orders concerning its storage. Then to the control room, stretching and bending hugely as he went, in vast relief at his freedom from the narrow and irksome confinement which he had endured so long. He wanted a shower badly—in fact, he needed one—but business came first.

Of all the men in that control room, only two knew Kinnison personally. All knew of him, however, and as the tall, gray-clad figure entered there was a loud, quick cheer.

"Hi, fellows—thanks." Kinnison waved a salute to the room as a whole. "Hi, Port Admiral! Hi, Commandant!" He saluted Haynes and von Hohendorff as perfunctorily, and greeted them as casually, as though he had last seen them an hour, instead of ten weeks, before; as though the intervening time had been spent in the veriest idleness, instead of in the fashion in which it actually had been spent.

Old von Hohendorff greeted his erstwhile pupil cordially enough, but:

"Out with it!" Haynes demanded. "What did you do? How did you do it? What does all this confounded rigmarole mean? Tell us all about it—all you can, I mean," he added, hastily.

"There's no need for secrecy now, I don't think," and in flashing thoughts the Gray Lensman went on to describe everything that had happened.

"So you see," he concluded, "I don't really *know* anything. It's all surmise, suspicion, and deduction. Maybe nothing at all will happen; in which case these precautions, while they will have been wasted effort, will have done us no harm. In case something *does* happen, however— and something will, for all the tea in China—we'll be ready for it."

"But if what you are beginning to suspect is really true, it means that Boskonia is inter-galactic in scope—wider-spread even than the Patrol!"

"Probably, but not necessarily—it may mean only that they have bases farther outside. And remember I'm arguing on a mighty slim thread of evidence. That screen was hard and tight, and I couldn't touch the external beam—if there was one—at all. I got just part of a thought, here and there. However, the thought was 'that' galaxy; not just 'galaxy,' or 'this' or 'the' galaxy—and why think that way if the guy was already in this galaxy?"

"But nobody has ever . . . but skip it for now—the boys are ready for you. Take over!"

"QX. First we'll go free again. Don't think much, if any, of the stuff can come out here, but no use taking chances. Cut your screens. Now, all you gamma-zeta men, throw out your fields, and if any of you get a puncture, or even a flash, measure its position. You recording observers, step your scanners up to fifty thousand. QX?"

"QX!" the observers and recorders reported, almost as one, and the Gray Lensman sat down at a plate.

His mind, free at last to make the investigation from which it had been so long and so sternly barred, flew down into and through the dome, to and into that cryptic globe so tantalizingly poised in the air of the Center.

The reaction was practically instantaneous; so rapid that any ordinary mind could have perceived nothing at all; so rapid that even Kinnison's consciousness recorded only a confusedly blurred impression. But he did see something: in that fleeting millionth of a second he sensed a powerful, malignant mental force; a force backing multiplex scanners and sub-ethereal stress-fields interlocked in peculiarly unidentifiable patterns.

For that ball was, as Kinnison had more than suspected, a potent agency indeed. It was, as he had thought, a communicator; but it was far more than that. Ordinarily harmless enough, it could be so set as to become an infernal machine at the vibrations of any thought not in a certain coded sequence; and Helmuth had so set it.

Therefore at the touch of the Patrolman's thoughts it exploded: liberating instantaneously the unimaginable forces with which it was charged. More, it sent out waves which, attuned to detonating receivers, touched off strategically-placed stores of duodecaplylatomate. "Duodec," the concentrated quintessence of atomic violence!

"Hell's . . . Jingling . . . Bells!" Port Admiral Haynes grunted in stunned amazement, then subsided into silence, eyes riveted upon his plate; for to the human eye dome, fortress, and planet had disappeared in one cataclysmically incandescent sphere of flame.

But the observers of the Galactic Patrol did not depend upon eyesight alone. Their scanners had been working at ultra-fast speed; and, as soon as it became clear that none of the ships of the Fleet had been endangered, Kinnison asked that certain of the spools be run into a visitank at normal tempo.

There, slowed to a speed at which the eye could clearly discern sequences of events, the two old Lensmen and the young one studied with care the three-dimensional pictures of what had happened; pictures taken from points of projection close to and even within the doomed structure itself.

Deliberately the ball of force opened up, followed an inappreciable instant later by the secondary centers of detonation; all expanding magically into spherical volumes of blindingly brilliant annihilation. There were as yet no flying fragments: no inert fragment *can* fly from duodec in the first few instants of its detonation. For the detonation of duodec is propagated at the velocity of light, so that the entire mass disintegrates in a period of time to be measured only in fractional trillionths of a second. Its detonation pressure and temperature have never been measured save indirectly, since nothing will hold it except a Q-type helix of pure force. And even those helices, which must be practically open at both ends, have to be designed and powered to withstand pressures and temperatures obtaining only in the cores of suns.

Imagine, if you can, what would happen if some fifty thousand metric tons of material from the innermost core of Sirius B were to be taken to Grand Base, separated into twenty-five packages, each package placed at a strategic point, and all restraint instantaneously removed. What would have happened then, was what actually *was* happening!

As has been said, for moments nothing moved except the ever-expanding spheres of destruction. Nothing *could* move—the inertia of matter itself held it in place until it was too late—everything close to those centers of action simply flared into turgid incandescence and added its contribution to the already hellish whole.

As the spheres expanded their temperatures and pressures decreased and the action became somewhat less violent. Matter no longer simply disappeared. Instead, plates and girders, even gigantic structural members, bent, buckled, and crumbled. Walls blew outward and upward. Huge chunks of metal and of masonry, many with fused and dripping edges, began to fly in all directions.

And not only, or principally, upward was directed the force of those inconceivable explosions. Downward the effect was, if possible, even more catastrophic, since conditions there approximated closely the oft-argued meeting between the irresistible force and the immovable object. The planet was to all intents and purposes immovable, the duodec to the same degree irresistible. The result was that the entire planet was momentarily blown apart. A vast chasm was blasted deep into its interior, and, gravity temporarily overcome, stupendous cracks and fissures began to yawn. Then, as the pressure decreased, the core-stuff of the planet became molten and began to wreak its volcanic havoc. Gravity, once more master of the situation, took hold. The cracks and chasms closed, extruding uncounted cubic miles of fiery lava and metal. The entire world shivered and shuddered in a Gargantuan cosmic ague.

The explosion blew itself out. The hot gases and vapors cooled. The steam condensed. The volcanic dust disappeared. There lay the planet; but changed—hideously and awfully changed. Where Grand Base had been there remained nothing whatever to indicate that anything wrought by man had ever been there. Mountains were leveled, valleys were filled. Continents and oceans had shifted, and were still shifting; visibly. Earthquakes, volcanoes, and other seismic disturbances, instead of decreasing, were increasing in violence, minute by minute.

Helmuth's planet was and would for years remain a barren and uninhabitable world.

"Well!" Haynes, who had been holding his breath unconsciously, released it in an almost explosive sigh. "That is inescapably and incontrovertibly *that*. I was going to use that base, but it looks as though we'll have to get along without it."

Without comment Kinnison turned to the gamma-zeta observers. "Any traces?" he asked.

It developed that three of the fields had shown activity. Not merely traces or flashes, but solid punctures showing the presence of a hard, tight beam. And those three punctures were in the same line; a line running straight out into inter-galactic space.

Kinnison took careful readings on the line, then stood motionless. Feet wide apart, hands jammed into pockets, head slightly bent, eyes distant, he stood there unmoving; thinking with all the power of his brain.

"I want to ask three questions," the old Commandant of Cadets interrupted his cogitations finally. "Was Helmuth Boskone, or not? Have we got them licked, or not? What do we do next, besides mopping up those eighteen super-maulers?"

"To all three the answer is 'I don't know.' " Kinnison's face was stern and hard. "You know as much about the whole thing as I do—I haven't held back anything I even suspect. I didn't tell you that Helmuth was Boskone; I said that everyone in any position to judge, including myself, was as sure of it as one could be about anything that couldn't be proved. The presence of this communicator line, and the other stuff I've told you about, makes me think he wasn't. However, we don't actually *know* any more than we did before. It is no more certain now that Helmuth was *not* Boskone than it was before that he *was*. The second question ties in with the first, and so does the third—but I see they've started to mop up."

While von Hohendorff and Kinnison had been talking, Haynes had issued orders and the Grand Fleet, divided roughly and with difficulty into eighteen parts, went raggedly outward to surround the eighteen outlying fortresses. But, and surprisingly enough to the Patrol forces, the reduction of those hulking monsters was to prove no easy task.

The Boskonians had witnessed the destruction of Helmuth's Grand Base. Their master plates were dead. Try as they would, they could get in touch with no one with authority to give them orders, with no one to whom they could report their present plight. Nor could they escape: the slowest mauler in the Patrol Fleet could have caught any one of them in five minutes.

To surrender was not even thought of—better far to die a clean death in the blazing holocaust of space-battle than to be thrown ignominiously into the lethal chambers of the Patrol. There was not, there could not be, any question of pardon or of sentence to any mere imprisonment, for the strife between Civilization and Boskonia in no respect resembled the wars between two fundamentally similar and friendly nations which small, green Terra knew so frequently of old. It was a galaxy-wide struggle for survival between two diametrically opposed, mutually exclusive, and absolutely incompatible cultures; a duel to the death in which quarter was neither asked nor given; a conflict which, except for the single instance which Kinnison himself had engineered, was and of stern necessity had to be one of ruthless, complete, and utter extinction.

Die, then, the pirates must; and, although adherents to a scheme of existence monstrous indeed to our way of thinking, they were in no sense cowards. Not like cornered rats did they conduct themselves, but fought like what they were; courageous beings hopelessly outnumbered and outpowered, unable either to escape or to choose the field of operations, grimly resolved that in their passing they would take full toll of the minions of that detested and despised Galactic Civilization. Therefore, in suicidal glee, Boskonian engineers rigged up a fantastically potent weapon of offense, tuned in their defensive screens, and hung poised in space, awaiting calmly the massed attack so sure to come.

Up flashed the heavy cruisers of the Patrol, serenely confident. Although of little offensive strength, these vessels mounted tractors and pressors of prodigious power, as well as defensive screens which—theoretically—no projector-driven beam of force could puncture. They had engaged mauler after mauler of Boskonia's mightiest, and never yet had one of those screens gone down. Theirs the task of immobilizing the opponent; since, as is of course well known, it is under any ordinary conditions impossible to wreak any hurt upon an object which is both inertialess and at liberty to move in space. It simply darts away from the touch of the harmful agent, whether it be immaterial beam or material substance.

Formerly the attachment of two or three tractors was all that was necessary to insure immobility, and thus vulnerability; but with the Velantian development of a shear-plane to cut tractor beams, a new technique became necessary. This was englobement, in which a dozen or more vessels surrounded the proposed victim in space and held it motionless at the center of a sphere by means of pressors, which could not be cut or evaded. Serene, then, and confident, the heavy cruisers rushed out to englobe the Boskonian fortress.

Flash! Flash! Flash! Three points of light, as unbearably brilliant as atomic vortices, sprang into being upon the fortress' side. Three needle-rays of inconceivable energy lashed out, hurtling through the cruisers' outer screens as though they had been so much inactive webbing. Through the second and through the first. Through the wall-shield, even that ultra-powerful field scarcely flashing as it went down. Through the armor, violating the prime tenet then held and which has just been referred to, that no object free in space can be damaged—in this case, so unthinkably vehement was the thrust, the few atoms of substance in the space surrounding the doomed cruisers afforded resistance enough. Through the ship itself, a ravening cylinder of annihilation.

For perhaps a second—certainly no longer—those incredible, those undreamed-of beams persisted before winking out into blackness; but that second had been long enough. Three riddled hulks lay dead in space, and as the three original projectors went black three more flared out. Then three more. Nine of the mightiest of Civilization's ships of war were riddled before the others could hurl themselves backward out of range!

Most of the officers of the flagship were stunned into temporary inactivity by that shocking development, but two reacted almost instantly.

"Thorndyke!" the admiral snapped. "What did they do, and how?"

And Kinnison, not speaking at all, leaped to a certain panel, to read for himself the analysis of those incredible beams of force.

"They made super-needle-rays out of their main projectors," Master Technician LaVerne Thorndyke reported, crisply. "They must have shorted everything they've got onto them to burn them out that fast."

"Those beams were hot—plenty hot," Kinnison corroborated the findings. "These recorders go to five billion and have a factor of safety of ten. Even that wasn't anywhere nearly enough—everything in the recorder circuits blew."

"But how could they handle them . . ." von Hohendorff began to ask.

"They didn't—they pointed them and died," Thorndyke explained, grimly. "They traded one projector and its crew for one cruiser and *its* crew—a good trade from their viewpoint."

"There will be no more such trades," Haynes declared.

Nor were there. The Patrol had maulers enough to englobe the enemy craft at a distance greater even than the effective range of those suicidal beams, and it did so.

Shielding screens cut off the Boskonians' intake of cosmic power and the relentless beaming of the bull-dog maulers began. For hour after hour it continued, the cordon ever tightening as the victims' power lessened. And finally even the gigantic accumulators of the immense fortresses were drained. Their screens went down under the hellish fury of the maulers' incessant attack, and in a space of minutes thereafter the structures and their contents ceased to exist save as cosmically atomic detritus.

The Grand Fleet of the Galactic Patrol remade its formation after a fashion and set off toward the galaxy at touring blast.

And in the control room of the flagship three Lensmen brought a very serious conference to a close.

"You saw what happened to Helmuth's planet," Kinnison's voice was oddly hard, "and I gave you all I could get of the thought about the destruction of all life on Sol III. A big enough duodec bomb in the bottom of an ocean would do it. I don't really *know* anything except that we hadn't better let them catch us asleep at the switch again—we've got to be on our toes every second."

And the Gray Lensman, face set and stern, strode off to his quarters.

2

WIDE-OPEN TWO-WAY

During practically all of the long trip back to Earth Kinnison kept pretty much to his cabin, thinking deeply, blackly, and, he admitted ruefully to himself, to very little purpose. And at Prime Base, through week after week of its feverish activity, he continued to think. Finally, however, he was snatched out of his dark abstraction by no less a personage than Surgeon-Marshal Lacy.

"Snap out of it, lad," that worthy advised, smilingly. "When you concentrate on one thing too long, you know, the vortices of thought occupy narrower and narrower loci, until finally the effective volume becomes infinitesimal. Or, mathematically, the then range of cogitation, integrated between the limits of plus and minus infinity, approaches zero as a limit . . ."

"Huh? What are you talking about?" the Lensman demanded.

"Poor mathematics, perhaps, but sound psychology," Lacy grinned. "It got your undivided attention, didn't it? That was what I was after. In plain English, if you keep on thinking around in circles you'll soon be biting yourself in the small of the back. Come on, you and I are going places."

"Where?"

"To the Grand Ball in honor of the Grand Fleet, my boy—old Doctor

Lacy prescribes it for you as a complete and radical change of atmosphere. Let's go!"

The city's largest ball-room was a blaze of light and color. A thousand polychromatic lamps flooded their radiance downward through draped bunting upon an even more colorful throng. Two thousand items of feminine loveliness were there, in raiment whose fabrics were the boasts of hundreds of planets, whose hues and shades put the spectrum itself to shame. There were over two thousand men, clad in plain or beribboned or bemedaled full civilian dress, or in the variously panoplied dress uniforms of the many Services.

"You're dancing with Miss Forrester first, Kinnison," the surgeon introduced them informally, and the Lensman found himself gliding away with a stunning blonde, ravishingly and revealingly dressed in a dazzlingly blue wisp of Manarkan glamorette—fashion's *dernier cri*.

To the uninformed, Kinnison's garb of plain gray leather might have seemed incongruous indeed in that brilliantly and fastidiously dressed assemblage. But to those people, as to us of today, the drab, starkly utilitarian uniform of the Unattached Lensman transcended far any other, however resplendent, worn by man: and literally hundreds of eyes followed the strikingly handsome couple as they slid rhythmically out upon the polished floor. But a measure of the tall beauty's customary poise had deserted her. She was slimly taut in the circle of the Lensman's arm, her eyes were downcast, and suddenly she missed a step.

" 'Scuse me for stepping on your feet," he apologized. "A fellow gets out of practice, flitting around in a speedster so much."

"Thanks for taking the blame, but it's my fault entirely—I know it as well as you do," she replied, flushing uncomfortably. "I *do* know how to dance, too, but . . . well, you're a Gray Lensman, you know."

"Huh?" he ejaculated, in honest surprise, and she looked up at him for the first time. "What has that fact got to do with the price of Venerian orchids in Chicago—or with my clumsy walking all over your slippers?"

"Everything in the world," she assured him. Nevertheless, her stiff young body relaxed and she fell into the graceful, accurate dancing which she really knew so well how to do. "You see, I don't suppose that any of us has ever seen a Gray Lensman before, except in pictures, and actually to be dancing with one is . . . well, it's really a kind of shock. I have to get used to it gradually. Why, I don't even know how to talk to you! One couldn't possibly call you plain Mister, as one would any ord . . ."

"It'll be QX if you just call me 'say,' " he informed her. "Maybe you'd rather not dance with a dub? What say we go get us a sandwich and a bottle of fayalin or something?"

"No—never!" she exclaimed. "I didn't mean it that way at all. I'm going to have this full dance with you, and enjoy every second of it. And later I'm going to pack this dance card—which I hope you will sign for me—away in lavender, so it will go down in history that in my youth I really did dance with Gray Lensman Kinnison. Perhaps I've recovered enough now to talk and dance at the same time. Do you mind if I ask you some silly questions about space?"

"Go ahead. They won't be silly, if I'm any judge. Elementary, perhaps, but not silly."

"I hope so, but I think you're being charitable again. Like most of the girls here, I suppose, I've never been out in deep space at all. Besides a few hops to the moon. I've taken only two flits, and they were both only interplanetary—one to Mars and one to Venus. I never could see how you deep-space men can really understand what you're doing—either the frightful speeds at which you travel, the distances you cover, or the way your communicators work. In fact, according to the professors, no human mind can understand figures of those magnitudes at all. But you must understand them, I should think . . . or, perhaps . . ."

"Or maybe the guy isn't human?" Kinnison laughed deeply, infectiously. "No, the professors are right. We can't understand the figures, but we don't have to—all we have to do is to work with 'em. And, now that it has just percolated through my skull who you really are, that you are *Gladys* Forrester, it's quite clear that you and I are in the same boat."

"Me? How?" she exclaimed.

"The human mind cannot really understand a million of anything. Yet your father, an immensely wealthy man, gave you clear title to a million credits in cash, to train you in finance in the only way that really produces results—the hard way of actual experience. You lost a lot of it at first, of course; but at last accounts you had got it all back, and some besides, in spite of all the smart guys trying to take it away from you. The fact that your brain can't envisage a million credits hasn't interfered with your manipulation of that amount, has it?"

"No, but that's entirely different!" she protested.

"Not in any essential feature," he countered. "I can explain it best, perhaps, by analogy. You can't visualize, mentally, the size of North America, either, yet that fact doesn't bother you in the least while you're driving around on it in an automobile. What do you drive? On the ground, I mean, not in the air?"

"A DeKhotinsky sporter."

"Um. Top speed a hundred and forty miles an hour, and I suppose you cruise between ninety and a hundred. We'll have to pretend that you drive a Crownover sedan, or some other big, slow jalopy, so that you tour at about sixty and have an absolute top of ninety. Also, you have a radio. On the broadcast bands you can hear a program from three or four thousand miles away; or, on short wave, from anywhere on Tellus . . ."

"I can get tight-beam short-wave programs from the moon," the girl broke in. "I've heard them lots of times."

"Yes," Kinnison assented dryly, "at such times as there didn't happen to be any interference."

"Static *is* pretty bad, lots of times," the heiress agreed.

"Well, change 'miles' to 'parsecs' and you've got the picture of deep-space speeds and operations," Kinnison informed her. "Our speed varies, of course, with the density of matter in space; but on the average—say one atom of substance per ten cubic centimeters of space—we tour at about sixty parsecs an hour, and full blast is about ninety. And our ultra-wave communicators, working below the level of the ether, in the sub-ether . . ."

"Whatever that is," she interrupted.

"That's as good a definition of it as any," he grinned at her. "We don't know what even the ether is, or whether or not it exists as an objective reality; to say nothing of what we so nonchalantly call the sub-ether. We can't understand gravity, even though we make it to order. Nobody yet has been able to say how it is propagated, or even whether or not it *is* propagated—no one has been able to devise any kind of an apparatus or meter or method by which its nature, period, or velocity can be determined. Neither do we know anything about time or space. In fact, fundamentally, we don't really *know* much of anything at all," he concluded.

"Says you . . . but that makes me feel better, anyway," she confided, snuggling a little closer. "Go on about the communicators."

"Ultra-waves are faster than ordinary radio waves, which of course travel through the ether with the velocity of light, in just about the same ratio as that of the speed of our ships to the speed of slow automobiles—that is, the ratio of a parsec to a mile. Roughly nineteen billion to one. Range, of course, is proportional to the square of the speed."

"Nineteen billion!" she exclaimed. "And you just said that nobody could understand even a million!"

"That's the point exactly," he went on, undisturbed. "You don't have to understand or visualize it. All you have to know is that deep-space vessels and communicators cover distances in parsecs at practically the same rate that Tellurian automobiles and radios cover miles. So, when some space-flea talks to you about parsecs, just think of miles in terms of an automobile and a teleset and you'll know as much as he does—maybe more."

"I never heard it explained that way before—it does make it ever so much simpler. Will you sign this, please?"

"Just one more point." The music had ceased and he was signing her card, preparatory to escorting her back to her place. "Like your supposedly tight-beam Luna-Tellus hookups, our long-range, equally tight-beam communicators are very sensitive to interference, either natural or artificial. So, while under perfect conditions we can communicate clear across the galaxy, there are times—particularly when the pirates are scrambling the channels—that we can't drive a beam from here to Alpha Centauri. . . . Thanks a lot for the dance."

The other girls did not quite come to blows as to which of them was to get him next; and shortly—he never did know exactly how it came about—he found himself dancing with a luscious, cuddly little brunette, clad—partially clad, at least—in a high-slitted, flame-colored sheath of some new fabric which the Lensman had never seen before. It looked like solidified, tightly-woven electricity!

"Oh, Mr. Kinnison!" his new partner cooed, ecstatically, "I think all spacemen, and you Lensmen particularly, are just too perfectly darn *heroic* for anything! Why, I think space is just *terrible!* I simply can't *cope* with it at *all!*"

"Ever been out, miss?" he grinned. He had never known many social butterflies, and temporarily he had forgotten that such girls as this one really existed.

"Why, of *course!*" The young woman kept on being exclamatory.

"Clear out to the moon, perhaps?" he hazarded.

"Don't be ridic—*ever* so much farther than that—why, I went clear to *Mars!* And it gave me the screaming *meamies,* no less—I thought I would *collapse!*"

That dance ended ultimately, and other dances with other girls followed; but Kinnison could not throw himself into the gayety surrounding him. During his cadet days he had enjoyed such revels to the full, but now the whole thing left him cold. His mind insisted upon reverting to its problem. Finally, in the throng of young people on the floor, he saw a girl with a mass of red-bronze hair and a supple, superbly molded figure. He did not need to await her turning to recognize his erstwhile nurse and later assistant, whom he had last seen just this side of far-distant Boyssia II.

"Mac!" To her mind alone he sent out a thought. "For the love of

Klono, lend a hand—rescue me! How many dances have you got ahead?"

"None at all—I'm not dating ahead." She jumped as though someone had jabbed her with a needle, then paused in panic; eyes wide, breath coming fast, heart pounding. She had felt Lensed thoughts before, but this was something else, something entirely different. Every cell of his brain was open to her—and what *was* she seeing! She could read his mind as fully and as easily as . . . as . . . as Lensmen were supposed to be able to read anybody's! She blanketed her thoughts desperately, tried with all her might not to think at all!

"QX, Mac," the thought went quietly on within her mind, quite as though nothing unusual were occurring. "No intrusion meant—you didn't think it; I already knew that if you started dating ahead you'd be tied up until day after tomorrow. Can I have the next one?"

"Surely, Kim."

"Thanks—the Lens is off for the rest of the evening." She sighed in relief as he snapped the telepathic line as though he were hanging up the receiver of a telephone.

"I'd like to dance with you all, kids," he addressed at large the group of buds surrounding him and eyeing him hungrily, "but I've got this next one. See you later, perhaps," and he was gone.

"Sorry, fellows," he remarked casually, as he made his way through the circle of men around the gorgeous red-head. "Sorry, but this dance is mine, isn't it, Miss MacDougall?"

She nodded, flashing the radiant smile which had so aroused his ire during his hospitalization. "I heard you invoke your spaceman's god, but I was beginning to be afraid that you had forgotten this dance."

"And she said she wasn't dating ahead—the diplomat!" murmured an ambassador, aside.

"Don't be a dope," a captain of Marines muttered in reply. "She meant with *us*—*that's* a Gray Lensman!"

Although the nurse, as has been said, was anything but small, she appeared almost petite against the Lensman's mighty frame as they took off. Silently the two circled the great hall once; lustrous, goldenly green gown—of Earthly silk, this one, and less revealing than most—swishing in perfect cadence against deftly and softly stepping high-zippered gray boots.

"This is better, Mac," Kinnison sighed, finally, "but I lack just seven thousand kilocycles of being in tune with this. Don't know what's the matter, but its clogging my jets. I must be getting to be a space-louse."

"A space-louse—you? Uh-uh!" She shook her head. "You know

very well what the matter is—you're just too much of a man to mention it."

"Huh?" he demanded.

"Uh-huh," she asserted, positively if obliquely. "Of course you're not in tune with this crowd—how could you be? I don't fit into it any more myself, and what I'm doing isn't even a baffled flare compared to your job. Not one in ten of these fluffs here tonight has ever been beyond the stratosphere; not one in a hundred has ever been out as far as Jupiter, or has ever had a serious thought in her head except about clothes or men; not one of them all has any more idea of what a Lensman really is than I have of hyper-space or of non-Euclidean geometry!"

"Kitty, kitty!" he laughed. "Sheathe the little claws, before you scratch somebody!"

"That isn't cattishness, it's the barefaced truth. Or perhaps," she amended, honestly, "it's both true and cattish, but it's certainly true. And that isn't half of it. No one in the Universe except yourself really *knows* what you are doing, and I'm pretty sure that only two others even suspect. And Doctor Lacy is *not* one of them," she concluded, surprisingly.

Though shocked, Kinnison did not miss a step. "You *don't* fit into this matrix, any more than I do," he agreed, quietly. "S'pose you and I could do a little flit somewhere?"

"Surely, Kim," and, breaking out of the crowd, they strolled out into the grounds. Not a word was said until they were seated upon a broad, low bench beneath the spreading foliage of a tree.

Then: "What did you come here for tonight, Mac—the *real* reason?" he demanded, abruptly.

"I . . . we . . . you . . . I mean—oh, skip it!" the girl stammered, a wave of scarlet flooding her face and down even to her superb, bare shoulders. Then she steadied herself and went on: "You see, I agree with you—as you say, I check you to nineteen decimals. Even Doctor Lacy, with all his knowledge, can be slightly screwy at times, I think."

"Oh, so that's it!" It was not, it was only a very minor part of her reason; but the nurse would have bitten her tongue off rather than admit that she had come to that dance solely and only because Kimball Kinnison was to be there. "You knew, then, that this was old Lacy's idea?"

"Of course. You would never have come, else. He thinks that you may begin wobbling on the beam pretty soon unless you put out a few braking jots."

"And you?"

"Not in a million, Kim. Lacy's as cockeyed as Trenco's ether, and I as good as told him so. He may wobble a bit, but *you* won't. You've got a job to do, and you're doing it. You'll finish it, too, in spite of all the vermin infesting all the galaxies of the macro-cosmic Universe!" she finished, passionately.

"Klono's brazen whiskers, Mac!" he turned suddenly and stared intently down into her wide, gold-flecked, tawny eyes. She stared back for a moment, then looked away.

"Don't look at me like that!" she almost screamed. "I can't stand it—you make me feel stark naked! I know your Lens is off—I'd simply die if it wasn't—but you're a mind-reader, even without it!"

She did know that that powerful telepath was off and would remain off, and she was glad indeed of the fact; for her mind was seething with thoughts which that Lensman must not know, then or ever. And for his part, the Lensman knew much better than she did that had he chosen to exert the powers at his command she would have been naked, mentally and physically, to his perception; but he did not exert those powers—then. The amenities of human relationship demanded that some fast-nesses of reserve remain inviolate, but he had to know what this woman knew. If necessary, he would take the knowledge away from her by force, so completely that she would never know that she had ever known it. Therefore:

"Just what do you know, Mac, and how did you find it out?" he demanded; quietly, but with a stern finality of inflection that made a quick chill run up and down the nurse's back.

"I know a lot, Kim." The girl shivered slightly, even though the evening was warm and balmy. "I learned it from your own mind. When you called me, back there on the floor, I didn't get just a single, sharp thought, as though you were speaking to me, as I always did before. Instead, it seemed as though I was actually inside your own mind—the whole of it. I've heard Lensmen speak of a wide-open two-way, but I never had even the faintest inkling of what such a thing would be like—no one could who has never experienced it. Of course I didn't—I couldn't—understand a millionth of what I saw, or seemed to see. It was too vast, too incredibly immense. I never dreamed any mortal *could* have a mind like that, Kim! But it was ghastly, too—it gave me the shrieking jitters and just about sent me down out of control. And you didn't even know it—I know you didn't! I didn't want to look, really, but I couldn't help seeing, and I'm glad I did—I wouldn't have missed it for the world!" she finished, almost incoherently.

"Hm . . . m. That changes the picture entirely." Much to her surprise, the man's voice was calm and thoughtful; not at all incensed. Not even disturbed. "So I spilled the beans myself, on a wide-open two-way, and didn't even realize it* . . . I knew you were backfiring about something, but thought it was because I might think you guilty of petty vanity. And I called *you* a dumbbell once!" he marveled.

"Twice," she corrected him, "and the second time I was never so glad to be called names in my whole life."

"Now I *know* I was getting to be a space-louse."

"Uh-uh, Kim," she denied again, gently. "And you aren't a brat or a lug or a clunker, either, even though I *have* called you such. But, now that I've actually got all this stuff, what can you—what can we—do about it?"

"Perhaps . . . probably . . . I think, since I gave it to you myself, I'll let you keep it," Kinnison decided, slowly.

"Keep it!" she exclaimed. "Of course I'll keep it! Why, it's in my mind—I'll *have* to keep it—nobody can take *knowledge* away from anyone!"

"Oh, sure—of course," he murmured, absently. There were a lot of things that Mac didn't know, and no good end would be served by enlightening her farther. "You see, there's a lot of stuff in my mind that I don't know much about myself, yet. Since I gave you an open channel, there must have been a good reason for it, even though, consciously, I don't know myself what it was." He thought intensely for moments, then went on: "Undoubtedly the subconscious. Probably it recognized the necessity of discussing the whole situation with someone having a fresh viewpoint, someone whose ideas can help me develop a fresh angle of attack. Haynes and I think too much alike for him to be of much help."

"You trust *me* that much?" the girl asked, dumbfounded.

"Certainly," he replied without hesitation. "I know enough about you to know that you can keep your mouth shut."

Thus unromantically did Kimball Kinnison, Gray Lensman, acknowledge the first glimmerings of the dawning perception of a vast fact—that this nurse and he were two between whom there never would nor could exist any iota of doubt or of question.

Then they sat and talked. Not idly, as is the fashion of lovers, of the minutiæ of their own romantic affairs, did these two converse, but cosmically, of the entire Universe and of the already existent conflict between the cultures of Civilization and Boskonia.

---

* Of course this was not the true explanation; but at that time only Mentor of Arisia had any idea of the real power of Clarrissa MacDougall's mind E.E.S.

They sat there, romantically enough to all outward seeming; their privacy assured by Kinnison's Lens and by his ever-watchful sense of perception. Time after time, completely unconsciously, that sense reached out to other couples who approached; to touch and to affect their minds so insidiously that they did not know that they were being steered away from the tree in whose black moon-shadow sat the Lensman and the nurse.

Finally the long conversation came to an end and Kinnison assisted his companion to her feet. His frame was straighter, his eyes held a new and brighter light.

"By the way, Kim," she asked idly as they strolled back toward the ball-room, "who is this Klono, by whom you were swearing a while ago? Another spaceman's god, like Noshabkeming, of the Valerians?"

"Something like him, only more so," he laughed. "A combination of Noshabkeming, some of the gods of the ancient Greeks and Romans, all three of the Fates, and quite a few other things as well. I think, originally, from Corvina, but fairly wide-spread through certain sections of the galaxy now. He's got so much stuff—teeth and horns, claws and whiskers, tail and everything—that he's much more satisfactory to swear by than any other space-god I know of."

"But why do men have to swear at all, Kim?" she queried, curiously. "It's so silly."

"For the same reason that women cry," he countered. "A man swears to keep from crying, a woman cries to keep from swearing. Both are sound psychology. Safety valves—means of blowing off excess pressure that would otherwise blow fuses or burn out tubes."

3

DEI EX MACHINA

In the library of the port Admiral's richly comfortable home, a room as heavily guarded against all forms of intrusion as was his private office, two old but active Gray Lensmen sat and grinned at each other like the two conspirators which in fact they were. One took a squat, red bottle of fayalin* from a cabinet and filled two small glasses. The glasses clinked, rim to rim.

"Here's to love!" Haynes gave the toast.

"Ain't it grand!" Surgeon-Marshal Lacy responded.

"Down the hatch!" they chanted in unison, and action followed word.

"You aren't asking if everything stayed on the beam." This from Lacy.

"No need—I had a spy-ray on the whole performance."

"You would—you're the type. However, I would have, too, if I had a panel full of them in *my* office. . . . Well, say it, you old space-hellion!" Lacy grinned again, albeit a trifle wryly.

"Nothing to say, saw-bones. You did a grand job, and you've got nothing to blow a jet about."

"No? How would you like to have a red-headed spitfire who's scarcely dry behind the ears yet tell you to your teeth that you've got

---

* A stimulating, although non-intoxicating beverage prepared from the fruit of a Crevenian shrub, *Fayaloclastus Augustifolius Barnstead;* much in favor as a ceremonial drink among those who can afford it. E.E.S.

softening of the brain? That you had the mental capacity of a gnat, the intellect of a Zabriskan fontema? And to have to take it, without even heaving the insubordinate young jade into the can for about twenty-five well-earned black spots?"

"Oh, come, now, you're just blasting. It wasn't that bad!"

"Perhaps not—quite—but it was bad enough."

"She'll grow up, some day, and realize that you were foxing her six ways from the origin."

"Probably. . . . In the meantime, it's all part of the bigger job. . . . Thank God I'm not young any more. They suffer so."

"Check. *How* they suffer!"

"But you saw the ending and I didn't. How did it turn out?" Lacy asked.

"Partly good, partly bad." Haynes slowly poured two more drinks and thoughtfully swirled the crimson, pungently aromatic liquid around and around in his glass before he spoke again. "Hooked—but she knows it, and I'm afraid she'll do something about it."

"She's a smart operator—I told you she was. She doesn't fox herself about anything. Hmm. . . . A bit of separation is indicated, it would seem."

"Check. Can you send out a hospital ship somewhere, so as to get rid of her for two or three weeks?"

"Can do. Three weeks be enough? We can't send him anywhere, you know."

"Plenty—he'll be gone in two." Then, as Lacy glanced at him questioningly, Haynes continued: "Ready for a shock? He's going to Lundmark's Nebula."

"But he *can't!* That would take years! Nobody has ever got back from there yet, and there's this new job of his. Besides, this separation is only supposed to last until you can spare him for a while!"

"If it takes very long he's coming back. The idea has always been, you know, that intergalactic matter may be so thin—one atom per liter or so—that such a flit won't take one-tenth the time supposed. We recognize the danger—he's going well heeled."

"How well?"

"The very best."

"I hate to clog their jets this way, but it's got to be done. We'll give her a raise when I send her out—make her sector chief. Huh?"

"Did I hear any such words lately as spitfire, hussy, and jade, or did I dream them?" Haynes asked, quizzically.

"She's all of them, and more—but she's one of the best nurses and one of the finest women that ever lived, too!"

"QX, Lacy, give her her raise. Of course she's good. If she wasn't, she wouldn't be in on this deal at all. In fact, they're about as fine a couple of youngsters as old Tellus ever produced."

"They are that. Man, *what* a pair of skeletons!"

And in the Nurses' Quarters a young woman with a wealth of red-bronze-auburn hair and tawny eyes was staring at her own reflection in a mirror.

"You half-wit, you ninny, you lug!" she stormed, bitterly if almost inaudibly, at that reflection. "You lamebrained moron, you red-headed, idiotic imbecile, you microcephalic dumb-bell, you *clunker!* Of all the men in this whole cockeyed galaxy, you *would* have to make a dive at Kimball Kinnison, the one man who thinks you're just part of the furniture. At a Gray Lensman. . . ." Her expression changed and she whispered softly, "A . . . Gray . . . Lensman. He *can't* love anybody as long as he's carrying that load. They can't let themselves be human . . . quite . . . perhaps loving *him* will be enough. . . ."

She straightened up, shrugged, and smiled; but even that pitiful travesty of a smile could not long endure. Shortly it was buried in waves of pain and the girl threw herself down upon her bed.

"Oh Kim, Kim!" she sobbed. "I wish . . . why can't you . . . Oh, why did I ever have to be born!"

Three weeks later, far out in space, Kimball Kinnison was thinking thoughts entirely foreign to his usual pattern. He was in his bunk, smoking dreamily, staring unseeing at the metallic ceiling. He was not thinking of Boskone.

When he had thought at Mac, back there at that dance, he had, for the first time in his life, failed to narrow down his beam to the exact thought being sent. Why? The explanation he had given the girl was totally inadequate. For that matter, why had he been so glad to see her there? And why, at every odd moment, did visions of her keep coming into his mind—her form and features, her eyes, her lips, her startling hair? . . . She was beautiful, of course, but not nearly such a seven-sector callout as that thionite dream he had met on Aldebaran II—and his only thought of *her* was an occasional faint regret that he hadn't half-wrung her lovely neck . . . why, she wasn't really as good-looking as, and didn't have half the *je ne sais quoi* of, that blonde heiress—what was her name?—oh, yes, Forrester. . . .

There was only one answer, and it jarred him to the core—he would not admit it, even to himself. He *couldn't* love anybody—it just simply was not in the cards. He had a job to do. The Patrol had spent a million credits making a Lensman out of him, and it was up to him to give them some kind of a run for their money. No Lensman had any business with a wife, especially a Gray Lensman. He couldn't sit down anywhere, and she couldn't flit with him. Besides, nine out of every ten Gray Lensmen got killed before they finished their jobs, and the one that did happen to live long enough to retire to a desk was almost always half machinery and artificial parts. . . .

No, not in seven thousand years. No woman deserved to have her life made into such a hell on earth as that would be—years of agony, of heart-breaking suspense, climaxed by untimely widowhood; or, at best, the wasting of the richest part of her life upon a husband who was half steel, rubber, and phenoline plastic. Red in particular was much too splendid a person to be let in for anything like that. . . .

But hold on—jet back! What made him think he rated any such girl? That there was even a possibility—especially in view of the way he had behaved while under her care in Base Hospital—that she would ever feel like being anything more to him than a strictly impersonal nurse? Probably not—he had Klono's own gadolinium guts to think that she would marry *him,* under any conditions, even if he made a full-power dive at her. . . .

Just the same, she might. Look at what women did fall in love with, sometimes. So he'd never make any kind of a dive at her; no, not even a pass. She was too sweet, too fine, too vital a woman to be tied to any space-louse; she deserved happiness, not heartbreak. She deserved the best there was in life, not the worst; the whole love of a whole man for a whole lifetime, not the fractions which were all that he could offer any woman. As long as he could think a straight thought he wouldn't make any motions toward spoiling her life. In fact, he hadn't better see Reddy again. He wouldn't go near any planet she was on, and if he saw her out in space he'd go somewhere else at a hundred parsecs an hour.

With a bitter imprecation Kinnison sprang out of his bunk, hurled his half-smoked cigarette at an ash-tray, and strode toward the control-room.

The ship he rode was of the Patrol's best. Superbly powered, for flight, defense, and offense, she was withal a complete space-laboratory and observatory; and her personnel, over and above her regular crew, was as varied as her equipment. She carried ten Lensmen, a circumstance unique in the annals of space, even for such trouble-shooting battle-wagon as the *Dauntless* was; and a scientific staff which was practically a cross-section of the Tree of Knowledge. She carried Lieutenant Peter vanBuskirk and his company of Valerian wildcats; Worsel of Velantia and three score of his reptilian kinsmen; Tregonsee, the blocky Rigellian Lensman, and a dozen or so of his fellows; Master Technician LaVerne Thorndyke and his crew. She carried three Master Pilots, Prime Base's best—Henderson, Schermerhorn and Watson.

The *Dauntless* was an immense vessel. She had to be, in order to carry, in addition to the men and the things requisitioned by Kinnison, the personnel and the equipment which Port Admiral Haynes had insisted upon sending with him.

"But great Klono, Chief, think of what a hole you're making in Prime Base if we don't get back!" Kinnison had protested.

"You're coming back, Kinnison," the Port Admiral had replied, gravely. "That is why I am sending these men and this stuff along—to be as sure as I possibly can that you *do* come back."

Now they were out in inter-galactic space, and the Gray Lensman, closing his eyes, sent his sense of perception out beyond the confining iron walls and let it roam the void. This was better than a visiplate; with no material barriers or limitations he was feasting upon a spectacle scarcely to be pictured in the most untrammeled imaginings of man.

There were no planets, no suns, no stars; no meteorites, no particles of cosmic debris. All nearby space was empty, with an indescribable perfection of emptiness at the very thought of which the mind quailed in incomprehending horror. And, accentuating that emptiness, at such mind-searing distances as to be dwarfed into buttons, and yet, because of their intrinsic massiveness, starkly apparent in their three-dimensional relationships, there hung poised and motionlessly stately the component galaxies of a Universe.

Behind the flying vessel the First Galaxy was a tiny, brightly-shining lens, so far away that such minutiæ as individual solar systems were invisible; so distant that even the gigantic masses of its accompanying globular star-clusters were merged indistinguishably into its sharply lenticular shape. In front of her, to right and to left of her, above and beneath her were other galaxies, never explored by man or by any other beings subscribing to the code of Galactic Civilization. Some, edge on, were thin, wafer-like. Others appeared as full disks, showing faintly or boldly the prodigious, mathematically inexplicable spiral arms by virtue of whose obscure functioning they had come into being. Between these two extremes there was every possible variant in angular displacement.

Utterly incomprehensible although the speed of the spaceflyer was, yet those galaxies remained relatively motionless, hour after hour. What distances! What magnificence! What grandeur! What awful, what poignantly solemn calm!

Despite the fact that Kinnison had gone out there expecting to behold that very scene, he felt awed to insignificance by the overwhelming, the cosmic immensity of the spectacle. What business had he, a sub-electronic midge from an ultra-microscopic planet, venturing out into macro-cosmic space, a demesne comprehensible only to the omniscient and omnipotent Creator?

He got up, shaking off the futile mood. This wouldn't get him to the first check-station, and he had a job to do. And after all, wasn't man as big as space? Could he have come out here, otherwise? He was. Yes, man was bigger even than space. Man, by his very envisionment of macro-cosmic space, had already mastered it.

Besides, the Boskonians, whoever they might be, had certainly mastered it; he was now certain that they were operating upon an inter-galactic scale. Even after leaving Tellus he had hoped and had really expected that his line would lead to a stronghold in some star-cluster belonging to his own galaxy, so distant from it or perhaps so small as to have escaped the notice of the chart-makers; but such was not the case. No possible error in either the determination or the following of that line placed it anywhere near any such cluster. It led straight to and only to Lundmark's Nebula; and that galaxy was, therefore, his present destination.

Man was certainly as good as the pirates; probably better, on the basis of past performance. Of all the races of the galaxy, man had always taken the initiative, had always been the leader and commander. And, with the exception of the Arisians, man had the best brain in the galaxy.

The thought of that eminently philosophical race gave Kinnison pause. His Arisian sponsor had told him that by virtue of the Lens the Patrol should be able to make Civilization secure throughout the galaxy. Just what did that mean—that it could not go outside? Or did even the Arisians suspect that Boskonia was in fact inter-galactic? Probably. Mentor had said that, given any one definite fact, a really competent mind could envisage the entire Universe; even though had added carefully that his own mind was not a really competent one.

But this, too, was idle speculation, and it was time to receive and to correlate some more reports. Therefore, one by one, he got in touch with scientists and observers.

The density of matter in space, which had been lessening steadily, was now approximately constant at one atom per four hundred cubic centimeters. Their speed was therefore about a hundred thousand parsecs per hour; and, even allowing for the slowing up at both ends due to the density of the medium, the trip should not take over ten days.

The power situation, which had been his gravest care, since it was almost the only factor not amenable to theoretical solution, was even better than anyone had dared hope; the cosmic energy available in space had actually been increasing as the matter content decreased—a fact which seemed to bear out the contention that energy was continually being converted into matter in such regions. It was taking much less excitation of the intake screens to produce a given flow of power than any figure ever observed in the denser media within the galaxy.

Thus, the atomic motors which served as exciters had a maximum power of four hundred pounds an hour; that is, each exciter could transform that amount of matter into pure energy and employ the output usefully in energizing the intake screen to which it was connected. Each screen, operating normally on a hundred thousand to one ratio, would then furnish its receptor on the ship with energy equivalent to the annihilation of four million pounds per hour of material substance. Out there, however, it was being observed that the intake-exciter ratio, instead of being less than a hundred thousand to one, was actually almost a million to one.

It would serve no useful purpose here to go further into the details of any more of the reports, or to dwell at any great length upon the remainder of the journey to the Second Galaxy. Suffice it to say that Kinnison and his highly-trained crew observed, classified, recorded, and conferred; and that they approached their destination with every possible precaution. Detectors were full out, observers were at every plate, the ship itself was as immune to detection as Hotchkiss' nullifiers could make it.

Up to the Second Galaxy the *Dauntless* flashed, and into it. Was this Island Universe essentially like the First Galaxy as to planets and peoples? If so, had they been won over or wiped out by the horrid culture of Boskonia or was the struggle still going on?

"If we assume, as we must, that the line we followed was the trace of Boskone's beam," argued the sagacious Worsel, "the probability is very great that the enemy is in virtual control of this entire galaxy. Otherwise—if they were in a minority or were struggling seriously for dominion—they could neither have spared the forces which invaded our galaxy, nor would they have been in condition to rebuild their vessels as they did to match the new armaments developed by the Patrol."

"Very probably true," agreed Kinnison, and that was the concensus of opinion. "Therefore we want to do our scouting very quietly. But in some ways that makes it all the better. If they're in control, they won't be unduly suspicious."

And thus it proved. A planet-bearing sun was soon located, and while the *Dauntless* was still light-years distant from it, several ships were detected. At least, the Boskonians were not using nullifiers!

Spy-rays were sent out. Tregonsee the Rigellian Lensman exerted to the full his powers of perception, and Kinnison hurled downward to the planet's surface a mental viewpoint and communications center. That the planet was Boskonian was soon learned, but that was all. It was scarcely fortified: no trace could he find of a beam communicating with Boskone.

Solar system after solar system was found and studied, with like result. But finally, out in space, one of the screens showed activity; a beam was in operation between a vessel then upon the plates and some other station. Kinnison tapped it quickly; and, while observers were determining its direction, hardness, and power, a thought flowed smoothly into the Lensman's brain.

". . . proceed at once to relieve vessel P4K730. Eichlan, speaking for Boskone, ending message."

"Follow that ship, Hen!" Kinnison directed, crisply. "Not too close, but don't lose him!" He then relayed to the others the orders which had been intercepted.

"The same formula, huh?" VanBuskirk roared, and "Just another lieutenant, that sounds like, not Boskone himself." Thorndyke added.

"Perhaps so, perhaps not." The Gray Lensman was merely thoughtful. "It doesn't prove a thing except that Helmuth was not Boskone, which was already fairly certain. If we can prove that there is such a being as Boskone, and that he isn't in this galaxy . . . well, in that case, we'll go somewhere else," he concluded, with grim finality.

The chase was comparatively short, leading toward a yellowish star around which swung eight average-sized planets. Toward one of these flew the unsuspecting pirate, followed by the Patrol vessel, and it soon became apparent that there was a battle going on. One spot upon the planet's surface, either a city or a tremendous military base, was domed over by a screen which was one blinding glare of radiance. And for miles in every direction ships of space were waging spectacularly devastating warfare.

Kinnison shot a thought down into the fortress, and with the least possible introduction or preamble, got into touch with one of its high officers. He was not surprised to learn that those people were more or less human in appearance, since the planet was quite similar to Tellus in age, climate, atmosphere, and mass.

"Yes, we are fighting Boskonia," the answering thought came coldly clear. "We need help, and badly. Can you . . . ?"

"We're detected!" Kinnison's attention was seized by a yell from the board. "They're all coming at us at once!"

Whether the scientists of Boskone developed the detector-nullifier before or after Helmuth's failure to deduce the Lensman's use of such an instrument is a nice question, and one upon which a great deal has been said. While interesting, the point is really immaterial here; the facts remaining the same—that the pirates not only had it at the time of the Patrol's first visit to the Second Galaxy, but had used it to such good advantage that the denizens of that recalcitrant planet had been forced, in sheer desperation of self-preservation, to work out a scrambler for that nullification and to surround their world with its radiations. They could not restore perfect detection, but the condition for complete nullification was so critical that it was a comparatively simple matter to upset it sufficiently so that an image of a sort was revealed. And, at that close range, any sort of an image was enough.

The *Dauntless,* approaching the planet, entered the zone of scrambling and stood revealed plainly enough upon the plates of the enemy vessels. They attacked instantly and viciously; within a second after the lookout had shouted his warning the outer screens of the Patrol ship were blazing incandescent under the furious assaults of a dozen Boskonian beams.

4

MEDON

For a moment all eyes were fixed apprehensively upon meters and recorders, but there was no immediate cause for alarm. The builders of the *Dauntless* had builded well; her outer screen, the lightest of her series of four, was carrying the attackers' load with no sign of distress.

"Strap down, everybody," the expedition's commander ordered then. "Inert her, Hen. Match velocity with that base," and as Master Pilot Henry Henderson cut his Bergenholm the vessel lurched wildly aside as its intrinsic velocity was restored.

Henderson's fingers swept over his board as rapidly and as surely as those of an organist over the banked keys of his console; producing, not chords and arpeggios of harmony, but roaring blasts of precisely-controlled power. Each key-like switch controlled one jet. Lightly and fleetingly touched, it produced a gentle urge; at sharp, full contact it yielded a mighty, solid shove; depressed still farther, so as to lock into any one of a dozen notches, it brought into being a torrent of propulsive force of any desired magnitude, which ceased only when its key-release was touched.

And Henderson was a virtuoso. Smoothly, effortlessly, but in a space of seconds the great vessel rolled over, spiraled and swung until her landing jets were in line and exerting five gravities of thrust. Then, equally smoothly, almost imperceptibly, the line of force was varied until the flame-enshrouded dome was stationary below them. Nobody, not even the two other Master Pilots, and least of all Henderson himself, paid any attention to the polished perfection, the consummate artistry, of the performance. That was his job. He was a Master Pilot, and one of the hallmarks of his rating was the habit of making difficult maneuvers look easy.

"Take 'em now, Chief? Can't we, huh?" Chatway, the Chief Firing Officer, did not say those words. He did not need to. The attitude and posture of the C.F.O. and his subordinates made the thought tensely plain.

"Not yet, Chatty," the Lensman answered the unsent thought. "We'll have to wait until they englobe us, so we can get 'em all. It's got to be all or none—if even one of them gets away or even has time to analyze and report on the stuff we're going to use it'll be just too bad."

He then got in touch with the officer within the beleagured base and renewed the conversation at the point at which it had been broken off.

"We can help you, I think; but to do so effectively we must have clear ether. Will you please order your ships away, out of even extreme range?"

"For how long? They can do us irreparable damage in one rotation of the planet."

"One-twentieth of that time, at most—if we can't do it in that time we can't do it at all. Nor will they direct many beams at you, if any. They'll be working on us."

Then, as the defending ships darted away, Kinnison turned to his C.F.O.

"QX, Chatty. Open up with your secondaries. Fire at will!"

Then from projectors of a power theretofore carried only by maulers there raved out against the nearest Boskonian vessels beams of a vehemence compared to which the enemies' own seemed weak, futile. And those were the secondaries!

As has been intimated, the *Dauntless* was an unusual ship. She was enormous. She was bigger even than a mauler in actual bulk and mass; and from needle-beaked prow to jet-studded stern she was literally packed with power—power for any emergency conceivable to the fertile minds of Port Admiral Haynes and his staff of designers and engineers. Instead of two, or at most three intake-screen exciters, she had two hundred. Her bus-bars, instead of being the conventional rectangular coppers, of a few square inches cross-sectional area, were laminated members built up of co-axial tubing of pure silver to a diameter of over a yard—multiple and parallel conductors, each of whose current-carrying capacity was to be measured only in millions of amperes. And everything else aboard that mighty engine of destruction was upon the same Gargantuan scale.

Titanic though those thrusts were, not a pirate ship was seriously hurt. Outer screens went down, and more than a few of the second lines of defense also failed. But that was the Patrolmen's strategy; to let the enemy know that they had weapons of offense somewhat superior to their own, but not quite powerful enough to be a real menace.

In minutes, therefore, the Boskonians rushed up and proceeded to englobe the newcomer; supposing, of course, that she was a product of the world below, that she was manned by the race who had so long and so successfully fought off Boskonian encroachment.

They attacked, and under the concentrated fury of their beams the outer screen of the Patrol ship began to fail. Higher and higher into the spectrum it radiated, blinding white . . . blue . . . an intolerable violet glare; then, patchily, through the invisible ultra-violet and into the black of extinction. The second screen resisted longer and more stubbornly, but finally it also went down; the third automatically taking up the burden of defense. Simultaneously the power of the *Dauntless'* projectors weakened, as though she were shifting her power from offense to defense in order to stiffen her third, and supposedly her last, shielding screen.

"Pretty soon, now, Chatway," Kinnison observed. "Just as soon as they can report that they've got us in a bad way; that it's just a matter of time until they blow us out of the ether. Better report now—I'll put you on the spool."

"We are equipped to energize simultaneously eight of the new, replaceable-unit primary projectors," the C.F.O. stated, crisply. "There are twenty-one vessels englobing us, and no others within detection. With a discharge period of point six zero and a switching interval of point zero nine, the entire action should occupy one point nine eight seconds."

"Chief Communications Officer Nelson on the spool. Can the last surviving ship of the enemy report enough in two seconds to do us material harm?"

"In my opinion it can not, sir," Nelson reported, formally. "The Communications Officer is neither an observer nor a technician; he merely transmits whatever material is given him by other officers for transmission. If he is already working a beam to his base at the moment of our first blast he might be able to report the destruction of vessels, but he could not be specific as to the nature of the agent used. Such a report could do no harm, as the fact of the destruction of the vessels will in any event become apparent shortly. Since we are apparently being overcome easily, however, and this is a routine action, the probability is that this detachment is not in direct communication with Base at any given moment. If not, he could not establish working control in two seconds."

"Kinnison now reporting. Having determined to the best of my ability that engaging the enemy at this time will not enable them to send Boskone any information regarding our primary armament, I now give the word to . . . FIRE!"

The underlying principle of the destructive beam produced by overloading a regulation projector had, it is true, been discovered by a Boskonian technician. Insofar as Boskonia was concerned, however, the secret had died with its inventor; since the pirates had at that time no headquarters in the First Galaxy. And the Patrol had had months of time in which to perfect it, for that work was begun before the last of Helmuth's guardian fortresses had been destroyed.

The projector was not now fatal to its crew, since they were protected from the lethal back-radiation, not only by shields of force, but also by foot after impenetrable foot of lead, osmium, carbon, cadmium, and paraffin. The refractories were of neo-carballoy, backed and permeated by M K R fields; the radiators were constructed of the most ultimately resistant materials known to the science of the age. But even so the unit had a useful life of but little over half a second, so frightful was the overload at which it was used. Like a rifle cartridge, it was good for only one shot. Then it was thrown away, to be replaced by a new unit.

Those problems were relatively simple of solution. Switching those enormous energies was the great stumbling block. The old Kimmerling block-dispersion circuit-breaker was prone to arc-over under loads much in excess of a hundred billion KVA, hence could not even be considered in this new application. However, the Patrol force finally succeeded in working out a combination of the immersed-antenna and the semipermeable-condenser types, which they called the Thorndyke heavy-duty switch. It was cumbersome, of course—any device to interrupt voltages and amperages of the really astronomical magnitudes in question could not at that time be small—but it was positive, fast-acting, and reliable.

At Kinnison's word of command eight of those indescribable primary beams lashed out; stilettoes of irresistibly penetrant energy which not even a Q-type helix could withstand. Through screens, through wall-shields, and through metal they hurtled in a space of time almost too brief to be measured. Then, before each beam expired, it was swung a little, so that the victim was literally split apart or carved into sections. Performance exceeded by far that of the hastily-improvised weapon which had so easily destroyed the heavy cruisers of the Patrol; in fact, it checked almost exactly with the theoretical figure of the designers.

As the first eight beams winked out eight more came into being, then five more; and meanwhile the mighty secondaries were sweeping the heavens with full-aperture cones of destruction. Metal meant no more to those rays than did organic material; everything solid or liquid whiffed into vapor and disappeared. The *Dauntless* lay alone in the sky of that new world.

"Marvelous—wonderful!" the thought beat into Kinnison's brain as soon as he re-established rapport with the being so far below. "We have recalled our ships. Will you please come down to our space-port at once, so that we can put into execution a plan which has been long in preparation?"

"As soon as your ships are down," the Tellurian acquiesced. "Not sooner, as your landing conventions are doubtless very unlike our own and we do not wish to cause disaster. Give me the word when your field is entirely clear."

That word came soon and Kinnison nodded to the pilots. Once more inertialess the *Dauntless* shot downward, deep into atmosphere, before her inertia was restored. Rematching velocity this time was a simple matter, and upon the towering, powerfully resilient pillars of her landing-jets the inconceivable mass of the Tellurian ship of war settled toward the ground, as lightly seeming as a wafted thistledown.

"Their cradles wouldn't fit us, of course, even if they were big enough—which they aren't, by half," Schermerhorn commented, "Where do they want us to put her?"

" 'Anywhere,' they say," the Lensman answered, "but we don't want to take that too literally—without a solid dock she'll make an awful hole, wherever we set her down. Won't hurt her any. She's designed for it—we couldn't expect to find cradles to fit her anywhere except on Tellus. I'd say to lay her down on her belly over there in that corner, out of the way; as close to that big hangar as you can work without blasting it out with your jets."

As Kinnison had intimated, the lightness of the vessel was indeed only seeming. Superbly and effortlessly the big boat seeped downward into the designated corner; but when she touched the pavement she did not stop. Still easily and without jar or jolt she settled—a full twenty feet into the concrete, re-enforcing steel, and hard-packed earth of the field before she came to a halt.

"What a monster! Who are they? Where could they have come from? . . ." Kinnison caught a confusion of startled thoughts as the real size and mass of the visitor became apparent to the natives. Then again came the clear thought of the officer.

"We would like very much to have you and as many as possible of your companions come to confer with us as soon as you have tested our atmosphere. Come in spacesuits if you must."

The air was tested and found suitable. True, it did not match exactly that of Tellus, or Rigel IV, or Velantia; but then, neither did that of the *Dauntless,* since that gaseous mixture was a compromise one, and mostly artificial to boot.

"Worsel, Tregonsee, and I will go to this conference," Kinnison decided. "The rest of you sit tight. I don't need to tell you to keep on your toes, that anything is apt to happen, anywhere, without warning. Keep your detectors full out and keep your noses clean—be ready, like the good little Endeavorers you are, 'to do with your might what your hands find to do.' Come on, fellows," and the three Lensmen strode, wriggled, and waddled across the field, to and into a spacious room of the Administration Building.

"Strangers, or, I should say friends, I introduce you to Wise, our President," Kinnison's acquaintance said, clearly enough, although it was plain to all three Lensmen that he was shocked at the sight of the Earth-man's companions.

"I am informed that you understand our language . . ." the President began, doubtfully.

He too was staring at Tregonsee and Worsel. He had been told that Kinnison, and therefore, supposedly the rest of the visitors, were beings fashioned more or less after his own pattern. But these two creatures!

For they were not even remotely human in form. Tregonsee, the Rigellian, with his leathery, multi-appendaged, oildrum-like body, his immobile dome of a head and his four blocky pillars of legs must at first sight have appeared fantastic indeed. And Worsel, the Velantian, was infinitely worse. He was repulsive, a thing materialized from sheer-est nightmare—a leather-winged, crocodile-headed, crooked-armed, thirty-foot-long, pythonish, reptilian monstrosity!

But the President of Medon saw at once that which the three out-landers had in common. The Lenses, each glowingly aflame with its own innate pseudo-vitality—Kinnison's clamped to his brawny wrist by a band of metallic alloy; Tregonsee's embedded in the glossy black flesh of one mighty, sinuous arm; Worsel's apparently driven deep and with cruel force into the horny, scaly hide squarely in the middle of his fore-head, between two of his weirdly stalked, repulsively extensible eyes.

"It is not your language we understand, but your thoughts, by virtue of these our Lenses which you have already noticed." The President gasped as Kinnison bulleted the information into his mind. "Go ahead . . . Just a minute!" as an unmistakable sensation swept through his being. "We've gone *free;* the whole planet, I perceive. In that respect, at least, you are in advance of us. As far as I know, no scientist of any of our races has even thought of a Bergenholm big enough to free a world."

"It was long in the designing; many years in the building of its units," Wise replied. "We are leaving this sun in an attempt to escape from our enemy and yours, Boskone. It is our only chance of survival. The means have long been ready, but the opportunity which you have just made for us is the first that we have had. This is the first time in many, many years that not a single Boskonian vessel is in position to observe our flight."

"Where are you going? Surely the Boskonians will be able to find you if they wish."

"That is possible, but we must run that risk. We must have a respite or perish; after a long lifetime of continuous warfare our resources are at the point of exhaustion. There is a part of this galaxy in which there are very few planets, and of those few none are inhabited or habitable. Since nothing is to be gained, ships seldom or never go there. If we can reach that region undetected, the probability is that we shall be unmolested long enough to recuperate."

Kinnison exchanged flashing thoughts with his two fellow Lensmen, then turned again to Wise.

"We come from a neighboring galaxy," he informed him, and pointed out to his mind just which galaxy he meant. "You are fairly close to the edge of this one. Why not move over to ours? You have no friends here, since you think that yours may be the only remaining independent planet. We can assure you of friendship. We can also give you some hope of peace—or at least semi-peace—in the near future, for we are driving Boskonia out of our galaxy."

"What you think of as 'semi-peace' would be tranquility incarnate to us," the old man replied with feeling. "We have in fact considered long that very move. We decided against it for two reasons: first, because we knew nothing about conditions there, and hence might be going from bad to worse; and second and more important, because of lack of reliable data upon the density of matter in inter-galactic space. Lacking that, we could not estimate the time necessary for the journey, and we could have no assurance that our sources of power, great as they are, would be sufficient to make up the heat lost by radiation."

"We have already given you an idea of conditions and we can give you the data you lack."

They did so, and for a matter of minutes the Medonians conferred. Meanwhile Kinnison went on a mental expedition to one of the power-plants. He expected to see super-colossal engines; bus-bars ten feet thick, perhaps cooled in liquid helium; and other things in proportion. But what he actually saw made him gasp for breath and call Tregonsee's attention. The Rigellian sent out his sense of perception with Kinnison's, and he also was almost stunned.

"What's the answer, Trig?" the Earthman asked, finally. "This is more down your alley than mine. That motor's about the size of my foot, and if it isn't eating a thousand pounds an hour I'm Klono's maiden aunt. And the whole output is going out on two wires no bigger than number four, jacketed together like ordinary parallel pair. Perfect insulator? If so, how about switching?"

"That must be it, a substance of practically infinite resistance," the Rigellian replied, absently, studying intently the peculiar mechanisms. "Must have a better conductor than silver, too, unless they can handle voltages of ten to the fifteenth or so, and don't see how they could break such potentials . . . Guess they don't use switches—don't see any—must shut down, the prime sources . . . No, there it is—so small that I over-looked it completely. In that little box there. Sort of a jam-plate type; a thin sheet of insulation with a knife on the leading edge, working in a slot to cut the two conductors apart—kills the arc by jamming into the tight slot at the end of the box. The conductors must fuse together at each make and burn away a little at each break, that's why they have renewable tips. Kim, they've really got something! I certainly am going to stay here and do some studying."

"Yes, and we'll have to rebuild the *Dauntless* . . ."

The two Lensmen were called away from their study by Worsel—the Medonians had decided to accept the invitation to move to the First Galaxy. Orders were given, the course was changed and the planet, now a veritable spaceship, shot away in the new direction.

"Not as many legs as a speedster, of course, but at that, she's no slouch—we're making plenty of lights," Kinnison commented, then turned to the president. "It seems rather presumptuous for us to call you simply 'Wise,' especially as I gather that that is not your name . . ."

"That is what I am called, and that is what you are to call me," the oldster replied. "We of Medon do not have names. Each has a number; or, rather, a symbol composed of numbers and letters of our alphabet—a symbol which gives his full classification. Since these things are too clumsy for regular use, however, each of us is given a nickname, usually an adjective, which is supposed to be more less descriptive. You of Earth we could not give a complete symbol; your two companions we could not give any at all. However, you may be interested in knowing that you three have already been named?"

"Very much so."

"You are to be called 'Keen.' He of Rigel IV is 'Strong,' and he of Velantia is 'Agile.' "

"Quite complimentary to me, but . . ."

"Not bad at all, I'd say," Tregonsee broke in. "But hadn't we better be getting on with more serious business?"

"We should indeed," Wise agreed. "We have much to discuss with you; particularly the weapon you used."

"Could you get an analysis of it?" Kinnison asked, sharply.

"No. No one beam was in operation long enough. However, a study of the recorded data, particularly the figures for intensity—figures so high as to be almost unbelievable—lead us to believe that the beam is the result of an enormous overload upon a projector otherwise of more or less conventional type. Some of us have wondered why we did not think of the idea ourselves . . ."

"So did we, when it was used on us," Kinnison grinned and went on to explain the origin of the primary. "We will give you the formulæ and also the working hook-up—including the protective devices, because they're mighty dangerous without plenty of force-backing—of the primaries, in exchange for some lessons in power-plant design."

"Such an exchange of knowledge would be helpful indeed," Wise agreed.

"The Boskonians know nothing whatever of this beam, and we do not want them to learn of it," Kinnison cautioned. "Therefore I have two suggestions to make.

"First, that you try everything else before you use this primary beam. Second, that you don't use it even then unless you can wipe out, as nearly simultaneously as we did out there, every Boskonian who may be able to report back to his base as to what really happened. Fair enough?"

"Eminently so. We agree without reservation—it is to our interest as much as yours that such a secret be kept from Boskone."

"QX. Fellows, let's go back to the ship for a couple of minutes." Then, aboard the *Dauntless:* "Tregonsee, you and your crew want to stay with the planet, to show the Medonians what to do and to help them along generally, as well as to learn about their power system. Thorndyke, you and your gang, and probably Lensman Hotchkiss, had better study these things too—you'll know what you want as soon as they show you the hook-up. Worsel, I'd like to have you stay with the ship. You're in command of her until further orders. Keep her here for say a week or ten days, until the planet is well out of the galaxy. Then, if Hotchkiss and Thorndyke haven't got all the dope they want, leave them here to ride back with Tregonsee on the planet and drill the *Dauntless* for Tellus. Keep yourself more or less disengaged for a while, and sort of keep tuned to me. I may not need an ultra-long-range communicator, but you never can tell."

"Why such comprehensive orders, Kim?" asked Hotchkiss. "Who ever heard of a commander abandoning his expedition? Aren't you sticking around?"

"Nope—got to do a flit. Think maybe I'm getting an idea. Break out my speedster, will you, Allerdyce?" and the Gray Lensman was gone.

5

DESSA DESPLAINES, ZWILNIK

Kinnison's speedster shot away and made an undetectable, uneventful voyage back to Prime Base.

"Why the foliage?" the Port Admiral asked, almost at sight, for the Gray Lensman was wearing a more-than-half-grown beard.

"I may need to be Chester Q. Fordyce for a while. If I don't, I can shave it off quick. If I do, a real beard is a lot better than an imitation," and he plunged into his subject.

"Very fine work, son, very fine indeed," Haynes congratulated the younger man at the conclusion of his report. "We shall begin at once, and be ready to rush things through when the technicians bring back the necessary data from Medon. But there's one more thing I want to ask you. How come you placed those spotting-screens so exactly? The beam practically dead-centered them. You claimed it was surmise and suspicion before it happened, but you must have had a much firmer foundation than any kind of a mere hunch. What was it?"

"Deduction, based upon an unproved, but logical, cosmogonic theory—but you probably know more about that stuff than I do."

"Highly improbable. I read just a smattering now and then of the doings of the astronomers and astrophysicists. I didn't know that that was one of your specialties, either."

"It isn't, but I had to do a little cramming. We'll have to go back quite a while to make it clear. You know, of course, that a long time ago, before even inter-planetary ships were developed, the belief was general that not more than about four planetary solar systems could be in existence at any one time in the whole galaxy?"

"Yes, in my youth I was exposed to Wellington's Theory. The theory itself is still good, isn't it?"

"Eminently so—every other theory was wrecked by the hard facts of angular momentum and filament energies. But you know already what I'm going to say."

"No, just let's say that a bit of light is beginning to dawn. Go ahead."

"QX. Well, when it was discovered that there were millions of times as many planets in the galaxy as could be accounted for by a Wellington Incident occurring once in two times ten to the tenth years or so, some way had to be figured out to increase, millionfold, the number of such occurrences. Manifestly, the random motion of the stars within the galaxy could not account for it. Neither could the vibration or oscillation of the globular clusters through the galaxy. The meeting of two galaxies—the passage of them completely through each other, edgewise—would account for it very nicely. It would also account for the fact that the solar systems on one side of the galaxy tend to be somewhat older than the ones on the opposite side. Question, find the galaxy. It was van der Schleiss, I believe, who found it. Lundmark's Nebula. It is edge on to us, with a receding velocity of thirty one hundred and sixteen kilometers per second—the exact velocity which, corrected for gravitational decrement, will put Lundmark's Nebula right here at the time when, according to our best geophysicists and geochemists, old Earth was being born. If that theory was correct, Lundmark's Nebula should also be full of planets. Four expeditions went out to check the theory, and none of them came back. We know why, now—Boskone got them. We got back, because of you, and only you."

"Holy Klono!" the old man breathed, paying no attention to the tribute. "It checks—*how* it checks!

"To nineteen decimals."

"But still it doesn't explain why you set your traps on that line."

"Sure it does. How many galaxies are there in the Universe, do you suppose, that are full of planets?"

"Why, all of them, I suppose—or no, not so many perhaps . . . I don't know—I don't remember having read anything on that question."

"No, and you probably won't. Only loose-screwed space detectives, like me, and crackpot science-fiction writers, like Wacky Williamson, have noodles vacuous enough to harbor such thin ideas. But, according to our admittedly highly tenuous reasoning, there are only two such galaxies—Lundmark's nebula and ours."

"Huh? Why?" demanded Haynes.

"Because galactic coalescences don't occur much, if any, oftener than Wellingtons within a galaxy do," Kinnison asserted. "True, they are closer together in space, relative to their actual linear dimensions, than are stars; but on the other hand their relative motions are slower— that is, a star will traverse the average interstellar distance much quicker than a galaxy will the inter-galactic one—so that the whole thing evens up. As nearly as Wacky and I could figure it, two galaxies will collide deeply enough to produce a significant number of planetary solar systems on an average of once in just about one point eight times ten to the tenth years. Pick up your slide rule and check me on it, if you like."

"I'll take your word for it," the old Lensman murmured, absently. "But any galaxy probably has at least a couple of solar systems all the time—but I see your point. The probability is overwhelmingly great that Boskone would be in a galaxy having hundreds of millions of planets rather than in one having only a dozen or less inhabitable worlds. But at that, they *could* all have lots of planets. Suppose that our wilder thinkers are right, that galaxies are grouped into Universes, which are spaced, roughly, about the same as the galaxies are. Two of them *could* collide, couldn't they?"

"They could, but you're getting 'way out of my range now. At this point the detective withdraws, leaving a clear field for you and the science-fiction imaginationeer."

"Well, finish the thought—that I'm wackier even than he is!" Both men laughed, and the Port Admiral went on: "It's a fascinating specu- lation . . . it does no harm to let the fancy roam at times . . . but at that, there are things of much greater importance. You think, then, that the thionite ring enters into this matrix?"

"Bound to. Everything ties in. Most of the intelligent races of this galaxy are oxygen-breathers, with warm, red blood: the only kind of physiques which thionite affects. The more of us who get the thionite habit the better for Boskone. It explains why we have never got to the first check-station in getting any of the real higher-ups in the thionite game; instead of being an ordinary criminal ring they've got all the brains and all the resources of Boskonia back of them. But if they're that big . . . and as good as we know they are . . . I wonder why . . ." Kinnison's voice trailed off into silence; his brain raced.

"I want to ask you a question that's none of my business," the young Lensman went on almost immediately, in a voice strangely altered. "Just how long ago was it that you started losing fifth-year men just before graduation? I mean, that boys sent to Arisia to be measured for their Lenses supposedly never got there? Or at least, they never came back and no Lenses were ever received for them?"

"About ten years. Twelve, I think, to be ex . . . ," Haynes broke off in the middle of the word and his eyes bored into those of the younger man. "What makes you think there were any such?"

"Deduction again, but this time I know I'm right. At least one every year. Usually two or three."

"Right, but there have always been space accidents . . . or they were caught by the pirates . . . you think, then, that . . . ?"

"I don't think. I *know!*" Kinnison declared. "They got to Arisia, and they died there. All I can say is, thank God for the Arisians. We can still trust our Lenses; they are seeing to that."

"But why didn't they tell us?" Haynes asked, perplexed.

"They wouldn't—that isn't their way," Kinnison stated, flatly and with conviction. "They have given us an instrumentality, the Lens, by virtue of which we should be able to do the job, and they are seeing to it that that instrumentality remains untarnished. We've got to learn how to handle it, though, ourselves. We've got to fight our own battles and bury our own dead. Now that we've smeared up the enemy's military organization in this galaxy by wiping out Helmuth and his headquarters, the drug syndicate seems to be my best chance of getting a line on the real Boskone. While you are mopping up and keeping them from establishing another war base here, I think I'd better be getting at it, don't you?"

"Probably so—you know your own oysters best. Mind if I ask where you're going to start in?" Haynes looked at Kinnison quizzically as he spoke. "Have you deduced that, too?"

The Gray Lensman returned the look in kind. "No. Deduction couldn't take me quite that far," he replied in the same tone. "You're going to tell me that, when you get around to it."

"Me? Where do I come in?" the Port Admiral feigned surprise.

"As follows. Helmuth probably had nothing to do with the dope running, so its organization must still be intact. If so, they would take over as much of the other branch as they could get hold of, and hit us harder than ever. I haven't heard of any unusual activity around here, so it must be somewhere else. Wherever it is, you would know about it, since you are a member of the Galactic Council; and Councillor Ellington, in charge of Narcotics, would hardly take any very important step without conferring with you. How near right am I?"

"On the center of the beam, all the way—your deducer is blasting at maximum," Haynes said, in admiration. "Radelix is the worst—they're hitting it mighty hard. We sent a full unit over there last week. Shall we recall them, or do you want to work independently?"

"Let them go on; I'll be of more use working on my own, I think. I did the boys over there a favor a while back—they would cooperate anyway, of course, but it's a little nicer to have them sort of owe it to me. We'll all be able to play together very nicely, if the opportunity arises."

"I'm mighty glad you're taking this on. The Radeligians are stuck, and we had no real reason for thinking that our men could do any better. With this new angle of approach, however, and with you working behind the scenes, the picture looks entirely different."

"I'm afraid that's unjustifiably high . . ."

"Not a bit of it, lad. Just a minute—I'll break out a couple of beakers of fayalin . . . Luck!"

"Thanks, chief!"

"Down the hatch!" and again the Gray Lensman was gone. To the spaceport, into his speedster, and away—hurtling through the void at the maximum blast of the fastest space-flyer then boasted by the Galactic Patrol.

During the long trip Kinnison exercised, thought, and studied spool after spool of tape—the Radeligian language. Thoughts of the red-headed nurse obtruded themselves strongly at times, but he put them aside resolutely. He was, he assured himself, off of women forever—all women. He cultivated his new beard; trimming it, with the aid of a triple mirror and four stereoscopic photographs, into something which, although neat and spruce enough, was too full and bushy by half to be a Van Dyke. Also, he moved his Lens-bracelet up his arm and rayed the white skin thus exposed until his whole wrist was the same even shade of tan.

He did not drive his speedster to Radelix, for that racy little fabrication would have been recognized anywhere for what she was; and private citizens simply did not drive ships of that type. Therefore, with every possible precaution of secrecy, he landed her in a Patrol base four solar systems away. In that base Kimball Kinnison disappeared; but the tall, shock-haired, bushy-bearded Chester Q. Fordyce—cosmopolite, man of leisure, and dilettante in science—who took the next space-liner for Radelix was not precisely the same individual who had come to that planet a few days before with that name and those unmistakable characteristics.

Mr. Chester Q. Fordyce, then, and not Gray Lensman Kimball Kinnison, disembarked at Ardith, the world-capital of Radelix. He took up his abode at the Hotel Ardith-Splendide and proceeded, with neither too much nor too little fanfare, to be his cosmopolitan self in those circles of society in which, wherever he might find himself, he was wont to move.

As a matter of course he entertained, and was entertained by, the Tellurian Ambassador. Equally as a matter of course he attended divers and sundry functions, at which he made the acquaintance of hundreds of persons, many of them personages. That one of these should have been Lieutenant-Admiral Gerrond, Lensman in charge of the Patrol's Radeligian base, was inevitable.

It was, then, a purely routine and logical development that at a reception one evening Lensman Gerrond stopped to chat for a moment with Mr. Fordyce; and it was purely accidental that the nearest bystander was a few yards distant. Hence, Mr. Fordyce's conduct was strange enough.

"Gerrond!" he said without moving his lips and in a tone almost inaudible, the while he was proffering an Alsakanite cigarette. "Don't look at me particularly right now, and don't show surprise. Study me for the next few minutes, then put your Lens on me and tell me whether you have ever seen me before or not." Then, glancing at the watch upon his left wrist—a timepiece just about as large and as ornate as a wrist-watch could be and still remain in impeccable taste—he murmured something conventional and strolled away.

Ten minutes passed and he felt Gerrond's thought. A peculiar sensation, this, being on the receiving end of a single beam, instead of using his own Lens.

"As far as I can tell, I have never seen you before. You are certainly not one of our agents, and if you are one of Haynes' whom I have ever worked with you have done a wonderful job of disguising. I must have met you somewhere, sometime, else there would be no point to your question; but beyond the evident—and admitted—fact that you are a white Tellurian, I can't seem to place you."

"Does this help?" This question was shot through Kinnison's own Lens.

"Since I have known so few Tellurian Lensmen it tells me that you must be Kinnison, but I do not recognize you at all readily. You seem changed—older—besides, who ever heard of an Unattached Lensman doing the work of an ordinary agent?"

"I am both older and changed—partly natural and partly artificial. As for the work, it's a job that no ordinary agent can handle—it takes a lot of special equipment . . ."

"You've got *that,* indubitably! I get goose-flesh yet every time I think of that trial."

"You think I'm proof against recognition, then, as long as I don't use my Lens?" Kinnison stuck to the issue.

"Absolutely so . . . You're here, then, on thionite?" No other issue, Gerrond knew, could be grave enough to account for this man's presence. "But your wrist? I studied it. You can't have worn your Lens there for months—those Tellurian bracelets leave white streaks an inch wide."

"I tanned it with a pencil-beam. Nice job, eh? But what I want to ask you about is a little cooperation—as you supposed, I'm here to work on this drug ring."

"Surely—anything we can do. But Narcotics is handling that, not us—but you know that, as well as I do . . ." the officer broke off, puzzled.

"I know. That's why I want you—that and because you handle the secret service. Frankly, I'm scared to death of leaks. For that reason I'm not saying anything to anyone except Lensmen, and I'm having no dealings with anyone connected with Narcotics. I have as unimpeachable an identity as Haynes could furnish. . . ."

"There's no question as to its adequacy, then," the Radeligian interposed.

"I'd like to have you pass the word around among your boys and girls that you know who I am and that I'm safe to play with. That way, if Boskone's agents spot me, it will be for an agent of Haynes's, and not for what I really am. That's the first thing. Can do?"

"Easily and gladly. Consider it done. Second?"

"To have a boat-load of good, tough marines on hand if I should call you. There are some Valerians coming over later but I may need help in the meantime. I may want to start a fight—quite possibly even a riot."

"They'll be ready, and they'll be big, tough, and hard. Anything else?"

"Not just now, except for one question. You know Countess Avondrin, the woman I was dancing with a while ago. Got any dope on her?"

"Certainly not—what do you mean?"

"Huh? Don't you know even that she's a Boskonian agent of some kind?"

"Man, you're crazy! She isn't an agent, she can't be. Why, she's the daughter of a Planetary Councillor, the wife of one of our most loyal officers."

"She would be—that's the type they like to get hold of."

"Prove it!" the Admiral snapped. "Prove it or retract it!" He almost lost his poise, almost looked toward the distant corner in which the bewhiskered gentleman was sitting so idly.

"QX. If she isn't an agent, why is she wearing a thought-screen? You haven't tested her, of course."

Of course not. The amenities, as has been said, demanded that certain reserves of privacy remain inviolate. The Tellurian went on:

"You didn't, but I did. On this job I can recognize nothing of good taste, of courtesy, of chivalry, or even of ordinary common decency. I suspect *everyone* who does not wear a Lens."

"A thought-screen!" exclaimed Gerrond. "How could she, without armor?"

"It's a late model—brand new. Just as good and just as powerful as the one I myself am wearing," Kinnison explained. "The mere fact that she's wearing it gives me a lot of highly useful information."

"What do you want me to do about her?" the Admiral asked. He was mentally a-squirm, but he was a Lensman.

"Nothing whatever—except possibly, for our own information, to find out how many of her friends have become thionite-sniffers lately. If you do anything you may warn them, although I know nothing definite about which to caution you. I'll handle her. Don't worry too much, though; I don't think she's anybody we really want. Afraid she's small fry—no such luck as that I'd get hold of a big one so soon."

"I hope she's small fry," Gerrond's thought was a grimace of distaste. "I hate Boskonia as much as anybody does, but I don't relish the idea of having to put that girl into the Chamber."

"If my picture is half right she can't amount to much," Kinnison replied. "A good lead is the best I can expect . . . I'll see what I can do."

For days, then, the searching Lensman pried into minds: so insidiously that he left no trace of his invasions. He examined men and women, of high and low estate. Waitresses and ambassadors, flunkeys and bankers, ermined prelates and truck-drivers. He went from city to city. Always, but with only a fraction of his brain, he played the part of Chester Q. Fordyce; ninety-nine percent of his stupendous mind was probing, searching, and analyzing. Into what charnel pits of filth and corruption he delved, into what fastnesses of truth and loyalty and high courage and ideals, must be left entirely to the imagination; for the Lensman never has spoken and never will speak of these things.

He went back to Ardith and, late at night, approached the dwelling of Count Avondrin. A servant arose and admitted the visitor, not knowing then or ever that he did so. The bedroom door was locked from the inside, but what of that? What resistance can any mechanism offer to a master craftsman, plentifully supplied with tools, who can perceive every component part, however deeply buried?

The door opened. The Countess was a light sleeper, but before she could utter a single scream one powerful hand clamped her mouth, another snapped the switch of her supposedly carefully concealed thought-screen generator. What followed was done very quickly.

Mr. Fordyce strolled back to his hotel and Lensman Kinnison directed a thought at Lensman Gerrond.

"Better fake up some kind of an excuse for having a couple of guards or policemen in front of Count Avondrin's town house at eight twenty-five this morning. The Countess is going to have a brainstorm."

"What *have* . . . er, what will she do?"

"Nothing much. Scream a bit, rush out-of-doors half dressed, and fight anything and everybody that touches her. Warn the officers that she'll kick, scratch, and bite. There will be plenty of signs of a prowler having been in her room, but if they can find him they're good—*very* good. She'll have all the signs and symptoms, even to the puncture, of having been given a shot in the arm of something the doctors won't be able to find or to identify. But there will be no question raised of insanity or of any other permanent damage—she'll be right as rain in a couple of months."

"Oh, that mind-ray machine of yours again, eh? And that's all you're going to do to her?"

"That's all. I can let her off easy and still be just, I think. She's helped me a lot. She'll be a good girl from now on, too; I've thrown a scare into her that will last her the rest of her life."

"Fine business, Gray Lensman! What else?"

"I'd like to have you at the Tellurian Ambassador's Ball day after tomorrow, if it's convenient."

"I've been planning on it, since it's on the 'must' list. Shall I bring anything or anyone special?"

"No. I just want you on hand to give me any information you can on a person who will probably be there to investigate what happened to the Countess."

"I'll be there," and he was.

It was a gay and colorful throng, but neither of the two Lensmen was in any mood for gayety. They acted, of course. They neither sought nor avoided each other; but, somehow, they were never alone together.

"Man or woman?" asked Gerrond.

"I don't know. All I've got is the recognition."

The Radeligian did not ask what that signal was to be. Not that he was not curious; but if the Gray Lensman wanted him to know it he would tell him—if not, he wouldn't tell him even if he asked.

Suddenly the Radeligian's attention was wrenched toward the doorway, to see the most marvelously, the most flawlessly beautiful woman he had ever seen. But not long did he contemplate that beauty, for the Tellurian Lensman's thoughts were fairly seething, despite his iron control.

"Do you mean . . . you can't mean . . ." Gerrond faltered.

"She's the one!" Kinnison rasped. "She looks like an angel, but take it from me, she isn't. She's one of the slimiest snakes that ever crawled—she's so low she could put on a tall silk hat and walk under a duck. I know she's beautiful. She's a riot, a seven-section callout, a thionite dream. So what? She is also Dessa Desplaines, formerly of Aldebaran II. Does that mean anything to you?"

"Not a thing, Kinnison."

"She's in it, clear to her neck. I had a chance to wring her neck once, too, damn it all, and didn't. She's got a carballoy crust, coming here now, with all our Narcotics on the job . . . wonder if they think they've got Enforcement so badly whipped that they can get away with stuff as rough as this . . . sure you don't know her, or know of her?"

"I never saw her before, or heard of her."

"Perhaps she isn't known, out this way. Or maybe they think they're ready for a show-down . . . or don't care. But her being here ties me up in hard knots—*she'll* recognize me, for all the tea in China. You know the Narcotics' Lensmen, don't you?"

"Certainly."

"Call one of them, right now. Tell him that Dessa Desplaines, the zwilnik* houri, is right here on the floor . . . What? He doesn't know her, either? And none of our boys are Lensmen! Make it a three-way. Lensman Winstead? Kinnison of Sol III, Unattached. Sure that none of you recognize this picture?" and he transmitted a perfect image of the ravishing creature then moving regally across the floor. "Nobody does? Maybe that's why she's here, then—they thought she could get away with it. She's your meat—come and get her."

"You'll appear against her, of course?"

"If necessary—but it won't be. As soon as she sees the game's up, all hell will be out for noon."

As soon as the connection had been broken, Kinnison realized that the thing could not be done that way; that he could not stay out of it. No man alive save himself could prevent her from flashing a warning— badly as he hated to, he had to do it. Gerrond glanced at him curiously: he had received a few of those racing thoughts.

---

* Any entity connected with the illicit drug traffic. E.E.S.

"Tune in on this." Kinnison grinned wryly. "If the last meeting I had with her is any criterion, it ought to be good. S'pose anybody around here understands Aldebaranian?"

"Never heard it mentioned if they do."

The Tellurian walked blithely up to the radiant visitor, held out his hand in Earthly—and Aldebaranian—greeting, and spoke:

"Madame Desplaines would not remember Chester Q. Fordyce, of course. It is of the piteousness that I should be so accursedly of the ordinariness; for to see Madame but the one time, as I did at the New Year's Ball in High Altamont, is to remember her forever."

"Such a flatterer!" the woman laughed. "I trust that you will forgive me, Mr. Fordyce, but one meets so many interesting . . ." her eyes widened in surprise, an expression which changed rapidly to one of flaming hatred, not unmixed with fear.

"So you *do* know me, you bedroom-eyed Aldebaranian hell-cat," he remarked, evenly. "I thought you would."

"Yes, you sweet, uncontaminated sissy, you overgrown superboy-scout, I do!" she hissed, malevolently, and made a quick motion toward her corsage. These two, as has been intimated, were friends of old.

Quick though she was, the man was quicker. His left hand darted out to seize her left wrist; his right, flashing around her body, grasped her right and held it rigidly in the small of her back. Thus they walked away.

"Stop!" she flared. "You're making a spectacle of me!"

"Now isn't that just too bad?" His lips smiled, for the benefit of the observers, but his eyes held no glint of mirth. "These folks will think that this is the way all Aldebaranian friends walk together. If you think for a second you've got any chance at all of touching that sounder—think again. Stop wiggling! Even if you can shimmy enough to work it I'll smash your brain to a pulp before it contacts once!"

Outside, in the grounds: "Oh, Lensman, let's sit down and talk this over!" and the girl brought into play everything she had. It was a distressing scene, but it left the Lensman cold.

"Save your breath," he advised her finally, wearily. "To me you're just another zwilnik, no more and no less. A female louse is still a louse; and calling a zwilnik a louse is insulting the whole louse family."

He said that; and, saying it, knew it to be the exact and crystal truth: but not even that knowledge could mitigate in any iota the recoiling of his every fiber from the deed which he was about to do. He could not even pray, with immortal Merritt's *Dwayanu:*

"Luka—turn your wheel so I need not slay this woman!"

It had to be. Why in all the nine hells of Valeria did he have to be a Lensman? Why did he have to be the one to do it? But it had to be done, and soon; they'd be here shortly.

"There's just one thing you can do to make me believe you're even partially innocent," he ground out, "that you have even one decent thought or one decent instinct anywhere in you."

"What is that, Lensman? I'll do it, whatever it is!"

"Release your thought-screen and send out a call to the Big Shot."

The girl stiffened. This big cop wasn't so dumb—he really *knew* something. He must die, and at once. How could she get word to . . . ?

Simultaneously Kinnison perceived that for which he had been waiting; the Narcotics men were coming.

He tore open the woman's gown, flipped the switch of her thought-screen, and invaded her mind. But, fast as he was, he was late—almost too late altogether. He could get neither direction line nor location; but only and faintly a picture of a space-dock saloon, of a repulsively obese man in a luxuriously-furnished back room. Then her mind went completely blank and her body slumped down, bonelessly.

Thus Narcotics found them; the woman inert and flaccid upon the bench, the man staring down at her in black abstraction.

6

ROUGH-HOUSE

Suicide? Or did you . . ." Gerrond paused, delicately. Winstead, the Lensman of Narcotics, said nothing, but looked on intently.

"Neither," Kinnison replied, still studying. "I would have had to, but she beat me to it."

"What d'you mean, 'neither'? She's dead, isn't she? How did it happen?"

"Not yet, and unless I'm more cockeyed even than usual, she won't be. She isn't the type to rub herself out. Ever, under any conditions. As to 'how,' that was easy. A hollow false tooth. Simple, but new . . . and clever. But why? WHY?" Kinnison was thinking to himself more than addressing his companions. "If they had killed her, yes. As it is, it doesn't make any kind of sense—any of it."

"But the girl's dying!" protested Gerrond. "What're you going to *do?*"

"I wish to Klono I knew." The Tellurian was puzzled, groping. "No hurry doing anything about her—what was done to her nobody can undo . . . BUT WHY? . . . unless I can fit these pieces together into some kind of a pattern I'll never know what it's all about . . . none of it makes sense . . ." He shook himself and went on: "One thing is plain. She won't die. If they had intended to kill her, she would've died right then. They figure she's worth saving; in which I agree with them. At the same time, they certainly aren't planning on letting me tap her knowledge, and they may be figuring on taking her away from us. Therefore, as long as she stays alive—or even not dead, the way she is now—guard her so heavily that an army can't get her. If she should happen to die, don't leave her body unguarded for a second until she's been autopsied and you know she'll stay dead. The minute she recovers, day or night, call me. Might as well take her to the hospital now, I guess."

The call came soon that the patient had indeed recovered.

"She's talking, but I haven't answered her," Gerrond reported. "There's something strange here, Kinnison."

"There would be—bound to be. Hold everything until I get there," and he hurried to the hospital.

"Good morning, Dessa," he greeted her in Aldebaranian. "You are feeling better, I hope?"

Her reaction was surprising. "You really know me?" she almost shrieked, and flung herself into the Lensman's arms. Not deliberately; not with her wonted, highly effective technique of bringing into play the equipment with which she was overpoweringly armed. No; this was the utterly innocent, the wholly unself-conscious abandon of a very badly frightened young girl. "What happened?" she sobbed, frantically, "Where am I? Why are all these strangers here?"

Her wide, child-like, tear-filled eyes sought his; and as he probed them, deeper and deeper into the brain behind them, his face grew set and hard. Mentally, she now *was* a young and innocent girl! Nowhere in her mind, not even in the deepest recesses of her subconscious, was there the slightest inkling that she had even existed since her fifteenth year. It was staggering; it was unheard of; but it was indubitably a fact. For her, now, the intervening time had lapsed instantaneously—had disappeared so utterly as never to have been!

"You have been very ill, Dessa," he told her gravely, "and you are no longer a child." He led her into another room and up to a triple mirror. "See for yourself."

"But that isn't I!" she protested. "It can't be! Why, she's beautiful!"

"You're all of that," the Lensman agreed casually. "You've had a bad shock. Your memory will return shortly, I think. Now you must go back to bed."

She did so, but not to sleep. Instead, she went into a trance; and so, almost, did Kinnison. For over an hour he lay intensely a-sprawl in an easy chair, the while he engraved, day by day, a memory of missing years into that bare storehouse of knowledge. And finally the task was done.

"Sleep, Dessa," he told her then. "Sleep. Waken in eight hours; whole."

"Lensman, you're a *man!*" Gerrond realized vaguely what had been done. "You didn't give her the truth, of course?"

"Far from it. Only that she was married and is a widow. The rest of it is highly fictitious—just enough like the real thing so she can square herself with herself if she meets old acquaintances. Plenty of lapses, of course, but they're covered by shock."

"But the husband?" queried the inquisitive Radeligian.

"That's her business," Kinnison countered, callously. "She'll tell you sometime, maybe, if she ever feels like it. One thing I did do, though—they'll never use her again. The next man that tries to hypnotize her will be lucky if he gets away alive."

The advent of Dessa Desplaines, however, and his curious adventure with her, had altered markedly the Lensman's situation. No one else in the throng had worn a screen, but there might have been agents . . . anyway, the observed facts would enable the higher-ups to link Fordyce up with what had happened . . . they would know, of course, that the real Fordyce hadn't done it . . . he could be Fordyce no longer . . .

Wherefore the real Chester Q. Fordyce took over and a stranger appeared. A Posenian, supposedly, since against the air of Radelix he wore that planet's unmistakable armor. No other race of even approximately human shape could "see" through a helmet of solid, opaque metal.

And in this guise Kinnison continued his investigations. That place and that man must be on this planet somewhere; the sending outfit worn by the Desplaines woman could not possibly reach any other. He had a good picture of the room and a fair picture—several pictures, in fact—of the man. The room was an actuality; all he had to do was to fill in the details which definitely, by unmistakable internal evidence, belonged there. The man was different. How much of the original picture was real, and how much of it was bias?

She was, he knew, physically fastidious in the extreme. He knew that no possible hypnotism could nullify completely the basic, the fundamental characteristics of the subconscious. The intrinsic ego could not be changed. Was the man really such a monster, or was the picture in the girl's mind partially or largely the product of her physical revulsion?

For hours he sat at a recording machine, covering yard after yard of tape with every possible picture of the man he wanted. Pictures ranging from a man almost of normal build up to a thing embodying every repulsive detail of the woman's mental image. The two extremes, he concluded, were highly improbable. Somewhere in between . . . the man *was* fat, he guessed. Fat, and had a mean pair of eyes. And, no matter how Kinnison had changed the man's physical shape he had found it impossible to eradicate a personality that was definitely bad.

"The guy's a louse," Kinnison decided, finally. "Needs killing. Glad of that—if I have to keep on fighting women much longer I'll go completely nuts. Got enough dope to identify the ape now, I think."

And again the Tellurian Lensman set out to comb the planet, city by city. Since he was not now dealing with Lensmen, every move he made had to be carefully planned and as carefully concealed. It was heartbreaking; but at long last he found a bartender who knew his quarry. He *was* fat, Kinnison discovered, and he was a bad egg. From that point on, progress was rapid. He went to the indicated city, which was, ironically enough, the very Ardith from which he had set out; and, from a bit of information here and a bit there, he tracked down his man.

Now what to do? The technique he had used so successfully upon Boysia II and in other bases could not succeed here; there were thousands of people instead of dozens, and someone would certainly catch him at it. Nor could he work at a distance. He was no Arisian, he had to be right beside his job. He would have to turn dock-walloper.

Therefore a dock-walloper he became. Not like one, but actually one. He labored prodigiously, his fine hands and his entire being becoming coarse and hardened. He ate prodigiously, and drank likewise. But, wherever he drank, his liquor was poured from the bartender's own bottle or from one of similarly innocuous contents; for then as now bartenders did not themselves imbibe the corrosively potent distillates in which they dealt. Nevertheless, Kinnison became intoxicated—boisterously, flagrantly, and pugnaciously so, as did his fellows.

He lived scrupulously within his dock-walloper's wages. Eight credits per week went to the company, in advance, for room and board; the rest he spent over the fat man's bar or gambled away at the fat man's crooked games—for Bominger, although engaged in vaster commerce far, nevertheless allowed no scruple to interfere with his esurient rapacity. Money was money, whatever its amount or source or however despicable its means of acquirement.

The Lensman knew that the games were crooked, certainly. He could see, however they were concealed, the crooked mechanisms of the wheels. He could see the crooked workings of the dealers' minds as they manipulated their crooked decks. He could read as plainly as his own the cards his crooked opponents held. But to win or to protest would have set him apart, hence he was always destitute before pay-day. Then, like his fellows, he spent his spare time loafing in the same saloon, vaguely hoping for a free drink or for a stake at cards, until one of the bouncers threw him out.

But in his every waking hour, working, gambling, or loafing, he studied Bominger and Bominger's various enterprises. The Lensman could not pierce the fat man's thought-screen, and he could never catch him without it. However, he could and did learn much. He read volume after volume of locked account books, page by page. He read secret documents, hidden in the deepest recesses of massive vaults. He listened in on conference after conference; for a thought-screen of course does not interfere with either sight or sound. The Big Shot did not own—legally—the saloon, nor the ornate, almost palatial back room which was his office. Nor did he own the dance-hall and boudoirs upstairs, nor the narrow, cell-like rooms in which addicts of twice a score of different noxious drugs gave themselves over libidinously to their addictions. Nevertheless, they were his; and they were only a part of that which was his.

Kinnison detected, traced, and identified agent after agent. With his sense of perception he followed passages, leading to other scenes, utterly indescribable here. One comparatively short gallery, however, terminated in a different setting altogether; for there, as here and perhaps everywhere, ostentation and squalor lie almost back to back. Nalizok's Cafe, the highlife hot-spot of Radelix! Downstairs innocuous enough; nothing rough—that is, too rough—was ever pulled there. Most of the robbery there was open and aboveboard, plainly written upon the checks. But there were upstairs rooms, and cellar rooms, and back rooms. And there were addicts, differing only from those others in wearing finer raiment and being of a self-styled higher stratum. Basically they were the same.

Men, women, girls even were there, in the rigid muscle-lock of thionite. Teeth hard-set, every muscle tense and straining, eyes jammed closed, fists clenched, faces white as though carved from marble, immobile in the frenzied emotion which characterizes the ultimately passionate fulfillment of every suppressed desire; in the release of their every inhibition crowding perilously close to the dividing line beyond which lay death from sheer ecstasy. That is the technique of the thionite-sniffer—to take every microgram that he can stand, to come to, shaken and too weak even to walk; to swear that he will never so degrade himself again; to come back after more as soon as he has recovered strength to do so; and finally, with an irresistible craving for stronger and ever stronger thrills, to take a larger dose than his rapidly-weakening body can endure and so to cross the fatal line.

There also were the idiotically smiling faces of the hadive smokers, the twitching members of those who preferred the Centralian nitrolabe-needle, the helplessly stupefied eaters of bentlam—but why go on? Suffice it to say that in that one city block could be found every vice and every drug enjoyed by Radeligians and the usual run of visitors; and if perchance you were an unusual visitor, desiring something unusual, Bominger could get it for you—at a price.

Kinnison studied, perceived, and analyzed. Also, he reported, via Lens, daily and copiously, to Narcotics, under Lensman's Seal.

"But Kinnison!" Winstead protested one day. "How much longer are you going to make us wait?"

"Until I get what I came after or until they get onto me," Kinnison replied, flatly. For weeks his Lens had been hidden in the side of his shoe, in a flat sheath of highly charged metal, proof against any except the most minutely searching spy-ray inspection; but this new location did not in any way interfere with its functioning.

"Any danger of that?" the Narcotics head asked, anxiously.

"Plenty—and getting worse every day. More actors in the drama. Some day I'll make a slip—I can't keep this up forever."

"Turn us loose, then," Winstead urged. "We've got enough now to blow this ring out of existence, all over the planet."

"Not yet. You're making good progress, aren't you?"

"Yes, but considering . . ."

"Don't consider it yet. Your present progress is normal for your increased force. Any more would touch off an alarm. You could take this planet's drug personnel, yes, but that isn't what I'm after. I want big game, not small fry. So sit tight until I give you the go ahead. QX?"

"Got to be QX if you say so, Kinnison. Be careful!"

"I am. Won't be long now, I'm sure. Bound to break very shortly, one way or the other. If possible, I'll give you and Gerrond warning."

Kinnison had everything lined up except the one thing he had come after—the real boss of the zwilniks. He knew where the stuff came in, and when, and how. He knew who received it, and the principal distributors of it. He knew almost all of the secret agents of the ring, and not a few even of the small-fry peddlers. He knew where the remittances went, and how much, and what for. But every lead had stopped at Bominger. Apparently the fat man was the absolute head of the drug syndicate; and that appearance didn't make sense—it *had* to be false. Bominger and the other planetary lieutenants—themselves only small fry if the Lensman's ideas were only half right—*must* get orders from, and send reports and, in all probability, payments to some Boskonian authority; of that Kinnison felt certain, but he had not been able to get even the slightest trace of that higher up.

That the communication would be established upon a thought-beam the Tellurian was equally certain. The Boskonian would not trust any ordinary, tappable communicator beam, and he certainly would not be such a fool as to send any written or taped or otherwise permanently recorded message, however coded. No, that message, when it came, would come as thought, and to receive it the fat man would have to release his screen. Then, and not until then, could Kinnison act. Action at that time might not prove simple—judging from the precautions Bominger was taking already, he would not release his screen without taking plenty more—but until then the Lensman could do nothing.

That screen had not yet been released, Kinnison could swear to that. True, he had had to sleep at times, but he had slept on a very hair-trigger, with his subconscious and his Lens set to guard that screen and to give the alarm at its first sign of weakening.

As the Lensman had foretold, the break came soon. Not in the middle of the night, as he had half-thought that it would come; nor yet in the quiet of the daylight hours. Instead, it came well before midnight, while revelry was at its height. It did not come suddenly, but was heralded by a long period of gradually increasing tension, of a mental stress very apparent to the mind of the watcher.

Agents of the drug baron came in, singly and in groups, to an altogether unprecedented number. Some of them were their usual viciously self-contained selves, others were slightly but definitely ill at ease. Kinnison, seated alone at a small table, playing a game of Radeligian solitaire, divided his attention between the big room as a whole and the office of Bominger; in neither of which was anything definite happening.

Then a wave of excitement swept over the agents as five men wearing thought-screen entered the room and, sitting down at a reserved table, called for cards and drinks; and Kinnison thought it time to send his warning.

"Gerrond! Winstead! Three-way! It's going to break soon, now, I think—tonight. Agents all over the place—five men with thought-screens here on the floor. Nervous tension high. Lots more agents outside, for blocks. General precaution, I think, not specific. Not suspicious of me, at least not exactly. Afraid of spies with a sense of perception—Rigellians or Posenians or such. Just killed an Ordovik on general principles, over on the next block. Get your gangs ready, but don't come too close—just close enough so you can be here in thirty seconds after I call you."

"What do you mean 'not exactly suspicious'? What have you done?"

"Nothing I know of—any one of a million possible small slips I may have made. Nothing serious, though, or they wouldn't have let me hang around this long."

"You're in danger. No armor, no DeLamater, no anything. Better come out of it while you can."

"And miss what I've spent all this time building up? Not a chance! I'll be able to take care of myself, I think . . . Here comes one of the boys in a screen, to talk to me. I'll leave my Lens open, so you can sort of look on."

Just then Bominger's screen went down and Kinnison invaded his mind; taking complete possession of it. Under his domination the fat man reported to the Boskonian, reported truly and fully. In turn he received orders and instructions. Had any inquisitive stranger been around, or anyone on the planet using any kind of a mind-ray machine since that quadruply-accursed Lensman had held that trial? (Oh, that was what had touched them off! Kinnison was glad to know it.) No, nothing unusual at all . . .

And just at that critical moment, when the Lensman's mind was so busy with its task, the stranger came up to his table and stared down at him dubiously, questioningly.

"Well, what's on *your* mind?" Kinnison growled. He could not spare much of his mind just then, but it did not take much of it to play his part as a dock-walloper. "You another of them slime-lizard house-numbers, snooping around to see if I'm trying to run a blazer? By Klono and all his cubs, if I hadn't lost so much money here already I'd tear up this deck and go over to Croleo's and *never* come near this crummy joint again—his rot-gut can't be any worse than yours is."

"Don't burn out a jet, pal." The agent, apparently reassured, adopted a conciliatory tone.

"Who in hell ever said you was a pal of mine, you Radelig-gig-gigian pimp?" The supposedly three-quarters-drunken, certainly three-quarters-naked Lensman got up, wobbled a little, and sat down again, heavily. "Don't 'pal' me, ape—I'm partic-hic-hicular about who I pal with."

"That's all right, big fellow; no offense intended," soothed the other. "Come on, I'll buy you a drink."

"Don't want no drink 'til I've finished this game," Kinnison grumbled, and took an instant to flash a thought via Lens. "All set, boys? Things're moving fast. If I have to take this drink—it's doped, of course—I'll bust this bird wide open. When I yell, shake the lead out of your pants!"

"Of course you want a drink!" the pirate urged. "Come and get it—it's on me, you know."

"And who are you to be buying me, a Tellurian gentleman, a drink?" the Lensman roared, flaring into one of the sudden, senseless rages of the character he had cultivated so assiduously. "Did I ask you for a drink? I'm educated, I am, and I've got money, I have. I'll buy myself a drink when I want one." His rage mounted higher and higher, visibly. "Did I *ever* ask you for a drink, you (unprintable here, even in a modern and realistic novel, for the space of two long breaths) . . . ?"

This was the blow-off. If the fellow was even half level, there would be a fight, which Kinnison could make last as long as necessary. If he did not start slugging after what Kinnison had just called him he was not what he seemed and the Lensman was surely suspect; for the Earthman had dredged the foulest vocabularies of space.

"If you weren't drunk I'd break every bone in your laxlo-soaked carcass." The other man's anger was sternly suppressed, but he looked at the dock-walloper with no friendship in his eyes. "I don't ask lousy space-port bums to drink with me every day, and when I do, they do—or else. Do you want to take that drink now or do you want a couple of the boys to work you over first? Barkeep! Bring two glasses of laxlo over here!"

Now the time was short indeed, but Kinnison would not—could not—act yet. Bominger's conference was still on; the Lensman didn't know enough yet. The fellow wasn't very suspicious, certainly, or he would have made a pass at him before this. Bloodshed meant less than nothing to these gentry; the stranger did not want to incur Bominger's wrath by killing a steady customer. The fellow probably thought the whole mind-ray story was hocuspocus, anyway—not a chance in a million of it being true. Besides he needed a machine, and Kinnison couldn't hide a thing, let alone anything as big as that "mind-ray machine" had been, because he didn't have clothes enough on to flag a hand-car with. But that free drink was certainly doped . . . Oh, they wanted to question him. It would be a truth-dope in the laxlo, then—he certainly couldn't take *that* drink!

Then came the all-important second; just as the bartender set the glasses down Bominger's interview ended. At the signing off, Kinnison got additional data, just as he had expected; and in that instant, before the drugmaster could restore his screen, the fat man died—his brain literally blasted. And in that same instant Kinnison's Lens fairly throbbed with the power of the call he sent out to his allies.

But not even Kinnison could hurl such a mental bolt without some outward sign. His face stiffened, perhaps, or his eyes may have lost their drunken, vacant stare, to take on momentarily the keen, cold ruthlessness that was for the moment his. At any rate, the enemy agent was now definitely suspicious.

"Drink that, bum, and drink it quick—or burn!" he snapped, De-Lameter out and poised.

The Tellurian's hand reached for the glass, but his mind also reached out, and faster by a second, to the brains of two nearby agents. Those worthies drew their own weapons and, with wild yells, began firing. Seemingly indiscriminately, yet in those blasts two of the thought-screened minions died. For a fraction of a second even the hard-schooled mind of Kinnison's opponent was distracted, and that fraction was time enough.

A quick flick of the wrist sent the potent liquor into the Boskonian's eyes; a lightning thrust of the knee sent the little table hurtling against his gun-hand, flinging the weapon afar. Simultaneously the Lensman's ham-like fist, urged by all the strength and all the speed of his two hundred and sixteen pounds of rawhide and whalebone, drove forward. Not for the jaw. Not for the head or the face. Lensmen know better than to mash bare hands, break fingers and knuckles, against bone. For the solar plexus. The big Patrolman's fist sank forearm-deep. The stricken zwilnik uttered one shrieking grunt, doubled up, and collapsed; never to rise again. Kinnison leaped for the fellow's DeLameter—too late, he was already hemmed in.

One—two—three—four of the nearest men died without having received a physical blow; again and again Kinnison's heavy fists and far heavier feet crashed deep into vital spots. One thought-screened enemy dived at him bodily in a Tomingan donganeur, to fall with a broken neck as the Lensman opposed instantly the only possible parry—a savage chop, edge-handed, just below the base of the skull; the while he disarmed the surviving thought-screened stranger with an accurately-hurled chair. The latter, feinting a swing, launched a vicious French kick. The Lensman, expecting anything, perceived the foot coming. His big hands shot out like striking snakes, closing and twisting savagely in the one fleeting instant, then jerking upward and backward. A hard and heavy dock-walloper's boot crashed thuddingly to a mark. A shriek rent the air and that foeman too was done.

Not fair fighting, no; nor clubby. Lensmen did not and do not fight according to the tenets of the square ring. They use the weapons provided by Mother Nature only when they must; but they can and do use them with telling effect indeed when body-to-body brawling becomes necessary. For they are skilled in the art—every Lensman has a completely detailed knowledge of all the lethal tricks of foul combat known to all the dirty fighters of ten thousand planets for twice ten thousand years.

And then the doors and windows crashed in, admitting those whom no other bifurcate race has ever faced willingly in hand-to-hand combat—full-armed Valerians, swinging their space-axes!

The gangsters broke, then, and fled in panic disorder; but escape from Narcotics' fine-meshed net was impossible. They were cut down to a man.

"QX, Kinnison?" came two hard, sharp thoughts. The Lensmen did not see the Tellurian, but Lieutenant Peter vanBuskirk did. That is, he saw him, but did not look at him.

"Hi, Kim, you little Tellurian wart!" That worthy's thought was a yell. "Ain't we got fun?"

"QX, fellows—thanks," to Gerrond and to Winstead, and "Ho, Bus! Thanks, you big, Valerian ape!" to the gigantic Dutch-Valerian with whom he had shared so many experiences in the past. "A good clean-up, fellows?"

"One hundred percent, thanks to you. We'll put you . . ."

"Don't, please. You'll clog my jets if you do. I don't appear in this anywhere—it's just one of your good, routine jobs of mopping up. Clear ether, fellows, I've got to do a flit."

"Where?" all three wanted to ask, but they didn't—the Gray Lensman was gone.

7

AMBUSCADE

Kinnison did start his flit, but he did not get far. In fact, he did not even reach his squalid room before cold reason told him that the job was only half done—yes, less than half. He had to give Boskone credit for having brains, and it was not at all likely that even such a comparatively small unit as a planetary headquarters would have only one string to its bow. They certainly would have been forced to install duplicate controls of some sort or other by the trouble they had had after Helmuth's supposedly impregnable Grand Base had been destroyed.

There were other straws pointing the same way. Where had those five strange thought-screened men come from? Bominger hadn't known of them apparently. If that idea was sound, the other headquarters would have had a spy-ray on the whole thing. Both sides used spy-rays freely, of course, and to block them was, ordinarily, worse than to let them come. The enemies' use of the thought-screen was different. They realized that it made it easy for the unknown Lensman to discover their agents, but they were forced to use it because of the deadliness of the supposed mind-ray. Why hadn't he thought of this sooner, and had the whole area blocked off? Too late to cry about it now, though.

Assume the idea correct. They certainly knew now that he was a Lensman; probably were morally certain that he was *the* Lensman. His instantaneous change from a drunken dock-walloper to a cold-sober, deadly-skilled rough-and-tumble brawler . . . and the unexplained deaths of half-a-dozen agents, as well as that of Bominger himself . . . this was bad. Very, *very* bad . . . a flare-lit tip-off, if there ever was one. Their spy-rays would have combed him, millimeter by plotted cubic millimeter: they knew exactly where his Lens was, as well as he did himself. He had put his tail right into the wringer . . . wrecked the whole job right at the start . . . unless he could get that other headquarters outfit, too, and get them before they reported in detail to Boskone.

In his room, then, he sat and thought, harder and more intensely than he had ever thought before. No ordinary method of tracing would do. It might be anywhere on the planet, and it certainly would have no connection whatever with the thionite gang. It would be a small outfit; just a few men, but under smart direction. Their purpose would be to watch the business end of the organization, but not to touch it save in an emergency. All that the two groups would have in common would be recognition signals, so that the reserves could take over in case anything happened to Bominger—as it already had. They had him, Kinnison, cold . . . What to do? WHAT TO DO?

The Lens. That must be the answer—it *had* to be. The Lens—what was it, really, anyway? Simply an aggregation of crystalloids. Not really alive; just a pseudo-life, a sort of reflection of his own life . . . he wondered . . . Great Klono's tungsten teeth, could *that* be it? An idea had struck him, an idea so stupendous in its connotations and ramifications that he gasped, shuddered, and almost went faint at the shock. He started to reach for his Lens, then forced himself to relax and shot a thought to Base.

"Gerrond! Send me a portable spy-ray block, quick!"

"But that would give everything away—that's why we haven't been using them."

"Are you telling me?" the Lensman demanded. "Shoot it along—I'll explain while it's on the way." He went on to tell the Radeligian everything he thought it well for him to know, concluding: "I'm as wide open as inter-galactic space—nothing but fast and sure moves will do us a bit of good."

The block arrived, and as soon as the messenger had departed Kinnison set it going. He was now the center of a sphere into which no spy-ray beam could penetrate. He was also an object of suspicion to anyone using a spy-ray, but that fact made no difference, then. Snatching off his shoe, he took out his Lens, wrapped it in a handkerchief, and placed it on the floor. Then, just as though he still wore it, he directed a thought at Winstead.

"All serene, Lensman?" he asked, quietly.

"Everything's on the beam," came instant reply. "Why?"

"Just checking, is all." Kinnison did not specify exactly what he was checking!

He then did something which, so far as he knew, no Lensman had ever before even thought of doing. Although he felt stark naked without his Lens, he hurled a thought three-quarters of the way across the galaxy to that dread planet Arisia; a thought narrowed down to the exact pattern of Mentor himself—the gigantic, fearsome Brain who had been his teacher and his sponsor.

"Ah, 'tis Kimball Kinnison, of Earth," that entity responded, in precisely the same modulation it had employed once before. "You have perceived, then, youth, that the Lens is not the supremely important thing you have supposed it to be?"

"I . . . you . . . I mean . . ." the flustered Lensman, taken completely aback, was cut off by a sharp rebuke.

"Stop! You are thinking muddily—conduct ordinarily inexcusable! Now, youth, to redeem yourself, you will explain the phenomenon to me, instead of asking me to explain it to you. I realize that you have just discovered another facet of the Cosmic Truth; I know what a shock it has been to your immature mind; hence for this once it may be permissible for me to overlook your crime. But strive not to repeat the offense, for I tell you again in all possible seriousness—I cannot urge upon you too strongly the fact—that in clear and precise thinking lies your only safeguard through that which you are attempting. Confused, wandering thought will assuredly bring disaster inevitable and irreparable."

"Yes, sir," Kinnison replied meekly; a small boy reprimanded by his teacher. "It must be this way. In the first stage of training the Lens is a necessity; just as is the crystal ball or some other hypnotic object in a seance. In the more advanced stage the mind is able to work without aid. The Lens, however, may be—in fact, it must be—endowed with uses other than that of a symbol of identification; uses about which I as yet know nothing. Therefore, while I can work without it, I should not do so except when it is absolutely necessary, as its help will be imperative if I am to advance to any higher stage. It is also clear that you were expecting my call. May I ask if I am on time?"

"You are—your progress has been highly satisfactory. Also, I note with approval that you are not asking for help in your admittedly difficult present problem."

"I know it wouldn't do me any good—and why." Kinnison grinned wryly. "But I'll bet that Worsel, when he comes up for his second treatment, will know on the spot what it has taken me all this time to find out."

"You deduce truly. He did."

"What? He has been back there already? And you told me . . ."

"What I told you was true and is. His mind is more fully developed and more responsive than yours; yours is of vastly greater latent capacity, capability, and force," and the line of communication snapped.

Calling a conveyance, Kinnison was whisked to Base, the spy-ray block full on all the way. There, in a private room, he put his heavily-insulated Lens and a full spool of tape into a ray-proof container, sealed it, and called in the base commander.

"Gerrond, here is a package of vital importance," he informed him. "Among other things, it contains a record of everything I have done to date. If I don't come back to claim it myself, please send it to Prime Base for personal delivery to Port Admiral Haynes. Speed will be no object, but safety very decidedly of the essence."

"QX—we'll send it in by special messenger."

"Thanks a lot. Now I wonder if I could use your visiphone a minute? I want to talk to the zoo."

"Certainly."

"Zoological Gardens?" and the image of an elderly, white-bearded man appeared upon the plate. "Lensman Kinnison of Tellus—Unattached. Have you as many as three oglons, caged together?"

"Yes. In fact, we have four of them in one cage."

"Better yet. Will you please send them over here to base at once? Lieutenant-Admiral Gerrond, here, will confirm."

"It is most unusual, sir," the graybeard began, but broke off at a curt word from Gerrond. "Very well, sir," he agreed, and disconnected.

"Oglons?" the surprised commander demanded. "OGLONS!"

For the oglon, or Radeligian cateagle, is one of the fiercest, most intractable beasts of prey in existence; it assays more concentrated villainy and more sheerly vicious ferocity to the gram than any other creature known to science. It is not a bird, but a winged mammal; and is armed not only with the gripping, tearing talons of the eagle, but also with the heavy, cruel, needle-sharp fangs of the wildcat. And its mental attitude toward all other forms of life is anti-social to the nth degree.

"Oglons." Kinnison confirmed, shortly. "I can handle them."

"You can, of course. But . . ." Gerrond stopped. This Gray Lensman was forever doing amazing, unprecedented, incomprehensible things. But, so far, he had produced eminently satisfactory results, and he could not be expected to spend all his time in explanations.

"But you think I'm screwy, huh?"

"Oh, no, Kinnison, I wouldn't say that. I only . . . well . . . after all, there isn't much real evidence that we didn't mop up one hundred percent."

"Much? Real evidence? There isn't any," the Tellurian assented, cheerfully enough. "But you've got the wrong slant entirely on these people. You are still thinking of them as gangsters, desperadoes, renegade scum of our own civilization. They're not. They are just as smart as we are; some of them are smarter. Perhaps I'm taking unnecessary precautions; but, if so, there's no harm done. On the other hand, there are two things at stake which, to me at least, are extremely important; this whole job of mine and my life: and remember this—the minute I leave this base both of those things are in your hands."

To that, of course, there could be no answer.

While the two men had been talking and while the oglons were being brought out, two trickling streams of men had been passing, one into and one out of the spy-ray-shielded confines of the base. Some of these men were heavily bearded, some were shaven clean, but all had two things in common. Each one was human in type and each one in some respect or other resembled Kimball Kinnison.

"Now remember, Gerrond," the Gray Lensman said impressively as he was about to leave, "They're probably right here in Ardith, but they may be anywhere on the planet. Keep a spy-ray on me wherever I go, and trace theirs if you can. That will take some doing, as he's bound to be an expert. Keep those oglons at least a mile—thirty seconds flying time—away from me; get all the Lensmen you can on the job; keep a cruiser and a speedster hot, but not too close. I may need any of them, or all, or none of them, I can't tell; but I do know this—if I need anything at all, I'll need it fast. Above all, Gerrond, by the Lens you wear, do nothing whatever, no matter what happens around me or to me, until I give you the word. QX?"

"QX, Gray Lensman. Clear ether!"

Kinnison took a ground-cab to the mouth of the narrow street upon which was situated his dock-walloper's mean lodging. This was a desperate, a foolhardy trick—but in its very boldness, in its insolubly paradoxical aspects, lay its strength. Probably Boskone could solve its puzzles, but—he hoped—this ape, not being Boskone, couldn't. And, paying off the cabman, he thrust his hands into his tattered pockets and, whistling blithely if a bit raucously through his stained teeth, he strode off down the narrow way as though he did not have a care in the world. But he was doing the finest job of acting of his short career; even though, for all he really knew, he might not have any audience at all. For inwardly, he was strung to highest tension. His sense of perception, sharply alert, was covering the full hemisphere around and above him; his mind was triggered to jerk any muscle of his body into instantaneous action.

Meanwhile, in a heavily guarded room, there sat a manlike being, humanoid to eight places. For two hours he had been sitting at his spy-ray plate, studying with ever-growing uneasiness the human beings so suddenly and so surprisingly numerously having business at the Patrol's base. For minutes he had been studying minutely a man in a ground-cab, and his uneasiness reached panic heights.

"It *is* the Lensman!" he burst out. "It's *got* to be, Lens or no Lens. Who else would have the cold nerve to go back there when he knows he's let the cat completely out of the bag?"

"Well, get him, then," advised his companion. "All set, ain't you?"

"But it *can't* be!" the chief went on, reversing himself in mid-flight. "A Lensman has *got* to have a Lens, and a Lens *can't* be invisible! And this fellow has not now, and never has had, a mind-ray machine. He hasn't got *anything!* And besides, the Lensman we're after wouldn't be sticking around—he disappears."

"Well, drop him and chase somebody else, then," the lieutenant advised, unfeelingly.

"But there's nobody nearly enough like him!" snarled the chief, in desperation. He was torn by doubt and indecision. This whole situation was a mess—it didn't add up right, from any possible angle. "It's got to be him—it can't be anybody else. I've checked and rechecked him. It *is* him, and not a double. He thinks he's safe enough; he can't know about us—can't even suspect. Besides, his only good double, Fordyce— and *he's* not good enough to stand the inspection I just gave him—hasn't appeared anywhere."

"Probably inside base yet. Maybe this is a better double. Perhaps this *is* the real Lensman pretending he isn't, or maybe the real Lensman is slipping out while you're watching the man in the cab," the junior suggested, helpfully.

"Shut up!" the superior yelled. He started to reach for a switch, but paused, hand in air.

"Go ahead. That's it, call District and toss it into their laps, if it's too hot for you to handle. I think myself whoever did this job is a warm number—plenty warm."

"And get my ears burned off with that 'your report is neither complete nor conclusive' of his?" the chief sneered. "And get reduced for incompetence besides? No, we've got to do it ourselves, and do it right . . . but that man there isn't the Lensman—he can't be!"

"Well, you'd better make up your mind—you haven't got all day. And nix on that 'we' stuff. It's *you* that's got to do it—you're the boss, not me," the underling countered, callously. For once, he was really glad that he was not the one in command. "And you'd better get busy and do it, too."

"I'll do it," the chief declared, grimly. "There's a way."

There was a way. One only. He must be brought in alive and compelled to divulge the truth. There was no other way.

The Boskonian touched a stud and spoke. "Don't kill him—bring him in alive. If you kill him even accidentally I'll kill both of you, myself."

The Gray Lensman made his carefree way down the alley-like thoroughfare, whistling inharmoniously and very evidently at peace with the Universe.

It takes something, friends, to walk knowingly into a trap; without betraying emotion or stress even while a black-jack, wielded by a strong arm, is descending toward the back of your head. Something of quality, something of fiber, something of *je ne sais quoi.* But whatever it took Kinnison in ample measure had.

He did not wink, flinch, or turn an eye as the billy came down. Only as it touched his hair did he act, exerting all his marvelous muscular control to jerk forward and downward, with the weapon and ahead of it, to spare himself as much as possible of the terrific blow.

The black-jack crunched against the base of the Lensman's skull in a shower of coruscating constellations. He fell. He lay there, twitching feebly.

8

CATEAGLES

As has been said, Kinnison rode the blow of the blackjack forward and downward, thus robbing it of some of its power. It struck him hard enough so that the thug did not suspect the truth; he thought that he had all but taken the Lensman's life. And, for all the speed with which the Tellurian had yielded before the blow, he was hurt; but he was not stunned. Therefore, although he made no resistance when the two bullies rolled him over, lashed his feet together, tied his hands behind him, and lifted him into a car, he was fully conscious throughout the proceedings.

When the cab was perhaps half an hour upon its way the Lensman struggled back, quite realistically, to consciousness.

"Take it easy, pal," the larger of his thought-screened captors advised, dandling the black-jack suggestively before his eyes. "One yelp out of you, or a signal, if you've got one of them Lenses, and I bop you another one."

"What the blinding blue hell's coming off here?" demanded the dock-walloper, furiously. "Wha'd'ya think you're doing, you lop-eared . . ." and he cursed the two, viciously and comprehensively.

"Shut up or he'll knock you kicking," the smaller thug advised from the driver's seat, and Kinnison subsided. "Not that it bothers me any, but you're making too damn much noise."

"But what's the matter?" Kinnison asked, more quietly. "What'd you slug me for and drag me off? I ain't done nothing and I ain't got nothing."

"I don't know nothing," the big agent replied. "The boss will tell you all you need to know when we get to where we're going. All I know is the boss says to bop you easy-like and bring you in alive if you don't act up. He says to tell you not to yell and not to use no Lens. If you yell we burn you out. If you use any Lens, the boss he's got his eyes on all the bases and spaceports and everything, and if any help starts to come this way he'll tell us and we fry you and buzz off. We can kill you and flit before any help can get near you, he says."

"Your boss ain't got the brains of a fontema," Kinnison growled. He knew that the boss, wherever he was, could hear every word. "Hell's hinges, if I was a Lensman you think I'd be walloping junk on a dock? Use your head, cully, if you got one."

"I wouldn't know nothing about that," the other returned, stolidly.

"But I ain't got no Lens!" the dock-walloper stormed, in exasperation. "Look at me—frisk me! You'll see I ain't!"

"All that ain't none of my dish." The thug was entirely unmoved. "I don't know nothing and I don't do nothing except what the boss tells me, see? Now take it easy, all nice and quiet-like. If you don't," and he flicked the black-jack lightly against the Lensman's knee, "I'll put out your landing-lights. I'll lay you like a mat, and I don't mean maybe. See?"

Kinnison saw, and relapsed into silence. The automobile rolled along. And, flitting industriously about upon its delivery duties, but never much more or less than one measured mile distant, a panel job pursued its devious way. Oddly enough, its chauffeur was a Lensman. Here and there, high in the heavens, were a few airplanes, gyros, and copters; but they were going peacefully and steadily about their business—even though most of them happened to have Lensmen as pilots.

And, not at the base at all, but high in the stratosphere and so thoroughly screened that a spy-ray observer could not even tell that his gaze was being blocked, a battle-cruiser, Lensman-commanded, rode poised upon flare-baffled, softly hissing under-jets. And, equally high and as adequately protected against observation, a keen-eyed Lensman sat at the controls of a speedster, jazzing her muffled jets and peering eagerly through a telescopic sight. As far as the Patrol was concerned, everything was on the trips.

The car approached the gates of a suburban estate and stopped. It waited. Kinnison knew that the Boskonian within was working his every beam, alert for any sign of Patrol activity; knew that if there were any such sign the car would be off in an instant. But there was no activity. Kinnison sent a thought to Gerrond, who relayed micrometric readings of the objective to various Lensmen. Still everyone waited. Then the gate opened of itself, the two thugs jerked their captive out of the car to the ground, and Kinnison sent out his signal.

Base remained quiet, but everything else erupted at once. The airplanes wheeled, cruiser and speedster plummeted downward at maximum blast. The panel job literally fell open, as did the cage within it, and four ravening cateagles, with the silent ferocity of their kind, rocketed toward their goal.

Although the oglons were not as fast as the flying ships they did not have nearly as far to go, wherefore they got there first. The thugs had no warning whatever. One instant everything was under control; in the next the noiselessly arrowing destroyers struck their prey with the mad fury that only a striking cateagle can exhibit. Barbed talons dug viciously into eyes, faces, mouths, tearing, rending, wrenching; fierce-driven fangs tore deeply, savagely into defenseless throats.

Once each the thugs screamed in mad, lethal terror, but no warning was given; for by that time every building upon that pretentious estate had disappeared in the pyrotechnic flare of detonating duodec. The pellets were small, of course—the gunners did not wish either to destroy the nearby residences or to injure Kinnison—but they were powerful enough for the purpose intended. Mansion and outbuildings disappeared, and not even the most thoroughgoing spy-ray search revealed the presence of anything animate or structural where those buildings had been.

The panel job drove up and Kinnison, perceiving that the cateagles had done their work, sent them back into their cage. The Lensman driver, after securely locking cage and truck, cut the Earthman's bonds.

"QX, Kinnison?" he asked.

"QX, Barknett—thanks," and the two Lensmen, one in the panel truck and the other in the gangsters' car, drove back to headquarters. There Kinnison recovered his package.

"This has got me all of a soapy dither, but you have called the turn on every play yet," Winstead told the Tellurian, later. "Is this all of the big shots, do you think, or are there some more of them around here?"

"Not around here, I'm pretty sure," Kinnison replied. "No, two main lines is all they would have had, I think . . . this time. Next time . . ."

"There won't be any next time," Winstead declared.

"Not on this planet, no. Knowing what to expect, you fellows can handle anything that comes up. I was thinking then of my next step."

"Oh. But you'll get 'em, Gray Lensman!"

"I hope so," soberly.

"Luck, Kinnison!"

"Clear ether, Winstead!" and this time the Tellurian really did flit.

As his speedster ripped through the void Kinnison did more thinking, but he was afraid that Menter would have considered the product muddy indeed. He couldn't seem to get to the first check-station. One thing was limpidly clear; this line of attack or any very close variation of it would never work again. He'd have to think up something new. So far, he had got away with his stuff because he had kept one lap ahead of them, but how much longer could he manage to keep up the pace?

Bominger had been no mental giant, of course; but this other lad was nobody's fool and this next higher-up, with whom he had had the interview via Bominger, would certainly prove to be a really shrewd number.

" 'The higher the fewer,' " he repeated to himself the old saying, adding, "and in this case, the smarter." He had to put out some jets, but where he was going to get the fuel he simply didn't know.

Again the trip to Tellus was uneventful, and the Gray Lensman, the symbol of his rank again flashing upon his wrist, sought interview with Haynes.

"Send him in, certainly—send him in!" Kinnison heard the communicator crackle, and the receptionist passed him along. He paused in surprise, however, at the doorway of the office, for Surgeon-Marshal Lacy and a Posenian were in conference with the Port Admiral.

"Come in, Kinnison," Haynes invited. "Lacy wants to see you a minute, too. Doctor Phillips—Lensman Kinnison, Unattached. His name isn't Phillips, of course; we gave him that in self-defense, to keep from trying to pronounce his real one."

Phillips, the Posenian, was as tall as Kinnison, and heavier. His figure was somewhat human in shape, but not in detail. He had four arms instead of two, each arm had two opposed hands, and each hand had two thumbs, one situated about where a little finger would be expected. He had no eyes, not even vestigial ones. He had two broad, flat noses and two toothful mouths; one of each in what would ordinarily be called the front of his round, shining, hairless head; the other in the back. Upon the sides of his head were large, volute, highly dirigible ears. And, like most races having the faculty of perception instead of that of sight, his head was relatively immobile, his neck being short, massive, and tremendously strong.

"You look well, very well," Lacy reported, after feeling and prodding vigorously the members which had been in his splints and casts so long. "Have to take a picture, of course, before saying anything definite. No, we won't either, now. Phillips, look at his . . ." an interlude of technical jargon . . . "and see what kind of a recovery he has made." Then, while the Posenian was examining Kinnison's interior mechanisms, the Surgeon-Marshal went on:

"Wonderful diagnosticians and surgeons, these Posenians—can see into the patient without taking him apart. In another few centuries every doctor will have to have the sense of perception. Phillips is doing a research in neurology—more particularly a study of the neural synapse and the proliferation of neural dendrites . . ."

"La—cy-y-y!" Haynes drawled the word in reproof. "I've told you a thousand times to talk English when you're talking to me. How about it, Kinnison?"

"Afraid I can't quite check you, chief," Kinnison grinned. "Specialists—precisionists—can't talk in Basic."

"Right, my boy—surprisingly and pleasingly right!" Lacy exclaimed. "Why can't you adopt that attitude, Haynes, and learn enough words so you can understand what a man's talking about? But to reduce it to monosyllabic simplicity, Phillips is studying a thing that has baffled us for thousands of years. The lower forms of cells are able to regenerate themselves; wounds heal, bones knit. Higher types, such as nerve cells, regenerate imperfectly, if at all; and the highest type, the brain cells, do not do so under any conditions." He turned a reproachful gaze upon Haynes. "This is terrible. Those statements are pitiful—inadequate—false. Worse than that—practically meaningless. What I wanted to say, and what I'm going to say, is that . . ."

"Oh no you aren't, not in this office," his old friend interrupted. "We got the idea perfectly. The question is, why can't human beings repair nerves or spinal cords, or grow new ones? If such a worthless beastie as a starfish can grow a whole new body to one leg, including a brain, if any, why can't a really intelligent victim of simple infantile paralysis—or a ray—recover the use of a leg that is otherwise in perfect shape?"

"Well, that's something like it, but I hope you can aim closer than that at a battleship," Lacy grunted. "We'll buzz off now, Phillips, and leave these two war-horses alone."

"Here is my report in detail." Kinnison placed the package upon the Port Admiral's desk as soon as the room was sealed behind the visitors. "I talked to you direct about most of it—this is for the record."

"Of course. Mighty glad you found Medon, for our sake as well as theirs. They have things that we need, badly."

"Where did they put them? I suggested a sun near Sol, so as to have them handy to Prime Base."

"Right next door—Alpha Centauri. Didn't get to do much scouting, did you?"

"I'll say we didn't. Boskonia owns that galaxy; lock, stock, and barrel. May be some other independent planets—bound to be, of course; probably a lot of them—but it's too dangerous, hunting them at this stage of the game. But at that, we did enough, for the time being. We proved our point. Boskone, if there is any such being, is certainly in the Second Galaxy. However, it will be a long time before we're ready to carry the war there to him, and in the meantime we've got a lot to do. Check?"

"To nineteen decimals."

"It seems to me, then, that while you are rebuilding our first-line ships, super-powering them with Medonian insulation and conductors, I had better keep on tracing Boskone along the line of drugs. I'm just about sure that they're back of the whole drug business."

"And in some ways their drugs are more dangerous to Civilization than their battleships. More insidious and, ultimately, more fatal."

"Check. And since I am perhaps as well equipped as any of the other Lensmen to cope with that particular problem . . . ?" Kinnison paused, questioningly.

"That certainly is no overstatement," the Port Admiral replied, dryly. You're the *only* one equipped to cope with it."

"None of the other boys except Worsel, then? . . . I heard that a couple . . ."

"They thought they had a call, but they didn't. All they had was a wish. They came back."

"Too bad . . . but I can see how it would be. It's a rough course, and if a man's mind isn't completely ready for it, it burns it out. It almost does, anyway . . . mind is a funny thing. But that isn't getting us anywhere. Can you take time to let me talk at you a few minutes?"

"I certainly can. You've got the most important assignment in the galaxy, and I'd like to know more about it, if it's anything you can pass on."

"Nothing that need be sealed from any Lensman. The main object of all of us, as you know, is to push Boskonia out of this galaxy. From a military standpoint they practically *are* out. Their drug syndicate, however, is very decidedly in, and getting in deeper all the time. Therefore we next push the zwilniks out. They have peddlers and such small fry, who deal with distributors and so on. These fellows form the bottom layer. Above them are the secret agents, the observers, and the wholesale handlers; runners and importers. All these folks are directed and controlled by one man, the boss of each planetary organization. Thus, Bominger was the boss of all zwilnik activities on the whole planet of Radelix.

"In turn the planetary bosses report to, and are synchronized and controlled by a Regional Director, who supervises the activities of a couple of hundred or so planetary outfits. I got a line on the one over Bominger, you know—Prellin, the Kalonian. By the way, you knew, didn't you, that Helmuth was a Kalonian, too?"

"I got it from the tape. Smart people, they must be, but not my idea of good neighbors."

"I'll say not. Well, that's all I really *know* of their organization. It seems logical to suppose, though, that the structure is coherent all the way up. If so, the Regional Directors would be under some higher-up, possibly a Galactic Director, who in turn might be under Boskone himself—or one of his cabinet officers, at least. Perhaps the Galactic Director might even be a cabinet officer in their government, whatever it is?"

"An ambitious program you've got mapped out for yourself. How are you figuring on swinging it?"

"That's the rub—I don't know," Kinnison confessed, ruefully. "But if it's done at all, that's the way I've got to go about it. Any other way would take a thousand years and more men than we'll ever have. This way works fine, when it works at all."

"I can see that—lop off the head and the body dies," Haynes agreed.

"That's the way it works—especially when the head keeps detailed records and books covering the activities of all the members of his body. With Bominger and the others gone, and with full transcripts of his accounts, the boys mopped up Radelix in a hurry. From now on it will be simple to keep it clean, except of course for the usual bootleg trickle, and that can be reduced to a minimum. Similarly, if we can put this Prellin away and take a good look at his ledgers, it will be easy to clear up his two hundred planets. And so on."

"Very clear, and quite simple . . . in theory." The older man was thoughtful and frankly dubious. "In practice, difficult in the extreme."

"But necessary," the younger insisted.

"I suppose so," Haynes assented finally. "Useless to tell you not to take chances—you'll have to—but for all our sakes, if not for your own, be as careful as you can."

"I'll do that, chief. I think a lot of me. As much as anybody—maybe more—and 'Careful' is my middle name."

"Ummmh," Haynes grunted, skeptically. "We've noticed that. Anything special you want done?"

"Yes, very special," Kinnison surprised him by answering in the affirmative. "You know that the Medonians developed a scrambler for a detector nullifier. Hotchkiss and the boys developed a new line of attack on that—against long-range stuff we're probably safe—but they haven't been able to do a thing on electromagnetics. Well, the Boskonians, beginning with Prellin, are going to start wondering what has been happening. Then, if I succeed in getting Prellin, they're bound to start doing things. One thing they'll do will be to fix up their headquarters so that they'll have about five hundred percent overlap on their electros. Perhaps they'll have outposts, too, close enough together to have the same thing there—possibly two or three hundred even on visuals."

"In that case you stay out."

"Not necessarily. What do electros work on?"

"Iron, I suppose—they did when I went to school last."

"The answer, then, is to build me a speedster that is inherently undetectable—absolutely non-ferrous. Berylumin and so on for all the structural parts . . ."

"But you've got to have silicon-steel cores for your electrical equipment!"

"I was coming to that. Have you? I was reading in the 'Transactions' the other day that force-fields had been used in big units, and were more efficient. Some of the smaller units, instruments and so on, might have to have some iron, but wouldn't it be possible to so saturate those small pieces with a dense field of detector frequencies that they wouldn't react?"

"I don't know. Never thought of it. Would it?"

"I don't know, either—I'm not telling you, I'm just making suggestions. I do know one thing, though. We've got to keep ahead of them—think of things first and oftenest, and be ready to abandon them for something else as soon as we've used them once."

"Except for those primary projectors." Haynes grinned wryly. "They can't be abandoned—even with Medonian power we haven't been able to develop a screen that will stop them. We've got to keep them secret from Boskone—and in that connection I want to compliment you on the suggestion of having Velantian Lensmen as mind-readers wherever those projectors are even being thought of."

"You caught spies, then? How many?"

"Not many—three or four in each base—but enough to have done the damage. Now, I believe, for the first time in history, we can be *sure* of our entire personnel."

"I think so. Mentor says the Lens is enough, if we use it properly. That's up to us."

"But how about visuals?" Haynes was still worrying, and to good purpose.

"Well, we have a black coating now that's ninety nine percent absorptive, and I don't need ports or windows. At that, though, one percent reflection would be enough to give me away at a critical time. How'd it be to put a couple of the boys on that job? Have them put a decimal point after the ninety nine and see how many nines they can tack on behind it?"

"That's a thought, Kinnison. They'll have lots of time to work on it while the engineers are trying to fill your specifications as to a speedster. But you're right, dead right. We—or rather, you—have got to outthink them; and it certainly is up to us to do everything we can to build the apparatus to put your thoughts into practice. And it isn't at some vague time in the future that Boskone is going to start doing something about you and what you've done. It's right now; or even, more probably, a week or so ago. But you haven't said a word yet about the really big job you have in mind."

"I've been putting that off until the last," the Gray Lensman's voice held obscure puzzlement. "The fact is that I simply can't get a tooth into it—can't get a grip on it anywhere. I don't know enough about math or physics. Everything comes out negative for me; not only inertia, but also force, velocity, and even mass itself. Final results always contain an 'i,' too, the square root of minus one. I can't get rid of it, and I don't see how it can be built into any kind of apparatus. It may not be workable at all, but before I give up the idea I'd like to call a conference, if it's QX with you and the Council."

"Certainly it is QX with us. You're forgetting again, aren't you, that you're a Gray Lensman?" Haynes' voice held no reproof, he was positively beaming with a super-fatherly pride.

"Not exactly." Kinnison blushed, almost squirmed. "I'm just too much of a cub to be sticking my neck out so far, is all. The idea may be—probably is—wilder than a Radeligian cateagle. The only kind of a conference that could even begin to handle it would cost a young fortune, and I don't want to spend that much money on my own responsibility."

"To date your ideas have worked out well enough so that the Council is backing you one hundred percent," the older man said, dryly. "Expense is no object." Then, his voice changing markedly, "Kim, have you any idea at all of the financial resources of the Patrol?"

"Very little, sir, if any, I'm afraid," Kinnison confessed.

"Here on Tellus alone we have an expendable reserve of over ten thousand million credits. With the restriction of government to its proper sphere and its concentration into our organization, resulting in the liberation of manpower into wealth-producing enterprise, and especially with the enormous growth of inter-world commerce, world-income increased to such a point that taxation could be reduced to a minimum; and the lower the taxes the more flourishing business became and the greater the income.

"Now the tax rate is the lowest in history. The total income tax, for instance, in the highest bracket, is only three point five nine two percent. At that, however, if it had not been for the recent slump, due to Boskonian interference with inter-systemic commerce, we would have had to reduce the tax rate again to avoid serious financial difficulty due to the fact that too much of the galactic total of circulating credit would have been concentrated in the expendable funds of the Galactic Patrol. So don't even think of money. Whether you want to spend a thousand credits, a million, or a thousand million; go ahead."

"Thanks, Chief; glad you explained. I'll feel better now about spending money that doesn't belong to me. Now if you'll give me, for about a week, the use of the librarian in charge of science files and a galactic beam, I'll quit bothering you."

"I'll do that." The Port Admiral touched a button and in a few minutes a trimly attractive blonde entered the room. "Miss Hostetter, this is Lensman Kinnison, Unattached. Please turn over your regular duties to an assistant and work with him until he releases you. Whatever he says, goes; the sky's the limit."

In the Library of Science Kinnison outlined his problem briefly to his new aide, concluding:

"I want only about fifty, as a larger group could not cooperate efficiently. Are your lists arranged so that you can skim off the top fifty?"

"Such a group can be selected, I think." The girl stood for a moment, lower lip held lightly between white teeth. "That is not a standard index, but each scientist has a rating. I can set the acceptor . . . no, the rejector would be better—to throw out all the cards above any given rating. If we take out all ratings over seven hundred we will have only the highest of the geniuses."

"How many, do you suppose?"

"I have only a vague idea—a couple of hundred, perhaps. If too many, we can run them again at a higher level, say seven ten. But there won't be very many, since there are only two galactic ratings higher than seven fifty. There will be duplications, too—such people as Sir Austin Cardynge will have two or three cards in the final rejects."

"QX—we'll want to hand-pick the fifty, anyway. Let's go!"

Then for hours bale after bale of cards went through the machine; thousands of records per minute. Occasionally one card would flip out into a rack, rejected. Finally:

"That's all, I think. Mathematicians, physicists," the librarian ticked off upon pink fingers. "Astronomers, philosophers, and this new classification, which hasn't been named yet."

"The H.T.T.'s." Kinnison glanced at the label, lightly lettered in pencil, fronting the slim packet of cards. "Aren't you going to run them through, too?"

"No. These are the two I mentioned a minute ago—the only ones higher than seven hundred fifty."

"A choice pair, eh? Sort of a *creme de la creme?* Let's look 'em over," and he extended his hand. "What do the initials stand for?"

"I'm awfully sorry, sir, really," the girl flushed in embarrassment as she relinquished the cards in high reluctance. "If I'd had any idea we wouldn't have dared—we call you, among ourselves, the 'High-Tension Thinkers.' "

"Us!" It was the Lensman's turn to flush. Nevertheless, he took the packet and read sketchily the facer: "Class XIX—Unclassifiable at present . . . lack of adequate methods . . . minds of range and scope far beyond any available indices . . . Ratings above high genius (750) . . . yet no instability . . . power beyond any heretofore known . . . assigned ratings tentative and definitely minimum."

He then read the cards.

"Worsel, Velantia, eight hundred."

And:

"Kimball Kinnison, Tellus, eight hundred seventy-five."

9

EICH AND ARISIAN

The Port Admiral was eminently correct in supposing that Boskone, whoever or whatever he or it might be, was already taking action upon what the Tellurian Lensman had done. For, even as Kinnison was at work in the Library of Science, a meeting which was indirectly to affect him no little was being called to order.

In the immensely distant Second Galaxy was that meeting being held; upon the then planet Jarnevon of the Eich; within that sullen fortress already mentioned briefly. Presiding over it was the indescribable entity known to history as Eichlan; or, more properly, Lan of the Eich.

"Boskone is now in session," that entity announced to the eight other similar monstrosities who in some fashion indescribable to man were stationed at the long, low, wide bench of stone-like material which served as a table of state. "Nine days ago each of us began to search for whatever new facts might bear upon the activities of the as yet entirely hypothetical Lensman who, Helmuth believed, was the real force back of our recent intolerable reverses in the Tellurian Galaxy.

"As First of Boskone I will report as to the military situation. As you know, our positions there became untenable with the fall of our Grand Base and all our mobile forces were withdrawn. In order to facilitate reorganization, coordinating ships were sent out. Some of these ships went to planets held in toto by us. Not one of these vessels has been able to report any pertinent facts whatever. Ships approaching bases of the Patrol, or encountering Patrol ships of war in space, simply ceased communicating. Even their automatic recorders ceased to function without transmitting any intelligible data, indicating complete destruction of those ships. A cascade system, in which one ship followed another at long range and with analytical instruments set to determine the nature of any beam or weapon employed, was attempted. The enemy, however, threw out blanketing zones of tremendous power; and we lost six more vessels without obtaining the desired data. These are the facts, all negative. Theorizing, deduction, summation, and integration will as usual come later. Eichmil, Second of Boskone, will now report."

"My facts are also entirely negative," the Second began. "Soon after our operations upon the planet Radelix became productive of results a contingent of Tellurian narcotic agents arrived; which may or may not have included the Lensman . . ."

"Stick to facts for the time being." Eichlan ordered, curtly.

"Shortly thereafter a minor agent, a female instructed to wear a thought-screen at all times, lost her usefulness by suffering a mental disorder which incapacitated her quite seriously. Then another agent, also a female, this time one of the third order and who had been very useful up to that time, ceased reporting. A few days later Bominger, the Planetary Director, failed to report, as did the Planetary Observer; who, as you know, was entirely unknown to, and had no connection with, the operating staff. Reports from other sources, such as importers and shippers—these, I believe, are here admissible as facts—indicate that all our personnel upon Radelix have been liquidated. No unusual developments have occurred upon any other planet, nor has any significant fact, however small, been discovered."

"Eichnor, Third of Boskone."

"Also negative. Our every source of information from within the bases of the Patrol has been shut off. Every one of our representatives, some of whom have been reporting regularly for many years, has been silent, and every effort to reach any of them has failed."

"Eichsnap, Fourth of Boskone."

"Utterly negative. We have been able to find no trace whatever of the planet Medon, or of any one of the twenty one warships investing it at the time of its disappearance."

And so on, through nine reports, while the tentacles of the mighty First of Boskone played intermittently over the keys of a complex instrument or machine before him.

"We will now reason, theorize, and draw conclusions," the First announced, and each of the organisms fed his ideas and deductions into the machine. It whirred briefly, then ejected a tape, which Eichlan took up and scanned narrowly.

"Rejecting all conclusions having a probability of less than ninety five percent," he announced, "we have: First, a set of three probabilities of a value of ninety nine and ninety nine one-hundredths—virtual certainties—that some one Tellurian Lensman is the prime mover behind what has happened; that he has acquired a mental power heretofore unknown to his race; and that he has been in large part responsible for the development of the Patrol's new and formidable weapons. Second, a probability of ninety nine percent that he and his organization are no longer on the defensive, but have assumed the offensive. Third, one of ninety seven percent that it is not primarily Tellus which is an obstacle, even though the Galactic Patrol and Civilization did originate upon that planet, but Arisia; that Helmuth's report was at least partially true. Fourth, one of ninety five and one half percent that the Lens is also concerned in the disappearance of the planet Medon. There is a lesser probability, but still of some ninety four percent, that that same Lensman is involved here.

"I will interpolate here that the vanishment of that planet is a much more serious matter than it might appear, on the surface, to be. *In situ,* it was a thing of no concern—gone, it becomes an affair of almost vital import. To issue orders impossible of fulfillment, as Helmuth did when he said 'Comb Trenco, inch by inch,' is easy. To comb this galaxy star by star for Medon would be an even more difficult and longer task; but what can be done is being done.

"To return to the conclusions, they point out a state of things which I do not have to tell you is really grave. This is the first major set-back which the culture of the Boskone has encountered since it began its rise. You are familiar with that rise; how we of the Eich took over in turn a city, a race, a planet, a solar system, a region, a galaxy. How we extended our sway into the Tellurian Galaxy, as a preliminary to the extension of our authority throughout all the populated galaxies of the macro-cosmic Universe.

"You know our creed; to the victor the power. He who is strongest and fittest shall survive and shall rule. This so-called Civilization which is opposing us, which began upon Tellus but whose driving force is that which dwells upon Arisia, is a soft, weak, puny-spirited thing indeed to resist the mental and material power of our culture. Myriads of beings upon each planet, each one striving for power and, so striving, giving of that power to him above. Myriads of planets, each, in return for our benevolently despotic control, delegating and contributing power to the

Eich. All this power, delegated to the thousands of millions of the Eich of this planet, culminates in and is wielded by the nine of us, who comprise Boskone.

"Power! Our forefathers thought that control of one planet was enough. Later it was declared that mastery of a galaxy, if realized, would sate ambition. We of Boskone, however, now know that our power shall be limited only by the bounds of the Material Cosmic All—every world that exists throughout space shall and must pay homage and tribute to Boskone! What, gentlemen, is the sense of this meeting?"

"Arisia must be visited!" There was no need of integrating this thought; it was dominant and unanimous.

"I would advise caution, however," the Eighth of Boskone amended his ballot. "We are an old race, it is true, and able. I cannot help but believe, however, that in Arisia there exists an unknown quality, an 'x' which we as yet are unable to evaluate. It must be borne in mind that Helmuth, while not of the Eich, was nevertheless an able being; yet he was handled so mercilessly there that he could not render a complete or conclusive report of his expedition, then or ever. With these thoughts in mind I suggest that no actual landing be made, but that the torpedo be launched from a distance."

"The suggestion is eminently sound," the First approved. "As to Helmuth, he was, for an oxygen-breather, fairly able. He was, however, mentally soft, as are all such. Do you, our foremost psychologist, believe that any existent or conceivable mind—even that of a Plooran—could break yours with no application of physical force or device, as Helmuth's reports seemed to indicate that his was broken? I use the word 'seemed' advisedly, for I do not believe that Helmuth reported the actual truth. In fact, I was about to replace him with an Eich, however unpleasant such an assignment would be to any of our race, because of that weakness."

"No," agreed the Eighth. "I do not believe that there exists in the universe a mind of sufficient power to break mine. It is a truism that no mental influence, however powerful, can affect a strong, definitely and positively opposed will. For that reason I voted against the use of thought-screens by our agents. Such screens expose them to detection and can be of no real benefit. Physical means were—must have been—used first, and, after physical subjugation, the screens were of course useless."

"I am not sure that I agree with you entirely," the Ninth put in. "We have here cogent evidence that there have been employed mental forces of a type or pattern with which we are entirely unfamiliar. While it is the consensus of opinion that the importance of Helmuth's report should be minimized, it seems to me that we have enough corroborative evidence to indicate that this mentality may be able to operate without material aid. If so, rigid screening should be retained, as offering the only possible safeguard from such force."

"Sound in theory, but in practice dubious," the psychologist countered. "If there were any evidence whatever that the screens had done any good I would agree with you. But have they? Screening failed to save Helmuth or his base; and there is nothing to indicate that the screens impeded, even momentarily, the progress of the suppositious Lensman upon Radelix. You speak of 'rigid' screening. The term is meaningless. Perfectly effective screening is impossible. If, as we seem to be doing, we postulate the ability of one mind to control another without physical, bodily contact—nor is the idea at all far-fetched, considering what I myself have done to the minds of many of our agents—the Lensman can work through any unshielded mentality whatever to attain his ends. As you know, Helmuth deduced, too late, that it must have been through the mind of a dog that the Lensman invaded Grand Base."

"Poppycock!" snorted the Seventh. "Or, if not, we can kill the dogs—or screen their minds, too," he sneered.

"Admitted," the psychologist returned, unmoved. "You might conceivably kill all the animals that run and all the birds that fly. You cannot, however, destroy all life in any locality at all extended, clear down to the worms in their burrows and the termites in their hidden retreats; and the mind does not exist which can draw a line of demarcation and say 'here begins intelligent life.' "

"This discussion is interesting, but futile," put in Eichlan, forestalling a scornful reply. "It is more to the point, I think, to discuss that which must be done; or, rather, who is to do it, since the thing itself admits of only one solution—an atomic bomb of sufficient power to destroy every trace of life upon that accursed planet. Shall we send someone, or shall some of us ourselves go? To overestimate a foe is at worst only an unnecessary precaution; to underestimate this one may well prove fatal. Therefore it seems to me that the decision in this matter should lie with our psychologist. I will, however, if you prefer, integrate our various conclusions."

Recourse to the machine was unnecessary; it was agreed by all that Eichamp, the Eighth of Boskone, should decide.

"My decision will be evident," that worthy said, measuredly, "when I say that I myself, for one, am going. The situation is admittedly a serious one. Moreover, I believe, to a greater extent than do the rest of you, that there is a certain amount of truth in Helmuth's version of his experiences. My mind is the only one in existence of whose power I am absolutely certain; the only one which I definitely *know* will not give way before any conceivable mental force, whatever its amount or whatever its method of application. I want none with me save of the Eich, and even those I will examine carefully before permitting them aboard ship with me."

"You decide as I thought," said the First. "I also shall go. My mind will hold, I think."

"It will hold—in your case examination is unnecessary," agreed the psychologist.

"And I! And I!" arose what amounted to a chorus.

"No," came curt denial from the First. "Two are enough to operate all machinery and weapons. To take any more of the Boskone would weaken us here injudiciously; well you know how many are working, and in what fashions, for seats at this table. To take any weaker mind, even of the Eich, might conceivably be to court disaster. We two should be safe; I because I have proven repeatedly my right to hold the title of First of this Council, the rulers and masters of the dominant race of the Universe; Eichamp because of his unparalleled knowledge of all intelligence. Our vessel is ready. We go."

As has been indicated, none of the Eich were, or ever had been, cowards. Tyrants they were, it is true, and dictators of the harshest, sternest, and most soulless kind; callous and merciless they were; cold as the rocks of their frigid world and as utterly ruthless and remorseless as the fabled Juggernaut: but they were as logical as they were hard. He who of them all was best fitted to do any thing did it unquestioningly and as a matter of course; did it with the calmly emotionless efficiency of the machine which in actual fact he was. Therefore it was the First and the Eighth of Boskone who went.

Through the star-studded purlieus of the Second Galaxy the black, airless, lightless vessel sped; through the reaches, vaster and more tenuous far, of inter-galactic space; into the Tellurian Galaxy; up to a solar system shunned then as now by all uninvited intelligences—dread and dreaded Arisia.

Not close to the planet did even the two of Boskone venture; but stopped at the greatest distance at which a torpedo could be directed surely against the target. But even so the vessel of the Eich had punctured a screen of mental force; and as Eichlan extended a tentacle toward the firing mechanism of the missiles, watched in as much suspense as they were capable of feeling by the planet-bound seven of Boskone, a thought as penetrant as a needle and yet as binding as a cable of tempered steel drove into his brain.

"Hold!" that thought commanded, and Eichlan held, as did also his fellow Boskonian.

Both remained rigid, unable to move any single voluntary muscle; while the other seven of the Council looked on in uncomprehending amazement. Their instruments remained dead—since those mechanisms were not sensitive to thought, to them nothing at all was occurring. Those seven leaders of the Eich knew that something was happening; something dreadful, something untoward, something very decidedly not upon the program they had helped to plan. They, however, could do nothing about it; they could only watch and wait.

"Ah, 'tis Lan and Amp of the Eich," the thought resounded within the minds of the helpless twain. "Truly, the Elders are correct. My mind is not yet competent, for, although I have had many facts instead of but a single one upon which to cogitate, and no dearth of time in which to do so, I now perceive that I have erred grievously in my visualization of the Cosmic All. You do, however, fit nicely into the now enlarged Scheme, and I am really grateful to you for furnishing new material with which, for many cycles of time to come, I shall continue to build.

"Indeed, I believe that I shall permit you to return unharmed to your own planet. You know the warning we gave Helmuth, your minion, hence your lives are forfeit for violating knowingly the privacy of Arisia; but wanton or unnecessary destruction is not conducive to mental growth. You are, therefore, at liberty to depart. I repeat to you the instructions given your underling; do not return, either in person or by any form whatever of proxy."

The Arisian had as yet exerted scarcely a fraction of his power; although the bodies of the two invaders were practically paralyzed, their minds had not been punished. Therefore the psychologist said, coldly:

"You are not now dealing with Helmuth, nor with any other weak, mindless oxygen-breather, but with the *Eich*," and, by sheer effort of will, he moved toward the controls.

"What boots it?" The Arisian compressed upon the Eighth's brain a searing force which sent shrieking waves of pain throughout all nearby space. Then, taking over the psychologist's mind, he forced him to move to the communicator panel, upon whose plate could be seen the other seven of Boskone, gazing in wonder.

"Set up planetary coverage," he directed, through Eichamp's organs of speech, "so that each individual member of the entire race of the Eich can understand what I am about to transmit." There was a brief pause, then the deep, measured voice rolled on;

"I am Eukonidor of Arisia, speaking to you through this mass of undead flesh which was once your Chief Psychologist, Eichamp, the Eighth of that high council which you call Boskone. I had intended to spare the lives of these two simple creatures, but I perceive that such action would be useless. Their minds and the minds of all you who listen to me are warped, perverted, incapable of reason. They and you would have misinterpreted the gesture completely; would have believed that I did not slay them only because I could not do so. Some of you would have offended again and again, until you were so slain; you can be convinced of such a fact only by an unmistakable demonstration of superior force. Force is the only thing you are able to understand. Your one aim in life is to gain material power; greed, corruption, and crime are your chosen implements.

"You consider yourselves hard and merciless. In a sense and according to your abilities you are, although your minds are too callow to realize that there are depths of cruelty and of depravity which you cannot even faintly envision.

"You love and worship power. Why? To any thinking mind it should be clear that such a lust intrinsically is, and forever must by its very nature be, futile. For, even if any one of you could command the entire material Universe, what good would it do him? None. What would he have? Nothing. Not even the satisfaction of accomplishment, for that lust is in fact insatiable—it would then turn upon itself and feed upon itself. I tell you as a fact that there is only one power which is at one and the same time illimitable and yet finite; insatiable yet satisfying; one which, while eternal, yet invariably returns to its possessor the true satisfaction of real accomplishment in exact ratio to the effort expended upon it. That power is the power of the mind. You, being so backward and so wrong of development, cannot understand how this can be, but if any one of you will concentrate upon one single fact, or small object, such as a pebble or the seed of a plant or other creature, for as short a period of time as one hundred of your years, you will begin to perceive its truth.

"You boast that your planet is old. What of that? We of Arisia dwelt in turn upon many planets, from planetary youth to cosmic old age, before we became independent of the chance formation of such celestial bodies.

"You prate that you are an ancient race. Compared to us you are sheerly infantile. We of Arisia did not originate upon a planet formed during the recent inter-passage of these two galaxies, but upon one which came into being in an antiquity so distant that the figure in years would be entirely meaningless to your minds. We were of an age to your mentalities starkly incomprehensible when your most remote ancestors began to wriggle about in the slime of your parent world.

" 'Do the men of the Patrol know . . . ?' I perceive the question in your minds. They do not. None save a few of the most powerful of their minds has the slightest inkling of the truth. To reveal any portion of it to Civilization as a whole would blight that Civilization irreparably. Though Seekers after Truth in the best sense, they are essentially juvenile and their life-spans are ephemeral indeed. The mere realization that there is in existence such a race as ours would place upon them such an inferiority complex as would make further advancement impossible. In your case such a course of events is not to be expected. You will close your minds to all that has happened, declaring to yourselves that it was impossible and that therefore it could not have taken place and did not. Nevertheless, you will stay away from Arisia henceforth.

"But to resume. You consider yourselves long-lived. Know then, insects, that your life-span of a thousand of your years is but a moment. I, myself, have already lived many such periods, and I am but a youth—a mere watchman, not yet to be entrusted with really serious thinking.

"I have spoken over long; the reason for my prolixity being that I do not like to see the energy of a race so misused, so corrupted to material conquest for its own sake. I would like to set your minds upon the Way of Truth, if perchance such a thing should be possible. I have pointed out that Way; whether or not you follow it is for you to decide. Indeed, I fear that most of you, in your short-sighted pride, have already cast my message aside; refusing point-blank to change your habits of thought. It is, however, in the hope that some few of you will perceive the Way and will follow it that I have discoursed at such length.

"Whether or not you change your habits of thought, I advise you to heed this, my warning. Arisia does not want and will not tolerate intrusion. As a lesson, watch these two violators of our privacy destroy themselves."

The giant voice ceased. Eichlan's tentacles moved toward the controls. The vast torpedo launched itself.

But instead of hurtling toward distant Arisia it swept around in a circle and struck, in direct central impact, the great cruiser of the Eich. There was an appalling crash, a space-wracking detonation, a flare of incandescence incredible and indescribable as the energy calculated to disrupt—almost to volatilize—a world expended itself upon the insignificant mass of one Boskonian battleship and upon the unresisting texture of the void.

10

THE NEGASPHERE

Considerably more than the stipulated week passed before Kinnison was done with the librarian and with the long-range communicator beam, but eventually he succeeded in enlisting the aid of the fifty three most eminent scientists and thinkers of all the planets of Galactic Civilization. From all over the galaxy were they selected; from Vandemar and Centralia and Alsakan; from Chickladoria and Radelix; from the solar systems of Rigel and Sirius and Antares. Millions of planets were not represented at all; and of the few which were, Tellus alone had more than one delegate.

This was necessary, Kinnison explained carefully to each of the chosen. Sir Austin Cardynge, the man whose phenomenal brain had developed a new mathematics to handle the positron and the negative energy levels, was the one who would do the work; he himself was present merely as a coordinator and observer. The meeting-place, even, was not upon Tellus, but upon Medon, the newly acquired and hence entirely neutral planet. For the Gray Lensman knew well the minds with which he would have to deal.

They were all geniuses of the highest rank, but in all too many cases their stupendous mentalities verged altogether too closely upon insanity for any degree of comfort. Even before the conclave assembled it became evident that jealousy was to be rife and rampant; and after the initial meeting, at which the problem itself was propounded, it required all of Kinnison's ability, authority, and drive: and all of Worsel's vast diplomacy and tact, to keep those mighty brains at work.

Time after time some essential entity, his dignity outraged and his touchy ego infuriated by some real or fancied insult, stalked off in high dudgeon to return to his own planet; only to be coaxed or bullied, or even mentally man-handled by Kinnison or Worsel, or both, into returning to his task.

Nor were those insults all, or even mostly, imaginary. Quarreling and bickering were incessant, violent flare-ups and passionate scenes of denunciation and vituperation were of almost hourly occurrence. Each of those minds had been accustomed to world-wide adulation, to the unquestioned acceptance as gospel of his every idea or pronouncement, and to have to submit his work to the scrutiny and to the unworshipful criticisms of lesser minds—actually to have to give way, at times, to those inferior mentalities—was a situation quite definitely intolerable.

But at length most of them began to work together, as they appreciated the fact that the problem before them was one which none of them singly had been able even partially to solve; and Kinnison let the others, the most fanatically non-cooperative, go home. Then progress began—and none too soon. The Gray Lensman had lost twenty five pounds in weight, and even the iron-thewed Worsel was a wreck. He could not fly, he declared, because his wings buckled in the middle; he could not crawl, because his belly-plates clashed against his back-bone!

And finally the thing was done; reduced to a set of equations which could be written upon a single sheet of paper. It is true that those equations would have been meaningless to almost anyone then alive, since they were based upon a system of mathematics which had been brought into existence at that very meeting, but Kinnison had taken care of that.

No Medonian had been allowed in the Conference—the admittance of one to membership would have caused a massed exodus of the high-strung, temperamental maniacs working so furiously there—but the Tellurian Lensman had had recorded every act, almost every thought, of every one of those geniuses. Those records had been studied for weeks, not only by Wise of Medon and his staff, but also by a corps of the less brilliant, but infinitely better balanced scientists of the Patrol proper.

"Now you fellows can really get to work." Kinnison heaved a sigh of profound relief as the last member of the Conference figuratively shook the dust of Medon off his robe as he departed homeward. "I'm going to sleep for a week. Call me, will you, when you get the model done?"

This was sheerest exaggeration, of course, for nothing could have kept the Lensman from watching the construction of that first apparatus. He watched the erection of a spherical shell of loosely latticed truss-work some twenty feet in diameter. He watched the installation, at its six cardinal points, of atomic exciters, each capable of transforming ten thousand pounds per hour of substance into pure energy. He knew that those exciters were driving their intake screens at a ratio of at least twenty thousand to one; that energy equivalent to the annihilation of at least six hundred thousand tons per hour of material was being hurled into the center of that web from the six small mechanisms which were in fact super-Bergenholms. Nor is that word adequate to describe them; their fabrication would have been utterly impossible without Medonian conductors and insulation.

He watched the construction of a conveyor and a chute, and looked on intently while a hundred thousand tons of refuse—rocks, sand, concrete, scrap iron, loose metal, debris of all kinds—were dropped into that innocuous-appearing sphere, only to vanish as though they had never existed.

"But we ought to be able to see it by this time, I should think!" Kinnison protested once.

"Not yet, Kim," Master Technician LaVerne Thorndyke informed him. "Just forming the vortex—microscopic yet. I haven't the faintest idea of what is going in there; but, man, dear man, *am* I glad I'm here to help make it go on!"

"But *when?*" demanded the Lensman. "How soon will you know whether it's going to work or not? I've got to do a flit."

"You can flit any time—now, if you like," the technician told him, brutally. "We don't need *you* any more—you've done your bit. It's working now. If it wasn't, do you think we could pack all that stuff into that little space? We'll have it done long before you'll need it."

"But I want to see it work, you big lug!" Kinnison retorted, only half playfully.

"Come back in three-four days—maybe a week; but don't expect to see anything but a hole."

"That's exactly what I want to see, a hole in space," and that was precisely what, a few days later, the Lensman did see.

The spherical framework was unchanged, the machines were still carrying easily their incredible working load. Material—any and all kinds of stuff—was still disappearing; instantaneously, invisibly, quietly, with no flash or fury to mark its passing.

But at the center of that massive sphere there now hung poised a . . . a *something*. Or was it a nothing? Mathematically, it was a sphere, or rather a negasphere, about the size of a baseball; but the eye, while it could see something, could not perceive it analytically. Nor could the mind envision it in three dimensions, for it was not essentially three-dimensional in nature. Light sank into the thing, whatever it was, and vanished. The peering eye could see nothing whatever of shape or of texture; the mind behind the eye reeled away before infinite vistas of nothingness.

Kinnison hurled his extra-sensory perception into it and jerked back, almost stunned. It was neither darkness nor blackness, he decided, after he recovered enough poise to think coherently. It was worse than that—worse than anything imaginable—an infinitely vast and yet non-existent realm of the total absence of everything whatever . . . ABSOLUTE NEGATION!

"That's it, I guess," the Lensman said then. "Might as well stop feeding it now."

"We would have to stop soon, in any case," Wise replied, "for our available waste material is becoming scarce. It will take the substance of a fairly large planet to produce that which you require. You have, perhaps, a planet in mind which is to be used for the purpose?"

"Better than that. I have in mind the material of just such a planet, but already broken up into sizes convenient for handling."

"Oh, the asteroid belt!" Thorndyke exclaimed. "Fine! Kill two birds with one stone, huh? Build this thing and at the same time clear out the menaces to inert interplanetary navigation? But how about the miners?"

"All covered. The ones actually in development will be let alone. They're not menaces, anyway, as they all have broadcasters. The tramp miners we send—at Patrol expense and grubstake—to some other system to do their mining. But there's one more point before we flit. Are you sure you can shift to the second stage without an accident?"

"Positive. Build another one around it, mount new Bergs, exciters, and screens on it, and let this one, machines and all, go in to feed the kitty—whatever it is."

"QX. Let's go, fellows!"

Two huge Tellurian freighters were at hand; and, holding the small framework between them in a net of tractors and pressors, they set off blithely toward Sol. They took a couple of hours for the journey—there was no hurry, and in the handling of this particular freight caution was decidedly of the essence.

Arrived at destination, the crews tackled with zest and zeal this new game. Tractors lashed out, seizing chunks of iron . . .

"Pick out the little ones, men," cautioned Kinnison. "Nothing over about ten feet in section-dimension will go into this frame. Better wait for the second frame before you try to handle the big ones."

"We can cut 'em up," Thorndyke suggested. "What've we got these shear-planes for?"

"QX if you like. Just so you keep the kitty fed."

"We'll feed her!" and the game went on.

Chunks of debris—some rock, but mostly solid meteoric nickel-iron—shot toward the vessels and the ravening sphere, becoming inertialess as they entered a wide-flung zone. Pressors seized them avidly, pushing them through the interstices of the framework, holding them against the voracious screen. As they touched the screen they disappeared; no matter how fast they were driven the screen ate them away, silently and unspectacularly, as fast as they could be thrown against it. A weird spectacle indeed, to see a jagged fragment of solid iron, having a mass of thousands of tons, drive against that screen and disappear! For it vanished, utterly, along a geometrically perfect spherical surface. From the opposite side the eye could see the mirror sheen of the metal at the surface of disintegration; it was as though the material were being shoved out of our familiar three-dimensional space into another universe—which, as a matter of cold fact, may have been the case.

For not even the men who were doing the work made any pretense of understanding what was happening to that iron. Indeed, the only entities who did have any comprehension of the phenomenon—the forty-odd geniuses whose mathematical wizardry had made it possible—thought of it and discussed it, not in the limited, three-dimensional symbols of every-day existence, but only in the language of high mathematics; a language in which few indeed are able really and readily to think.

And while the crews became more and more expert at the new technique, so that metal came in faster and faster—huge, hot-sliced bars of iron ten feet square and a quarter of a mile long were being driven into that enigmatic sphere of extinction—an outer framework a hundred and fifty miles in diameter was being built. Nor, contrary to what might be supposed, was a prohibitive amount of metal or of labor necessary to fabricate that mammoth structure. Instead of six there were six cubed—two hundred sixteen—working stations, complete with generators and super-Bergenholms and screen generators, each mounted upon a massive platform; but, instead of being connected and supported by stupendous beams and trusses of metal, those platforms were linked by infinitely stronger bonds of pure force. It took a lot of ships to do the job, but the technicians of the Patrol had at call enough floating machine shops and to spare.

When the sphere of negation grew to be about a foot in apparent diameter it had been found necessary to surround it with a screen opaque to all visible light, for to look into it long or steadily then meant insanity. Now the opaque screen was sixteen feet in diameter, nearing dangerously the sustaining framework, and the outer frame was ready. It was time to change.

The Lensman held his breath, but the Medonians and the Tellurian technicians did not turn a hair as they mounted their new stations and tested their apparatus.

"Ready," "Ready," "Ready." Station after station reported; then, as Thorndyke threw in the master switch, the primary sphere—invisible now, through distance, to the eye, but plain upon the visiplates—disappeared; a mere morsel to those new gigantic forces.

"Swing into it, boys!" Thorndyke yelled into his transmitter. "We don't have to feed her with a teaspoon any more. Let her have it!"

And "let her have it" they did. No more cutting up of the larger meteorites; asteroids ten, fifteen, twenty miles in diameter, along with hosts of smaller stuff, were literally hurled through the black screen into the even lusher blackness of that which was inside it, without complaint from the quietly humming motors.

"Satisfied, Kim?" Thorndyke asked.

"Uh-*huh!*" the Lensman assented, vigorously. "Nice! . . . Slick, in fact," he commended. "I'll buzz off now, I guess."

"Might as well—everything's on the green. Clear ether, space-hound!"

"Same to you, big fella. I'll be seeing you, or sending you a thought. There's Tellus, right over there. Funny, isn't it, doing a flit to a place you can actually see before you start?"

The trip to Earth was scarcely a hop, even in a supply-boat. To Prime Base the Gray Lensman went, where he found that his new non-ferrous speedster was done; and during the next few days he tested it out thoroughly. It did not register at all, neither upon the regular, long-range ultra-instruments nor upon the short-range emergency electros. Nor could it be seen in space, even in a telescope at point-blank range. True, it occulted an occasional star; but since even the direct rays of a search-light failed to reveal its shape to the keenest eye—the Lensmen-chemists who had worked out that ninety nine point nine nine percent absolute black coating had done a wonderful job—the chance of discovery through that occurrence was very slight.

"QX, Kim?" the Port Admiral asked. He was accompanying the Gray Lensman on a last tour of inspection.

"Fine, chief. Couldn't be better—thanks a lot."

"Sure you're non-ferrous yourself?"

"Absolutely. Not even an iron nail in my shoes."

"What is it, then? You look worried. Want something expensive?"

"You hit the thumb, Admiral, right on the nail. But it's not only expensive—we may never have any use for it."

"Better build it, anyway. Then if you want it you'll have it, and if you don't want it we can always use it for something. What is it?"

"A nut-cracker. There are a lot of cold planets around, aren't there, that aren't good for anything?"

"Thousands of them—millions."

"The Medonians put Bergenholms on their planet and flew it from Lundmark's Nebula to here in a few weeks. Why wouldn't it be a sound idea to have the planetographers pick out a couple of useless worlds which, at some points in their orbits, have diametrically opposite velocities, to within a degree or two?"

"You've got something there, my boy. Will do. Very much worth having, just for its own sake, even if we never have any use for it. Anything else?"

"Not a thing in the universe. Clear ether, chief!"

"Light landings, Kinnison!" and gracefully, effortlessly, the dead-black sliver of semi-precious metal lifted herself away from Earth.

Through Bominger, the Radeligian Big Shot, Kinnison had had a long and eminently satisfactory interview with Prellin, the regional director of all surviving Boskonian activities. Thus he knew where he was, even to the street address, and knew the name of the firm which was his alias—Ethan D. Wembleson and Sons, Inc., 4627 Boulevard Dezalies, Cominoche, Quadrant Eight, Bronseca. That name had been his first shock, for that firm was one of the largest and most conservative houses in galactic trade; one having an unquestioned AA-A1 rating in every mercantile index.

However, that was the way they worked, Kinnison reflected, as his speedster reeled off the parsecs. It wasn't far to Bronseca—easy Lens distance—he'd better call somebody there and start making arrangements. He had heard about the planet, although he'd never been there. Somewhat warmer than Tellus, but otherwise very Earth-like. Millions of Tellurians lived there and liked it.

His approach to the planet Bronseca was characterized by all possible caution, as was his visit to Cominoche, the capital city. He found that 4627 Boulevard Dezalies was a structure covering an entire city block and some eighty stories high, owned and occupied exclusively by Wembleson's. No visitors were allowed except by appointment. His first stroll past it showed him that an immense cylinder, comprising almost the whole interior of the building, was shielded by thought screens. He rode up and down in the elevators of nearby buildings—no penetration. He visited a dozen offices in the neighborhood upon various errands, choosing his time with care so that he would have to wait in each an hour or so in order to see his man.

These leisurely scrutinies of his objective failed to reveal a single fact of value. Ethan D. Wembleson and Sons, Inc., did a tremendous business, but every ounce of it was legitimate! That is, the files in the outer offices covered only legitimate transactions, and the men and women busily at work there were all legitimately employed. And the inner offices—vastly more extensive than the outer, to judge by the number of employees entering in the morning and leaving at the close of business—were sealed against his prying, every second of every day.

He tapped in turn the minds of dozens of those clerks, but drew only blanks. As far as they were concerned, there was nothing "queer" going on anywhere in the organization. The "Old Man"—Howard Wembleson, a grand-nephew or something of Ethan—had developed a complex lately that his life was in danger. Scarcely ever left the building—not that he had any need to, as he had always had palatial quarters there—and then only under heavy guard.

A good many thought-screened persons came and went, but a careful study of them and their movements convinced the Gray Lensman that he was wasting his time.

"No soap," he reported to a Lensman at Bronseca's Base. "Might as well try to stick a pin quietly into a cateagle. He's been told that he's the next link in the chain, and he's got the jitters right. I'll bet he's got a dozen loose observers, instead of only one. I'll save time, I think, by tracing another line. I have thought before that my best bet is in the asteroid dens instead of on the planets. I let them talk me out of it—it's a dirty job and I've got to establish an identity of my own, which will be even dirtier—but it looks as though I'll have to go back to it."

"But the others are warned, too," suggested the Bronsecan. "They'll probably be just as bad. Let's blast it open and take a chance on finding the data you want."

"No," Kinnison said, emphatically. "Not a chance—that's not the way to get anything I'm looking for. The others are probably warned, yes, but since they aren't on my direct line to the throne, they probably aren't taking it as seriously as this Prellin—or Wembleson—is. Or if they are, they won't keep it up as long. They can't, and get any joy out of life at all.

"And you can't say a word to Prellin about his screens, either," the Tellurian went on in reply to a thought. "They're legal enough; just as much so as spy-ray blocks. Every man has a right to privacy. Just one question here, or just one suspicious move, is apt to blow everything into a cocked hat. You fellows keep on working along the lines we laid out and I'll try another line. If it works I'll come back and we'll open this can the way you want to. That way, we may be able to get the low-down on about four hundred planetary organizations at one haul."

Thus it came about that Kinnison took his scarcely-used indetectable speedster back to Prime Base; and that, in a solar system prodigiously far removed from both Tellus and Bronseca there appeared another tramp meteor-miner.

Peculiar people, these toilers in the inter-planetary voids; flotsam and jetsam; for the most part the very scum of space. Some solar systems contain more asteroidal and meteoric debris than did ours of Sol, others less, but few if any have none at all. In the main this material is either nickel-iron or rock, but some of these fragments carry prodigious values in platinum, osmium, and other noble metals, and occasionally there are discovered diamonds and other gems of tremendous size and value. Hence, in the asteroid belts of every solar system there are to be found those universally despised, but nevertheless bold and hardy souls who, risking life and limb from moment to moment though they are, yet live in hope that the next lump of cosmic detritus will prove to be Bonanza.

Some of these men are the sheer misfits of life. Some are petty criminals, fugitives from the justice of their own planets, but not of sufficient importance to be upon the "wanted" lists of the Patrol. Some are of those who for some reason or other—addiction to drugs, perhaps, or the overwhelming urge occasionally to go on a spree—are unable or unwilling to hold down the steady jobs of their more orthodox brethren. Still others, and these are many, live that horridly adventurous life because it is in their blood; like the lumberjacks who in ancient times dwelt upon Tellus, they labor tremendously and unremittingly for weeks, only and deliberately to "blow in" the fruits of their toil in a few wild days and still wilder nights of hectic, sanguine, and lustful debauchery in one or another of the spacemen's hells of which every inhabited solar system has its quota.

But, whatever their class, they have much in common. They all live for the moment only, from hand to mouth. They all are intrepid space-men. They have to be—no others last long. They all live hardly, dangerously, violently. They are men of red and gusty passions, and they have, if not an actual contempt, at least a loud-voiced scorn of the law in its every phase and manifestation. "Law ends with atmosphere" is the galaxy-wide creed of the clan, and it is a fact that no law save that of the ray-gun is even yet really enforced in the badlands of the asteroid belts.

Indeed, the meteor miners as a matter of course take their innate lawlessness with them into their revels in the crimson-lit resorts already referred to. In general the nearby Planetary Police adopt a *laissez-faire* attitude, particularly since the asteroids are not within their jurisdictions, but are independent worlds, each with its own world-government. If they kill a dozen or so of each other and of the bloodsuckers who batten upon them, what of it? If everybody in those hells could be killed at once, the universe would be that much better off!—and if the Galactic Patrol is compelled, by some unusually outrageous performance, to intervene in the revelry, it comes in, not as single policemen, but in platoons or in companies of armed, full-armored infantry going to war!

Such, then, were those among whom Kinnison chose to cast his lot, in a new effort to get in touch with the Galactic Director of the drug ring.

11

HI-JACKERS

Although Kinnison left Bronseca, abandoning that line of attack completely—thereby, it might be thought, forfeiting all the work he had theretofore done upon it—the Patrol was not idle, nor was Prellin-Wembleson of Cominoche, the Boskonian Regional Director, neglected. Lensman after Lensman came and went, unobtrusively, but grimly determined. There came Tellurians, Venerians, Manarkans, Borovans; Lensmen of every human breed, any of whom might have been, as far as the minions of Boskone knew, the one foe whom they had such good cause to fear.

Rigellian Lensmen came also, and Posenians, and Ordoviks; representatives, in fact, of almost every available race possessing any type or kind of extra-sensory perception, came to test out their skill and cunning. Even Worsel of Velantia came, hurled for days his mighty mind against those screens, and departed.

Whether or not business went on as usual no one could say, but the Patrol was certain of three things. First, that while the Boskonians might be destroying some of their records, they were moving none away, by air, land, or tunnel; second, that there was no doubt in any zwilik mind that the Lensmen were there to stay until they won, in one way or another; and third, that Prellin's life was not a happy one!

And while his brothers of the Lens were so efficiently pinch-hitting for him—even though they were at the same time trying to show him up and thereby win kudos for themselves—in mentally investing the Regional stronghold of Boskone, Kinnison was establishing an identity as a wandering hellion of the asteroid belts.

There would be no slips this time. He would *be* a meteor miner in every particular, down to the last, least detail. To this end he selected his equipment with the most exacting care. It must be thoroughly adequate and dependable, but neither new nor of such outstanding quality or amount as to cause comment.

His ship, a stubby, powerful space-tug with an oversized air-lock, was a used job—hard-used, too—some ten years old. She was battered, pitted, and scarred; but it should be noted here, perhaps parenthetically, that when the Patrol technicians finished their rebuilding she was actually as staunch as a battleship. His space-armor, Spalding drills, De-Lameters, tractors and pressors, and "spee-gee" (torsion specific-gravity apparatus) were of the same grade. All bore unmistakable evidence of years of hard use, but all were in perfect working order. In short, his outfit was exactly that which a successful meteor-miner—even such a one as he was going to become—would be expected to own.

He cut his own hair, and his whiskers too, with ordinary shears, as was good technique. He learned the polyglot of the trade; the language which, made up of words from each of hundreds of planetary tongues, was and is the everyday speech of human or near-human meteor miners, where-ever found. By "near-human" is meant a six-place classification of AAAAAA—meaning oxygen-breathing, warm-blooded, erect, and having more or less humanoid heads, arms, and legs. For, even in meteor-mining, like runs with like. Warm-blooded oxygen-breathers find neither welcome nor enjoyment in a pleasure-resort operated by and for such a race, say, as the Trocanthers, who are cold-blooded, quasi-reptilian beings who abhor light of all kinds and who breathe a gaseous mixture not only paralyzingly cold but also chemically fatal to man.

Above all he had to learn how to drink strong liquors and how to take drugs, for he knew that no drink that had ever been distilled, and no drug, with the possible exception of thionite, could enslave the mind he then had. Thionite was out, anyway. It was too scarce and too expensive for meteor miners; they simply didn't go for it. Hadive, heroin, opium, nitrolabe, bentlam—that was it, bentlam. He could get it anywhere, all over the galaxy, and it was very much in character. Easy to take, potent in results, and not as damaging—if you didn't become a real addict—to the system as most of the others. He would become a bentlam-eater.

Bentlam, known also to the trade by such nicknames as "benny," "ben-weed," "happy-sleep," and others, is a shredded, moistly fibrous material of about the same consistency and texture as fine-cut chewing tobacco. Through his friends of Narcotics the Gray Lensman obtained a supply of "the clear quill, first chop, in the original tins" from a prominent bootlegger, and had it assayed for potency.

The drinking problem required no thought; he would learn to drink, and apparently to like, anything and everything that would pour. Meteor miners did.

Therefore, coldly, deliberately, dispassionately, and with as complete a detachment as though he were calibrating a burette or analyzing an unknown solution, he set about the task. He determined his capacity as impersonally as though his physical body were a volumetric flask; he noted the effect of each measured increment of high-proof beverage and of habit-forming drug as precisely as though he were studying a chemical reaction in which he himself was not concerned save as a purely scientific observer.

He detested the stuff. Every fiber of his being rebelled at the sensations evoked—the loss of coordination and control, the inflation, the aggrandizement, the falsity of values, the sheer hallucinations—nevertheless he went through with the whole program, even to the extent of complete physical helplessness for periods of widely varying duration. And when he had completed his researches he was thoroughly well informed.

He knew to a nicety, by feel, how much active principle he had taken, no matter how strong, how weak, or how adulterated the liquor or the drug had been. He knew to a fraction how much more he could take; or, having taken too much, almost exactly how long he would be incapacitated. He learned for himself what was already widely known, that it was better to get at least moderately illuminated before taking the drug; that bentlam rides better on top of liquor than vice versa. He even determined roughly the rate of increase with practice of his tolerances. Then, and only then, did he begin working as a meteor miner.

Working in an asteroid belt of one solar system might have been enough, but the Gray Lensman took no chances at all of having his new identity traced back to its source. Therefore he worked, and caroused, in five; approaching stepwise to the solar system of Borova which was his goal.

Arrived at last, he gave his chunky space-boat the average velocity of an asteroid belt just outside the orbit of the fourth planet, shoved her down into it, turned on his Bergenholm, and went to work. His first job was to "set up"; to install in the extra-large air-lock, already equipped with duplicate controls, his tools and equipment. He donned space-armor, made sure that his DeLameters were sitting pretty—all meteor miners go armed as routine, and the Lensman had altogether too much at stake in any case to forego his accustomed weapons—pumped the air of the lock back into the body of the ship, and opened the outer port. For meteor miners do not work inside their ships. It takes too much time to bring the metal in through the air-locks. It also wastes air, and air is precious; not only in money, although that is no minor item, but also because no small ship, stocked for a six-weeks run, can carry any more air than is really needed.

Set up, he studied his electros and flicked his tractor beams out to a passing fragment of metal, which flashed up to him, almost instantaneously. Or, rather, the inertialess tugboat flashed across space to the comparatively tiny, but inert, bit of metal which he was about to investigate. With expert ease Kinnison clamped the meteorite down and rammed into it his Spalding drill, the tool which in one operation cuts out and polishes a cylindrical sample exactly one inch in diameter and exactly one inch long. Kinnison took the sample, placed it in the jaw of his spee-gee, and cut his Berg. Going inert in an asteroid belt is dangerous business, but it is only one of a meteor miner's hazards and it is necessary; for the torsiometer is the quickest and simplest means of determining the specific gravity of metal out in space, and no torsion instrument will work upon inertialess matter.

He read the scale even as he turned on the Berg. Seven point nine. Iron. Worthless. Big operators could use it—the asteroid belts had long since supplanted the mines of the worlds as sources of iron—but it wouldn't do him a bit of good. Therefore, tossing it aside, he speared another. Another, and another. Hour after hour, day after day; the backbreaking, lonely labor of the meteor miner. But very few of the bona-fide miners had the Gray Lensman's physique or his stamina, and not one of them all had even a noteworthy fraction of his brain. And brain counts, even in meteor-mining. Hence Kinnison found pay-metal; quite a few really good, although not phenomenally dense, pieces.

Then one day there happened a thing which, if it was not in actual fact premeditated, was as mathematically improbable, almost, as the formation of a planetary solar system; an occurrence that was to exemplify in startling and hideous fashion the doctrine of tooth and fang which is the only law of the asteroid belts. Two tractor beams seized, at almost the same instant, the same meteor! Two ships, flashing up to zone contact in the twinkling of an eye, the inoffensive meteor squarely between them! And in the air lock of the other tug there were two men, not one; two men already going for their guns with the practiced ease of space-hardened veterans to whom the killing of a man was the veriest bagatelle!

They must have been hi-jackers, killing and robbing as a business, Kinnison concluded, afterward. Bona-fide miners almost never work two to a boat, and the fact that they actually beat him to the draw, and yet were so slow in shooting, argued that they had not been taken by surprise, as had he. Indeed, the meteor itself, the bone of contention, might very well have been a bait.

He could not follow his natural inclination to let go, to let them have it. The tale would have spread far and wide, branding him as a coward and a weakling. He would have had to kill, or have been killed by, any number of lesser bullies who would have attacked him on sight. Nor could he have taken over their minds quickly enough to have averted death. One, perhaps, but not two; he was no Arisian. These thoughts, as has been intimated, occurred to him long afterward. During the actual event there was no time to think at all. Instead, he acted; automatically and instantaneously.

Kinnison's hands flashed to the worn grips of his DeLamters, sliding them from the leather and bringing them to bear at the hip with one smoothly flowing motion that was a marvel of grace and speed. But, fast as he was, he was almost too late. Four bolts of lightning blasted, almost as one. The two desperadoes dropped, cold; the Lensman felt a stab of agony sear through his shoulder and the breath whistled out of his mouth and nose as his space-suit collapsed. Gasping terribly for air that was no longer there, holding onto his senses doggedly and grimly, he made shift to close the outer door of the lock and to turn a valve. He did not lose consciousness—quite—and as soon as he recovered the use of his muscles he stripped off his suit and examined himself narrowly in a mirror.

Eyes, plenty bloodshot. Nose, bleeding copiously. Ears, bleeding, but not too badly; drums not ruptured, fortunately—he had been able to keep the pressure fairly well equalized. Felt like some internal bleeding, but he could see nothing really serious. He hadn't breathed space long enough to do any permanent damage, he guessed.

Then, baring his shoulder, he treated the wound with Zinsmaster burn-dressing. This was no trifle, but at that, it wasn't so bad. No bone gone—it'd heal in two or three weeks. Lastly, he looked over his suit. If he'd only had his G-P armor on—but that, of course, was out of the question. He had a spare suit, but he'd rather . . . Fine, he could replace the burned section easily enough. QX.

He donned his other suit, re-entered the air lock, neutralized the screens, and crossed over; where he did exactly what any other meteor miner would have done. He divested the bloated corpses of their space-suits and shoved them off into space. He then ransacked the ship, trans-ferring from it to his own, as well as four heavy meteors, every other item of value which he could move and which his vessel could hold. Then, inerting her, he gave her a couple of notches of drive and cut her loose, for so a real miner would have done. It was not compunction or scruple that would have prevented any miner from taking the ship, as well as the supplies. Ships were registered, and otherwise were too hot to be handled except by organized criminal rings.

As a matter of routine he tested the meteor which had been the innocent cause of all this strife—or had it been a bait?—and found it worthless iron. Also as routine he kept on working. He had almost enough metal now, even at Miners' Rest prices, for a royal binge, but he couldn't go in until his shoulder was well. And a couple of weeks later he got the shock of his life.

He had brought in a meteor; a mighty big one, over four feet in its smallest dimension. He sampled it, and as soon as he cut the Berg and flicked the sample experimentally from hand to hand, his skilled muscles told him that that metal was astoundingly dense. Heart racing, he locked the test-piece into the spee-gee; and that vital organ almost stopped beating entirely as the indicator needle went up and up and up—stopping at a full twenty two, and the scale went only to twenty four!

"Klono's brazen hoofs and diamond-tipped horns!" he ejaculated. He whistled stridently through his teeth, then measured his find as accurately as he could. Then, speaking aloud "Just about thirty thou-sand kilograms of something noticeably denser than pure platinum—thirty million credits or I'm a Zabriskan fontema's maiden aunt. What to do?"

This find, as well it might, gave the Gray Lensman pause. It upset all his calculations. It was unthinkable to take that meteor to such a fence's hideout as Miners' Rest. Men had been murdered, and would be again, for a thousandth of its value. No matter where he took it, there would be publicity galore, and that wouldn't do. If he called a Patrol ship to take the white elephant off his hands he might be seen; and he had put in too much work on this identity to jeopardize it. He'd have to bury it, he guessed—he had maps of the system, and the fourth planet was close by.

He cut off a chunk of a few pounds' weight and made a nugget—a tiny meteor—of it, then headed for the planet, a plainly visible disk some fifteen degrees from the sun. He had a fairly large-scale chart of the system, with notes. Borova IV was uninhabited, except by low forms of life, and by outposts. Cold. Atmosphere thin—good, that meant no clouds. No oceans. No volcanic activity. Very good! He'd look it over, and the first striking landmark he saw, from one diameter out, would be his cache.

He circled the planet once at the equator, observing a formation of five mighty peaks arranged in a semi-circle, cupped toward the world's north pole. He circled it again, seeing nothing as prominent, and nothing else resembling it at all closely. Scanning his plate narrowly, to be sure nothing was following him, he drove downward in a screaming dive toward the middle mountain.

It was an extinct volcano, he discovered, with a level-floored crater more than a hundred miles in diameter. Practically level, that is, except for a smaller cone which reared up in the center of that vast, desolate plain of craggy, tortured lava. Straight down into the cold vent of the inner cone the Lensman steered his ship; and in its exact center he dug a hole and buried his treasure. He then lifted his tug-boat fifty feet and held her there, poised on her raving under-jets, until the lava in the little crater again began sluggishly to flow, and thus to destroy all evidence of his visit. This detail attended to, he shot out into space and called Haynes, to whom he reported in full.

"I'll bring the meteor in when I come—or do you want to send somebody out here after it? It belongs to the Patrol, of course."

"No, it doesn't, Kim—it belongs to you."

"Huh? Isn't there a law that any discoveries made by any employees of the Patrol belong to the Patrol?"

"Nothing as broad as that. Certain scientific discoveries, by scientists assigned to an exact research, yes. But you're forgetting again that you're an Unattached Lensman, and as such are accountable to no one in the Universe. Even the ten-percent treasure-trove law couldn't touch you. Besides, your meteor is not in that category, as you are its first owner, as far as we know. If you insist I'll mention it to the Council, but I know in advance what the answer will be."

"QX, Chief—thanks," and the connection was broken.

There, that was that. He had got rid of the white elephant, yet it wouldn't be wasted. If the zwilniks got him, the Patrol would dig it up; if he lived long enough to retire to a desk job he wouldn't have to take any more of the Patrol's money as long as he lived. Financially, he was all set.

And physically, he was all set for his first real binge as a meteor-miner. His shoulder and arm were as good as new. He had a lot of metal; enough so that its proceeds would finance, not only his next venture into space, but also a really royal celebration in the spaceman's resort he had already picked out.

For the Lensman had devoted a great deal of thought to that item. For his purpose, the bigger the resort—within limits—the better. The man he was after would not be a small operator, nor would he deal directly with such. Also, the big king-pins did not murder drugged miners for their ships and outfits, as the smaller ones sometimes did. The big ones realized that there was more long-pull profit in repeat business.

Therefore Kinnison set his course toward the great asteroid Euphrosyne and its festering hell-hole, Miners' Rest. Miners' Rest, to all highly moral citizens the disgrace not only of a solar system but of a sector; the very name of which was (and is) a by-word and a hissing to the blue-noses of twice a hundred inhabited and civilized worlds.

12

WILD BILL WILLIAMS, METEOR MINER

As has been implied, Miners' Rest was the biggest, widest-open, least restrained joint in that entire sector of the galaxy. And through the underground activities of his fellows of the Patrol, Kinnison knew that of all the king-snipes of that lawless asteroid, the man called Strongheart was the Big Shot.

Therefore the Lensman landed his battered craft at Strongheart's Dock, loaded the equipment of the hi-jacker's boat into a hand truck, and went into to talk to Strongheart himself. "Supplies—Equipment—Metal—Bought and Sold" the sign read; but to any experienced eye it was evident that the sign was conservative indeed; that it did not cover Strongheart's business, by half. There were dance-halls, there were long and ornate bars, there were rooms in plenty devoted to various games of so-called chance, and most significant, there were scores of those unmistakable cubicles.

"Welcome, stranger! Glad to see you—have a good trip?" The dive-keeper always greeted new customers effusively. "Have a drink on the house!"

"Business before pleasure," Kinnison replied, tersely. "Pretty good, yes. Here's some stuff I don't need any more that I aim to sell. What'll you gimme for it?"

The dealer inspected the suits and instruments, then bored a keen stare into the miner's eyes; a scrutiny under which Kinnison neither flushed nor wavered.

"Two hundred and fifty credits for the lot," Strongheart decided.

"Best you can do?"

"Tops. Take it or leave it."

"QX, they're yours. Gimme it."

"Why, this just starts our business, don't it? Ain't you got cores? Sure you have."

"Yeah, but not for no"—doubly and unprintably qualified—"damn robber. I like a louse, but you suit me altogether too damn well. Them suits alone, just as they lay, are worth a thousand."

"So what? For why go to insult me, a business man? Sure I can't give what that stuff is worth—who could? You ought to know how I got to get rid of hot goods. You killed, ain't it, the guys what owned it, so how could I treat it except like it's hot? Now be your age—don't burn out no jets," as the Lensman turned with a blistering, sizzling deep-space oath. "I know they shot first, they always do, but how does that change things? But keep your shirt on yet, I don't tell nobody nothing. For why should I? How could I make any money on hot stuff if I talk too much with my mouth, huh? But on cores, that's something else again. Meteors is legitimate merchandise, and I pay you as much as anybody, maybe more."

"QX," and Kinnison tossed over his cores. He had sold the bandits' space-suits and equipment deliberately, in order to minimize further killing.

This was his first visit to Miners' Rest, but he intended to become an habitue of the place; and before he would be accepted as a "regular" he knew that he would have to prove his quality. Buckos and bullies would be sure to try him out. This way was much better. The tale would spread; and any gunman who had drilled two hi-jackers, dead-center through the face-plates, was not one to be challenged lightly. He might have to kill one or two, but not many, nor frequently.

And the fellow was honest enough in his buying of the metal. His Spaldings cut honest cores—Kinnison put micrometers on them to be sure of that fact. He did not under-read his torsiometer, and he weighed the meteors upon certified balances. He used Galactic Standard average-value-density tables, and offered exactly half of the calculated average value; which, Kinnison knew, was fair enough. By taking his metal to a mint or a rare-metals station of the Patrol, any miner could get the precise value of any meteor, as shown by detailed analysis. However, instead of making the long trip and waiting—and paying—for the exact analyses, the miners usually preferred to take the "fifty-percent-of-average-density-value" which was the customary offer of the outside dealers.

Then, the meteors unloaded and hauled away, Kinnison dickered with Strongheart concerning the supplies he would need during his next trip; the hundred-and-one items which are necessary to make a tiny space-ship a self-contained, self-sufficient, warm and inhabitable worldlet in the immense and unfriendly vacuity of space. Here, too, the Lensman was overcharged shamelessly; but that, too, was routine. No one would, or could be expected to, do business in any such place as Miners' Rest at any sane or ordinary percentage of profit.

When Strongheart counted out to him the net proceeds of the voyage, Kinnison scratched reflectively at his whiskery chin.

"That ain't hardly enough, I don't think, for the real, old-fashioned, stem-winding bender I was figuring on," he ruminated. "I been out a long time and I was figuring on doing the thing up brown. Have to let go of my nugget, too, I guess. Kinda hate to—been packing it round quite a while—but here she is." He reached into his kit-bag and tossed over the lump of really precious metal. "Let you have it for fifteen hundred credits."

"Fifteen hundred! An idiot you must be, or you should think I'm one, I don't know!" Strongheart yelped, as he juggled the mass lightly from hand to hand. "Two hundred, you mean . . . well two fifty, then, but that's an awful high bid, mister, believe me . . . I tell you, I couldn't give my own mother over three hundred—I'd lose money on the goods. You ain't tested it, what makes you think it's such a much?"

"No, and I notice you ain't testing it, neither," Kinnison countered. "Me and you both know metal well enough so we don't need to test no such nugget as that. Fifteen hundred or I flit to a mint and get full value for it. I don't have to stay here, you know, by all the nine hells of Valeria. They's millions of other places where I can get just as drunk and have just as good a time as I can here."

There ensued howls of protest, but Strongheart finally yielded, as the Lensman had known that he would. He could have forced him higher, but fifteen hundred was enough.

"Now, sir, just the guarantee and you're all set for a lot of fun." Strongheart's anguish had departed miraculously upon the instant of the deal's closing. "We take your keys, and when your money's gone and you come back to get 'em, to sell your supplies or your ship or whatever, we takes you, without hurting you a bit more than we have to, and sober you up, quick as scat. A room here, whenever you want it, included. Padded, sir, very nice and comfortable—you can't hurt yourself, possibly. We been in business here for years, with perfect satisfaction. Not one of our customers, and we got hundreds who never go nowhere else, have we ever let sell any of the stuff he had laid in for his next trip, and we never steal none of his supplies, neither. Only two hundred credits for the whole service, sir. Cheap, sir—very, *very* cheap at the price."

"Um . . . m . . . m." Kinnison again scratched meditatively, this time at the nape of his neck.

"I'll take your guarantee, I guess, because sometimes, when I get to going real good, I don't know just exactly when to stop. But I won't need no padded cell. Me, I don't never get violent—I always taper off on twenty four units of benny. That gives me twenty four hours on the shelf, and then I'm all set for another stretch out in the ether. You couldn't get me no benny, I don't suppose, and if you could it wouldn't be no damn good."

This was the critical instant, the moment the Lensman had been approaching so long and so circuitously. Mind was already reading mind; Kinnison did not need the speech which followed.

"Twenty four units!" Strongheart exclaimed. That was a heroic jolt—but the man before him was of heroic mold. "Sure of that?"

"Sure I'm sure; and if I get cut weight or cut quality I cut the guy's throat that peddles it to me. But I ain't out. I got a couple of belts left—guess I'll use my own, and when it gets gone go buy me some from a fella I know that's about half honest."

"Don't handle it myself," this, the Lensman knew, was at least partially true, "but I know a man who has a friend who can get it. Good stuff, too, in the original tins; special import from Corvina II. That'll be four hundred altogether. Gimme it and you can start your helling around."

"Whatja mean, four hundred?" Kinnison snorted. "Think I'm just blasting off about having some left, huh? Here's two hundred for your guarantee, and that's all I want out of you."

"Wait a minute—jet back, brother!" Strongheart had thought that the newcomer was entirely out of his drug, and could therefore be charged eight prices for it. "How much do you get it for, mostly, the clear quill?"

"One credit per unit—twenty four for the belt," Kinnison replied, tersely and truly. That was the prevailing price charged by retail peddlers. "I'll pay you that, and I don't mean twenty five, neither."

"QX, gimme it. You don't need to be afraid of being bumped off or rolled here, neither. We got a reputation, we have."

"Yeah, I been told you run a high-class joint," Kinnison agreed, amiably. "That's why I'm here. But you wanna be mighty sure the ape don't gyp me on the heft of the belt—looky here!"

As the Lensman spoke he shrugged his shoulders and the dive-keeper leaped backward with a shriek; for faster than sight two ugly DeLameters had sprung into being in the miner's huge, dirty paws and were pointing squarely at his midriff!

"Put 'em away!" Strongheart yelled.

"Look 'em over first," and Kinnison handed them over, butts first. "These ain't like them buzzards' cap-pistols what I sold you. These is my own, and they're hot and tight. You know guns, don't you? Look 'em over, pal—real close."

The renegade did know weapons, and he studied these two with care, from the worn, rough-checkered grips and full-charged magazines to the burned, scarred, deeply-pitted orifices. Definitely and unmistakably they were weapons of terrific power; weapons, withal, which had seen hard and frequent service; and Strongheart personally could bear witness to the blinding speed of this miner's draw.

"And remember this," the Lensman went on. "I never yet got so drunk that anybody could take my guns away from me, and if I don't get a full belt of benny I get mighty peevish."

The publican knew that—it was a characteristic of the drug—and he certainly did not want that miner running amok with those two weapons in his highly capable hands. He would, he assured him, get his full dose.

And, for his part, Kinnison knew that he was reasonably safe, even in this hell of hells. As long as he was active he could take care of himself, in any kind of company; and he was fairly certain that he would not be slain, during his drug-induced physical helplessness, for the value of his ship and supplies. This one visit had yielded Strongheart a profit at least equal to everything he had left, and each subsequent visit should yield a similar amount.

"The first drink's on the house, always," Strongheart derailed his guest's train of thought. "What'll it be? Tellurian, ain't you—whiskey?"

"Uh-uh. Close, though—Aldebaran II. Got any good old Aldebaranian bolega?"

"No, but we got some good old Tellurian whiskey, about the same thing."

"QX—gimme a shot." He poured a stiff three fingers, downed it at a gulp, shuddered ecstatically, and emitted a wild yell. "Yip-yip-yippee! I'm Wild Bill Williams, the ripping, roaring, ritoodolorum from Aldebaran II, and this is my night to howl. Whee . . . yow . . . owrie-e-e!" Then, quieting down, "This rot-gut wasn't never within a million parsecs of Tellus, but it ain't bad—not bad at all. Got the teeth and claws of holy old Klono himself—goes down your throat just like swallowing a cateagle. Clear ether, pal, I'll be back shortly."

For his first care was to tour the entire Rest, buying scrupulously one good stiff drink, of whatever first came to hand, at each hot spot as he came to it.

"A good-will tour," he explained joyously to Strongheart upon his return. "Got to do it, pal, to keep 'em from calling down the curse of Klono on me, but I'm going to do all my serious drinking right here."

And he did. He drank various and sundry beverages, mixing them with a sublime disregard for consequences which surprised even the hard-boiled booze-fighters assembled there. "Anything that'll pour," he declared, loud and often, and acted accordingly. Potent or mild; brewed, fermented, or distilled; loaded, cut, or straight, all one. "Down the hatch!" and down it went. Here was a two-fisted drinker whose like had not been seen for many a day, and his fame spread throughout the Rest.

Being a "happy jag," the more he drank the merrier he became. He bestowed largess hither and yon, in joyous abandon. He danced blithely with the "hostesses" and tipped them extravagantly. He did not gamble, explaining frequently and painstakingly that that wasn't none of his dish; he wanted to have fun with his money.

He fought, even, without anger or rancor; but gayly, laughing with Homeric gusto the while. He missed with terrific swings that would have felled a horse had they landed; only occasionally getting in, as though by chance, a paralyzing punch. Thus he accumulated an entirely unnecessary mouse under each eye and a sadly bruised nose.

However, his good humor was, as is generally the case in such instances, quite close to the surface, and was prone to turn into passionate anger with less real cause even than the trivialities which started the friendly fist-fights. During various of these outbursts of wrath he smashed four chairs, two tables, and assorted glassware.

But only once did he have to draw a deadly weapon—the news, as he had known it would, had spread abroad that with a DeLameter he was nobody to monkey with—and even then he didn't have to kill the guy. Just winging him—a little bit of a burn through his gun-arm—had been enough.

So it went for days. And finally, it was in immense relief that the hilariously drunken Lensman, his money gone to the last millo, went roistering up the street with a two-quart bottle in each hand; swigging now from one, then from the other; inviting bibulously the while any and all chance comers to join him in one last, fond drink. The sidewalk was not wide enough for him, by half; indeed, he took up most of the street. He staggered and reeled, retaining any semblance of balance only by a miracle and by his rigorous spaceman's training.

He threw away one empty bottle, then the other. Then, as he strode along, so purposefully and yet so futilely, he sang. His voice was not particularly musical, but what it lacked in quality of tone it more than made up in volume. Kinnison had a really remarkable voice, a bass of tremendous power, timbre, and resonance; and, pulling out all the stops, in tones audible for two thousand yards against the wind, he poured out his zestfully lusty reveler's soul. His song was a deep-space chanty that would have blistered the ears of any of the gentler spirits who had known him as Kimball Kinnison, of Earth; but which, in Miners' Rest, was merely a humorous and sprightly ballad.

Up the full length of the street he went. Then back, as he put it, to "Base." Even if this final bust did make him sicker at the stomach than a ground-gripper going free for the first time, the Lensman reflected, he had done a mighty good job. He had put Wild Bill Williams, meteor miner, of Aldebaran II, on the map in a big way. It wasn't a faked and therefore fragile identity, either; it was solidly, definitely his own.

Staggering up to his friend Strongheart he steadied himself with two big hands upon the latter's shoulders and breathed a forty-thousand-horsepower breath into his face.

"I'm boiled like a Tellurian hoot-owl," he announced, still happily. "When I'm this stewed I can't say 'partic-hic-hicular-ly' without hic-hicking, but I would partic-hic-hicularly like just one more quart. How about me borrowing a hundred on what I'm going to bring in next time, or selling you . . ."

"You've had plenty, Bill. You've had lots of fun. How about a good chew of sleepy-happy, huh?"

"That's a thought!" the miner exclaimed eagerly. "Lead me to it!"

A stranger came up unobtrusively and took him by one elbow. Strongheart took the other, and between them they walked him down a narrow hall and into a cubicle. And while he walked flabbily along

Kinnison studied intently the brain of the newcomer. *This* was what he was after!

The ape had had a screen; but it was such a nuisance he took it off for a rest whenever he came here. No Lensmen on Euphrosyne! They had combed everybody, even this drunken bum here. This was one place that no Lensman would ever come to; or, if he did, he wouldn't last long. Kinnison had been pretty sure that Strongheart would be in cahoots with somebody bigger than a peddler, and so it had proved. This guy knew plenty, and the Lensman was taking the information—all of it. Six weeks from now, eh? Just right—time to find enough metal for another royal binge here . . . And during that binge he would really do things . . .

Six weeks. Quite a while . . . but . . . QX. It would take some time yet, anyway, probably, before the Regional Directors would, like this fellow, get over their scares enough to relax a few of their most irksome precautions. And, as has been intimated, Kinnison, while impatient enough at times, could hold himself in check like a cat watching a mousehole whenever it was really necessary.

Therefore, in the cell, he seated himself upon the bunk and seized the packet from the hand of the stranger. Tearing it open, he stuffed the contents into his mouth; and, eyes rolling and muscles twitching, he chewed vigorously; expertly allowing the potent juice to trickle down his gullet just fast enough to keep his head humming like a swarm of angry bees. Then, the cud sucked dry, he slumped down upon the mattress, physically dead to the world for the ensuing twenty four G-P hours.

He awakened; weak, flimsy, and supremely wretched. He made heavy going to the office, where Strongheart returned to him the keys of his boat.

"Feeling low, sir." It was a statement, not a question.

"I'll say so," the Lensman groaned. He was holding his spinning head, trying to steady the gyrating universe. "I'd have to look up—'way, 'way up, with a number nine visiplate—to see a snake's belly in a swamp. Make that damn cat quit stomping his feet, can't you?'

"Too bad, but it won't last long." The voice was unctuous enough, but totally devoid of feeling. "Here's a pick-up—you need it."

The Lensman tossed off the potion, without thanks, as was good technique in those parts. His head cleared miraculously, although the stabbing ache remained.

"Come in again next time. Everything's been on the green here, ain't it, sir?"

"Uh-huh, very nice," the Lensman admitted. "Couldn't ask for better. I'll be back in five or six weeks, if I have any luck at all."

As the battered but staunch and powerful meteor-boat floated slowly upward a desultory conversation was taking place in the dive he had left. At that early hour business was slack to the point of non-existence, and Strongheart was chatting idly with a bartender and one of the hostesses.

"If more of the boys was like him we wouldn't have no trouble at all," Strongheart stated with conviction. "Nice, quiet, easy-going—a right guy, I say."

"Yeah, but at that maybe it's a good gag nobody riled him up too much," the barkeep opined. "He could be rough if he wanted to, I bet a quart. Drunk or sober, he's chain lightning with them DeLameters."

"He's so refined, such a perfect gentleman," sighed the woman. "He's nice." To her, he had been. She had had plenty of credits from the big miner, without having given anything save smiles and dances in return. "Them two guys he drilled must have needed killing, or he wouldn't have burned 'em."

And that was that. As the Lensman had intended, Wild Bill Williams was an old, known, and highly respected resident of Miners' Rest!

Out among the asteroids again; more muscle-tearing, back-breaking, lonesome labor. Kinnison did not find any more fabulously rich meteors—such things happen only once in a hundred lifetimes—but he was getting his share of heavy stuff. Then one day when he had about half a load there came screaming in upon the emergency wave a call for help; a call so loud that the ship broadcasting it must be very close indeed. Yes, there she was, right in his lap; startlingly large even upon the low-power plates of his space-tramp.

"Help! Space-ship 'Kahlotus', position . . ." a rattling string of numbers. "Bergenholm dead, meteorite screens practically disabled, intrinsic velocity throwing us into the asteroids. Any space-tugs, any vessels with tractors—help! And hurry!"

At the first word Kinnison had shoved his blast-lever full over. A few seconds of free flight, a minute of inert maneuvering that taxed to the utmost his Lensman's skill and powerful frame, and he was within the liner's air-lock.

"I know something about Bergs!" he snapped. "Take this boat of mine and pull! Are you evacuating passengers?" he shot at the mate as they ran toward the engine room.

"Yes, but afraid we haven't boats enough—overloaded," was the gasped reply.

"Use mine—fill 'er up!" If the mate was surprised at such an offer from a despised space-rat he did not show it. There were many more surprises in store.

In the engine room Kinnison brushed aside a crew of helplessly futile gropers and threw in switch after switch. He looked. He listened. Above all, he pried into that sealed monster of power with all his sense of perception. How glad he was now that he and Thorndyke had struggled so long and so furiously with a balky Bergenholm on that trip to tempestuous Trenco! For as a result of that trip he *did* know Bergs, with a sure knowledge possessed by few other men in space.

"Number four lead is shot somewhere," he reported. "Must be burned off where it clears the pilaster. Careless overhaul last time—got to take off the lower port third cover. No time for wrenches—get me a cutting beam, and get the lead out of your pants!"

The beam was brought on the double and the Lensman himself blasted away the designated cover. Then, throwing an insulated plate over the red-hot casing he lay on his back—"Hand me a light!"—and peered briefly upward into the bowels of the gargantuan mechanism.

"Thought so," he grunted. "Piece of four-oh stranded, eighteen inches long. Ditmars number six clip ends, twenty inches on centers. Myerbeer insulation on center section, doubled. Snap it up! One of you other fellows, bring me a short, heavy screw-driver and a pair of Ditmars six wrenches!"

The technicians worked fast and in a matter of seconds the stuff was there. The Lensman labored briefly but hugely; and much more surely than if he were dependent upon the rays of the hand-lamp to penetrate the smoky, steamy, greasy murk in which he toiled. Then:

"QX—give her the juice!" he snapped.

They gave it, and to the stunned surprise of all, she took it. The liner again was free!

"Kind of a jury rigging I gave it, but it'll hold long enough to get you into port, sir," he reported to the captain in his sanctum, saluting crisply. He was in for it now, he knew, as the officer stared at him. But he *couldn't* have let that shipload of passengers get ground up into hamburger. Anyway, there was a way out.

In apparent reaction he turned pale and trembled, and the officer hastily took from his medicinal stores a bottle of choice old brandy.

"Here, drink this," he directed, proferring the glass.

Kinnison did so. More, he seized the bottle and drank that, too—all of it—a draft which would have literally turned him inside out a few months since. Then, to the captain's horrified disgust, he took from his filthy dungarees a packet of bentlam and began to chew it, idiotically blissful. Thence, and shortly, into oblivion.

"Poor devil . . . you poor, poor devil," the commander murmured, and had him put into a bunk.

When he had come to and had had his pickup, the captain came and regarded him soberly.

"You were a man once. An engineer—a top-bracket engineer—or I'm an oiler's pimp," he said levelly.

"Maybe," Kinnison replied, white and weak. "I'm all right yet, except once in a while . . ."

"I know," the captain frowned. "No cure?"

"Not a chance. Tried dozens. So . . ." and the Lensman spread out his hands in a hopeless gesture.

"Better tell me your name, anyway—your real name. That'll let your planet know you aren't . . ."

"Better not," the sufferer shook his aching head. "Folks think I'm dead. Let them keep on thinking so. Williams is the name, sir; William Williams, of Aldabaran II."

"As you say."

"How far are we from where I boarded you?"

"Close. Less than half a billion miles. This, the second, is our home planet; your asteroid belt is just outside the orbit of the fourth."

"I'll do a flit, then."

"As you say," the officer agreed, again. "But we'd like to . . ." and he extended a sheaf of currency.

"Rather not, sir, thanks. You see, the longer it takes me to earn another stake, the longer it'll be before . . ."

"I see. Thanks, anyway, for us all," and captain and mate helped the derelict embark. They scarcely looked at him, scarcely dared look at each other . . . but . . .

Kinnison, for his part, was content. This story, too, would get around. It would be in Miners' Rest before he got back there, and it would help . . . help a lot.

He could not possibly let those officers know the truth, even though he realized full well that at that very moment they were thinking, pityingly:

"The poor devil . . . the poor, brave devil!"

13

ZWILNIK CONFERENCE

The Gray Lensman went back to his mining with a will and with un-impaired vigor, for his distress aboard the ship had been sheerest acting. One small bottle of good brandy was scarcely a cocktail to the physique that had stood up under quart after quart of the crudest, wickedest, fieri-est beverages known to space; that tiny morsel of bentlam—scarcely half a unit—affected him no more than a lozenge of licorice.

Three weeks. Twenty one days, each of twenty four G-P hours. At the end of that time, he had learned from the mind of the zwilnik, the Boskonian director of this, the Borovan solar system, would visit Miners' Rest, to attend some kind of meeting. His informant did not know what the meeting was to be about, and he was not unduly curious about it. Kinnison, however, did and was.

The Lensman knew, or at least very shrewdly suspected, that that meeting was to be a regional conference of big-shot zwilniks; he was intensely curious to know all about everything that was to take place; and he was determined to be present.

Three weeks was lots of time. In fact, he should be able to complete his quota of heavy metal in two, or less. It was there, there was no question of that. Right out there were the meteors, uncountable thou-sands of millions of them, and a certain proportion of them carried values. The more and the harder he worked, the more of these worthwhile wanderers of the void he would find. Wherefore he labored long, hard, and rapidly, and his store of high-test meteors grew apace. To such good purpose did he use beam and Spalding drill that he was ready more than a week ahead of time. That was QX—he'd much rather be early than late. Something might have happened to hold him up—things did happen, too often—and he *had* to be at that meeting!

Thus it came about that, a few days before the all-important date, Kinnison's battered treasure-hunter blasted herself down to her second landing at Strongheart's Dock. This time the miner was welcomed, not as a stranger, but as a friend of long standing.

"Hi, Wild Bill!" Strongheart yelled at sight of the big space-hound. "Right on time, I see—glad to see you! Luck, too, I hope—lots of luck, and all good, I bet me—ain't it?"

"Ho, Strongheart!" the Lensman roared in return, pummeling the divekeeper affectionately. "Had a good trip, yeah—a fine trip. Struck a rich sector—twice as much as I got last time. Told you I'd be back in five or six weeks, and made it in five weeks and four days."

"Keeping tabs on the days, huh?"

"I'll say I do. With a thirst like mine a guy can't do nothing else—I tell you all my guts're dryer than any desert on the whole of Rhylce. Well, what're we waiting for? Check this plunder of mine in and let me get to going places and doing things!"

The business end of the visit was settled with neatness and dispatch. Dealer and miner understood each other thoroughly; each knew what could and what could not be done to the other. The meteors were tested and weighed. Supplies for the ensuing trip were bought. The guarantee and twenty four units of benny—QX. No argument. No hysterics. No bickering or quarreling or swearing. Everything on the green, all the way. Gentlemen and friends. Kinnison turned over his keys, accepted a thick sheaf of currency, and, after the first formal drink with his host, set out upon the self-imposed, superstitious tour of the other hot spots which would bring him the favor—or at least would avert the active disfavor—of Klono, his spaceman's deity.

This time, however, that tour took longer. Upon his first ceremonial round he had entered each saloon in turn, had bought one drink of whatever was nearest, had tossed it down, and had gone on to the next place; unobserved and inconspicuous. Now, how different it all was! Wherever he went he was the center of attention.

Men who had met him before flung themselves upon him with whoops of welcome; men who had never seen him clamored to drink with him; women, whether or not they knew him, fawned upon him and brought into play their every lure and wile. For not only was this man a hero and a celebrity of sorts; he was a lucky—or a skillful—miner whose every trip resulted in wads of money big enough to clog the under-jets of a freighter! Moreover, when he was lit up he threw it round regardless, and he was getting stewed as fast as he could swallow. Let's keep him here—or, if we can't do that, let's go along, wherever he goes! This, too, was strictly according to the Lensman's expectations. Everybody knew that he did not do any serious drinking glass by glass at the bar, but bottle by bottle; that he did not buy individual drinks for his friends, but let them drink as deeply as they would from whatever container chanced then to be in hand; and his vast popularity gave him a sound excuse to begin his bottle-buying at the start instead of waiting until he got back to Strongheart's. He bought, then, several or many bottles and tins in each place, instead of a single drink. And, since everybody knew for a fact that he was a practically bottomless drinker, who was even to suspect that he barely moistened his gullet while the hangers-on were really emptying the bottles, cans, and flagons?

And during his real celebration at Strongheart's, while he drank enough, he did not drink too much. He waxed exceedingly happy and frolicsome, as before. He was as profligate, as extravagant in tips. He had the same sudden flashes of hot anger. He fought enthusiastically and awkwardly, as Wild Bill Williams did, although only once or twice, that time; and he did not have to draw his DeLameter at all—he was so well known and so beloved! He sang as loudly and as raucously, and with the same fine taste in madrigals.

Therefore, when the infiltration of thought-screened men warned him that the meeting was about to be called Kinnison was ready. He was in fact cold sober when he began his tuneful, last-two-bottles trip up the street, and he was almost as sober when he returned to "Base," empty of bottles and pockets, to make the usual attempt to obtain more money from Strongheart and to compromise by taking his farewell chew of bentlam instead.

Nor was he unduly put out by the fact that both Strongheart and the zwilnik were now wearing screens. He had taken it for granted that they might be, and had planned accordingly. He seized the packet as avidly as before, chewed its contents as ecstatically, and slumped down as helplessly and as idiotically. That much of the show, at least, was real. Twenty four units of that drug will paralyze *any* human body, make it assume the unmistakable pose and stupefied mien of the bentlam eater. But Kinnison's mind was not an ordinary one; the dose which would have rendered any bona-fide miner's brain as helpless as his body did not affect the Lensman's new equipment at all. Alcohol and bentlam together were bad, but the Lensman was sober. Therefore, if anything, the drugging of his body only made it easier to dissociate his new mind from it. Furthermore, he need not waste any thought in making it act. There was only one way it could act, now, and Kinnison let his new senses roam abroad without even thinking of the body he was leaving behind him.

In view of the rigorous orders from higher up the conference room was heavily guarded by screened men; no one except old and trusted employees were allowed to enter it, and they were also protected. Nevertheless, Kinnison got in, by proxy.

A clever pick-pocket brushed against a screened waiter who was about to enter the sacred precincts, lightning fingers flicking a switch. The waiter began to protest—then forgot what he was going to say, even as the pick-pocket forgot completely the deed he had just done. The waiter in turn was a trifle clumsy in serving a certain Big Shot, but earned no rebuke thereby; for the latter forgot the offense almost instantly. Under Kinnison's control the director fumbled at his screen-generator for a moment, loosening slightly a small but important resistor. That done, the Lensman withdrew delicately and the meeting was an open book.

"Before we do anything," the director began, "show me that all your screens are on." He bared his own—it would have taken an expert service man an hour to find that it was not functioning perfectly.

"Poppycock!" snorted the zwilnik. "Who in all the hells of space thinks that a Lensman would—or *could*—come to Euphrosyne?"

"Nobody can tell what this particular Lensman can or can't do, and nobody knows what he's doing until just before he dies. Hence the strictness. You've searched everybody here, of course?"

"Everybody," Strongheart averred, "even the drunks and the dopes. The whole building is screened, besides the screens we're wearing."

"The dopes don't count, of course, provided they're really doped." No one except the Gray Lensman himself could possibly conceive of a Lensman being—not seeming to be, but actually *being*—a drunken sot, to say nothing of being a confirmed addict of any drug. "By the way, who is this Wild Bill Williams we've been hearing about?"

Strongheart and his friend looked at each other and laughed.

"I checked up on him early," the zwilnik chuckled. "He isn't the Lensman, of course, but I thought at first he might be an agent. We frisked him and his ship thoroughly—no dice—and checked back on him as a miner, four solar systems back. He's clean, anyway; this is his second bender here. He's been guzzling everything in stock for a week, getting more pie-eyed every day, and Strongheart and I just put him to bed with twenty four units of benny. You know what *that* means, don't you?"

"Your own benny or his?" the director asked.

"My own. That's why I know he's clean. All the other dopes are too. The drunks we gave the bum's rush, like you told us to."

"QX. I don't think there's any danger, myself—I think the hot-shot Lensman they're afraid of is still working Bronseca—but these orders not to take any chances at all come from 'way, 'way up."

"How about this new system they're working on, that nobody knows his boss any more? Hooey, I call it."

"Not ready yet. They haven't been able to invent an absolutely safe one that'll handle the work. In the meantime, we're using these books. Cumbersome, but absolutely safe, they say, unless and until the enemy gets onto the idea. Then one group will go into the lethal chambers of the Patrol and the rest of us will use something else. Some say this code can't be cracked; others say any code can be read in time. Anyway here's your orders. Pass them along. Give me your stuff and we'll have supper and a few drinks."

They ate. They drank. They enjoyed an evening and a night of high revelry and low dissipation, each to his taste; each secure in the knowledge that his thought-screen was one hundred percent effective against the one enemy he really feared. Indeed, the screens were that effective— then—since the Lensman, having learned from the director all he knew, had restored the generator to full efficiency in the instant of his relinquishment of control.

Although the heads of the zwilniks, and therefore their minds, were secure against Kinnison's prying, the books of record were not. And, though his body was lying helpless, inert upon a drug-fiend's cot, his sense of perception read those books; if not as readily as though they were in his hands and open, yet readily enough. And, far off in space, a power-brained Lensman yclept Worsel recorded upon imperishable metal a detailed account, including names, dates, facts, and figures, of all the doings of all the zwilniks of a solar system!

The information was coded, it is true; but, since Kinnison knew the key, it might just as well have been printed in English. To the later consternation of Narcotics, however, that tape was sent in under Lensman's Seal—it could not be read until the Gray Lensman gave the word.

In twenty four hours Kinnison recovered from the effects of his debauch. He got his keys from Strongheart. He left the asteroid. He knew the mighty intellect with whom he had next to deal, he knew where that entity was to be found; but, sad to say, he had positively no idea at all as to what he was going to do or how he was going to do it.

Wherefore it was that a sense of relief tempered the natural apprehension he felt upon receiving, a few days later, an insistent call from Haynes. Truly this must be something really extraordinary, for while during the long months of his service Kinnison had called the Port Admiral several times, Haynes had never before Lensed him.

"Kinnison! Haynes calling!" the message beat into his consciousness.

"Kinnison acknowledging, sir!" the Gray Lensman thought back.

"Am I interrupting anything important?"

"Not at all. I'm just doing a little flit."

"A situation has come up which we feel you should study, not only in person, but also without advance information or pre-conceived ideas. Can you come in to Prime Base immediately?"

"Yes, sir. In fact, a little time right now might do me good in two ways—let me mull a job over, and let a nut mellow down to a point where maybe I can crack it. At your orders, sir!"

"Not orders, Kinnison!" the old man reprimanded him sharply. "No one gives Unattached Lensmen orders. We request or suggest, but you are the sole judge as to where your greatest usefulness lies."

"Please believe, sir, that your requests are orders, to me," Kinnison replied in all seriousness. Then, more lightly, "Your calling me in suggests an emergency, and travelling in this miner's scow of mine is just a trifle faster than going afoot. How about sending out something with some legs to pick me up?"

"The *Dauntless,* for instance?"

"Oh—you've got her rebuilt already?"

"Yes."

"I'll bet she's a sweet clipper! She was a mighty slick stepper before; now she must have more legs than a centipede!"

And so it came about that in a region of space entirely empty of all other vessels as far as ultra-powerful detectors could reach, the *Dauntless* met Kinnison's tugboat. The two went inert and maneuvered briefly, then the immense warship engulfed her tiny companion and flashed away.

"Hi, Kim, you old son-of-a-space-flea!" A general yell arose at sight of him, and irrepressible youth rioted, regardless of Regs, in this reunion of old comrades in arms who were yet scarcely more than boys in years.

"His Nibs says for you to call him, Kim, when we're about an hour out from Prime Base," Maitland informed his class-mate irreverently, as the *Dauntless* neared the Solarian system.

"Plate or Lens?"

"Didn't say—as you like, I suppose."

"Plate then, I guess—don't want to butt in," and in moments Port Admiral and Gray Lensman were in image face to face.

"How are you making out, Kinnison?" Haynes studied the young man's face intently, gravely, line by line. Then, via Lens, "We heard about the shows you put on, clear over here on Tellus. A man can't drink and dope the way you did without suffering consequences. I've been wondering if even you can fight it off. How about it? How do you feel now?"

"Some craving, of course," Kinnison replied, shrugging his shoulders. "That can't be helped—you can't make an omelette without breaking eggs. However, it's nothing I can't lick. I've got it pretty well boiled out of my system already."

"Mighty glad to hear that, son. Only Ellison and I know who Wild Bill Williams really is. You had us scared stiff for a while." Then, speaking aloud:

"I would like to have you come to my office as soon as possible."

"I'll be there, chief, two minutes after we hit the bumpers," and he was.

"The admiral busy, Ruby?" he asked, waving an airy salute at the attractive young woman in Haynes' outer office.

"Go right in, Lensman Kinnison, he's waiting for you," and opening the door for him, she stood aside as he strode into the sanctum.

The Port Admiral returned the younger man's punctilious salute, then the two shook hands warmly before Haynes referred to the third man in the room.

"Navigator Xylpic, this is Lensman Kinnison, Unattached. Sit down, please; this may take some time. Now, Kinnison, I want to tell you that ships have been disappearing, right and left, disappearing without sending out an alarm or leaving a trace. Convoying makes no difference, as the escorts also disappear . . ."

"Any with the new projectors?" Kinnison flashed the question via Lens—this was nothing to talk about aloud.

"No," came the reassuring thought in reply. "Every one bottled up tight until we find out what it's all about. Sending out the *Dauntless* after you was the only exception."

"Fine. You shouldn't have taken even that much chance." This interplay of thought took but an instant; Haynes went on with scarcely a break in his voice:

". . . with no more warning or report than the freighters and liners they are supposed to be protecting. Automatic reporting also fails—instruments simply stop sending. The first and only sign of light—if it *is* such a sign; which frankly, I doubt—came shortly before I called you in, when Xylpic here came to me with a tall story."

Kinnison looked then at the stranger. Pink. Unmistakably a Chickladorian—pink all over. Bushy hair, triangular eyes, teeth, skin; all that same peculiar color. Not the flush of red blood showing through translucent skin, but opaque pigment; the brick-reddish pink so characteristic of the near-humanity of that planet.

"We have investigated this Xylpic thoroughly," Haynes went on, discussing the Chickladorian as impersonally as though he were upon his home planet instead of there in the room, listening. "The worst of it is that the man is absolutely honest—or at least, he thinks he is—in telling this yarn. Also, except for this one thing—this obsession, fixed idea, hallucination, call it what you like; it seems incredible that it *can* be a fact—he not only seems to be, but actually *is*, sane. Now, Xylpic, tell Kinnison what you told the rest of us. And Kinnison, I hope you can make sense of it—none of the rest of us can."

"QX. Go ahead, I'm listening." But Kinnison did far more than listen. As the fellow began to talk the Gray Lensman insinuated his mind into that of the Chickladorian. He groped for moments, seeking the wave-length; then he, Kimball Kinnison, was actually re-living with the pink man an experience which harrowed his very soul.

"The second navigator of a Radeligian vessel died in space, and when it landed on Chickladoria I took the berth. About a week out, the whole crew went crazy, all at once. The first I knew of it was when the pilot on duty beside me left his board, picked up a stool, and smashed the automatic recorder. Then he went inert and neutralized all the controls.

"I yelled at him, but he didn't answer me, and all the men in the control room acted funny. They just milled around like men in a trance. I buzzed the captain, but he didn't acknowledge either. Then the men around me left the control room and went down the companionway toward the main lock. I was scared—my skin prickled and the hair on the back of my neck stood straight up—but I followed along, quite a ways behind, to see what they were going to do. The captain, all the rest of the officers, and the whole crew joined them in the lock. Everybody was in an awful hurry to get somewhere.

"I didn't go any nearer—I wasn't going to go out into space without a suit on. I went back into the control room to get at a spy-ray, then changed my mind. That was the first place they would come to if they boarded us, as they probably would—other ships had disappeared in space, plenty of them. Instead, I went over to a life-boat and used its spy. And I tell you, sirs, there was nothing there—nothing at all!" The stranger's voice rose almost to a shriek, his mind quivered in an ecstasy of horror.

"Steady, Xylpic, steady," the Gray Lensman said, quietingly. "Everything you've said so far makes sense. It all fits right into the matrix. Nothing to go off the beam about, at all."

"What! You believe me!" the Chickladorian stared at Kinnison in amazement, an emotion very evidently shared by the Port Admiral.

"Yes," the man in gray leather asserted. "Not only that, but I have a very fair idea of what's coming next. Shoot!"

"The men walked out into space." The pink man offered this information diffidently, although positively—an oft-repeated but starkly incredible statement. "They did not float outward, sirs, they *walked;* and they acted as if they were breathing air, not space. And as they walked they sort of faded out; became thin, misty-like. This sounds crazy, sir," to Kinnison alone, "I thought then maybe I was cuckoo, and everybody around here thinks I am now, too. Maybe I *am* nuts, sir—I don't know."

"I do. You aren't," Kinnison said calmly.

"Well, and here comes the worst of it, they walked around just as though they were in a ship, growing fainter all the time. Then some of them lay down and something began to *skin* one of them—skin him alive, sir—but there was nothing there at all. I ran, then. I got into the fastest lifeboat on the far side and gave her all the oof she'd take. That's all, sir."

"Not quite all, Xylpic, unless I'm badly mistaken. Why didn't you tell the rest of it while you were at it?"

"I didn't dare to, sir. If I'd told any more they would have *known* I was crazy instead of just thinking so . . ." He broke off sharply, his voice altering strangely as he went on: "What makes you think there was anything more, sir? Do you . . . ?" The question trailed off into silence.

"I do. If what I think happened really did happen there was more— quite a lot more—and worse. Wasn't there?"

"I'll say there was!" The navigator almost exploded in relief. "Or rather, I think now that there was. But I can't describe any of it very well—everything was getting fainter all the time, and I thought I must be imagining most of it."

"You weren't imagining a thing . . ." the Lensman began, only to be interrupted by Haynes.

"Hell's jingling bells!" that worthy shouted. "If you know what it was, spill it!"

"Think I know, but not quite sure yet—got to check it. Can't get it from him—he's told everything he really knows. He didn't really see anything, it was practically invisible. Even if he had tried to describe the whole performance you wouldn't have recognized it. Nobody could have except Worsel and I, and possibly vanBuskirk. I'll tell you the rest of what actually happened and Xylpic can tell us if it checks." His features grew taut, his voice became hard and chill. "I saw it done, once. Worse, I heard it. Saw it and heard it, clear and plain. Also, I knew what it was all about, so I can describe it a lot better than Xylpic possibly can.

"Every man of that crew was killed by torture. Some were flayed alive, as Xylpic said; then they were carved up, slowly and piecemeal. Some were stretched, pulled apart by chains and hooks, on racks. Others twisted on frames. Boiled, little by little. Picked apart, bit by bit. Gassed. Eaten away by corrosives, one molecule at a time. Pressed out flat, as though between two plates of glass. Whipped. Scourged. Beaten gradually to a pulp. Other methods, lots of them—indescribable. All slow, though, and extremely painful. Greenish-yellow light, showing the aura of each man as he died. Beams from somewhere—possibly invisible—consuming the auras. Check, Xylpic?"

"Yes, sir, it checks!" The Chickladorian exclaimed in profound relief; then added, carefully: "That is, that's the way the torture was, exactly, sir, but there was something funny, a difference, about their fading away. I can't describe what was funny about it, but it didn't seem so much that they became invisible as that they went away, sir, even though they didn't go any place."

"That's the way their system of invisibility works. Got to be—nothing else will fit into . . ."

"The Overlords of Delgon!" Haynes rasped, sharply. "But if that's a true picture how in all the hells of space did this Xylpic, alone of all the ship's personnel, get away clean? Tell me that!"

"Simple!" the Gray Lensman snapped back sharply. "The rest were all Radeligians—he was the only Chickladorian aboard. The Overlords simply didn't know he was there—didn't feel him at all. Chickladorians think on a wave nobody else in the galaxy uses—you must have noticed that when you felt of him with your Lens. It took me half a minute to synchronize with him.

"As for his escape, that makes sense, too. The Overlords are slow workers and when they're playing that game they really concentrate on it—they don't pay any attention to anything else. By the time they got done and were ready to take over the ship, he could be almost anywhere."

"But he says that there was no ship there—nothing at all!" Haynes protested.

"Invisibility isn't hard to understand." Kinnison countered. "We've almost got it ourselves—we undoubtedly could have it as good as that, with a little more work on it. There was a ship there, beyond question. Close. Hooked on with magnets, and with a space-tube, lock to lock.

"The only peculiar part of it, and the bad part, is something you haven't mentioned yet. What would the Overlords—if, as we must assume, some of them got away from Worsel and his crew—be doing with a ship? They never had any space-ships that I ever knew anything about, nor any other mechanical devices requiring any advanced engineering skill. Also, and most important, they never did and never could invent or develop such an invisibility apparatus as that."

Kinnison fell silent; and while he frowned in thought Haynes dismissed the Chickladorian, with orders that his every want be supplied.

"What do you deduce from those facts?" the Port Admiral presently asked.

"Plenty," the Gray Lensman said, darkly. "I smell a rat. In fact, it stinks to high Heaven. Boskone."

"You may be right," Haynes conceded. It was hopeless, he knew, for him to try to keep up with this man's mental processes. "But why, and above all, how?"

" 'Why' is easy. They both owe us a lot, and want to pay us in full. Both hate us to hell and back. 'How' is immaterial. One found the other, some way. They're together, just as sure as hell's a man-trap, and that's what matters. It's bad. Very, *very* bad, believe me."

"Orders?" asked Haynes. He was a big man; big enough to ask instructions from anyone who knew more than he did—big enough to make no bones of such asking.

"One does not give orders to the Port Admiral," Kinnison mimicked him lightly, but meaningly. "One may request, perhaps, or suggest, but . . ."

"Skip it! I'll take a club to you yet, you young hellion! You said you'd take orders from me. QX—I'll take 'em from you. What are they?"

"No orders yet, I don't think . . ." Kinnison ruminated. "No . . . not until after we investigate. I have to have Worsel and vanBuskirk; we're the only three who have had experience. We'll take the *Dauntless*,

I think—it'll be safe enough. Thought-screens will stop the Overlords cold, and a scrambler will take care of the invisibility business."

"Safe enough, then, you think, to let traffic resume, if they're all protected with screens?"

"I wouldn't say so. They've got Boskonian super-dreadnoughts now to use if they want to, and that's something else to think about. Another week or so won't hurt much—better wait until we see what we can see. I've been wrong once or twice before, too, and I may be again."

He was. Although his words were conservative enough, he was certain in his own mind that he knew all the answers. But how wrong he was—how terribly, how tragically wrong! For even his mentality had not as yet envisaged the incredible actuality; his deductions and perceptions fell far, far short of the appalling truth!

14

EICH AND OVERLORD

The fashion in which the Overlords of Delgon had come under the ægis of Boskone, while obscure for a time, was in reality quite simple and logical; for upon distant Jarnevon the Eich had profited signally from Eichlan's disastrous raid upon Arisia. Not exactly in the sense suggested by Eukonidor the Arisian Watchman, it is true, but profited nevertheless. They had learned that thought, hitherto considered only a valuable adjunct to achievement, was actually an achievement in itself; that it could be used as a weapon of surpassing power.

Eukonidor's homily, as he more than suspected at the time, might as well never have been uttered, for all the effect it had upon the life or upon the purpose in life of any single member of the race of the Eich. Eichmil, who had been Second of Boskone, was now First; the others were advanced correspondingly; and a new Eighth and Ninth had been chosen to complete the roster of the Council which was Boskone.

"The late Eichlan," Eichmil stated harshly after calling the new Boskone to order—which event took place within a day after it became apparent that the two bold spirits had departed to a bourne from which there was to be no returning—"erred seriously, in fact fatally, in underestimating an opponent, even though he himself was prone to harp upon the danger of that very thing.

"We are agreed that our objectives remain unchanged; and also that greater circumspection must be used until we have succeeded in discovering the hitherto unsuspected potentialities of pure thought. We will now hear from one of our new members, the Ninth, also a psychologist, who most fortunately had been studying this situation even before the inception of the expedition which yesterday came to such a catastrophic end."

"It is clear," the Ninth of Boskone began, "that Arisia is at present out of the question. Perceiving the possibility of some such dénouement—an idea to which I repeatedly called the attention of my predecessor psychologist, the late Eighth—I have been long at work upon certain alternative measures.

"Consider, please, the matter of the thought-screens. Who developed them first is immaterial—whether Arisia stole them from Ploor, or vice versa, or whether each developed them independently. The pertinent facts are two:

"First, that the Arisians can break such screens by the application of mental force, either of greater magnitude than they can withstand or of some new and as yet unknown composition or pattern.

"Second, that such screens were and probably still are used largely and commonly upon the planet Velantia. Therefore they must have been both necessary and adequate. The deduction is, I believe, defensible that they were used as a protection against entities who were, and who still may be, employing against the Velantians the weapons of pure thought which we wish to investigate and to acquire.

"I propose, therefore, that I and a few others of my selection continue this research, not upon Arisia, but upon Velantia and perhaps elsewhere."

To this suggestion there was no demur and a vessel set out forthwith. The visit to Velantia was simple and created no disturbance whatever. In this connection it must be remembered that the natives of Velantia, then in the early ecstasies of discovery by the Galactic Patrol and the consequent acquisition of inertialess flight, were fairly reveling in visits to and from the widely-variant peoples of the planets of hundreds of other suns. It must be borne in mind that, since the Eich were physically more like the Velantians than were the men of Tellus, the presence of a group of such entities upon the planet would create less comment than that of a group of human beings. Therefore that fateful visit went unnoticed at the time, and it was only by long and arduous research, after Kinnison had deduced that some such visit must have been made, that it was shown to have been an actuality.

Space forbids any detailed account of what the Ninth of Boskone and his fellows did, although that story of itself would be no mean epic. Suffice it to say, then, that they became well acquainted with the friendly Velantians; they studied and they learned. Particularly did they seek information concerning the noisome Overlords of Delgon, although the natives did not care to dwell at any length upon the subject.

"Their power is broken," they were wont to inform the questioners, with airy flirtings of tail and wing. "Every known cavern of them, and not a few hitherto unknown caverns, have been blasted out of existence. Whenever one of them dares to obtrude his mentality upon any one of us he is at once hunted down and slain. Even if they are not all dead, as we think, they certainly are no longer a menace to our peace and security."

Having secured all the information available upon Velantia, the Eich went to Delgon, where they devoted all the power of their admittedly first-grade minds and all the not inconsiderable resources of their ship to the task of finding and uniting the remnants of what had once been a flourishing race, the Overlords of Delgon.

The Overlords! That monstrous, repulsive, amoral race which, not excepting even the Eich themselves, achieved the most universal condemnation ever to have been given in the long history of the Galactic Union. The Eich, admittedly deserving of the fate which was theirs, had and have their apologists. The Eich were wrong-minded, all admit. They were anti-social, blood-mad, obsessed with an insatiable lust for power and conquest which nothing except complete extinction could extirpate. Their evil attributes were legion. They were, however, brave. They were organizers par excellence. They were, in their own fashion, creators and doers. They had the courage of their convictions and followed them to the bitter end.

Of the Overlords, however, nothing good has ever been said. They were debased, cruel, perverted to a degree starkly unthinkable to any normal intelligence, however housed. In their native habitat they had no weapons, nor need of any. Through sheer power of mind they reached out to their victims, even upon other planets, and forced them to come to the gloomy caverns in which they had their being. There the victims were tortured to death in numberless unspeakable fashions, and while they died the captors *fed*, ghoulishly, upon the departing life-principle of the sufferers.

The mechanism of that absorption is entirely unknown; nor is there any adequate evidence as to what end was served by it in the economy of that horrid race. That these orgies were not essential to their physical well-being is certain, since many of the creatures survived for a long time after the frightful rites were rendered impossible.

Be that as it may, the Eich sought out and found many surviving Overlords. The latter tried to enslave the visitors and to bend them to their hideously sadistic purposes, but to no avail. Not only were the Eich protected by thought-screens; they had minds stronger even than the Overlord's own. And, after the first overtures had been made and channels of communication established, the alliance was a natural.

Much has been said and written of the binding power of love. That, and other noble emotions, have indeed performed wonders. It seems to this historian, however, that all too little has been said of the effectiveness of pure hate as a cementing material. Probably for good and sufficient moral reasons; perhaps because—and for the best—its application has been of comparatively infrequent occurrence. Here, in the case in hand, we have history's best example of two entirely dissimilar peoples working efficiently together under the urge, not of love or of any other lofty sentiment, but of sheer, stark, unalloyed and corrosive, but common, hate.

Both hated Civilization and everything pertaining to it. Both wanted revenge; wanted it with a searing, furious need almost tangible: a gnawing, burning lust which neither countenanced palliation nor brooked denial. And above all, both hated vengefully, furiously, esuriently—every way except blindly—an as yet unknown and unidentified wearer of the million-times-accursed Lens of the Galactic Patrol!

The Eich were hard, ruthless, cold; not even having such words in their language as "conscience," "mercy," or "scruple." Their hatred of the Lensmen was then a thing of an intensity unknowable to any human mind. Even that emotion however, grim as it was and fearsome, paled beside the passionately vitriolic hatred of the Overlords of Delgon for the being who had been the Nemesis of their race.

And when the sheer mental power of the Overlords, unthinkably great as it was and operative withal in a fashion utterly incomprehensible to us of Civilization, was combined with the ingenuity, resourcefulness, and drive, as well as with the scientific ability of the Eich, the results would in any case have been portentous indeed.

In this case they were more than portentous, and worse. Those prodigious intellects, fanned into fierce activity by fiery blasts of hatred, produced a thing incredible.

15

OVERLORDS OF DELGON

Before his ship was serviced for the flight into the unknown Kinnison changed his mind. He was vaguely troubled about the trip. It was nothing as definite as a "hunch"; hunches are, the Gray Lensman knew, the results of the operation of an extra-sensory perception possessed by all of us in greater or lesser degree. It was probably not an obscure warning to his super-sense from an other, more pervasive dimension. It was, he thought, a repercussion of the doubt in Xylpic's mind that the fading out of the men's bodies had been due to simple invisibility.

"I think I'd better go alone, chief," he informed the Port Admiral one day. "I'm not quite as sure as I was as to just what they've got."

"What difference does that make?" Haynes demanded.

"Lives," was the terse reply.

"Your life is what I'm thinking about. You'll be safer with the big ship, you can't deny that."

"We-ll, perhaps. But I don't want . . ."

"What you want is immaterial."

"How about a compromise? I'll take Worsel and vanBuskirk. When the Overlords hypnotized him that time it made Bus so mad that he's been taking treatments from Worsel. Nobody can hypnotize him now, Worsel says, not even an Overlord."

"No compromise. I can't order you to take the *Dauntless,* since your authority is transcendent. You can take anything you like. I can, however, and shall, order the *Dauntless* to ride your tail wherever you go."

"QX, I'll have to take her then." Kinnison's voice grew somber. "But suppose half the crew don't get back . . . and that I do?"

"Isn't that what happened on the *Brittania?*"

"No," came the flat answer. "We were all taking the same chance then—it was the luck of the draw. This is different."

"How different?"

"I've got better equipment than they have . . . I'd be a murderer, cold."

"Not at all, no more than then. You had better equipment then, too, you know, although not as much of it. Every commander of men has that same feeling when he sends men to death. But put yourself in my place. Would you send one of your best men, or let him go, alone on a highly dangerous mission when more men or ships would improve his chances? Answer that, honestly."

"Probably I wouldn't," Kinnison admitted, reluctantly.

"QX. Take all the precautions you can—but I don't have to tell you that. I know you will."

Therefore it was the *Dauntless* in which Kinnison set out a day or two later. With him were Worsel and vanBuskirk, as well as the vessel's full operating crew of Tellurians. As they approached the region of space in which Xylpic's vessel had been attacked every man in the crew got his armor in readiness for instant use, checked his sidearms, and took his emergency battle-station. Kinnison turned then to Worsel.

"How d'you feel, fellow old snake?" he asked.

"Scared," the Velantian replied, sending a rippling surge of power the full length of the thirty-foot-long cable of supple, leather-hard flesh that was his body. "Scared to the tip of my tail. Not that they can treat me as they did before—we three, at least, are safe from their minds—but at what they will *do*. Whatever it is to be, it will not be what we expect. They certainly will not do the obvious."

"That's what's clogging my jets," the Lensman agreed. "As a girl told me once, I'm getting the screaming meamies."

"Thats what you mugs get for being so brainy," vanBuskirk put in. With a flick of his massive wrist he brought his thirty-pound space-axe to the "ready" as lightly as though it were a Tellurian dress saber. "Bring on your Overlords—squish! Just like that!" and a whistling sweep of his atrocious weapon was illustration enough.

"May be something in that, too, Bus," he laughed. Then, to the Velantian, "About time to tune in on 'em, I guess."

He was in no doubt whatever as to Worsel's ability to reach them. He knew that that incredibly powerful mind, without Lens or advanced Arisian instruction, had been able to cover eleven solar systems: he knew that, with his present ability, Worsel could cover half of space!

Although every fiber of his being shrieked protest against contact with the hereditary foe of his race, the Velantian put his mind en rapport with the Overlords and sent out his thought. He listened for seconds, motionless, then glided across the room to the thought-screened pilot and hissed directions. The pilot altered his course sharply and gave her the gun.

"I'll take her over now," Worsel said, presently. "It'll look better that way—more as though they had us all under control."

He cut the Bergenholm, then set everything on zero—the ship hung, inert and practically motionless, in space. Simultaneously twenty unscreened men—volunteers—dashed toward the main airlock, overcome by some intense emotion.

"Now! Screens on! Scramblers!" Kinnison yelled; and at his words a thought-screen enclosed the ship; high-powered scramblers, within whose fields no invisibility apparatus could hold, burst into action. There the vessel was, right beside the *Dauntless,* a Boskonian in every line and member! "Fire!"

But even as she appeared, before a firing-stud could be pressed, the enemy craft almost disappeared again; or rather, she did not really appear at all, except as the veriest wraith of what a good, solid ship of space-alloy ought to be. She was a ghost-ship, as unsubstantial as fog. Misty, tenuous, immaterial; the shadow of a shadow. A dream-ship, built of the gossamer of dreams, manned by figments of horror recruited from sheerest nightmare. Not invisibility this time, Kinnison knew with a profound shock. Something else—something entirely different—something utterly incomprehensible. Xylpic had said it as nearly as it could be put into understandable words—the Boskonian ship was *leaving,* although it was standing still! It was monstrous—it *couldn't be done!*

Then, at a range of only feet instead of the usual "pointblank" range of hundreds of miles, the tremendous secondaries of the *Dauntless* cut loose. At such a ridiculous range as that—why, the screens themselves kept anything further away from them than that ship was—they *couldn't* miss. Nor did they; but neither did they hit. Those ravening beams went through and through the tenuous fabrication which should have been a vessel, but they struck nothing whatever. They went *past*—entirely harmlessly past—both the ship itself and the wraithlike but unforgettable figures which Kinnison recognized at a glance as Overlords of Delgon. His heart sank with a thud. He knew when he had had enough; and this was altogether too much.

"Go free!" he rasped. "Give 'er the oof!"

Energy poured into and through the great Bergenholm, but nothing happened; ship and contents remained inert. Not exactly inert, either, for the men were beginning to feel a new and unique sensation.

Energy raved from the driving jets, but still nothing happened. There was none of the thrust, none of the reaction of an inert start; there was none of the lashing, quivering awareness of speed which affects every mind, however hardened to free flight, in the instant of change from rest to a motion many times faster than that of light.

"Armor! Thought-screen! Emergency stations all!" Since they could not run away from whatever it was that was coming, they would face it.

And something was happening now, there was no doubt of that. Kinnison had been seasick and airsick and spacesick. Also, since cadets must learn to be able to do without artificial gravity, pseudo-inertia, and those other refinements which make space-liners so comfortable, he had known the nausea and the queasily terrifying endless-fall sensations of weightlessness, as well as the even worse outrages to the sensibilities incident to inertialessness in its crudest, most basic applications. He thought that he was familiar with all the untoward sensations of every mode of travel known to science. This, however, was something entirely new.

He felt as though he were being compressed; not as a whole, but atom by atom. He was being twisted—corkscrewed in a monstrously obscure fashion which permitted him neither to move from his place nor to remain where he was. He hung there, poised, for hours—or was it for a thousandth of a second? At the same time he felt a painless, but revolting transformation progress in a series of waves throughout his entire body; a rearrangement, a writhing, crawling distortion, an incomprehensibly impossible extrusion of each ultimate corpuscle of his substance in an unknowable and non-existent direction!

As slowly—or as rapidly?—as the transformation had waxed, it waned. He was again free to move. As far as he could tell, everything was almost as before. The *Dauntless* was about the same; so was the almost-invisible ship attached to her so closely. There was, however, a difference. The air seemed thick . . . familiar objects were seen blurrily, dimly . . . distorted . . . outside the ship there was nothing except a vague blur of grayness . . . no stars, no constellations . . .

A wave of thought came beating into his brain. He *had* to leave the

Dauntless. It was most vitaily important to get into that dimly-seen companion vessel without an instant's delay! And even as his mind instinctively reared a barrier, blocking out the intruding thought, he recognized it for what it was—the summons of the Overlords!

But how about the thought screens, he thought in a semi-daze, then reason resumed accustomed sway. He was no longer in space—at least, not in the space he knew. That new, indescribable sensation had been one of *acceleration*—when they attained constant velocity it stopped. Acceleration—velocity—in what? To what? He did not know. Out of space as he knew it, certainly. Time was distorted, unrecognizable. Matter did not necessarily obey the familiar laws. Thought? QX—thought, lying in the sub-ether, probably was unaffected. Thought-screen generators, however, being material might not—in fact, did not—work. Worsel, vanBuskirk, and he did not need them, but those other poor devils . . .

He looked at them. The men—all of them, officers and all—had thrown off their armor, thrown away their weapons, and were again rushing toward the lock. With a smothered curse Kinnison followed them, as did the Velantian and the giant Dutch-Valerian. Into the lock. Through it, into the almost invisible space-tube, which, he noticed, was floored with a solider-appearing substance. The air felt heavy; dense, like water, or even more like metallic mercury. It breathed, however, QX. Into the Boskonian ship, along corridors, into a room which was precisely such a torture-chamber as Kinnison had described. There they were, ten of them; ten of the dragon-like, reptilian Overlords of Delgon!

They moved slowly, sluggishly, as did the Tellurians, in that thick, dense medium which was not, could not be, air. Ten chains were thrown, like pictures in slow motion, about ten human necks; ten entranced men were led unresistingly to anguished doom. This time the Gray Lensman's curse was not smothered—with a blistering deep-space oath he pulled his DeLameter and fired—once, twice, three times. No soap—he knew it, but he had to try. Furious, he launched himself. His taloned fingers, ravening to tear, went past, not around, the Overlord's throat; and the scimitared tail of the reptile, fierce-driven, apparently went through the Lensman, screens, armor, and brisket, but touched none of them in passing. He hurled a thought, a more disastrous bolt by far than he had sent against any mind since he had learned the art. In vain—the Overlords, themselves masters of mentality, could not be slain or even swerved by any forces at his command.

Kinnison reared back then in thought. There must be some ground, some substance common to the planes or dimensions involved, else they could not be here. The deck, for instance, was as solid to his feet as it was to the enemy. He thrust out a hand at the wall beside him—it was not there. The chains, however, held his suffering men, and the Overlords held the chains. The knives, also, and the clubs, and the other implements of torture being wielded with such peculiarly horrible slowness.

To think was to act. He leaped forward, seized a maul and made as though to swing it in terrific blow; only to stop, shocked. The maul did not move! Or rather, it moved, but *so* slowly, as though he were hauling it through putty! He dropped the handle, shoving it back, and received another shock, for it kept on coming under the urge of his first mighty heave—kept coming, knocking him aside as it came!

Mass! Inertia! The stuff must be a hundred times as dense as platinum!

"Bus!" he flashed a thought to the staring Valerian. "Grab one of these clubs here—a little one, even *you* can't swing a big one—and get to work!"

As he thought, he leaped again; this time for a small, slender knife, almost a scalpel, but with a long, keenly thin blade. Even though it was massive as a dozen broadswords he could swing it and he did so; plunging lethally as he swung. A full-arm sweep—razor edge shearing, crunching through plated, corded throat—grisly head floating one way, horrid body the other!

Then an attack in waves of his own men! The Overlords knew what was toward. They commanded their slaves to abate the nuisance, and the Gray Lensman was buried under an avalanche of furious, although unarmed, humanity.

"Chase 'em off me, will you, Worsel?" Kinnison pleaded. "You're husky enough to handle 'em all—I'm not. Hold 'em off while Bus and I polish off this crowd, huh?" And Worsel did so.

VanBuskirk, scorning Kinnison's advice, had seized the biggest thing in sight, only to relinquish it sheepishly—he might as well have attempted to wield a bridge-girder! He finally selected a tiny bar, only half an inch in diameter and scarcely six feet long; but he found that even this sliver was more of a bludgeon than any space-axe he had ever swung.

Then the armed pair went joyously to war, the Tellurian with his knife, the Valerian with his magic wand. When the Overlords saw that a fight to the finish was inevitable they also seized weapons and fought with the desperation of the cornered rats they were. This, however, freed Worsel from guard duty, since the monsters were fully occupied in defending themselves. He seized a length of chain, wrapped six feet of tail in an unbreakable anchorage around a torture rack, and set viciously to work.

Thus again the intrepid three, the only minions of Civilization theretofore to have escaped alive from the clutches of the Overlords of Delgon, fought side by side. VanBuskirk particularly was in his element. He was used to a gravity almost three times Earth's, he was accustomed to enormously heavy, almost viscous air. This stuff, thick as it was, tasted infinitely better than the vacuum that Tellurians liked to breathe. It let a man *use* his strength; and the gigantic Dutchman waded in happily, swinging his frightfully massive weapon with devastating effect. Crunch! Splash! THWUCK! When that bar struck it did not stop. It went through; blood, brains, smashed heads and dismembered limbs flying in all directions. And Worsel's lethal chain, driven irresistibly at the end of the twenty-five-foot lever of his free length of body, clanked, hummed, and snarled its way through reptilian flesh. And, while Kinnison was puny indeed in comparison with his two brothers-in-arms, he had selected a weapon which would make his skill count; and his wicked knife stabbed, sheared, and trenchantly bit.

And thus, instead of dealing out death, the Overlords died.

16

OUT OF THE VORTEX

The carnage over, Kinnison made his way to the control board, which was more or less standard in type. There were, however, some instruments new to him; and these he examined with care, tracing their leads throughout their lengths with his sense of perception before he touched a switch. Then he pulled out three plungers, one after the other.

There was a jarring "thunk"! and a reversal of the inexplicable, sickening sensations he had experienced previously. They ceased; the ships, solid now and still locked side by side, lay again in open, familiar space.

"Back to the *Dauntless*," Kinnison directed, tersely, and they went; taking with them the bodies of the slain Patrolmen. The ten who had been tortured were dead; twelve more had perished under the mental forces or the physical blows of the Overlords. Nothing could be done for any of them save to take their remains back to Tellus.

"What do we do with this ship—let's burn her out, huh?" asked vanBuskirk.

"Not on Tuesdays—the College of Science would fry me to a crisp in my own lard if I did," Kinnison retorted. "We take her in, as is. Where are we, Worsel? Have you and the navigator found out yet?"

" 'Way, 'way out—almost out of the galaxy," Worsel replied, and one of the computers recited a string of numbers, then added, "I don't see how we could have come so far in that short a time."

"How much time was it—got any idea?" Kinnison asked, pointedly.

"Why, by the chronometers . . . Oh . . ." the man's voice trailed off.

"You're getting the idea. Wouldn't have surprised me much if we'd been clear out of the known Universe. Hyperspace is funny that way, they say. Don't know a thing about it myself, except that we were in it for a while, but that's enough for me."

Back to Tellus they drove at the highest practicable speed, and at Prime Base scientists swarmed over and throughout the Boskonian vessel. They tore down, rebuilt, measured, analyzed, tested, and conferred.

"They got some of it, but they say you missed a lot," Thorndyke reported to his friend Kinnison one day. "Old Cardynge is mad as a cateagle about your report on that vortex or tunnel or whatever it was. He says your lack of appreciation of the simplest fundamentals is something pitiful, or words to that effect. He's going to blast you to a cinder as soon as he can get hold of you."

"Vell, ve can't all be first violiners in der orchestra, some of us got to push vind t'rough der trombone," Kinnison quoted, philosophically. "I done my damndest—how's a guy going to report accurately on something he can't hear, see, feel, taste, smell, or sense? But I heard that they've solved that thing of the interpenetrability of the two kinds of matter. What's the low-down on that?"

"Cardynge says it's simple. Maybe it is, but I'm a technician myself, not a mathematician. As near as I can get it, the Overlords and their stuff were treated or conditioned with an oscillatory of some kind, so that under the combined action of the fields generated by the ship and the shore station all their substance was rotated almost out of space. Not out of space, exactly, either, more like, say, very nearly one hundred eighty degrees out of phase; so that two bodies—one untreated, our stuff—could occupy the same place at the same time without perceptible interference. The failure of either force, such as your cutting the ship's generators, would relieve the strain."

"It did more than that—it destroyed the vortex . . . but it might, at that," the Lensman went on, thoughtfully. "It could very well be that only that one special force, exerted in the right place relative to the home-station generator, could bring the vortex into being. But how about that heavy stuff, common to both planes, or phases, of matter?"

"Synthetic, they say. They're working on it now."

"Thanks for the dope. I've got to flit—got a date with Haynes. I'll see Cardynge later and let him get it off his chest," and the Lensman strode away toward the Port Admiral's office.

Haynes greeted him cordially; then, at sight of the storm signals flying in the younger man's eyes, he sobered.

"QX," he said, wearily. "If we have to go over this again, unload it, Kim."

"Twenty two good men," Kinnison said, harshly. "I murdered them. Just as surely, if not quite as directly, as though I brained them with a space-axe."

"In one way, if you look at it fanatically enough, yes," the older man admitted, much to Kinnison's surprile. "I'm not asking you to look at it in a broader sense, because you probably can't—yet. Some things you can do alone; some things you can do even better alone than with help. I have never objected, nor shall I ever object to your going alone on such missions, however dangerous they may be. That is, and will be, your job. What you are forgetting in the luxury of giving way to your emotions is that the Patrol comes first. The Patrol is of vastly greater importance than the lives of any man or group of men in it."

"But I know that, sir," protested Kinnison. "I . . ."

"You have a peculiar way of showing it, then," the admiral broke in. "You say that you killed twenty two men. Admitting it for the moment, which would you say was better for the Patrol—to lose those twenty two good men in a successful and productive operation, or to lose the life of one Unattached Lensman without gaining any information or any other benefit whatever thereby?"

"Why . . . I . . . If you look at it that way, sir . . ." Kinnison still knew that he was right, but in that form the question answered itself.

"That is the only way it can be looked at," the old man returned, flatly. "No heroics on your part, no maudlin sentimentality. Now, as a Lensman, is it your considered judgment that it is best for the Patrol that you traverse that hyperspatial vortex alone, or with all the resources of the *Dauntless* at your command?"

Kinnison's face was white and strained. He could not lie to the Port Admiral. Nor could he tell the truth, for the dying agonies of those fiendishly tortured boys still racked him to the core.

"But I *can't* order men into any such death as that," he broke out, finally.

"You must," Haynes replied, inexorably. "Either you take the ship as she is or else you call for volunteers—and you know what that would mean."

Kinnison did, too well. The surviving personnel of the two *Brit-*

tanias, the full present complement of the *Dauntless,* the crews of every other ship in Base, practically everybody on the Reservation—Haynes himself certainly, even Lacy and old von Hohendorff, everybody, even or especially if they had no business on such a trip as that—would volunteer; and every man jack of them would yell his head off at being left out. Each would have a thousand reasons for going.

"QX, I suppose. You win." Kinnison submitted, although with ill grace, rebelliously. "But I don't like it, nor any part of it. It clogs my jets."

"I know it, Kim," Haynes put a hand upon the boy's shoulder, tightening his fingers. "We all have it to do; it's part of the job. But remember always, Lensman, that the Patrol is not an army of mercenaries or conscripts. Any one of them, just as would you yourself, would go out there, *knowing* that it meant death in the torture-chambers of the Overlords, if in so doing he knew that he could help to end the torture and the slaughter of non-combatant men, women, and children that is now going on."

Kinnison walked slowly back to the field; silenced, but not convinced. There was something screwy somewhere, but he couldn't . . ."

"Just a moment, young man!" came a sharp, irritated voice. "I have been looking for you. At what time do you propose to set out for that which is being so loosely called the 'hyperspatial vortex'?"

He pulled himself out of his abstraction to see Sir Austin Cardynge. Testy, irascible, impatient, and vitriolic of tongue, he had always reminded Kinnison of a frantic hen attempting to mother a brood of ducklings.

"Hi, Sir Austin! Tomorrow—hour fifteen. Why?" The Lensman had too much on his mind to be ceremonious with this mathematical nuisance.

"Because I find that I must accompany you, and it is most damnably inconvenient, sir. The Society meets Tuesday week, and that ass Weingarde will . . ."

"Huh?" Kinnison ejaculated. "Who told you that you had to go along, or that you even *could,* for that matter?"

"Don't be a fool, young man!" the peppery scientist advised. "It should be apparent even to your feeble intelligence that after your fiasco, your inexcusable negligence in not reporting even the most elementary vectorial-tensorial analysis of that extremely important phenomenon, someone with a brain should . . ."

"Hold on, Sir Austin!" Kinnison interrupted the harangue, "You want to come along just to study the *mathematics* of that damn . . . ?"

"Just to study it!" shrieked the old man, almost tearing his hair. "You dolt—you blockhead! My God, why should anything with such a

brain be permitted to live? Don't you even know, Kinnison, that in that vortex lies the solution of one of the greatest problems in all science?"

"Never occurred to me," the Lensman replied, unruffled by the old man's acid fury. He had had weeks of it, at the Conference.

"It is imperative that I go," Sir Austin was still acerbic, but the intensity of his passion was abating. "I must analyze those fields, their patterns, interactions and reactions, myself. Unskilled observations are useless, as you learned to your sorrow, and this opportunity is priceless—possibly it is unique. Since the data must be not only complete but also entirely authoritative, I myself must go. That is clear, is it not, even to you?"

"No. Hasn't anybody told you that everybody aboard is simply flirting with the undertaker?"

"Nonsense! I have subjected the affair, every phase of it, to a rigid statistical analysis. The probability is significantly greater than zero— oh, ever so much greater, almost point one nine, in fact—that the ship will return, with my notes."

"But listen, Sir Austin," Kinnison explained patiently. "You won't have time to study the generators at the other end, even if the folks there felt inclined to give us the chance. Our object is to blow the whole thing clear out of space."

"Of course, of course—certainly! The mere generating mechanisms are immaterial. Analyses of the forces themselves are the sole desiderata. Vectors—tensors—performance of mechanisms in reception—ethereal and sub-ethereal phenomena—propagation—extinction—phase angles—complete and accurate data upon hundreds of such items—slighting even one would be calamitous. Having this material, however, the mechanism of energization becomes a mere detail—complete solution and design inevitable, absolute—childishly simple."

"Oh." The Lensman was slightly groggy under the barrage. "The ship may get back, but how about you, personally?"

"What difference does that make?" Cardynge snapped fretfully. "Even if, as is theoretically probable, we find that communication is impossible, my notes have a very good chance—very good indeed—of getting back. You do not seem to realize, young man, that to science that data is *necessary*. I *must* accompany you."

Kinnison looked down at the wispy little man in surprise. Here was something he had never suspected. Cardynge was a scientific wizard, he knew. That he had a phenomenal mind there was no shadow of doubt, but the Lensman had never thought of him as being physically brave. It was not merely courage, he decided. It was something bigger—better.

Transcendent. An utter selflessness, a devotion to science so complete that neither physical welfare nor even life itself could be given any consideration whatever.

"You think, then, that this data is worth sacrificing the lives of four hundred men, including yours and mine, to get?" Kinnison asked, earnestly.

"Certainly, or a hundred times that many," Cardynge snapped, testily. "You heard me say, did you not, that this opportunity is priceless, and may very well be unique?"

"QX, you can come," and Kinnison went on into the *Dauntless*.

He went to bed wondering. Maybe the chief was right. He woke up, still wondering. Perhaps he was taking himself too seriously. Perhaps he was, as Haynes had more than intimated, indulging in mock heroics.

He prowled about. The two ships of space were still locked together. They would fly together to and along that dread tunnel, and he had to see that everything was on the green.

He went into the wardroom. One young officer was thumping the piano right tunefully and a dozen others were rending the atmosphere with joyous song. In that room any formality or "as you were" signal was unnecessary; the whole bunch fell upon their commander gleefully and with a complete lack of restraint, in a vociferous hilarity very evidently neither forced nor assumed.

Kinnison went on with his tour. "What was it?" he demanded of himself. Haynes didn't feel guilty. Cardynge was worse—he would kill forty thousand men, including the Lensman and himself, without batting an eye. These kids didn't give a damn. Their fellows had been slain by the Overlords, the Overlords had in turn been slain. All square—QX. Their turn next? So what? Kinnison himself did not want to die—he wanted to live—but if his number came up that was part of the game.

What was it, this willingness to give up life itself for an abstraction? Science, the Patrol, Civilization—notoriously ungrateful mistresses. Why? Some inner force—some compensation defying sense, reason, or analysis?

Whatever it was, he had it, too. Why deny it to others? What in all the nine hells of Valeria was he griping about?

"Maybe *I'm* nuts!" he concluded, and gave the word to blast off.

To blast off—to find and to traverse wholly that awful hyper-tube, at whose far terminus there would be lurking no man knew what.

17

DOWN THE HYPER-SPATIAL TUBE

Out in open space Kinnison called the entire crew to a mass meeting, in which he outlined to them as well as he could that which they were about to face.

"The Boskonian ship will undoubtedly return automatically to her dock," he concluded. "That there is probably docking-space for only one ship is immaterial, since the *Dauntless* will remain free. That ship is not manned, as you know, because no one knows what is going to happen when the fields are released in the home dock. Consequences may be disastrous to any foreign, untreated matter within her. Some signal will undoubtedly be given upon landing, although we have no means of knowing what that signal will be and Sir Austin has pointed out that there can be no communication between that ship and her base until her generators have been cut.

"Since we also will be in hyper-space until that time, it is clear that the generator must be cut from within the vessel. Electrical and mechanical relays are out of the question. Therefore two of our personnel will keep alternate watches in her control-room, to pull the necessary switches. I am not going to order any man to such a duty, nor am I going to ask for volunteers. If the man on duty is not killed outright—this is a distinct possibility, although perhaps not a probability—speed in getting back here will be decidedly of the essence. It seems to me that the best interests of the Patrol will be served by having the two fastest members of our force on watch. Time trials from the Boskonian panel to our airlock are, therefore, now in order."

This was Kinnison's device for taking the job himself. He was, he knew, the fastest man aboard, and he proved it. He negotiated the distance in seven seconds flat, over half a second faster than any other member of the crew. Then:

"Well, if you small, slow runts are done playing creepie-mousie, get out of the way and let folks run that really can," vanBuskirk boomed. "Come on, Worsel, I see where you and I are going to get ourselves a job."

"But see here, you can't!" Kinnison protested, aghast. "I said members of the crew."

"No, you didn't," the Valerian contradicted. "You said 'two of our personnel,' and if Worsel and I ain't personnel, what are we? We'll leave it to Sir Austin."

"Indubitably 'personnel,' " the arbiter decided, taking a moment from the apparatus he was setting up. "Your statement that speed is a prime requisite is also binding."

Whereupon the winged Velantian flew and wriggled the distance in two seconds, and the giant Dutch-Valerian ran it in three!

"You big, knot-headed Valerian ape!" Kinnison hissed a malevolent thought; not as the expedition's commander to a subordinate, but as an outraged friend speaking plainly to friend. "You knew I wanted that job myself, you clunker—damn your thick, hard crust!"

"Well, so did I, you poor, spindly little Tellurian wart, and so did Worsel," vanBuskirk shot back in kind. "Besides, it's for the good of the Patrol—you said so yourself! Comb *that* out of your whiskers, half-portion!" he added, with a wide and toothy grin, as he swaggered away, lightly brandishing his ponderous mace.

The run to the point in space where the vortex had been was made on schedule. Switches drove home, most of the fabric of the enemy vessel went out of phase, the voyagers experienced the weirdly uncomfortable acceleration along an impossible vector, and the familiar firmament disappeared into an impalpable but impenetrable murk of featureless, textureless gray.

Sir Austin was in his element. Indeed, he was in a seventh heaven of rapture as he observed, recorded, and calculated. He chuckled over his interferometers, he clucked over his meters, now and again he emitted shrill whoops of triumph as a particularly abstruse bit of knowledge was torn from its lair. He strutted, he gloated, he practically purred as he recorded upon the tape still another momentous conclusion or a gravid equation, each couched in terms of such incomprehensibly formidable mathematics that no one not a member of the Conference of Scientists could even dimly perceive its meaning.

Cardynge finished his work; and, after doing everything that could be done to insure the safe return to Science of his priceless records, he simply preened himself. He wasn't like an old hen, after all, Kinnison decided. More like a lean, gray tomcat. One that has just eaten the canary and, contemplatively smoothing his whiskers, is full of pleasant, if somewhat sanguine visions of what he is going to do to those other felines at that next meeting.

Time wore on. A long time? Or a short? Who could tell? What possible measure of that unknown and intrinsically unknowable concept exists or can exist in that fantastic region of—hyper-space? Inter-space? Pseudo-space? Call it what you like.

Time, as has been said, wore on. The ships arrived at the enemy base, the landing signal was given. Worsel, on duty at the time, recognized it for what it was—with his brain that was a foregone conclusion. He threw the switches, then flew and wriggled as even he had never done before, hurling a thought as he came.

And as the Velantian, himself in the throes of weird deceleration, tore through the thinning atmosphere, the queasy Gray Lensman watched the development about them of a forbiddingly inimical scene.

They were materializing upon a landing field of sorts, a smooth and level expanse of black igneous rock. Two suns, one hot and close, one pale and distant, cast the impenetrable shadows so characteristic of an airless world. Dwarfed by distance, but still massively, craggily tremendous, there loomed the encircling rampart of the volcanic crater upon whose floor the fortress lay.

And what a fortress; New—raw—crude . . . but fanged with armament of might. There was the typically Boskonian dome of control, there were powerful ships of war in their cradles, there beside the *Dauntless* was very evidently the power-plant in which was generated the cryptic force which made inter-dimensional transit an actuality. But, and here was the saving factor which the Lensman had dared only half hope to find, those ultra-powerful defensive mechanisms were mounted to resist attack from without, not from within. It had not occurred to the foe, even as a possibility, that the Patrol might come upon them in panoply of war through their own hyper-spatial tube!

Kinnison knew that it was useless to assault that dome. He could, perhaps, crack its screens with his primaries, but he did not have enough stuff to reduce the whole establishment and therefore could not use the primaries at all. Since the enemy had been taken completely by surprise, however, he had a lot of time—at least a minute, perhaps a trifle more— and in that time the old *Dauntless* could do a lot of damage. The power-plant came first; that was what they had come out here to get.

"All secondaries fire at will!" Kinnison barked into his microphone. He was already at his conning board; every man of the crew was at his station. "All of you who can reach twenty-seven three-oh-eight, hit it— hard. The rest of you do as you please."

Every beam which could be brought to bear upon the power-house, and there were plenty of them, flamed out practically as one. The building stood for an instant, starkly outlined in a raging inferno of incandescence, then slumped down flabbily; its upper, nearer parts flaring away in clouds of sparklingly luminous vapor even as its lower members flowed sluggishly together in streams of molten metal. Deeper and deeper bore the frightful beams; foundations, sub-cellars, structural members and gargantuan mechanisms uniting with the obsidian of the crater's floor to form a lake of bubbling, frothing lava.

"QX—that's good!" Kinnison snapped. "Scatter your stuff, fel-lows—hit 'em!" He then spoke to Henderson, his chief pilot. "Lift us up a bit, Hen, to give the boys a better sight. Be ready to flit, fast; all hell's going to be out for noon any second now!"

The time of the *Dauntless* was short, but she was working fast. Her guns were not being tripped. Instead, every firing lever was jammed down into its last notch and was locked there. Into the plates stared hard-faced young firing officers, keen eyes glued to crossed hair-lines, grimly steady right and left hands spinning controller-rheostats by touch alone, tensely crouched as though by sheer driving force of will they could energize to even higher levels the ravening beams which were weaving beneath and around the Patrol's super-dreadnought a writhing, flaming pattern of death and destruction.

Ships—warships of Boskone's mightiest—caught cold. Some crewless; some half-manned; none ready for the stunning surprise attack of the Patrolmen. Through and through them the ruthless beams tore; leaving, not ships, but nondescript masses of half-fused metal. Hangars, machine-shops, supply depots suffered the same fate; a good third of the establishment became a smoking, smouldering heap of junk.

Then, one by one, the fixed-mount weapons of the enemy, by dint of what Herculean efforts can only be surmised, were brought to bear upon the bold invader. Brighter and brighter flamed her prodigiously powerful defensive screens. Number One faded out; crushed flat by the hellish energies of Boskone's projectors. Number Two flared into even more spectacular pyrotechnics, until soon even its tremendous resources of power became inadequate—blotchily, in discrete areas, clinging to existence with all the might of its Medonian generators and transmitters, it, too, began to fail.

"Better we flit, Hen, while we're all in one piece—right now," Kinnison advised the pilot then. "And I don't mean loaf, either—let's see you burn a hole in the ether."

Henderson's fingers swept over his board, depressing to maximum and locking down key after key. From her jets flared blast after blast of energies whose intensity paled the brilliance of the madly warring screens, and to Boskone's observers the immense Patrol raider vanished from all ken.

At that drive, the *Dauntless'* incomprehensible maximum, there was little danger of pursuit: for, as well as being the biggest and the most powerfully armed, she was also the fastest thing in space.

Out in open inter-galactic space—safe—discipline went by the board as though on signal and all hands joined in a release of pent-up emotion. Kinnison threw off his armor and, seizing the scandalized and highly outraged Cardynge, spun him around in dizzying, though effort-less circles.

"Didn't lose a man—NOT A MAN!" he yelled, exuberantly.

He plucked the now idle Henderson from his board and wrestled with him, only to drift lightly away, ahead of a tremendous slap aimed at his back by vanBuskirk. Inertialessness takes most of the edge off of rough-housing, but the performance did relieve the tension and soon the ebullient youths quieted down.

The enemy base was located well outside the galaxy. Not, as Kinnison had feared, in the Second Galaxy, but in a star cluster not too far removed from the First. Hence the flight to Prime Base did not take long.

Sir Austin Cardynge was more like a self-satisfied tomcat than ever as he gathered up his records, gave a corps of aides minute instructions regarding the packing of his equipment, and set out, figuratively but very evidently licking his chops, rehearsing the scene in which he would confound his allegedly learned fellows, especially that insufferable puppy, that upstart Weingarde . . .

"And that's that," Kinnison concluded his informal report to Haynes. "They're all washed up, there, at least. Before they can rebuild, you can wipe out the whole nest. If there should happen to be one or two more such bases, the boys know now how to handle them. I think I'd better be getting back onto my own job, don't you?"

"Probably so," Haynes thought for moments, then continued: "Can you use help, or can you work better alone?"

"I've been thinking about that. The higher the tougher, and it might not be a bad idea at all to have Worsel standing by in my speedster: close by and ready all the time. He's pretty much of an army himself, mental and physical. QX?"

"Can do," and thus it came about that the good ship *Dauntless* flew again, this time out Borova way; her sole freight a sleek black speedster and a rusty, battered meteor-tug, her passengers a sinuous Velantian and a husky Tellurian.

"Sort of a thin time for you, old man, I'm afraid." Kinnison leaned unconcernedly against the towering pillar of his friend's tail, whereupon four or five grotesquely stalked eyes curled out at him speculatively. To these two, each other's appearance and shape were neither repulsive nor strange. They were friends, in the deepest, truest sense. "He's so hideous that he's positively distinguished-looking," each had boasted more than once of the other to friends of his own race.

"Nothing like that." The Velantian flashed out a leather wing and flipped his tail aside in a playfully unsuccessful attempt to catch the Earthman off balance. "Some day, if you ever learn really to think, you will discover that a few weeks' solitary, undisturbed and concentrated thought is a rare treat. To have such an opportunity in the line of duty makes it a pleasure unalloyed."

"I always did think that you were slightly screwy at times, and now I know it," Kinnison retorted, unconvinced. "Thought is—or should be—a means to an end, not an end in itself; but if that's your idea of a wonderful time I'm glad to be able to give it to you."

They disembarked carefully in far space, the complete absence of spectators assured by the warship's fullest reach of detectors, and Kinnison again went down to Miners' Rest. Not, this time, to carouse. Miners were not carousing there. Instead, the whole asteroid was buzzing with news of the fabulously rich finds which were being made in the distant solar system of Tressilia.

Kinnison had known that the news would be there, for it was at his instructions that those rich meteors had been placed there to be found. Tressilia III was the home of the regional director with whom the Gray Lensman had important business to transact; he had to have a solid reason, not a mere excuse, for Bill Williams to leave Borova for Tressilia.

The lure of wealth, then as ever, was stronger even than that of drink or of drug. Miners came to revel, but instead they outfitted in haste and hied themselves to the new Klondike. Nor was this anything out of the ordinary. Such stampedes occurred every once in a while, and Strongheart and his minions were not unduly concerned. They'd be back, and in the meantime there was the profit on a lot of metal and an excess profit due to the skyrocketing prices of supplies.

"You too, Bill?" Strongheart asked without surprise.

"I'll tell the Universe!" came ready answer. "If they's metal there I'll find it, pal." In making this declaration he was not boasting, he was merely voicing a simple truth. By this time the meteor belts of a hundred solar systems knew for a fact that Wild Bill Williams of Aldebaran II could find metal if metal was there to be found.

"If it's a bloomer, Bill, come back," the dive-keeper urged. "Come back anyway when you've worked it a couple of drunks."

"I'll do that, Strongheart, old pal, I sure will," the Lensman agreed, amiably enough. "You run a nice joint here and I like it."

Thus Kinnison went to the asteroid belts of Tressilia and there Bill Williams found rich metal. Or, more precisely, he dumped out into space and then recovered a very special meteor indeed—one in whose fabrication Kinnison's own treasure-trove had played the leading part. He did not find it the first day, of course, nor during the first week—it would be a trifle smelly to have even Wild Bill strike it rich too soon—but after a decent interval of time.

His Tressilian find had to be very much worth while, far too much so to be left to chance; for Edmund Crowninshield, the Regional Director, inhabited no such rawly obvious dive as Miners' Rest. He catered only to the upper crust; meteor miners and other similar scum were never permitted to enter his door.

When Kinnison repaired the Bergenholm of the Borovan space-liner he had, by sheerest accident, laid the groundwork of a perfect approach, and now he was taking advantage of the circumstance. That incident had been reported widely: it was well known that Wild Bill Williams had been a gentleman once. If he should strike it rich—really rich—what would be more natural than that he should forsake the noisome space-hells he had been wont to frequent in favor of such gilded palaces of sin as the Crown-On-Shield?

In due time, then, Kinnison "found" his special meteor, which was big enough and rich enough so that any miner would have taken it to a Patrol station instead of to a space-robber. He disposed of his whole load by analysis; then, with more money in the bank than William Williams had ever dreamed of having, he hesitated visibly before embarking upon one of the gorgeous, spectacular sprees from which he had derived his nickname. He hesitated; then, with an effort apparent to all observers, he changed his mind.

He had been a gentleman once, he would be again. He had his hair cut, he had himself shaved every day. Manicurists dug away and scrubbed away the ingrained grime from his hardened, meteor-miner's paws. His nails, even, became pink and glossy. He bought clothes, including the full-dress shorts, barrel-top jacket, and voluminous cloak of the Aldebaranian gentleman, and wore them with easy grace. And in the meantime he was drinking steadily. He drank, however, only the choicest beverages; decorously and—for him—sparingly. Thus, while he was seldom what would be called strictly sober, he was never really drunk. He shunned low resorts, living in the best hotel and frequenting only the finest taverns. The finest, that is, with one exception, the Crown-On-Shield. Not only did he not go there, he never spoke of or would discuss the place. It was as though for him it did not exist.

Occasionally he escorted—oh, so correctly!—a charming companion to supper or to the theater, but ordinarily he was alone. Alone by choice. Aloof, austere, possibly not quite sure of himself. He rebuffed all attempts to inveigle him into any one of the numerous cliques with which the "upper crust" abounded. He waited for what he knew would come.

Underlings of gradually increasing numbers and importance came to him with invitations to the Crown-On-Shield, but he refused them all; curtly, definitely and without giving reason or excuse. In the light of what he was going to do there he could not be seen in the place unless and until it was clear to all that the visit was not of his design. Finally Crowninshield himself met the ex-miner as though by accident.

"Why haven't you been out to our place, Mr. Williams?" he asked, heartily.

"Because I didn't want to, and don't want to," Kinnison replied, flatly and definitely.

"But why?" demanded the Boskonian director, this time in genuine surprise. "It's getting talked about—*everybody* comes to the Crown!— people are wondering why you never even look in on us."

"You know who I am, don't you?" The Lensman's voice was coldly level, uninflected.

"Certainly. William Williams, formerly of Aldebaran II."

"No. Wild Bill Williams, meteor-miner. The Crown-On-Shield boasts that it does not solicit the patronage of men of my profession. If I go there some dim-wit will start blasting off about miners. Then you'll have the job of mopping him up off the floor with a sponge and the

Patrol will be after me with a speedster. Thanks just the same, but none of that for me."

"Oh, is *that* all?" Crowinshield smiled in relief. "Perhaps a natural misapprehension, Mr. Williams, but you are entirely mistaken. It is true that practicing miners do not find our society congenial, but you are no longer a miner and we never refer to any man's past. As an Aldebaranian gentleman we would welcome you. And, in the extremely remote contingency to which you refer, I assure you that you would not have to act. Any guest so boorish would be expelled."

"In that case I would really enjoy spending a little time with you. It has been a long time since I associated with persons of breeding," he explained, with engaging candor.

"I'll have a boy see to the transfer of your things," and thus the Gray Lensman allowed the zwilnik to persuade him to visit the one place in the Universe where he most ardently wished to be.

For days in the new environment everything went on with the utmost decorum and circumspection, but Kinnison was not deceived. They would feel him out some way, just as effectively if not as crassly as did the zwilniks of Miners' Rest. They would have to—this was Regional Headquarters. At first he had been suspicious of thionite, but since the high-ups were not wearing anti-thionite plugs in their nostrils, he wouldn't have to either.

Then one evening a girl—young, pretty, vivacious—approached him, a pinch of purple powder between her fingers. As the Gray Lensman he knew that the stuff was not thionite, but as William Williams he did not.

"*Do* have a tiny smell of thionite, Mr. Williams!" she urged, coquettishly, and made as though to blow it into his face.

Williams reacted strangely, but instantaneously. He ducked with startling speed and the flat of his palm smacked ringingly against the girl's cheek. He did not slap her hard—it looked and sounded much worse than it really was—the only actual force was in the follow-up push that sent her flying across the room.

"Wha'ja mean, you? You can't slap girls around like that here!" and the chief bouncer came at him with a rush.

This time the Lensman did not pull his punch. He struck with everything he had, from heels to finger-tips. Such was the sheer brute power of the blow that the bouncer literally somersaulted half the length of the room, bringing up with a crash against the wall; so accurate was its placement that the victim, while not killed outright, would be unconscious for hours to come.

Others turned then, and paused; for Williams was not running away; he was not even giving ground. Instead, he stood lightly poised upon the balls of his feet, knees bent the veriest trifle, arms hanging at ready, eyes as hard and as cold as the iron meteorites of the space he knew so well.

"Any others of you damn zwilniks want to make a pass at me?" he demanded, and a concerted gasp arose: the word "zwilnik" was in those circles far worse than a mere fighting word. It was absolutely tabu: it was *never,* under any circumstance, uttered.

Nevertheless, no action was taken. At first the cold arrogance, the sheer effrontery of the man's pose held them in check; then they noticed one thing and remembered another, the combination of which gave them most emphatically to pause.

No garment, even by the most deliberate intent, could possibly have been designed as a better hiding-place for DeLameters than the barrel-topped full-dress jacket of Aldebaran II; and—

Mr. William Williams, poised there in steel-spring readiness for action; so coldly self-confident; so inexplicably, so scornfully derisive of that whole roomful of men not a few of whom he knew must be armed; was also the Wild Bill Williams, meteor miner, who was widely known as the fastest and deadliest performer with twin DeLameters who had ever infested space!

18

CROWN ON SHIELD

Edmund Crowninshield sat in his office and seethed quietly, the all-pervasive blueness of the Kalonian brought out even more prominently than usual by his mood. His plan to find out whether or not the ex-miner was a spy had back-fired, badly. He had had reports from Euphrosyne that the fellow was not—*could* not be—a spy, and now his test had confirmed that conclusion, too thoroughly by far. He would have to do some mighty quick thinking and perhaps some salve-spreading or lose him. He certainly didn't want to lose a client who had over a quarter of a million credits to throw away, and who could not possibly resist his cravings for alcohol and bentlam very much longer! But curse him, what had the fellow meant by having a kit-bag built of indurite, with a lock on it that not even his cleverest artists could pick?

"Come in," he called, unctuously, in answer to a tap. "Oh, it's you! What did you find out?"

"Janice isn't hurt. He didn't make a mark on her—just gave her a shove and scared hell out of her. But Clovis was nudged, believe me. He's still out—will be for an hour, the doctor says. What a sock that guy's got! He looks like he'd been hit with a tube-maul."

"You're sure he was armed?"

"Must have been. Typical gun-fighters crouch. He was ready, not bluffing, believe me. The man don't live that could bluff a roomful of us like that. He was betting he could whiff us all before we could get a gun out, and I wouldn't wonder if he was right."

"QX. Beat it, and don't let anyone come near here except Williams."

Therefore the ex-miner was the next visitor.

"You wanted to see me, Crowinshield, before I flit." Kinnison was fully dressed, even to his flowing cloak, and he was carrying his own kit. This, in an Aldebaranian, implied the extremest height of dudgeon.

"Yes, Mr. Williams, I wish to apologize for the house. However," somewhat exasperated, "it does seem that you were abrupt, to say the least, in your reaction to a childish prank."

"Prank!" The Aldebaranian's voice was decidedly unfriendly. "Sir, to me thionite is no prank. I don't mind nitrolabe or heroin, and a little bentlam now and then is good for a man, but when anyone comes around me with thionite I object, sir, vigorously, and I don't care who knows it."

"Evidently. But that wasn't really thionite—we would never permit it—and Miss Carter is an exemplary young lady . . ."

"How was I to know it wasn't thionite?" Williams demanded. "And as for your Miss Carter, as long as a woman acts like a lady I treat her like a lady, but if she acts like a zwilnik . . ."

"Please, Mr. Williams . . . !"

"I treat her like a zwilnik, and that's that."

"Mr. Williams, please! Not that word, ever!"

"No? A planetary idiosyncrasy, perhaps?" The ex-miner's towering wrath abated into curiosity. "Now that you mention it, I do not recall having heard it lately, nor hereabouts. For its use please accept my apology."

Oh, this was better. Crowninshield was making headway. The big Aldebaranian didn't even know thionite when he saw it, and he had a rabid fear of it.

"There remains, then, only the very peculiar circumstance of your wearing arms here in a quiet hotel . . ."

"Who says I was armed?" Kinnison demanded.

"Why . . . I . . . it was assumed . . ." The proprietor was flabbergasted.

The visitor threw off his cloak and removed his jacket, revealing a shirt of sheer glamorette through which could be plainly seen his hirsute chest and the smooth, bronzed skin of his brawny shoulders. He strode over to his kit-bag, unlocked it, and took out a double DeLameter harness and his weapons. He donned them, put on jacket and cloak—open, now, this latter—shrugged his shoulders a few times to settle the burden into its wonted position, and turned again to the hotel-keeper.

"This is the first time I have worn this hardware since I came here," he said, quietly. "Having the name, however, you may take it upon the very best of authority that I will be armed during the remaining minutes of my visit here. With your permission, I shall leave now."

"Oh, no, that won't do, sir, really." Crowinshield was almost abject at the prospect. "We should be desolated. Mistakes will happen, sir—planetary prejudices—misunderstandings . . . Give us a little more time to get really acquainted, sir . . ." and thus it went.

Finally Kinnison let himself be mollified into staying on. With true Aldebaranian mulishness, however, he wore his armament, proclaiming to all and sundry his sole reason therefore: "An Aldebaranian gentleman, sir, keeps his word; however lightly or under whatever circumstances given. I said that I would wear these things as long as I stay here; therefore wear them I must and I shall. I will leave here any time, sir, gladly; but while here I remain armed, every minute of every day."

And he did. He never drew them, was always and in every way a gentleman. Nevertheless, the zwilniks were always uncomfortably conscious of the fact that those grim, formidable portables were there—always there and always ready. The fact that they themselves went armed with weapons deadly enough was all too little reassurance.

Always the quintessence of good behavior, Kinnison began to relax his barriers of reserve. He began to drink—to buy, at least—more and more. He had taken regularly a little bentlam; now, as though his will to moderation had begun to go down, he took larger and larger doses. It was not a significant fact to any one except himself that the nearer drew the time for a certain momentous meeting the more he apparently drank and the larger the doses of bentlam became.

Thus it was a purely unnoticed coincidence that it was upon the afternoon of the day during whose evening the conference was to be held that Williams' quiet and gentlemanly drunkenness degenerated into a noisy and obstreperous carousal. As a climax he demanded—and obtained—the twenty four units of bentlam which, his host knew, comprised the highest-ceiling dose of the old, unregenerate mining days. They gave him the Titanic jolt, undressed him, put him carefully to bed upon a soft mattress covered with silken sheets, and forgot him.

Before the meeting every possible source of interruption or spying was checked, rechecked, and guarded against; but no one even thought of suspecting the free-spending, hard-drinking, drug-soaked Williams. How could they?

And so it came about that the Gray Lensman attended that meeting also; as insidiously and as successfully as he had the one upon Euphrosyne. It took longer, this time, to read the reports, notes, orders, addresses, and so on, for this was a regional meeting, not merely a local one. However, the Lensman had ample time and was a fast reader withal; and in Worsel he had an aide who could tape the stuff as fast as he could send it in. Wherefore when the meeting broke up Kinnison was well content. He had forged another link in his chain—was one link nearer to Boskone, his goal.

As soon as Kinnison could walk without staggering he sought out his host. He was ashamed, embarrassed, bitterly and painfully humiliated; but he was still—or again—an Aldebaranian gentleman. He had made a resolution, and gentlemen of that planet did not take their gentlemanliness lightly.

"First, Mr. Crowninshield, I wish to apologize, most humbly, most profoundly, sir, for the fashion in which I have outraged your hospitality." He could slap down a girl and half-kill a guard without loss of self-esteem, but no gentleman, however inebriated, should descend to such depths of commonness and vulgarity as he had plumbed here. Such conduct was inexcusable. "I have nothing whatever to say in defense or palliation of my conduct. I can only say that in order to spare you the task of ordering me out, I am leaving."

"Oh, come, Mr. Williams, that is not at all necessary. Anyone is apt to take a drop too much occasionally. Really, my friend, you were not at all offensive: we have not even entertained the thought of your leaving us." Nor had he. The ten thousand credits which the Lensman had thrown away during his spree would have condoned behavior a thousand times worse; but Crowinshield did not refer to that.

"Thank you for your courtesy, sir, but I remember some of my actions, and I blush with shame," the Aldebaranian rejoined, stiffly. He was not to be mollified. "I could never look your other guests in the face again. I think, sir, that I can still be a gentleman; but until I am certain of the fact—until I know I can get drunk as a gentleman should—I am going to change my name and disappear. Until a happier day, sir, goodbye."

Nothing could make the stiff-necked Williams change his mind, and leave he did, scattering five-credit notes abroad as he departed. However, he did not go far. As he had explained so carefully to Crowninshield, William Williams did disappear—forever, Kinnison hoped; he was all done with him—but the Gray Lensman made connections with Worsel.

"Thanks, old man," Kinnison shook one of the Velantian's gnarled, hard hands, even though Worsel never had had much use for that peculiarly human gesture. "Nice work. I won't need you for a while now, but I probably will later. If I succeed in getting the data I'll Lens it to you as usual for record—I'll be even less able than usual, I imagine, to take recording apparatus with me. If I can't get it I'll call you anyway, to help me make other arrangements. Clear ether, big fella!"

"Luck, Kinnison," and the two Lensmen went their separate ways; Worsel to Prime Base, the Tellurian on a long flit indeed. He had not been surprised to learn that the galactic director was not in the galaxy proper, but in a star cluster; nor at the information that the entity he wanted was one Jalte, a Kalonian. Boskone, Kinnison thought, was a highly methodical sort of a chap—he marked out the best way to do anything, and then stuck by it through thick and thin.

Kinnison was almost wrong there, for not long afterward Boskone was called in session and that very question was discussed seriously and at length.

"Granted that the Kalonians are good executives," the new Ninth of Boskone argued. "They are strong of mind and do produce results. It cannot be claimed, however, that they are in any sense comparable to us of the Eich. Eichlan was thinking of replacing Helmuth, but he put off acting until it was too late."

"There are many factors to consider," the First replied, gravely. "The planet is uninhabitable save for warm-blooded oxygen-breathers. The base is built for such, and such is the entire personnel. Years of time went into the construction there. One of us could not work efficiently alone, insulated against its heat and its atmosphere. If the whole dome were conditioned for us, we must needs train an entire new organization to man it. Then, too, the Kalonians have the work well in hand and, with all due respect to you and others of your mind, it is by no means certain that even Eichlan could have saved Helmuth's base had he been there. Eichlan's own doubt upon this point had much to do with his delay in acting. In the end it comes down to efficiency, and some Kalonians are efficient. Jalte is one. And, while it may seem as though I am boasting of my own selection of directors, please note that Prellin, the Kalonian director upon Bronseca, seems to have been able to stop the advance of the Patrol."

" 'Seems to' may be too exactly descriptive for comfort," said another, darkly.

"That is always a possibility," was conceded, "but whenever that Lensman has been able to act, he has acted. Our keenest observers can find no trace of his activities elsewhere, with the possible exception of the misfunctioning of the experimental hyper-spatial tube of our allies of Delgon. Some of us have from the first considered that venture ill-advised, premature; and its seizure by the Patrol smacks more of their able mathematical physicists than of a purely hypothetical, super-human Lensman. Therefore it seems logical to assume that Prellin has stopped him. Our observers report that the Patrol is loath to act illegally without evidence, and no evidence can be obtained. Business was hurt, but Jalte is reorganizing as rapidly as may be."

"I still say that the galactic base should be rebuilt and manned by the Eich," Nine insisted. "It is our sole remaining Grand Headquarters there, and since it is both the brain of the peaceful conquest and the nucleus of our new military organization, it should not be subjected to any unnecessary risk."

"And you will, of course, be glad to take that highly important command, man the dome with your own people, and face the Lensman— if and when he comes—backed by the forces of the Patrol?"

"Why . . . ah . . . no," the Ninth managed. "I am of so much more use here . . ."

"That's what we all think," the First said, cynically. "While I would like very much to welcome that hypothetical Lensman here, I do not care to meet him upon any other planet. I really believe, however, that any change in our organization would weaken it seriously. Jalte is capable, energetic, and is as well informed as is any of us as to the possibilities of invasion by the Lensman or his Patrol. Beyond asking him whether he needs anything, and sending him everything he may wish of supplies and of reinforcements, I do not see how we can improve matters."

They argued pro and con, bringing up dozens of points which cannot be detailed here, then voted. The decision sustained the First: they would send, if desired, munitions and men to Jalte.

But even before the question was put, Kinnison's blackly invisible, indetectable speedster was well within the star cluster. The guardian fortresses were closer spaced by far than Helmuth's had been. Electro-magnetics had a three hundred percent overlap; ether and sub-ether alike were suffused with vibratory fields in which nullification of detection was impossible, and the observers were alert and keen. To what avail? The speedster was non-ferrous, intrinsically indetectable; the Lensman slipped through the net with ease.

Sliding down the edge of the world's black shadow he felt for the expected thought-screen, found it, dropped cautiously through it, and poised there; observing during one whole rotation. This had been a fair, green world—once. It had had forests. It had once been peopled by intelligent, urban dwellers, who had had roads, works, and other evi-dences of advancement. But the cities had been melted down into vast lakes of lava and slag. Cold now for years, cracked, fissured, weathered; yet to Kinnison's probing sense they told tales of horror, revealed all too clearly the incredible ferocity and ruthlessness with which the conquerors had wiped out all the population of a world. What had been roads and works were jagged ravines and craters of destruction. The forests of the planet had been burned, again and again; only a few charred stumps remaining to mark where a few of the mightiest monarchs had stood. Except for the Boskonian base the planet was a scene of desolation and ravishment indescribable.

"They'll pay for that, too," Kinnison gritted, and directed his attention toward the base. Forbidding indeed it loomed; thrice a hundred square miles of massively banked offensive and defensive armament, with a central dome of such colossal mass as to dwarf even the stupendous fabrications surrounding it. Typical Boskonian layout, Kinnison thought, very much like Helmuth's Grand Base. Fully as large and as strong, or stronger . . . but he had cracked that one and he was pretty sure that he could crack this. Exploringly he sent out his sense of perception; nor was he surprised to find that the whole aggregation of structures was screened. He had not thought that it would be as easy as that!

He did not need to get inside the dome this time, as he was not going to work directly upon the personnel. Inside the screen anywhere would do. But how to get there? The ground all around the thing was flat, as level as molten lava would cool, and every inch of it was bathed in the white glare of flood-lights. They had observers, of course, and photo-cells, which were worse.

Approach then, either through the air or upon the ground, did not look so promising. That left only underground. They got water from somewhere—wells, perhaps—and their sewage went somewhere unless they incinerated it, which was highly improbable. There was a river over there; he'd see if there wasn't a trunk sewer running into it somewhere. There was. There was also a place within easy flying distance to hide his speedster, an overhanging bank of smooth black rock. The risk of his being seen was nil, anyway, for the only intelligent life left upon the planet inhabited the Boskonian fortress and did not leave it.

Donning his space-black, indetectable armor, Kinnison flew down the river to the sewer's mouth. He lowered himself into the placid stream and against the sluggish current of the sewer he made his way. The drivers of his suit were not as efficient in water as they were in air or in space, and in the dense medium his pace was necessarily slow. But he was in no hurry. It was fast enough—in a few hours he was beneath the stronghold.

Here the trunk began to divide into smaller and smaller mains. The tube running toward the dome, however, was amply large to permit the passage of his armor. Close enough to his objective, he found a long-disused manhole and, bracing himself upright, so that he would be under no muscular strain, he prepared to spend as long a time as would prove necessary.

He then began his study of the dome. It was like Helmuth's in some ways, entirely different from it in others. There were fully as many firing stations, each with its operators ready at signal to energize and to direct the most terrifically destructive agencies known to the science of the time. There were fewer visiplates and communicators, fewer catwalks; but there were vastly more individual offices and there were ranks and tiers of filing cabinets. There would have to be; this was headquarters for the organized illicit commerce of an entire galaxy. There was the familiar center, in which Jalte sat at his great desk; and near that desk there sparkled the peculiar globe of force which the Lensman now knew was an intergalactic communicator.

"Ha!" Kinnison exclaimed triumphantly if inaudibly to himself, "the real boss of the outfit—Boskone—*is* in the Second Galaxy!"

He would have to wait until that communicator went into action, if it took a month. But in the meantime there was plenty to do. Those cabinets at least were not thought-screened, they held all the really vital secrets of the drug ring, and it would take many days to transmit the information which the Patrol must have if it were to make a one hundred percent clean-up of the whole zwilnik organization.

He called Worsel, and, upon being informed that the recorders were ready, he started in. Characteristically, he began with Prellin of Bronseca, and memorized the data covering that wight as he transmitted it. The next one to go down upon the steel tape was Crowninshield of Tressilia. Having exhausted all the filed information upon the organizations controlled by those two regional directors, he took the rest of them in order.

He had finished his real task and had practically finished a detailed survey of the entire base when the forceball communicator burst into activity. Knowing approximately the analysis of the beam and exactly its location in space, it took only seconds for Kinnison to tap it; but the longer the interview went on the more disappointed the Lensman grew. Orders, reports, discussions of broad matters of policy—it was simply a conference between two high executives of a vast business firm. It was interesting enough, but in it there was no grist for the Lensman's mill. There was no new information except a name. There was no indication as to who Eichmil was, or where, there was no mention whatever of Boskone. There was nothing even remotely of a personal nature until the very last.

"I assume from lack of mention that the Lensman has made no farther progress," Eichmil concluded.

"Not so far as our best men can discover," Jalte replied, carefully, and Kinnison grinned like the Cheshire cat in his secure, if uncomfortable, retreat. It tickled his vanity immensely to be referred to so matter-of-factly as "the" Lensman, and he felt very smart and cagy indeed to be within a few hundred feet of Jalte as the Boskonian uttered the words. "Lensmen by the score are still working Prellin's base in Cominoche. Some twelve of these—human or approximately so—have been returning again and again. We are checking those with care, because of the possibility that one of them may be the one we want, but as yet I can make no conclusive report."

The connection was broken, and the Lensman's brief thrill of elated self-satisfaction died away.

"No soap," he growled to himself in disgust. "I've *got* to get into that guy's mind, some way or other!"

How could he make the approach? Every man in the base wore a screen, and they were mighty careful. No dogs or other pet animals. There were a few birds, but it would smell very cheesy indeed to have a bird flying around, pecking at screen generators. To anyone with half a brain that would tell the whole story, and these folks were really smart. What, then?

There was a nice spider up there in a corner. Big enough to do light work, but not big enough to attract much, if any, attention. Did spiders have minds? He could soon find out.

The spider had more of a mind than he had supposed, and he got into it easily enough. She could not really think at all, and at the starkly terrible savagery of her tiny ego the Lensman actually winced, but at that she had redeeming features. She was willing to work hard and long for a comparatively small return of food. He could not fuse his mentality with hers smoothly, as he could do in the case of creatures of greater brain power, but he could handle her after a fashion. At least she knew that certain actions would result in nourishment.

Through the insect's compound eyes the room and all its contents were weirdly distorted, but the Lensman could make them out well enough to direct her efforts. She crawled along the ceiling and dropped upon a silken rope to Jalte's belt. She could not pull the plug of the power-pack— it loomed before her eyes, a gigantic metal pillar as immovable as the Rock of Gibraltar—therefore she scampered on and began to explore the mazes of the set itself. She could not see the thing as a whole, it was far too immense a structure for that; so Kinnison, to whom the device was no larger than a hand, directed her to the first grid lead.

A tiny thing, thread-thin in gross; yet to the insect it was an ordinary cable of stranded soft-metal wire. Her powerful mandibles pried loose one of the component strands and with very little effort pulled it away from its fellows beneath the head of a binding screw. The strand bent easily, and as it touched the metal of the chassis the thought-screen vanished.

Instantly Kinnison insinuated his mind into Jalte's and began to dig for knowledge. Eichmil was his chief—Kinnison knew that already. His office was in the Second Galaxy, on the planet Jarnevon. Jalte had been there . . . coordinates so and so, courses such and such . . . Eichmil reported to Boskone . . .

The Lensman stiffened. Here was the first positive evidence he had found that his deductions were correct—or even that there really *was* such an entity as Boskone! He bored anew.

Boskone was not a single entity, but a council . . . probably of the Eich, the natives of Jarnevon . . . weird impressions of coldly intellectual reptilian monstrosities, horrific, indescribable . . . Eichmil must know exactly who and where Boskone was. Jalte did not. Kinnison finished his research and abandoned the Kalonian's mind as insidiously as he had entered it. The spider opened the short, restoring the screen to usefulness. Then, before he did anything else, the Lensman directed his small ally to a whole family of young grubs just under the cover of his manhole. Lensmen paid their debts, even to spiders.

Then, with a profound sigh of relief, he dropped down into the sewer. The submarine journey to the river was made without incident, as was the flight to his speedster. Night fell, and through its blackness there darted the even blacker shape which was the Lensman's little ship. Out into inter-galactic space she flashed, and homeward. And as she flew the Tellurian scowled.

He had gained much, but not enough by far. He had hoped to get all the data on Boskone, so that the zwilniks' headquarters could be stormed by Civilization's armada, invincible in its newly-devised might.

No soap. Before he could do that he would have to scout Jarnevon . . . in the Second Galaxy . . . alone. Alone? Better not. Better take the flying snake along. Good old dragon! That was a mighty long flit to be doing alone, and one with some mighty high-powered opposition at the other end of it.

19

PRELLIN IS ELIMINATED

Before you go anywhere; or, rather, whether you go anywhere or not, we want to knock down that Bronsecan base of Prellin's," Haynes declared to Kinnison in no uncertain voice. "It's a galactic scandal, the way we've been letting them thumb their noses at us. Everybody in space thinks that the Patrol has gone soft all of a sudden. When are you going to let us smack them down? Do you know what they've done now?"

"No—what?"

"Gone out of business. We've been watching them so closely that they couldn't do any queer business—goods, letters, messages, or anything—so they closed up the Bronseca branch entirely. 'Unfavorable conditions,' they said. Locked up tight—telephones disconnected, communicators cut, everything."

"Hm . . . m . . . In that case we'd better take 'em, I guess. No harm done, anyway, now—maybe all the better. Let Boskone think that our strategy failed and we had to fall back on brute force."

"You say it easy. You think it'll be a push-over, don't you?"

"Sure—why not?"

"You noticed the shape of their screens?"

"Roughly cylindrical," in surprise. "They're hiding a lot of stuff, of course, but they can't possibly. . . ."

"I'm afraid that they can, and will. I've been checking up on the building. Ten years old. Plans and permits QX except for the fact that nobody knows whether or not the building resembles the plans in any way."

"Klono's whiskers!" Kinnison was aghast, his mind was racing. "How could that be, chief? Inspections—builders—contractors—workmen?"

"The city inspector who had the job came into money later, retired, and nobody has seen him since. Nobody can locate a single builder or workman who saw it constructed. No competent inspector has been in it since. Cominoche is lax—all cities are, for that matter—with an outfit as big as Wembleson's, who carries its own insurance, does its own inspecting, and won't allow outside interference. Wembleson's isn't alone in that attitude—they're not all zwilniks, either."

"You think it's really fortified, then?"

"Sure of it. That's why we ordered a gradual, but complete, evacuation of the city, beginning a couple of months ago."

"How could you?" Kinnison was growing more surprised by the minute. "The businesses—the houses—the expense!"

"Martial law—the Patrol takes over in emergencies, you know. Businesses moved, and mostly carrying on very well. People ditto—very nice temporary camps, lake- and river-cottages, and so on. As for expense, the Patrol pays damages. We'll pay for rebuilding the whole city if we have to—much rather that than leave that Boskonian base there alone."

"What a mess! Never thought of it that way, but you're right, as usual. They wouldn't be there at all unless they thought . . . but they must know, chief, that they can't hold off the stuff you can bring to bear."

"Probably betting that we won't destroy our own city to get them—if so, they're wrong. Or possibly they hung on a few days too long."

"How about the observers?" Kinnison asked. "They have four auxiliaries there, you know."

"That's strictly up to you." Haynes was unconcerned. "Smearing that base is the only thing I insist on. We'll wipe out the observers or let them observe and report, whichever you say; but that base goes—it has been there far too long already."

"Be nicer to let them alone," Kinnison decided. "We're not supposed to know anything about them. You won't have to use primaries, will you?"

"No. It's a fairly large building, as business blocks go, but it lacks a lot of being big enough to be a first class base. We can burn the ground out from under its deepest possible foundations with our secondaries."

He called an adjutant. "Get me Sector Nineteen." Then, as the seamed, scarred face of an old Lensman appeared upon a plate:

"You can go to work on Cominoche now, Parker. Twelve maulers. Twenty heavy caterpillars and about fifty units of Q-type mobile screen, remote control. Supplies and service. Have them muster all available fire-fighting apparatus. If desirable, import some—we want to save as much of the place as we can. I'll come over in the *Dauntless*."

He glanced at Kinnison, one eyebrow raised quizzically.

"I feel as though I rate a little vacation; I think I'll go and watch this," he commented. "The *Dauntless* can get us there soon enough. Got time to come along?"

"I think so. It's more or less on my way to Lundmark's Nebula."

Upon Bronseca then, as the *Dauntless* ripped her way through protesting space, there converged structures of the void from a dozen nearby systems. There came maulers; huge, ungainly flying fortresses of stupendous might. There came transports, bearing the commissariat and the service units. Vast freighters, under whose unimaginable mass the Gargantuanly braced and latticed and trussed docks yielded visibly and groaningly, crushed to a standstill and disgorged their varied cargoes.

What Haynes had so matter-of-factly referred to as "heavy" caterpillars were all of that, and the mobile screens were even heavier. Clanking and rumbling, but with their weight so evenly distributed over huge, flat treads that they sank only a foot or so into even ordinary ground, they made their ponderous way along Cominoche's deserted streets.

What thoughts seethed within the minds of the Boskonians can only be imagined. They knew that the Patrol had landed in force, but what could they do about it? At first, when the Lensmen began to infest the place, they could have fled in safety; but at that time they were too certain of their immunity to abandon their richly established position. Even now, they would not abandon it until that course became absolutely necessary.

They could have destroyed the city, true; but it was not until after the noncombatant inhabitants had unobstrusively moved out that that course suggested itself as an advisability. Now the destruction of mere property would be a gesture worse than meaningless; it would be a waste of energy which would all too certainly be needed badly and soon.

Hence, as the Patrol's land forces ground clangorously into position the enemy made no demonstration. The mobile screens were in place, surrounding the doomed section with a wall of force to protect the rest of the city from the hellish energies so soon to be unleashed. The heavy caterpillars, mounting projectors quite comparable in size and power with the warships' own—weapons similar in purpose and function to the railway-carriage coast-defense guns of an earlier day—were likewise ready. Far back of the line, but still too close, as they were to discover later, heavily armored men crouched at their remote controls behind their shields; barriers both of hard-driven, immaterial fields of force and of solid, grounded, ultra-refrigerated walls of the most refractory materials possible of fabrication. In the sky hung the maulers, poised stolidly upon the towering pillars of flame erupting from their under-jets.

Cominoche, Bronseca's capital city, witnessed then what no one there present had ever expected to see; the warfare designed for the illimitable reaches of empty space being waged in the very heart of its business district!

For Port Admiral Haynes had directed the investment of this minor stronghold almost as though it were a regulation base, and with reason. He knew that from their coigns of vantage afar four separate Boskonian observers were looking on, charged with the responsibility of recording and reporting everything that transpired, and he wanted that report to be complete and conclusive. He wanted Boskone, whoever and wherever he might be, to know that when the Galactic Patrol started a thing it finished it; that the mailed fist of Civilization would not spare an enemy base simply because it was so located within one of humanity's cities that its destruction must inevitably result in severe property damage. Indeed, the Port Admiral had massed there thrice the force necessary, specifically and purposely to drive that message home.

At the word of command there flamed out almost as one a thousand lances of energy intolerable. Masonry, brick-work, steel, glass, and chromium trim disappeared; flaring away in sparkling, hissing vapor or cascading away in brilliantly mobile streams of fiery, corrosive liquid. Disappeared, revealing the unbearably incandescent surface of the Boskonian defensive screen.

Full-driven, that barrier held, even against the Titanic thrusts of the maulers above and of the heavy defense-guns below. Energy rebounded in scintillating torrents, shot off in blinding streamers, released itself in bolts of lightning hurling themselves frantically to ground.

Nor was that superbly-disguised citadel designed for defense alone. Knowing now that the last faint hope of continuing in business upon Bronseca was gone, and grimly determined to take full toll of the hated Patrol, the defenders in turn loosed their beams. Five of them shot out simultaneously, and five of the panels of mobile screen flamed instantly into eye-tearing violet. Then black. These were not the comparatively feeble, antiquated beams which Haynes had expected, but were the output of up-to-the-minute, first-line space artillery!

Defenses down, it took but a blink of time to lick up the caterpillars. On, then, the destroying beams tore, each in a direct line for a remote-control station. Through tremendous edifices of masonry and steel they drove, the upper floors collapsing into the cylinder of annihilation only to be consumed almost as fast as they could fall.

"All screen-control stations, back! Fast!" Haynes directed, crisply. "Back, dodging. Put your screens on automatic block until you get back beyond effective range. Spy-ray men! See if you can locate the enemy observers directing fire!"

Three or four of the crews were caught, but most of the men were able to get away, to move back far enough to save their lives and their equipment. But no matter how far back they went, Boskonian beams still sought them out in grimly persistent attempts to slay. Their shielding fields blazed white, their refractories wavered in the high blue as the over-driven refrigerators strove mightily to cope with the terrific load. The operators, stifling, almost roasting in their armor of proof, shook sweat from the eyes they could not reach as they drove themselves and their mechanisms on to even greater efforts; cursing luridly, fulminantly the while at carrying on a space-war in the hotly reeking, the hellishly reflecting and heat-retaining environment of a metropolis!

And all around the embattled structure, within the Patrol's now partially open wall of screen, spread holocaust supreme, holocaust spreading wider and wider during each fractional split second. In an instant, it seemed, nearby buildings burst into flame. The fact that they were fireproof meant nothing whatever. The air inside them, heated in moments to a point far above the ignition temperature of organic material, fed furiously upon furniture, rugs, drapes, and whatever else had been left in place. Even without such adventitious aids the air itself, expanding tremendously, irresistibly, drove outward before it the glass of windows and the solid brickwork of walls. And as they fell glass and brick ceased to exist as such. Falling, they fused; coalescing and again splashing apart as they descended through the inferno of annihilatory vibrations in an appalling rain which might very well have been sprinkled from the hottest middle of the central core of hell itself. And in this fantastically potent, this incredibly corrosive flood the very ground, the metaled pavement, the sturdily immovable foundations of sky-scrapers, dissolved as do lumps of sugar in boiling coffee. Dissolved, slumped down, flowed away in blindingly turbulent streams. Superstructures toppled into disintegration, each discrete particle contributing as it fell to the utterly indescribable fervency of the whole.

More and more panels of mobile screen went down. They were not designed to stand up under such heavy projectors as "Wembleson's" mounted, and the Boskonians blasted them down in order to get at the remote-control operators back of them. Swath after swath of flaming ruin was cut through the Bronsecan metropolis as the enemy gunners followed the dodging caterpillar tractors.

"Drop down, maulers!" Haynes ordered. "Low enough so that your screens touch ground. Never mind damage—they'll blast the whole city if we don't stop those beams. Surround him!"

Down the maulers came, ringwise; mighty protective envelopes overlapping, down until the screens bit ground. Now the caterpillar and mobile-screen crews were safe; powerful as Prellin's weapons were, they could not break through those maulers' screens.

Now holocaust waxed doubly infernal. The wall was tight, the only avenue of escape of all that fiercely radiant energy was straight upward; adding to the furor were the flaring underjets—themselves destructive agents by no means to be despised!

Inside the screens, then, raged pure frenzy. At the line raved the maulers' prodigious lifting blasts. Out and away, down every avenue of escape, swept torrents of super-heated air at whose touch anything and everything combustible burst into flame. But there could be no fire-fighting—yet. Outlying fires, along the line of destruction previously cut, yes; but personal armor has never been designed to enable life to exist in such an environment as that near those screens then was.

"Burn out the ground under them!" came the order. "Tip them over—slag them down!"

Sharply downward angled two-score of the beams which had been expending their energies upon Boskone's radiant defenses. Downward into the lake of lava which had once been pavement. That lake had already been seething and bubbling; from moment to moment emitting bursts of lambent flame. Now it leaped into a frenzy of its own, a transcendent fury of volatilization. High-explosive shells by the hundred dropped also into the incandescent mess, hurling the fiery stuff afar; deepening, broadening the sulphurous moat.

"Deep enough," Haynes spoke calmly into his microphone. "Tractors and pressors as assigned—tip him over."

The intensity of the bombardment did not slacken, but from the maulers to the north there reached out pressors, from those upon the south came tractors: each a beam of terrific power, each backed by all the mass and all the driving force of a veritable flying fortress.

Slowly that which had been a building leaned from the perpendicular, its inner defensive screen still intact.

"Chief?" From his post as observer Kinnison flashed a thought to Haynes. "Are you beginning to think any funny thoughts about that ape down there?"

"No. Are you? What?" asked the Port Admiral in surprise.

"Maybe I'm nuts, but it wouldn't surprise me if he'd start doing a flit pretty quick. I've got a CRX tracer on him, just in case, and it might be smart to caution Henderson to be on his toes."

"Your diagnosis—'nuts'—is correct, I think," came the answering thought; but the Port Admiral followed the suggestion, nevertheless.

And none too soon. Deliberately, grandly the Colossus was leaning over, bowing in stately fashion toward the awful lake in which it stood. But only so far. Then there was a flash, visible even in the inferno of energies already there at war, and the already coruscant lava was hurled to all points of the compass as the full-blast drive of a super-dreadnought was cut loose beneath its surface!

To the eye the thing simply and instantly disappeared; but not to the ultra-vision of the observers' plates, and especially not to the CRX tracers solidly attached by Kinnison and by Henderson. They held, and the chief pilot, already warned, was on the trail as fast as he could punch his keys.

Through atmosphere, through stratosphere, into interplanetary space flew pursued and pursuer at ever-increasing speed. The *Dauntless* overtook her proposed victim fairly easily. The Boskonian was fast, but the Patrol's new flyer was the fastest thing in space. But tractors would not hold against the now universal standard equipment of shears, and the heavy secondaries served only to push the fleeing vessel along all the faster. And the dreadful primaries could not be used—yet.

"Not yet," cautioned the admiral. "Don't get too close—wait until there's nothing detectable in space."

Finally an absolutely empty region was entered, the word to close up was given and Prellin drank of the bitter cup which so many commanders of vessels of the Patrol had had to drain—the gallingly fatal necessity of engaging a ship which was both faster and more powerful than his own. The Boskonian tried, of course. His beams raged out at full power against the screens of the larger ship, but without effect. Three primaries lashed out as one. The fleeing vessel, structure and contents, ceased to be. The *Dauntless* returned to the torn and ravaged city.

The maulers had gone. The lumbering caterpillars—what were left of them—were clanking away; reeking, smoking hot in every plate and member. Only the firemen were left, working like Trojans now with explosives, rays, water, carbon-dioxide snow, clinging and smothering chemicals; anything and everything which would isolate, absorb, or dissipate any portion of the almost incalculable heat energy so recently and so profligately released.

Fire apparatus from four planets was at work. There were pumpers, ladder-trucks, hose- and chemical-trucks. There were men in heavily-insulated armor. Vehicles and men alike were screened against the specific wave-lengths of heat; and under the direction of a fire-marshal in his red speedster high in air they fought methodically and efficiently the conflagration which was the aftermath of battle. They fought, and they were winning.

And then it rained. As though the heavens themselves had been outraged by what had been done they opened and rain sluiced down in level sheets. It struck hissingly the nearby structures, but it did not touch the central area at all. Instead it turned to steam in midair, and, rising or being blown aside by the tempestuous wind, it concealed the redly glaring, raw wound beneath a blanket of crimson fog.

"Well, that's that," the Port Admiral said, slowly. His face was grim and stern. "A good job of clean-up . . . expensive, in men and money, but well worth the price . . . so be it to every pirate base and every zwilnik hideout in the galaxy . . . Henderson, land us at Cominoche Space-Port."

And from four other cities of the planet four Boskonian observers, each unknown to all the others, took off in four spaceships for four different destinations. Each had reported fully and accurately to Jalte everything that had transpired until the two flyers faded into the distance. Then, highly elated—and probably, if the truth could be known, no little surprised as well—at the fact that he was still alive, each had left Bronseca at maximum blast.

The galactic director had done all that he could, which was little enough. At the Patrol's first warlike move he had ordered a squadron of Boskone's ablest fighting ships to Prellin's aid. It was almost certainly a useless gesture, he knew as he did it. Gone were the days when pirate bases dotted the Tellurian Galaxy; only by a miracle could those ships reach the Bronsecan's line of flight in time to be of service.

Nor could they. The howl of interfering vibrations which was smothering Prellin's communicator beam snapped off into silence while the would-be rescuers were many hours away. For minutes then Jalte sat immersed in thought, his normally bluish face turning a sickly green, before he called the planet Jarnevon to report to Eichmil, his chief.

"There is, however, a bright side to the affair," he concluded. "Prellin's records were destroyed with him. Also there are two facts—that the Patrol had to use such force as practically to destroy the city of

Cominoche, and that our four observers escaped unmolested—which furnish conclusive proof that the vaunted Lensman failed completely to penetrate with his mental powers the defenses we have been using against him."

"Not conclusive proof," Eichmil rebuked him harshly. "Not proof at all, in any sense—scarcely a probability. Indeed, the display of force may very well mean that he has already attained his objective. He may have allowed the observers to escape, purposely, to lull our suspicions. You yourself are probably the next in line. How certain are you that your own base has not already been invaded?"

"Absolutely certain, sir." Jalte's face, however, turned a shade greener at the thought.

"You use the term 'absolutely' very loosely—but I hope that you are right. Use all the men and all the equipment we have sent you to make sure that it remains impenetrable."

20

DISASTER

In their non-magnetic, practically invisible speedster Kinnison and Worsel entered the terra incognita of the Second Galaxy and approached the solar system of the Eich, slowing down to a crawl as they did so. They knew as much concerning dread Jarnevon, the planet which was their goal, as did Jalte, from whom the knowledge had been acquired; but that was all too little.

They knew that it was the fifth planet out from the sun and that it was bitterly cold. It had an atmosphere, but one containing no oxygen, one poisonous to oxygen-breathers. It had no rotation—or, rather, its day coincided with its year—and its people dwelt upon its eternally dark hemisphere. If they had eyes, a point upon which there was doubt, they did not operate upon the frequencies ordinarily referred to as "visible" light. In fact, about the Eich as persons or identities they knew next to nothing. Jalte had seen them, but either he did not perceive them clearly or else his mind could not retain their true likeness; his only picture of the Eichian physique being a confusedly horrible blue.

"I'm scared, Worsel," Kinnison declared. "Scared purple, and the closer we come the worse scared I get."

And he was scared. He was afraid as he had never before been afraid in all his short life. He had been in dangerous situations before, certainly; not only that, he had been wounded almost fatally. In those instances, however, peril had come upon him suddenly. He had reacted to it automatically, having had little if any time to think about it beforehand.

Never before had he gone into a place in which he knew in advance that the advantage was all upon the other side; from which his chance of getting out alive was so terrifyingly small. It was worse, much worse, than going into that vortex. There, while the road was strange, the enemy was known to be one he had conquered before, and furthermore, he had had the *Dauntless,* its eager young crew, and the scientific self-abnegation of old Cardynge to back him. Here he had the speedster and Worsel—and Worsel was just as scared as he was.

The pit of his stomach felt cold, his bones seemed bits of rubber tubing. Nevertheless the two Lensman were going in. That was their job. They had to go in, even though they knew that the foe was at least their equal mentally, was overwhelmingly their superior physically and was upon his own ground.

"So am I," Worsel admitted. "I'm scared to the tip of my tail. I have one advantage over you, however—I've been that way before." He was referring to the time when he had gone to Delgon, abysmally certain that he would not return. "What is fated, happens. Shall we prepare?"

They had spent many hours in discussion of what could be done, and in the end had decided that the only possible preparation was to make sure that if Kinnison failed his failure would not bring disaster to the Patrol.

"Might as well. Come in, my mind's wide open."

The Velantian insinuated his mind into Kinnison's and the Earthman slumped down, unconscious. Then for many minutes Worsel wrought within the plastic brain. Finally:

"Thirty seconds after you leave me these inhibitions will become operative. When I release them your memory and your knowledge will be exactly as they were before I began to operate," he thought; slowly, intensely, clearly. "Until that time you know nothing whatever of any of these matters. No mental search, however profound; no truth-drug, however potent; no probing even of the subconscious will or can discover them. They do not exist. They have never existed. They shall not exist until I so allow. These other matters have been, are, and shall be facts until that instant. Kimball Kinnison, awaken!"

The Tellurian came to, not knowing that he had been out. Nothing had occurred, for him no time whatever had elapsed. He could not perceive even that his mind had been touched.

"Sure it's done, Worsel? I can't find a thing!" Kinnison, who had himself operated tracelessly upon so many minds, could scarcely believe his own had been tampered with.

"It is done. If you could detect any trace of the work it would have been poor work, and wasted."

Down dropped the speedster, as nearly as the Lensmen dared toward Jarnevon's tremendous primary base. They did not know whether they were being observed or not. For all they knew these incomprehensible beings might be able to see or to sense them as plainly as though their ship were painted with radium and were landing openly, with searchlights ablaze and with bells a-clang. Muscles tense, ready to hurl their tiny flyer away at the slightest alarm, they wafted downward.

Through the screens they dropped. Power off, even to the gravity-pads; thought, even, blanketed to zero. Nothing happened. They landed. They disembarked. Foot by foot they made their cautious way forward.

In essence the plan was simplicity itself. Worsel would accompany Kinnison until both were within the thought-screens of the dome. Then the Tellurian would get, some way or other, the information which the Patrol had to have, and the Velantian would get it back to Prime Base. If the Gray Lensman could go too, QX. And after all, there was no real reason to think that he couldn't—he was merely playing safe on general principles. But, if worst came to worst . . . well . . .

They arrived.

"Now remember, Worsel, no matter what happens to me, or around me, you stay out. Don't come in after me. Help me all you can with your mind, but not otherwise. Take everything I get, and at the first sign of danger you flit back to the speedster and give her the oof, whether I'm around or not. Check?"

"Check," Worsel agreed, quietly. Kinnison's was the harder part. Not because he was the leader, but because he was the better qualified. They both knew it. The Patrol came first. It was bigger, vastly more important, than any being or any group of beings in it.

The man strode away and in thirty seconds underwent a weird and striking mental transformation. Three-quarters of his knowledge disappeared so completely that he had no inkling that he had ever had it. A new name, a new personality were his, so completely and indisputably his that he had no faint glimmering of a recollection that he had ever been otherwise.

He was wearing his Lens. It could do no possible harm, since it was almost inconceivable that the Eich could be made to believe that any ordinary agent could have penetrated so far, and the fact should not be revealed to the foe that any Lensman could work without his Lens.

That would explain far too much of what had already happened. Furthermore, it was a necessity in the only really convincing role which Kinnison could play in the event of capture.

As he neared his objective he slowed down. There were pits beneath the pavement, he observed, big enough to hold a speedster. Traps. He avoided them. There were various mechanisms within the blank walls he skirted. More traps. He avoided them. Photo-cells, trigger-beams, invisible rays, networks. He avoided them all. Close enough.

Delicately he sent out a mental probe, and almost in the instant of its sending cables of steel came whipping from afar. He perceived them as they came, but could not dodge them. His projectors flamed briefly, only to be sheared away. The cables wrapped about his arms, binding him fast. Helpless, he was carried through the atmosphere, into the dome, through an airlock into a chamber containing much grimly unmistakable apparatus. And in the council chamber, where the nine of Boskone and one armored Delgonian Overlord held meeting, a communicator buzzed and snarled.

"Ah!" exclaimed Eichmil. "Our visitor has arrived and is awaiting us in the Delgonian hall of question. Shall we meet again, there?"

They did so; they of the Eich armored against the poisonous oxygen, the Overlord naked. All wore screens.

"Earthling, we are glad indeed to see you here," the First of Boskone welcomed the prisoner. "For a long time we have been anxious indeed . . ."

"I don't see how that can be," the Lensman blurted. "I just graduated. My first big assignment, and I have failed," he ended, bitterly.

A start of surprise swept around the circle. Could this be?

"He is lying." Eichmil decided. "You of Delgon, take him out of his armor." The Overlord did so, the Tellurian's struggles meaningless to the reptile's superhuman strength. "Release your screen and see whether or not you can make him tell the truth."

After all, the man might not be lying. The fact that he could understand a strange language meant nothing. All Lensmen could.

"But in case he *should* be the one we seek . . ." the Overlord hesitated.

"We will see to it that no harm comes to you . . ."

"We cannot," the Ninth—the psychologist—broke in. "Before any screen is released I suggest that we question him verbally, under the influence of the drug which renders it impossible for any warm-blooded oxygen-breather to tell anything except the complete truth."

The suggestion, so eminently sensible, was adopted forthwith.

"Are you the Lensman who has made it possible for the Patrol to drive us out of the Tellurian Galaxy?" came the sharp demand.

"No," was the flat and surprising reply.

"Who are you, then?"

"Philip Morgan, Class of . . ."

"Oh, this will take forever!" snapped the Ninth. "Let me question him. Can you control minds at a distance and without previous treatment?"

"If they are not too strong, yes. All of us specialists in psychology can do that."

"Go to work upon him, Overlord!"

The now reassured Delgonian snapped off his screen and a battle of wills ensued which made the sub-ether boil. For Kinnison, although he no longer knew what the truth was, still possessed the greater part of his mental power, and the Delgonian's mind, as has already been made clear, was a capable one indeed.

"Desist!" came the command. "Earthman, what happened?"

"Nothing," Kinnison replied, truthfully. "Each of us could resist the other; neither could penetrate or control."

"Ah!" and nine Boskonian screens snapped off. Since the Lensman could not master one Delgonian, he would not be a menace to the massed minds of the Nine of Boskone and the questioning need not wait upon the slowness of speech. Thoughts beat into Kinnison's brain from all sides.

This power of mind was relatively new, yes. He did not know what it was. He went to Arisia, fell asleep, and woke up with it. A refinement, he thought, of hypnotism. Only advanced students in psychology could do it. He knew nothing except by hearsay of the old *Brittania*—he was a cadet then. He had never heard of Blakeslee, or of anything unusual concerning any one hospital ship. He did not know who had scouted Helmuth's base, or put the thionite into it. He had no idea who it was who had killed Helmuth. As far as he knew, nothing had ever been done about any Boskonian spies in Patrol bases. He had never happened to hear of the planet Medon, or of anyone named Bominger, or Madame Desplaines, or Prellin. He was entirely ignorant of any unusual weapons of offense—he was a psychologist, not an engineer or a physicist. No, he was not unusually adept with DeLameters . . .

"Hold on!" Eichmil commanded. "Stop questioning him, everybody! Now, Lensman, instead of telling us what you do not know, give us positive information, in your own way. How do you work? I am beginning to suspect that the man we really want is a director, not an operator."

That was a more productive line. Lensmen, hundreds of them, each worked upon definite assignment. None of them had ever seen or ever would see the man who issued orders. He had not even a name, but was a symbol—Star A Star. They received orders through their Lenses, wherever they might be in space. They reported back to him in the same way. Yes, Star A Star knew what was going on there, he was reporting constantly . . .

A knife descended viciously. Blood spurted. The stump was dressed, roughly but efficiently. They did not wish their victim to bleed to death when he died, and he was not to die in any fashion—yet.

And in the instant that Kinnison's Lens went dead Worsel, from his safely distant nook, reached out direct to the mind of his friend, thereby putting his own life in jeopardy. He knew that there was an Overlord in that room, and the grue of a thousand helplessly-sacrificed generations of forebears swept his sinuous length at the thought, despite his inward certainty of the new powers of his mind. He knew that of all the entities in the Universe the Delgonians were most sensitive to the thought-vibrations of Velantians. Nevertheless, he did it.

He narrowed the beam down to the smallest possible coverage, employed a frequency as far as possible from that ordinarily used by the Overlords, and continued to observe. It was risky, but it was necessary. It was beginning to appear as though the Earthman might not be able to escape, and he must not die in vain.

"Can you communicate now?" In the ghastly chamber the relentless questioning went on.

"I can not communicate."

"It is well. In one way I would not be averse to letting your Star A Star know what happens when one of his minions dares to spy upon the Council of Boskone itself, but the information is as yet a trifle premature. Later, he shall learn . . ."

Kinnison did not consciously thrill at that thought. He did not know that the news was going beyond his brain; that he had achieved his goal. Worsel, however, did; and Worsel thrilled for him. The Gray Lensman had finished his job; all that was left to do was to destroy that base and the power of Boskone would be broken. Kinnison could die, now, content.

But no thought of leaving entered Worsel's mind. He would of course stand by as long as there remained the slightest shred of hope, or until some development threatened his ability to leave the planet with his priceless information. And the pitiless inquisition went on.

Star A Star had sent him to investigate their planet, to discover whether or not there was any connection between it and the zwilnik organization. He had come alone, in a speedster. No, he could not tell them even approximately where the speedster was. It was so dark, and he had come such a long distance on foot. In a short time, though, it would start sending out a thought-signal which he could detect . . .

"But you must have some ideas about this Star A Star!" This director was the man they want so desperately to get. They believed implicitly in this figment of a Lensman-Director. Fitting in so perfectly with their own ideas of efficient organization, it was more convincing by far than the actual truth would have been. They knew now that he would be hard to find. They did not now insist upon facts; they wanted every possible crumb of surmise. "You must have wondered who and where Star A Star is? You must have tried to trace him?"

Yes, he had tried, but the problem could not be solved. The Lens was non-directional, and the signals came in at practically the same strength, anywhere in the galaxy. They were, however, very much fainter out here. That might be taken to indicate that Star A Star's office was in a star cluster, well out in either zenith or nadir direction . . .

The victim sucked dry, eight of the Council departed, leaving Eichmil and the Overlord with the Lensman.

"What you have in mind to do, Eichmil, is childish. Your basic idea is excellent, but your technique is pitifully inadequate."

"What could be worse?" Eichmil demanded. "I am going to dig out his eyes, smash his bones, flay him alive, roast him, cut him up into a dozen pieces, and send him back to his Star A Star with a warning that every creature he sends into this galaxy will be treated the same way. What would *you* do?"

"You of the Eich lack finesse," the Delgonian sighed. "You have no subtlety, no conception of the nicer possibilities of torture, either of an individual or of a race. For instance, to punish Star A Star adequately this man must be returned to him alive, not dead."

"Impossible! He dies, *here!*"

"You misunderstand me. Not alive as he is now—but not entirely dead. Bones broken, yes, and eyes removed; but those minor matters are but a beginning. If I were doing it, I should then apply several of these devices here, successively; but none of them to the point of complete incompatibility with life. I should inoculate the extremities of his four limbs with an organism which grows—shall we say unpleasantly? Finally, I should extract his life force and consume it—as you know, that material is a rarely satisfying delicacy with us—taking care to leave just enough to maintain a bare existence. I should then put what is left of him aboard his ship, start it toward the Tellurian Galaxy, and send notice to the Patrol as to its exact course and velocity."

"But they would find him *alive!*" Eichmil stormed.

"Exactly. For the fullest vengeance they must, as I have said. Which is worse, think you? To find a corpse, however dismembered, and to dispose of it with full military honors, or to find and to have to take care of for a full lifetime a something that has not enough intelligence even to swallow food placed in its mouth? Remember also that the organism will be such that they themselves will be obliged to amputate all four of the creature's limbs to save its life."

While thinking thus the Delgonian shot out a slender tentacle which, slithering across the floor, flipped over the tiny switch of a small mechanism in the center of the room. This entirely unexpected action almost stunned Worsel. He had been debating for moments whether or not to release the Gray Lensman's inhibitions. He would have done so instantly if he had had any warning of what the Delgonian was about to do. Now it was too late.

"I have set up a thought-screen about the room. I do not wish to share this tid-bit with any of my fellows, as there is not enough to divide," the monster explained, parenthetically. "Have you any suggestion as to how my plan may be improved?"

"No. You have shown that you understand torture better than we do."

"I should, since we Overlords have practiced it as a fine art since our beginnings as a race. Do you wish the pleasure of breaking his bones now?"

"I do not break bones for pleasure. Since you do, you may carry out the procedure as outlined. All I want is the assurance that he will be an object-lesson and a warning to Star A Star of the Patrol."

"I can assure you definitely that it will be both. More, I will show you the results when I have finished my work. Or, if you like, I would be glad to have you stay and look on—you will find the spectacle interesting, entertaining, and highly instructive."

"No, thanks." Eichmil left the room and the Delgonian turned his attention to the bound and helpless Lensman.

It is best, perhaps, to draw a kindly veil over the events of the next two hours. Kinnison himself refuses positively to discuss it, except to say:

"I knew how to set up a nerve-block then, so I can't say that any of it really hurt me. I wouldn't let myself feel it. But all the time I knew what he was doing to me and it made me sick. Did you ever watch a surgeon while he was taking out your appendix? Like that, only worse. It wasn't funny. I didn't like it a bit. Your readers wouldn't like it, either, so you'd better lay off that stuff entirely."

The mere fact that the Overlord had established coverage was of course sufficient to set up in the Lensman's mind a compulsion to knock it down. He *had* to break that screen! But there were no birds here; no spiders. Was there any life at all? There was. That torture room had been used fully and often; the muck in its drains was rich pasture for the Jarnevonian equivalent of worms.

Selecting a big one, long and thick, Kinnison tuned down to its mental level and probed. This took time—much, much too much time. The creature did not have nearly the intelligence of a spider, but it did have a dim consciousness of being, and therefore an ego of a sort. Also, when Kinnison finally got in touch with that ego, it reacted very favorably to his suggestion of food.

"Hurry, worm! Snap it up!" and the little thing really did hurry. Scrambling, squirming, almost leaping along the floor it hurried, in a very grotesquerie of haste.

The Delgonian's leisurely preliminary work was done. The feast was ready. The worm reached the generator while the Overlord was warming up the tubes of the apparatus which was to rive away that which made the man Kinnison everything that he was.

Curling one end of its sinuous shape around a convenient anchorage, Kinnison's small proxy reached up and looped the other about the handle of the switch. Then, visions of choice viands suffusing its barely existent consciousness, it contracted convulsively. There was a snap and the mental barrier went out of existence.

At the tiny sound the Delgonian whirled—and stopped. Worsel's gigantic mentality had been beating ceaselessly against that screen ever since its erection, and in the instant of its fall Kinnison again became the Gray Lensman of old. And in the next instant both those prodigious minds—the two most powerful then known to Civilization—had hurled themselves against that of the Delgonian. Bitter though the ensuing struggle was, it was brief. Nothing short of an Arisian mind could have withstood the venomous fury, the Berserk power, of that concerted and synchronized attack.

Brain half burned out, the Overlord wilted; and, docility itself, he energized the communicator.

"Eichmil? The work is done. Thoroughly done and well. Do you wish to inspect it before I put what is left of the Lensman into his ship?"

"No." Eichmil, as a high executive, was accustomed to delegating far more important matters than that to competent underlings. "If you are satisfied, I am."

Weirdly enough to any casual observer, the Overlord's first act was to deposit the worm, carefully and tenderly, in a spot in which the muck was particularly rich and toothsome. Then, picking up the hideously mangled thing that was Kinnison's body, he encased it in its armor and, donning his own, wriggled boldly away with his burden.

"Clear the way for me, please," he requested of Eichmil. "I go to place this residuum within its ship and to return it to Star A Star."

"You will be able to find the speedster?"

"Certainly. He was to find it. Whatever he could have done I, working through the cells of his brain, can likewise do."

"Can you handle him alone, Kinnison?" Worsel asked presently. "Can you hold out to the speedster?"

"Yes to both. I can handle him—we whittled him down to a nub. I'll last—I'll make myself last long enough."

"I go, then, lest they be observing with spy-rays."

To the black flyer, then, the completely subservient Delgonian carried his physically disabled master, and carefully he put him aboard. Worsel helped openly there, for he had screened the speedster against all forms of intrusion. The vessel took off and the Overlord wriggled blithely back toward the dome. He was full of the consciousness of a good job well done. He even felt the sensation of repletion concomitant with having consumed practically all of Kinnison's life force!

"I hate to let him go!" Worsel's thought was a growl of baffled hatred. "It gripes me to let him think that he did everything he set out to do, even though I know it had to be that way. I wanted—I still want—to tear him apart for what he has done to you, my friend."

"Thanks, old snake." Kinnison's thought came faintly. "Just temporary. He's living on borrowed time. He'll get his. You've got everything under control, haven't you?"

"On the green. Why?"

"Because I can't hold this nerve-block any longer . . . It hurts . . . I'm sick. I think I'm going to . . ."

He fainted. More, he plunged parsecs deep into the blackest depths of oblivion as outraged Nature took the toll she had been so long denied.

Worsel hurled a call to Earth, then turned to his maimed and horribly broken companion. He applied splints to the shattered limbs, he dressed and bandaged the hideous wounds and the raw sockets which had once held eyes, he ministered to the raging, burning thirst. Whenever Kinnison's mind wearied he held for him the nerve-block; the priceless anodyne without which the Gray Lensman must have died from sheerest agony.

"Why not allow me, friend, to relieve you of all consciousness until help arrives?" the Velantian asked, pityingly.

"Can you do it without killing me?"

"If you so allow, yes. If you offer any resistance, I do not believe that any mind in the universe could."

"I won't resist. Come in," and Kinnison's suffering ended.

But kindly Worsel could do nothing about the fantastically atrocious growth which were transforming the Earthman's legs and arms into monstrosities out of nightmare.

He could only wait—wait for the skilled assistance which he knew must be so long in coming.

21

AMPUTATION

When Worsel's hard-driven call impinged upon the Port Admiral's Lens he dropped everything to take the report himself. Characteristically Worsel sent first and Haynes first recorded a complete statement of the successful mission to Jarnevon. Last came personalities, the tale of Kinnison's ordeal and his present plight.

"Are they following you in force, or can't you tell?"

"Nothing detectable, and at the time of our departure there had been no suggestion of any such action," Worsel replied, carefully.

"We'll come in force, anyway, and fast. Keep him alive until we meet you," Haynes urged, and disconnected.

It was an unheard-of occurrence for the Port Admiral to turn over his very busy and extremely important desk to a subordinate without notice and without giving him instructions, but Haynes did it now.

"Take charge of everything, Southworth!" he snapped. "I'm called away—emergency. Kinnison found Boskone—got away—hurt—I'm going after him in the *Dauntless*. Taking the new flotilla with me. Indefinite time—probably a few weeks."

He strode toward the communicator desk. The *Dauntless* was, as always, completely serviced and ready for any emergency. Where was that fleet of her sister-ships, on its shake-down cruise? He'd shake them down! They had with them the new hospital-ship, too—the only Red Cross ship in space that could leg it, parsec for parsec, with the *Dauntless*.

"Get me Navigations . . . Figure best point of rendezvous for *Dauntless* and Flotilla ZKD, both at full blast, en route to Lundmark's Nebula. Fifteen minutes departure. Figure approximate time of meeting with speedster, also at full blast, leaving that nebula hour nine fourteen today. Correction! Cancel speedster meeting, we can compute that more accurately later. Advise adjutant. Admiral Southworth will send order, through channels. Get me Base Hospital . . . Lacy, please . . . Kinnison's hurt, sawbones, bad. I'm going out after him. Coming along?"

"Yes. How about . . ."

"On the green. Flotilla ZKD, including your new two-hundred-million-credit hospital, is going along. Slip twelve, *Dauntless,* eleven and one-half minutes from now. Hipe!" and the Surgeon-Marshal "hiped."

Two minutes before the scheduled take-off Base Navigations called the chief navigating officer of the *Dauntless.*

"Course to rendezvous with Flotilla ZKD latitude three fifty four dash thirty longitude nineteen dash forty two time approximately twelve dash seven dash twenty six place one dash three dash zero outside arbitrary galactic rim check and repeat" rattled from the speaker without pause or punctuation. Nevertheless the chief navigator got it, recorded it, checked and repeated it.

"Figures only approximations because of lack of exact data on variations in density of medium and on distance necessarily lost in detouring stars" the speaker chattered on "suggest instructing your second navigator to communicate with navigating officers Flotilla ZKD at time twelve dash zero to correct courses to compensate unavoidably erroneous assumptions in computation Base Navigations off."

"I'll say he's off! 'Way off!" growled the Second. "What does he think I am—a complete nitwit? Pretty soon he'll be telling me two plus two equals four point zero."

The fifteen-second warning bell sounded. Every man came to the ready at his post, and precisely upon the designated second the super-dreadnought blasted off. For four or five miles she rose inert upon her under-jets, sirens and flaring lights clearing her way. Then she went free, her needle prow slanted sharply upward, her full battery of main driving projectors burst into action, and to all intents and purposes she vanished.

The Earth fell away from her at an incredible rate, dwindling away into invisibility in less than a minute. In two minutes the sun itself was merely a bright star, in five it had merged indistinguishably into the sharply-defined, brilliantly white belt of the Milky Way.

Hour after hour, day after day the *Dauntless* hurtled through space, swinging almost imperceptibly this way and that to avoid the dense ether in the neighborhood of suns through which the designated course would have led; but never leaving far or for long the direct line, almost exactly in the equatorial plane of the galaxy, between Tellus and the place of meeting. Behind her the Milky Way clotted, condensed, gathered itself together; before her and around her the stars began rapidly to thin out. Finally there were no more stars in front of her. She had reached the "arbitrary rim" of the galaxy, and the second navigator, then on duty, plugged into Communications.

"Please get me Flotilla ZKD, Flagship Navigations," he requested; and, as a clean-cut young face appeared upon his plate, "Hi, Harvey, old spacehound! Fancy meeting you out here! It's a small Universe, ain't it? Say, did that crumb back there at Base tell you, too, to be sure and start checking course before you over-ran the rendezvous? If he was singling me out to make that pass at, I'm going to take steps, and not through channels, either."

"Yeah, he told me the same. I thought it was funny, too—an oiler's pimp would know enough to do that without being told. We figured maybe he was jittery on account of us meeting the admiral or something. What's burned out all the jets, Paul, to get the big brass hats 'way out here and all dithered up, and to pull us offa the cruise this way? Must be a hell of an important flit! You're computing the Old Man himself, you must know something. What's this speedster that we're going to escort, and why? Give us the dope!"

"I don't know anything, Harvey, honest, any more than you do. They didn't put out a thing. Well, we'd better be getting onto the course— 'to compensate unavoidably erroneous assumptions in computation,' " he mimicked, caustically. "What do you read on my lambda? Fourteen— three—point zero six—decrement . . ."

The conversation became a technical jargon; because of which, however, the courses of the flying space-ships changed subtly. The flotilla swung around, through a small arc of a circle of prodigious radius, decreasing by a tenth its driving force. Up to it the *Dauntless* crept; through it and into the van. Then again in cone formation, but with fifty five units instead of fifty four, the flotilla screamed forward at maximum blast.

Well before the calculated time of meeting the speedster a Velantian Lensman who knew Worsel well put himself en rapport with him and sent a thought out far ahead of the flying squadron. It found its goal— Lensmen of that race, as has been brought out, have always been extraordinarily capable communicators—and once more the course was

altered slightly. In due time Worsel reported that he could detect the
fleet, and shortly thereafter:

"Worsel says to cut your drive to zero," the Velantian transmitted.
"He's coming up . . . He's close . . . He's going to go inert and start
driving . . . We're to stay free until we see what his intrinsic velocity
is . . . Watch for his flare."

It was a weird sensation, this of knowing that a speedster—quite a
sizable chunk of boat, really—was almost in their midst, and yet having
all their instruments, even the electros, register empty space . . .

There it was! The flare of the driving blast, a brilliant streamer of
fierce white light, sprang into being and drifted rapidly away to one side
of their course. When it had attained a safe distance:

"All ships of the flotilla except the *Dauntless* go inert," Haynes
directed. Then, to his own pilot. "Back us off a bit, Henderson, and do
the same," and the new flagship, too, went inert.

"How can I get onto the *Pasteur* the quickest, Haynes?" Lacy demanded.

"Take a gig," the Admiral grunted, "and tell the boys how much
you want to take. Three G's is all we can use without warning and
preparation."

There followed a curious and fascinating spectacle, for the hospital
ship had an intrinsic velocity entirely different from that of either Kinnison's speedster or Lacy's powerful gig. The *Pasteur,* gravity pads cut
to zero, was braking down by means of her under-jets at a conservative
one point four gravities—hospital ships were not allowed to use the
brutal accelerations employed as a matter of course by ships of war.

The gig was on her brakes at five gravities, all that Lacy wanted to
take—but the speedster! Worsel had put his patient into a pressure-pack
and had hung him on suspension, and was "balancing her down on her
tail" at a full eleven gravities!

But even at that, the gig first matched the velocity of the hospital
ship. The intrinsics of those two were at least of the same order of
magnitude, since both had come from the same galaxy. Therefore Lacy
boarded the Red Cross vessel and was escorted to the office of the chief
nurse while Worsel was still blasting at eleven G's—fifty thousand miles
distant then and getting farther away by the second—to kill the speedster's Lundmarkian intrinsic velocity. Nor could the tractors of the warships be of any assistance—the speedster's own vicious jets were fully
capable of supplying more acceleration than even a pressure-packed human body could endure.

"How do you do, Doctor Lacy? Everything is ready." Clarrissa Mac-

Dougal met him, hand outstretched. Her saucy white cap was worn as perkily cocked as ever: perhaps even more so, now that it was emblazoned with the cross-surmounted wedge which is the insignia of sector chief nurse. Her flaming hair was as gorgeous, her smile as radiant, her bearing as confidently—Kinnison has said of her more than once that she is the only person he has ever known who can strut sitting down !—as calmly poised. "I'm very glad to see you, doctor. It's been quite a while . . ." Her voice died away, for the man was looking at her with an expression defying analysis.

For Lacy was thunder-struck. If he had ever known it—and he must have—he had completely forgotten that MacDougall had this ship. This was awful—terrible!

"Oh, yes . . . yes, of course. How do you do? Mighty glad to see you again. How's everything going?" He pumped her hand vigorously, thinking frantically the while what he would—what he *could* say next. "Oh, by the way, who is to be in charge of the operating room?"

"Why, I am, of course," she replied in surprise. "Who else would be?"

"*Anyone* else!" he wanted to say, but did not—then. "Why, that isn't at all necessary . . . I would suggest . . ."

"You'll suggest nothing of the kind!" She stared at him intently; then, as she realized what his expression really meant—she had never before seen such a look of pitying anguish upon his usually sternly professional face—her own turned white and both hands flew to her throat.

"Not Kim, Lacy!" she gasped. Gone now was everything of poise, of insouciance, which had so characterized her a moment before. She who had worked unflinchingly upon all sorts of dismembered, fragmentary, maimed and mangled men was now a pleading, stricken, desperately frightened girl. "Not Kim—please! Oh, merciful God, don't let it be my Kim!"

"You *can't* be there, Mac." He did not need to tell her. She knew. He knew that she knew. "Somebody else—*anybody* else."

"No!" came the hot negative, although the blood drained completely from her face, leaving it as white as the immaculate uniform she wore. Her eyes were black, burning holes. "It's my job, Lacy, in more ways than one. Do you think I'd let anyone else work on *him?*" she finished passionately.

"You'll have to," he declared. "I didn't want to tell you this, but he's a mess." This, from a surgeon of Lacy's long and wide experience, was an unthinkable statement. Nevertheless:

"All the more reason why I've got to do it. No matter what shape he's in I'll let no one else work on my Kim!"

"I say no. That's an order—official!"

"Damn such orders!" she flamed. "There's nothing back of it—you know that as well as I do!"

"See here, young woman . . . !"

"Do you think you can order me not to perform the very duties I swore to do?" she stormed. "And even if it were not my job, I'd come in and work on him if I had to get a torch and cut my way in to do it. The only way you can keep me out is to have about ten of your men put me into a strait-jacket—and if you do that I'll have you kicked out of the Service bodily!"

"QX, MacDougall, you win." She had him there. This girl could and would do exactly that. "But if you faint I'll make you wish. . . ."

"You know me better than that, doctor." She was cold now as a woman of marble. "If he dies I'll die too, right then; but if he lives I'll stand by."

"You would, at that," the surgeon admitted. "Probably you would be able to hold together better than any one else could. But there'll be after-effects in your case, you know."

"I know." Her voice was bleak. "I'll live through them . . . if Kim lives." She became all nurse in the course of a breath. White, cold, inhuman; strung to highest tension and yet placidly calm, as only a truly loving woman in life's great crises can be. "You have had reports on him, doctor. What is your provisional diagnosis?"

"Something like elephantiasis, only worse, affecting both arms and both legs. Drastic amputations indicated. Eye-sockets. Burns. Multiple and compound fractures. Punctured and incised wounds. Traumatism, ecchymosis, extensive extravasations, œdema. Profound systemic shock. The prognosis, however, seems to be favorable, as far as we can tell."

"Oh, I'm glad of that," she breathed, the woman for a moment showing through the armor of the nurse. She had not dared even to think of prognosis. Then she had a thought. "Is that really true, or are you just giving me a shot in the arm?" she demanded.

"The truth—strictly," he assured her. "Worsel has an excellent sense of perception, and has reported fully and clearly. His brain, mind, and spine are not affected in any way, and we should be able to save his life. That is the one good feature of the whole thing."

The speedster finally matched the intrinsic velocity of the hospital ship. She went free, flashed up to the *Pasteur,* inerted, and maneuvered briefly. The larger vessel engulfed the smaller. The Gray Lensman was carried into the operating room. The anæsthetist approached the table and Lacy was stunned at a thought from Kinnison.

"Never mind the anæsthetic, Doctor Lacy. You can't make me unconscious without killing me. Just go ahead with your work. I held a nerve-block while the Delgonian was doing his stuff and I can hold it while you're doing yours."

"But we can't, man!" Lacy exclaimed. "You've got to be under a general for this job—we can't have you conscious. You're raving, I think. It will work—it always has. Let us try it, anyway, won't you?"

"Sure. It'll save me the trouble of holding the block, even though it won't do anything else. Go ahead."

The attendant doctor did so, with the same cool skill and to the same end-point as in thousands of similar and successful undertakings. At its conclusion, "Gone now, aren't you, Kinnison?" Lacy asked, through his Lens.

"No," came the surprising reply. "Physically, it worked. I can't feel a thing and I can't move a muscle, but mentally I'm still here."

"But you shouldn't be!" Lacy protested. "Perhaps you were right, at that—we can't give you much more without danger of collapse. But you've *got* to be unconscious! Isn't there some way in which you can be made so?"

"Yes, there is. But why do I have to be unconscious?" he asked, curiously.

"To avoid mental shock—seriously damaging," the surgeon explained. "In your case particularly the mental aspect is graver than the purely physical one."

"Maybe you're right, but you can't do it with drugs. Call Worsel; he has done it before. He had me unconscious most of the way over here except when he had to give me a drink or something to eat. He's the only man this side of Arisia who can operate on my mind."

Worsel came. "Sleep, my friend," he commanded, gently but firmly. "Sleep profoundly, body and mind, with no physical or mental sensations, no consciousness, no perception even of the passage of time. Sleep so until someone having authority to do so bids you awaken."

And Kinnison slept; so deeply that even Lacy's probing Lens could elicit no response.

"He will *stay* that way?" Lacy asked in awe.

"Yes."

"For how long?"

"Indefinitely. Until one of you doctors or nurses tells him to wake up, or until he dies for lack of food or water."

"He'll get nourishment. He would make a much better recovery if we could keep him in that state until his injuries are almost healed. Would that hurt him?"

"Not at all."

Then the surgeons and the nurses went to work. Since it has already been made amply plain what had to be done to the Gray Lensman, no good end is to be served by following in revolting detail the stark hideousness of its actual doing. Suffice it to say, then, that Lacy was not guilty of exaggeration when he described Kinnison as being a "mess." He was. The job was long and hard. It was heart-breaking, even for those to whom Kinnison was merely another case, not a beloved personality. What they had to do they did, and the white-marble chief nurse carried on through every soul-wrenching second, through every shocking, searing motion of it. She did her part, stoically, unflinchingly, as efficiently as though the patient upon the table were a total stranger undergoing a simple appendectomy and not the one man in her entire Universe undergoing radical dismemberment. Nor did she faint—then.

"Three or four of the girls fainted dead away, and a couple of the internes turned sort of green around the gills," she explained to your historian in reply to a direct question. She can bring herself to discuss the thing, now that it is so happily past, although she does not like to do so. "But I held on until it was all over. I did more than faint then." She smiled wryly at the memory. "I went into such a succession of hysterical cat-fits that they had to give me hypos and keep me in bed, and they didn't let me see Kim again until we had him back in Base Hospital, on Tellus. But even old Lacy himself was so woozy that he had to have a couple of snifters of brandy, so the show I put on wasn't too much out of order, at that."

Back in Base Hospital, then, time wore on until Lacy decided that the Lensman could be aroused from his trance. Clarrissa woke him up. She had fought for the privilege: first claiming it as a right and then threatening to commit mayhem upon the person of anyone else who dared even to think of doing it.

"Wake up, Kim dear," she whispered. "The worst of it is over now. You are getting well."

The Gray Lensman came to instantly, in full command of every faculty; knowing everything that had happened up to the instant of his hypnosis by Worsel. He stiffened, ready to establish again the nerveblock against the intolerable agony to which he had been subjected so long, but there was no need. His body was, for the first time in untold eons, free from pain; and he relaxed blissfully, reveling in the sheer comfort of it.

"I'm *so* glad that you're awake, Kim," the nurse went on. "I know that you can't talk to me—we can't unbandage your jaw until next week—and you can't think at me, either, because your new Lens hasn't come yet. But I can talk to you and you can listen. Don't be discouraged, Kim. Don't let it get you down. I love you just as much as I ever did, and as soon as you can talk we're going to get married. I am going to take care of you . . ."

"Don't 'poor dear' me, Mac," he interrupted her with a vigorous thought. "You didn't say it, I know, but you were thinking it. I'm not half as helpless as you think I am. I can still communicate, and I can see as well as I ever could, or better. And if you think I'm going to let you marry me to take care of me, you're crazy."

"You're raving! Delirious! Stark, staring mad!" She started back, then controlled herself by an effort. "Maybe you can think at people without a Lens—of course you can, since you just did, at me—but you *can't* see, Kim, possibly. Believe me, boy, I *know* you can't. I was there . . ."

"I can, though," he insisted. "I got a lot of stuff on my second trip to Arisia that I couldn't let anybody know about then, but I can now. I've got as good a sense of perception as Tregonsee has—maybe better. To prove it, you look thin, worn—whittled down to a nub. You've been working too hard—on me."

"Deduction," she scoffed. "You'd know I would."

"QX. How about those roses over there on the table? White ones, yellow ones, and red ones? With ferns?"

"You can smell them, perhaps," dubiously. Then, with more assurance, "You would know that practically all the flowers known to botany would be here."

"Well, I'll count 'em and point 'em out to you, then—or better, how about that little gold locket, with 'CM' engraved on it, that you're wearing under your uniform? I can't smell that, nor the picture in it . . ." The man's thought faltered in embarrassment. *"My* picture! Klono's whiskers, Mac, where did you get that—and why?"

"It's a reduction that Admiral Haynes let me have made. I am wearing it because I love you—I've said that before."

The girl's entrancing smile was now in full evidence. She knew now that he *could* see, that he would never be the helpless hulk which she had so gallingly thought him doomed to become, and her spirits rose in ecstatic relief. But he would *never* take the initiative now. QX, then—she would; and this was as good an opening as she would ever have with the stubborn brute. Therefore:

"More than that, as I also said before, I am going to marry you, whether you like it or not." She blushed a heavenly (and discordant) magenta, but went on unfalteringly: "And not out of pity, either, Kim, or just to take care of you. It's older than that—much older."

"It can't be done, Mac." His thought was a protest to high Heaven at the injustice of Fate. "I've thought it over out in space a thousand times—thought until I was black in the face—but I get the same result every time. It's just simply no soap. You are much too fine a woman—too splendid, too vital, too much of everything a woman should be—to be tied down for life to a thing that's half steel, rubber, and phenoline. It just simply isn't on the wheel, that's all."

"You're full of pickles, Kim." Gone was all her uncertainty and nervousness. She was calm, poised; glowing with a transcendent inward beauty. "I didn't really *know* until this minute that you love me, too, but I do now. Don't you realize, you big, dumb, wonderful clunker, that as long as there's one single, little bit of a piece of you left alive I'll love that piece more than I ever could any other man's entire being?"

"But I *can't*, I tell you!" He groaned the thought. "I can't and I won't! My job isn't done yet, either, and next time they'll probably get me. I *can't* let you waste yourself, Mac, on a fraction of a man for a fraction of a lifetime!"

"QX, Gray Lensman." Clarrissa was serene, radiantly untroubled. She could make things come out right now; everything was on the green. "We'll put this back up on the shelf for a while. I'm afraid that I have been terribly remiss in my duties as nurse. Patients mustn't be excited or quarreled with, you know."

"That's another thing. How come you, a sector chief, to be doing ordinary room duty, and night duty at that?"

"Sector chiefs assign duties, don't they?" she retorted sunnily. "Now I'll give you a rub and change some of these dressings."

22

REGENERATION

Hi, skeleton-gazer!"

"Ho, Big Chief Feet-on-the-Desk!"

"I see your red-headed sector chief is still occupying all strategic salients in force." Haynes had paused in the Surgeon-Marshal's office on his way to another of his conferences with the Gray Lensman. "Can't you get rid of her or don't you want to?"

"Don't want to. Couldn't, anyway, probably. The young vixen would tear down the hospital—she might even resign, marry him out of hand, and lug him off somewhere. You want him to recover, don't you?"

"Don't be any more of an idiot than you have to. What a question!"

"Don't work up a temperature about MacDougall, then. As long as she's around him—and that's twenty four hours a day—he'll get everything in the universe that he can get any good out of."

"That's so, too. This other thing's out of our hands now, anyway. Kinnison can't hold his position long against her and himself both—overwhelmingly superior force. Just as well, too—Civilization needs more like those two."

"Check, but the affair isn't out of our hands, by any means—we've got quite a little fine work to do there yet, as you'll see, before it'll be a really good job. But about Kinnison . . ."

"Yes. When are you going to fit arms and legs on him? He should be practising with them at this stage of the game, I should think—I was."

"You *should* think—but unfortunately, you don't," was the surgeon's dry rejoinder. "If you did, you would have paid more attention to what Phillips has been doing. He's making the final test today. Come along and we'll explain it to you again—your conference with Kinnison can wait half an hour."

In the research laboratory which had been assigned to Phillips they found von Hohendorff with the Posenian. Haynes was surprised to see the old Commandant of Cadets, but Lacy quite evidently had known that he was to be there.

"Phillips," the Surgeon-Marshal began, "explain to this warhorse, in words of as few syllables as possible, what you are doing."

"The original problem was to discover what hormone or other agent caused proliferation of neural tissue . . ."

"Wait a minute, I'd better do it," Lacy broke in. "Besides, you wouldn't do yourself justice. The first thing he found out was that the problem of repairing damaged nervous tissue was inextricably involved with several other unknown things, such as the original growth of such tissue, its relationship to growth in general, the regeneration of lost members in lower forms, and so on. You see, Haynes, it's a known fact that nerves do grow, or else they could not exist; and in lower forms of life they regenerate. Those facts were all he had, at first. In higher forms, even during the growth stage, regeneration does not occur spontaneously. Phillips set out to find out why.

"The thyroid controls growth, but does not initiate it, he learned. This fact seemed to indicate that there was an unknown hormone involved—that certain lower types possess an endocrine gland which is either atrophied or non-existent in higher types. If the latter, it was no landing. He reasoned, however, since higher types evolved from lower, that the gland in question might very well exist in a vestigial state. He studied animals, thousands of them, from the germ upward. He exhausted the patience of the Posenian authorities; and when they cut off his appropriation, on the ground that the thing was impossible, he came here. We felt that if he were so convinced of the importance of the work as to be willing to spend his whole life on it, the least we could do would be to support him. We gave him carte blanche.

"The man is a miracle of perseverance, a keen observer, a shrewd reasoner, and a mechanic par excellence—a born researcher. So he finally found out what it must be—the pineal. Then he had to find the stimulant. Drugs, chemicals, the spectrum of radiation; singly and in combination.

Years of plugging, with just enough progress to keep him at it. Visits to other planets peopled by races human to two places or more; learning everything that had been done along that line. When you fellows moved Medon over here he visited it as routine, and there he hit the jackpot. Wise himself is a surgeon, and the Medonians have had warfare and grief enough to develop the medical and surgical arts no end.

"They knew how to stimulate the pineal, but their method was dangerous. With Phillips' fresh viewpoint, his wide knowledge, and his mechanical genius, they worked out a new and highly satisfactory technique. He was going to try it out on a pirate slated for the lethal chamber, but von Hohendorff heard about it and insisted on being the guinea pig. Got up on his Unattached Lensman's high horse and won't come down. So here we are."

"Hm . . . m . . . interesting!" The admiral had listened attentively. "You're pretty sure it'll work, then, I gather?"

"As sure as we can be of any technique so new. Ninety percent probability, say—perhaps ninety five."

"Good enough odds." Haynes turned to von Hohendorff. "What do you mean, you old reprobate, by sneaking around behind my back and horning in on my reservation? I rate Unattached too, you know, and it's mine. You're out, Von."

"I saw it first and I refuse to relinquish." Von Hohendorff was adamant.

"You've got to," Haynes insisted. "He isn't your cub any more, he's my Lensman. Besides, I'm a better test than you are—I've got more parts to replace than you have."

"Four or five make just as good a test as a dozen," the commandant declared.

"Gentlemen, think!" the Posenian pleaded. "Please consider that the pineal is actually inside the brain. It is true that I have not been able to discover any brain injury so far, but the process has not yet been applied to a Tellurian brain and I can offer no assurance whatever that some obscure injury will not result."

"What of it?" and the two old Unattached Lensmen resumed their battle, hammer and tongs. Neither would yield a millimeter.

"Operate on them both, then, since they're both above law or reason," Lacy finally ordered in exasperation. "There ought to be a law to reduce Gray Lensmen to the ranks when they begin to suffer from ossification of the intellect."

"Starting with yourself, perhaps?" the admiral shot back, not at all abashed.

Haynes relented enough to let von Hohendorff go first, and both were given the necessary injections. The commandant was then strapped solidly into a chair; his head was immobilized with clamps.

The Posenian swung his needle-rays into place; two of them, each held rigidly upon micrometered racks and each operated by two huge, double, rock-steady hands. The operator *looked* entirely aloof—being eyeless and practically headless, it is impossible to tell from a Posenian's attitude or posture anything about the focal point of his attention—but the watchers knew that he was observing in microscopic detail the tiny gland within the old Lensman's skull.

Then Haynes. "Is this all there is to it, or do we come back for more?" he asked, when he was released from his shackles.

"That's all," Lacy answered. "One stimulation lasts for life, as far as we know. But if the treatment was successful you'll come back—about day after tomorrow, I think—to go to bed here. Your spare equipment won't fit and your stumps may require surgical attention."

Sure enough, Haynes did come back to the hospital, but not to go to bed. He was too busy. Instead, he got a wheel-chair and in it he was taken back to his now boiling office. And in a few more days he called Lacy in high exasperation.

"Know what you've done?" he demanded. "Not satisfied with taking my perfectly good parts away from me, you took my teeth too! They don't fit—I can't eat a thing! And I'm hungry as a wolf—I don't think I was ever so hungry in my life! I *can't* live on soup, man; I've got work to do. What are you going to do about it?"

"Ho-ho-haw!" Lacy roared. "Serves you right—von Hohendorff is taking it easy here, sitting on top of the world. Easy, now, sailor, don't rupture your aorta. I'll send a nurse over with a soft-boiled egg and a spoon. *Teething*—at *your* age—*Haw-ho-haw!"*

But it was no ordinary nurse who came, a few minutes later, to see the Port Admiral; it was the sector chief herself. She looked at him pityingly as she trundled him into his private office and shut the door, thereby establishing complete coverage.

"I had no idea, Admiral Haynes, that you . . . that there . . ." she paused.

"That I was so much of a rebuild?" complacently. "Except in the matter of eyes—which he doesn't need anyway—our mutual friend Kinnison has very little on me, my dear. I got so handy with the replacements that very few people knew how much of me was artificial. But it's these teeth that are taking all the joy out of life. I'm hungry, confound it! Have you got anything really satisfying that I can eat?"

"I'll say I have!" She fed him; then, bending over, she squeezed him tight and kissed him emphatically. "You and the commandant are just perfectly wonderful old darlings, and I *love* you!" she declared. "Lacy was simply poisonous to laugh at you the way he did. Why, you're two of the world's very best! And he knew perfectly well all the time, the lug, that of course you'd be hungry; that you'd have to eat twice as much as usual while your legs and things are growing. Don't worry, admiral, I'll feed you until you bulge. I want you to hurry up with this, so they'll do it to Kim."

"Thanks, Mac," and as she wheeled him back into the main office he considered her anew. A ravishing creature, but sound. Rash, and a bit stubborn, perhaps; impetuous and headstrong; but clean, solid metal all the way through. She had what it takes—she qualified. She and Kinnison would make a mighty fine couple when the lad got some of that heroic damn nonsense knocked out of his head . . . but there was work to do.

There was. The Galactic Council had considered thoroughly Kinnison's reports; its every member had conferred with him and with Worsel at length. Throughout the First Galaxy the Patrol was at work in all its prodigious might, preparing to wipe out the menace to Civilization which was Boskone. First-line super-dreadnoughts—no others would go upon that mission—were being built and armed, rebuilt and re-armed.

Well it was that the Galactic Patrol had previously amassed an almost inexhaustible supply of wealth, for its "reserves of expendable credit" were running like water.

Weapons, supposedly already of irresistible power, were made even more powerful. Screens already "impenetrable" were stiffened into even greater stubbornness. Primary projectors were made to take even higher loads for longer times. New and heavier Q-type helices were designed and built. Larger and more destructive duodec bombs were hurled against already ruined, torn, and quivering test-planets. Uninhabited worlds were being equipped with super-Bergenholms and with driving projectors. The negasphere, the most incredible menace to navigation which had ever existed in space, was being patrolled by a cordon of guard-ships.

And all this activity centered in one vast building and culminated in one man—Port Admiral Haynes, Galactic Councillor. And Haynes could not get enough to eat because he was cutting a new set of teeth!

He cut them, all thirty two of them. Arm and leg, foot and hand grew perfectly, even to the nails. Hair grew upon what had for years been a shining expanse of pate. But, much to Lacy's relief, it was old skin, not young, that covered the new limbs. It was white hair, not brown, that was dulling the glossiness of Haynes' bald old head. His tri-focals, unchanged, were still necessary if he were to see anything clearly, near or far.

"Our experimental animals aged and died normally," he explained graciously, "but I was beginning to wonder if we had rejuvenated you two, or perhaps endowed you with eternal life. Glad to see that the new parts have the same physical age as the rest of you—It would be mildly embarrassing to have to kill two Gray Lensmen to get rid of them."

"You're about as funny as a rubber crutch," Haynes grunted. "When are you going to give Kinnison the works? Don't you realize we need him?"

"Pretty quick now. Just as soon as we give you and Von your psychological examinations."

"Bah! That isn't necessary—my brain's QX!"

"That's what you think, but what do you know about brains? Worsel will tell us what shape your mind—if any—is in."

The Velantian put both Haynes and von Hohendorff through a gruelling examination, finding that their minds had not been affected in any way by the stimulants applied to their pineal glands.

Then and only then did Phillips operate upon Kinnison; and in his case, too, the operation was a complete success. Arms and legs and eyes replaced themselves flawlessly. The scars of his terrible wounds disappeared, leaving no sign of ever having been.

He was a little slower, however; somewhat clumsy, and woefully weak. Therefore, instead of discharging him from the hospital as cured, which procedure would have restored to him automatically all the rights and privileges of an Unattached Lensman, the Council decided to transfer him to a physical-culture camp. A few weeks there would restore to him entirely the strength, speed, and agility which had formerly been his, and he would then be allowed to resume active duty.

Just before he left the hospital, Kinnison strolled with Clarrissa out to a bench in the grounds.

". . . and you're making a perfect recovery," the girl was saying. "You'll be exactly as you were. But things between us aren't just as they were, and they never can be again. You know that, Kim. We've got unfinished business to transact—let's take it down off the shelf before you go."

"Better let it lay, Mac." All the new-found joy of existence went out of the man's eyes. "I'm whole, yes, but that angle was really the least important of all. You never yet have faced squarely the fact that my job isn't done and that my chance of living through it is just about one in ten. Even Phillips can't do anything about a corpse."

"I won't face it, either, unless and until I must." Her reply was tranquility itself. "Most of the troubles people worry about in advance never do materialize. And even if it did, you ought to know that I . . . that any woman would rather . . . well, that half a loaf is better than no bread."

"QX. I haven't mentioned the worst thing. I didn't want to—but if you've got to have it, here it is," the man wrenched out. "Look at what I am. A bar-room brawler. A rum-dum. A hard-boiled egg. A cold-blooded, ruthless murderer; even of my own men . . ."

"Not that, Kim, ever, and you know it," she rebuked him.

"What else can you call it?" he grated. "A killer besides—a red-handed butcher if there ever was one; then, now, and forever. I've got to be. I can't get away from it. Do you think that you, or any other decent woman, could stand it to live with me? That you could feel my arms around you, feel my gory paws touching you, without going sick at the stomach?"

"Oh, so *that's* what's been really griping you all this time?" Clarrissa was surprised, but entirely unshaken. "I don't have to think about that, Kim—I *know.* If you were a murderer or had the killer instinct, that would be different, but you aren't and you haven't. You are hard, of course. You have to be . . . but do you think I'd be running a temperature over a softy? You brawl, yes—like the world's champion you are. Anybody you ever killed needed killing, there's no question of that. You don't do these things for fun; and the fact that you can drive yourself to do the things that have to be done shows your real size.

"Nor have you even thought of the obverse; that you lean over backwards in wielding that terrific power of yours. The Desplaines woman, the countess—lots of other instances. I respect and honor you more than any other man I have ever known. Any woman who really knew you would—she *must!*

"Listen, Kim. Read my mind, all of it. You'll really know me then, and understand me better than I can ever explain myself."

"Have you got a picture of me doing that?" he asked, flatly.

"No, you big, unreasonable clunker, I haven't!" she flared, "and that's just what's driving me mad!" Then, voice dropping to a whisper, almost sobbing; "Cancel that, Kim—I didn't mean it. You wouldn't—you *couldn't,* I suppose, and still be you, the man I love. But isn't there something—*anything*—that will make you understand what I really am?"

"I know what you are." Kinnison's voice was uninflected, weary. "As I told you before—the universe's best. It's what I am that's clogging the jets—what I have been and what I've got to keep on being. I simply don't rate up, and you'd better lay off me, Mac, while you can. There's a poem by one of the ancients—Kipling—the 'Ballad of Boh Da Thone'—that describes it exactly. You wouldn't know it . . ."

"You just think I wouldn't," nodding brightly. "The only trouble is, you always think of the wrong verses. Part of it really *is* descriptive of you. You know, where all the soldiers of the Black Tyrone thought so much of their captain?"

She recited:

" 'And worshipped with fluency, fervor, and zeal
" 'The mud on the boot-heels of "Crook" O'Neil.'

"That describes you to a 'T.' "

"You're crazy for the lack of sense," he demurred. "I don't rate like that."

"Sure you do," she assured him. "All the men think of you that way. And not only men. Women, too, darn 'em—and the next time I catch one of them at it I'm going to kick her cursed teeth out, one by one!"

Kinnison laughed, albeit a trifle sourly. "You're raving, Mac. Imagining things. But to get back to that poem, what I was referring to went like this . . ."

"I know how it goes. Listen:

" 'But the captain had quitted the long-drawn strife
" 'And in far Simoorie had taken a wife;

" 'And she was a damsel of delicate mold,
" 'With hair like the sunshine and heart of gold.

" 'And little she knew the arms that embraced
" 'Had cloven a man from the brow to the waist:

" 'And little she knew that the loving lips
" 'Had ordered a quivering life's eclipse,

" 'And the eyes that lit at her lightest breath
" 'Had glared unawed in the Gates of Death.

" '(For these be matters a man would hide,
" 'As a general thing, from an innocent bride.)'

"That's what you mean, isn't it?" she asked, quietly.

"Mac, you know a lot of things you've got no business knowing." Instead of answering her question, he stared at her speculatively. "My sprees and brawls, Dessa Desplaines and the Countess Avondrin, and now this. Would you mind telling me how you get the stuff?"

"I'm closer to you than you suspect, Kim—I've always been. Worsel calls it being 'en rapport.' You don't need to think at me—in fact, you have to put up a conscious block to keep me out. So I know a lot that I shouldn't, but Lensmen aren't the only ones who don't talk. You'd been thinking about that poem a lot—it worried you—so I checked with Archeology on it. I memorized most of it."

"Well, to get the true picture of me you'll have to multiply that by a thousand. Also, don't forget that loose heads might be rolling out onto your breakfast table almost any morning instead of only once."

"So what?" she countered evenly. "Do you think I could sit for Kipling's portrait of Mrs. O'Neil? Nobody ever called my mold delicate, and Kipling, if he had been describing me, would have said:

" 'With hair like a conflagration,

" 'And a heart of solid brass!'

"Captain O'Neil's bride, as well as being innocent and ignorant, strikes me as having been a good deal of a sissy, something of a weeping willow, and no little of a shrinking violet. Tell me, Kim, do you think she would have made good as a sector chief nurse?"

"No, but that's neither . . ."

"It is, too," she interrupted. "You've got to consider that I did, and that it's no job for any girl with a weak stomach. Besides, the Boh's head took the fabled Mrs. O'Neil by surprise. She didn't know that her husband used to be in the wholesale mayhem-and-killing business. I do.

"And lastly, you big lug, do you think I'd be making such bare-faced passes at you unless I knew exactly what the score is—exactly where *you* stand? You're too much of a gentleman to read my mind; but I'm not that sque . . . I *had* to know."

"Huh?" he demanded, blushing fiercely. "You really know, then, that . . ." he would not say it, even then.

"Of course I know!" She nodded; then, as the man spread his hands helplessly, she abandoned her attempt to keep the conversation upon a light level.

"I know, my dear. There's nothing we can do about it yet." Her voice was unsteady, her heart in every word. "You have to do your job, and I honor you for that, even if it does take you away from me. It'll be easier for you, though, I think, and I *know* it will be easier for me, to have it out in the open. Whenever you're ready, Kim, I'll be here—or somewhere—waiting. Clear ether, Gray Lensman!" and, rising to her feet, she turned back toward the hospital.

"Clear ether, Chris!" Unconsciously he used the pet name by which he had thought of her so long. He stared after her for a minute, hungrily. Then, squaring his shoulders, he strode away.

And upon far Jarnevon Eichmil, the First of Boskone, was conferring with Jalte via communicator. Long since, the Kalonian had delivered through devious channels the message of Boskone to an imaginary director of Lensmen; long since had he received this cryptically direful reply:

"Morgan lives, and so does—Star A Star."

Jalte had not been able to report to his chief any news concerning the fate of that which the speedster bore, since spies no longer existed within the reservations of the Patrol. He had learned of no discovery that any Lensman had made. He could not venture a hypothesis as to how this Star A Star had heard of Jarnevon or had learned of its location. He was sure of only one thing, and that was a grimly disturbing fact indeed. The Patrol was re-arming throughout the galaxy, upon a scale theretofore unknown. Eichmil's thought was cold:

"That means but one thing. A Lensman invaded you and learned of us here—in no other way could knowledge of Jarnevon have come to them."

"Why me?" Jalte demanded. "If there exists a mind of power sufficient to break my screens and tracelessly to invade my mind, what of yours?"

"It is proven by the outcome." The Boskonian's statement was a calm summation of fact. "The messenger sent against you succeeded; the one against us failed. The Patrol intends and is preparing: certainly to wipe out our remaining forces within the Tellurian Galaxy; probably to attack your stronghold; eventually to invade our own galaxy."

"Let them come!" snarled the Kalonian. "We can and will hold this planet forever against anything they can bring through space!"

"I would not be too sure of that," cautioned the superior. "In fact, if—as I am beginning to regard as a probability—the Patrol does make a concerted drive against any significant number of our planetary organizations, you should abandon your base there and return to Kalonia, after disbanding and so preserving for future use as many as possible of the planetary units."

"Future use? In that case there will be no future."

"There will so," Eichmil replied, coldly vicious. "We are strengthening the defenses of Jarnevon to withstand any conceivable assault. If they do not attack us here of their own free will we shall compel them to do so. Then, after destroying their every mobile force, we shall again take over their galaxy. Arms for the purpose are even now in the building. Is the matter clear?"

"It is clear. We shall warn all our groups that such an order may issue, and we shall prepare to abandon this base should such a step become desirable."

So it was planned; neither Eichmil nor Jalte even suspecting two startling truths:

First, that when the Patrol was ready it would strike hard and without warning, and

Second, that it would strike, not low, but high!

23

ANNIHILATION

Kinnison played, worked, rested, ate, and slept. He boxed, strenuously and viciously, with masters of the craft. He practiced with his DeLameters until he had regained his old-time speed and dead-center accuracy. He swam for hours at a time, he ran in cross-country races. He lolled, practically naked, in hot sunshine. And finally, when his muscles were writhing and rippling as of yore beneath the bronzed satin of his skin, Lacy answered his insistent demands by coming to see him.

The Gray Lensman met the flyer eagerly, but his face fell when he saw that the surgeon-marshal was alone.

"No, MacDougall didn't come—she isn't around any more," he explained, guilefully.

"Huh?" came startled query. "How come?"

"Out in space—out Borova way somewhere. What do you care? After the way you acted you've got the crust of a rhinoceros to . . ."

"You're crazy, Lacy. Why, we . . . she . . . it's all fixed up."

"Funny kind of fixing. Moping around Base, crying her red head off. Finally, though, she decided she had some Scotch pride left, and I let her go aboard again. If she isn't all done with you, she ought to be." This, Lacy figured, would be good for what ailed the big sap-head. "Come on, and I'll see whether you're fit to go back to work or not."

He was fit. "QX, lad—flit!" Lacy discharged him informally with a slap upon the back. "Get dressed and I'll take you back to Haynes—he's been snapping at me like a turtle ever since you've been out here."

At Prime Base Kinnison was welcomed enthusiastically by the admiral.

"Feel those fingers, Kim!" he exclaimed. "Perfect! Just like the originals!"

"Mine, too. They do feel good."

"It's a pity you got your new ones so quick. You'd appreciate 'em much more after a few years without 'em. But to get down to business. The fleets have been taking off for weeks—we're to join up as the line passes. If you haven't anything better to do I'd like to have you aboard the Z9M9Z."

"I don't know of any place I'd rather be, sir—thanks."

"QX. Thanks should be the other way. You can make yourself mighty useful between now and zero time." He eyed the younger man speculatively.

Haynes had a special job for him, Kinnison knew. As a Gray Lensman, he could not be given any military rank or post, and he could not conceive of the admiral of Grand Fleet wanting him around as an aide-de-camp.

"Spill it, chief," he invited. "Not orders, of course—I understand that perfectly. Requests or—ah-hum—suggestions."

"I *will* crown you with something yet, you whelp!" Haynes sorted, and Kinnison grinned. These two were very close, in spite of their disparity in years; and very much of a piece. "As you get older you'll realize that it's good tactics to stick pretty close to Gen Regs. Yes, I *have* got a job for you, and a nasty one. Nobody has been able to handle it, not even two companies of Rigellians. Grand Fleet Operations."

"Grand Fleet Operations!" Kinnison was aghast. "Holy—Klono's—Iridium—Intestines! What makes you think I've got jets enough to swing *that* load?"

"I haven't any idea whether you can or not. If you can't, though, nobody can; and in spite of all the work we've done on the thing we'll have to operate as a mob, the way we did before; not as a fleet. If so, I shudder to think of the results."

"QX. If you'll send for Worsel we'll try it a fling or two. It'd be a shame to build a whole ship around an Operations tank and then not be able to use it. By the way, I haven't seen my head nurse—Miss MacDougall, you know—around any place lately. Have you? I ought to tell her 'thanks' or something—maybe send her a flower."

"Nurse? MacDougall? Oh, yes, the red-head. Let me see—did hear something about her the other day. Married? No . . . took a hospital ship somewhere. Alsakan? Vandemar? Didn't pay any attention. She doesn't need thanks—or flowers, either—getting paid for her work. Much more important, don't you think, to get Operations straightened out?"

"Undoubtedly, sir," Kinnison replied, stiffly; and as he went out Lacy came in.

The two old conspirators greeted each other with knowing grins. *Was* Kinnison taking it big! He was falling, like ten thousand bricks down a well.

"Do him good to undermine his position a bit. Too cocky altogether. But *how* they suffer!"

"Check!"

The Gray Lensman rode toward the flagship in a mood which even he could not have described. He had expected to see her, as a matter of course . . . he wanted to see her . . . confound it, he *had* to see her! Why did she have to do a flit now, of all the times on the calendar? She knew the fleet was shoving off, and that he'd have to go along . . . and nobody knew where she was. When he got back he'd find her if he had to chase her all over the galaxy. He'd put an end to this. Duty was duty, of course . . . but Chris was CHRIS . . . and half a loaf *was* better than no bread!

He jerked back to reality as he entered the gigantic tear-drop which was technically the Z9M9Z, socially the *Directrix,* and ordinarily GFHQ. She had been designed and built specifically to be Grand Fleet Headquarters, and nothing else. She bore no offensive armament, but since she had to protect the presiding geniuses of combat she had every possible defense.

Port Admiral Haynes had learned a bitter lesson during the expedition to Helmuth's base. Long before that relatively small fleet got there he was sick to the core, realizing that fifty thousand vessels simply could not be controlled or maneuvered as a group. If that base had been capable of an offensive or even of a real defense, or if Boskone could have put their fleets into that star-cluster in time, the Patrol would have been defeated ignominiously; and Haynes, wise old tactician that he was, knew it.

Therefore, immediately after the return from that "triumphant" venture, he gave orders to design and to build, at whatever cost, a flagship capable of directing efficiently a million combat units.

The "tank"—the minutely cubed model of the galaxy which is a necessary part of every pilot room—had grown and grown as it became evident that it must be the prime agency in Grand Fleet Operations. Finally, in this last rebuilding, the tank was seven hundred feet in diameter and eighty feet thick in the middle—over seventeen million cubic feet of space in which more than two million tiny lights crawled hither and thither in helpless confusion. For, after the technicians and designers had put that tank into actual service, they had discovered that it was useless. No available mind had been able either to perceive the situation as a whole or to identify with certainty any light or group of lights needing correction; and as for linking up any particular light with its individual, blanket-proof communicator in time to issue orders in space-combat . . . !

Kinnison looked at the tank, then around the full circle of the million-plug board encircling it. He observed the horde of operators, each one trying frantically to do something. Next he shut his eyes, the better to perceive everything at once, and studied the problem for an hour.

"Attention, everybody!" he thought then. "Open all circuits—do nothing at all for a while." He then called Haynes.

"I think we can clean this up if you'll send over some Simplex analyzers and a crew of technicians. Helmuth had a nice set-up on multiplex controls, and Jalte had some ideas, too. If we add them to this we may have something."

And by the time Worsel arrived, they did.

"Red lights are fleets already in motion," Kinnison explained rapidly to the Velantian. "Greens are fleets still at their bases. Ambers are the planets the reds took off from—connected, you see, by Ryerson string-lights. The white star is us, the *Directrix*. That violet cross 'way over there is Jalte's planet, our first objective. The pink comets are our free planets, their tails showing their intrinsic velocities. Being so slow, they had to start long ago. The purple circle is the negasphere. It's on its way, too. You take that side, I'll take this. They were supposed to start from the edge of the twelfth sector. The idea was to make it a smooth, bowl-shaped sweep across the galaxy, converging upon the objective, but each of the system marshals apparently wants to run this war to suit himself. Look at that guy there—he's beating the gun by nine thousand parsecs. Watch me pin his ears back!"

He pointed his Simplex at the red light which had so offendingly sprung into being. There was a whirring click and the number 449276 flashed above a board. An operator flicked a switch.

"Grand Fleet Operations!" Kinnison's thought snapped across space. "Why are you taking off without orders?"

"Why, I . . . I'll give you the marshal, sir . . ."

"No time! Tell your marshal that one more such break will put him in irons. Land at once! GFO—off.

"With around a million fleets to handle we can't spend much time on any one," he thought at Worsel. "But after we get them lined up and get our Rigellians broken in, it won't be so bad."

The breaking in did not take long; definite and meaningful orders flew faster and faster along the tiny, but steel-hard beams of the communicators.

"Take off . . . Increase drive four point five . . . Decrease drive two point eight . . . Change course to . . ." and so it went, hour after hour and day after day.

And with the passage of time came order out of chaos. The red lights formed a gigantically sweeping, curving wall; its almost imperceptible forward crawl representing an actual velocity of almost a hundred parsecs an hour. Behind that wall blazed a sea of amber, threaded throughout with the brilliant filaments which were the Ryerson lights. Ahead of it lay a sparkling, almost solid blaze of green. Closer and closer the wall crept toward the bright white star.

And in the "reducer"—the standard, ten-foot tank in the lower well—the entire spectacle was reproduced in miniature. It was plainer there, clearer and much more readily seen: but it was so crowded that details were indistinguishable.

Haynes stood beside Kinnison's padded chair one day, staring up into the immense lens and shaking his head. He went down the flight of stairs to the reducer, studied that, and again shook his head.

"This is very pretty, but it doesn't mean a thing," he thought at Kinnison. "It begins to look as though I'm going along just for the ride. You—or you and Worsel—will have to do the fighting, too, I'm afraid."

"Uh-uh," Kinnison demurred. "What do we—or anyone else—know about tactics, compared to you? You've got to be the brains. That's why we had the boys rig up the original working model there, for a reducer. On that you can watch the gross developments and tell us in general terms what to do. Knowing that, we'll know who ought to do what, from the big chart here, and pass your orders along."

"Say, that *will* work, at that!" and Haynes brightened visibly. "Looks as though a couple of those reds are going to knock our star out of the tank, doesn't it?"

"It'll be close in that reducer—they'll probably touch. Close enough in real space—less than three parsecs."

The zero hour came and the Tellurian armada of eighty one sleek space-ships—eighty super-dreadnoughts and the *Directrix*—spurned Earth and took its place in that hurtling wall of crimson. Solar system after solar system was passed: fleet after fleet leaped into the ether and fitted itself into the smoothly geometrical pattern which Grand Fleet Operations was nursing along so carefully.

Through the galaxy the formation swept and out of it, toward a star cluster. It slowed its mad pace, the center hanging back, the edges advancing and folding in.

"Surround the cluster and close in," the admiral directed; and, under the guidance now of two hundred Rigellians, Civilization's vast Grand Fleet closed smoothly in and went inert. Drivers flared white as they fought to match the intrinsic velocity of the cluster.

"Marshals of all system-fleets, attention! Using secondaries only, fire at will upon any enemy object coming within range. Engage outlying structures and such battle craft as may appear. Keep assigned distance from planet and stiffen cosmic screens to maximum. Haynes—off!"

From millions upon millions of projectors there raved out gigantic rods, knives, and needles of force, under the impact of which the defensive screens of Jalte's guardian citadels flamed into terrible refulgence. Duodec bombs were hurled—tight-beam-directed monsters of destruction which, looping around in vast circles to attain the highest possible measure of momentum, flung themselves against Boskone's defenses in Herculean attempts to smash them down. They exploded; each as it burst filling all nearby space with blindingly intense violet light and with flying scraps of metal. Q-type helices, driven with all the frightful kilowattage possible to Medonian conductors and insulation, screwed in; biting, gouging, tearing in wild abandon. Shear-planes, hellish knives of force beside which Tellurian lightning is pale and wan, struck and struck and struck again—fiendishly, crunchingly.

But those grimly stolid fortresses could take it. They had been repowered; their defenses stiffened to such might as to defy, in the opinion of Boskone's experts, any projectors capable of being mounted upon mobile bases. And not only could they take it—those formidably armed and armored planetoids could dish it out as well. The screens of the Patrol ships flared high into the spectrum under the crushing force of sheer enemy power. Not a few of those defenses were battered down, clear to the wall-shields, before the unimaginable ferocity of the Boskonian projectors could be neutralized.

And at this spectacularly frightful deep-space engagement Galactic Director Jalte, and through him Eichmil, First of Boskone itself, stared in stunned surprise.

"It is insane!" Jalte gloated. "The fools judged our strength by that of Helmuth, not considering that we, as well as they, would be both learning and doing during the intervening time. They have a myriad of ships, but mere numbers will never conquer my outposts, to say nothing of my works here."

"They are not fools. I am not so sure . . ." Eichmil cogitated.

He would have been even less sure could he have listened to a conversation which was even then being held.

"QX, Thorndyke?" Kinnison asked.

"On the green," came instant reply. "Intrinsic, placement, releases—everything on the green."

"Cut!" and the lone purple circle disappeared from tank and from reducer. The master technician had cut his controls and every pound of metal and other substance surrounding the negasphere had fallen into that enigmatic realm of nothingness. No connection or contact with it was now possible; and with its carefully established intrinsic velocity it rushed engulfingly toward the doomed planet. One of the mastodonic fortresses, lying in its path, vanished utterly, with nothing save a burst of invisible cosmics to mark its passing. It approached its goal. It was almost upon it before any of the defenders perceived it, and even then they could neither understand nor grasp it. All detectors and other warning devices remained static, but:

"Look! There! Something's *coming!*" an observer jittered, and Jalte swung his plate. He saw—nothing. Eichmil saw the same thing. There was nothing to see. A vast, intangible nothing—yet a nothing tangible enough to occult everything material in a full third of the cone of vision! Jalte's operators hurled into it their mightiest beams. Nothing happened. They struck nothing and disappeared. They loosed their heaviest duodec torpedoes; gigantic missiles whose warheads contained enough of that frightfully violent detonate to disrupt a world. Nothing happened—not even an explosion. Not even the faintest flash of light. Shell and contents alike merely—and Oh! so incredibly peacefully!—ceased to exist. There were important bursts of cosmics, but they were invisible and inaudible; and neither Jalte nor any member of his force was to live long enough to realize how terribly he had already been burned.

Gigantic pressors shoved against it: beams of power sufficient to deflect a satellite; beams whose projectors were braced, in steel-laced concrete down to bedrock, against any conceivable thrust. But this was *negative,* not positive matter—matter negative in every respect of mass, inertia, and force. To it a push was a pull. Pressors to it were tractors—at contact they pulled themselves up off their massive foundations and hurtled into the appalling blackness.

Then the negasphere struck. Or did it? Can nothing strike anything? It would be better, perhaps, to say that the spherical hyper-plane which

was the three-dimensional cross-section of the negasphere began to occupy the same volume of space as that in which Jalte's unfortunate world
already was. And at the surface of contact of the two the materials of
both disappeared. The substance of the planet vanished, the incomprehensible nothingness of the negasphere faded away into the ordinary
vacuity of empty space.

Jalte's base, the whole three hundred square miles of it, was taken
at the first gulp. A vast pit opened where it had been, a hole which
deepened and widened with horrifying rapidity. And as the yawning
abyss enlarged itself the stuff of the planet fell into it, in turn to vanish.
Mountains tumbled into it, oceans dumped themselves into it. The hot,
frightfully compressed and nascent material of the planet's core sought
to erupt—but instead of moving, it, too, vanished. Vast areas of the
world's surface crust, tens of thousands of square miles in extent, collapsed into it, splitting off along crevasses of appalling depth, and became nothing. The stricken globe shuddered, trembled, ground itself to
bits in paroxysm after ghastly paroxysm of disintegration.

What was happening? Eichmil did not know, since his "eye" was
destroyed before any really significant developments could eventuate. He
and his scientists could only speculate and deduce—which, with surprising accuracy, they did. The officers of the Patrol ships, however, *knew*
what was going on, and they were scanning with tensely narrowed eyes
the instruments which were recording instant by instant the performance
of the new cosmic super-screens which were being assaulted so brutally.

For, as has been said, the negasphere was composed of negative matter. Instead of electrons its building-blocks were positrons—the "Dirac
holes" in an infinity of negative energy. Whenever the field of a positron
encountered that of an electron the two neutralized each other, giving rise
to two quanta of hard radiation. And, since those encounters were occurring at the rate of countless trillions per second, there was tearing at the
Patrol's defenses a flood of cosmics of an intensity which no space-ship
had ever before been called upon to withstand. But the new screens had
been figured with a factor of safety of five, and they stood up.

The planet dwindled with soul-shaking rapidity to a moon, to a
moonlet, and finally to a discretely conglomerate aggregation of meteorites before the mutual neutralization ceased.

"Primaries now," Haynes ordered briskly, as the needles of the
cosmic-ray-screen meters dropped back to the green lines of normal
functioning. The probability was that the defenses of the Boskonian
citadels would now be automatic only, that no life had endured through
that awful flood of lethal radiation; but he was taking no chances. Out

flashed the penetrant super-rays and the fortresses, too, ceased to exist save as the impalpable infra-dust of space.

And the massed Grand Fleet of the Galactic Patrol, remaking its formation, hurtled outward through the intergalactic void.

24

PASSING OF THE EICH

They are not fools. I am not so sure . . ." Eichmil had said; and when the last force-ball, his last means of inter-galactic communication, went dead the First of Boskone became very unsure indeed. The Patrol undoubtedly had something new—he himself had had glimpses of it—but what was it?

That Jalte's base was gone was obvious. That Boskone's hold upon the Tellurian Galaxy was gone followed as a corollary. That the Patrol was or soon would be wiping out Boskone's regional and planetary units was a logical inference. Star A Star, that accursed Director of Lensmen, had—must have—succeeded in stealing Jalte's records, to be willing to destroy out of hand the base which housed them.

Nor could Boskone do anything to help the underlings, now that the long-awaited attack upon Jarnevon itself was almost certainly coming. Let the Patrol come—they were ready. Or were they, quite? Jalte's defenses were strong, but they had not withstood that unknown weapon even for seconds.

Eichmil called a joint meeting of Boskone and the Academy of Science. Coldly and precisely he told them everything that he had seen. Discussion followed.

"Negative matter beyond a doubt," a scientist summed up. "It has long been surmised that in some other, perhaps hyper-spatial, universe there must exist negative matter of mass sufficient to balance the positive material of the universe we know. It is conceivable that by hyper-spatial explorations and manipulations the Tellurians have discovered that other universe and have transported some of its substance into ours."

"Can they manufacture it?" Eichmil demanded.

"The probability that such material can be manufactured is exceedingly small," was the studied reply. "An entirely new mathematics would be necessary. In all probability they found it already existent."

"We must find it also, then, and at once."

"We will try. Bear in mind, however, that the field is large, and do not be optimistic of an early success. Note also that that substance is not necessary—perhaps not even desirable—in a defensive action."

"Why not?"

"Because, by directing pressors against such a bomb, Jalte actually pulled it into his base, precisely where the enemy wished it to go. As a surprise attack, against those ignorant of its true nature, such a weapon would be effective indeed; but against us it will prove a boomerang. All that is needful is to mount tractor heads upon pressor bases, and thus drive the bombs back upon those who send them." It did not occur, even to the coldest scientist of them all, that that bomb had been of planetary mass. Not one of the Eich suspected that all that remained of the entire world upon which Jalte's base had stood was a handful of meteorites.

"Let them come, then," said Eichmil, grimly. "Their dependence upon a new and supposedly unknown weapon explains what would otherwise be insane tactics. With that weapon impotent they cannot possibly win a long war waged so far from their bases. We can match them ship for ship, and more; and our supplies and munitions are close at hand. We will wear them down—blast them out—the Tellurian Galaxy shall yet be ours!"

Admiral Haynes spent almost every waking hour setting up and knocking down tactical problems in the practice tank, and gradually his expression changed from one of strained anxiety to one of pleased satisfaction. He went over to his sealed-band transmitter, called all communications officers to attention, and thought:

"Each vessel will direct its longest-range detector, at highest possible power, centrally upon the objective galaxy. The first observer to find detectable activity, however faint, will report it instantly to GHQ. We will send out a general C.B., at which every vessel in Grand Fleet will cease blasting at once; remaining motionless in space until further orders." He then called Kinnison.

"Look here," he directed the attention of the younger man into the reducer, which now represented inter-galactic space, with a portion of the Second Galaxy filling one edge. "I have a solution, but its practicability depends upon whether or not it calls for the impossible from you, Worsel, and your Rigellians. You remarked at the start that I knew my tactics. I wish I knew more—or at least could be certain that Boskone and I agree on what constitutes good tactics. I feel quite safe in assuming, however, that we shall meet their Grand Fleet well outside the galaxy . . ."

"Why?" asked the startled Kinnison. "If I were Eichmil I'd pull every ship I had in around Jarnevon and keep it there! They can't force engagement with us!"

"Poor tactics. The very presence of their fleet out in space will force engagement, and a decisive one at that. From his viewpoint, if he defeats us there, that ends it. If he loses, that's only his first line of defense. His observers will have reported fully. He will have invaluable data to work upon, and much time before even his outlying fortresses can be threatened.

"From our viewpoint, we can't refuse battle if his fleet is there. It would be suicidal for us to enter that galaxy, leaving intact outside it a fleet as powerful as that one is bound to be."

"Why? Harrying us from the rear might be bothersome, but I don't see how it could be disastrous."

"Not that. They could, and would, attack Tellus."

"Oh—I never thought of that. But couldn't they anyway—two fleets?"

"No. He knows that Tellus is very strongly held, and that this is no ordinary fleet. He will have to concentrate everything he has upon either one or the other—it is almost inconceivable that he would divide his forces."

"QX. I said that you're the brains of the outfit. You are!"

"Thanks, lad. At the first sign of detection, we stop. They may be able to detect us, but I doubt it, since we're looking for them with special instruments. But that's immaterial. What I want to know is, can you and your crew split Grand Fleet, making two big, hollow hemispheres of it? Let this group of ambers represent the enemy. Since they know we'll have to carry the battle to them, they'll probably be in fairly close formation. Set your two hemispheres—the reds—there, and there. Close them in, thus englobing their whole fleet. Can you do it?"

Kinnison whistled through his teeth, a long, low, unmelodious whistle. "Yes—but Klono's carballoy claws, chief, suppose they catch you at it?"

"How can they? If you were using detectors, instead of double-end, tight-beam binders, how many of our own vessels could you locate?"

"That's right, too—about two percent of them. They couldn't tell that they were being englobed until long after it was done. They could, however, globe up inside us . . ."

"Yes—and that would give them the tactical advantage of position," the admiral admitted. "We probably have, however, enough superiority in fire-power, if not in actual tonnage, to make up the difference. Also, we have speed enough, I think, so that we could retire in good order. But you're assuming that they can maneuver as rapidly and as surely as we can, a condition which I do not consider at all probable. If, as I believe much more likely, they have no better Grand Fleet Operations than we had in Helmuth's star-cluster—if they haven't the equivalent of you and Worsel and this super-tank here—then what?"

"In that case it'd be just too bad. Just like pushing baby chicks into a pond." Kinnison saw the possibilities very clearly after they had been explained to him.

"How long will it take you?"

"With Worsel and me and both full crews of Rigellians I would guess it at about ten hours—eight to compute and assign positions and two to get there."

"Fast enough—faster than I would have thought possible. Oil up your Simplexes and calculating machines and get ready."

In due time the enemy fleet was detected and the "cease blasting" signal was given. Civilization's prodigious fleet stopped dead; hanging motionless in space at the tantalizing limit of detectability from the warships awaiting them. For eight hours two hundred Rigellians stood at whirring calculators, each solving course-and-distance problems at the rate of ten per minute. Two hours or less of free flight and Haynes rejoiced audibly in the perfection of the two red hemispheres shown in his reducer. The two huge bowls flashed together, rim to rim. The sphere began inexorably to contract. Each ship put out a red K6T screen as a combined battle flag and identification, and the greatest naval engagement of the age was on.

It soon became evident that the Boskonians could not maneuver their forces efficiently. The fleet was too huge, too unwieldy for their Operations officers to handle. Against an equally uncontrollable mob of battle craft it would have made a showing, but against the carefully-planned, chronometer-timed attack of the Patrol individual action, however courageous or however desperate, was useless.

Each red-sheathed destroyer hurtled along a definite course at a definite force of drive for a definite length of time. Orders were strict; no ship was to be lured from course, pace, or time. They could, however, fight *en passant* with their every weapon if occasion arose; and occasion did arise, some thousands of times. The units of Grand Fleet flashed inward, lashing out with their terrible primaries at everything in space not wearing the crimson robe of Civilization. And whatever those beams struck did not need striking again.

The warships of Boskone fought back. Many of the Patrol's defensive screens blazed hot enough almost to mask the scarlet beacons; some of them went down. A few Patrol ships were englobed by the concerted action of two or three sub-fleet commanders more cooperative or more farsighted than the rest, and were blasted out of existence by an overwhelming concentration of power. But even those vessels took toll with their primaries as they went out: few indeed were the Boskonians who escaped through holes thus made.

At a predetermined instant each dreadnought stopped: to find herself one unit of an immense, red-flaming hollow sphere of ships packed almost screen to screen. And upon signal every primary projector that could be brought to bear hurled bolt after bolt, as fast as the burned-out shells could be replaced, into the ragingly incandescent inferno which that sphere's interior instantly became. For two hundred million discharges such as those will convert a very large volume of space into something utterly impossible to describe.

The raving torrents of energy subsided and keen-eyed observers swept the scene of action. Nothing was there except jumbled and tumbling white-hot wreckage. A few vessels had escaped during the closing in of the sphere, but none inside it had survived this climactic action—not one in five thousand of Boskone's massed fleet made its way back to Jarnevon.

"Maneuver fifty-eight—hipe!" Haynes ordered, and again Grand Fleet shot away. There was no waiting, no hesitation. Every course and time had been calculated and assigned.

Into the Second Galaxy the scarcely diminished armada of the Patrol hurtled—to Jarnevon's solar system—around it. Once again the crimson sheathing of Civilization's messengers almost disappeared in blinding coruscance as the outlying fortresses unleashed their mighty weapons; once again a few ships, subjected to such concentrations of force as to overload their equipment, were lost; but this conflict, though savage in its intensity, was brief. Nothing mobile *could* withstand for long the utterly hellish energies of the primaries, and soon the armored planetoids, too, ceased to be.

"Maneuver fifty-nine—hipe!" and Grand Fleet closed in upon dark Jarnevon.

"Sixty!" It rolled in space, forming an immense cylinder; the doomed planet the mid-point of its axis.

"Sixty-one!" Tractors and pressors leaped out from ship to ship and from ship to shore. The Patrolmen did not know whether or not the scientists of the Eich could render their planet inertialess, and now it made no difference. Planet and fleet were for the time being one rigid system.

"Sixty-two—Blast!" And against the world-girdling battlements of Jarnevon there flamed out in all their appalling might the dreadful beams against which the defensive screens of battleships and of mobile citadels alike had been so pitifully inadequate.

But these which they were attacking now were not the limited installations of a mobile structure. The Eich had at their command all the resources of a galaxy. Their generators and conductors could be of any desired number and size. Hence Eichmil, in view of prior happenings, had strengthened Jarnevon's defenses to a point which certain of his fellows derided as being beyond the bounds of sanity or reason.

Now those unthinkably powerful screens were being tested to the utmost. Bolt after bolt of quasi-solid lightning struck against them, spitting mile-long sparks in baffled fury as they raged to ground. Plain and encased in Q-type helices they came: biting, tearing, gouging. Often and often, under the thrust of half a dozen at once, local failures appeared; but these were only momentary and even the newly devised shells of the Patrol's projectors could not stand the load long enough to penetrate effectively Boskone's indescribably capable defenses. Nor were Jarnevon's offensive weapons less capable.

Rods, cones, planes, and shears of pure force bored, cut, stabbed, and slashed. Bombs and dirigible torpedoes charged to the skin with duodec sought out the red-cloaked ships. Beams, sheathed against atmosphere in Q-type helices, crashed against and through their armoring screens; beams of an intensity almost to rival that of the Patrol's primary weapons and of a hundred times their effective aperture. And not singly did those beams come. Eight, ten, twelve at once they clung to and demolished dreadnought after dreadnought of the Expeditionary Force.

Eichmil was well content. "We can hold them and we are burning them down," he gloated. "Let them loose their negative-matter bombs! Since they are burning out projectors they cannot keep this up indefinitely. We will blast them out of space!"

He was wrong. Grand Fleet did not stay there long enough to suffer serious losses. For even while the cylinder was forming Kinnison was in rapid but careful consultation with Thorndyke, checking intrinsic velocities, directions, and speeds. "QX, Verne, *cut!*" he yelled.

Two planets, one well within each end of the combat cylinder, went inert at the word; resuming instantaneously their diametrically opposed intrinsic velocities of some thirty miles per second. And it was these two very ordinary, but utterly irresistible planets, instead of the negative-matter bombs with which the Eich were prepared to cope, which hurtled then along the axis of the immense tube of warships toward Jarnevon. Whether or not the Eich could make their planet inertialess has never been found out. Free or inert, the end would have been the same.

"Every Y14M officer of every ship of the Patrol, attention!" Haynes ordered. "Don't get all tensed up. Take it easy, there's lots of time. Any time within a second after I give the word will be p-l-e-n-t-y o-f t-i-m-e . . . CUT!"

The two worlds rushed together, doomed Jarnevon squarely between them. Haynes snapped out his order as the three were within two seconds of contact; and as he spoke all the pressors and all the tractors were released. The ships of the Patrol were already free—none had been inert since leaving Jalte's ex-planet—and thus could not be harmed by flying debris.

The planets touched. They coalesced, squishingly at first, the encircling warships drifting lightly away before a cosmically violent blast of superheated atmosphere. Jarnevon burst open, all the way around, and spattered; billions upon billions of tons of hot core-magma being hurled afar in gouts and streamers. The two planets, crashing through what had been a world, met, crunched, crushed together in all the unimaginable momentum of their masses and velocities. They subsided, crashingly. Not merely mountains, but entire halves of worlds disrupted and fell, in such Gargantuan paroxysms as the eye of man had never elsewhere beheld. And every motion generated heat. The kinetic energy of translation of two worlds became heat. Heat added to heat, piling up ragingly, frantically, unable to escape!

The masses, still falling upon and through and past themselves and each other melted—boiled—vaporized incandescently. The entire mass, the mass of three fused worlds, began to equilibrate; growing hotter and hotter as more and more of its terrific motion was converted into pure heat. Hotter! *Hotter!* HOTTER!

And as the Grand Fleet of the Galactic Patrol blasted through intergalactic space toward the First Galaxy and home, there glowed behind it a new, small, comparatively cool, and probably short-lived companion to an old and long-established star.

25

ATTACHED

The uproar of the landing was over; the celebration of victory had not yet begun. Haynes had, peculiarly enough, set a definite time for a conference with Kinnison and the two of them were in the admiral's private office, splitting a bottle of fayalin and discussing—apparently—nothing at all.

"Narcotics has been yelling for you," Haynes finally got around to business. "But they don't need you to help them clean up the zwilnik mess; they just want to work with you. So I told Ellington, as diplomatically as possible, to take a swan-dive off of an asteroid. Hicks wants you, too; and Spencer and Frelinghuysen and thousands of others. See that basket-full of junk? All requests for you, to be submitted to you for your consideration. I submit 'em, thus—into the circular file. You see, there's something really important . . ."

"Nix, chief, nix—jet back a minute, please!" Kinnison implored. "Unless it's something that's got to be done right away, gimme a break, can't you? I've got a couple of things to do—stuff to attend to. Maybe a little flit somewhere, too, I don't know yet."

"More important than Patrol business?" dryly.

"Until it's cleaned up, yes." Kinnison's face burned scarlet and his eyes revealed the mental effort necessary to make that statement. "The most important thing in the universe," he finished, quietly but doggedly.

"Well, of course I can't give you orders . . ." Haynes' frown was instinct with disappointment.

"Don't, chief—that hurts. I'll be back, honest, as soon as I possibly can, and I'll do anything you want me to . . ."

"That's enough, son." Haynes stood up and grasped Kinnison's hands—hard—in both his own. "I know. Forgive me for taking you for this little ride, but you and Mac suffer so! You're so young, so intense, so insistent upon carrying the entire Cosmos on your shoulders—I couldn't help it. You won't have to do much of a flit." He glanced at his chronometer. "You'll find all your unfinished business in Room 7295, Base Hospital."

"Huh? You know, then?"

"Who doesn't? There may be a few members of some backward race somewhere who don't know all about you and your red-headed sector riot, but I don't know . . ." He was addressing empty air.

Kinnison shot out of the building and, exerting his Gray Lensman's authority, he did a thing which he had always longed boyishly to do but which he had never before really considered doing. He whistled, shrill and piercingly, and waved a Lensed arm, even while he was directing a Lensed thought at the driver of the fast ground-car always in readiness in front of Haynes' office.

"Base Hospital—full emergency blast!" he ordered, and the Jehu obeyed. That chauffeur loved emergency stuff and the long, low, wide racer took off with a deafening roar of unmuffled exhaust and a scream of tortured, burning rubber. Two projectors flamed, sending out for miles ahead of the bellowing roadster twin beams of a redness so thick as to be felt, not merely seen. Simultaneously the mighty, four-throated siren began its ululating, raucously overpowering yell, demanding and obtaining right of way over any and all traffic—particularly over police, fire, and other ordinary emergency apparatus—which might think it had some rights upon the street!

"Thanks, Jack—you needn't wait." At the hospital's door Kinnison rendered tribute to fast service and strode along a corridor. An express elevator whisked him up to the seventy-second floor, and there his haste departed completely. This was Nurse's Quarters, he realized suddenly. He had no more business there than . . . yes he did, too. He found Room 7295 and rapped upon its door. Boldly, he intended, but the resultant sound was surprisingly small.

"Come in!" called a clear contralto. Then, after a moment: *"Come in!"* more sharply; but the Lensman did not, could not obey the summons. She might be . . . dammit all, he *didn't* have any business on this floor! Why hadn't he called her up or sent her a thought or something . . . ? Why didn't he think at her now?

The door opened, revealing the mildly annoyed sector chief. At what she saw her hands flew to her throat and her eyes widened in starkly unbelieving rapture.

"KIM!" She shrieked in ecstasy.

"Chris . . . my Chris!" Kinnison whispered unsteadily, and for minutes those two uniformed minions of the Galactic Patrol stood motionless upon the room's threshold, strong young arms straining; nurse's crisp and spotless white crushed unregarded against Lensman's pliant gray.

"Oh . . . I've missed you so terribly, my darling," she crooned. Her voice, always sweetly rich, was pure music.

"You don't know the half of it. This can't be real—nothing *can* feel this good!"

"You *did* come back to me—you really did!" she lilted. "I didn't dare hope you could come so soon."

"I had to." Kinnison drew a deep breath, "I simply couldn't stand it. It'll be tough, maybe, but you were right—half a loaf *is* better than no bread."

"Of course it is!" She released herself—partially—after the first transports of their first embrace and eyed him shrewdly. "Tell me, Kim, did Lacy have a hand in this surprise?"

"Uh-uh," he denied. "I haven't seen him for ages—but jet back! Haynes told me—say, what'll you bet those two old hard-heads haven't been giving us the works?"

"Who are old hard-heads?" Haynes—in person—demanded. So deeply immersed had Kinnison been in his rapturous delirium that even his sense of perception was in abeyance; and there, not two yards from the entranced couple, stood the two old Lensmen under discussion!

The culprits sprang apart, flushing guiltily, but Haynes went on imperturbably, quite as though nothing out of the ordinary had been either said or done:

"We gave you fifteen minutes, then came up to be sure to catch you before you flitted off to the celebration or somewhere. We have matters to discuss."

"QX. Come in, all of you." As she spoke the nurse stood aside in invitation. "You know, don't you, that it's exceedingly much contra Regs for nurses to entertain visitors of the opposite sex in their rooms? Fifty demerits per offense. Most girls never get a chance at even one Gray Lensman, and here I've got three!" She giggled infectiously. "Wouldn't it be one for the book for me to get a hundred and fifty black spots for this? And to have Surgeon-Marshal Lacy, Port Admiral Haynes, and Unattached Lensman Kimball Kinnison, all heaved into the clink to boot? Boy, oh boy, ain't we got fun?"

"Lacy's too old and I'm too moral to be affected by the wiles even of the likes of you, my dear," Haynes explained equably, as he seated himself upon the davenport—the most comfortable thing in the room.

"Old? Moral? Tommyrot!" Lacy glared an "I'll-see-you-later" look at the admiral, then turned to the nurse. "Don't worry about that, Mac-Dougall. No penalties accrue—Regulations apply only to nurses in the Service . . ."

"And what . . ." she started to blaze, but checked herself and her tone changed instantly. "Go on—you interest me strangely, sir. I'm just going to love this!" Her eyes sparkled, her voice was vibrant with unconcealed eagerness.

"Told you she was quick on the uptake," Lacy gloated. "Didn't fox her for a second!"

"But say—listen—what's this all about, anyway?" Kinnison demanded.

"Never mind, you'll learn soon enough," from Lacy, and:

"Kinnison, you are very urgently invited to attend a meeting of the Galactic Council tomorrow afternoon," from Haynes.

"Huh? What's up now?" Kinnison protested. His arm tightened about the girl's supple waist and she snuggled closer, a trace of foreboding beginning to dim the eagerness in her eyes.

"Promotion. We want to make you something—galactic coordinator, director, something like that—the job hasn't been named yet. In plain language, the Big Shot of the Second Galaxy, formerly known as Lundmark's Nebula."

"But listen, chief! I couldn't handle such a job as that—I simply haven't got the jets!"

"You always yelp about a dynage deficiency whenever a new job is mentioned, but you deliver the goods. Who else could we wish it onto?"

"Worsel," Kinnison declared with hesitation. "He's . . ."

"Balloon-juice!" snorted the older man.

"Well, then . . . ah . . . er . . ." he stopped. Clarrissa opened her mouth, then shut it, ridiculously, without having uttered a word.

"Go ahead, MacDougall. You're an interested party, you know."

"No." She shook her spectacular head. "I'm not saying a word nor thinking a thought to sway his decision one way or the other. Besides, he'd have to flit around then as much as now."

"Some travel involved, of course," Haynes admitted. "All over that galaxy, some in this one, and back and forth between the two. However, the *Dauntless*—or something newer, bigger, and faster—will be his private yacht, and I don't see why it is either necessary or desirable that his flits be solo."

"Say, I never thought of that!" Kinnison blurted; and as thoughts began to race through his mind of what he could do, with Chris beside him all the time, to straighten out the mess in the Second Galaxy:

"Oh, Kim!" Clarrissa squealed in ecstasy, squeezing his arm even tighter against her side.

"Hooked!" Lacy chortled in triumph.

"But I'd have to retire!" That thought was the only thorn in Kinnison's whole wreath of roses. "I wouldn't like that."

"Certainly you wouldn't," Haynes agreed. "But remember that all such assignments are conditional, subject to approval, and with a very definite cancellation agreement in case of what the Lensman regards as an emergency. If a Gray Lensman had to give up his right to serve the Patrol in any way he considered himself most able, they'd have to shoot us all before they could make executives out of us. And finally, I don't see how the job we're talking about can be figured as any sort of a retirement. You'll be as active as you are now—yes, more so, unless I miss my guess."

"QX. I'll be there—I'll try it," Kinnison promised.

"Now for some more news," Lacy announced. "Haynes didn't tell you, but he has been made president of the Galactic Council. You are his first appointment. I hate to say anything good about the old scoundrel, but he has one outstanding ability. He doesn't know much or do much himself, but he certainly can pick the men who have to do the work for him!"

"There's something vastly more important than that." Haynes steered the acclaim away from himself.

"Just a minute," Kinnison interposed. "I haven't got this all straight yet. What was the crack about active nurses awhile ago?"

"Why, Doctor Lacy was just intimating that I had resigned, goose," Clarrissa chuckled. "I didn't know a thing about it myself, but I imagine it must have been just before this conference started. Am I right, doctor?" she asked innocently.

"Or tomorrow, or even yesterday—any convenient time will do," Lacy blandly assented. "You see, young man, MacDougall has been a mighty busy girl, and wedding preparations take time, too. Therefore we have very reluctantly accepted her resignation."

"Especially preparations take time when it's going to be such a wedding as the Patrol is going to throw," Haynes commented. "That was what I was starting to talk about when I was so rudely interrupted."

"Nix! Not in seven thousand years!" Kinnison exploded. "Cancel that, right now—I won't stand for it—I'll not . . ."

"Cancel nothing. Baffle your jets, Kim," the admiral said, firmly. "Bridegrooms are to be seen—just barely visible—but that's all. No voice. Weddings are where the girls really strut their stuff. How about it, you gorgeous young menace to Civilization?"

"I'll say so!" she exclaimed in high animation. "I'd just *love* it, admiral . . ." She broke off, aghast. Her face fell. "No, I'll take that back. Kim's right. Thanks a million, just the same, but . . ."

"But nothing!" Haynes broke in. "I know what's the matter. Don't try to fox an old campaigner, and don't be silly. I said the Patrol was throwing this wedding. All you have to do is participate in the action. Got any money, Kinnison? On you, I mean?"

"No," in surprise. "What would I be doing with money?"

"Here's ten thousand credits—Patrol funds. Take it and . . ."

"He will not!" the nurse stormed. "No! You can't, admiral, really. Why, a bride has *got* to buy her own clothes!"

"She's right, Haynes," Lacy announced. The admiral stared at him in wrathful astonishment and even Clarrissa seemed disappointed at her easy victory. "But listen to this. As surgeon-marshal, et cetera, in recognition of the unselfish services, et cetera, unflinching bravery under fire, et cetera, performances beyond and above requirements or reasonable expectations, et cetera, et cetera; Sector Chief Nurse Clarrissa May Mac-Dougall, upon the occasion of her separation from the Service, is hereby granted a bonus of ten thousand credits. That goes on the record as of hour twelve, today.

"Now, you red-headed young spit-fire, if you refuse to accept that bonus I'll cancel your resignation and put you back to work. What do you say?"

"I say thanks, Doctor Lacy. Th . . . thanks a million . . . both of you . . . you're two of the most wonderful men that ever lived, and I . . . I . . . I just *love* you!" The happy girl kissed them both, then turned to Kinnison.

"Let's go and hike about ten miles, shall we, Kim? I've got to do *something* or I'll explode!"

And the tall Lensman—no longer unattached—and the radiant nurse swung down the hall.

Side by side; in step; heads up; laughing: a beginning symbolical indeed of the life they were to live together.

Second Stage Lensmen

To
F. Edwin Counts

CONTENTS

FOREWORD

A couple of billion years ago, when the First and Second Galaxies were passing through each other and when myriads of planets were coming into being where only a handful had existed before, two races of beings were already ancient. Each had become independent of the chance formation of planets upon which to live. Each had won a large measure of power over its environment; the Arisians by force of mind alone, the Eddorians by employing both mind and mechanism.

The Arisians were native to this, our normal space-time continuum. They had lived in it since the unthinkably remote time of their origin. The original Arisia was very much like Earth. Thus all our normal space was permeated by Arisian life-spores, and thus upon all Earth-like planets there came into being races more or less like what the Arisians had been in the days of their racial youth.

The Eddorians, on the other hand, were interlopers. They came to our space-time continuum from some horribly different plenum. For eons they had been exploring the Macrocosmic All; moving their planets from plenum to plenum; seeking that which at last they found—one in which there were enough planets, soon to be inhabited by intelligent life, to sate even the Eddorian lust for dominance. Here, in our own universe, they would stay; and here supreme they would rule.

The Elders of Arisia, however, the ablest thinkers of the race, had known of and had studied the Eddorians for many cycles of time. Their integrated Visualization of the Cosmic All showed what was to happen. No more than the Arisians themselves could the Eddorians be slain by any physical means; nor could the Arisians, unaided, kill all the invaders by mental force. Eddore's All-Highest and his Innermost Circle, in their ultrashielded citadel, could be destroyed only by a mental bolt of such nature and magnitude that its generator, which was to become known as the Galactic Patrol, would require several long Arisian lifetimes for its building.

Nor would that building be easy. The Eddorians must be kept in ignorance, both of Arisia and of the proposed generator, until too late to take effective counter-measures. Also, no entity below the third level of intelligence could ever be allowed to learn the truth, for that knowledge would set up an inferiority complex that would rob the generator of its ability to do the work.

On the four most promising planets of the First Galaxy—our Earth or Sol Three, Velantia, Rigel Four, and Palain Seven—breeding programs, to develop the highest mentality of which each race was capable, were begun as soon as intelligent life appeared.

On our Earth there were only two blood lines, since humanity has only two sexes. One was a straight male line of descent, and was always named Kinnison or its equivalent. Civilizations rose and fell; Arisia surreptitiously lifting them up, Eddore callously knocking them down. Pestilences raged, and wars, and famines, and holocausts and disasters that decimated entire populations again and again; but the direct male line of descent of the Kinnisons was never broken.

The other line, sometimes male and sometimes female, which was to culminate in the female penultimate of the Arisian program, was equally persistent and was characterized throughout its prodigious length by a peculiarly spectacular shade of red-bronze-auburn hair and equally striking gold-flecked, tawny eyes. Atlantis fell, but the red-headed, yellow-eyed child of red-haired Captain Phryges had been sent to North Maya, and lived. Patroclus, the red-headed gladiator, begot a red-haired daughter before he was cut down. And so it went.

World Wars One, Two, and Three, occupying as they did only a few moments of Arisian-Eddorian time, formed merely one incident in the eons-long game. Immediately after that incident, Gharlane of Eddore made what proved to be an error. Knowing nothing of the Arisians, he assumed that the then completely ruined Tellus would not require his personal attention again for many hundreds of Tellurian years, and went elsewhere; to Rigel Four, to Palain Seven, and to Velantia Two, or Delgon, where he found that his creatures, the Overlords, were not progressing satisfactorily. He spent quite a little time there; during which the men of Earth, aided by the Arisians, made a rapid recovery from the ravages of atomic warfare and very rapid advances in both sociology and technology.

Virgil Samms, the auburn-haired, tawny-eyed Crusader who was to become the first wearer of Arisia's Lens, took advantage of the demoralization to institute an effective planetary police force. Then, with the advent of interplanetary flight, he was instrumental in forming the Interplanetary League. As head of the Triplanetary Service he took a leading part in the brief war with the Nevians, a race of highly intelligent amphibians who used allotropic iron as a source of atomic power.*

Gharlane of Eddore came back to the Solarian System as Gray Roger, the enigmatic and practically immortal scourge of space, only to find his every move so completely blocked that he could not kill two ordinary human beings, Conway Costigan and Clio Marsden. Nor were these two, in spite of some belief to the contrary, anything but what they seemed. Neither of them ever knew that they were being protected. Gharlane's blocker was in fact an Arisian fusion; the four-ply mentality which was to become known to every Lensman of the Patrol as Mentor of Arisia.

The inertialess drive, which made an interstellar trip a matter of minutes instead of lifetimes brought with it such an increase in crime, and made detection of criminals so difficult, that law enforcement broke down almost completely. As Samms himself expressed it:

"How can legal processes work efficiently—work at all, for that matter—when a man can commit a murder or a pirate can loot a spaceship and be a hundred parsecs away before the crime is even discovered? How can a Tellurian John Law find a criminal on a strange world that knows nothing of our Patrol, with a completely alien language—maybe no language at all—when it takes months even to find out who and where—if any—the native police officers are?"

Also there was the apparently insuperable difficulty of identification of authorized personnel. Triplanetary's best scientists had done their best in the way of a non-counterfeitable badge—the historic Golden Meteor, which upon touch impressed upon the toucher's consciousness an unpronounceable, unspellable syllable—but that best was not enough. What physical science could devise and synthesize, physical science could analyze and duplicate; and that analysis and duplication had caused trouble indeed.

Triplanetary needed something vastly better than its meteor. In fact, without a better, its expansion into an intersystemic organization would probably be impossible. It needed something to identify a Patrolman,

---

*For a complete treatment of matters up to this point, including the discovery of the inertialess—"free"—space-drive, the Nevian War, and the mind-to-mind meeting of Mentor of Arisia and Gharlane of Eddore, see *Triplanetary*, Fantasy Press, Reading, Pa.

anytime and anywhere. This something must be impossible of duplication or imitation—ideally, it should kill, painfully, any entity attempting imposture. It should operate as a telepath or endow its wearer with telepathic power—how else could a Tellurian converse with peoples such as the Rigellians, who could not talk, see, or hear?

Both Solarian Councillor Virgil Samms and his friend of old, Commissioner of Public Safety Roderick Kinnison, knew these things; but they also knew how utterly preposterous their thoughts were; how utterly and self-evidently impossible such a device was.

But Arisia again came to the rescue. The scientist working on the meteor problem, one Dr. Nels Bergenholm—who, all unknown to even his closest associates, was a form of flesh energized at various times by various Arisians—reported to Virgil Samms that:

(1) Physical science could not then produce what was needed, and probably could never do so. (2) Although it could not be explained by any symbology known to man, there was—there *must* be—a science of the mind; a science whose tangible products physical science could neither analyze nor imitate. (3) Virgil Samms, by going to Arisia, could obtain *exactly* what was needed.

"Arisia! Of all the hells in space, why Arisia?" Kinnison demanded. "How? Don't you know that nobody can get anywhere near that damn planet?"

"I *know* that the Arisians are very well versed in that science. I *know* that if Virgil Samms goes to Arisia he will obtain the symbol he needs. I *know* that he will never obtain it otherwise. As to *how* I know these things—I can't—I just—I *know* them, I tell you!"

And since Bergenholm was already as well known for uncannily accurate "hunches" as for a height of genius bordering on insanity, the two leaders of Civilization did not press him farther, but went immediately to the hitherto forbidden planet. They were—apparently—received hospitably enough, and were given Lenses by Mentor of Arisia; Lenses which, it developed, were all that Bergenholm had indicated, and more.

The Lens is a lenticular structure of hundreds of thousands of tiny crystalloids, built and tuned to match the individual life force—the ego, the personality—of one individual entity. While not, strictly speaking, alive, it is endowed with a sort of pseudo-life by virtue of which it gives off a strong, characteristically-changing, polychromatic light as long as it is in circuit with the living mentality with which it is in synthronization. Conversely, when worn by anyone except its owner, it not only remains dark, but it kills; so strongly does its pseudo-life interfere with any life to which it is not attuned. It is also a telepathic communicator of astounding power and range—and other things.

Back on Earth, Samms set out to find people of Lensman caliber to send to Arisia. Kinnison's son, Jack, Jack's friend Mason Northrop, Conway Costigan, and Samms' daughter Virgilia—who had inherited her father's hair and eyes and who was the most accomplished muscle-reader of her time—went first. The boys got Lenses, but Jill did not. Mentor, who was to her senses a woman seven feet tall—it should be mentioned here that no two entities who ever saw Mentor ever saw the same thing—told her that she did not then and never would need a Lens.

Frederick Rodebush, Lyman Cleveland, young Bergenholm and a couple of commodores of the Patrol—Clayton of North America and Schweikert of Europe—just about exhausted Earth's resources. Nor were the other Solarian planets very helpful, yielding only three Lensmen— Knobos of Mars, DalNalten of Venus, and Rularion of Jove. Lensman material was very scarce stuff.

Knowing that his proposed Galactic Council would have to be made up exclusively of Lensmen, and that it should represent as many solar systems as possible, Samms visited the various systems which had been colonized by humanity, then went on: to Rigel Four, where he found Dronvire the Explorer, who was of Lensman grade; and next to Pluto, where he found Pilinixi the Dexitroboper, who very definitely was not; and finally to Palain Seven, an ultra-frigid world where he found Tallick, who might—or might not—go to Arisia some day. And Virgil Samms, being physically tough and mentally a real crusader, survived these various ordeals.

For some time the existence of the newly-formed Galactic Patrol was precarious indeed. Archibald Isaacson, head of Interstellar Space-ways, wanting a monopoly of interstellar trade, first tried bribery; then, joining forces with the machine of Senator Morgan and Boss Towne, assassination. The other Lensmen and Jill saved Samms' life; after which Kinnison took him to the safest place on Earth—deep underground beneath the Hill; the tremendously fortified, superlatively armed fortress which had been built to be the headquarters of the Triplanetary Service.

But even there the First Lensman was attacked, this time by a fleet of space-ships in full battle array. By that time, however, the Galactic Patrol had a fleet of its own, and again the Lensmen won.

Knowing that the final and decisive struggle would of necessity be a political one, the Patrol took over the Cosmocrat party and set out to gather detailed and documentary evidence of corrupt and criminal activities of the Nationalists, the party then in power. Roderick ("Rod the

Rock") Kinnison ran for President of North America against the incumbent Witherspoon; and after a knock-down-and-drag-out political battle with Senator Morgan, the voice of the Morgan-Towne-Isaacson machine, he was elected.

And Morgan was murdered—supposedly by disgruntled gangsters; actually by his Kalonian boss, who was in turn a minion of Eddore—simply because he had failed.*

North America was the most powerful continent of Earth; Earth was the mother planet, the leader and the boss. Hence, under the sponsorship of the Cosmocratic government of North America, the Galactic Council and its arm, the Galactic Patrol, came into their own. At the end of R. K. Kinnison's term of office, at which time he resumed his interrupted duties as Port Admiral of the Patrol, there were a hundred planets adherent to Civilization. In ten years there were a thousand; in a hundred years a million; and it is sufficient characterization of the government of the Galactic Council to say that in the long history of Civilization no planet has ever withdrawn from it.

Time went on. The prodigiously long blood-lines, so carefully manipulated by Mentor of Arisia, neared culmination. Lensman Kimball Kinnison was graduated Number One of his class—as a matter of fact, although he did not know it, he was Number One of his time. And his female counterpart and complement, Clarrissa MacDougall of the red-bronze-auburn hair and the gold-flecked tawny eyes, was a nurse in the Patrol's Hospital at Prime Base.

Shortly after graduation Kinnison was called in by Port Admiral Haynes. Space piracy had become an organized force; and, under the leadership of someone or something known as "Boskone," had risen to such heights of power as to threaten seriously the Patrol itself. In one respect Boskonia was ahead of the Patrol; its scientists having developed a source of power vastly greater than any known to Civilization. Pirate ships, faster than the Patrol's fastest cruisers and yet more heavily armed than its most powerful battleships, had been doing as they pleased throughout all space.

For one particular purpose the engineers of the Patrol had designed and built one ship—the *Brittania*. She was the fastest thing in space, but for offense she had only one weapon, the "Q-gun." Kinnison was put in command of this vessel, with orders to: (1) Capture a late-model pirate vessel; (2) Learn her secrets of power; and (3) Transmit the information to Prime Base.

---

* *First Lensman*, Fantasy Press, Reading, Pa.

He found and took such a ship. Sergeant Peter vanBuskirk led the storming party of Valerians—men of human ancestry, but of extraordinary size, strength, and agility because of the enormous gravitation of the planet Valeria—in wiping out those of the pirate crew not killed in the battle between the two vessels.

The *Brittania's* scientists secured the desired data. It could not be transmitted to Prime Base, however, as the pirates were blanketing all channels of communication. Boskonian warships were gathering for the kill, and the crippled Patrol ship could neither run nor fight. Therefore each man was given a spool of tape bearing a complete record of everything that had occurred; and, after setting up a director-by-chance to make the empty ship pursue an unpredictable course in space, and after rigging bombs to destroy her at the first touch of a ray, the Patrolmen paired off by lot and took to the lifeboats.

The erratic course of the cruiser brought her near the lifeboat manned by Kinnison and vanBuskirk, and there the pirates tried to stop her. The ensuing explosion was so violent that flying wreckage disabled practically the entire personnel of one of the attacking ships, which did not have time to go free before the crash. The two Patrolmen boarded the pirate vessel and drove her toward Earth, reaching the solar system of Velantia before the Boskonians headed them off. Again taking to their lifeboat, they landed on the planet Delgon, where they were rescued from a horde of Catlats by one Worsel—later to become Lensman Worsel of Velantia—a highly intelligent winged reptile.

By means of improvements upon Velantian thought-screens the three destroyed a group of the Overlords of Delgon, a sadistic race of monsters who had been preying upon the other peoples of the system by sheer power of mind. Worsel then accompanied the two Patrolmen to Velantia, where all the resources of the planet were devoted to the preparation of defenses against the expected attack of the Boskonians. Several other lifeboats reached Velantia, guided by Worsel's mind working through Kinnison's ego and Lens.

Kinnison intercepted a message from Helmuth, who "spoke for Boskone," and traced his communicator beam, thus getting his first line on Boskone's Grand Base. The pirates attacked Velantia, and six of their warships were captured. In these six ships, manned by Velantian crews, the Patrolmen again set out for Earth and Prime Base.

Then Kinnison's Bergenholm, the generator of the force which makes inertialess flight possible, broke down, so that he had to land upon Trenco for repairs. Trenco, the tempestuous, billiard-ball-smooth planet where it rains forty seven feet and five inches every night and where the wind blows at over eight hundred miles per hour—Trenco, the source of thionite, the deadliest of all deadly drugs—Trenco, whose weirdly-charged ether and atmosphere so distort beams and vision that it can be policed only by such beings as the Rigellians, who possess the sense of perception instead of those of sight and hearing!

Lensman Tregonsee, of Rigel Four, then in command of the Patrol's wandering base on Trenco, supplied Kinnison with a new Bergenholm and he again set out for Tellus.

Meanwhile Helmuth had decided that some one particular Lensman must be the cause of all his set-backs; and that the Lens, a complete enigma to all Boskonians, was in some way connected with Arisia. That planet had always been dreaded and shunned by all spacemen. No Boskonian who had ever approached that planet could be compelled, even by the certainty of death, to go near it again.

Thinking himself secure by virtue of thought-screens given him by a being from a higher-echelon planet named Ploor, Helmuth went alone to Arisia, determined to learn all about the Lens. There he was punished to the verge of insanity, but was permitted to return to his Grand Base alive and sane: "Not for your own good, but for the good of that struggling young Civilization which you oppose."

Kinnison reached Prime Base with the all-important data. By building super-powerful battleships, called "maulers", the Patrol gained a temporary advantage over Boskonia, but a stalemate soon ensued. Kinnison developed a plan of action whereby he hoped to locate Helmuth's Grand Base, and asked Port Admiral Haynes for permission to follow it. In lieu of that, however, Haynes told him that he had been given his Release; that he was an Unattached Lensman—a "Gray" Lensman, popularly so-called, from the color of the plain leather uniforms they wear. Thus he earned the highest honor possible for the Galactic Patrol to give, for the Gray Lensman works under no supervision or direction whatever. He is responsible to no one; to nothing save his own conscience. He is no longer a cog in the immense machine of the Galactic Patrol: wherever he may go he *is* the Patrol!

In quest of a second line to Grand Base, Kinnison scouted a pirate stronghold on Aldebaran I. Its personnel, however, were not even near-human, but were Wheelmen, possessed of the sense of perception; hence Kinnison was discovered before he could accomplish anything and was very seriously wounded. He managed to get back to his speedster and to send a thought to Port Admiral Haynes, who rushed ships to his aid. In Base Hospital Surgeon-Marshal Lacy put him back together; and, during a long and quarrelsome convalescence, Nurse Clarissa MacDougall held him together. And Lacy and Haynes connived to promote a romance between nurse and Lensman.

As soon as he could leave the hospital he went to Arisia in the hope that he might be given advanced training; something which had never before been attempted. Much to his surprise he learned that he had been expected to return for exactly such training. Getting it almost killed him, but he emerged from the ordeal vastly stronger of mind than any human being had ever been before; and possessed of a new sense as well—the sense of perception, a sense somewhat analogous to sight, but of much greater power, depth, and scope, and not dependent on light.

After trying out his new mental equipment by solving a murder mystery on Radelix, he went to Boyssia II, where he succeeded in entering an enemy base. He took over the mind of a communications officer and waited for a chance to get his second, all-important line to Grand Base. An enemy ship captured a hospital ship of the Patrol and brought it in to Boyssia. Nurse MacDougall, head nurse of the ship, working under Kinnison's instructions, stirred up trouble which soon became mutiny. Helmuth took a hand from Grand Base, thus enabling the Lensman to get his second line.

The hospital ship, undetectable by virtue of Kinnison's nullifier, escaped from Boyssia II and headed for Earth at full blast. Kinnison, convinced that Helmuth was really Boskone himself, found that the intersection of the two lines, and therefore the pirates' Grand Base, lay in Star Cluster AC 257-4736, well outside the galaxy. Pausing only long enough to destroy the Wheelmen of Aldebaran I, he set out to investigate Helmuth's headquarters. He found a stronghold impregnable to any attack the Patrol could throw against it; manned by thought-screened personnel. His sense of perception was suddenly cut off—the pirates had erected a thought-screen around their whole planet. He then returned to Prime Base, deciding en route that boring from within was the only possible way to take that stupendous fortress.

In consultation with the Port Admiral the zero hour was set, at which time the massed Grand Fleet of the Patrol was to attack Grand Base with every projector it could bring to bear.

Pursuant to his plan, Kinnison again visited Trenco, where the Patrol forces extracted for him some fifty kilograms of thionite; the noxious drug which, in microgram inhalations, makes the addict experience all the sensations of doing whatever it is that he wishes most ardently to do. The larger the dose, the more intense and exquisite the sensations—resulting, sooner or later, in a super-ecstatic death.

Thence to Helmuth's planet; where, working through the unshielded brain of a dog, he let himself into the central dome. Here, just before the zero minute, he released his thionite into the air-stream, thus wiping out all the pirates except Helmuth himself, who, in his ultra-shielded inner bomb-proof, could not be affected.

The Patrol attacked precisely on schedule, but Helmuth would not leave his retreat, even to try to save his base. Therefore Kinnison had to go in after him. Poised in the air of the inner dome there was an enigmatic, sparkling ball of force which the Lensman could not understand, and of which he was therefore very suspicious.

But the storming of that quadruply-defended inner stronghold was exactly the task for which Kinnison's new and ultra-cumbersome armor had been designed; so in he went. He killed Helmuth in armor-to-armor combat.*

Kinnison was pretty sure that that force-ball was keyed to some particular pattern, and suspected—correctly—that it was in part an intergalactic communicator. Hence he did not think into it until he was in the flagship with Port Admiral Haynes; until all kinds of recorders and analyzers had been set up. Then he did so—and Grand Base was blasted out of existence by duodec bombs placed by the pirates themselves and triggered by the force-ball. The detectors showed a hard, tight communications line running straight out toward the Second Galaxy. Helmuth was not Boskone.

Scouting the Second Galaxy in his super-powerful battleship *Dauntless,* Kinnison met and defeated a squadron of Boskonian war-vessels. He landed upon the planet Medon, whose people had been fighting a losing war against Boskone. The Medonians, electrical wizards who had already installed inertia-neutralizers and a space-drive, moved their world across inter-galactic space to our First Galaxy.

With the cessation of military activity, however, the illicit traffic in habit-forming drugs had increased tremendously, and Kinnison, deducing that Boskone was back of the drug syndicate, decided that the best way to find the real leader of the enemy was to work upward through the drug ring.

Disguised as a dock walloper, he frequented the saloon of a drug baron, and helped to raid it; but, although he secured much information, his disguise was penetrated.

---

* *Galactic Patrol,* Fantasy Press, Reading, Pa.

He called a Conference of Scientists to devise means of building a gigantic bomb of negative matter. Then, impersonating a Tellurian secret-service agent who lent himself to the deception, he tried to investigate the stronghold of Prellin of Bronseca, one of Boskone's regional directors. This disguise also failed and he barely managed to escape.

Ordinary disguises having proved useless, Kinnison became Wild Bill Williams; once a gentleman of Aldebaran II, now a space-rat meteor miner. He made of himself an almost bottomless drinker of the hardest beverages known to space. He became a drug fiend—a bentlam eater—discovering that his Arisian-trained mind could function at full efficiency even while his physical body was completely stupefied. He became widely known as the fastest, deadliest performer with twin DeLameters ever to strike the asteroid belts.

Through solar system after solar system he built up an unimpeachable identity as a hard-drinking, wildly-carousing, bentlam-eating, fast-shooting space-hellion; a lucky or a very skillful meteor miner; a derelict who had been an Aldebaranian gentleman once and who would be again if he should ever strike it rich.

Physically helpless in a bentlam stupor, he listened in on a zwilnik conference and learned that Edmund Crowninshield, of Tressilia III, was also a regional director of the enemy.

Boskone formed an alliance with the Overlords of Delgon, and through a hyper-spatial tube the combined forces again attacked humanity. Not simple slaughter this time, for the Overlords tortured their captives and consumed their life forces in sadistic orgies. The Conference of Scientists solved the mystery of the tube and the *Dauntless* counter-attacked through it, returning victorious.

Wild Bill Williams struck it rich at last. Abandoning the low dives in which he had been wont to carouse, he made an obvious effort to become again an Aldebaranian gentleman. He secured an invitation to visit Crowninshield's resort—the Boskonian, believing that Williams was basically a booze- and drug-soaked bum, wanted to get his quarter-million cridits.

In a characteristically wild debauch, Kinnison-Williams did squander a large part of his new fortune; but he learned from Crowninshield's mind that one Jalte, a Kalonian by birth, was Boskone's galactic director; and that Jalte had his headquarters in a star cluster just outside the First Galaxy. Pretending bitter humiliation and declaring that he would change his name and disappear, the Gray Lensman left the planet—to investigate Jalte's base.

He learned that Boskone was not a single entity, but a council. Jalte did not know very much about it, but his superior, one Eichmil, who lived on the planet Jarnevon, in the Second Galaxy, would know who and what Boskone really was.

Therefore Kinnison and Worsel went to Jarnevon. Kinnison was captured and tortured—there was at least one Overlord there—but Worsel rescued him before his mind was damaged and brought him back with his knowledge intact. Jarnevon was peopled by the Eich, a race almost as monstrous as the Overlords. The Council of Nine which ruled the planet was in fact the long-sought Boskone.

The greatest surgeons of the age—Phillips of Posenia and Wise of Medon—demonstrated that they could grow new nervous tissue; even new limbs and organs if necessary. Again Clarrissa MacDougall nursed Kinnison back to health, and this time the love between them could not be concealed.

The Grand Fleet of the Patrol was assembled, and with Kinnison in charge of Operations, swept outward from the First Galaxy. Jalte's planet was destroyed by means of the negasphere—the negative-matter bomb— then on to the Second Galaxy.

Jarnevon, the planet of the Eich, was destroyed by smashing it between two barren planets which had been driven there in the "free" (inertialess) condition. These planets, having exactly opposite intrinsic velocities, were inerted, one upon each side of the doomed world; and when that frightful collision was over a minor star had come into being.

Grand Fleet returned to our galaxy. Galactic Civilization rejoiced. Prime Base was a center of celebration. Kinnison, supposing that the war was over and that his problem was solved, threw off Lensman's Load. Marrying his Cris, he declared, was the most important thing in the universe.

But how wrong he was! For even as Lensman and nurse were walking down a corridor of Base Hospital after a conference with Haynes and Lacy regarding that marriage—*

---

* *Gray Lensman,* Fantasy Press, Reading, Pa.

1

RECALLED

Stop, youth!" The Voice of Mentor the Arisian thundered silently, deep within the Lensman's brain.

He stopped convulsively, almost in mid-stride, and at the rigid, absent awareness in his eyes Nurse MacDougall's face went white.

"This is not merely the loose and muddy thinking of which you have all too frequently been guilty in the past," the deeply resonant, soundless voice went on, "it is simply not thinking at all. At times, Kinnison of Tellus, we almost despair of you. Think, youth, *think!* For know, Lensman, that upon the clarity of your thought and upon the trueness of your perception depends the whole future of your Patrol and of your Civilization; more so now by far than at any time in the past."

"What'dy'mean, 'think'?" Kinnison snapped back thoughtlessly. His mind was a seething turmoil, his emotions an indescribable blend of surprise, puzzlement, and incredulity.

For moments, as Mentor did not reply, the Gray Lensman's mind raced. Incredulity . . . becoming tinged with apprehension . . . turning rapidly into rebellion.

"Oh, Kim!" Clarrissa choked. A queer enough tableau they made, these two, had any been there to see; the two uniformed figures standing there so strainedly, the nurse's two hands gripping those of the Lensman.

She, completely en rapport with him, had understood his every fleeting thought. "Oh, Kim! They *can't* do that to us . . ."

"I'll say they can't!" Kinnison flared. "By Klono's tungsten teeth, I won't do it! We have a right to happiness, you and I, and we'll . . ."

"We'll what?" she asked, quietly. She knew what they had to face; and, strong-souled woman that she was, she was quicker to face it squarely than was he. "You were just blasting off, Kim, and so was I."

"I suppose so," glumly. "Why in all the nine hells of Valeria did I have to be a Lensman? Why couldn't I have stayed a . . . ?"

"Because you are you," the girl interrupted, gently. "Kimball Kinnison, the man I love. You couldn't do anything else." Chin up, she was fighting gamely. "And if I rate Lensman's Mate I can't be a sissy, either. It won't last forever, Kim. Just a little longer to wait, that's all."

Eyes, steel-gray now, stared down into eyes of tawny, gold-flecked bronze. "QX, Cris? *Really* QX?" What a world of meaning there was in that cryptic question!

"Really, Kim." She met his stare unfalteringly. If not entirely unafraid, at least with whole-hearted determination. "On the beam and on the green, Gray Lensman, all the way. Every long, last millimeter. There, wherever it is—to the very end of whatever road it has to be—and back again. Until it's over. I'll be here. Or somewhere, Kim. Waiting."

The man shook himself and breathed deep. Hands dropped apart—both knew consciously as well as subconsciously that the less of physical demonstration the better for two such natures as theirs—and Kimball Kinnison, Unattached Lensman, came to grips with his problem.

He began really to think; to think with the full power of his prodigious mind; and as he did so he began to see what the Arisian could have—what he must have—meant. He, Kinnison, had gummed up the works. He had made a colossal blunder in the Boskonian campaign. He knew that Mentor, although silent, was still en rapport with him; and as he coldly, grimly, thought the thing through to its logical conclusion he knew, with a dull, sick certainty, what was coming next. It came:

"Ah, you perceive at last some portion of the truth. You see that your confused, superficial thinking has brought about almost irreparable harm. I grant that, in specimens so young of such a youthful race, emotion has its place and its function; but I tell you now in all solemnity that for you the time of emotional relaxation has not yet come. *Think, youth—THINK!*" and the ancient Arisian snapped the telepathic line.

As one, without a word, nurse and Lensman retraced their way to the room they had left so shortly before. Port Admiral Haynes and Surgeon-

Marshal Lacy still sat upon the nurse's davenport, scheming roseate schemes having to do with the wedding they had so subtly engineered.

"Back so soon? Forget something, MacDougall?" Lacy asked, amiably. Then, as both men noticed the couple's utterly untranslatable expression:

"What happened? Break it out, Kim!" Haynes commanded.

"Plenty, chief," Kinnison answered, quietly. "Mentor stopped us before we got to the elevator. Told me I'd put my foot in it up to my neck on that Boskonian thing. That instead of being all buttoned up, my fool blundering has put us farther back than we were when we started."

"Mentor!"

"*Told* you!"

"Put us back!"

It was an entirely unpremeditated, unconscious duet. The two old officers were completely dumbfounded. Arisians never had come out of their shells, they never would. Infinitely less disturbing would have been the authentic tidings that a brick house had fallen upstairs. They had nursed this romance along *so* carefully, had timed it *so* exactly, and now it had gone *p-f-f-f-t*—it had been taken out of their hands entirely. That thought flashed through their minds first. Then, as catastrophe follows lightning's flash, the real knowledge exploded within their consciousnesses that, in some unguessable fashion or other, the whole Boskonian campaign had gone *p-f-f-f-t*, too.

Port Admiral Haynes, master tactician, reviewed in his keen strategist's mind every phase of the recent struggle, without being able to find a flaw in it.

"There wasn't a loop-hole anywhere," he said aloud. "Where do they figure we slipped up?"

"We didn't slip—*I* slipped," Kinnison stated, flatly. "When we took Bominger—the fat Chief Zwilnik of Radelix, you know—I took a bop on the head to learn that Boskone had more than one string per bow. Observers, independent, for every station at all important. I learned that fact thoroughly then, I thought. At least, we figured on Boskone's having lines of communication past, not through, his Regional Directors, such as Prellin of Bronseca. Since I changed my line of attack at that point, I did not need to consider whether or not Crowninshield of Tressilia III was by-passed in the same way; and when I had worked my way up through Jalte in his star-cluster to Boskone itself, on Jarnevon, I had forgotten the concept completely. Its possibility didn't even occur to me. That's where I fell down."

"I still don't see it!" Haynes protested. "Boskone was the top!"

"Yeah?" Kinnison asked, pointedly. "That's what I thought—but prove it."

"Oh." The Port Admiral hesitated. "We had no reason to think otherwise . . . looked at in that light, this intervention would seem to be conclusive . . . but before that there was no . . ."

"There were so," Kinnison contradicted, "but I didn't see them then. That's where my brain went sour; I should have seen them. Little things, mostly, but significant. Not so much positive as negative indices. Above all, there was nothing whatever to indicate that Boskone actually was the top. That idea was the product of my own wishful and very low-grade thinking, with no basis or foundation in fact or in theory. And now," he concluded bitterly, "because my skull is so thick that it takes an idea a hundred years to filter through it—because a sheer, bare fact has to be driven into my brain with a Valerian maul before I can grasp it—we're sunk without a trace."

"Wait a minute, Kim, we aren't sunk yet," the girl advised, shrewdly. "The fact that, for the first time in history, an Arisian has taken the initiative in communicating with a human being, means something big—*really* big. Mentor does not indulge in what he calls 'loose and muddy' thinking. Every part of every thought he sent carries meaning—plenty of meaning."

"What do you mean?" As one, the three men asked substantially the same question; Kinnison, by virtue of his faster reactions, being perhaps half a syllable in the lead.

"I don't know, exactly," Clarrissa admitted. "I've got only an ordinary mind, and it's firing on half its jets or less right now. But I do know that his thought was 'almost' irreparable, and that he meant precisely that—nothing else. If it had been wholly irreparable he not only would have expressed his thought that way, but he would have stopped you before you destroyed Jarnevon. I know that. Apparently it would have become wholly irreparable if we had got . . ." she faltered, blushing, then went on, ". . . if we had kept on about our own personal affairs. That's why he stopped us. We can win out, he meant, if you keep on working. It's your oyster, Kim . . . it's up to you to open it. You can do it, too—I just *know* you can."

"But why didn't he stop you before you fellows smashed Boskone?" Lacy demanded, exasperated.

"I hope you're right, Cris—it sounds reasonable," Kinnison said, thoughtfully. Then, to Lacy:

"That's an easy one to answer, doctor. Because knowledge that comes the hard way is knowledge that really sticks with you. If he had drawn me a diagram before, it wouldn't have helped, the next time I get into a jam. This way it will. I've got to learn how to think, if it cracks my skull.

"*Really* think," he went on, more to himself than to the other three. "To think so it counts."

"Well, what are we going to do about it?" Haynes was—he had to be, to get where he was and to stay where he was—quick on the uptake. "Or, more specifically, what are you going to do and what am I going to do?"

"What I am going to do will take a bit of mulling over," Kinnison replied, slowly. "Find some more leads and trace them up, is the best that occurs to me right now. Your job and procedure are rather clearer. You remarked out in space that Boskone knew that Tellus was very strongly held. That statement, of course, is no longer true."

"Huh?" Haynes half-pulled himself up from the davenport, then sank back. "Why?" he demanded.

"Because we used the negasphere—a negative-matter bomb of planetary anti-mass—to wipe out Jalte's planet, and because we smashed Jarnevon between two colliding planets," the Lensman explained, concisely. "Can the present defenses of Tellus cope with either one of those offensives?"

"I'm afraid not . . . no," the Port Admiral admitted. "But . . ."

"We can admit no 'buts', admiral," Kinnison declared, with grim finality. "Having used those weapons, we must assume that the Boskonian scientists—we'll have to keep on calling them 'Boskonians', I suppose, until we find a truer name—had recorders on them and have now duplicated them. Tellus must be made safe against anything we have ever used; against, as well, everything that, by the wildest stretch of the imagination, we can conceive of the enemy using."

"You're right . . . I can see that," Haynes nodded.

"We've been underestimating them right along," Kinnison went on. "At first we thought they were merely organized outlaws and pirates. Then, when it was forced upon us that they could match us—overmatch us in some things—we still wouldn't admit that they must be as large and as wide-spread as we are—galactic in scope. We know now that they were wider-spread than we are. Inter-galactic. They penetrated into our galaxy, riddled it, before we knew that theirs was inhabited or inhabitable. Right?"

"To a hair, although I never thought of it in exactly that way before."

"None of us have—mental cowardice. And they have the advantage," Kinnison continued, inexorably, "in knowing that our Prime Base is on Tellus; whereas, if Jarnevon was not in fact theirs, we have no idea whatever where it is. And another point. Was that fleet of theirs a planetary outfit?"

"Well, Jarnevon was a big planet, and the Eich were a mighty warlike race."

"Quibbling a bit, aren't you, chief?"

"Uh-huh," Haynes admitted, somewhat sheepishly. "The probability is very great that no one planet either built or maintained that fleet."

"And that leads us to expect what?"

"Counter-attack. In force. Everything they can shove this way. However, they've got to rebuild their fleet, besides designing and building the new stuff. We'll have time enough, probably, if we get started right now."

"But, after all, Jarnevon *may* have been their vital spot," Lacy submitted.

"Even if that were true, which it probably isn't," the now thoroughly convinced Port Admiral sided in with Kinnison, "it doesn't mean a thing, Sawbones. If they should blow Tellus out of space it wouldn't kill the Galactic Patrol. It would hurt it, of course, but it wouldn't cripple it seriously. The other planets of Civilization could, and certainly would, go ahead with it."

"My thought exactly," from Kinnison. "I check you to the proverbial nineteen decimals."

"Well, there's a lot to do and I'd better be getting at it." Haynes and Lacy got up to go. "See you in my office when convenient?"

"I'll be there as soon as I tell Clarrissa goodbye."

At about the same time that Haynes and Lacy went to Nurse Mac-Dougall's room, Worsel the Velantian arrowed downward through the atmosphere toward a certain flat roof. Leather wings shot out with a snap and in a blast of wind—Velantians can stand eleven Tellurian gravities—he came in to his customary appalling landing and dived unconcernedly down a nearby shaft. Into a corridor, along which he wriggled blithely to the office of his old friend, Master Technician LaVerne Thorndyke.

"Verne, I have been thinking," he announced, as he coiled all but about six feet of his sinuous length into a tight spiral upon the rug and thrust out half a dozen weirdly stalked eyes.

"That's nothing new," Thorndyke countered. No human mind can sympathize with or even remotely understand the Velantian passion for solid weeks of intense, uninterrupted concentration upon a single thought. "What about this time? The whichness of the why?"

"That is the trouble with you Tellurians," Worsel grumbled. "Not only do you not know how to think, but you . . ."

"Hold on!" Thorndyke interrupted, unimpressed. "If you've got anything to say, old snake, why not say it? Why circumnavigate total space before you get to the point?"

"I have been thinking about thought . . ."

"So what?" The technician derided. "That's even worse. That's a logarithmic spiral if there ever was one."

"Thought—and Kinnison," Worsel declared, with finality.

"Kinnison? Oh—that's different. I'm interested—very much so. Go ahead."

"And his weapons. His DeLameters, you know."

"No, I don't know, and you know I don't know. What about them?"

"They are so . . . so . . . so *obvious.*" The Velantian finally found the exact thought he wanted. "So big, and so clumsy, and so obtrusive. So inefficient, so wasteful of power. No subtlety—no finesse."

"But that's far and away the best hand-weapon that has ever been developed!" Thorndyke protested.

"True. Nevertheless, a millionth of that power, properly applied, could be at least a million times as deadly."

"How?" The Tellurian, although shocked, was dubious.

"I have reasoned it out that thought, in any organic being, is and must be connected with one definite organic compound—this one," the Velantian explained didactically, the while there appeared within the technician's mind the space formula of an incredibly complex molecule; a formula which seemed to fill not only his mind, but the entire room as well. "You will note that it is a large molecule, one of very high molecular weight. Thus it is comparatively unstable. A vibration at the resonant frequency of any one of its component groups would break it down, and thought would therefore cease."

It took perhaps a minute for the full import of the ghastly thing to sink into Thorndyke's mind. Then, every fiber of him flinching from the idea, he began to protest.

"But he doesn't need it, Worsel. He's got a mind already that can . . ."

"It takes much mental force to kill," Worsel broke in equably. "By that method one can slay only a few at a time, and it is exhausting work. My proposed method would require only a minute fraction of a watt of power and scarcely any mental force at all."

"And it would *kill*—it would have to. That reaction could not be made reversible."

"Certainly," Worsel concurred. "I never could understand why you soft-headed, soft-hearted, soft-bodied human beings are so reluctant to kill your enemies. What good does it do merely to stun them?"

"QX—skip it." Thorndyke knew that it was hopeless to attempt to convince the utterly unhuman Worsel of the fundamental rightness of human ethics. "But nothing has ever been designed small enough to project such a wave."

"I realize that. Its design and construction will challenge your inventive ability. Its smallness is its great advantage. He could wear it in a ring, in the bracelet of his Lens; or, since it will be actuated, controlled, and directed by thought, even imbedded surgically beneath his skin."

"How about backfires?" Thorndyke actually shuddered. "Projection . . . shielding . . ."

"Details—mere details," Worsel assured him, with an airy flip of his scimitared tail.

"That's nothing to be running around loose," the man argued. "Nobody could tell what killed them, could they?"

"Probably not." Worsel pondered briefly. "No. Certainly not. The substance must decompose in the instant of death, from any cause. And it would not be 'loose', as you think; it should not become known, even. You would make only the one, of course."

"Oh. You don't want one, then?"

"Certainly not. What do I need of such a thing? Kinnison only—and only for his protection."

"Kim can handle it . . . but he's the only being this side of Arisia that I'd trust with one . . . QX, give me the dope on the frequency, waveform, and so on, and I'll see what I can do."

2

INVASION VIA TUBE

Port Admiral Haynes, newly chosen President of the Galactic Council and by virtue of his double office the most powerful entity of Civilization, set instantly into motion the vast machinery which would make Tellus safe against any possible attack. He first called together his Board of Strategy; the same keen-minded tacticians who had helped him plan the invasion of the Second Galaxy and the eminently successful attack upon Jarnevon. Should Grand Fleet, many of whose component fleets had not yet reached their home planets, be recalled? Not yet—lots of time for that. Let them go home for a while first. The enemy would have to rebuild before they could attack, and there were many more pressing matters.

Scouting was most important. The planets near the galactic rim could take care of that. In fact, they should concentrate upon it, to the exclusion of everything else of warfare's activities. Every approach to the galaxy—yes, the space between the two galaxies and as far into the Second Galaxy as it was safe to penetrate—should be covered as with a blanket. That way, they could not be surprised.

Kinnison, when he heard that, became vaguely uneasy. He did not really have a thought; it was as though he should have had one, but didn't. Deep down, far off, just barely above the threshold of perception an indefinite, formless something obtruded itself upon his consciousness. Tug and haul at it as he would, he could not get the drift. There was *something* he ought to be thinking of, but what in all the iridescent hells from Vandemar to Alsakan was it? So, instead of flitting about upon his declared business, he stuck around; helping the General Staff—and thinking.

And Defense Plan BBT went from the idea men to the draftsmen, then to the engineers. This was to be, primarily, a war of planets. Ships could battle ships, fleets fleets; but, postulating good tactics upon the other side, no fleet, however armed and powered, could stop a planet. That had been proved. A planet had a mass of the order of magnitude of one times ten to the twenty fifth kilograms, and an intrinsic velocity of somewhere around forty kilometers per second. A hundred probably, relative to Tellus, if the planet came from the Second Galaxy. Kinetic energy, roughly, about five times ten to the forty first ergs. No, that was nothing for any possible fleet to cope with.

Also, the attacking planets would of course be inertialess until the last strategic instant. Very well, they must be made inert prematurely, when the Patrol wanted them that way, not the enemy. How? HOW? The Bergenholms upon those planets would be guarded with everything the Boskonians had.

The answer to that question, as worked out by the engineers, was something they called a "super-mauler". It was gigantic, cumbersome, and slow; but little faster, indeed, than a free planet. It was like Helmuth's fortresses of space, only larger. It was like the special defense cruisers of the Patrol, except that its screens were vastly heavier. It was like a regular mauler, except that it had only one weapon. All of its incomprehensible mass was devoted to one thing—*power!* It could defend itself; and, if it could get close enough to its objective, it could do plenty of damage—its dreadful primary was the first weapon ever developed capable of cutting a Q-type helix squarely in two.

And in various solar systems, uninhabitable and worthless planets were converted into projectiles. Dozens of them, possessing widely varying masses and intrinsic velocities. One by one they flitted away from their parent suns and took up positions—not too far away from our Solar System, but not too near.

And finally Kinnison, worrying at his tantalizing thought as a dog worries a bone, crystallized it. Prosaically enough, it was an extremely short and flamboyantly waggling pink skirt which catalyzed the reaction; which acted as the seed of the crystallizaton. Pink—a Chickladorian—Xylpic the Navigator—Overlords of Delgon. Thus flashed the train of thought, culminating in:

"Oh, so *that's* it!" he exclaimed, aloud. "A TUBE—just as sure as hell's a mantrap!" He whistled raucously at a taxi, took the wheel himself, and broke—or at least bent—most of the city's traffic ordinances in getting to Haynes' office.

The Port Admiral was always busy, but he was never too busy to see Gray Lensman Kinnison; especially when the latter demanded the right of way in such terms as he used then.

"The whole defense set-up is screwy," Kinnison declared. "I thought I was overlooking a bet, but I couldn't locate it. Why should they fight their way through inter-galactic space and through sixty thousand parsecs of planet-infested galaxy when they don't have to?" he demanded. "Think of the length of the supply line, with our bases placed to cut it in a hundred places, no matter how they route it. It doesn't make sense. They'd have to out-weigh us in an almost impossibly high ratio, unless they have an improbably superior armament."

"Check." The old warrior was entirely unperturbed. "Surprised you didn't see that long ago. We did. I'll be very much surprised if they attack at all."

"But you're going ahead with all this just as though . . ."

"Certainly. Something *may* happen, and we can't be caught off guard. Besides, it's good training for the boys. Helps morale, no end." Haynes' nonchalant air disappeared and he studied the younger man keenly for moments. "But Mentor's warning certainly meant something, and you said 'when they don't have to'. But even if they go clear around the galaxy to the other side—an impossibly long haul—we're covered. Tellus is far enough in so they can't possibly take us by surprise. So—spill it!"

"How about a hyperspatial tube? They know exactly where we are, you know."

"Um . . . m . . . m." Haynes was taken aback. "Never thought of it . . . possible, distinctly a possibility. A duodec bomb, say, just far enough underground . . ."

"Nobody else thought of it, either, until just now," Kinnison broke in. "However, I'm not afraid of duodec—don't see how they could control it accurately enough at this three dimensional distance. Too deep, it wouldn't explode at all. What I don't like to think of, though, is a negasphere. Or a planet, perhaps."

"Ideas? Suggestions?" the admiral snapped.

"No—I don't know anything about that stuff. How about putting our Lenses on Cardynge?"

"That's a thought!" and in seconds they were in communication with Sir Austin Cardynge, Earth's mightiest mathematical brain.

"Kinnison, how many times must I tell you that I am not to be interrupted?" the aged scientist's thought was a crackle of fury. "How can I concentrate upon vital problems if every young whippersnapper in the System is to perpetrate such abominable, such outrageous intrusions . . ."

"Hold it, Sir Austin—hold everything!" Kinnison soothed. "I'm sorry. I wouldn't have intruded if it hadn't been a matter of life or death. But it would be worse intrusion, wouldn't it, if the Boskonians sent a planet about the size of Jupiter—or a negasphere—through one of their extra-dimensional vortices into your study? That's exactly what they're figuring on doing."

"What-what-what?" Cardynge snapped, like a string of firecrackers. He quieted down, then, and thought. And Sir Austin Cardynge *could* think, upon occasion and when he felt so inclined; could think in the abstruse symbology of pure mathematics with a cogency equalled by few minds in the universe. Both Lensmen perceived those thoughts, but neither could understand or follow them. No mind not a member of the Conference of Scientists could have done so.

"They can't!" of a sudden the mathematician cackled, gleefully disdainful. "Impossible—quite definitely impossible. There are laws governing such things, Kinnison, my impetuous and ignorant young friend. The terminus of the necessary hyper-tube could not be established within such proximity to the mass of the sun. This is shown by . . ."

"Never mind the proof—the fact is enough," Kinnison interposed, hastily. "How close to the sun could it be established?"

"I couldn't say, off-hand," came the cautiously scientific reply. "More than one astronomical unit, certainly, but the computation of the exact distance would require some little time. It would, however, be an interesting, if minor, problem. I will solve it for you, if you like, and advise you of the exact minimum distance."

"Please do so—thanks a million," and the Lensmen disconnected.

"The conceited old goat!" Haynes snorted. "I'd like to smack him down!"

"I've felt like it more than once, but it wouldn't do any good. You've got to handle him with gloves—besides, you can afford to make concessions to a man with a brain like that."

"I suppose so. But how about that infernal tube? Knowing that it can not be set up within or very near Tellus helps some, but not enough. We've got to know where it is—*if* it is. Can you detect it?"

"Yes. That is, I can't, but the specialists can, I think. Wise of Medon would know more about that than anyone else. Why wouldn't it be a thought to call him over here?"

"It would that," and it was done.

Wise of Medon and his staff came, conferred, and departed.

Sir Austin Cardynge solved his minor problem, reporting that the minimum distance from the sun's center to the postulated center of the terminus of the vortex—actually, the geometrical origin of the three-dimensional figure which was the hyper-plane of intersection—was one point two six four seven, approximately, astronomical units; the last figure being tentative and somewhat uncertain because of the rapidly-moving masses of Jupiter . . .

Haynes cut the tape—he had no time for an hour of mathematical dissertation—and called in his execs.

"Full-globe detection of hyper-spatial tubes," he directed, crisply. "Kinnison will tell you exactly what he wants. Hipe!"

Shortly thereafter, five-man speedsters, plentifully equipped with new instruments, flashed at full drive along courses carefully calculated to give the greatest possible coverage in the shortest possible time.

Unobstrusively the loose planets closed in; close enough so that at least three or four of them could reach any designated point in one minute or less. The outlying units of Grand Fleet, too, were pulled in. That fleet was not actually mobilized—yet—but every vessel in it was kept in readiness for instant action.

"No trace," came the report from the Medonian surveyors, and Haynes looked at Kinnison, quizzically.

"QX, chief—glad of it," the Gray Lensman answered the unspoken query. "If it was up, that would mean they were on the way. Hope they don't get a trace for two months yet. But I'm next-to-positive that that's the way they're coming and the longer they put it off the better—there's a possible new projector that will take a bit of doping out. I've got to do a flit—can I have the *Dauntless?*"

"Sure—anything you want—she's yours anyway."

Kinnison went. And, wonder of wonders, he took Sir Austin Cardynge with him. From solar system to solar system, from planet to planet, the mighty *Dauntless* hurtled at the incomprehensible velocity of her full maximum blast; and every planet so visited was the home world of one of the most cooperative—or, more accurately, one of the least non-cooperative—members of the Conference of Scientists. For days brilliant but more or less unstable minds struggled with new and obdurate problems; struggled heatedly and with friction, as was their wont. Few if any of those mighty intellects would have really enjoyed a quietly studious session, even had such a thing been possible.

Then Kinnison returned his guests to their respective homes and shot his flying warship-laboratory back to Prime Base. And, even before the *Dauntless* landed, the first few hundreds of a fleet which was soon to be numbered in the millions of meteor-miners' boats began working like beavers to build a new and exactly-designed system of asteroid belts of iron meteors.

And soon, as such things go, new structures began to appear here and there in the void. Comparatively small, these things were; tiny, in fact, compared to the Patrol's maulers. Unarmed, too; carrying nothing except defensive screen. Each was, apparently, simply a power-house; stuffed skin full of atomic motors, exciters, intakes, and generators of highly peculiar design and pattern. Unnoticed except by gauntly haggard Thorndyke and his experts, who kept dashing from one of the strange craft to another, each took its place in a succession of precisely-determined relationships to the sun.

Between the orbits of Mars and of Jupiter, the new, sharply-defined rings of asteroids moved smoothly. Most of Grand Fleet formed an enormous hollow hemisphere. Throughout all nearby space the surveying speedsters and flitters rushed madly hither and yon. Uselessly, apparently, for not one needle of the vortex-detectors stirred from its zero-pin.

As nearly as possible at the Fleet's center there floated the flagship. Technically the *Z9M9Z,* socially the *Directrix,* ordinarily simply *GFHQ,* that ship had been built specifically to control the operations of a million separate flotillas. At her million-plug board stood—they had no need, ever, to sit—two hundred blocky, tentacle-armed Rigellians. They were waiting, stolidly motionless.

Inter-galactic space remained empty. Interstellar ditto, ditto. The flitters flitted, fruitlessly.

But if everything out there in the threatened volume of space seemed quiet and serene, things in the *Z9M9Z* were distinctly otherwise. Haynes and Kinnison, upon whom the heaviest responsibilities rested, were tensely ill at ease.

The admiral had his formation made, but he did not like it at all. It was too big, too loose, too cumbersome. The Boskonian fleet might appear anywhere, and it would take him far, far too long to get any kind of a fighting formation made, anywhere. So he worried. Minutes dragged—he wished that the pirates would hurry up and start something!

Kinnison was even less easy in his mind. He was not afraid of nega-spheres, even if Boskonia should have them; but he was afraid of fortified, mobile planets. The super-maulers were big and powerful, of course, but they very definitely were not planets; and the big, new idea was mighty hard to jell. He didn't like to bother Thorndyke by calling him—the master technician had troubles of his own—but the reports that were coming in were none too cheery. The excitation was wrong or the grid action was too unstable or the screen potentials were too high or too low or too something. Sometimes they got a concentration, but it was just as apt as not to be a spread flood instead of a tight beam. To Kinnison, therefore, the minutes fled like seconds—but every minute that space remained clear was one more precious minute gained.

Then, suddenly, it happened. A needle leaped into significant figures. Relays clicked, a bright red light flared into being, a gong clanged out its raucous warning. A fractional instant later ten thousand other gongs in ten thousand other ships came brazenly to life as the discovering speedster automatically sent out its number and position; and those other ships—surveyors all—flashed toward that position and dashed frantically about. Theirs the task to determine, in the least number of seconds possible, the approximate location of the center of emergence.

For Port Admiral Haynes, canny old tactician that he was, had planned his campaign long since. It was standing plain in his tactical tank—to englobe the entire space of emergence of the foe and to blast them out of existence before they could maneuver. If he could get into formation before the Boskonians appeared it would be a simple slaughter—if not, it might be otherwise. Hence seconds counted; and hence he had had high-speed computers working steadily for weeks at the computation of courses for every possible center of emergence.

"Get me that center—fast!" Haynes barked at the surveyors, already blasting at maximum.

It came in. The chief computer yelped a string of numbers. Selected loose-leaf binders were pulled down, yanked apart, and distributed on the double, leaf by leaf. And:

"Get it over there! Especially the shock-globe!" the Port Admiral yelled.

For he himself could direct the engagement only in broad; details must be left to others. To be big enough to hold in any significant relationship the millions of lights representing vessels, fleets, planets, structures, and objectives, the Operations tank of the *Directrix* had to be seven hundred feet in diameter; and it was a sheer physical impossibility for any ordinary mind either to perceive that seventeen million cubic feet of space as a whole or to make any sense at all out of the stupendously bewildering maze of multi-colored lights crawling and flashing therein.

Kinnison and Worsel had handled Grand Fleet Operations during the battle of Jarnevon, but they had discovered that they could have used some help. Four Rigellian Lensmen had been training for months for that all-important job, but they were not yet ready. Therefore the two old masters and one new one now labored at GFO: three tremendous minds, each supplying something that the others lacked. Kinnison of Tellus, with his hard, flat driving urge, his unconquerable, unstoppable will to do. Worsel of Velantia, with the prodigious reach and grasp which had enabled him even without the Lens, to scan mentally a solar system eleven light-years distant. Tregonsee of Rigel IV, with the vast, calm certainty, the imperturbable poise peculiar to his long-lived, solemn race. Second Stage Lensmen all, graduates of Arisian advanced training; minds linked, basically, together into one mind by a wide-open three-way; superficially free, each to do his assigned third of the gigantic task.

Smoothly, effortlessly, those three linked minds went to work at the admiral's signal. Orders shot out along tight beams of thought to the stolid hundreds of Rigellian switchboard operators, and thence along communicator beams to the pilot rooms, wherever stationed. Flotillas, squadrons, sub-fleets flashed smoothly toward their newly-assigned positions. Super-maulers moved ponderously toward theirs. The survey ships, their work done, vanished. They had no business anywhere near what was coming next. Small they were, and defenseless; a speedster's screens were as efficacious as so much vacuum against the forces about to be unleashed. The power houses also moved. Maintaining rigidly their cryptic mathematical relationships to each other and the sun, they went as a whole into a new one with respect to the circling rings of tightly-packed meteors and the invisible, non-existent mouth of the Boskonian vortex.

Then, before Haynes' formation was nearly complete, the Boskonian fleet materialized. Just that—one instant space was empty; the next it was full of warships. A vast globe of battle-wagons, in perfect fighting formation. They were not free, but inert and deadly.

Haynes swore viciously under his breath, the Lensmen pulled themselves together more tensely; but no additional orders were given. Everything that could possibly be done was already being done.

Whether the Boskonians expected to meet a perfectly-placed fleet or whether they expected to emerge into empty space, to descend upon a defenseless Tellus, is not known or knowable. It is certain, however, that they emerged in the best possible formation to meet anything that could be brought to bear. It is also certain that, had the enemy had a $Z9M9Z$ and a Kinnison-Worsel-Tregonsee combination scanning its Operations tank, the outcome might well have been otherwise than it was.

For that ordinarily insignificant delay, that few minutes of time necessary for the Boskonians' orientation, was exactly that required for those two hundred smoothly-working Rigellians to get Civilization's shock-globe into position.

A million beams, primaries raised to the hellish heights possible only to Medonian conductors and insulation, lashed out almost as one. Screens stiffened to the urge of every generable watt of defensive power. Bolt after bolt of quasi-solid lightning struck and struck and struck again. Q-type helices bored, gouged, and searingly bit. Rods and cones, planes and shears of incredibly condensed pure force clawed, tore, and ground in mad abandon. Torpedo after torpedo, charged to the very skin with duodec, loosed its horribly detonant cargo against flinching wall-shields, in such numbers and with such violence as to fill all circumambient space with an atmosphere of almost planetary density.

Screen after screen, wall-shield after wall-shield, in their hundreds and their thousands, went down. A full eighth of the Patrol's entire count of battleships was wrecked, riddled, blown apart, or blasted completely out of space in the paralyzingly cataclysmic violence of the first, seconds-long, mind-shaking, space-wracking encounter. Nor could it have been otherwise; for this encounter had not been at battle range. Not even at point-blank range; the warring monsters of the void were packed practically screen to screen.

But not a man died—upon Civilization's side at least—even though practically all of the myriad of ships composing the inner sphere, the shock-globe, was lost. For they were automatics, manned by robots; what little superintendence was necessary had been furnished by remote control. Indeed it is possible, although perhaps not entirely probable, that the shock-globe of the foe was similarly manned.

That first frightful meeting gave time for the reserves of the Patrol to get there, and it was then that the superior Operations control of the *Z9M9Z* made itself tellingly felt. Ship for ship, beam for beam, screen for screen, the Boskonians were, perhaps equal to the Patrol; but they did not have the perfection of control necessary for unified action. The field was too immense, the number of contending units too enormously vast. But the mind of each of the three Second Stage Lensmen read aright the flashing lights of his particular volume of the gigantic tank and spread their meaning truly in the infinitely smaller space-model beside which Port Admiral Haynes, Master Tactician, stood. Scanning the entire space of battle as a whole, he rapped out general orders—orders applying, perhaps, to a hundred or to five hundred planetary fleets. Kinnison and his fellows broke these orders down for the operators, who in turn told the admirals and vice-admirals of the fleets what to do. They gave detailed orders to the units of their commands, and the line officers, knowing exactly what to do and precisely how to do it, did it with neatness and dispatch.

There was no doubt, no uncertainty, no indecision or wavering. The line officers, even the admirals, knew nothing, could know nothing of the progress of the engagement as a whole. But they had worked under the *Z9M9Z* before. They knew that the maestro Haynes did know the battle as a whole. They knew that he was handling them as carefully and as skillfully as a master at chess plays his pieces upon the square-filled board. They knew that Kinnison or Worsel or Tregonsee was assigning no task too difficult of accomplishment. They knew that they could not be taken by surprise, attacked from some unexpected and unprotected direction; knew that, although in those hundreds of thousands of cubic miles of space there were hundreds of thousands of highly inimical and exceedingly powerful ships of war, none of them were or shortly could be in position to do them serious harm. If there had been, they would have been pulled out of there, *beaucoup* fast. They were as safe as anyone in a warship in such a war could expect, or even hope, to be. Therefore they acted instantly; directly, wholeheartedly and efficiently; and it was the Boskonians who were taken, repeatedly and by the thousands, by surprise.

For the enemy, as has been said, did not have the Patrol's smooth perfection of control. Thus several of Civilization's fleets, acting in full synchronization, could and repeatedly did rush upon one unit of the foe; englobing it, blasting it out of existence, and dashing back to stations; all before the nearest-by fleets of Boskone knew even that a threat was being made. Thus ended the second phase of the battle, the engagement of the two Grand Fleets, with the few remaining thousands of Boskone's battleships taking refuge upon or near the phalanx of planets which had made up their center.

Planets. Seven of them. Armed and powered as only a planet can be armed and powered; with fixed-mount weapons impossible of mounting upon a lesser mobile base, with fixed-mount intakes and generators which only planetary resources could excite or feed. Galactic Civilization's war-vessels fell back. Attacking a full-armed planet was not part of their job. And as they fell back the super-maulers moved ponderously up and went to work. This was their dish; for this they had been designed. Tubes, lances, stillettoes of unthinkable energies raved against their mighty screens; bouncing off, glancing away, dissipating themselves in space-torturing discharges as they hurled themselves upon the nearest ground. In and in the monsters bored, inexorably taking up their positions directly over the ultra-protected domes which, their commanders knew, sheltered the vitally important Bergenholms and controls. They then loosed forces of their own. Forces of such appalling magnitude as to burn out in a twinkling of an eye projector-shells of a refractoriness to withstand for ten full seconds the maximum output of a first-class battleship's primary batteries!

The resultant beam was of very short duration, but of utterly intolerable poignancy. No material substance could endure it even momentarily. It pierced instantly the hardest, tightest wall-shield known to the scientists of the Patrol. It was the only known thing which could cut or rupture the ultimately stubborn fabric of a Q-type helix. Hence it is not to be wondered at that as those incredible needles of ravening energy stabbed and stabbed and stabbed again at Boskonian domes every man of the Patrol, even Kimball Kinnison, fully expected those domes to go down.

But those domes held. And those fixed-mount projectors hurled back against the super-maulers forces at the impact of which course after course of fierce-driven defensive screen flamed through the spectrum and went down.

"Back! Get them back!" Kinnison whispered, white-lipped, and the attacking structures sullenly, stubbornly gave way.

"Why?" gritted Haynes. "They're all we've got."

"You forget the new one, chief—give us a chance."

"What makes you think it'll work?" the old admiral flashed the searing thought. "It probably won't—and if it doesn't . . ."

"If it doesn't," the younger man shot back, "we're no worse off than now to use the maulers. But we've got to use the sunbeam *now* while those planets are together and before they start toward Tellus."

"QX," the admiral assented; and, as soon as the Patrol's maulers were out of the way:

"Verne?" Kinnison flashed a thought. "We can't crack 'em. Looks like it's up to you—what do you say?"

"Jury-rigged—don't know whether she'll light a cigarette or not—but here she comes!"

The sun, shining so brightly, darkened almost to the point of invisibility. War-vessels of the enemy disappeared, each puffing out into a tiny but brilliant sparkle of light.

Then, before the beam could effect the enormous masses of the planets, the engineers lost it. The sun flashed up—dulled—brightened—darkened—wavered. The beam waxed and waned irregularly; the planets began to move away under the urgings of their now thoroughly scared commanders.

Again, while millions upon millions of tensely straining Patrol officers stared into their plates, haggard Thorndyke and his sweating crews got the sunbeam under control—and, in a heart-stopping wavering fashion, held it together. It flared—sputtered—ballooned out—but very shortly, before they could get out of its way, the planets began to glow. Ice-caps melted, then boiled. Oceans boiled, their surfaces almost exploding into steam. Mountain ranges melted and flowed sluggishly down into valleys. The Boskonian domes of force went down and stayed down.

"QX, Kim—let be," Haynes ordered. "No use overdoing it. Not bad-looking planets; maybe we can use them for something."

The sun brightened to its wonted splendor, the planets began visibly to cool—even the Titanic forces then at work had heated those planetary masses only superficially.

The battle was over.

"What in all the purple hells of Palain did you do, Haynes, and how?" demanded the *Z9M9Z's* captain.

"He used the whole damned solar system as a vacuum tube!" Haynes explained, gleefully. "Those power stations out there, with all their motors and intake screens, are simply the power leads. The asteroid belts, and maybe some of the planets, are the grids and plates. The sun is . . ."

"Hold on, chief!" Kinnison broke in. "That isn't quite it. You see, the directive field set up by the . . ."

"Hold on yourself!" Haynes ordered, briskly. "You're too damned scientific, just like Sawbones Lacy. What do Rex and I care about technical details that we can't understand anyway? The net result is what counts—and that was to concentrate upon those planets practically the whole energy output of the sun. Wasn't it?"

"Well, that's the main idea," Kinnison conceded. "The energy equivalent, roughly, of four million one hundred and fifty thousand tons per second of disintegrating matter."

"Whew!" the captain whistled. "No wonder it frizzled 'em up."

"I can say now, I think, with no fear of successful contradiction, that Tellus *is* strongly held," Haynes stated, with conviction. "What now, Kim old son?"

"I think they're done, for a while," the Gray Lensman pondered. "Cardynge can't communicate through the tube, so probably they can't; but if they managed to slip an observer through they may know how almighty close they came to licking us. On the other hand, Verne says that he can get the bugs out of the sunbeam in a couple of weeks—and when he does, the next zwilnik he cuts loose at is going to get a surprise."

"I'll say so," Haynes agreed. "We'll keep the surveyors on the prowl, and some of the Fleet will always be close by. Not all of it, of course—we'll adopt a schedule of reliefs—but enough of it to be useful. That ought to be enough, don't you think?"

"I think so—yes," Kinnison answered, thoughtfully. "I'm just about positive that they won't be in shape to start anything here again for a long time. And I had better get busy, sir, on my own job—I've got to put out a few jets."

"I suppose so," Haynes admitted.

For Tellus *was* strongly held, now—so strongly held that Kinnison felt free to begin again the search upon whose successful conclusion depended, perhaps, the outcome of the struggle between Boskonia and Galactic Civilization.

3

LYRANE THE MATRIARCHY

When the forces of the Galactic Patrol blasted Helmuth's Grand Base out of existence and hunted down and destroyed his secondary bases throughout this galaxy, Boskone's military grasp upon Civilization was definitely broken. Some minor bases may have escaped destruction, of course. Indeed, it is practically certain that some of them did so, for there are comparatively large volumes of our Island Universe which have not been mapped, even yet, by the planetographers of the Patrol. It is equally certain, however, that they were relatively few and of no real importance. For warships, being large, cannot be carried around or concealed in a vest pocket—a war-fleet must of necessity be based upon a celestial object not smaller than a very large asteroid. Such a base, lying close enough to any one of Civilization's planets to be of any use, could not be hidden successfully from the detectors of the Patrol.

Reasoning from analogy, Kinnison quite justifiably concluded that the back of the drug syndicate had been broken in similar fashion when he had worked upward through Bominger and Strongheart and Crowninshield and Jalte to the dread council of Boskone itself. He was, however, wrong.

For, unlike the battleship, thionite is a vest-pocket commodity. Unlike the space-fleet base, a drug-baron's headquarters can be and frequently is small, compact, and highly mobile. Also, the galaxy is huge, the number of planets in it immense, the total count of drug addicts utterly incomprehensible. Therefore it had been found more efficient to arrange the drug hook-up in multiple series-parallel, instead of in the straight encascade sequence which Kinnison thought that he had followed up.

He thought so at first, that is, but he did not think so long. He had thought, and he had told Haynes, as well as Gerrond of Radelix, that the situation was entirely under control; that with the zwilnik headquarters blasted out of existence and with all of the regional heads and many of the planetary chiefs dead or under arrest, all that the Enforcement men would have to cope with would be the normal bootleg trickle. In that, too, he was wrong. The lawmen of Narcotics had had a brief respite, it is true; but in a few days or weeks, upon almost as many planets as before, the illicit traffic was again in full swing.

After the Battle of Tellus, then, it did not take the Gray Lensman long to discover the above facts. Indeed, they were pressed upon him. He was, however, more relieved than disappointed at the tidings, for he knew that he would have material upon which to work. If his original opinion had been right, if all lines of communication with the now completely unknown ultimate authorities of the zwilniks had been destroyed, his task would have been an almost hopeless one.

It would serve no good purpose here to go into details covering his early efforts, since they embodied, in principle, the same tactics as those which he had previously employed. He studied, he analyzed, he investigated. He snooped and he spied. He fought; upon occasion he killed. And in due course—and not too long a course—he cut into the sign of what he thought must be a key zwilnik. Not upon Bronseca or Radelix or Chickladoria, or any other distant planet, but right upon Tellus!

But he could not locate him. He never saw him on Tellus. As a matter of cold fact, he could not find a single person who had ever seen him or knew anything definite about him. These facts, of course, only whetted Kinnison's keenness to come to grips with the fellow. He might not be a very big shot, but the fact that he was covering himself up so thoroughly and so successfully made it abundantly evident that he was a fish well worth landing.

This wight, however, proved to be as elusive as the proverbial flea. He was never there when Kinnison pounced. In London he was a few minutes late. In Berlin he was a minute or so too early, and the ape didn't show up at all. He missed him in Paris and in San Francisco and in Shanghai. The guy sat down finally in New York, but still the Gray Lensman could not connect—it was always the wrong street, or the wrong house, or the wrong time, or something.

Then Kinnison set a snare which should have caught a microbe—and *almost* caught his zwilnik. He missed him by one mere second when he blasted off from New York Space-Port. He was so close that he saw his flare, so close that he could slap onto the fleeing vessel the beam of the CRX tracer which he always carried with him.

Unfortunately, however, the Lensman was in mufti at the time, and was driving a rented flitter. His speedster—altogether too spectacular and obvious a conveyance to be using in a hush-hush investigation—was at Prime Base. He didn't want the speedster, anyway, except inside the *Dauntless.* He'd go organized this time to chase the lug clear out of space, if he had to. He shot in a call for the big cruiser, and while it was coming he made luridly sulphurous inquiry.

Fruitless. His orders had been carried out to the letter, except in the one detail of not allowing any vessel to take off. This take-off absolutely could not be helped—it was just one of those things. The ship was a Patrol speedster from Deneb V, registry number so-and-so. Said he was coming in for servicing. Came in on the north beam, identified himself properly—Lieutenant Quirkenfal, of Deneb V, he said it was, and it checked . . .

It would check, of course. The zwilnik that Kinnison had been chasing so long certainly would not be guilty of any such raw, crude work as a faulty identification. In fact, right then he probably looked just as much like Quirkenfal as the lieutenant himself did.

"He wasn't in any hurry at all," the information went on. "He waited around for his landing clearance, then slanted in on his assigned slide to the service pits. In the last hundred yards, though, he shot off to one side and sat down, *plop,* broadside on, clear over there in the far corner of the field. But he wasn't down but a second, sir. Long before anybody could get to him—before the cruisers could put a beam on him, even—he blasted off as though the devil was on his tail. Then you came along, sir, but we did put a CRX tracer on him . . ."

"I did that much, myself," Kinnison stated, morosely. "He stopped just long enough to pick up a passenger—my zwilnik, of course—then flitted . . . and you fellows let him get away with it."

"But we couldn't help it, sir," the official protested. "And anyway, he couldn't possibly have . . ."

"He sure could. You'd be surprised no end at what that bimbo can do."

Then the *Dauntless* flashed in; not asking but demanding instant right of way.

"Look around, fellows, if you like, but you won't find a damned thing," Kinnison's uncheering conclusion came back as he sprinted toward the dock into which his battleship had settled. "The lug hasn't left a loose end dangling yet."

By the time the great Patrol ship had cleared the stratosphere Kinnison's CRX, powerful and tenacious as it was, was just barely registering a line. But that was enough. Henry Henderson, Master Pilot, stuck the *Dauntless'* needle nose into that line and shoved into the driving projectors every watt of "oof" that those Brobdingnagian creations would take.

They had been following the zwilnik for three days now, Kinnison reflected, and his CRX's were none too strong yet. They were overhauling him mighty slowly; and the *Dauntless* was supposed to be the fastest thing in space. That bucket up ahead had plenty of legs—must have been souped up to the limit. This was apt to be a long chase, but he'd get that bozo if he had to chase him on a geodesic line along the hyper-dimensional curvature of space clear back to Tellus where he started from!

They did not have to circumnavigate total space, of course, but they did almost leave the galaxy before they could get the fugitive upon their plates. The stars were thinning out fast; but still, hazily before them in a vastness of distance, there stretched a milky band of opalescence.

"What's coming up, Hen—a rift?" Kinnison asked.

"Uh-huh, Rift Ninety Four," the pilot replied. "And if I remember right, that arm up ahead is Dunstan's Region and it has never been explored. I'll have the chart-room check up on it."

"Never mind; I'll go check it myself—I'm curious about this whole thing."

Unlike any smaller vessel, the *Dauntless* was large enough so that she could—and hence as a matter of course did—carry every space-chart issued by all the various Boards and Offices and Bureaus concerned with space, astronomy, astrogation, and planetography. She had to, for there were usually minds aboard which were apt at any time to become intensely and unpredictably interested in anything, anywhere. Hence it did not take Kinnison long to obtain what little information there was.

The vacancy they were approaching was Rift Ninety Four, a vast space, practically empty of stars, lying between the main body of the galaxy and a minor branch of one of its prodigious spiral arms. The opalescence ahead was the branch—Dunstan's Region. Henderson was right; it had never been explored.

The Galactic Survey, which has not even yet mapped at all completely the whole of the First Galaxy proper, had of course done no systematic work upon such outlying sections as the spiral arms. Some such regions

were well known and well mapped, it is true; either because its own population, independently developing means of space-flight, had come into
contact with our Civilization upon its own initative or because private
exploration and investigation had opened up profitable lines of commerce. But Dunstan's Region was bare. No people resident in it had ever
made themselves known; no private prospecting, if there had ever been
any such, had revealed anything worthy of exploitation or development.
And, with so many perfectly good uninhabited planets so much nearer to
Galactic Center, it was of course much too far out for colonization.

Through the rift, then, and into Dunstan's Region the *Dauntless*
bored at the unimaginable pace of her terrific full-blast drive. The tracers' beams grew harder and more taut with every passing hour; the fleeing speedster itself grew large and clear upon the plates. The opalescence
of the spiral arm became a firmament of stars. A sun detached itself
from that firmament; a dwarf of Type G. Planets appeared.

One of these in particular, the second out, looked so much like Earth
that it made some of the observers homesick. There were the familiar
polar ice-caps, the atmosphere and stratosphere, the high-piled, billowy
masses of clouds. There were vast blue oceans, there were huge, unfamiliar continents glowing with chlorophyllic green.

At the spectroscopes, at the bolometers, at the many other instruments men went rapidly and skillfully to work.

"Hope the ape's heading for Two, and I think he is," Kinnison remarked, as he studied the results. "People living on that planet would
be human to ten places, for all the tea in China. No wonder he was so
much at home on Tellus . . . Yup, it's Two—there, he's gone inert."

"Whoever is piloting that can went to school just one day in his
life and that day it rained and the teacher didn't come," Henderson
snorted. "And he's trying to balance her down on her tail—look at her
bounce and flop around! He's just begging for a crack-up."

"If he makes it it'll be bad—plenty bad," Kinnison mused. "He'll
gain a lot of time on us while we're rounding the globe on our landing
spiral."

"Why spiral, Kim? Why not follow him down, huh? Our intrinsic
is no worse than his—it's the same one, in fact."

"Get conscious, Hen. This is a superbattlewagon—just in case you
didn't know it before."

"So what? I can certainly handle this super a damn sight better than
that ground-gripper is handling that scrap-heap down there." Henry Henderson, Master Pilot Number One of the Service, was not bragging. He
was merely voicing what to him was the simple and obvious truth.

"Mass is what. Mass and volume and velocity and inertia and power. You never stunted this much mass before, did you?"

"No, but what of it? I took a course in piloting once, in my youth." He was then a grand old man of twenty-eight or thereabouts. "I can line up the main rear center pipe onto any grain of sand you want to pick out on that field, and hold her there until she slags it down."

"If you think you can spell 'able', hop to it!"

"QX, this is going to be fun." Henderson gleefully accepted the challenge, then clicked on his general-alarm microphone. "Strap down, everybody, for inert maneuvering, Class Three, on the tail. Tail over to belly landing. Hipe!"

The Bergenholms were cut and as the tremendously massive super-dreadnought, inert, shot off at an angle under its Tellurian intrinsic velocity, Master Pilot Number One proved his rating. As much a virtuoso of the banks and tiers of blast keys and levers before him as a concert organist is of his instrument, his hands and feet flashed hither and yon. Not music?—the bellowing, crescendo thunders of those jets *were* music to the hard-boiled space-hounds who heard them. And in response to the exact placement and the precisely-measured power of those blasts the great sky-rover spun, twisted, and bucked as her prodigious mass was forced into motionlessness relative to the terrain beneath her.

Three G's, Kinnison reflected, while this was going on. Not bad—he'd guessed it at four or better. He could sit up and take notice at three, and he did so.

This world wasn't very densely populated, apparently. Quite a few cities, but all just about on the equator. Nothing in the temperate zones at all; even the highest power revealed no handiwork of man. Virgin forest, untouched prairie. Lots of roads and things in the torrid zone, but nothing anywhere else. The speedster was making a rough and un-skillful, but not catastrophic landing.

The field which was their destination lay just outside a large city. Funny—it wasn't a space-field at all. No docks, no pits, no ships. Low, flat buildings—hangars. An air-field, then, although not like any air-field he knew. Too small. Gyros? 'Copters? Didn't see any—all little ships. Crates—biplanes and tripes. Made of wire and fabric. Wotta woil, wotta woil!

The *Dauntless* landed, fairly close to the now deserted speedster.

"Hold everything, men," Kinnison cautioned. "Something funny here. I'll do a bit of looking around before we open up."

He was not surprised that the people in and around the airport were human to at least ten places of classification; he had expected that from the planetary data. Nor was he surprised at the fact that they wore no clothing. He had learned long since that, while most human or near-human races—particularly the women—wore at least a few ornaments, the wearing of clothing as such, except when it was actually needed for protection, was far more the exception than the rule. And, just as a Martian, out of deference to conventions, wears a light robe upon Tellus, Kinnison as a matter of course stripped to his evenly-tanned hide when visiting planets upon which nakedness was *de rigueur.* He had attended more than one state function, without a quibble or a qualm, tastefully attired in his Lens.

No, the startling fact was that there was not a man in sight anywhere around the place; there was nothing male perceptible as far as his sense of perception could reach. Women were laboring, women were supervising, women were running the machines. Women were operating the airplanes and servicing them. Women were in the offices. Women and girls and little girls and girl babies filled the waiting rooms and the automobile-like conveyances parked near the airport and running along the streets.

And, even before Kinnison had finished uttering his warning, while his hand was in the air reaching for a spy-ray switch, he felt an alien force attempting to insinuate itself into his mind.

Fat chance! With any ordinary mind it would have succeeded, but in the case of the Gray Lensman it was just like trying to stick a pin unobtrusively into a panther. He put up a solid block automatically, instantaneously; then, a fraction of a second later, a thought-tight screen enveloped the whole vessel.

"Did any of you fellows . . ." he began, then broke off. They wouldn't have felt it, of course; their brains could have been read completely with them none the wiser. He was the only Lensman aboard, and even most Lensmen couldn't . . . this was his oyster. But *that* kind of stuff, on such an apparently backward planet as this? It didn't make sense, unless that zwilnik . . . ah, this *was* his oyster, absolutely!

"Something funnier even than I thought—thought-waves," he calmly continued his original remark. "Thought I'd better undress to go out there, but I'm not going to. I'd wear full armor, except that I may need my hands or have to move fast. If they get insulted at my clothes I'll apologize later."

"But listen, Kim, you can't go out there alone—especially without armor!"

"Sure I can. I'm not taking any chances. You fellows couldn't do me much good out there, but you can here. Break out a 'copter and keep a spy-ray on me. If I give you the signal, go to work with a couple of narrow needle-beams. Pretty sure that I won't need any help, but you can't always tell."

The airlock opened and Kinnison stepped out. He had a high-powered thought-screen, but he did not need it—yet. He had his DeLameters. He had also a weapon deadlier by far even than those mighty portables; a weapon so utterly deadly that he had not used it. He did not need to test it—since Worsel had said that it would work, it would. The trouble with it was that it could not merely disable: if used at all it killed, with complete and grim finality. And behind him he had the full awful power of the *Dauntless*. He had nothing to worry about.

Only when the space-ship had settled down upon and into the hard packed soil of the airport could those at work there realize just how big and how heavy the visitor was. Practically everyone stopped work and stared, and they continued to stare as Kinnison strode toward the office. The Lensman had landed upon many strange planets, he had been met in divers fashions and with various emotions; but never before had his presence stirred up anything even remotely resembling the sentiments written so plainly upon these women's faces and expressed even more plainly in their seething thoughts.

Loathing, hatred, detestation—not precisely any one of the three, yet containing something of each. As though he were a monstrosity, a revolting abnormality that should be destroyed on sight. Beings such as the fantastically ugly, spider-like denizens of Dekanore VI had shuddered at the sight of him, but their thoughts were mild compared to these. Besides, that was natural enough. Any human being would appear a monstrosity to such as those. But these women were human; as human as he was. He didn't get it, at all.

Kinnison opened the door and faced the manager, who was standing at that other-worldly equivalent of a desk. His first glance at her brought to the surface of his mind one of the peculiarities which he had already unconsciously observed. Here, for the first time in his life, he saw a woman without any touch whatever of personal adornment. She was tall and beautifully proportioned, strong and fine; her smooth skin was tanned to a rich and even brown. She was clean, almost blatantly so.

But she wore no jewelry, no bracelets, no ribbons; no decoration of any sort or kind. No paint, no powder, no touch of perfume. Her heavy, bushy eyebrows had never been plucked or clipped. Some of her teeth had been expertly filled, and she had a two-tooth bridge that would have done credit to any Tellurian dentist—but her hair! It, too, was painfully clean, as was the white scalp beneath it, but aesthetically it was a mess. Some of it reached almost to her shoulders, but it was very evident that whenever a lock grew long enough to be a bother she was wont to grab it and hew it off, as close to the skull as possible, with whatever knife, shears, or other implement came readiest to hand.

These thoughts and the general inspection did not take any appreciable length of time, of course. Before Kinnison had taken two steps toward the manager's desk, he directed a thought:

"Kinnison of Sol III—Lensman, Unattached. It is possible, however, that neither Tellus nor the Lens are known upon this planet?"

"Neither is known, nor does anyone of Lyrane care to know anything of either," she replied, coldly. Her brain was keen and clear; her personality vigorous, striking, forceful. But, compared with Kinnison's doubly-Arisian-trained mind, hers was woefully slow. He watched her assemble the mental bolt which was intended to slay him then and there. He let her send it, then struck back. Not lethally, not even paralyzingly, but solidly enough so that she slumped down, almost unconscious, into a nearby chair.

"It's good technique to size a man up before you tackle him, sister," he advised her when she had recovered. "Couldn't you tell from the feel of my mind-block that *you* couldn't crack it?"

"I was afraid so," she admitted, hopelessly, "but I had to kill you if I possibly could. Since you are the stronger you will of course kill me." Whatever else these peculiar women were, they were stark realists. "Go ahead—get it over with . . . But it *can't* be!" Her thought was a wail of protest. "I do not grasp your thought of a 'man', but you are certainly a male; and no mere *male* can be—can *possibly* be, ever—as strong as a person."

Kinnison got that thought perfectly, and it rocked him. She did not think of herself as a woman, a female, at all. She was simply a *person*. She could not understand even dimly Kinnison's reference to himself as a man. To her, "man" and "male" were synonymous terms. Both meant sex, and nothing whatever except sex.

"I have no intention of killing you, or anyone else upon this planet," he informed her levelly, "unless I absolutely have to. But I have chased that speedster over there all the way from Tellus, and I intend to get the man that drove it here, if I have to wipe out half of your population to do it. Is that perfectly clear?"

"That is perfectly clear, male." Her mind was fuzzy with a melange of immiscible emotions. Surprise and relief that she was not to be slain out of hand; disgust and repugnance at the very idea of such a horrible, monstrous male creature having the audacity to exist; stunned, disbelieving wonder at his unprecedented power of mind; a dawning comprehension that there were perhaps some things which she did not know: these and numerous other conflicting thoughts surged through her mind. "But there was no male within the space-traversing vessel which you think of as a 'speedster'," she concluded, surprisingly.

And he knew that she was not lying. "Damnation!" he snorted to himself. "Fighting *women* again!"

"Who was she, then—it, I mean," he hastily corrected the thought. "It was our elder sister . . ."

The thought so translated by the man was not really "sister". That term, having distinctly sexual connotations and implications, would never have entered the mind of any "person" of Lyrane II. "Elder child of the same heritage" was more like it.

". . . and another person from what it claimed was another world," the thought flowed smoothly on. "An entity, rather, not really a person, but you would not be interested in that, of course."

"Of course I would," Kinnison assured her. "In fact, it is this other person, and not your elderly relative, in whom I am interested. But you say that it is an entity, not a person. How come? Tell me all about it."

"Well, it looked like a person, but it wasn't. Its intelligence was low, its brain power was small. And its mind was upon things . . . its thoughts were so . . ."

Kinnison grinned at the Lyranian's efforts to express clearly thoughts so utterly foreign to her mind as to be totally incomprehensible.

"You don't know what that entity was, but I do," he broke in upon her floundering. "It was a person who was also, and quite definitely, a female. Right?"

"But a person couldn't—couldn't possibly—be a female!" she protested. "Why, even biologically, it doesn't make sense. There are no such things as females—there can't be!" and Kinnison saw her viewpoint clearly enough. According to her sociology and conditioning there could not be.

"We'll go into that later," he told her. "What I want now is this female zwilnik. Is she—or it—with your elder relative now?"

"Yes. They will be having dinner in the hall very shortly."

"Sorry to bother, but you'll have to take me to them—right now."

"Oh, may I? Since I could not kill you myself, I must take you to them so they can do it. I have been wondering how I could force you to go there," she explained, naively.

"Henderson?" The Lensman spoke into his microphone—thought-screens, of course, being no barrier to radio waves. "I'm going after the zwilnik. This woman here is taking me. Have the 'copter stay over me, ready to needle anything I tell them to. While I'm gone go over that speeder with a fine-tooth comb, and when you get everything we want, blast it. It and the *Dauntless* are the only spacecraft on the planet. These janes are man-haters and mental killers, so keep your thought-screens up. Don't let them down for a fraction of a second, because they've got plenty of jets and they're just as sweet and reasonable as a cageful of cateagles. Got it?"

"On the tape, chief," came an instant answer. "But don't take any chances, Kim. Sure you can swing it alone?"

"Jets enough and to spare," Kinnison assured him, curtly. Then, as the Tellurians' helicopter shot into the air, he again turned his thought to the manager.

"Let's go," he directed, and she led him across the way to a row of parked ground-cars. She manipulated a couple of levers and smoothly, if slowly, the little vehicle rolled away.

The distance was long and the pace was slow. The woman was driving automatically, the while her every sense was concentrated upon finding some weak point, some chink in his barrier, through which to thrust at him. Kinnison was amazed—stumped—at her fixity of purpose; at her grimly single-minded determination to make an end of him. She was out to get him, and she wasn't fooling.

"Listen, sister," he thought at her, after a few minutes of it; almost plaintively, for him. "Let's be reasonable about this thing. I told you I didn't want to kill you; why in all the iridescent hells of space are you so dead set on killing me? If you don't behave yourself, I'll give you a treatment that will make your head ache for the next six months. Why don't you snap out of it, you dumb little lug, and be friends?"

This thought jarred her so that she stopped the car, the better to stare directly and viciously into his eyes.

"Be *friends*? With a *male*?" The thought literally seared its way into the man's brain.

"Listen, half-wit!" Kinnison stormed, exasperated. "Forget your narrow-minded, one-planet prejudices and think for a minute, if you can think—use that pint of bean soup inside your skull for something besides hating me all over the place. Get this—I am no more a male than you are the kind of a female that you think, by analogy, such a creature would have to be if she could exist in a sane and logical world."

"Oh." The Lyranian was taken aback at such cavalier instruction. "But the others, those in your so-immense vessel, they are of a certainly males," she stated with conviction. "I understood what you told them via your telephone-without-conductors. You have mechanical shields against the thought which kills. Yet you do not have to use it, while the others—males indubitably—do. You yourself are not entirely male; your brain is almost as good as a person's."

"Better, you mean," he corrected her. "You're wrong. All of us of the ship are men—all alike. But a man on a job can't concentrate all the time on defending his brain against attack, hence the use of thought-screens. I can't use a screen out here, because I've got to talk to you people. See?"

"You fear us, then, so little?" she flared, all of her old animosity blazing out anew. "You consider our power, then, so small a thing?"

"Right. Right to a hair," he declared, with tightening jaw. But he did not believe it—quite. This girl was just about as safe to play around with as five-feet-eleven of coiled bushmaster, and twice as deadly.

She could not kill him mentally. Nor could the elder sister—whoever she might be—and her crew; he was pretty sure of that. But if they couldn't do him in by dint of brain it was a foregone conclusion that they would try brawn. And brawn they certainly had. This jade beside him weighed a hundred sixty five or seventy, and she was trained down fine. Hard, limber, and fast. He might be able to lick three or four of them—maybe half a dozen—in a rough-and-tumble brawl; but more than that would mean either killing or being killed. Damn it all! He'd never killed a woman yet, but it looked as though he might have to start in pretty quick now.

"Well, let's get going again," he suggested, "and while we're en route let's see if we can't work out some basis of cooperation—a sort of live-and-let-live arrangement. Since you understood the orders I gave the crew, you realize that our ship carries weapons capable of razing this entire city in a space of minutes." It was a statement, not a question.

"I realize that." The thought was muffled in helpless fury. "Weapons, weapons—always *weapons!* The eternal *male!* If it were not for your huge vessel and the peculiar airplane hovering over us I would claw your eyes out and strangle you with my bare hands!"

"That would be a good trick if you could do it," he countered, equably enough. "But listen, you frustrated young murderess. You have already shown yourself to be, basically, a realist in facing physical facts. Why not face mental, intellectual facts in the same spirit?"

"Why, I do, of course. I *always* do!"

"You do not," he contradicted, sharply. "Males, according to your lights, have two—and only two—attributes. One, they breed. Two, they fight. They fight each other, and everything else, to the death and at the drop of a hat. Right?"

"Right, but . . ."

"But nothing—let me talk. Why didn't you breed the combativeness out of your males, hundreds of generations ago?"

"They tried it once, but the race began to deteriorate," she admitted.

"Exactly. Your whole set-up is cock-eyed—unbalanced. You can think of me only as a male—one to be destroyed on sight, since I am not like one of yours. Yet, when I could kill you and had every reason to do so, I didn't. We can destroy you all, but we won't unless we must. What's the answer?"

"I don't know," she confessed, frankly. Her frenzied desire for killing abated, although her ingrained antipathy and revulsion did not. "In some ways, you do seem to have some of the instincts and qualities of a . . . almost of a person."

"I am a person . . ."

"You are *not!* Do you think that I am to be misled by the silly coverings you wear?"

"Just a minute. I am a person of a race having two *equal* sexes. Equal in every way. Numbers, too—one man and one woman . . ." and he went on to explain to her, as well as he could, the sociology of Civilization.

"Incredible!" she gasped the thought.

"But true," he assured her. "And now are you going to lay off me and behave yourself, like a good little girl, or am I going to have to do a bit of massaging on your brain? Or wind that beautiful body of yours a couple of times around a tree? I'm asking this for your own good, kid, believe me."

"Yes, I do believe you," she marveled. "I am becoming convinced that . . . that perhaps you are a person—at least of a sort—after all."

"Sure I am—that's what I've been trying to tell you for an hour. And cancel that 'of a sort', too . . ."

"But tell me," she interrupted, "a thought you used—'beautiful'. I do not understand it. What does it mean, 'beautiful body'?"

"Holy Klono's whiskers!" If Kinnison had never been stumped before, he was now. How could he explain beauty, or music, or art, to this . . . this matriarchal savage? How to explain cerise to a man born blind? And above all, who had ever heard of having to explain to a woman—to any woman, anywhere in the whole macrocosmic universe—that she in particular was beautiful?

But he tried. In her mind he spread a portrait of her as he had seen her first. He pointed out to her the graceful curves and lovely contours, the lithely flowing lines, the perfection of proportion and modeling and symmetry, the flawlessly smooth, firm-textured skin, the supple, hard-trained fineness of her whole physique. No soap. She tried, in brow-furrowing concentration, to get it, but in vain. It simply did not register.

"But that is merely efficiency, everything you have shown," she declared. "Nothing else. I must be so, for my own good and for the good of those to come. But I think that I have seen some of your beauty," and in turn she sent into his mind a weirdly distorted picture of a human woman. The zwilnik he was following, Kinnison decided instantly.

She would be jeweled, of course, but not that heavily—a horse couldn't carry that load. And no woman ever born put paint on that thick, or reeked so of violent perfume, or plucked her eyebrows to such a thread, or indulged in such a hair-do.

"If that is *beauty,* I want none of it," the Lyranian declared.

Kinnison tried again. He showed her a waterfall, this time, in a stupendous gorge, with appropriate cloud formations and scenery. That, the girl declared, was simply erosion. Geological formations and mete-orological phenomena. Beauty still did not appear. Painting, it appeared to her, was a waste of pigment and oil. Useless and inefficient—for any purpose of record the camera was much faster and much more accurate. Music—vibrations in the atmosphere—would of necessity be simply a noise; and noise—any kind of noise—was not efficient.

"You poor little devil." The Lensman gave up. "You poor, ignorant, soul-starved little devil. And the worst of it is that you don't even real-ize—and never can realize—what you are missing."

"Don't be silly." For the first time, the woman actually laughed. "You are utterly foolish to make such a fuss about such trivial things."

Kinnison quit, appalled. He knew, now, that he and this apparently human creature beside him were as far apart as the Galactic Poles in every essential phase of life. He had heard of matriarchies, but he had never considered what a real matriarchy, carried to its logical conclusion, would be like.

This was it. For ages there had been, to all intents and purposes, only one sex; the masculine element never having been allowed to rise above the fundamental necessity of reproducing the completely domi-nant female. And that dominant female had become, in every respect save the purely and necessitously physical one, absolutely and utterly sexless. Men, upon Lyrane II, were dwarfs about thirty inches tall. They had the temper and the disposition of a mad Radeligian cateagle, the intellectual capacity of a Zabriskan fontema. They were not regarded as people, either at birth or at any subsequent time. To maintain a static population, each person gave birth to one person, on the grand average. The occasional male baby—about one in a hundred—did not count. He was not even kept at home, but was taken immediately to the "maletorium", in which he lived until attaining maturity.

One man to a hundred or so women for a year, then death. The hundred persons had their babies at twenty-one or twenty-two years of age—they lived to an average age of a hundred years—then calmly blasted their male's mind and disposed of his carcass. The male was not exactly an outcast; not precisely a pariah. He was tolerated as a necessary adjunct to the society of persons, but in no sense whatever was he a member of it.

The more Kinnison pondered this hook-up the more appalled he became. Physically, these people were practically indistinguishable from human, Tellurian, Caucasian women. But mentally, intellectually, in every other way, how utterly different! Shockingly, astoundingly so to any really human being, whose entire outlook and existence is fundamentally, however unconsciously or subconsciously, based upon and conditioned by the prime division of life into two cooperant sexes. It didn't seem, at first glance, that such a cause could have such terrific effects; but here they were. In cold reality, these women were no more human than were the . . . the Eich. Take the Posenians, or the Rigellians, or even the Velantians. Any normal, stay-at-home Tellurian woman would pass out cold if she happened to stumble onto Worsel in a dark alley at night. Yet the members of his repulsively reptilian-appearing race, merely because of having a heredity of equality and cooperation between the sexes, were in essence more nearly human than were these tall, splendidly-built, actually and intrinsically beautiful creatures of Lyrane II!

"This is the hall," the person informed him, as the car came to a halt in front of a large structure of plain gray stone. "Come with me."

"Gladly," and they walked across the peculiarly bare grounds. They were side by side, but a couple of feet apart. She had been altogether too close to him in the little car. She did not want this male—or *any* male—to touch her or to be near her. And, considerably to her surprise, if the truth were to be known, the feeling was entirely mutual. Kinnison would have preferred to touch a Borovan slime-lizard.

They mounted the granite steps. They passed through the dull, weather-beaten portal. They were still side by side—but they were now a full yard apart.

4

KINNISON CAPTURES . . .

Listen, my beautiful but dumb guide," Kinnison counseled the Lyranian girl as they neared their objective. "I see that you're forgetting all your good girl-scout resolutions and are getting all hot and bothered again. I'm telling you now for the last time to watch your step. If that zwilnik person has even a split second's warning that I'm on her tail all hell will be out for noon, and I don't mean perchance."

"But I must notify the Elder One that I am bringing you in," she told him. "One simply does not intrude unannounced. It is not permitted."

"QX. Stick to the announcement, though, and don't put out any funny ideas or I'll lay you out cold. I'll send a thought along, just to make sure."

But he did more than that, for even as he spoke his sense of perception was already in the room to which they were going. It was a large room, and bare; filled with tables except for a clear central space upon which at the moment a lithe and supple person was doing what seemed to be a routine of acrobatic dancing, interspersed with suddenly motionless posings and posturings of extreme technical difficulty. At the tables were seated a hundred or so Lyranians, eating.

Kinnison was not interested in the floor show, whatever it was, nor in the massed Lyranians. The zwilnik was what he was after. Ah, there she was, at a ringside table—a small, square table seating four—near the door. Her back was to it—good. At her left, commanding the central view of the floor, was a redhead, sitting in a revolving, reclining chair, the only such seat in the room. Probably the Big Noise herself—the Elder One. No matter, he wasn't interested in her, either—yet. His attention flashed back to his proposed quarry and he almost gasped.

For she, like Dessa Desplaines, was an Aldebaranian, and she was everything that the Desplaines woman had been—more so, if possible. She was a seven-sector callout, a thionite dream if there ever was one. And jewelry! This Lyranian tiger hadn't exaggerated that angle very much, at that. Her breast-shields were of gold and platinum filigree, thickly studded with diamonds, emeralds, and rubies, in intricate designs. Her shorts, or rather trunks, made of something that looked like glamorette, blazed with gems. A cleverly concealed dagger, with a jeweled haft and a vicious little fang of a blade. Rings, even a thumb-ring. A necklace which was practically a collar flashed all the colors of the rainbow. Bracelets, armlets, anklets and knee-bands. High-laced dress boots, jeweled from stem to gudgeon. Ear-rings, and a meticulous, micrometrically precise coiffure held in place by at least a dozen glittering buckles, combs and barrettes.

"Holy Klono's brazen tendons!" the Lensman whistled to himself, for every last, least one of those stones was the clear quill. "Half a million credits if it's a millo's worth!"

But he was not particularly interested in this jeweler's vision of what the well-dressed lady zwilnik will wear. There were other, far more important things. Yes, she had a thought-screen. It was off, and its battery was mighty low, but it would still work; good thing he had blocked the warning. And she had a hollow tooth, too, but he'd see to it that she didn't get a chance to swallow its contents. She knew plenty, and he hadn't chased her this far to let her knowledge be obliterated by that hellish Boskonian drug.

They were at the door now. Disregarding the fiercely-driven mental protests of his companion, Kinnison flung it open, stiffening up his mental guard as he did so. Simultaneously he invaded the zwilnik's mind with a flood of force, clamping down so hard that she could not move a single voluntary muscle. Then, paying no attention whatever to the shocked surprise of the assembled Lyranians, he strode directly up to the Aldebaranian and bent her head back into the crook of his elbow. Forcibly but gently he opened her mouth. With thumb and forefinger he deftly removed the false tooth. Releasing her then, mentally and physically, he dropped his spoil to the cement floor and ground it savagely to bits under his hard and heavy heel.

The zwilnik screamed wildly, piercingly at first. However, finding that she was getting no results, from Lensman or Lyranian, she subsided quickly into alertly watchful waiting.

Still unsatisfied, Kinnison flipped out one of his DeLameters and flamed the remains of the capsule of worse than paralyzing fluid, caring not a whit that his vicious portable, even in that brief instant, seared a hole a foot deep into the floor. Then and only then did he turn his attention to the redhead in the boss's chair.

He had to hand it to Elder Sister—through all this sudden and to her entirely unprecedented violence of action she hadn't turned a hair. She had swung her chair around so that she was facing him. Her back was to the athletic dancer who, now holding a flawlessly perfect pose, was going on with the act as though nothing out of the ordinary were transpiring. She was leaning backward in the armless swivel chair, her right foot resting upon its pedestal. Her left ankle was crossed over her right knee, her left knee rested lightly against the table's top. Her hands were clasped together at the nape of her neck, supporting her red-thatched head; her elbows spread abroad in easy, indolent grace. Her eyes, so deeply, darkly green as to be almost black stared up unwinkingly into the Lensman's— "insolently" was the descriptive word that came first to his mind.

If the Elder Sister was supposed to be old, Kinnison reflected as he studied appreciatively the startlingly beautiful picture which the artless Chief Person of this tribe so unconsciously made, she certainly belied her looks. As far as looks went, she really qualified—whatever it took, she in abundant measure had. Her hair was not really red, either. It was a flamboyant, gorgeous auburn, about the same color as Clarrissa's own, and just as thick. And it wasn't all haggled up. Accidently, of course, and no doubt because on her particular job her hair didn't get in the way very often, it happened to be a fairly even, shoulder-length bob. What a mop! And damned if it wasn't wavy! Just as she was, with no dolling up at all, she'd be a primary beam on any man's planet. She had this zwilnik houri here, knockout that she was and with all her war-paint and feathers, blasted clear out of the ether. But this queen bee had a sting; she was still boring away at his shield. He'd better let her know that she didn't even begin to have enough jets to swing *that* load.

"QX, ace, cut the gun!" he directed, crisply. "Ace", from him, was a complimentary term indeed. "Pipe down—that's all of that kind of stuff from you. I stood for this much of it, just to show you that you can't get to the first check-station with that kind of fuel, but enough is a great plenty." At the sheer cutting power of the thought, rebroadcast no doubt by the airport manager, Lyranian activity throughout the room came to a halt. This was decidedly out of the ordinary. For a male mind—any male mind—to be able even momentarily to resist that of the meanest person of Lyrane was starkly unthinkable. The Elder's graceful body tensed, into her eyes there crept a dawning doubt, a peculiar, wondering uncertainty. Of fear there was none; all these sexless Lyranian women were brave to the point of foolhardiness.

"You tell her, draggle-pate," he ordered his erstwhile guide. "It took me hell's own time to make you understand that I mean business, but you talk her language—see how fast you can get the thing through Her Royal Nibs's skull."

It did not take long. The lovely, dark-green eyes held conviction, now; but also a greater uncertainty.

"It will be best, I think, to kill you now, instead of allowing you to leave . . ." she began.

"*Allow* me to leave!" Kinnison exploded. "Where do you get such funny ideas as that killing stuff? Just who, Toots, is going to keep me from leaving?"

"This." At the thought a weirdly conglomerate monstrosity which certainly had not been in the dining hall an instant before leaped at Kinnison's throat. It was a frightful thing indeed, combining the worst features of the reptile and the feline, a serpent's head upon a panther's body. Through the air it hurtled, terrible claws unsheathed to rend and venomous fangs out-thrust to stab.

Kinnison had never before met that particular form of attack, but he knew instantly what it was—knew that neither leather nor armor of proof nor screen of force could stop it. He knew that the thing was real only to the woman and himself, that it was not only invisible, but non-existent to everyone else. He also knew how ultimately deadly the creature was, knew that if claw or fang should strike him he would die then and there.

Ordinarily very efficient, to the Lensman this method of slaughter was crude and amateurish. No such figment of any other mind could harm him unless he knew that it was coming; unless his mind was given ample time in which to appreciate—in reality, to manufacture—the danger he was in. And in *that* time *his* mind could negate it. He had two defenses. He could deny the monster's existence, in which case it would simply disappear. Or, a much more difficult, but technically a much nicer course, would be to take over control and toss it back at her.

Unhesitatingly he did the latter. In mid-leap the apparition swerved, in a full right-angle turn, directly toward the quietly-poised body of the Lyranian. She acted just barely in time; the madly-reaching claws were within scant inches of her skin when they vanished. Her eyes widened in frightened startlement; she was quite evidently shaken to the core by the Lensman's viciously skillful riposte. With an obvious effort she pulled herself together.

"Or these, then, if I must," and with a sweeping gesture of thought she indicated the roomful of her Lyranian sisters.

"How?" Kinnison asked, pointedly.

"By force of numbers; by sheer weight and strength. You can kill many of them with your weapons, of course, but not enough or quickly enough."

"You yourself would be the first to die," he cautioned her; and, since she was en rapport with his very mind, she knew that it was not a threat, but the stern finality of fact.

"What of that?" He in turn knew that she, too, meant precisely that and nothing else.

He had another weapon, but she would not believe it without a demonstration, and he simply could not prove that weapon upon an unarmed, defenseless woman, even though she was a Lyranian.

Stalemate.

No, the 'copter. "Listen, Queen of Sheba, to what I tell my boys," he ordered, and spoke into his microphone.

"Ralph? Stick a one-second needle down through the floor here; close enough to make her jump, but far enough away so as not to blister her fanny."

At his word a narrow, but ragingly incandescent pencil of destruction raved downward through ceiling and floor. So inconceivably hot was it that if it had been a fraction larger, it would have ignited the Elder Sister's very chair. Effortlessly, insatiably it consumed everything in its immediate path, radiating the while the entire spectrum of vibrations. It was unbearable, and the auburn-haired creature did indeed jump, in spite of herself—half-way to the door. The rest of the hitherto imperturbable persons clustered together in panic-stricken knots.

"You see, Cleopatra," Kinnison explained, as the dreadful needle-beam expired, "I've got plenty of stuff if I want to—or have to—use it. The boys up there will stick a needle like that through the brain of any one or everyone in this room if I give the word. I don't want to kill any of you unless it's necessary, as I explained to your misbarbered friend here, but I am leaving here alive and all in one piece, and I'm taking this Aldebaranian along with me, in the same condition. If I must, I'll lay down a barrage like that sample you just saw, and only the zwilnik and I will get out alive. How about it?"

"What are you going to do with the stranger?" the Lyranian asked, avoiding the issue.

"I'm going to take some information away from her, that's all. Why? What were you going to do with her yourselves?"

"We were—and are going to kill it," came a flashing reply. The lethal

bolt came even before the reply; but, fast as the Elder One was, the Gray
Lensman was faster. He blanked out the thought, reached over and flipped
on the Aldebaranian's thought-screen.

"Keep it on until we get to the ship, sister," he spoke aloud in the
girl's native tongue. "Your battery's low, I know, but it'll last long enough.
These hens seem to be strictly on the peck."

"I'll say they are—you don't know the half of it." Her voice was low,
rich, vibrant. "Thanks, Kinnison."

"Listen, Red-Top, what's the percentage in playing so dirty?" the
Lensman complained then. "I'm doing my damndest to let you off easy, but
I'm all done dickering. Do we go out of here peaceably, or do we fry you
and your crew to cinders in your own lard, and walk out over the grease
spots? It's strictly up to you, but you'll decide right here and right now."

The Elder One's face was hard, her eyes flinty. Her fingers were
curled into ball-tight fists. "I suppose, since we cannot stop you, we must
let you go free," she hissed, in helpless but controlled fury. "If by giving
my life and the lives of all these others we could kill you, here and now
would you two die . . . but as it is, you may go."

"But why all the rage?" the puzzled Lensman asked. "You strike me
as being, on the whole, reasoning creatures. You in particular went to
Tellus with this zwilnik here, so you should know . . ."

"I *do* know," the Lyranian broke in. "That is why I would go to any
length, pay any price whatever, to keep you from returning to your own
world, to prevent the inrush of your barbarous hordes here . . ."

"Oh! So *that's* it!" Kinnison exclaimed. "You think that some of our
people might want to settle down here, or to have traffic with you?"

"Yes." She went into a eulogy concerning Lyrane II, concluding, "I
have seen the planets and the races of your so-called Civilization, and I
detest them and it. Never again shall any of us leave Lyrane; nor, if I can
help it, shall any stranger ever come here."

"Listen, angel-face!" the man commanded. "You're as mad as a
Radeligian cateagle—you're as cockeyed as Trenco's ether. Get this, and
get it straight. To any really intelligent being of any one of forty million
planets, your whole Lyranian race would be a total loss with no insurance.
You're a God-forsaken, spiritually and emotionally starved, barren, mentally ossified, and completely monstrous mess. If I, personally, never see
either you or your planet again, that will be exactly twenty seven minutes
too soon. This girl here thinks the same of you as I do. If anybody else
ever hears of Lyrane and thinks he wants to visit it, I'll take him out
of—I'll knock a hip down on him if I have to, to keep him away from
here. Do I make myself clear?"

"Oh, yes—perfectly!" she fairly squealed in school-girlish delight.

The Lensman's tirade, instead of infuriating her further, had been sweet music to her peculiarly insular mind. "Go, then, at once—hurry! Oh, please, hurry! Can you drive the car back to your vessel, or will one of us have to go with you?"

"Thanks. I could drive your car, but it won't be necessary. The 'copter will pick us up."

He spoke to the watchful Ralph, then he and the Aldebaranian left the hall, followed at a careful distance by the throng. The helicopter was on the ground, waiting. The man and the woman climbed aboard.

"Clear ether, persons!" The Lensman waved a salute to the crowd and the Tellurian craft shot into the air.

Thence to the *Dauntless,* which immediately did likewise, leaving behind her, upon the little airport, a fused blob of metal that had once been the zwilniks' speedster. Kinnison studied the white face of his captive, then handed her a tiny canister.

"Fresh battery for your thought-screen generator; yours is about shot." Since she made no motion to accept it, he made the exchange himself and tested the result. It worked. "What's the matter with you, kid, anyway? I'd say you were starved, if I hadn't caught you at a full table."

"I am starved," the girl said, simply. "I couldn't eat there. I knew they were going to kill me, and it . . . it sort of took away my appetite."

"Well, what are we waiting for? I'm hungry, too—let's go eat."

"Not with you, either, any more than with them. I thanked you, Lensman, for saving my life there, and I meant it. I thought then and still think that I would rather have you kill me than those horrible, monstrous women, but I simply can't eat."

"But I'm not even thinking of killing you—can't you get that through your skull? I don't make war on women; you ought to know that by this time."

"You will have to." The girl's voice was low and level. "You didn't kill any of those Lyranians, no, but you didn't chase them a million parsecs, either. We have been taught ever since we were born that you Patrolmen always torture people to death. I don't quite believe that of you personally, since I have had a couple of glimpses into your mind, but you'll kill me before I'll talk. At least, I hope and I believe that I can hold out."

"Listen, girl." Kinnison was in deadly earnest. "You are in no danger whatever. You are just as safe as though you were in Klono's hip pocket. You have some information that I want, yes, and I will get it, but in the process I will neither hurt you nor do you mental or physical harm. The only torture you will undergo will be that which, as now, you give yourself."

"But you called me a . . . a zwilnik, and they *always* kill them," she protested.

"Not always. In battles and in raids, yes. Captured ones are tried in court. If found guilty, they used to go into the lethal chambers. Sometimes they do yet, but not usually. We have mental therapists now who can operate on a mind if there's anything there worth saving."

"And you think that I will wait to stand trial, in the entirely negligible hope that your bewhiskered, fossilized therapists will find something in me worth saving?"

"You won't have to," Kinnison laughed. "Your case has already been decided—in your favor. I am neither a policeman nor a Narcotics man; but I happen to be qualified as judge, jury, and executioner. I am a therapist to boot. I once saved a worse zwilnik than you are, even though she wasn't such a knockout. Now do we eat?"

"Really? You aren't just . . . just giving me the needle?"

The Lensman flipped off her screen and gave her unmistakable evidence. The girl, hitherto so unmovedly self-reliant, broke down. She recovered quickly, however, and in Kinnison's cabin she ate ravenously.

"Have you a cigarette?" She sighed with repletion when she could hold no more food.

"Sure. Alsakanite, Venerian, Tellurian, most anything—we carry a couple of hundred different brands. What would you like?"

"Tellurian, by all means. I had a package of Camerfields once—they were gorgeous. Would you have those, by any chance?"

"Uh-huh," he assured her. "Quartermaster! Carton of Camerfields, please." It popped out of the pneumatic tube in seconds. "Here you are sister."

The glittery girl drew the fragrant smoke deep down into her lungs.

"Ah, that tastes good! Thanks, Kinnison—for everything. I'm glad you kidded me into eating; that was the finest meal I ever ate. But it won't take, really. I've never broken yet, and I won't break now. If I do, I won't be worth a damn, to myself or to anybody else, from then on." She crushed out the butt. "So let's get on with the third degree. Bring on your rubber hose and your lights and your drip-can."

"You're still on the wrong foot, Toots," Kinnison said, pityingly. What a frightful contrast there was between her slimly rounded body, in its fantastically gorgeous costume, and the stark somberness of her eyes! "There'll be no third degree, no hose, no lights, nothing like that. In fact, I'm not even going to talk to you until you've had a good long sleep. You don't look hungry any more, but you're still not in tune, by seven thousand kilocycles. How long has it been since you really slept?"

"A couple of weeks, at a guess. Maybe a month."

"Thought so. Come on; you're going to sleep now."

The girl did not move. "With whom?" she asked, quietly. Her voice did not quiver, but stark terror lay in her mind and her hand crept unconsciously toward the hilt of her dagger.

"Holy Klono's claws!" Kinnison snorted, staring at her in wide-eyed wonder. "Just what kind of a bunch of hyenas do you think you've got into, anyway?"

"Bad," the girl replied, gravely. "Not the worst possible, perhaps, but from my standpoint plenty bad enough. What can I expect from the Patrol except what I do expect? You don't need to kid me along, Kinnison. I can take it, and I'd a lot rather take it standing up, facing it, than have you sneak up on me with it after giving me your shots in the arm."

"What somebody has done to you is a sin and a shrieking shame," Kinnison declared, feelingly. "Come on, you poor little devil." He picked up sundry pieces of apparatus, then, taking her arm, he escorted her to another, almost luxuriously furnished cabin.

"That door," he explained carefully, "is solid chrome-tungsten-molybdenum steel. The lock can't be picked. There are only two keys to it in existence, and here they are. There's a bolt, too, that's proof against anything short of a five-hundred-ton hydraulic jack, or an atomic-hydrogen cutting torch. Here's a full-coverage screen, and a twenty-foot spy-ray block. There is your stuff out of the speedster. If you want help, or anything to eat or drink, or anything else that can be expected aboard a ship like this, there's the communicator. QX?"

"Then you really mean it? That I . . . that you . . . I mean . . ."

"Absolutely," he assured her. "Just that. You are completely the master of your destiny, the captain of your soul. Good-night."

"Good-night, Kinnison. Good-night, and th . . . thanks." The girl threw herself face downward upon the bed in a storm of sobs.

Nevertheless, as Kinnison started back toward his own cabin, he heard the massive bolt click into its socket and felt the blocking screens go on.

5

. . . ILLONA OF LONABAR

Some twelve or fourteen hours later, after the Aldebaranian girl had had her breakfast, Kinnison went to her cabin.

"Hi, Cutie, you look better. By the way, what's your name, so we'll know what to call you?"

"Illona."

"Illona what?"

"No what—just Illona, that's all."

"How do they tell you from other Illonas, then?"

"Oh, you mean my registry number. In the Aldebaranian language there are not the symbols—it would have to be 'The Illona who is the daughter of Porlakent the potter who lives in the house of the wheel upon the road of . . .' "

"Hold everything—we'll call you Illona Potter." He eyed her keenly. "I thought your Aldebaranian wasn't so hot—didn't seem possible that I could have got *that* rusty. You haven't been on Aldebaran II for a long time, have you?"

"No, we moved to Lonabar when I was about six."

"Lonabar? Never heard of it—I'll check up on it later. Your stuff was all here, wasn't it? Did any of the red-headed person's things get mixed in?"

"Things?" She giggled sunnily, then sobered in quick embarrassment. "She didn't carry any. They're horrid, I think—positively *inde-cent*—to run around that way."

"Hm . . . m. Glad you brought the point up. You've got to put on some clothes aboard this ship, you know."

"Me?" she demanded. "Why, I'm fully dressed . . ." She paused, then shrank together visibly. "Oh! Tellurians—I remember, all those coverings! You mean, then . . . you think I'm shameless and indecent too?"

"No. Not at all—yet." At his obvious sincerity Illona unfolded again. "Most of us—especially the officers—have been on so many different planets, had dealings with so many different types and kinds of entities, that we're used to anything. When we visit a planet that goes naked, we do also, as a matter of course; when we hit one that muffles up to the smothering point we do that, too. 'When in Rome, be a Roman candle', you know. The point is that we're at home here, you're the visitor. It's all a matter of convention, of course; but a rather important one. Don't you think so?"

"Covering up, certainly. Uncovering is different. They told me to be sure to, but I simply *can't*. I tried it back there, but I felt *naked!*"

"QX—we'll have the tailor make you a dress or two. Some of the boys haven't been around very much, and you'd look pretty bare to them. Everything you've got on, jewelry and all, wouldn't make a Tellurian sun-suit, you know."

"Then have them hurry up the dress, please. But this isn't jewelry, it is . . ."

"Jet back, beautiful. I know gold, and platinum, and . . ."

"The metal is expensive, yes," Illona conceded. "These alone," she tapped one of the delicate shields, "cost five days of work. But base metal stains the skin blue and green and black, so what can one do? As for the beads, they are synthetics—junk. Poor girls, if they buy it themselves, do not wear jewelry, but beads, like these. Half a day's work buys the lot."

"What!" Kinnison demanded.

"Certainly. Rich girls only, or poor girls who do not work, wear real jewelry, such as . . . the Aldebaranian has not the words. Let me think at you, please?"

"Sorry, nothing there that I recognize at all," Kinnison answered, after studying a succession of thought-images of multi-colored, spectacular gems. "That's one to file away in the book, too, believe me. But as to that 'junk' you've got draped all over yourself—half a day's pay—what do you work at for a living, when you work?"

"I'm a dancer—like this." She leaped lightly to her feet and her left boot whizzed past her ear in a flashingly fast high kick. Then followed a series of gyrations and contortions, for which the Lensman knew no names, during which the girl seemed a practically boneless embodiment of suppleness and grace. She sat down; meticulous hairdress scarcely rumpled, not a buckle or bracelet awry, breathing hardly one count faster.

"Nice." He applauded briefly. "Hard for me to evaluate such talent as that—I thought you were a pilot. However, on Tellus or any one of a thousand other planets I could point out to you, you can sell that 'junk' you're wearing for—at a rough guess—about fifty thousand days' work."

"Impossible!"

"True, nevertheless. So, before we land, you'd better give them to me, so that I can send them to a bank for you, under guard."

"If I land." As Kinnison spoke Illona's manner changed; darkened as though an inner light had been extinguished. "You have been so friendly and nice, I was forgetting where I am and the business ahead. Putting it off won't make it any easier. Better be getting on with it, don't you think?"

"Oh, that? That's all done, long ago."

"What?" she almost screamed. "It isn't! It *couldn't* be!"

"Sure. I got most of the stuff I wanted last night, while I was changing your thought-screen battery. Menjo Bleeko, your big-shot boss, and so on."

"You didn't! But . . . you must have, at that, to know it . . . but you didn't hurt me, or anything . . . you couldn't have operated—changed me, because I have all my memories . . . or seem to . . . I'm not an idiot, I mean any more than usual . . ."

"You've been taught a good many sheer lies, and quite a few half truths," he informed her, evenly. "For instance, what did they tell you that hollow tooth would do to you when you broke the seal?"

"Make my mind a blank. But one of their doctors would get hold of me very soon and give me the antidote that would restore me exactly as I was before."

"That is one of the half truths. It would certainly have made your mind a blank, but only by blasting most of your memory files out of existence. Their therapists would 'restore' you by substituting other memories for your real ones—whatever other ones they pleased."

"How horrible! How perfectly ghastly! That was why you treated it so, then; as though it were a snake. I wondered at your savagery toward it. But how, really, do I know that you are telling the truth?"

"You don't," he admitted. "You will have to make your own decisions after acquiring full information."

"You are a therapist," she remarked, shrewdly. "But if you operated on my mind you didn't 'save' me, because I still think exactly the same as I always did about the Patrol and everything pertaining to it . . . or do I? . . . Or is this . . ." her eyes widened with a startling possibility.

"No, I didn't operate," he assured her. "No such operation can possibly be done without leaving scars—breaks in the memory chains—that you can find in a minute if you look for them. There are no breaks or blanks in any chain in your mind."

"No—at least, I can't find any," she reported after a few minutes' thought. "But why didn't you? You can't turn me loose this way, you know—a z . . . an enemy of your society."

"You don't need saving," he grinned. "You believe in absolute good and absolute evil, don't you?"

"Why of course—certainly! *Everybody* must!"

"Not necessarily. Some of the greatest thinkers in the universe do not." His voice grew somber, then lightened again. "Such being the case, however, all you need to 'save' yourself is experience, observation, and knowledge of both sides of the question. You're a colossal little fraud, you know."

"How do you mean?" She blushed vividly, her eyes wavered.

"Pretending to be such a hard-boiled egg. 'Never broke yet'. Why should you break, when you've never been under pressure?"

"I have so!" she flared. "What do you suppose I'm carrying this knife for?"

"Oh, that." He mentally shrugged the wicked little dagger aside as he pondered. "You little lamb in wolf's clothing . . . but at that, your memories may, I think, be altogether too valuable to monkey with . . . there's something funny about this whole matrix—*damned* funny. Come clean, baby-face—why?"

"They told me to," she admitted, wriggling slightly. "To act tough—really tough. As though I were an adventuress who had been everywhere and had done . . . done everything. That the worse I acted the better I would get along in your Civilization."

"I suspected something of the sort. And what did you zwil—excuse me, you folks—go to Lyrane for, in the first place?"

"I don't know. From chance remarks I gathered that we were to land on one of the planets—any one, I supposed—and wait for somebody."

"What were you, personally, going to do?"

"I don't know that, either—not exactly, that is. I was to take some kind of a ship somewhere, but I don't know what, or when, or where,

or why, or whether I was to go alone or take somebody. Whoever it was
that we were going to meet was going to give us orders."

"How come those women killed your men? Didn't they have
thought-screens, too?"

"No. They weren't agents—just soldiers. They shot about a dozen
of the Lyranians when we first landed, just to show their authority, then
they dropped dead."

"Um. Poor technique, but typically Boskonian. Your trip to Tellus
was more or less accidental, then?"

"Yes. I wanted her to take me back to Lonabar, but she wouldn't.
She couldn't have, anyway, because she didn't know any more about
where it is than I did."

"Huh?" Kinnison blurted. "You don't know where your own home
planet is? What the hell kind of a pilot are you, anyway?"

"Oh, I'm not really a pilot. Just what they made me learn after we
left Lonabar, so I'd be able to make that trip. Lonabar wasn't shown on
any of the charts we had aboard. Neither was Lyrane—that was why I
had to make my own chart, to get back there from Tellus."

"But you *must* know *something!*" Kinnison fumed. "Stars? Constellations? The Galaxy—the Milky Way?"

"The Milky Way, yes. By its shape, Lonabar isn't anywhere near
the center of the galaxy. I've been trying to remember if there were any
noticeable star configurations, but I can't. You see, I wasn't the least bit
interested in such things, then."

"Hell's Brazen Hinges! You can't be *that* dumb—*nobody* can! Any
Tellurian infant old enough to talk knows either the Big Dipper or the
Southern Cross! Hold it—I'm coming in and find out for myself."

He came—but he did not find out.

"Well, I guess people can be that dumb, since you so indubitably
are," he admitted then. "Or—maybe—aren't there any?"

"Honestly, Lensman, I don't know. There were lots of stars, of
course . . . if there were any striking configurations I might have noticed
them; but I might not have, too. As I said, I wasn't the least bit interested."

"That was very evident," dryly. "However, excuse me, please, for
talking so rough."

"Rough? Of course, sir," Illona giggled. "That wasn't rough, comparatively—and nobody ever apologized before—I'd like awfully well
to help you, sir, if I possibly can."

"I know you would, Toots, and thanks. To get back onto the beam,
what put it into Helen's mind to go to Tellus?"

"She learned about Tellus and the Patrol from our minds—none of them could believe at first that there were any inhabited worlds except their own—and wanted to study them at first hand. She took our ship and made me fly it."

"I see. I'm not surprised. I thought that there was something remarkably screwy about those activities—they seemed so aimless and so barren of results—but I couldn't put my finger on it. And we crowded her so close that she decided to flit for home. You could see her, but nobody else could—that she didn't want to."

"That was it. She said that she was being hampered by a mind of power. That was you, of course?"

"And others. Well, that's that, for a while."

He called the tailor in. No, he didn't have a thing to make a girl's dress out of, especially not a girl like that. She should wear glamorette, and sheer—very sheer. He didn't know a thing about ladies' tailoring, either; he hadn't made a gown since he was knee-high to a duck. All he had in the shop was coat-linings. Perhaps nylon would do, after a fashion. He remembered now, he did have a bolt of nylon that wasn't any good for linings—not stiff enough, and red. Too heavy, of course, but it would drape well.

It did. She came swaggering back, an hour or so later, the hem of her skirt swishing against the tops of her high-laced boots.

"Do you like it?" she asked, pirouetting gayly.

"Fine!" he applauded, and it was. The tailor had understated tremendously both his ability and the resources of his shop.

"Now what? I don't have to stay in my room all the time now, please?"

"I'll say not. The ship is yours. I want you to get acquainted with every man on board. Go anywhere you like—except the private quarters, of course—even to the control room. The boys all know that you're at large."

"The language—but I'm talking English now!"

"Sure. I've been giving it to you right along. You know it as well as I do."

She stared at him in awe. Then, her natural buoyancy asserting itself, she flitted out of the room with a wave of her hand.

And Kinnison sat down to think. A girl—a kid who wasn't dry behind the ears yet—wearing beads worth a full grown fortune, sent somewhere . . . to do what? Lyrane II, a perfect matriarchy. Lonabar, a planet of zwilniks that knew all about Tellus, but wasn't on any Patrol chart, sending expeditions to Lyrane. To the system, perhaps not specifically to Lyrane II. Why? For what? To do what? Strange, new jewels of fabulous value. What was the hookup? It didn't make any kind of sense yet . . . not enough data . . .

And faintly, waveringly, barely impinging upon the outermost, most tenuous fringes of his mind he felt something: the groping, questing summons of an incredibly distant thought.

"Male of Civilization . . . Person of Tellus . . . Kinnison of Tellus . . . Lensman Kinnison of Sol III . . . Any Lens-bearing officer of the Galactic Patrol . . ." Endlessly the desperately urgent, almost imperceptible thought implored.

Kinnison stiffened. He reached out with the full power of his mind, seized the thought, tuned to it, and hurled a reply—and when *that* mind really pushed a thought, it traveled.

"Kinnison of Tellus acknowledging!" His answer fairly crackled on its way.

"You do not know my name," the stranger's thought came clearly now. "I am the 'Toots', the 'Red-Top', the 'Queen of Sheba', the 'Cleopatra', the Elder Person of Lyrane II. Do you remember me, Kinnison of Tellus?"

"I certainly do!" he shot back. What a brain—what a *terrific* brain—that sexless woman had!

"We are invaded by manlike beings in ships of space, who wear screens against our thoughts and who slay without cause. Will you help us with your ship of might and your mind of power?"

"Just a sec, Toots—*Henderson!*" Orders snapped. The *Dauntless* spun end-for-end.

"QX, Helen of Troy," he reported then. "We're on our way back there at maximum blast. Say, that name 'Helen of Troy' fits you better than anything else I have called you. You don't know it, of course, but that other Helen launched a thousand ships. You're launching only one; but believe me, Babe, the old *Dauntless* is SOME ship!"

"I hope so." The Elder Person, ignoring the by-play, went directly to the heart of the matter in her usual pragmatic fashion. "We have no right to ask; you have every reason to refuse . . ."

"Don't worry about that, Helen. We're all good little Boy Scouts at heart. We're supposed to do a good deed every day, and we've missed a lot of days lately."

"You are what you call 'kidding', I think." A matriarch could not be expected to possess a sense of humor. "But I do not lie to you or pretend. We did not, do not now, and never will like you or yours. With us now, however, it is that you are much the lesser of two terrible evils.

If you will aid us now we will tolerate your Patrol; we will even promise to endure others of your kind."

"And that's big of you, Helen, no fooling." The Lensman was really impressed. The plight of the Lyranians must be desperate indeed. "Just keep a stiff upper lip, all of you. We're coming loaded for bear, and we are not exactly creeping."

Nor were they. The big cruiser had plenty of legs and she was using them all; the engineers were giving her all the oof her drivers would take. She was literally blasting a hole through space; she was traveling so fast that the atoms of substance in the interstellar vacuum, merely wave-forms though they were, simply could not get out of the flyer's way. They were being blasted into nothingness against the *Dauntless'* wall-shields.

And throughout her interior the Patrol ship, always in complete readiness for strife, was being gone over again with microscopic thoroughness, to be put into more readiness, if possible, even than that.

After a few hours Illona danced back to Kinnison's "con" room, fairly bubbling over.

"Why, they're marvelous, Lensman!" she cried, "simply *marvelous!*"

"What are marvelous?"

"The boys," she enthused. "All of them. They're here because they *want* to be—why, the officers don't even have whips! They *like* them, actually! The officers who push the little buttons and things and those who walk around and look through the little glass things and even the gray-haired old man with the four stripes, why they like them all! And the boys were all putting on guns when I left—why, I never heard of such a thing!—and they're just simply *crazy* about you. I thought it was awfully funny you took off your guns as soon as the ship left Lyrane and you don't have guards around you all the time because I thought sure somebody would stab you in the back or something but they don't even want to and that's what's so marvelous and Hank Henderson told me . . ."

"Save it!" he ordered. "Jet back, angel-face, before you blow a fuse." He had been right in not operating—this girl was going to be a mine of information concerning Boskonian methods and operations, and all without knowing it. "That's what I've been trying to tell you about our Civilization; that it's based on the freedom of the individual to do pretty much as he pleases, as long as it is not to the public harm. And, as far as possible, equality of all the entities of Civilization."

"Uh-huh, I know you did," she nodded brightly, then sobered quickly, "but I couldn't understand it. I can't understand it yet; I can scarcely believe that you all are so . . . you know, don't you, what would happen if this were a Lonabarian ship and I would go running around talking to officers as though I were their equal?"

"No—what?"

"It's inconceivable, of course; it simply couldn't happen. But if it did, I would be punished terribly—perhaps though, at a first offense, I might be given only a twenty-scar whipping." At his lifted eyebrow she explained, "One that leaves twenty scars that show for life.

"That's why I'm acting so intoxicated, I think. You see, I . . ." she hesitated shyly, "I'm not used to being treated as anybody's equal, except of course other girls like me. Nobody is, on Lonabar. Everybody is higher or lower than you are. I'm going to simply love this when I get used to it." She spread both arms in a sweeping gesture. "I'd like to *squeeze* this whole ship and everybody in it—I just can't wait to get to Tellus and really *live* there!"

"That's a thing that has been bothering me," Kinnison confessed, and the girl stared wonderingly at his serious face. "We're going into battle, and we can't take time to land you anywhere before the battle starts."

"Of course not. Why should you?" she paused, thinking deeply. "You're not worrying about *me,* surely? Why, you're a high officer! Officers don't care whether a girl gets shot or not, do they?" The thought was obviously, utterly new.

"We do. It's extremely poor hospitality to invite a guest aboard and then have her killed. All I can say, though, is that if our number goes up . . . I still don't see how I could have done anything else."

"Oh . . . thanks, Gray Lensman. Nobody ever spoke to me like that before. But I wouldn't land if I could. I like Civilization. If you . . . if you don't win, I couldn't go to Tellus anyway, so I'd much rather take my chances here than not, sir, really. I'll *never* go back to Lonabar, in any case."

"At-a-girl, Toots!" He extended his hand. She looked at it dubiously, then hesitantly stretched out her own. But she learned fast; she put as much pressure into the brief handclasp as Kinnison did. "You'd better flit now, I've got work to do."

"Can I go up top? Hank Henderson is going to show me the primaries."

"Sure. Go anywhere you like. Before the trouble starts I'll take you down to the center and put you into a suit."

"Thanks, Lensman!" The girl hurried away and Kinnison Lensed the master pilot.

"Henderson? Kinnison. Official. Illona just told me about the primaries. They're QX—but no etchings."

"Of course not, sir."

"And please pass a word around for me. I know as well as anybody does that she doesn't belong aboard; but it couldn't be helped and I'm getting rid of her as soon as I possibly can. In the meantime she's my personal responsibility. So—no passes. She's strictly off limits."

"I'll pass the word, sir."

"Thanks." The Gray Lensman broke the connection and got into communication with Helen of Lyrane, who gave him a resume of everything that had happened.

Two ships—big ships, immense space-cruisers—appeared near the airport. Nobody saw them coming, they came so fast. They stopped, and without warning or parley destroyed all the buildings and all the people nearby with beams like Kinnison's needle-beam, except much larger. Then the ships landed and men disembarked. The Lyranians killed ten of them by direct mental impact or by monsters of the mind, but after that everyone who came out of the vessel wore thought-screens and the persons were quite helpless. The enemy had burned down and melted a part of the city, and as a further warning were then making formal plans to execute publicly a hundred leading Lyranians—ten for each man they had killed.

Because of the screens no communication was possible, but the invaders had made it clear that if there was one more sign of resistance, or even of non-cooperation, the entire city would be beamed; every living thing in it blasted out of existence. She herself had escaped so far. She was hidden in a crypt in the deepest sub-cellar of the city. She was, of course, one of the ones they wanted to execute, but finding any of Lyrane's leaders would be extremely difficult, if not impossible. They were still searching, with many persons as highly unwilling guides. They had indicated that they would stay there until the leaders were found; that they would make the Lyranians tear down their city, stone by stone, until they *were* found.

"But how could they know who your leaders are?" Kinnison wanted to know.

"Perhaps one of our persons weakened under their torture," Helen replied equably. "Perhaps they have among them a mind of power. Perhaps in some other fashion. What matters it? The thing of importance is that they do know."

"Another thing of importance is that it'll hold them there until we get there," Kinnison thought. "Typical Boskonian technique, I gather. It won't be many hours now. Hold them off if you can."

"I think that I can," came a tranquil reply. "Through mental contact each person acting as guide knows where each of us hidden ones is, and is avoiding all our hiding-places."

"Good. Tell me all you can about those ships, their size, shape, and armament."

She could not, it developed, give him any reliable information as to size. She thought that the present invaders were smaller than the *Dauntless,* but she could not be sure. Compared to the little airships which were the only flying structures with which she was familiar, both Kinnison's ship and those now upon Lyrane were so immensely huge that trying to tell which was larger was very much like attempting to visualize the difference between infinity squared and infinity cubed. On shape, however, she was much better; she spread in the Lensman's mind an accurately detailed picture of the two space-ships which the Patrolman intended to engage.

In shape they were ultra-fast, very much like the *Dauntless* herself. Hence they certainly were not maulers. Nor, probably, were they first-line battleships, such as had composed the fleet which had met Civilization's Grand Fleet off the edge of the Second Galaxy. Of course, the Patrol had had in that battle ultra-fast shapes which were ultra-powerful as well—such as this same *Dauntless*—and it was a fact that while Civilization was designing and building, Boskonia could very well have been doing the same thing. On the other hand, since the enemy could not logically be expecting real trouble in Dunstan's Region, these buckets might very well be second-line or out-of-date stuff . . .

"Are those ships lying on the same field we landed on?" he asked at that point in his cogitations.

"Yes."

"You can give me pretty close to an actual measurement of the difference, then," he told her. "We left a hole in that field practically our whole length. How does it compare with theirs?"

"I can find that out, I think," and in due time she did so; reporting that the *Dauntless* was the longer, by some twelve times a person's height.

"Thanks, Helen." Then, and only then, did Kinnison call his officers into consultation in the control room.

He told them everything he had learned and deduced about the two Boskonian vessels which they were about to attack. Then, heads bent over a visitank, the Patrolmen began to discuss strategy and tactics.

6

BACK TO LYRANE

As the *Dauntless* approached Lyrane II so nearly that the planet showed a perceptible disk upon the plates, the observers began to study their detectors carefully. Nothing registered, and a brief interchange of thoughts with the Chief Person of Lyrane informed the Lensman that the two Boskonian warships were still grounded. Indeed, they were going to stay grounded until after the hundred Lyranian leaders, most of whom were still safely hidden, had been found and executed, exactly as per announcement. The strangers had killed many persons by torture and were killing more in attempts to make them reveal the hiding-places of the leaders, but little if any real information was being obtained.

"Good technique, perhaps, from a bull-headed, dictatorial stand-point, but it strikes me as being damned poor tactics," grunted Malcolm Craig, the *Dauntless'* grizzled captain, when Kinnison had relayed the information.

"I'll say it's poor tactics," the Lensman agreed. "If anybody of Helmuth's caliber were down there one of those heaps would be out on guard, flitting all over space."

"But how could they be expecting trouble 'way out here, nine thousand parsecs from anywhere?" argued Chatway, the Chief Firing Officer.

"They ought to be—that's the point." This from Henderson. "Where do we land, Kim, did you find out?"

"Not exactly; they're on the other side of the planet from here, now. Good thing we don't have to get rid of a Tellurian intrinsic this time—it'll be a near thing as it is." And it was.

Scarcely was the intrinsic velocity matched to that of the planet when the observers reported that the airport upon which the enemy lay was upon the horizon. Inertialess, the *Dauntless* flashed ahead, going inert and into action simultaneously when within range of the zwilnik ships. Within range of one of them, that is; for, short as the time had been, the crew of one of the Boskonian vessels had been sufficiently alert to get her away. The other one did not move; then or ever.

The Patrolmen acted with the flawless smoothness of long practice and perfect teamwork. At the first sign of zwilnik activity as revealed by his spy-rays, Nelson the Chief Communications Officer loosed a barrage of ethereal and sub-ethereal interference through which no communications beam or signal could be driven. Captain Craig barked a word into his microphone and every dreadful primary that could be brought to bear erupted as one weapon. Chief Pilot Henderson, after a casual glance below, cut in the Bergenholms, tramped in his blasts, and set the cruiser's narrow nose into his tracer's line. One glance was enough. He needed no orders as to what to do next. It would have been apparent to almost anyone, even to one of the persons of Lyrane, that that riddled, slashed, three-quarters fused mass of junk never again would be or could contain aught of menace. The Patrol ship had not stopped: had scarcely even paused. Now, having destroyed half of the opposition *en passant,* she legged it after the remaining half.

"Now what, Kim?" asked Captain Craig. "We can't englobe him and he no doubt mounts tractor shears. We'll have to use the new tractor zone, won't we?" Ordinarily the gray-haired four-striper would have made his own decisions, since he and he alone fought his ship; but these circumstances were far from ordinary. First, any Unattached Lensman, wherever he was, was the boss. Second, the tractor zone was new; so brand new that even the *Dauntless* had not as yet used it. Third, the ship was on detached duty, assigned directly to Kinnison to do with as he willed. Fourth, said Kinnison was high in the confidence of the Galactic Council and would know whether or not the present situation justified the use of the new mechanism.

"If he can cut a tractor, yes," the Lensman agreed. "Only one ship. He can't get away and he can't communicate—safe enough. Go to it."

The Tellurian ship was faster than the Boskonian; and, since she had been only seconds behind at the start, she came within striking distance of her quarry in short order. Tractor beams reached out and seized; but only momentarily did they hold. At the first pull they were cut cleanly away. No one was surprised; it had been taken for granted that all Boskonian ships would by this time have been equipped with tractor shears.

These shears had been developed originally by the scientists of the Patrol. Immediately following that invention, looking forward to the time when Boskone would have acquired it, those same scientists set themselves to the task of working out something which would be just as good as a tractor beam for combat purposes, but which could not be cut. They got it finally—a globular shell of force, very much like a meteorite screen except double in phase. That is, it was completely impervious to matter moving in either direction, instead of only to that moving inwardly. Even if exact data as to generation, gauging, distance, and control of this weapon were available—which they very definitely are not—it would serve no good end to detail them here. Suffice it to say that the *Dauntless* mounted tractor zones, and had ample power to hold them.

Closer up the Patrol ship blasted. The zone snapped on, well beyond the Boskonian, and tightened. Henderson cut the Bergenholms. Captain Craig snapped out orders and Chief Firing Officer Chatway and his boys did their stuff.

Defensive screens full out, the pirate stayed free and tried to run. No soap. She merely slid around upon the frictionless inner surface of the zone. She rolled and she spun. Then she went inert and rammed. Still no soap. She struck the zone and bounced; bounced with all of her mass and against all the power of her driving thrust. The impact jarred the *Dauntless* to her very skin; but the zone's anchorages had been computed and installed by top-flight engineers and they held. And the zone itself held. It yielded a bit, but it did not fail and the shear-planes of the pirates could not cut it.

Then, no other course being possible, the Boskonians fought. Of course, theoretically, surrender was possible, but it simply was not done. No pirate ship ever had surrendered to a Patrol force, however large; none ever would. No Patrol ship had ever surrendered to Boskone—or would. That was the unwritten, but grimly understood code of this internecine conflict between two galaxy-wide and diametrically-opposed cultures; it was and had to be a war of utter and complete extermination. Individuals or small groups might be captured bodily, but no ship, no individual, even, ever, under any conditions, surrendered. The fight was—always and everywhere—to the death.

So this one was. The enemy was well-armed of her type, but her type simply did not carry projectors of sufficient power to crush the *Dauntless'* hard-held screens. Nor did she mount screens heavy enough to withstand for long the furious assault of the Patrolship's terrific primaries.

As soon as the pirate's screens went down the firing stopped; that order had been given long since. Kinnison wanted information, he wanted charts, he wanted a few living Boskonians. He got nothing. Not a man remained alive aboard the riddled hulk, the chart-room contained only heaps of fused ash. Everything which might have been of use to the Patrol had been destroyed, either by the Patrol's own beams or by the pirates themselves after they saw they must lose.

"Beam it out," Craig ordered, and the remains of the Boskonian warship disappeared.

Back toward Lyrane II, then, the *Dauntless* went, and Kinnison again made contact with Helen, the Elder Sister. She had emerged from her crypt and was directing affairs from her—"office" is perhaps the word—upon the top floor of the city's largest building. The search for the Lyranian leaders, the torture and murder of the citizens, and the destruction of the city had stopped, all at once, when the grounded Boskonian cruiser had been blasted out of commission. The directing intelligences of the raiders had remained, it developed, within the "safe" confines of their vessel's walls; and when they ceased directing, their minions in the actual theater of operations ceased operating. They had been grouped uncertainly in an open square, but at the first glimpse of the returning *Dauntless* they had dashed into the nearest large building, each man seizing one, or sometimes two persons as he went. They were now inside, erecting defenses and very evidently intending to use the Lyranians both as hostages and as shields.

Motionless now, directly over the city, Kinnison and his officers studied through their spy-rays the number, armament, and disposition of the enemy force. There were one hundred and thirty of them, human to about six places. They were armed with the usual portable weapons carried by such parties. Originally they had had several semi-portable projectors, but since all heavy stuff must be powered from the mother-ship, it had been abandoned long since. Surprisingly, though, they wore full armor. Kinnison had expected only thought-screens, since the Lyranians had no offensive weapons save those of the mind; but apparently either the pirates did not know that or else were guarding against surprise.

Armor was—and is—heavy, cumbersome, a handicap to fast action, and a nuisance generally; hence for the Boskonians to have dispensed with it would not have been poor tactics. True, the Patrol *did* attack, but that could not have been what was expected. In fact, had such an attack been in the cards, that Boskonian punitive party would not have been on the ground at all. It was equally true that canny old Helmuth, who took nothing whatever for granted, would have had his men in armor. However, he would have guarded much more completely against surprise . . . but few commanders indeed went to such lengths of precaution as Helmuth did. Thus Kinnison pondered.

"This ought to be as easy as shooting fish down a well—but you'd better put out space-scouts just the same," he decided, as he Lensed a thought to Lieutenant Peter vanBuskirk. "Bus? Do you see what we see?"

"Uh-huh, we've been peeking a bit," the huge Dutch-Valerian responded, happily.

"QX. Get your gang wrapped up in their tinware. I'll see you at the main lower stabbard lock in ten minutes." He cut off and turned to an orderly. "Break out my G-P cage for me, will you, Spike? And I'll want the 'copters—tell them to get hot."

"But listen, Kim!" and

"You can't do that, Kinnison!" came simultaneously from Chief Pilot and Captain, neither of whom could leave the ship in such circumstances as these. They, the vessel's two top officers, were bound to her; while the Lensman, although ranking both of them, even aboard the ship, was not and could not be bound by anything.

"Sure I can—you fellows are just jealous, that's all," Kinnison retorted, cheerfully. "I not only can, I've *got* to go with the Valerians. I need a lot of information, and I can't read a dead man's brain—yet."

While the storming party was assembling the *Dauntless* settled downward, coming to rest in the already devastated section of the town, as close as possible to the building in which the Boskonians had taken refuge.

One hundred and two men disembarked: Kinnison, vanBuskirk, and the full company of one hundred Valerians. Each of those space-fighting wild-cats measured seventy eight inches or more from sole to crown; each was composed of four hundred or more pounds of the fantastically powerful, rigid, and reactive brawn, bone, and sinew necessary for survival upon a planet having a surface gravity almost three times that of small, feeble Terra.

Because of the women held captive by the pirates, the Valerians carried no machine rifles, no semi-portables, no heavy stuff at all; only their DeLameters and of course their space-axes. A Valerian trooper without his space-axe? Unthinkable! A dire weapon indeed, the space-axe. A combination and sublimation of battle-axe, mace, bludgeon, and lumberman's picaroon; thirty pounds of hard, tough, space-tempered alloy; a weapon of potentialities limited only by the physical strength and bodily agility of its wielder. And vanBuskirk's Valerians had both—plenty of both. One-handed, with simple flicks of his incredible wrist, the smallest Valerian of the *Dauntless'* boarding party could manipulate his atrocious weapon as effortlessly as, and almost unbelievable faster than, a fencing master handles his rapier or an orchestra conductor waves his baton.

With machine-like precision the Valerians fell in and strode away; vanBuskirk in the lead, the helicopters hovering overhead, the Gray Lensman bringing up the rear. Tall and heavy, strong and agile as he was—for a Tellurian—he had no business in that front line, and no one knew that fact better than he did. The puniest Valerian of the company could do in full armor a standing high jump of over fourteen feet against one Tellurian gravity; and could dodge, feint, parry, and swing with a blinding speed starkly impossible to any member of any of the physically lesser breeds of man.

Approaching the building they spread out, surrounded it; and at a signal from a helicopter that the ring was complete the assault began. Doors and windows were locked, barred, and barricaded, of course; but what of that? A few taps of the axes and a few blasts of the DeLameters took care of things very nicely; and through the openings thus made there leaped, dove, rolled, or strode the space-black-and-silver warriors of the Galactic Patrol. Valerians, than whom no fiercer race of hand to hand fighters has ever been known—no bifurcate race, and but very few others, however built or shaped, have ever willingly come to grips with the armored axe-men of Valeria!

Not by choice, then, but of necessity and in sheer desperation the pirates fought. In the vicious beams of their portables the stone walls of the room glared a baleful red; in spots even were pierced through. Old-fashioned pistols barked, spitting steel-jacketed lead. But the G-P suits were screened against lethal beams by generators capable of withstanding anything of lesser power than a semi-portable projector; G-P armor was proof against any projectile possessing less energy than that hurled by the high-caliber machine rifle. Thus the Boskonian beams splashed off the Valerians' screens in torrents of man-made lightning and in pyrotechnic displays of multi-colored splendor, their bullets ricocheted harmlessly as spent, mis-shapen blobs of metal.

The Patrolmen did not even draw their DeLameters during their inexorable advance. They knew that the pirates' armor was as capable as theirs, and the women were not to die if death for them could possibly be avoided. As they advanced the enemy fell back toward the center of the great room; holding there with the Lyranians forming the outer ring of their roughly-circular formation; firing over the women's heads and between their naked bodies.

Kinnison did not want those women to die. It seemed, however, that die they must, from the sheer, tremendous reflection from the Valerians' fiercely radiant screens, if the Patrolmen persisted in their advance. He studied the enemy formation briefly, then flashed an order.

There ensued a startling and entirely unorthodox maneuver, one possible only to the troopers there at work, as at Kinnison's command every Valerian left the floor in a prodigious leap. Over the women's heads, over the heads of the enemy; but in mid-leap, as he passed over, each Patrolman swung his axe at a Boskonian helmet with all the speed and all the power he could muster. Most of the enemy died then and there, for the helmet has never been forged which is able to fend the beak of a space-axe driven as each of those was driven. The fact that the Valerians were nine or ten feet off the floor at the time made no difference whatever. They were space-fighters, trained to handle themselves and their weapons in any position or situation; with or without gravity, with or without even inertia.

"You persons—run! Get out of here! SCRAM!" Kinnison fairly shouted the thought as the Valerians left the floor, and the matriarchs obeyed—frantically. Through doors and windows they fled, in all directions and at the highest possible speed.

But in their enthusiasm to strike down the foe, not one of the Valerians had paid any attention to the exact spot upon which he was to land; or, if he did, some one else got there either first or just barely second. Besides, there was not room for them all in the center of the ring. For seconds, therefore, confusion reigned and a boiler-works clangor resounded for a mile around as a hundred and one extra-big and extra-heavy men, a writhing, kicking, pulling tangle of armor, axes, and equipment, jammed into a space which half their number would have filled over-full. Sulphurous Valerian profanity and sizzling deep-space oaths blistered the very air as each warrior struggled madly to right himself, to get one more crack at a pirate before somebody else beat him to it.

During this terrific melee some of the pirates released their screens and committed suicide. A few got out of the room, but not many. Nor far; the men in the helicopters saw to that. They had needle-beams, powered from the *Dauntless,* which went through the screens of personal armor as a knife goes through ripe cheese.

"Save it, guys—hold everything!" Kinnison yelled as the tangled mass of Valerians resolved itself into erect and warlike units. "No more axe-work—don't let them kill themselves—catch them ALIVE!"

They did so, quickly and easily. With the women out of the way, there was nothing to prevent the Valerians from darting right up to the muzzles of the foes' DeLameters. Nor could the enemy dodge, or run, half fast enough to get away. Armored, shielded hands batted the weapons away—if an arm or leg broke in the process, what the hell?—and the victim was held motionless until his turn came to face the mind-reading Kinnison.

Nothing. Nothing, flat. A string of zeros. And, bitterly silent, Kinnison led the way back to the *Dauntless*. The men he wanted, the ones who knew anything, were the ones who killed themselves, of course. Well, why not? In like case, officers of the Patrol had undoubtedly done the same. The live ones didn't know where their planet was, could give no picture even of where it lay in the galaxy, did not know where they were going, nor why. Well, so what? Wasn't ignorance the prime characteristic of the bottom layers of dictatorships everywhere? If they had known anything, they would have been under compulsion to kill themselves, too, and would have done it.

In his own room in the *Dauntless* his black mood lightened somewhat and he called the Elder Person.

"Helen of Troy? I suppose that the best thing we can do now, for your peace of mind, prosperity, well-being, et cetera, is to drill out of here as fast as Klono and Noshabkeming will let us. Right?"

"Why, I . . . you . . . um . . . that is . . ." The matriarch was badly flustered at the Lensman's bald summation of her attitude. She did not want to agree, but she certainly did not want these males around a second longer than was necessary.

"Just as well say it, because it goes double for me—you can play it clear across the board, Toots, that if I ever see you again it will be because I can't get out of it." Then, to his chief pilot:

"QX, Hen, give her the oof—back to Tellus."

7

WIDE-OPEN N-WAY

Serenely the mighty *Dauntless* bored her way homeward through the ether, at the easy touring blast—for her—of some eighty parsecs an hour. The engineers inspected and checked their equipment, from instrument-needles to blast-nozzles; relining, repairing, replacing anything and everything which showed any signs of wear or strain because of what the big vessel had just gone through. Then they relaxed into their customary routine of killing time—the games of a dozen planets and the vying with each other in the telling of outrageously untruthful stories.

The officers on watch lolled at ease in their cushioned seats, making much ado of each tiny thing as it happened, even the changes of watch. The Valerians, as usual, remained invisible in their own special quarters. There the gravity was set at twenty seven hundred instead of at the Tellurian normal of nine hundred eighty, there the atmospheric pressure was forty pounds to the square inch, there the temperature was ninety six degrees Fahrenheit, and there vanBuskirk and his fighters lived and moved and had their drills of fantastic violence and stress. They were irked less than any of the others by monotony; being, as has been intimated previously, neither mental nor intellectual giants.

And Kinnison, mirror-polished gray boots stacked in all their majestic size upon a corner of his desk, leaned his chair precariously backward and thought in black concentration. It *still* didn't make any kind of sense. He had just enough clues—fragments of clues—to drive a man nuts. Menjo Bleeko was the man he wanted. On Lonabar. To find one was to find the other, but how in the steaming hells of Venus was he going to find either of them? It might seem funny not to be able to find a thing as big as a planet—but since nobody knew where it was, by fifty thousand parsecs, and since there were millions and skillions and whillions of planets in the galaxy, a random search was quite definitely out. Bleeko was a zwilnik, or tied in with zwilniks, of course; but he could read a million zwilnik minds without finding, except by merest chance, one having any contact with or knowledge of the Lonabarian.

The Patrol had already scoured—fruitlessly—Aldebaran II for any sign, however slight, pointing toward Lonabar. The planetographers had searched the files, the charts, the libraries thoroughly. No Lonabar. Of course, they had suggested—what a help!—they might know it under some other name. Personally, he didn't think so, since no jeweler throughout the far-flung bounds of Civilization had as yet been found who could recognize or identify any of the items he had described.

Whatever avenue or alley of thought Kinnison started along, he always ended up at the jewels and the girl. Illona, the squirrel-brained, romping, joyous little imp who by now owned in fee simply half of the ship and nine-tenths of the crew. Why in Palain's purple hells couldn't she have had a brain? How could *anybody* be dumb enough not to know the galactic coordinates of their own planet? Not even to know *anything* that could help locate it? But at that, she was probably about as smart as most—you couldn't expect any other woman in the galaxy to have a mind like Mac's . . .

For minutes, then, he abandoned his problem and reveled in visions of the mental and physical perfections of his fiancee. But this was getting him nowhere, fast. The girl or the jewels—which? They were the only real angles he had.

He sent out a call for her, and in a few minutes she came swirling in. How different she was from what she had been! Gone were the somberness, the dread, the terror which had oppressed her; gone were the class-conscious inhibitions against which she had been rebelling, however subconsciously, since childhood. Here she was *free!* The boys were free, *everybody* was free! She had expanded tremendously—unfolded. She was living as she had never dreamed it possible to live. Each new minute was an adventure in itself. Her black eyes, once so dull, sparkled with animation; radiated her sheer joy in living. Even her jet-black hair seemed to have taken on a new luster and gloss, in its every, precisely-arranged wavelet.

"Hi, Lensman!" she burst out, before Kinnison could say a word or think a thought in greeting. "I'm *so* glad you sent for me, because there's something I've been wanting to ask you since yesterday. The boys are going to throw a blow-out, with all kinds of stunts, and they want me to do a dance. QX, do you think?"

"Sure. Why not?"

"Clothes," she explained. "I told them I couldn't dance in a dress, and they said I wasn't supposed to, that acrobats didn't wear dresses when they performed on Tellus, that my regular clothes were just right. I said they were trying to string me and they swore they weren't—said to ask the Old Man . . ." she broke off, two knuckles jammed into her mouth, expressive eyes wide in sudden fright. "Oh, excuse me, sir," she gasped. "I didn't . . ."

" 'Smatter? What bit you?" Kinnison asked, then got it. "Oh—the 'Old Man', huh? QX, angel-face, that's standard nomenclature in the Patrol. Not with you folks, though, I take it?"

"I'll say not," she breathed. She acted as though a catastrophe had been averted by the narrowest possible margin. "Why, if anybody got caught even *thinking* such a thing, the whole crew would go into the steamer that very minute. And if I would dare to say 'Hi' to Menjo Bleeko . . . !" she shuddered.

"Nice people," Kinnison commented.

"But are you sure that the . . . that I'm not getting any of the boys into trouble?" she pleaded. "For, after all, none of them ever dare call you that to your face, you know."

"You haven't been around enough yet," he assured her. "On duty, no; that's discipline—necessary for efficiency. And I haven't hung around the wardrooms much of late—been too busy. But at the party you'll be surprised at some of the things they call me—if you happen to hear them. You've been practicing—keeping in shape?"

"Uh-huh," she confessed. "In my room, with the spy-ray-block on."

"Good. No need to hide, though, and no need to wear dresses any time you're practicing—the boys were right on that. But what I called you in about is that I want you to help me. Will you?"

"Yes, sir. In anything I can—*anything,* sir," she answered, instantly.

"I want you to give me every scrap of information you possibly can about Lonabar; its customs and habits, its work and its play—everything, even its money and its jewelry." This last apparently an after-thought. "To do so, you'll have to let me into your mind of your own free will—you'll have to cooperate to the limit of your capability. QX?"

"That will be quite all right, Lensman," she agreed, shyly. "I know now that you aren't going to hurt me."

Illona did not like it at first, there was no question of that. And small wonder. It is an intensely disturbing thing to have your mind invaded, knowingly, by another; particularly when that other is the appallingly powerful mind of Gray Lensman Kimball Kinnison. There were lots of things she did not want exposed and the very effort not to think of them brought them ever and ever more vividly to the fore. She squirmed mentally and physically: her mind was for minutes a practically illegible turmoil. But she soon steadied down and, as she got used to the new sensations, she went to work with a will. She could not increase the planetographical knowledge which Kinnison had already obtained from her, but she was a mine of information concerning Lonabar's fine gems. She knew all about every one of them, with the completely detailed knowledge one is all too apt to have of a thing long and intensely desired, but supposedly forever out of reach.

"Thanks, Illona." It was over; the Lensman knew as much as she did about everything which had any bearing upon his quest. "You've helped a lot—now you can flit."

"I'm glad to help, sir, really—any time. I'll see you at the party, then, if not before." Illona left the room in a far more subdued fashion than she had entered it. She had always been more than half afraid of Kinnison; just being near him did things to her which she did not quite like. And this last thing, this mind-searching interview, did not operate to quiet her fears. It gave her the screaming meamies, no less!

And Kinnison, alone in his room, started to call for a tight beam to Prime Base, then changed his mind and Lensed a thought—gingerly and diffidently enough—to Port Admiral Haynes.

"Certainly I'm free!" came instant response. "To *you*, I'm free twenty four hours of every day. Go ahead."

"I want to try something that I don't know whether can be done or not. A wide-open, Lens-to-Lens conference with all the Lensmen, especially all Unattached Lensmen, who can be reached. Can it be done?"

"Whew!" Haynes whistled. "I've been in such things up to a hundred or so . . . no reason why it wouldn't work. Most of the people you want know me, and those who don't can tune in through someone who does. If everybody tunes to me at the same time, we'll all be en rapport with each other."

"It's QX, then? The reason I . . ."

"Skip it, son. No use explaining twice—I'll get it when the others do. I'll take care of it. It'll take some little time . . . Would hour twenty, tomorrow, be soon enough?"

"That'll be fine. Thanks a lot, chief."

The next day dragged, even for the always-busy Kinnison. He prowled about, aimlessly. He saw the spectacular Aldebaranian several times, noticing something which tied in very nicely with a fact he had half-seen in the girl's own mind before he could dodge it—that whenever she made a twosome with any man, the man was Henry Henderson.

"Blasted, Hen?" he asked, casually, when he came upon the pilot in a corner of a ward-room, staring fixedly at nothing.

"Out of the ether," Henderson admitted. "However, I *haven't* been making any passes. No use telling you that, though."

There wasn't. Unattached Lensmen, as well as being persons of supreme authority, are supremely able mind-readers. Verbum sap.

"I know you haven't." Then, answering the unasked question: "No, I haven't been reading your mind. Nor anybody else's, except Illona's. I've read hers, up and down and crosswise."

"Oh . . . so you know, then . . . say, Kim, can I talk to you for a minute? *Really* talk, I mean?"

"Sure. On the Lens?"

"That'd be better."

"Here you are. About Illona, the beautiful Aldebaranian zwilnik, I suppose."

"Don't, Kim." Henderson actually flinched, physically. "She isn't a zwilnik, really—she *can't* be—I'd bet my last millo on that?"

"Are you telling me or asking me?"

"I don't know." Henderson hesitated. "I've been wanting to ask you . . . you've got a lot of stuff we haven't, you know . . . whether she . . . I mean if I . . . Oh, hell! Kim, is there any reason why I shouldn't . . . well, er . . . get married?"

"Millions of reasons why you should, Hen. Everybody ought to."

"Damnation, Kim! That isn't what I meant, and you know it!"

"Think straight, then."

"QX. Sir, would Unattached Lensman Kimball Kinnison approve of my marriage to Illona Potter, if I've got jets enough to swing it?"

Mighty clever, the Lensman thought. Since the men of the Patrol were notoriously averse to going sloppy about it, he had wondered just how the pilot was going to phrase his question. He had done it very neatly, by tossing the buck right back at him. But he wouldn't go sloppy, either. This "untarnished-meteors-upon-the-collars-of-our-heroes" stuff was QX for swivel-tongued spellbinders, but not for anybody else. So:

"As far as I know—and I bashfully admit that I know it all—the answer is yes."

"Great!" Henderson came to life with a snap. "Now, if . . . but I don't suppose you'd . . ." the thought died away.

"I'll say I wouldn't. Unethical no end. I might cheat just a little bit, though. She probably won't do much worse than beat your brains out with a two-inch spanner if you ask her. And only about half of the twenty one hundred or so other guys aboard this heap are laying awake nights trying to figure out ways of beating your time."

"Huh? *Those* apes? Watch my jets!" Henderson strode away, doubts all resolved; and Kinnison, seeing that hour twenty was very near, went to his own room.

It is difficult for any ordinary mind to conceive of its being in complete accord with any other, however closely akin. Consider, then, how utterly impossible it is to envision that merging of a hundred thousand, or five hundred thousand, or a million—nobody ever did know how many Lensmen tuned in that day—minds so utterly different that no one human being can live long enough even to see each of the races there represented! Probably less than half of them were even approximately human. Many were not mammals, many were not warm-blooded. Not all, by far, were even oxygen-breathers—oxygen, to many of those races, was sheerest poison. Nevertheless, they had much in common. All were intelligent; most of them very highly so; and all were imbued with the principles of freedom and equality for which Galactic Civilization stood and upon which it was fundamentally based.

That meeting was staggering, even to Kinnison's mind. It was appalling—yet it was ultimately thrilling, too. It was one of the greatest, one of the most terrific thrills of the Lensman's long life.

"Thanks, fellows, for coming in," he began simply. "I will make my message very short. As Haynes may have told you, I am Kinnison of Tellus. It will help greatly in locating the head of the Boskonian culture if I can find a certain planet, known to me only by the name of Lonabar. Its people are human beings to the last decimal; its rarest jewels are these," and he spread in the collective mind a perfect, exactly detailed and pictured description of the gems. "Does any one of you know of such a planet? Has any one of you ever seen a stone like any of these?"

A pause—a heart-breakingly long pause. Then a faint, soft, diffident thought appeared; appeared as though seeping slowly from a single cell of that incredibly linked, million-fold-composite Lensman's BRAIN.

"I waited to be sure that no one else would speak, as my information is very meager, and unsatisfactory, and old," the thought apologized.

Kinnison started, but managed to conceal his surprise from the linkage. That thought, so diamond-clear, so utterly precise, must have come from a Second Stage Lensman—and since it was neither Worsel nor Tregonsee, there must be another one he had never heard of!

"Whatever its nature, any information at all is very welcome," Kinnison replied, without perceptible pause. "Who is speaking, please?"

"Nadreck of Palain VII, Unattached. Many cycles ago I secured, and still have in my possession, a crystal—or rather, a fragment of a super-cooled liquid—like one of the red gems you showed us; the one having practically all its transmittance in a very narrow band centering at point seven zero zero."

"But you do not know what planet it came from—is that it?"

"Not exactly," the soft thought went on. "I saw it upon its native planet, but unfortunately I do not now know just what or where that planet was. We were exploring at the time, and had visited many planets. Not being interested in any world having an atmosphere of oxygen, we paused but briefly, nor did we map it. I was interested in the fusion because of its peculiar filtering effect. A scientific curiosity merely."

"Could you find that planet again?"

"By checking back upon the planets we did map, and by retracing our route, I should be able to—yes, I am certain that I can do so."

"And when Nadreck of Palain VII admits to being certain of anything," another thought appeared, "nothing in the macrocosmic universe is more certain."

"I thank you, Twenty Four of Six, for the expression of confidence."

"And I thank both of you particularly, as well as all of you collectively," Kinnison broadcast. Intelligences by the millions broke away from the linkage. As soon as the two were alone:

"You're Second Stage, aren't you?"

"Yes. I felt a need. I was too feeble. A certain project was impossible, since it was so dangerous as to involve a distinct possibility of personal harm. Therefore Mentor gave me advanced treatment, to render me somewhat less feeble than I theretofore was."

"I see."

Kinnison didn't see, at all, since this was his first contact with a Palainian mind. Who ever heard of a Lensman refusing a job because of personal risk? Lensmen *always* went in . . . no matter how scared he was, *of course* he went in . . . that was the Code . . . human Lensmen, that is . . . There were a lot of things he didn't know, and other races could be—*must* be—different. He was astounded that there could be *that* much difference; but after all, since the guy was an L2, he certainly had enough of what it took to more than make up for any lacks. How did he know how short of jets he himself looked, in the minds of other Second Stage Lensmen? These thoughts flashed through his mind, behind his impervious shield, and after only the appropriate slight pause his thought went smoothly on:

"I had known of only Worsel of Velantia and Tregonsee of Rigel Four, besides myself. I don't need to tell you how terrifically glad I am that there are four of us instead of three. But at the moment the planet Lonabar is, I believe, more important to my job than anything else in existence. You will map it for me, and send the data to me at Prime Base?"

"I will map the planet and will myself bring the data to you at Prime Base. Do you want some of the gems, also?"

"I don't think so." Kinnison thought swiftly. "No, better not. They'll be harder to get now, and it might tip our hand too much. I'll get them myself, later. Will you inform me, through Haynes, when to expect you?"

"I will so inform you. I will proceed at once, with speed."

"Thanks a million, Nadreck—clear ether!"

The ship sped on, and as it sped Kinnison continued to think. He attended the "blow-out." Ordinarily he would have been right in the thick of it; but this time, young though he was and enthusiastic, he simply could not tune in. Nothing fitted, and until he could see a picture that made some kind of sense he could not let go. He listened to the music with half an ear, he watched the stunts with only half an eye.

He forgot his problem for a while when, at the end, Illona Potter danced. For Lonabarian acrobatic dancing is not like the Tellurian art of the same name. Or rather, it is like it, except more so—much more so. An earthly expert would be scarcely a novice on Lonabar, and Illona was a Lonabarian expert. She had been training, intensively, all her life, and even in Lonabar's chill social and psychological environment she had loved her work. Now, reveling as she was in the first realization of liberty of thought and of person, and inspired by the heart-felt applause of the space-hounds so closely packed into the hall, she put on something more than an exhibition of coldly impersonal skill and limberness. And the feelings, both of performer and of spectators, were intensified by the fact that, of all the repertoire of the *Dauntless'* superb orchestra, Illona liked best to dance to the stirring strains of "Our Patrol," "Our Patrol," which any man who has ever worn the space-black-and-silver will say is the greatest, grandest, most glorious, most terrific piece of music that ever was or ever will be written, played, or sung! Small wonder, then, that the dancer really "gave"; or that the mighty cruiser's walls almost bulged under the applause of Illona's "boys" at the end of her first number.

They kept her at it until the captain stopped it, to keep the girl from killing herself. "She's worn down to a nub," he declared, and she was. She was trembling. She was panting, her almost-lacquered-down hair stood out in wild disorder. Her eyes were starry with tears—happy tears. Then the ranking officers made short speeches of appreciation and the spectators carried the actors—actual carrying, in Illona's case, upon an improvised throne—off for refreshments.

Back in his quarters, Kinnison tackled his problem again. He could work out something on Lonabar now, but what about Lyrane? It tied in, too—there was an angle there, somewhere. To get it, though, somebody would have to get close—really friendly with—the Lyranians. Just looking on from the outside wouldn't do. Somebody they could trust and would confide in—and they were so damnably, so fanatically non-cooperative! A man couldn't get a millo's worth of real information—he could read any one mind by force, but he'd never get the right one. Neither could Worsel or Tregonsee or any other non-human Lensman; the Lyranians just simply didn't have the galactic viewpoint. No, what he wanted was a human woman Lensman, and there weren't any . . .

At the thought he gasped; the pit of his stomach felt cold. Mac! She was more than half Lensman already—she was the only un-Lensed human being who had ever been able to read his thoughts . . . But he didn't have the gall, the sheer, brazen crust, to shove a load like that onto *her* . . . or did he? Didn't the job come first? Wouldn't she be big enough to see it that way? Sure she would! As to what Haynes and the rest of the Lensmen would think . . . let them think! In this, he had to make his own decisions . . .

He couldn't. He sat there for an hour; teeth locked until his jaws ached, fists clenched.

"I can't make that decision alone," he breathed, finally. "Not jets enough by half," and he shot a thought to distant Arisia and Mentor the Sage.

"This intrusion is necessary," he thought coldly, precisely. "It seems to me to be wise to do this thing which has never before been done. I have no data, however, upon which to base a decision and the matter is grave. I ask, therefore—is it wise?"

"You do not ask as to repercussions—consequences, either to yourself or to the woman?"

"I ask what I asked."

"Ah, Kinnison of Tellus, you truly grow. You at last learn to think. It is wise," and the telepathic link snapped.

Kinnison slumped down in relief. He had not known what to expect.

He would not have been surprised if the Arisian had pinned his ears back; he certainly did not expect either the compliment or the clear-cut answer. He knew that Mentor would give him no help whatever in any problem which he could possibly solve alone; he was just beginning to realize that the Arisian *would* aid him in matters which were absolutely, intrinsically, beyond his reach.

Recovering, he flashed a call to Surgeon-Marshal Lacy.

"Lacy? Kinnison. I would like to have Sector Chief Nurse Clarrissa MacDougall detached at once. Please have her report to me here aboard the *Dauntless,* en route, at the earliest possible moment of rendezvous."

"Huh? What? You can't . . . you wouldn't . . ." the old Lensman gurgled.

"No, I wouldn't. The whole Corps will know it soon enough, so I might as well tell you now. I'm going to make a Lensman out of her."

Lacy exploded then, but Kinnison had expected that.

"Seal it!" he counseled, sharply. "I'm not doing it entirely on my own—Mentor of Arisia made the final decision. Prefer charges against me if you like, but in the meantime please do as I request."

And that was that.

8

CARTIFF THE JEWELER

A few hours before the time of rendezvous with the cruiser which was bringing Clarrissa out to him, the detectors picked up a vessel whose course, it proved, was set to intersect their own. A minute or so later a sharp, clear thought came through Kinnison's Lens.

"Kim? Raoul. Been flitting around out Arisia way, and they called me in and asked me to bring you a package. Said you'd be expecting it. QX?"

"Hi, Spacehound! QX." Kinnison had very decidedly not been expecting it—he had been intending to do the best he could without it—but he realized instantly, with a thrill of gladness, what it was. "Inert? Or can't you stay?"

"Free. Got to make a rendezvous. Can't take time to inert—that is, if you'll inert the thing in your cocoon. Don't want it to hole out on you, though."

"Can do. Free it is. Pilot room! Prepare for inertialess contact with vessel approaching. Magnets. Messenger coming aboard—free."

The two speeding vessels flashed together, at all their unimaginable velocities, without a thump or jar. Magnetic clamps locked and held. Airlock doors opened, shut, opened; and at the inner port Kinnison met Raoul LaForge, his classmate through the four years at Wentworth Hall.

Brief but hearty greetings were exchanged, but the visitor could not stop. Lensmen are busy men.

"Fine seeing you, Kim—be sure and inert the thing—clear ether!"

"Same to you, ace. Sure I will—think I want to vaporize half of my ship?"

Indeed, inerting the package was the Lensman's first care, for in the free condition it was a frightfully dangerous thing. Its intrinsic velocity was that of Arisia, while the ship's was that of Lyrane II. They might be forty or fifty miles per second apart; and if the *Dauntless* should go inert that harmless-looking package would instantly become a meteorite inside the ship. At the thought of that velocity he paused. The cocoon would stand it—but would the Lens? Oh, sure, Mentor knew what was coming; the Lens would be packed to stand it.

Kinnison wrapped the package in heavy gauze, then in roll after roll of spring-steel mesh. He jammed heavy steel springs into the ends, then clamped the whole thing into a form with high-alloy bolts an inch in diameter. He poured in two hundred pounds of metallic mercury, filling the form to the top. Then a cover, also bolted on. This whole assembly went into the "cocoon," a cushioned, heavily-padded affair suspended from all four walls, ceiling, and floor by every shock-absorbing device known to the engineers of the Patrol.

The *Dauntless* inerted briefly at Kinnison's word and it seemed as though a troop of elephants were running silently amuck in the cocoon room. The package to be inerted weighed no more than eight ounces— but eight ounces of mass, at a relative velocity of fifty miles per second, possesses a kinetic energy by no means to be despised.

The frantic lurchings and bouncings subsided, the cruiser resumed her free flight, and the man undid all that he had done. The Arisian package looked exactly as before, but it was harmless now; it had the same intrinsic velocity as did everything else aboard the vessel.

Then the Lensman pulled on a pair of insulating gloves and opened the package; finding, as he had expected, that the packing material was a dense, viscous liquid. He poured it out and there was the Lens—Cris's Lens! He cleaned it carefully, then wrapped it in heavy insulation. For of all the billions of unnumbered billions of living entities in existence, Clarrissa MacDougall was the only one whose flesh could touch that apparently innocuous jewel with impunity. Others could safely touch it while she wore it, while it glowed with its marvelously polychromatic cold flame; but until she wore it and unless she wore it its touch meant death to any life to which it was not attuned.

Shortly thereafter another Patrol cruiser hove in sight. This meeting, however, was to be no casual one, for the nurse could not be inerted from the free state in the *Dauntless'* cocoon. No such device ever built could stand it—and those structures are stronger far than is the human frame. Any adjustment which even the hardest, toughest space-hound can take in a cocoon is measured in feet per second, not in miles.

Hundreds of miles apart, the ships inerted and their pilots fought with supreme skill to make the two intrinsics match. And even so the vessels did not touch, even nearly. A space-line was thrown; the nurse and her space-roll were quite unceremoniously hauled aboard.

Kinnison did not meet her at the airlock, but waited for her in his con room; and the details of that meeting will remain unchronicled. They were young, they had not seen each other for a long time, and they were very much in love. It is evident, therefore, that Patrol affairs were not the first matters to be touched upon. Nor, if the historian has succeeded even partially in portraying truly the characters of the two persons involved, is it either necessary or desirable to go at any length into the argument they had as to whether or not she should be inducted so cavalierly into a service from which her sex had always, automatically, been barred. He did not want to make her carry that load, but he had to; she did not—although for entirely different reasons—want to take it.

He shook out the Lens and, holding it in a thick-folded corner of the insulating blanket, flicked one of the girl's fingertips across the bracelet. Satisfied by the fleeting flash of color which swept across the jewel, he snapped the platinum-iridium band around her left wrist, which it fitted exactly.

She stared for a minute at the smoothly, rythmically flowing colors of the thing so magically sprung to life upon her wrist; awe and humility in her glorious eyes. Then:

"I can't, Kim. I simply can't. I'm not worthy of it," she choked.

"None of us are, Cris. We can't be—but we've got to do it, just the same."

"I suppose that's true—it would be so, of course . . . I'll do my best . . . but you know perfectly well, Kim, that I'm not—can't ever be—a real Lensman."

"Sure you can. Do we have to go over all that again? You won't have some of the technical stuff that we got, of course, but you carry jets that no other Lensman ever has had. You're a real Lensman; don't worry about that—if you weren't, do you think they would have made that Lens for you?"

"I suppose not . . . it must be true, even though I can't understand it. But I'm simply scared to death of the rest of it, Kim."

"You needn't be. It'll hurt, but not more than you can stand. Don't think we'd better start that stuff for a few days yet, though; not until you get used to using your Lens. Coming at you, Lensman!" and he went into Lens-to-Lens communication, broadening it gradually into a wide-open two-way.

She was appalled at first, but entranced some thirty minutes later, when he called the lesson to a halt.

"Enough for now," he decided. "It doesn't take much of that stuff to be a great plenty, at first."

"I'll say it doesn't," she agreed. "Put this away for me until next time, will you, Kim? I don't want to wear it all the time until I know more about it."

"Fair enough. In the meantime I want you to get acquainted with a new girl-friend of mine," and he sent out a call for Illona Potter.

*"Girl-*friend!"

"Uh-huh. Study her. Educational no end, and she may be important. Want to compare notes with you on her later, is why I'm not giving you any advance dope on her—here she comes."

"Mac, this is Illona," he introduced them informally. "I told them to give you the cabin next to hers," he added, to the nurse. "I'll go with you to be sure everything's on the green."

It was, and the Lensman left the two together.

"I'm awfully glad you're here," Illona said, shyly. "I've heard *so* much about you, Miss . . ."

" 'Mac' to you, my dear—all my friends call me that," the nurse broke in. "And you don't want to believe everything you hear, especially aboard this space-bucket." Her lips smiled, but her eyes were faintly troubled.

"Oh, it was nice," Illona assured her. "About what a grand person you are, and what a wonderful couple you and Lensman Kinnison make—why, you really *are* in love with him, aren't you?" This in surprise, as she studied the nurse's face.

"Yes," unequivocally. "And you love him, too, and that makes it . . ."

"Good heavens, no!" the Aldebaranian exclaimed, so positively that Clarrissa jumped.

"What? You don't? *Really?*" Gold-flecked, tawny eyes stared intensely into engagingly candid eyes of black. The nurse wished then that she had left her Lens on, so she could tell whether this bejeweled brunette hussy was telling the truth or not.

"Certainly not. That's what I meant—I'm simply scared to death of him. He's so . . . well, so overpowering—he's so much more—tremendous—than I am. I didn't see how any girl could possibly love him—but I understand now how you could, perhaps. You're sort of—terrific— yourself, you know. I feel as though I ought to call you 'Your Magnificence' instead of just plain 'Mac'."

"Why, I'm no such thing!" Clarrissa exclaimed; but she softened noticeably, none the less. "And I think that I'm going to like you a lot."

"Oh . . . h . . . h—honestly?" Illona squealed. "It sounds too good to be true, you're so marvelous. But if you do, I think that Civilization will be everything that I've been afraid—*so* afraid—that it couldn't possibly be!"

No longer was it a feminine Lensman investigating a female zwilnik; it was two girls—two young, intensely alive, human girls—who chattered on and on.

Days passed. Clarrissa learned some of the uses of her Lens. Then Kimball Kinnison, Second Stage Lensman, began really to bear down. Since such training has been described in detail elsewhere, it need be said here only that Clarrissa MacDougall had mental capacity enough to take it without becoming insane. He suffered as much as she did; after every mental bout he was as spent as she was; but both of them stuck relentlessly to it.

He did not make a Second Stage Lensman of her, of course. He couldn't. Much of the stuff was too hazy yet; more of it did not apply. He gave her everything, however, which she could handle and which would be of any use to her in the work she was to do; including the sense of perception. He did it, that is, with a modicum of help; for, once or twice, when he faltered or weakened, not knowing exactly what to do or not being quite able to do it, a stronger mind than his was always there.

At length, approaching Tellus fast, the nurse and Kinnison had a final conference; the consultation of two Lensmen settling the last details of procedure in a long-planned and highly important campaign.

"I agree with you that Lyrane II is a key planet," she was saying, thoughtfully. "It must be, to have those expeditions from Lonabar and the as yet unknown planet 'X' centering there."

" 'X' certainly, and don't forget the possibility of 'Y' and 'Z' and maybe others," he reminded her. "The Lyrane-Lonabar linkage is the only one we're sure of. With you on one end of that and me on the other, it'll be funny if we can't trace out some more. While I'm building up an authentic identity to tackle Bleeko, you'll be getting chummy with Helen of Lyrane. That's about as far ahead as we can plan definitely right now, since this groundwork can't be hurried too much."

"And I report to you often—frequently, in fact." Clarrissa widened her expressive eyes at her man.

"At least," he agreed. "And I'll report to you between times."

"Oh, Kim, it's nice, being a Lensman!" She snuggled closer. Some way or other, the conference had become somewhat personal. "Being en rapport will be almost as good as being together—we can stand it, that way, at least."

"It'll help a lot, ace, no fooling. That was why I was afraid to go ahead with it on my own hook. I couldn't be sure that my feelings were not in control, instead of my judgment—if any."

"I'd have been certain that it was your soft heart instead of your hard head if it hadn't been for Mentor," she sighed, happily. "As it is, though, everything's on the green."

"All done with Illona?"

"Yes, the darling . . . she's the *sweetest* thing, Kim . . . and a storehouse of information if there ever was one. You and I know more of Boskonian life than anyone of Civilization ever knew before, I'm sure. And it's *so* ghastly! We *must* win, Kim . . . we simply *must,* for the good of all creation!"

"We will." Kinnison spoke with grim finality.

"But back to Illona. She can't go with me, and she can't stay here with Hank aboard the *Dauntless* taking me back to Lyrane, and you can't watch her. I'd hate to think of anything happening to her, Kim."

"It won't," he replied, comfortably. "Ilyowicz won't sleep nights until he has her as the top-flight solo dancer in his show—even though she doesn't have to work for a living any more . . ."

"She will, though, I think. Don't you?"

"Probably. Anyway, a couple of Haynes' smart girls are going to be her best friends, wherever she goes. Sort of keep an eye on her until she learns the ropes—it won't take long. We owe her that much, I figure."

"That much, at least. You're seeing to the selling of her jewelry yourself, aren't you?"

"No, I had a new thought on that. I'm going to buy it myself—or rather, Cartiff is. They're making up a set of paste imitations. Cartiff has to buy a stock somewhere; why not hers?"

"That's a thought—there's certainly enough of them to stock a wholesaler . . . 'Cartiff'—I can see that sign," she snickered. "Almost microscopic letters, severely plain, in the lower right-hand corner of an immense plate-glass window. One gem in the middle of an acre of black velvet. Cartiff, the most peculiar, if not quite the most exclusive, jeweler in the galaxy. And nobody except you and me knows anything about him. Isn't that something?"

"Everybody will know about Cartiff pretty soon," he told her. "Found any flaws in the scheme yet?"

"Nary a flaw." She shook her head. "That is, if none of the boys over-do it, and I'm sure they won't. I've got a picture of it," and she giggled merrily. "Think of a whole gang of sleuths from the Homicide Division chasing poor Cartiff, and never quite catching him!"

"Uh-huh—a touching picture indeed. But there goes the signal, and there's Tellus. We're about to land."

"Oh, I want to see!" and she started to get up.

"Look, then," pulling her down into her original place at his side. "You've got the sense of perception now, remember; you don't need visiplates."

And side by side, arms around each other, the two Lensmen watched the docking of their great vessel.

It landed. Jewelers came aboard with their carefully-made wares. Assured that the metal would not discolor her own skin, Illona made the exchange willingly enough. Beads were beads, to her. She could scarcely believe that she was now independently wealthy—in fact, she forgot all about her money after Ilyowicz had seen her dance.

"You see," she explained to Kinnison, "there were two things I wanted to do until Hank gets back—travel around a lot and learn all I can about your Civilization. I wanted to dance, too, but I didn't see how I could. Now I can do all three, and get paid for doing them besides—isn't that *marvelous?*—and Mr. Ilyowicz said you said it was QX. Is it, really?"

"Right," and Illona was off.

The *Dauntless* was serviced and Clarrissa was off, to far Lyrane.

Lensman Kinnison was supposedly off somewhere, also, when Cartiff appeared. Cartiff, the ultra-ultra; the Oh! so exclusive! Cartiff did not advertise. He catered, word spread fast, to only the very upper flakes of the upper crust. Simple dignity was Cartiff's key-note, his insidiously-spread claim; the dignified simplicity of immense wealth and impeccable social position.

What he actually achieved, however, was something subtly different. His simplicity was just a hair off-beam; his dignity was an affected, not a natural, quality. Nobody with less than a million credits ever got past his door, it is true. However, instead of being the real *creme de la creme* of Earth, Cartiff's clients were those who pretended to belong to, or who were trying to force an entrance into, that select stratum. Cartiff was a snob of snobs; he built up a clientele of snobs; and, even more than in his admittedly flawless gems, he dealt in equally high-proof snobbery.

Betimes came Nadreck, the Second Stage Lensman of Palain VII, and Kinnison met him secretly at Prime Base. Soft-voiced, apologetic, diffident; even though Kinnison now knew that the Palainian had a record of accomplishment as long as any one of his arms. But it was not an act, not affectation. It was simply a racial trait, for the intelligent and civilized race of that planet is in no sense human. Nadreck was utterly, startlingly unhuman. In his atmosphere there was no oxygen, in his body there flowed no aqueous blood. At his normal body temperature neither liquid water nor gaseous oxygen could exist.

The seventh planet out from any sun would of course be cold, but Kinnison had not thought particularly about the point until he felt the bitter radiation from the heavily-insulated suit of his guest; perceived how fiercely its refrigerators were laboring to keep its internal temperature down.

. "If you will permit it, please, I will depart at once," Nadreck pleaded, as soon as he had delivered his spool and his message. "My heat dissipators, powerful though they are, cannot cope much longer with this frightfully high temperature."

"QX, Nadreck, I won't keep you. Thanks a million. I'm mighty glad to have had this chance of getting acquainted with you. We'll see more of each other, I think, from now on. Remember, Lensman's Seal on all this stuff."

"Of course, Kinnison. You will understand, however, I am sure, that none of our races of Civilization are even remotely interested in Lonabar—it is as hot, as poisonous, as hellish generally as is Tellus itself!" The weird little monstrosity scuttled out.

Kinnison went back to Cartiff's; and very soon thereafter it became noised abroad that Cartiff was a crook. He was a cheat, a liar, a robber. His stones were synthetic; he made them himself. The stories grew. He was a smuggler; he didn't have an honest gem in his shop. He was a zwilnik, an out-and-out pirate; a red-handed murderer who, if he wasn't there already, certainly ought to be in the big black book of the Galactic Patrol. This wasn't just gossip, either; everybody saw and spoke to men who had seen unspeakable things with their own eyes.

Thus Cartiff was arrested. He blasted his way out, however, before he could be brought to trial, and the newscasters blazed with that highly spectacular, murderous jail-break. Nobody actually saw any lifeless bodies. Everybody, however, saw the Telenews broadcasts of the shattered walls and the sheeted forms; and, since such pictures are and always have been just as convincing as the real thing, everybody knew that there had been plenty of mangled corpses in those ruins and that Cartiff was a fugitive murderer. Also, everybody knew that the Patrol never gives up on a murderer.

Hence it was natural enough that the search for Cartiff, the jeweler-murderer, should spread from planet to planet and from region to region. Not exactly obtrusively, but inexorably, it did so spread; until finally anyone interested in the subject could find upon any one of a hundred million planets unmistakable evidence that the Patrol wanted one Cartiff, description so-and-so, for murder in the first degree.

And the Patrol was thorough. Wherever Cartiff went or how, they managed to follow him. At first he disguised himself, changed his name, and stayed in the legitimate jewelry business; apparently the only business he knew. But he never could get even a start. Scarcely would his shop open than he would be discovered and forced again to flee.

Deeper and deeper he went, then, into the noisome society of crime. A fence now—still and always he clung to jewelry. But always and ever the bloodhounds of the law were baying at his heels. Whatever name he used was nosed aside and "Cartiff!" they howled; so loudly that a thousand million worlds came to know that hated name.

Perforce he became a traveling fence, always on the go. He flew a dead-black ship, ultra-fast, armed and armored like a super-dreadnought, crewed—according to the newscasts—by the hardest-boiled gang of cut-throats in the known universe. He traded in, and boasted of trading in, the most blood-stained, the most ghost-ridden gems of a thousand worlds. And, so trading, hurling defiance the while into the teeth of the Patrol, establishing himself ever more firmly as one of Civilization's cleverest and most implacable foes, he worked zig-zag-wise and not at all obviously toward the unexplored spiral arm in which the planet Lonabar lay. And as he moved farther and farther away from the Solarian System his stock of jewels began to change. He had always favored pearls—the lovely, glorious things so characteristically Tellurian—and those he kept. The diamonds, however, he traded away; likewise the emeralds, the rubies, the sapphires, and some others. He kept and accumulated Borovan fire-stones, Manarkan star-drops, and a hundred other gorgeous gems, none of which would be "beads" upon the planet which was his goal.

As he moved farther he also moved faster; the Patrol was hopelessly outdistanced. Nevertheless, he took no chances. His villainous crew guarded his ship; his bullies guarded him wherever he went—surrounding him when he walked, standing behind him while he ate, sitting at either side of the bed in which he slept. He was a king-snipe now.

As such he was accosted one evening as he was about to dine in a garish restaurant. A tall, somewhat fish-faced man in faultless evening dress approached. His arms were at his sides, fingers bent into the "I'm not shooting" sign.

"Captain Cartiff, I believe. May I seat myself at your table, please?" the stranger asked, politely, in the lingua franca of deep space.

Kinnison's sense of perception frisked him rapidly for concealed weapons. He was clean. "I would be very happy, sir, to have you as my guest," he replied, courteously.

The stranger sat down, unfolded his napkin, and delicately allowed it to fall into his lap, all without letting either of his hands disappear from sight, even for an instant, beneath the table's top. He was an old and skillful hand. And during the excellent meal the two men conversed brilliantly upon many topics, none of which were of the least importance. After it Kinnison paid the check, despite the polite protestations of his *vis-a-vis*. Then:

"I am simply a messenger, you will understand, nothing else," the guest observed. "Number One has been checking up on you and has decided to let you come in. He will receive you tonight. The usual safe-guards on both sides, of course—I am to be your guide and guarantee."

"Very kind of him, I'm sure." Kinnison's mind raced. Who could this Number One be? The ape had a thought-screen on, so he was flying blind. Couldn't be a real big shot, though, so soon—no use monkeying with him at all. "Please convey my thanks, but also my regrets."

"What?" the other demanded. His veneer of politeness had sloughed off, his eyes were narrow, keen, and cold. "You know what happens to independent operators around here, don't you? Do you think you can fight *us?*"

"Not fight you, no." The Lensman elaborately stifled a yawn. He now had a clue. "Simply ignore you—if you act up, squash you like bugs, that's all. Please tell your Number One that I do not split my take with anybody. Tell him also that I am looking for a choicer location to settle down upon than any I have found as yet. If I do not find such a place near here, I shall move on. If I do find it I shall take it, in spite of God, man, or the devil."

The stranger stood up, glaring in quiet fury, but with both hands still above the table. "You want to make it a war, then, Captain Cartiff!" he gritted.

"Not 'Captain' Cartiff, please," Kinnison begged, dipping one paw delicately into his finger-bowl. " 'Cartiff' merely, my dear fellow, if you don't mind. Simplicity, sir, and dignity; those two are my key-words."

"Not for long," prophesied the other. "Number One'll blast you out of the ether before you swap another stone."

"The Patrol has been trying to do that for some time now, and I'm still here," Kinnison reminded him, gently. "Caution him, please, in order to avoid bloodshed, not to come after me in only one ship, but a fleet; and suggest that he have something hotter than Patrol primaries before he tackles me at all."

Surrounded by his bodyguards, Kinnison left the restaurant, and as he walked along he reflected. Nice going, this. It would get around fast. This Number One couldn't be Bleeko; but the king-snipe of Lonabar and its environs would hear the news in short order. He was now ready to go. He would flit around a few more days—give this bunch of zwilniks a chance to make a pass at him if they felt like calling his bluff—then on to Lonabar.

9

CARTIFF THE FENCE

Kinnison did not walk far, nor reflect much, before he changed his mind and retraced his steps; finding the messenger still in the restaurant.

"So you got wise to yourself and decided to crawl while the crawling's good, eh?" he sneered, before the Lensman could say a word. "I don't know whether the offer is still good or not."

"No—and I advise you to muffle your exhaust before somebody pulls one of your legs off and rams it down your throat." Kinnison's voice was coldly level. "I came back to tell you to tell your Number One that I'm calling his bluff. You know Checuster?"

"Of course." The zwilnik was plainly discomfited.

"Come along, then, and listen, so you'll know I'm not running a blazer."

They sought a booth, wherein the native himself got Checuster on the visiplate.

"Checuster, this is Cartiff." The start of surprise and the expression of pleased interest revealed how well that name was known. "I'll be down at your old warehouse day after tomorrow night about this time. Pass the word around that if any of the boys have any stuff too hot for them to handle conveniently, I'll buy it; paying for it in either Patrol credits or bar platinum, whichever they like."

He then turned to the messenger. "Did you get that straight, Lizard-Puss?"

The man nodded.

"Relay it to Number One," Kinnison ordered and strode off. This time he got to his ship, which took off at once.

Cartiff had never made a habit of wearing visible arms, and his guards, while undoubtedly fast gun-men, were apparently only that. Therefore there was no reason for Number One to suppose that his mob would have any noteworthy difficulty in cutting this upstart Cartiff down. He was, however, surprised; for Cartiff did not come afoot or unarmed.

Instead, it was an armored car that brought the intruding fence through the truck-entrance into the old warehouse. Not a car, either; it was more like a twenty-ton tank except for the fact that it ran upon wheels, not treads. It was screened like a cruiser; it mounted a battery of projectors whose energies, it was clear to any discerning eye, nothing short of battle-screen could handle. The thing rolled quietly to a stop, a door swung open, and Kinnison emerged. He was neither unarmed nor unarmored now. Instead, he wore a full suit of G-P armor or a reasonable facsimile thereof, and carried a semi-portable projector.

"You will excuse the seeming discourtesy, men," he announced, "when I tell you that a certain Number One has informed me that he will blast me out of the ether before I swap a stone on this planet. Stand clear, please, until we see whether he meant business or was just warming up his jets. Now, Number One, if you're around, come and get it!"

Apparently the challenged party was not present, for no overt move was made. Neither could Kinnison's sense of perception discover any sign of unfriendly activity within its range. Of mind-reading there was none, for every man upon the floor was, as usual, both masked and screened.

Business was slack at first, for those present were not bold souls and the Lensman's overwhelmingly superior armament gave them very seriously to doubt his intentions. Many of them, in fact, had fled precipitately at the first sight of the armored truck, and of these more than a few—Number One's thugs, no doubt—did not return. The others, however, came filtering back as they perceived that there was to be no warfare and as cupidity overcame their timorousness. And as it became evident to all that the stranger's armament was for defense only, that he was there to buy or to barter and not to kill and thus to steal, Cartiff trafficked ever more and more briskly, as the evening wore on, in the hottest gems of the planet.

Nor did he step out of character for a second. He was Cartiff the fence, all the time. He drove hard bargains, but not too hard. He knew jewels thoroughly by this time, he knew the code, and he followed it rigorously. He would give a thousand Patrol credits, in currency good upon any planet of Civilization or in bar platinum good anywhere, for an article worth five thousand, but which was so badly wanted by the law that its then possessor could not dispose of it at all. Or, in barter, he would swap for that article another item, worth fifteen hundred or so, but which was not hot—at least, not upon that planet. Fair enough— so fair that it was almost morning before the silently-running truck slid into its storage inside the dead-black space-ship.

Then, insofar as Number One, the Patrol, and Civilization was concerned, Cartiff and his outfit simply vanished. The zwilnik sub-chief hunted him viciously for a space, then bragged of how he had run him out of the region. The Patrol, as usual, was on a cold scent. The general public forgot him completely in the next sensation to arise.

Fairly close although he then was to the rim of the galaxy, Kinnison did not take any chances at all of detection in a line toward that rim. The spiral arm beyond Rift Eighty Five was unexplored. It had been of so little interest to Civilization that even its various regions were nameless upon the charts, and the Lensman wanted it to remain that way, at least for the time being. Therefore he left the galaxy in as nearly a straight nadir line as he could without coming within detection distance of any trade route. Then, making a prodigious loop, so as to enter the spiral arm from the nadir direction, he threw Nadreck's map into the pilot tank and began the computations which would enable him to place correctly in that three-dimensional chart the brilliant point of light which represented his ship.

In this work he was ably assisted by his chief pilot. He did not have Henderson now, but he did have Watson, who rated Number Two only by the hair-splitting of the supreme Board of Examiners. Such hair-splitting was, of course, necessary; otherwise no difference at all could have been found within the ranks of the first fifty of the Patrol's Master Pilots, to say nothing of the first three or four. And the rest of the crew did whatever they could.

For it was only in the newscasts that Cartiff's crew was one of murderous and villainous pirates. They were in fact volunteers; and, since everyone is familiar with what that means in the Patrol, that statement is as informative as a book would be.

The chart was sketchy and incomplete, of course; around the flying ships were hundreds, yes thousands, of stars which were not in the chart at all; but Nadreck had furnished enough reference points so that the pilots could compute their orientation. No need to fear detectors now, in these wild, waste spaces; they set a right-line course for Lonabar and followed it.

As soon as Kinnison could make out the continental outlines of the planet he took over control, as he alone of the crew was upon familiar ground. He knew everything about Lonabar that Illona had ever learned; and, although the girl was a total loss as an astronaut, she did know her geography.

Kinnison docked his ship boldly at the spaceport of Lonia, the planet's largest city and its capital. With equal boldness he registered as "Cartiff"; filling in some of the blank spaces in the space-port's routine registry form—not quite truthfully, perhaps—and blandly ignoring others. The armored truck was hoisted out of the hold and made its way to Lonia's largest bank, into which it disgorged a staggering total of bar platinum, as well as sundry coffers of hard, gray steel. These last items went directly into a private vault, under the watchful eyes and ready weapons of Kinnison's own guards.

The truck rolled swiftly back to the spaceport and Cartiff's ship took off—it did not need servicing at the time—ostensibly for another planet unknown to the Patrol, actually to go, inert, into a closed orbit around Lonabar and near enough to it to respond to a call in seconds.

Immense wealth can command speed of construction and service. Hence, in a matter of days, Cartiff was again in business. His salon was, upon a larger and grander scale, a repetition of his Tellurian shop. It was simple, and dignified, and blatantly expensive. Costly rugs covered the floor, impeccable works of art adorned the walls, and three precisely correct, flawlessly groomed clerks displayed, with the exactly right air of condescending humility, Cartiff's wares before those who wished to view them. Cartiff himself was visible, ensconced within a magnificent plate-glass-and-gold office in the rear, but he did not ordinarily have anything to do with customers. He waited; nor did he wait long before there happened that which he expected.

One of the super-perfect clerks coughed slightly into a microphone.

"A gentleman insists upon seeing you personally, sir," he announced.

"Very well, I will see him now. Show him in, please," and the visitor was ceremoniously ushered into the Presence.

"This is a very nice place you have here, Mr. Cartiff, but did it ever occur to you that . . ."

"It never did and it never will," Kinnison snapped. He still lolled at ease in his chair, but his eyes were frosty and his voice carried an icy sting. "I quit paying protection to little shots a good many years ago. Or are you from Menjo Bleeko?"

The visitor's eyes widened. He gasped, as though even to utter that dread name was sheer sacrilege. "No, but Number . . ."

"Save it, slob!" The cold venom of that crisp but quiet order set the fellow back onto his heels. "I am thoroughly sick of this thing of every half-baked tin-horn zwilnik in space calling himself Number One as soon as he can steal enough small change to hire an ape to walk around behind him packing a couple of blasters. If that louse of a boss of yours has a name, use it. If he hasn't call him 'The Louse'. But cancel that Number One stuff. In my book there is no Number One in the whole damned universe. Doesn't your mob know yet who and what Cartiff is?"

"What do we care?" the visitor gathered courage visibly. "A good big bomb . . ."

"Clam it, you squint-eyed slime-lizard!" The Lensman's voice was still low and level, but his tone bit deep and his words drilled in. "That stuff?" he waved inclusively at the magnificent hall. "Sucker-bait, nothing more. The whole works cost only a hundred thousand. Chicken feed. It wouldn't even nick the edge of the roll if you blew up ten of them. Bomb it any time you feel the urge. But take notice that it would make me sore—plenty sore—and that I would do things about it; because I'm in a big game, not this petty-larceny racketeering and chiseling your mob is doing, and when a toad gets in my way I step on it. So go back and tell that"—sulphurously and copiously qualified—"Number One of yours to case a job a lot more thoroughly than he did this one before he starts throwing his weight around. Now scram, before I feed your carcass to the other rats around here!"

Kinnison grinned inwardly as the completely deflated gangster slunk out. Good going. It wouldn't take long for *that* blast to get action. This little-shot Number One wouldn't dare to lift a hand, but Bleeko would have to. That was axiomatic, from the very nature of things. It was very definitely Bleeko's move next. The only moot point was as to which His Nibs would do first—talk or act. He would talk, the Lensman thought. The prime reward of being a hot-shot was to have people know it and bend the knee. Therefore, although Cartiff's salon was at all times in complete readiness for any form of violence, Kinnison was practically certain that Menjo Bleeko would send an emissary before he started the rough stuff.

He did, and shortly. A big, massive man was the messenger; a man wearing consciously an aura of superiority, of boundless power and force. He did not simply come into the shop—he made an entrance. All three of the clerks literally cringed before him, and at his casually matter-of-fact order they hazed the already uncomfortable customers out of the shop and locked the doors. Then one of them escorted the visitor, with a sickening servility he had never thought of showing toward his employer and with no thought of consulting Cartiff's wishes in the matter, into Cartiff's private sanctum. Kinnison knew at first glance that this was Ghundrith Khars, Bleeko's right-hand man. Khars, the notorious, who knelt only to His Supremacy, Menjo Bleeko himself; and to whom everyone else upon Lonabar and its subsidiary planets kneeled. The visitor waved a hand and the clerk fled in disorder.

"Stand up, worm, and give me that . . ." Khars began, loftily.

"Silence, fool! Attention!" Kinnison rasped, in such a drivingly domineering tone that the stupefied messenger obeyed involuntarily. The Lensman, psychologist par excellence that he was, knew that this man, with a background of twenty years of blind, dumb obedience to Bleeko's every order, simply could not cope with a positive and self-confident opposition. "You will not be here long enough to sit down, even if I permitted it in my presence, which I definitely do not. You came here to give me certain instructions and orders. Instead, you are going to listen merely; I will do all the talking.

"First. The only reason you did not die as you entered this place is that neither you nor Menjo Bleeko knows any better. The next one of you to approach me in this fashion dies in his tracks.

"Second. Knowing as I do the workings of that which your bloated leech of a Menjo Bleeko calls his brain, I know that he has a spy-ray on us now. I am not blocking it out as I want him to receive ungarbled—and I know that you would not have the courage to transmit it accurately to His Foulness—everything I have to say.

"Third. I have been searching for a long time for a planet that I like. This is it. I fully intend to stay here as long as I please. There is plenty of room here for both of us without crowding.

"Fourth. Being essentially a peaceable man, I came in peace and I prefer a peaceable arrangement. However, let it be distinctly understood that I truckle to no man or entity; dead, living, or yet to be born.

"Fifth. Tell Bleeko from me to consider very carefully and very thoroughly an iceberg; its every phase and aspect. That is all—you may go."

"Bub-bub-but," the big man stammered. "An *iceberg?*"

"An iceberg, yes—just that," Kinnison assured him. "Don't bother to try to think about it yourself, since you've got nothing to think with. But His Putrescence Bleeko, even though he is a mental, moral, and intellectual slime-lizard, can think—at least in a narrow, mean, small-souled sort of way—and I advise him in all seriousness to do so. Now get the hell out of here, before I burn the seat of your pants off."

Khars got, gathering together visibly the shreds of his self-esteem as he did so; the clerks staring the while in dumbfounded amazement. Then they huddled together, eyeing the owner of the establishment with a brand-new respect—a subservient respect, heavily laced with awe.

"Business as usual, boys," he counseled them, cheerfully enough. "They won't blow up the place until after dark."

The clerks resumed their places then and trade did go on, after a fashion; but Cartiff's force had not recovered its wonted blasé aplomb even at closing time.

"Just a moment." The proprietor called his employees together and, reaching into his pocket, distributed among them a sheaf of currency. "In case you don't find the shop here in the morning, you may consider yourselves on vacation at full pay until I call you."

They departed, and Kinnison went back to his office. His first care was to set up a spy-ray block—a block which had been purchased upon Lonabar and which was therefore certainly pervious to Bleeko's instruments. Then he prowled about, apparently in deep and anxious thought. But as he prowled, the eavesdroppers did not, could not, know that his weight set into operation certain devices of his own highly secret installation, or that when he finally left the shop no really serious harm could be done to it except by an explosion sufficiently violent to demolish the neighborhood for blocks around. The front wall would go, of course. He wanted it to go; otherwise there would be neither reason nor excuse for doing that which for days he had been ready to do.

Since Cartiff lived rigorously to schedule and did not have a spy-ray block in his room, Bleeko's methodical and efficient observers always turned off their beams when the observee went to sleep. This night, however, Kinnison was not really asleep, and as soon as the ray went off he acted. He threw on his clothes and sought the street, where he took a taxi to a certain airport. There he climbed into a prop-and-rocket job already hot and waiting.

Hanging from her screaming props the fantastically powerful little plane bulleted upward in a vertical climb, and as she began to slow down from lack of air her rockets took over. A tractor reached out, seizing her gently. Her wings retracted and she was drawn into Cartiff's great space-ship; which, a few minutes later, hung poised above one of the largest, richest jewel-mines of Lonabar.

This mine was, among others, Menjo Bleeko's personal property. Since over-production would glut the market, it was being worked by only one shift of men; the day-shift. It was now black night; the usual guards were the only men upon the premises. The big black ship hung there and waited.

"But suppose they don't, Kim?" Watson asked.

"Then we'll wait here every night until they do," Kinnison replied, grimly. "But they'll do it tonight, for all the tea in China. They'll have to, to save Bleeko's face."

And they did. In a couple of hours the observer at a high-powered plate reported that Cartiff's salon had just been blown to bits. Then the Patrolmen went into action.

Bleeko's mobsmen hadn't killed anybody at Cartiff's, therefore the Tellurians wouldn't kill anybody here. Hence, while ten immense beam-dirigible torpedoes were being piloted carefully down shafts and along tunnels into the deepest bowels of the workings, the guards were given warning that, if they got into their flyers fast enough, they could be fifty miles away and probably safe by zero time. They hurried.

At zero time the torpedoes let go as one. The entire planet quivered under the trip-hammer shock of detonating duodec. For those frightful, those appalling charges had been placed, by computations checked and rechecked, precisely where they would wreak the most havoc, the utmost possible measure of sheer destruction. Much of the rock, however hard, around each one of those incredible centers of demolition was simply blasted out of existence. That is the way duodec, in massive charges, works. Matter simply cannot get out of its way in the first instants of its detonation; matter's own inherent inertia forbids.

Most of the rock between the bombs was pulverized the merest fraction of a second later. Then, the distortedly-spherical explosion fronts merging, the total incomprehensible pressure was exerted as almost pure lift. The field above the mine-works lifted, then; practically as a mass at first. But it could not remain as such. It could not move fast enough as a whole; nor did it possess even a minute fraction of the tensile strength necessary to withstand the stresses being applied. Those stresses, the forces of the explosions, were to all intents and purposes irresistible. The crust disintegrated violently and almost instantaneously. Rock crushed grindingly against rock; practically the whole mass reducing in the twinkling of an eye to an impalpable powder.

Upward and outward, then, the ragingly compressed gases of detonation drove, hurling everything before them. Chunks blew out sidewise, flying for miles; the mind-staggeringly enormous volume of dust was hurled upward clear into the stratosphere.

Finally that awful dust-cloud was wafted aside, revealing through

its thinning haze a strangely and hideously altered terrain. No sign remained of the buildings or the mechanisms of Bleeko's richest mine.
No vestige was left to show that anything built by or pertaining to man
had ever existed there. Where those works had been there now yawned
an absolutely featureless crater; a crater whose sheer geometrical perfection of figure revealed with shocking clarity the magnitude of the
cataclysmic forces which had wrought there.

Kinnison, looking blackly down at that crater, did not feel the glow
of satisfaction which comes of a good deed well done. He detested it—it
made him sick at the stomach. But, since he had had it to do, he had done
it. Why in all the nine hells of Valeria did he have to be a Lensman,
anyway?

Back to Lonia, then, the Lensman made his resentful way, and back
to bed.

And in the morning, early, workmen began the reconstruction of
Cartiff's place of business.

10

BLEEKO AND THE ICEBERG

Since Kinnison's impenetrable shields of force had confined the damage to the store's front, it was not long before Cartiff's reopened. Business was and remained brisk; not only because of what had happened, but also because Cartiff's top-lofty and arrogant snobbishness had an irresistible appeal to the upper layers of Lonabar's peculiarly stratified humanity. The Lensman, however, paid little enough attention to business. Outwardly, seated at his ornate desk in haughty grandeur, he was calmness itself, but inwardly he was far from serene.

If he had figured things right, and he was pretty sure that he had, it was up to Bleeko to make the next move, and it would pretty nearly have to be a peaceable one. There was enough doubt about it, however, to make the Lensman a bit jittery inside. Also, from the fact that everybody having any weight at all wore thought-screens, it was almost a foregone conclusion that they had been warned against, and were on the lookout for, THE Lensman—that never-to-be-sufficiently-damned Lensman who had already done so much hurt to the Boskonian cause. That they now thought that one to be a well-hidden, unknown Director of Lensmen, and not an actual operative, was little protection. If he made one slip they'd have him, cold.

He hadn't slipped yet, they didn't suspect him yet; he was sure of those points. With these people to suspect was to act, and his world-circling ship, equipped with every scanning, spying, and eavesdropping device known to science, would have informed him instantly of any untoward development anywhere upon or near the planet. And his fight with Bleeko was, after all, natural enough and very much in character. It was of the very essence of Boskonian culture that king-snipes should do each other to death with whatever weapons came readiest to hand. The underdog was always trying to kill the upper, and if the latter was not strong enough to protect his loot, he deserved everything he got. A callous philosophy, it is true, but one truly characteristic of Civilization's inveterate foes.

The higher-ups never interfered. Their own skins were the only ones in which they were interested. They would, Kinnison reflected, probably check back on him, just to insure their own safety, but they would not take sides in this brawl if they were convinced that he was, as he appeared to be, a struggling young racketeer making his way up the ladder of fame and fortune as best he could. Let them check—Cartiff's past had been fabricated especially to stand up under precisely that investigation, no matter how rigid it were to be!

Hence Kinnison waited, as calmly as might be, for Bleeko to move. There was no particular hurry, especially since Cris was finding heavy going and thick ether at her end of the line, too. They had been in communication at least once every day, usually oftener; and Clarrissa had reported seethingly, in near-masculine, almost-deep-space verbiage, that that damned red-headed hussy of a Helen was a hard nut to crack.

Kinnison grinned sourly every time he thought of Lyrane II. Those matriarchs certainly were a rum lot. They were a pig-headed, self-centered, mulishly stubborn bunch of cock-eyed knotheads, he decided. Non-galaxy-minded; as short-sightedly anti-social as a flock of mad Radeligian cateagles. He'd better . . . no, he hadn't better, either— he'd have to lay off. If Cris, with all her potency and charm, with all her drive and force of will, with all her sheer power of mind and of Lens, couldn't pierce their armor, what chance did any other entity of Civilization have of doing it? Particularly any male creature? He'd like to half-wring their beautiful necks, all of them; but that wouldn't get him to the first check-station, either. He'd just have to wait until she broke through the matriarchs' crust—she'd do it, too, by Klono's prehensile tail!—and then they'd really ride the beam.

So Kinnison waited . . . and waited . . . and waited. When he got tired of waiting he gave a few more lessons in snobbishness and in the gentle art of self-preservation to the promising young Lonabarian thug whom he had selected to inherit the business, lock, stock, and barrel—

including good-will, if any—if, as, and when he was done with it. Then he waited some more; waited, in fact, until Bleeko was forced, by his silent pressure, to act.

It was not an overt act, nor an unfriendly—he simply called him up on the visiphone.

"What do you think you're trying to do?" Bleeko demanded, his darkly handsome face darker than ever with wrath.

"You." Kinnison made succinct answer. "You should have taken my advice about pondering the various aspects of an iceberg."

"Bah!" the other snorted. "That silliness?"

"Not as silly as you think. That was a warning, Bleeko, that the stuff showing above the surface is but a very small portion of my total resources. But you could not or would not learn by precept. You had to have it the hard way. Apparently, however, you have learned. That you have not been able to locate my forces I am certain. I am almost as sure that you do not want to try me again, at least until you have found out what you do not know. But I can give you no more time—you must decide now, Bleeko, whether it is to be peace or war between us. I still prefer a peaceful settlement, with an equitable division of the spoils; but if you want war, so be it."

"I have decided upon peace," the Lonabarian said, and the effort of it almost choked him. "I, Menjo Bleeko the Supreme, will give you a place beside me. Come to me here, at once, so that we may discuss the terms of peace."

"We will discuss them now," Kinnison insisted.

"Impossible! Barred and shielded as this room is . . ."

"It would be," Kinnison interrupted with a nod, "for you to make such an admission as you have just made."

". . . I do not trust unreservedly this communication line. If you join me now, you may do so in peace. If you do not come to me, here and now, it is war to the death."

"Fair enough, at that," the Lensman admitted. "After all, you've got to save your face, and I haven't—yet. And if I team up with you I can't very well stay out of your palace forever. But before I come there I want to give you three things—a reminder, a caution, and a warning. I remind you that our first exchange of amenities cost you a thousand times as much as it did me. I caution you to consider again, and more carefully this time, the iceberg. I warn you that if we again come into conflict you will lose not only a mine, but everything you have, including your life. So see to it that you lay no traps for me. I come."

He went out into the shop. "Take over, Sport," he told his gangster protege. "I'm going up to the palace to see Menjo Bleeko. If I'm not back in two hours, and if your grapevine reports that Bleeko is out of the picture, what I've left in the store here is yours until I come back and take it away from you."

"I'll take care of it, Boss—thanks," and the Lensman knew that in true Lonabarian gratitude the youth was already, mentally, slipping a long, keen knife between his ribs.

Without a qualm, but with every sense stretched to the limit and in instant readiness for any eventuality, Kinnison took a cab to the palace and entered its heavily-guarded portals. He was sure that they would not cut him down before he got to Bleeko's room—that room would surely be the one chosen for the execution. Nevertheless, he took no chances. He was supremely ready to slay instantly every guard within range of his sense of perception at the first sign of inimical activity. Long before he came to them, he made sure that the beams which were set to search him for concealed weapons were really search-beams and not lethal vibrations.

And as he passed those beams each one of them reported him clean. Rings, of course; a stick-pin, and various other items of adornment. But Cartiff, the great jeweler, would be expected to wear very large and exceedingly costly gems. And the beam has never been projected which could penetrate those Worsel-designed, Thorndyke-built walls of force; to show that any one of those flamboyant gems was not precisely what it appeared to be.

Searched, combed minutely, millimeter by cubic millimeter, Kinnison was escorted by a heavily-armed quartette of Bleeko's personal guards into His Supremacy's private study. All four bowed as he entered—but they strode in behind him, then shut and locked the door.

"You fool!" Bleeko gloated from behind his massive desk. His face flamed with sadistic joy and anticipation. "You trusting, greedy fool! I have you exactly where I want you now. How easy! How simple! This entire building is screened and shielded—by *my* screens and shields. Your friends and accomplices, whoever or wherever they are, can neither see you nor know what is to happen to you. If your ship attempts your rescue it will be blasted out of the ether. I will, personally, gouge out your eyes, tear off your nails, strip your hide from your quivering carcass . . ." Bleeko was now, in his raging exaltation, fairly frothing at the mouth.

"That would be a good trick if you could do it," Kinnison remarked, coldly. "But the real fact is that you haven't even tried to use that pint of blue mush that you call a brain. Do you think me an utter idiot? I put on an act and you fell for it . . ."

"Seize him, guards! Silence his yammering—tear out his tongue!" His Supremacy shrieked, leaping out of his chair as though possessed.

The guards tried manfully, but before they could touch him—before any one of them could take one full step—they dropped. Without being touched by material object or visible beam, without their proposed victim having moved a muscle, they died and fell. Died instantly, in their tracks; died completely, effortlessly, painlessly, with every molecule of the all-important compound without which life cannot even momentarily exist shattered instantaneously into its degradation products; died not knowing even that they died.

Bleeko was shaken, but he was not beaten. Needle-ray men, sharp-shooters all, were stationed behind those walls. Gone now the dictator's intent to torture his victim to death. Slaying him out of hand would have to suffice. He flashed a signal to the concealed marksmen, but that order too went unobeyed. For Kinnison had perceived the hidden gunmen long since, and before any of them could align his sights or press his firing stud each one of them ceased to live. The zwilnik then flipped on his communicator and gobbled orders. Uselessly; for death sped ahead. Before any mind at any switchboard could grasp the meaning of the signal, it could no longer think.

"You fiend from hell!" Bleeko screamed, in mad panic now, and wrenched open a drawer in order to seize a weapon of his own. Too late. The Lensman had already leaped, and as he landed he struck—not gently. Lonabar's tyrant collapsed upon the thick-piled rug in a writhing, gasping heap; but he was not unconscious. To suit Kinnison's purpose he could not be unconscious; he had to be in full possession of his mind.

The Lensmen crooked one brawny arm around the zwilnik's neck in an unbreakable strangle-hold and flipped off his thought-screen. Physical struggles were of no avail: the attacker knew exactly what to do to certain nerves and ganglia to paralyze all such activity. Mental resistance was equally futile against the overwhelmingly superior power of the Tellurian's mind. Then, his subject quietly passive, Kinnison tuned in and began his search for information. Began it—and swore soulfully. This *couldn't* be so . . . it didn't make any kind of sense . . . but there it was.

The ape simply didn't know a thing about any ramification whatever of the vast culture to which Civilization was opposed. He knew all about Lonabar and the rest of the domain which he had ruled with such an iron hand. He knew much—altogether too much—about humanity and Civilization, and plainly to be read in his mind were the methods by which he had obtained those knowledges and the brutally efficient precautions he had taken to make sure that Civilization would not in turn learn of him.

Kinnison scowled blackly. His deductions simply *couldn't* be that far off . . . and besides, it wasn't reasonable that this guy was the top or that he had done all that work on his own account . . . He pondered deeply, staring unseeing at Bleeko's placid face; and as he pondered, some of the jigsaw blocks of the puzzle began to click into a pattern.

Then, ultra-carefully, with the utmost nicety of which he was capable, he again fitted his mind to that of the dictator and began to trace, one at a time, the lines of memory. Searching, probing, coursing backward and forward along those deeply-buried time-tracks, until at last he found the breaks and the scars. For, as he had told Illona, a radical mind-operation cannot be performed without leaving marks. It is true that upon cold, unfriendly Jarnevon, after Worsel had so operated upon Kinnison's mind, Kinnison himself could not perceive that any work had been done. But that, be it remembered, was before any actual change had occurred; before the compulsion had been applied. The false memories supplied by Worsel were still latent, non-existent; the true memory chains, complete and intact, were still in place.

The lug's brain had been operated upon, Kinnison now knew, and by an expert. What the compulsion was, what combination of thought-stimuli it was that would restore those now non-existent knowledges, Kinnison had utterly no means of finding out. Bleeko himself, even subconsciously, did not know. It was, it had to be, something external, a thought-pattern impressed upon Bleeko's mind by the Boskonian higher-up whenever he wanted to use him; and to waste time in trying to solve *that* problem would be the sheerest folly. Nor could he discover how that compulsion had been or could be applied. If he got his orders from the Boskonian high command direct, there would have to be an inter-galactic communicator; and it would in all probability be right here, in Bleeko's private rooms. No force-ball, or anything else that could take its place, was to be found. Therefore Bleeko was, probably, merely another Regional Director, and took orders from someone here in the First Galaxy.

Lyrane? The possibility jarred Kinnison. No real probability pointed that way yet, however; it was simply a possibility, born of his own anxiety. He couldn't worry about it—yet.

His study of the zwilnik's mind, unproductive although it was of the desired details of things Boskonian, had yielded one highly important fact. His Supremacy of Lonabar had sent at least one expedition to Lyrane II; yet there was no present memory in his mind that he had ever done so. Kinnison had scanned those files with surpassing care, and knew positively that Bleeko did not now know even that such a planet as Lyrane II existed.

Could he, Kinnison, be wrong? Could somebody other than Menjo Bleeko have sent that ship? Or those ships, since it was not only possible, but highly probable, that that voyage was not an isolated instance? No, he decided instantly. Illona's knowledge was far too detailed and exact. Nothing of such importance would be or could be done without the knowledge and consent of Lonabar's dictator. And the fact that he did not now remember it was highly significant. It meant—it *must* mean—that the new Boskone or whoever was back of Boskone considered the solar system of Lyrane of such vital importance that knowledge of it must never, under any circumstances, get to Star A Star, the detested, hated, and feared Director of Lensmen of the Galactic Patrol! And Mac was on Lyrane II—ALONE! She had been safe enough so far, but . . .

"Cris!" he sent her an insistent thought.

"Yes, Kim?" came a flashing answer.

"Thank Klono and Noshabkeming! You're QX, then?"

"Of course. Why shouldn't I be, the same as I was this morning?"

"Things have changed since then," he assured her, grimly. "I've finally cracked things open here, and I find that Lonabar is simply a dead end. It's a feeder for Lyrane, nothing else. It's not a certainty, of course, but there's a very distinct possibility that Lyrane is IT. If it is, I don't need to tell you that you're on a mighty hot spot. So I want you to quit whatever you're doing and run. Hide. Crawl into a hole and pull it in after you. Get into one of Helen's deepest crypts and have somebody sit on the lid. And do it right now—five minutes ago would have been better."

"Why, Kim!" she giggled. "Everything here is exactly as it has always been. And surely, you wouldn't have a Lensman hide, would you? Would you, yourself?"

That question was, they both knew, unanswerable. "That's different," he of course protested, but he knew that it was not. "Well, anyway, be careful," he insisted. "More careful than you ever were before in your life. Use everything you've got, every second, and if you notice anything, however small, the least bit out of the way, let me know, right then."

"I'll do that. You're coming, of course." It was a statement, not a question.

"I'll say I am—in force! 'Bye, Cris—BE CAREFUL!" and he snapped the line. He had a lot to do. He had to act fast, and had to be right—and he couldn't take all day in deciding, either.

His mind flashed back over what he had done. Could he cover up? Should he cover up, even if he could? Yes and no. Better not even try to cover Cartiff up, he decided. Leave that trail just as it was; wide and plain—up to a certain point. This point, right here. Cartiff would disappear here, in Bleeko's palace.

He was done with Cartiff, anyway. They would smell a rat, of course—it stunk to high heaven. They might not—they probably would not—believe that he had died in the ruins of the palace, but they wouldn't know that he hadn't. And they would think that he hadn't found out a thing, and he would keep them thinking so as long as he could. The young thug in Cartiff's would help, too, all unconsciously. He would assume the name and station, of course, and fight with everything Kinnison had taught him. That *would* help—Kinnison grinned as he realized just how much it would help.

The real Cartiff would have to vanish as completely, as absolutely without a trace as was humanly possible. They would figure out in time that Cartiff had done whatever was done in the palace, but it was up to him to see to it that they could never find out how it was done. Wherefore he took from Menjo's mind every iota of knowledge which might conceivably be of use to him thereafter. Then Menjo Bleeko died and the Lensman strode along corridors and down stairways. And wherever he went, there went Death.

This killing griped Kinnison to the core of his being, but it had to be. The fate of all Civilization might very well depend upon the completeness of his butchery this day; upon the sheer mercilessness of his extermination of every foe who might be able to cast any light, however dim, upon what he had just done.

Straight to the palace arsenal he went, where he labored briefly at the filling of a bin with bombs. A minute more to set a timer and he was done. Out of the building he ran. No one stayed him; nor did any, later, say that they had seen him go. He dumped a dead man out of a car and drove it away at reckless speed. Even at that, however, he was almost too slow—hurtling stones from the dynamited palace showered down scarcely a hundred feet behind his screeching wheels.

He headed for the space-port; then, changing his mind, braked savagely as he sent Lensed instructions to Watson. He felt no compunction about fracturing the rules and regulations made and provided for the landing of space-ships at space-ports everywhere by having his vessel make a hot-blast, unauthorized, and quite possibly highly destructive landing to pick him up. Nor did he fear pursuit. The big shots were, for the most part, dead. The survivors and the middle-sized shots were too busy by far to waste time over an irregular incident at a space-port. Hence nobody would give anybody any orders, and without explicit orders no Lonabarian officer would act. No, there would be no pursuit. But They—the Ones Kinnison was after—would interpret truly every such irregular incident; wherefore there must not be any.

Thus it came about that when the speeding ground-car was upon an empty stretch of highway, with nothing in sight in any direction, a space-ship eased down upon muffled under-jets directly above it. A tractor beam reached down; car and man were drawn upward and into the vessel's hold. Kinnison did not want the car, but he could not leave it there. Since many cars had been blown out of existence with Bleeko's palace, for this one to disappear would be natural enough; but for it to be found abandoned out in the open country would be a highly irregular and an all too revealing occurrence.

Upward through atmosphere and stratosphere the black cruiser climbed; out into interstellar space she flashed. Then, while Watson coaxed the sleek flyer to do even better than her prodigious best, Kinnison went to his room and drilled a thought to Prime Base and Port Admiral Haynes.

"Kinnison. Are you too busy to give me a couple of minutes?"

"You always have the right-of-way, Kim, you know that—you're the most important thing in the galaxy right now," Haynes said, soberly.

"Well, a minute or so wouldn't make any difference—not *that* much difference, anyway," Kinnison replied, uncomfortably. "I don't like to Lens you unless I have to," and he began his report.

Scarcely had he started, however, when he felt a call impinge upon his own Lens. Clarrissa was calling him from Lyrane II.

"Just a sec, admiral! Come in, Cris—make it a three-way with Admiral Haynes!"

"You told me to report anything unusual, no matter what," the girl began. "Well, I finally managed to get chummy enough with Helen so she'd really talk to me. The death-rate from airplane crashes went up sharply a while ago and is still rising. I am reporting that fact as per instructions."

"Hm . . . m . . . m. What kind of crashes?" Kinnison asked.

"That's the unusual feature of it. Nobody knows—they just disappear."

"WHAT?" Kinnison yelled the thought, so forcibly that both Clarrissa and Haynes winced under its impact.

"Why, yes," she replied, innocently—somewhat too innocently. "But as to what it means . . ."

"You know what it means, don't you?" Kinnison snapped.

"I don't *know* anything. I can do some guessing, of course, but for the present I'm reporting a fact, not personal opinions."

"QX. That fact means that you *do,* right now, crawl into the deepest, most heavily thought-screened hole in Lyrane and stay there until I, personally, come and dig you out," he replied, grimly. "It means, Admiral Haynes, that I want Worsel and Tregonsee as fast as I can get them—not orders, of course, but very, *very* urgent requests. And I want vanBuskirk and his gang of Valerians, and Grand Fleet, with all the trimmings, within easy striking distance of Dunstan's Region as fast as you can possibly get them there. And I want . . ."

"Why all the excitement, Kim?" Haynes demanded. "You're 'way ahead of me, both of you. Give!"

"I don't *know* anything, either," Kinnison emphasized the verb very strongly. "However, I suspect a lot. Everything, in fact, grading downward from the Eich. I'd say Overlords, except that I don't see how . . . what do you think, Cris?"

"What I think is too utterly fantastic for words—my visualization of the Cosmic All calls for another Eich-Overlord alliance."

"Could be, I guess. That would . . ."

"But they were all destroyed, weren't they?" Haynes interrupted.

"Far from it." This from the nurse. "Would the destruction of Tellus do away with all mankind? I am beginning to think that the Eich are to Boskonia exactly what we are to Civilization."

"So am I," Kinnison agreed. "And, such being the case, I'm going to get in touch with Nadreck of Palain Seven—I think I know his pattern well enough to Lens him from here."

"Nadreck? Your new playfellow? Why?" Clarissa asked, curiously.

"Because he's a frigid-blooded, poison-breathing, second-stage Gray Lensman," Kinnison explained. "As such he is much closer to the Eich, in every respect, than we are, and may very well have an angle that we haven't." And in a few minutes the Palanian Lensman became en rapport with the group.

"An interesting development, truly," his soft thought came in almost wistfully when the situation had been made clear to him. "I fear greatly that I cannot be of any use, but I am not doing anything of importance at the moment and will be very glad indeed to give you whatever slight assistance may be possible to one of my small powers. I come at speed to Lyrane II."

11

ALCON OF THRALE

Kinnison had not underestimated the power and capacity of his as yet unknown opposition. Well it was for him and for his Patrol that he was learning to think; for, as has already been made clear, this phase of the conflict was not essentially one of physical combat. Material encounters did occur, it is true, but they were comparatively unimportant. Basically, fundamentally, it was brain against brain; the preliminary but nevertheless prodigious skirmishing of two minds—or, more accurately, two teams of minds—each trying, even while covering up its own tracks and traces, to get at and to annihilate the other.

Each had certain advantages.

Boskonia—although we know now that Boskone was by no means the prime mover in that dark culture which opposed Civilization so bitterly, nevertheless "Boskonia" it was and still is being called—for a long time had the initiative, forcing the Patrol to wage an almost purely defensive fight. Boskonia knew vastly more about Civilization than Civilization knew about Boskonia. The latter, almost completely unknown, had all the advantages of stealth and of surprise; her forces could and did operate from undeterminable points against precisely-plotted objectives. Boskonia had the hyper-spatial tube long before the Conference of Scientists solved its mysteries; and even after the Patrol could use it it could do Civilization no good unless and until something could be found at which to aim it.

Civilization, however, had the Lens. It had the backing of the Arisians; maddeningly incomplete and unsatisfactory though that backing seemed at times to be. It had a few entities, notably one Kimball Kinnison, who were learning to think really efficiently. Above all, it had a massed purpose, a loyalty, an esprit de corps back-boning a morale which the whip-driven ranks of autocracy could never match and which the whip-wielding drivers could not even dimly understand.

Kinnison, then, with all the powers of his own mind and the minds of his friends and co-workers, sought to place and to identify the real key mentality at the destruction of which the mighty Boskonian Empire must begin to fall apart; that mentality in turn was trying with its every resource to find and to destroy the intellect which, pure reason showed, was the one factor which had enabled Civilization to throw the fast-conquering hordes of Boskonia back into their own galaxy.

Now, from our point of vantage in time and space, we can study at leisure and in detail many things which Kimball Kinnison could only surmise and suspect and deduce. Thus, he knew definitely only the fact that the Boskonian organization did not collapse with the destruction of the planet Jarnevon.

We know now, however, all about the Thrallian solar system and about Alcon of Thrale, its unlamented Tyrant. The planet Thrale—planetographically speaking, Thrallis II—so much like Tellus that its natives, including the unspeakable Alcon, were human practically to the limit of classification; and about Onlo, or Thrallis IX, and its monstrous natives. We know now that the duties and the authorities of the Council of Boskone were taken over by Alcon of Thrale; we now know how, by reason of his absolute control over both the humanity of Thrale and the monstrosities of Onlo, he was able to carry on.

Unfortunately, like the Eich, the Onlonians simply cannot be described by or to man. This is, as is already more or less widely known, due to the fact that all such non-aqueous, sub-zero-blooded, non-oxygen-breathing peoples have of necessity a metabolic extension into the hyper dimension; a fact which makes even their three-dimensional aspect subtly incomprehensible to any strictly three-dimensional mind.

Not all such races, it may be said here, belonged to Boskonia. Many essentially similar ones, such as the natives of Palain VII, adhered to our culture from the very first. Indeed, it has been argued that sexual equality is the most important criterion of that which we know as Civilization. But, since this is not a biological treatise, this point is merely mentioned, not discussed.

The Onlonians, then, while not precisely describable to man, were very similar to the Eich—as similar, say, as a Posenian and a Tellurian are to each other in the perception of a Palainian. That is to say practically identical; for to the unknown and incomprehensible senses of those frigid beings the fact that the Posenian possess four arms, eight hands, and no eyes at all, as compared with the Tellurian's simply paired members, constitutes a total difference so slight as to be negligible.

But to resume the thread of history, we are at liberty to know things that Kinnison did not. Specifically, we may observe and hear a conference which tireless research has reconstructed in toto. The place was upon chill, dark Onlo, in a searingly cold room whose normal condition of utter darkness was barely ameliorated by a dim blue glow. The time was just after Kinnison had left Lonabar for Lyrane II. The conferees were Alcon of Thrale and his Onlonian cabinet officers. The armor-clad Tyrant, in whose honor the feeble illumination was, lay at ease in a reclining chair; the pseudo-reptilian monstrosities were sitting or standing in some obscure and inexplicable fashion at a long, low bench of stone.

"The fact is," one of the Onlonians was radiating harshly, "that our minions in the other galaxy could not or would not or simply did not think. For years things went so smoothly that no one had to think. The Great Plan, so carefully worked out, gave every promise of complete success. It was inevitable, it seemed, that that entire galaxy would be brought under our domination, its Patrol destroyed, before any inkling of our purpose could be perceived by the weaklings of humanity.

"The Plan took cognizance of every known factor of any importance. When, however, an unknown, unforeseeable factor, the Lens of the Patrol, became of real importance, that Plan of course broke down. Instantly upon the recognition of an unconsidered factor the Plan should have been revised. All action should have ceased until that factor had been evaluated and neutralized. But no—no one of our commanders in that galaxy or handling its affairs ever thought of such a thing . . ."

"It is you who are not thinking now," the Tyrant of Thrale broke in. "If any underling had dared any such suggestion you yourself would have been among the first to demand his elimination. The Plan should have been revised, it is true; but the fault does not lie with the underlings. Instead, it lies squarely with the Council of Boskone . . . by the way, I trust that those six of that Council who escaped destruction upon Jarnevon by means of their hyper-spatial tube have been dealt with?"

"They have been liquidated," another officer replied.

"It is well. They were supposed to think, and the fact that they neither coped with the situation nor called it to your attention until it was too late to mend matters, rather than any flaw inherent in the Plan, is what has brought about the present intolerable situation.

"Underlings are not supposed to think. They are supposed to report facts; and, if so requested, opinions and deductions. Our representatives there were well-trained and skillful. They reported accurately, and that was all that was required of them. Helmuth reported truly, even though Boskone discredited his reports. So did Prellin, and Crowninshield, and Jalte. The Eich, however, failed in their duties of supervision and correlation; which is why their leaders have been punished and their operators have been reduced in rank—why we have assumed a task which, it might have been supposed and was supposed, lesser minds could have and should have performed.

"Let me caution you now that to underestimate a foe is a fatal error. Lan of the Eich prated largely upon this very point, but in the eventuality he did in fact underestimate very seriously the resources and the qualities of the Patrol; with what disastrous consequences we are all familiar. Instead of thinking he attempted to subject a purely philosophical concept, the Lens, to a mathematical analysis. Neither did the heads of our military branch think at all deeply, or they would not have tried to attack Tellus until after this new and enigmatic factor had been resolved. Its expeditionary force vanished without sign or signal—in spite of its primaries, its negative-matter bombs, its supposedly irresistible planets—and Tellus still circles untouched about Sol its sun. The condition is admittedly not to be borne; but I have always said, and I now do and shall insist, that no further action be taken until the Great Plan shall have been so revised as reasonably to take into account the Lens . . . What of Arisia?" he demanded of a third cabineteer.

"It is feared that nothing can be done about Arisia at present," that entity replied. "Expeditions have been sent, but they were dealt with as simply and as effectively as were Lan and Amp of the Eich. Planets have also been sent, but they were detected by the Patrol and were knocked out by far-ranging dirigible planets of the enemy. However, I have concluded that Arisia, of and by itself, is not of prime immediate importance. It is true that the Lens did in all probability originate with the Arisians. It is hence true that the destruction of Arisia and its people would be highly desirable, in that it would insure that no more Lenses would be produced. Such destruction would not do away, however, with the myriads of the instruments which are already in use and whose wearers are operating so powerfully against us. Our most pressing business, it seems to me, is to hunt down and exterminate all Lensmen; particularly the one whom Jalte called THE Lensman; whom Eichmil was informed by Lensman Morgan, was known to even other Lensmen only as Star A Star. In that connection, I am forced to wonder—is Star A Star in reality only one mind?"

"That question has been considered both by me and by your chief psychologist," Alcon made answer. "Frankly, we do not know. We have not enough reliable data upon which to base a finding of fact. Nor does it matter in the least. Whether one of two or a thousand, we must find and we must slay until it is feasible to resume our orderly conquest of the universe. We must also work unremittingly upon a plan to abate the nuisance which is Arisia. Above all, we must see to it with the utmost diligence that no iota of information concerning us ever reaches any member of the Galactic Patrol—I do not want either of our worlds to become as Jarnevon now is."

"Hear! Bravo! Nor I!" came a chorus of thoughts, interrupted by an emanation from one of the sparkling force-ball inter-galactic communicators.

"Yes? Alcon acknowledging," the Tyrant took the call.

It was a zwilnik upon far Lonabar, reporting through Lyrane VIII everything that Cartiff had done. "I do not know—I have no idea—whether or not this matter is either unusual or important," the observer concluded. "I would, however, rather report ten unimportant things than miss one which might later prove to have had significance."

"Right. Report received," and discussion raged. Was this affair actually what it appeared upon the surface to be, or was it another subtle piece of the work of that never-to-be-sufficiently-damned Lensman?

The observer was recalled. Orders were given and were carried out. Then, after it had been learned that Bleeko's palace and every particle of its contents had been destroyed, that Cartiff had vanished utterly, and that nobody could be found upon the face of Lonabar who could throw any light whatever upon the manner or the time of his going; then, after it was too late to do anything about it, it was decided that this must have been the work of THE Lensman. And it was useless to storm or to rage. Such a happening could not have been reported sooner to so high an office; the routine events of a hundred million worlds simply could not be considered at that level. And since this Lensman never repeated—his acts were always different, alike only in that they were drably routine acts until their crashing finales—the Boskonian observers never had been and never would be able to report his activities in time.

"But he got nothing *this* time, I am certain of that," the chief psychologist exulted.

"How can you be so sure?" Alcon snapped.

"Because Menjo Bleeko of Lonabar knew nothing whatever of our activities or of our organization except at such times as one of my men was in charge of his mind," the scientist gloated. "I and my assistants know mental surgery as those crude hypnotists the Eich never will know it. Even our lowest agents are having those clumsy and untrustworthy false teeth removed as fast as my therapists can operate upon their minds."

"Nevertheless, you are even now guilty of underestimating," Alcon reproved him sharply, energizing a force-ball communicator. "It is quite eminently possible that he who wrought so upon Lonabar may have been enabled—by pure chance, perhaps—to establish a linkage between that planet and Lyrane . . ."

The cold, crisply incisive thought of an Eich answered the Tyrant's call.

"Have you of Lyrane perceived or encountered any unusual occurrences or indications?" Alcon demanded.

"We have not."

"Expect them, then," and the Thrallian despot transmitted in detail all the new developments.

"We always expect new and untoward things," the Eich more than half sneered. "We are prepared momently for anything that can happen, from a visitation by Star A Star and any or all of his Lensmen up to an attack by the massed Grand Fleet of the Galactic Patrol. Is there anything else, Your Supremacy?"

"No. I envy you your self-confidence and assurance, but I mistrust exceedingly the soundness of your judgment. That is all." Alcon turned his attention to the psychologist. "Have you operated upon the minds of those Eich and those self-styled Overlords as you did upon that of Menjo Bleeko?"

"No!" the mind-surgeon gasped. "Impossible! Not physically, perhaps, but would not such a procedure interfere so seriously with the work that it . . ."

"That is your problem—solve it," Alcon ordered, curtly. "See to it, however it is solved, that no traceable linkage exists between any of those minds and us. Any mind capable of thinking such thoughts as those which we have just received is not to be trusted."

As has been said, Kinnison-ex-Cartiff was en route for Lyrane II while the foregoing conference was taking place. Throughout the trip he kept in touch with Clarrissa. At first he tried, with his every artifice of diplomacy, cajolery, and downright threats, to make her lay off; he finally invoked all his Unattached Lensman's transcendental authority and ordered her summarily to lay off.

No soap. How did he get that way, she wanted furiously to know, to be ordering her around as though she were an uncapped probe? She was a Lensman, too, by Klono's curly whiskers! Solving this problem was her job—nobody else's—and she was going to do it. She was on a definite assignment—his own assignment, too, remember—and she wasn't going to be called off of it just because he had found out all of a sudden that it might not be quite as safe as dunking doughnuts at a down-river picnic. What kind of a sun-baked, space-tempered crust did he have to pull a crack like that on *her?* Would he have the bare-faced, unmitigated gall to spring a thing like that on any other Lensman in the whole cockeyed universe?

That stopped him—cold. Lensmen always went in; that was the Code. For any Tellurian Lensman, anywhere, to duck or to dodge because of any personal danger was sheerly, starkly unthinkable. The fact that she was, to him, the sum total of all the femininity of the galaxy could not be allowed any weight whatever; any more than the converse aspect had ever been permitted to sway him. Fair enough. Bitter, but inescapable. This was one—just one—of the consequences which Mentor had foreseen. He had foreseen it, too, in a dimly unreal sort of way, and now that it was here he'd simply have to take it. QX.

"But be careful, anyway," he surrendered. "Awfully careful—as careful as I would myself."

"I could be ever so much more careful than that and still be pretty reckless." Her low, entrancing chuckle came through as though she were present in person. "And by the way, Kim, did I ever tell you that I am fast getting to be a gray Lensman?"

"You always were, ace—you couldn't very well be anything else."

"No—I mean actually gray. Did you ever stop to consider what the laundry problem would be on this heathenish planet?"

"Cris, I'm surprised at you—what do you need of a laundry?" he derided her, affectionately. "Here you've been blasting me to a cinder about not taking your Lensmanship seriously enough, and yet you are violating one of the prime tenets—that of conformation to planetary customs. Shame on you!"

He felt her hot blush across all those parsecs of empty space. "I tried it at first, Kim, but it was just simply *terrible!"*

"You've got to learn how to be a Lensman or else quit throwing your weight around like you did a while back. No back chat, either, you insubordinate young jade, or I'll take that Lens away from you and heave you into the clink."

"You and what regiment of Valerians? Besides, it didn't make any difference," she explained, triumphantly. "These matriarchs don't like me one bit better, no matter what I wear or don't wear."

Time passed, and in spite of Kinnison's highly disquieting fears, nothing happened. Right on schedule the Patrol ship eased down to a landing at the edge of the Lyranian airport. Clarrissa was waiting; dressed now, not in nurse's white, but in startlingly nondescript gray shirt and breeches.

"Not the gray leather of my station, but merely dirt color," she explained to Kinnison after the first fervent greetings. "These women are clean enough physically, but I simply haven't got a thing fit to wear. Is your laundry working?"

It was, and very shortly Sector Chief Nurse Clarrissa MacDougall appeared in her wonted immaculately-white, stiffly-starched uniform. She would not wear the Grays to which she was entitled; nor would she— except when defying Kinnison—claim as her right any one of the per- quisites or privileges which were so indubitably hers. She was not, never had been, and never would or could be a *real* Lensman, she insisted. At best, she was only a synthetic—or an imitation—or a sort of amateur— maybe a "Red" Lensman—handy to have around, perhaps, for certain kinds of jobs, but absolutely and definitely not a regular Lensman. And it was this attitude which was to make the Red Lensman not merely tol- erated, but loved as she was loved by Lensmen, Patrolmen, and civilians alike throughout the length, breadth, and thickness of Civilization's bounds.

The ship lifted from the airport and went north into the uninhabited temperate zone. The matriarchs did not have anything the Tellurians either needed or wanted; the Lyranians disliked visitors so openly and so intensely that to move away from the populated belt was the only logical and considerate thing to do.

The *Dauntless* arrived a day later, bringing Worsel and Tregonsee; followed closely by Nadreck in his ultra-refrigerated speedster. Five Lensmen, then, studied intently a globular map of Lyrane II which Clar- rissa had made. Four of them, the oxygen-breathers, surrounded it in the flesh, while Nadreck was with them only in essence. Physically he was far out in the comfortably sub-zero reaches of the stratosphere, but his mind was en rapport with theirs; his sense of perception scanned the markings upon the globe as carefully and as accurately as did theirs.

"This belt which I have colored pink," the female Lensman explained, "corresponding roughly to the torrid zone, is the inhabited area of Lyrane II. Nobody lives anywhere else. Upon it I have charted every unexplained disappearance that I have been able to find out about. Each of these black crosses is where one such person lived. The black circle—or circles, for frequently there are more than one—connected to each cross by a black line, marks the spot—or spots—where that person was seen for the last time or times. If the black circle is around the cross it means that she was last seen at home."

The crosses were distributed fairly evenly all around the globe and throughout the populated zone. The circles, however, tended markedly to concentrate upon the northern edge of that zone; and practically all of the encircled crosses were very close to the northern edge of the populated belt.

"Almost all the lines intersect at this point here," she went on, placing a finger-tip near the north pole of the globe. "The few that don't could be observational errors, or perhaps the person was seen there before she really disappeared. If it *is* Overlords, their cavern must be within about fifty kilometers of the spot I've marked here. However, I couldn't find any evidence that any Eich have ever been here; and if they haven't I don't see how the Overlords could be here, either. That, gentlemen of the Second Stage, is my report; which, I fear, is neither complete nor conducive."

"You err, Lensman MacDougall." Nadreck was the first to speak. "It is both. A right scholarly and highly informative piece of work, eh, friend Worsel?"

"It is so . . . it is indeed so," the Velantian agreed, the while a shudder rippled along the thirty-foot length of his sinuous body. "I suspected many things, but not this . . . certainly not this, ever, away out here."

"Nor I." Tregonsee's four horn-lipped, toothless mouths snapped open and shut; his cabled arms writhed.

"Nor I," from Kinnison. "If I had, you'd never've got that Lens, Clarrissa May MacDougall."

His voice was the grimmest she had ever heard it. He was picturing to himself her lovely body writhing in torment; stretched, twisted, broken; forgetting completely that his thoughts were as clear as a tri-di to all the others.

"If they had detected *you* . . . you know what they'd do to get hold of a mind and a vital force such as yours . . ."

He shook himself and drew a tremendously deep breath of relief. "But thank God they didn't. So all I've got to say is that if we ever have any kids and they don't bawl when I tell 'em about this, I'll certainly give 'em something to bawl about!"

12

HELEN GOES NORTH

But listen, Kim!" Clarrissa protested. "All four of you are assuming that I've dead-centered the target. I thought probably I was right, but since I couldn't find any Eich traces, I expected a lot of argument."

"No argument," Kinnison assured her. "You know how they work. They tune in on some one mind, the stronger and more vital the better. In that connection, I wonder that Helen is still around—the ones who disappeared were upper-bracket minds, weren't they?"

She thought a space. "Now that you mention it, I believe so. Most of them, certainly."

"Thought so. That clinches it, if it needed clinching. They tune in; then drag 'em in in a straight line."

"But that would be so *obvious!*" she objected.

"It was not obvious, Clarrissa," Tregonsee observed, "until your work made it so: a task which, I would like to say here, could not have been accomplished by any other entity of Civilization."

"Thanks, Tregonsee. But they're smart enough to . . . you'd think they'd vary their technique, at least enough to get away from those dead straight lines."

"They probably can't," Kinnison decided. "A racial trait, bred into 'em for ages. They've always worked that way; probably can't work any other way. The Eich undoubtedly told 'em to lay off those orgies, but they probably couldn't do it—the vice is too habit-forming to break, would be my guess. Anyway, we're all in agreement that it's the Overlords?"

They were.

"And there's no doubt as to what we do next?"

There was none. Two great ships, the incomparable *Dauntless* and the camouflaged warship which had served Kinnison-Cartiff so well, lifted themselves into the stratosphere and headed north. The Lensman did not want to advertise their presence and there was no great hurry, therefore both vessels had their thought-screens out and both rode upon baffled jets.

Practically all of the crewmen of the *Dauntless* had seen Overlords in the substance; so far as is known they were the only human beings who had ever seen an Overlord and had lived to tell of it. Twenty two of their former fellows had seen Overlords and had died. Kinnison, Worsel, and vanBuskirk had slain Overlords in unscreened hand-to-hand combat in the fantastically incredible environment of a hyper-spatial tube—that uncanny medium in which man and monster could and did occupy the same space at the same time without being able to touch each other; in which the air or pseudo-air is thick and viscous; in which the only substance common to both sets of dimensions and thus available for combat purposes is dureum—a synthetic material so treated and so saturated as to be of enormous mass and inertia.

It is easier to imagine, then, than to describe the emotion which seethed through the crew as the news flew around that the business next in order was the extirpation of a flock of Overlords.

"How about a couple or three nice duodec torpedoes, Kim, steered right down into the middle of that cavern and touched off—POWIE!— slick, don't you think?" Henderson insinuated.

"Aw, let's not, Kim!" protested vanBuskirk, who, as one of the three Overlord-slayers, had been called into the control room. "This ain't going to be in a tube, Kim; it's in a cavern on a planet—made to order for axe-work. Let me and the boys put on our screens and bash their ugly damn skulls in for 'em—how about it, huh?"

"Not duodec, Hen . . . not yet, anyway," Kinnison decided. "As for axe-work, Bus—maybe, maybe not. Depends. We want to catch some of them alive, so as to get some information . . . but you and your boys will be good for that, too, so you might as well go and start getting them ready." He turned his thought to his snakish comrade-in-arms.

"What do you think, Worsel, is this hide-out of theirs heavily fortified, or just hidden?"

"Hidden, I would say from what I know of them—well hidden,"

the Velantian replied, promptly. "Unless they have changed markedly; and, like you, I do not believe that a race so old can change that much. I could tune them in, but it might very well do more harm than good."

"Certain to, I'm afraid." Kinnison knew as well as did Worsel that a Velantian was the tastiest dish which could be served up to any Overlord. Both knew also, however, the very real mental ability of the foe; knew that the Overlords would be sure to suspect that any Velantian so temptingly present upon Lyrane II must be there specifically for the detriment of the Delgonian race; knew that they would almost certainly refuse the proffered bait. And not only would they refuse to lead Worsel to their caverns, but in all probability they would cancel even their ordinary activities, thus making it impossible to find them at all, until they had learned definitely that the hook-bearing tid-bit and its accomplices had left the Lyranian solar system entirely. "No, what we need right now is a good, strong-willed Lyranian."

"Shall we go back and grab one? It would take only a few minutes," Henderson suggested, straightening up at his board.

"Uh-uh," Kinnison demurred. "That might smell a bit on the cheesy side, too, don't you think, fellows?" and Worsel and Tregonsee agreed that such a move would be ill-advised.

"Might I offer a barely tenable suggestion?" Nadreck asked diffidently.

"I'll say you can—come in."

"Judging by the rate at which Lyranians have been vanishing of late, it would seem that we would not have to wait too long before another one comes hither under her own power. Since the despised ones will have captured her themselves, and themselves will have forced her to come to them, no suspicion will be or can be aroused."

"That's a thought, Nadreck—that *is* a thought!" Kinnison applauded. "Shoot us up, will you, Hen? 'Way up, and hover over the center of the spread of intersections of those lines. Put observers on every plate you've got here, and have Communications alert all observers aboard ship. Have half of them search the air all around as far as they can reach for an airplane in flight; have the rest comb the terrain below, both on the surface and underground, with spy-rays, for any sign of a natural or artificial cave."

"What kind of information do you think they may have, Kinnison?" asked Tregonsee the Rigellian.

"I don't know." Kinnison pondered for minutes. "Somebody—around here somewhere—has got some kind of a tie up with some Boskonian entity or group that is fairly well up the ladder; I'm pretty sure of that. Bleeko sent ships here—one speedster, certainly, and there's no reason to suppose that it was an isolated case . . ."

"There is nothing to show, either, that it was not an isolated case," Tregonsee observed, quietly, "and the speedster landed, not up here near the pole, but in the populated zone. Why? To secure some of the women?" The Rigellian was not arguing against Kinnison; he was, as they all knew, helping to subject every facet of the matter to scrutiny.

"Possibly—but this is a transfer point," Kinnison pointed out. "Illona was to start out from here, remember. And those two ships . . . coming to meet her, or perhaps each other, or . . ."

"Or perhaps called there by the speedster's crew, for aid," Tregonsee completed the thought.

"One, but quite possibly not both," Nadreck suggested. "We are agreed, I think, that the probability of a Boskonian connection is sufficiently large to warrant the taking of these Overlords alive in order to read their minds?"

They were; hence the discussion then turned naturally to the question of how this none-too-easy feat was to be accomplished. The two Patrol ships had climbed and were cruising in great, slow circles; the spy-ray men and the other observers were hard at work. Before they had found anything upon or in the ground, however:

"Plane, ho!" came the report, and both vessels, with spy-ray blocks out now as well as thought-screens, plunged silently into a flatly-slanting dive. Directly over the slow Lyranian craft, high above it, they turned as one to match its course and slowed to match its pace.

"Come to life, Kim—don't let them have her!" Clarrissa exclaimed. Being en rapport with them all, she knew that both unhuman Worsel and monstrous Nadreck were perfectly willing to let the helpless Lyranian become a sacrifice; she knew that neither Kinnison nor Tregonsee had as yet given that angle of the affair a single thought. "Surely, Kim, you don't have to let them kill her, do you? Isn't showing you the gate or whatever it is, enough? Can't you rig up something to do something with when she gets almost inside?"

"Why . . . uh . . . I s'pose so." Kinnison wrenched his attention away from a plate. "Oh, sure, Cris. Hen! Drop us down a bit, and have the boys get ready to spear that crate with a couple of tractors when I give the word."

The plane held its course, directly toward a range of low, barren, precipitous hills. As it approached them it dropped, as though to attempt a landing upon a steep and rocky hillside.

"She can't land there," Kinnison breathed, "and Overlords would want her alive, not dead . . . suppose I've been wrong all the time? Get ready, fellows!" he snapped. "Take her at the very last possible instant—before—she—crashes—NOW!"

As he yelled the command the powerful beams leaped out, seizing the disaster-bound vehicle in a gently unbreakable grip. Had they not done so, however, the Lyranian would not have crashed; for in that last split second a section of the rugged hillside fell inward. In the very mouth of that dread opening the little plane hung for an instant; then:

"Grab the woman, quick!" Kinnison ordered, for the Lyranian was very evidently going to jump. And, such was the awful measure of the Overlords' compulsion, she did jump; without a parachute, with knowing or caring what, if anything, was to break her fall. But before she struck ground a tractor beam had seized her, and passive plane and wildly struggling pilot were both borne rapidly aloft.

"Why, Kim, it's *Helen!*" Clarrissa shrieked in surprise, then voice and manner became transformed. "The poor, poor thing," she crooned. "Bring her in at number six lock. I'll meet her there—you fellows keep clear. In the state she's in a shock—especially such a shock as seeing such a monstrous lot of males—would knock her off the beam, sure."

Helen of Lyrane ceased struggling in the instant of being drawn through the thought-screen surrounding the *Dauntless*. She had not been unconscious at any time. She had known exactly what she had been doing; she had wanted intensely—such was the insidiously devastating power of the Delgonian mind—to do just that and nothing else. The falseness of values, the indefensibility of motivation, simply could not register in her thoroughly suffused, completely blanketed mind. When the screen cut off the Overlord's control, however, thus restoring her own, the shock of realization of what she had done—what she had been forced to do—struck her like a physical blow. Worse than a physical blow, for ordinary physical violence she could understand.

This mischance, however, she could not even begin to understand. It was utterly incomprehensible. She knew what had happened; she knew that her mind had been taken over by some monstrously alien, incredibly powerful mentality, for some purpose so obscure as to be entirely beyond her ken. To her narrow philosophy of existence, to her one-planet insularity of viewpoint and outlook, the very existence, anywhere, of such a mind with such a purpose was in simple fact impossible. For it actually to exist upon her own planet, Lyrane II, was sheerly, starkly unthinkable.

She did not recognize the *Dauntless,* of course. To her all spaceships were alike. They were all invading warships, full of enemies. All things and all beings originating elsewhere than upon Lyrane II were, perforce, enemies. Those outrageous males, the Tellurian Lensman and his cohorts, had pretended not to be inimical, as had the peculiar, white-swathed Tellurian near-person who had been worming itself into her confidence in order to study the disappearances; but she did not trust even them.

She now knew the manner of, if not the reason for, the vanishment of her fellow Lyranians. The tractors of the space-ship had saved her from whatever fate it was that impended. She did not, however, feel any thrill of gratitude. One enemy or another, what difference did it make? Therefore, as she went through the blocking screen and recovered control of her mind, she set herself to fight; to fight with every iota of her mighty mind and with every fiber of her lithe, hard-schooled, tigress' body. The air-lock doors opened and closed—she faced, not an armed and armored male all set to slay, but the white-clad near-person whom she already knew better than she ever would know any other non-Lyranian.

"Oh, Helen!" the girl half sobbed, throwing both arms around the still-braced Chief Person. "I'm *so* glad that we got to you in time! And there will be no more disappearances, dear—the boys will see to that!"

Helen did not know, really, what disinterested friendship meant. Since the nurse had put her into a wide-open two-way, however, she knew beyond all possibility of doubt that these Tellurians wished her and all her kind well, not ill; and the shock of that knowledge, super-imposed upon the other shocks which she had so recently undergone, was more than she could bear. For the first and only time in her hard, busy, purposeful life, Helen of Lyrane fainted; fainted dead away in the circle of the Earth-girl's arms.

The nurse knew that this was nothing serious; in fact, she was professionally quite in favor of it. Hence, instead of resuscitating the Lyra-nian, she swung the pliant body into a carry—as has been previously intimated, Clarrissa MacDougall was no more a weakling physically than she was mentally—and without waiting for orderlies and stretcher she bore it easily away to her own quarters.

13

IN THE CAVERN

In the meantime the more warlike forces of the *Dauntless* had not been idle. In the instant of the opening of the cavern's doors the captain's talker issued orders, and as soon as the Lyranian was out of the line of fire keen-eyed needle-ray men saw to it that those doors were in no mechanical condition to close. The *Dauntless* settled downward; landed in front of the entrance to the cavern. The rocky, broken terrain meant nothing to her; the hardest, jaggedest boulders crumbled instantly to dust as her enormous mass drove the file-hard, inflexible armor of her mid-zone deep into the ground. Then, while alert beamers watched the entrance and while spy-ray experts combed the interior for other openings which Kinnison and Worsel were already practically certain did not exist, the forces of Civilization formed for the attack.

Worsel was fairly shivering with eagerness for the fray. His was, and with plenty of reason, the bitterest by far of all the animosities there present against the Overlords. For Delgon and his own native planet, Velantia, were neighboring worlds, circling about the same sun. Since the beginning of Velantian space-flight the Overlords of Delgon had preyed upon the Velantians; in fact, the Overlords had probably caused the first Velantian space-ship to be built. They had called them, in a never-ending stream, across the empty gulf of space. They had pinned them against their torture screens, had flayed them and had tweaked

them to bits, had done them to death in every one of the numberless
slow and hideous fashions which had been developed by a race of sadists
who had been specializing in the fine art of torture for thousands upon
thousands of years. Then, in the last minutes of the long-drawn-out agony of death, the Overlords were wont to feed, with a passionate, greedy,
ineradicably ingrained lust utterly inexplicable to any civilized mind,
upon the life-forces which the mangled bodies could no longer contain.

This horrible parasitism went on for ages. The Velantians fought
vainly; their crude thought-screens were almost useless until after the
coming of the Patrol. Then, with screens that were of real use, and with
ships of power and with weapons of might, Worsel himself had taken
the lead in the clean-up of Delgon. He was afraid, of course. Any Velantian was and is frightened to the very center of his being by the mere
thought of an Overlord. He cannot help it; it is in his heredity, bred into
the innermost chemistry of his body; the cold grue of a thousand thousand fiendishly tortured ancestors simply will not be denied or cast aside.

Many of the monsters had succeeded in fleeing Delgon, of course.
Some departed in the ships which had ferried their victims to the planet,
some were removed to other solar systems by the Eich. The rest were
slain; and as the knowledge that a Velantian *could* kill an Overlord gained
headway, the emotions toward the oppressors generated within minds
such as the Velantians' became literally indescribable. Fear was there yet
and in abundance—it simply could not be eradicated. Horror and revulsion. Sheer, burning hatred; and, more powerful than all, amounting almost to an obsession, a clamoring, shrieking, driving urge for revenge
which was almost tangible. All these, and more, Worsel felt as he waited,
twitching.

The Valerians wanted to go in because it meant a hand-to-hand fight.
Fighting was their business, their sport, and their pleasure; they loved it
for its own sweet sake, with a simple, whole-hearted devotion. To die in
combat was a Valerian soldier's natural and much-to-be-desired end; to
die in any peaceful fashion was a disgrace and a calamity. They did and
do go into battle with very much the same joyous abandon with which a
sophomore goes to meet his date in Lover's Lane. And now, to make
physical combat all the nicer and juicier, they carried semi-portable tractors and pressors, for the actual killing was not to take place until after
the battle proper was over. Blasting the Overlords out of existence would
have been simplicity itself; but they were not to die until after they had
been forced to divulge whatever they might have of knowledge or of
information.

Nadreck of Palain wanted to go in solely to increase his already vast store of knowledge. His thirst for facts was a purely scientific one; the fashion in which it was to be satisfied was the veriest, the most immaterial detail. Indeed, it is profoundly impossible to portray to any human intelligence the serene detachment, the utterly complete indifference to suffering exhibited by practically all of the frigid-blooded races, even those adherent to Civilization, especially when the suffering is being done by an enemy. Nadreck did know, academically and in a philological sense, from his reading, the approximate significance of such words as "compunction", "sympathy", and "squeamishness"; but he would have been astounded beyond measure at any suggestion that they would apply to any such matter-of-fact business as the extraction of data from the mind of an Overlord of Delgon, no matter what might have to be done to the unfortunate victim in the process.

Tregonsee went in simply because Kinnison did—to be there to help out in case the Tellurian should need him.

Kinnison went in because he felt that he had to. He knew full well that he was not going to get any kick at all out of what was going to happen. He was not going to like it, any part of it. Nor did he. In fact, he wanted to be sick—violently sick—before the business was well started. And Nadreck perceived his mental and physical distress.

"Why stay, friend Kinnison, when your presence is not necessary?" he asked, with the slightly pleased, somewhat surprised, hellishly placid mental immobility which Kinnison was later to come to know so well. "Even though my powers are admittedly small, I feel eminently qualified to cope with such minor matters as the obtainment and the accurate transmittal of that which you wish to know. I cannot understand your emotions, but I realize fully that they are essential components of that which makes you what you fundamentally are. There can be no justification for your submitting yourself needlessly to such stresses, such psychic traumata."

And Kinnison and Tregonsee, realizing the common sense of the Palainian's statement and very glad indeed to have an excuse for leaving the outrageous scene, left it forthwith.

There is no need to go into detail as to what actually transpired within that cavern's dark and noisome depths. It took a long time, nor was any of it gentle. The battle itself, before the Overlords were downed, was bad enough in any Tellurian eyes. Clad in armor of proof although they were, more than one of the Valerians died. Worsel's armor was shattered and rent, his leather-hard flesh was slashed, burned, and mangled before the last of the monstrous forms was pinned down and helpless. Nadreck alone escaped unscathed—he did so, he explained quite truthfully, because he did not go in there to fight, but to learn.

What followed the battle, however, was infinitely worse. The Delgonians, as has been said, were hard, cold, merciless, even among themselves; they were pitiless and unyielding and refractory in the extreme. It need scarcely be emphasized then, that they did not yield to persuasion either easily or graciously; that their own apparatus and equipment had to be put to its fullest grisly use before those stubborn minds gave up the secrets so grimly and so implacably sought. Worsel, the raging Velantian, used those torture-tools with a vengeful savagery and a snarling ferocity which are at least partially understandable; but Nadreck employed them with a calm capability, a coldly, emotionlessly efficient callousness the mere contemplation of which made icy shivers chase each other up and down Kinnison's spine.

At long last the job was done. The battered Patrol forces returned to the *Dauntless,* bringing with them their spoils and their dead. The cavern and its every molecule of contents was bombed out of existence. The two ships took off; Cartiff's heavily-armed "merchantman" to do the long flit back to Tellus, the *Dauntless* to drop Helen and her plane off at her airport and then to join her sister super-dreadnoughts which were already beginning to assemble in Rift Ninety Four.

"Come down here, will you please, Kim?" came Clarrissa's thought. "I've been keeping her pretty well blocked out, but she wants to talk to you—in fact, she insists on it—before she leaves the ship."

"Hm . . . that *is* something!" the Lensman exclaimed, and hurried to the nurse's cabin.

There stood the Lyranian queen; a full five inches taller than Clarrissa's five feet six, a good thirty-five pounds heavier than her not inconsiderable one hundred and forty five. Hard, fine, supple; erectly poised she stood there, an exquisitely beautiful statue of pale bronze, her flaming hair a gorgeous riot. Head held proudly high, she stared only slightly upward into the Earth-man's quiet, understanding eyes.

"Thanks, Kinnison, for everything that you and yours have done for me and mine," she said, simply; and held out her right hand in what she knew was the correct Tellurian gesture.

"Uh-uh, Helen," Kinnison denied, gently, making no motion to grasp the proffered hand—which was promptly and enthusiastically withdrawn. "Nice, and it's really big of you, but don't strain yourself to like us men too much or too soon; you've got to get used to us gradually. We like you a lot, and we respect you even more, but we've been around and you haven't. You can't be feeling friendly enough yet to enjoy shaking hands with me—you certainly haven't got jets enough to swing *that* load—so this time we'll take the thought for the deed. Keep trying, though, Toots old girl, and you'll make it yet. In the meantime we're all pulling for you, and if you ever need any help, shoot us a call on the communicator we've put aboard your plane. Clear ether, ace!"

"Clear ether, MacDougall and Kinnison!" Helen's eyes were softer than either of the Tellurians had ever seen them before. "There is, I think, something of wisdom, of efficiency, in what you have said. It may be . . . that is, there is a possibility . . . you of Civilization are, perhaps, persons—of a sort, that is—after all. Thanks—*really* thanks, I mean, this time—good-bye."

Helen's plane had already been unloaded. She disembarked and stood beside it; watching, with a peculiarly untranslatable expression, the huge cruiser until it was out of sight.

"It was just like pulling teeth for her to be civil to me," Kinnison grinned at his fiancee, "but she finally made the lift. She's a grand girl, that Helen, in her peculiar, poisonous way."

"Why, Kim!" Clarrissa protested. "She's nice, really, when you get to know her. And she's so stunningly, so ravishingly beautiful!"

"Uh-huh," Kinnison agreed, without a trace of enthusiasm. "Cast her in chilled stainless steel—she'd just about do as she is, without any casting—and she'd make a mighty fine statue."

"Kim! Shame on you!" the girl exclaimed. "Why, she's the most *perfectly* beautiful thing I ever saw in my whole life!" Her voice softened. "I wish I looked like that," she added wistfully.

"She's beautiful enough—in her way—of course," the man admitted, entirely unimpressed. "But then, so is a Radelegian cateagle, so is a spire of frozen helium, and so is a six-foot-long, armor-piercing punch. As for you wanting to look like her—that's sheer tripe, Cris, and you know it. Beside you, all the Helens that ever lived, with Cleopatra, Dessa Desplaines, and Illona Potter thrown in, wouldn't make a baffled flare . . ."

That was, of course, what she wanted him to say; and what followed is of no particular importance here.

Shortly after the *Dauntless* cleared the stratosphere, Nadreck reported that he had finished assembling and arranging the data, and Kinnison called the Lensmen together in his con room for an ultra-private conference. Worsel, it appeared, was still in surgery.

" 'Smatter, Doc?" Kinnison asked, casually. He knew that there was nothing really serious the matter—Worsel had come out of the cavern under his own power, and a Velantian recovers with startling rapidity from any wound which does not kill him outright. "Having trouble with your stitching?"

"I'll say we are!" the surgeon grunted. "Have to bore holes with an electric drill and use linemen's pliers. Just about through now, though—he'll be with you in a couple of minutes," and in a very little more than the stipulated time the Velantian joined the other Lensmen.

He was bandaged and taped, and did not move at his customary headlong pace, but he fairly radiated self-satisfaction, bliss, and contentment. He felt better, he declared, than he had at any time since he cleaned out the last of Delgon's caverns.

Kinnison stopped the inter-play of thoughts by starting up his Lensman's projector. This mechanism was something like a tri-di machine, except that instead of projecting sound and three-dimensional color, it operated via pure thought. Sometimes the thoughts of one or more Overlords, at other times the thoughts of the Eich or other beings as registered upon the minds of the Overlords, at still others the thoughts of Nadreck or of Worsel amplifying a preceding thought-passage or explaining some detail of the picture which was being shown at the moment. The spool of tape now being run, with others, formed the Lensmen's record of what they had done. This record would go to Prime Base under Lensman's Seal; that is, only a Lensman could handle it or see it. Later, after the emergency had passed, copies of it would go to various Central Libraries and thus become available to properly accredited students. Indeed, it is only from such records, made upon the scene and at the time by keen-thinking, logical, truth-seeking Lensmen, that such a factual, minutely-detailed history as this can be compiled; and your historian is supremely proud that he was the first person other than a Lensman to be allowed to study a great deal of this priceless data.

Worsel knew the gist of the report, Nadreck the compiler knew it all; but to Kinnison, Clarrissa, and Tregonsee the unreeling of the tape brought shocking news. For, as a matter of fact, the Overlords had known more, and there was more in the Lyranian solar system to know, than Kinnison's wildest imaginings had dared to suppose. That system was one of the main focal points for the zwilnik business of an immense volume of space; Lyrane II was the meeting-place, the dispatcher's office, the nerve-center from which thousands of invisible, immaterial lines reached out to thousands of planets peopled by warm-blooded oxygen-breathers. Menjo Bleeko had sent to Lyrane II not one expedition, but hundreds of them; the affair of Illona and her escorts had been the veriest, the most trifling incident.

The Overlords, however, did not know of any Boskonian group in the Second Galaxy. They had no superiors, anywhere. The idea of anyone or any thing anywhere being superior to an Overlord was unthinkable. They did, however, cooperate with—here came the really stunning fact—

certain of the Eich who lived upon eternally dark Lyrane VIII, and who managed things for the frigid-blooded, poison-breathing Boskonians of the region in much the same fashion as the Overlords did for the warm-blooded, light-loving races. To make the cooperation easier and more efficient, the two planets were connected by a hyper-spatial tube.

"Just a sec!" Kinnison interrupted, as he stopped the machine for a moment. "The Overlords were kidding themselves a bit there, I think—they must have been. If they didn't report to or get orders from the Second Galaxy or some other higher-up office, the Eich must have; and since the records and plunder and stuff were not in the cavern, the Eich must have them on Eight. Therefore, whether they realized it or not, the Overlords must have been inferior to the Eich and under their orders. Check?"

"Check," Nadreck agreed. "Worsel and I concluded that they knew the facts, but were covering up even in their own minds, to save face. Our conclusions, and the data from which they were derived, are in the introduction—another spool. Shall I get it?"

"By no means—just glad to have the point cleared up, is all. "Thanks," and the showing went on.

The principal reason why the Lyranian system had been chosen for that important headquarters was that it was one of the very few outlying solar systems, completely unknown to the scientists of the Patrol, in which both the Eich and the Overlords could live in their natural environments. Lyrane VIII was, of course, intensely, bitterly cold. This quality is not rare, since nearly all Number Eight planets are; its uniqueness lay in the fact that its atmosphere was almost exactly like that of Jarnevon.

And Lyrane II suited the Overlords perfectly. Not only did it have the correct temperature, gravity, and atmosphere, but also is offered that much rarer thing without which no cavern of Overlords would have been content for long—a native life-form possessing strong and highly vital minds upon which they could prey.

There was more, much more; but the rest of it was not directly pertinent to the immediate questions. The tape ran out, Kinnison snapped off the projector, and the Lensmen went into a five-way.

Why was not Lyrane II defended? Worsel and Kinnison had already answered that one. Secretiveness and power of mind, not armament, had always been the natural defenses of all Overlords. Why hadn't the Eich interfered? That was easy, too. The Eich looked after themselves—if the Overlords couldn't, that was just too bad. The two ships that had come to aid and had remained to revenge had certainly not come from Eight—their crews had been oxygen-breathers. Probably a rendezvous—immaterial anyway. Why wasn't the whole solar system ringed with outposts and screens? Too obvious. Why hadn't the *Dauntless* been detected? Because of her nullifiers; and if she had been spotted by any short-range stuff she had been mistaken for another zwilnik ship. They hadn't detected anything out of the way on Eight because it hadn't occurred to anybody to swing an analyzer toward that particular planet. If they did they'd find that Eight was defended plenty. Had the Eich had time to build defenses? They must have had, or they wouldn't be there—they certainly were not taking that kind of chance. And by the way, hadn't they better do a bit of snooping around Eight before they went back to join the *Z9M9Z* and the Fleet? They had.

Thereupon the *Dauntless* faced about and retraced her path toward the now highly important system of Lyrane. In their previous approaches the Patrolmen had observed the usual precautions to avoid revealing themselves to any zwilnik vessel which might have been on the prowl. Those precautions were now intensified to the limit, since they knew that Lyrane VIII was the site of a base manned by the Eich themselves.

As the big cruiser crept toward her goal, nullifiers full out and every instrument of detection and reception as attentively out-stretched as the whiskers of a tomcat slinking along a black alley at midnight, the Lensmen again pooled their brains in conference.

The Eich. This was going to be NO pushover. Even the approach would have to be figured to a hair; because, since the Boskonians had decided that it would be poor strategy to screen in their whole solar system, it was a cold certainty that they would have their own planets guarded and protected by every device which their inhuman ingenuity could devise. The *Dauntless* would have to stop just outside the range of electro-magnetic detection, for the Boskonians would certainly have a five hundred percent overlap. Their nullifiers would hash up the electros somewhat, but there was no use in taking too many chances. Previously, on right-line courses to and from Lyrane II, that had not mattered, for two reasons—not only was the distance extreme for accurate electro work, but also it would have been assumed that their ship was a zwilnik. Laying a course for Eight, though, would be something else entirely. A zwilnik would take the tube, and they would not, even if they had known where it was.

That left the visuals. The cruiser was a mighty small target at interplanetary distances; but there were such things as electronic telescopes, and the occultation of even a single star might prove disastrous. Kinnison called the chief pilot.

"Stars must be thin in certain regions of the sky out here, Hen.

Suppose you can pick us out a line of approach along which we will occult no stars and no bright nebulae?"

"I should think so, Kim—just a sec; I'll see . . . Yes, easily. There's a lot of black background, especially to the nadir," and the conference was resumed.

They'd have to go through the screens of electros in Kinnison's inherently indetectable black speedster. QX, but she was nobody's fighter—she didn't have a beam hot enough to light a match. And besides, there were the thought-screens and the highly-probable other stuff about which the Lensmen could know nothing.

Kinnison quite definitely did not relish the prospect. He remembered all too vividly what had happened when he had scouted the Eich's base on Jarnevon; when it was only through Worsel's aid that he had barely—*just* barely—escaped with his life. And Jarnevon's defenders had probably been exerting only routine precautions, whereas these fellows were undoubtedly cocked and primed for THE Lensman. He would go in, of course, but he'd probably come out feet first—he didn't know any more about their defenses than he had known before, and that was nothing, flat . . .

"Excuse the interruption, please," Nadreck's thought apologized, "but it would seem to appear more desirable, would it not, to induce the one of them possessing the most information to come out to us?"

"Huh?" Kinnison demanded. "It would, of course—but how in all your purple hells do you figure on swinging *that* load?"

"I am, as you know, a person of small ability," Nadreck replied in his usual circuitous fashion. "Also, I am of almost negligible mass and strength. Of what is known as bravery I have no trace—in fact, I have pondered long over that to be incomprehensible quality and have decided that it has no place in my scheme of existence. I have found it much more efficient to perform the necessary tasks in the easiest and safest possible manner, which is usually by means of stealth, deceit, indirection, and other cowardly artifices."

"Any of those, or all of them, would be QX with me," Kinnison assured him. "Anything goes, with gusto and glee, as far as the Eich are concerned. What I don't see is how we can put it across."

"Thought-screens interfered so seriously with my methods of procedure," the Palainian explained, "that I was forced to develop a means of puncturing them without upsetting their generators. The device is not generally known, you understand." Kinnison understood. So did the other Lensmen.

"Might I suggest that the four of you put on heated armor and come with me to my vessel in the hold? It will take some little time to transfer my apparatus and equipment to your speedster."

"Is it non-ferrous—undetectable?" Kinnison asked.

"Of course," Nadreck replied in surprise. "I work, as I told you, by stealth. My vessel is, except for certain differences necessitated by racial considerations, a duplicate of your own."

"Why didn't you say so?" Kinnison wanted to know. "Why bother to move the gadget? Why not use your speedster?"

"Because I was not asked. We should not bother. The only reason for using your vessel is so that you will not suffer the discomfort of wearing armor," Nadreck replied, categorically.

"Cancel it, then," Kinnison directed. "You've been wearing armor all the time you were with us—turn about for a while will be QX. Better that way, anyway, as this is very definitely your party, not ours. Not?"

"As you say; and with your permission," Nadreck agreed. "Also it may very well be that you will be able to suggest improvements in my device whereby its efficiency may be increased."

"I doubt it." The Tellurian's already great respect for this retiring, soft-spoken, "cowardly" Lensman was increasing constantly. "But we would like to study it, and perhaps copy it, if you so allow."

"Gladly," and so it was arranged.

The *Dauntless* crept along a black-background pathway and stopped. Nadreck, Worsel, and Kinnison—three were enough and neither Clarrissa nor Tregonsee insisted upon going—boarded the Palainian speedster.

Away from the mother-ship it sped upon muffled jets, and through the far-flung, heavily overlapped electro-magnetic detector zones. Through the outer thought-screens. Then, ultra-slowly, as space-speeds go, the speedster moved forward, feeling for whatever other blocking screens there might be.

All three of those Lensmen were in fact detectors themselves—their Arisian-imparted special senses made ethereal, even sub-ethereal, vibrations actually visible or tangible—but they did not depend only upon their bodily senses. That speedster carried instruments unknown to space-pilotry, and the Lensmen used them unremittingly. When they came to a screen they opened it, so insidiously that its generating mechanisms gave no alarms. Even a meteorite screen, which was supposed to forbid the passage of any material object, yielded without protest to Nadreck's subtle manipulation.

Slowly, furtively, a perfectly absorptive black body sinking through blackness so intense as to be almost palpable, the Palainian speedster settled downward toward the Boskonian fortress of Lyrane VIII.

14

NADRECK AT WORK

This is perhaps as good a place as any to glance in passing at the fashion in which the planet Lonabar was brought under the aegis of Civilization. No attempt will or can be made to describe it in any detail, since any adequate treatment of it would fill a volume—indeed, many volumes have already been written concerning various phases of the matter—and since it is not strictly germane to the subject in hand. However, some knowledge of the *modus operandi* in such cases is highly desirable for the full understanding of this history, in view of the vast number of planets which Coordinator Kinnison and his associates did have to civilize before the Second Galaxy was made secure.

Scarcely had Cartiff-Kinnison moved out than the Patrol moved in. If Lonabar had been heavily fortified, a fleet of appropriate size and power would have cleared the way. As it was, the fleet which landed was one of transports, not of battleships, and all the fighting from then on was purely defensive.

Propagandists took the lead; psychologists; Lensmen skilled not only in languages but also in every art of human relationships. The case of Civilization was stated plainly and repeatedly, the errors and the fallacies of autocracy were pointed out. A nucleus of government was formed; not of Civilization's imports, but of solid Lonabarian citizens who had passed the Lensmen's tests of ability and trustworthiness.

Under this local government a pseudo-democracy began haltingly to function. At first its progress was painfully slow; but as more and more of the citizens perceived what the Patrol actually was doing, it grew apace. Not only did the invaders allow—yes, foster—free speech and statutory liberty; they suppressed ruthlessly any person or any faction seeking to build a new dictatorship, whatever its nature, upon the ruins of the old. *That* news traveled fast; and laboring always and mightily upon Civilization's side were the always-present, however deeply-buried, urges of all intelligent entities toward self-expression.

There was opposition, of course. Practically all of those who had waxed fat upon the old order were very strongly in favor of its continuance. There were the hordes of the down-trodden who had so long and so dumbly endured oppression that they could not understand anything else; in whom the above-mentioned urges had been beaten and tortured almost out of existence. They themselves were not opposed to Civilization—for them it meant at worst only a change of masters—but those who sought by the same old wiles to re-enslave them were foes indeed.

Menjo Bleeko's sycophants and retainers were told to work or starve. The fat hogs could support the new order—or else. The thugs and those who tried to prey upon and exploit the dumb masses were arrested and examined. Some were cured, some were banished, some were shot.

Little could be done, however, about the dumb themselves, for in them the spark was feeble indeed. The new government nursed that spark along, the while ruling them as definitely, although not as harshly, as had the old; the Lensmen backing the struggling young Civilization knowing full well that in the children or in the children's children of these unfortunates the spark would flame up into a great white light.

It is seen that this government was not, and could not for many years become, a true democracy. It was in fact a benevolent semi-autocracy; autonomous in a sense, yet controlled by the Galactic Council through its representatives, the Lensmen. It was, however, so infinitely more liberal than anything theretofore known by the Lonabarians as to be a political revelation, and since corruption, that cosmos-wide curse of democracy, was not allowed a first fingerhold, the principles of real democracy and of Civilization took deeper root year by year.

To get back into the beam of narrative, Nadreck's blackly indetectable speedster settled to ground far from the Boskonians' central dome; well beyond the far-flung screens. The Lensmen knew that no life existed outside that dome and they knew that no possible sense of perception could pierce those defenses. They did not know, however, what other resources of detection, of offense, or of defense the foe might possess; hence the greatest possible distance at which they could work efficiently was the best distance.

"I realize that it is useless to caution any active mind not to think at all," Nadreck remarked as he began to manipulate various and sundry controls, "but you already know from the nature of our problem that any extraneous thought will wreak untold harm. For that reason I beg of you to keep your thought-screens up at all times, no matter what happens. It is, however, imperative that you be kept informed, since I may require aid or advice at any moment. To that end I ask you to hold these electrodes, which are connected to a receptor. Do not hesitate to speak freely to each other or to me; but please use only a spoken language, as I am averse to Lensed thoughts at this juncture. Are we agreed? Are we ready?"

They were agreed and ready. Nadreck actuated his peculiar drill—a tube of force somewhat analogous to a Q-type helix except in that it operated within the frequency-range of thought—and began to increase, by almost infinitesimal increments, its power. Nothing, apparently, happened; but finally the Palainian's instruments registered the fact that it was through.

"This is none too safe, friends," the Palainian announced from one part of his multi-compartmented brain, without distracting any part of his attention from the incredibly delicate operation he was performing. "May I suggest, Kinnison, in my cowardly way, that you place yourself at the controls and be ready to take us away from this planet at speed and without notice?"

"I'll say you may!" and the Tellurian complied, with alacrity. "Right now, cowardice is indicated—copiously!"

But through course after course of screen the hollow drill gnawed its cautious way without giving alarm; until at length there began to come through the interloping tunnel a vague impression of foreign thought. Nadreck stopped the helix, then advanced it by tiny steps until the thoughts came in coldly clear—the thoughts of the Eich going about their routine businesses. In the safety of their impregnably shielded dome the proudly self-confident monsters did not wear their personal thought-screens; which, for Civilization's sake, was just as well.

It had been decided previously that the mind they wanted would be that of a psychologist; hence the thought sent out by the Palainian was one which would appeal only to such a mind; in fact, one practically imperceptible to any other. It was extremely faint; wavering uncertainly upon the very threshold of perception. It was so vague, so formless, so inchoate that it required Kinnison's intensest concentration even to recognize it as a thought. Indeed, so starkly unhuman was Nadreck's mind and that of his proposed quarry that it was all the Tellurian Lensman could do to recognize it. It dealt, fragmentarily and in the merest glimmerings, with the nature and the mechanisms of the First Cause; with the fundamental ego, its *raison d'etre,* its causation, its motivation, its differentiation; with the stupendously awful concepts of the Prime Origin of all things ever to be.

Unhurried, monstrously patient, Nadreck neither raised the power of the thought nor hastened its slow tempo. Stolidly, for minute after long minute he held it, spraying it throughout the vast dome as mist is sprayed from an atomizer nozzle. And finally he got a bite. A mind seized upon that wistful, homeless, incipient thought; took it for its own. It strengthened it, enlarged upon it, built it up. And Nadreck followed it.

He did not force it; he did nothing whatever to cause any suspicion that the thought was or ever had been his. But as the mind of the Eich busied itself with that thought he all unknowingly let down the bars to Nadreck's invasion.

Then, perfectly in tune, the Palainian subtly insinuated into the mind of the Eich the mildly disturbing idea that he had forgotten something, or had neglected to do some trifling thing. This was the first really critical instant, for Nadreck had no idea whatever of what his victim's duties were or what he could have left undone. It had to be something which would take him out of the dome and toward the Patrolman's concealed speedster, but what it was, the Eich would have to develop for himself; Nadreck could not dare to attempt even a partial control at this stage and at this distance.

Kinnison clenched his teeth and held his breath, his big hands clutching fiercely the pilot's bars; Worsel unheedingly coiled his supple body into an ever smaller, ever harder and more compact bale.

"Ah!" Kinnison exhaled explosively. "It worked!" The psychologist, at Nadreck's impalpable suggestion, had finally thought of the thing. It was a thought-screen generator which had been giving a little trouble and which really should have been checked before this.

Calmly, with the mild self-satisfaction which comes of having successfully recalled to mind a highly elusive thought, the Eich opened one of the dome's unforceable doors and made his unconcerned way directly toward the waiting Lensmen; and as he approached Nadreck stepped up by logarithmic increments the power of his hold.

"Get ready, please, to cut your screens and to synchronize with me in case anything slips and he tries to break away," Nadreck cautioned; but nothing slipped.

The Eich came up unseeing to the speedster's side and stopped. The drill disappeared. A thought-screen encompassed the group narrowly. Kinnison and Worsel released their screens and also tuned in to the creature's mind. And Kinnison swore briefly, for what they found was meager enough.

He knew a great deal concerning the zwilnik doings of the First Galaxy; but so did the Lensmen; they were not interested in them. Neither were they interested, at the moment, in the files or in the records. Regarding the higher-ups, he knew of two, and only two, personalities. By means of an inter-galactic communicator he received orders from, and reported to, a clearly-defined, somewhat Eich-like entity known to him as Kandron; and vaguely, from occasional stray and unintentional thoughts of this Kandron, he had visualized as being somewhere in the background a human being named Alcon. He supposed that the planets upon which these persons lived were located in the Second Galaxy, but he was not certain, even of that. He had never seen either of them; he was pretty sure that none of his group ever would be allowed to see them. He had no means of tracing them and no desire whatsoever to do so. The only fact he really knew was that at irregular intervals Kandron got into communication with this base of the Eich.

That was all. Kinnison and Worsel let go and Nadreck, with a minute attention to detail which would be wearisome here, jockeyed the unsuspecting monster back into the dome. The native knew full where he had been, and why. He had inspected the generator and found it in good order. Every second of elapsed time was accounted for exactly. He had not the slightest inkling that anything out of the ordinary had happened to him or anywhere around him.

As carefully as the speedster had approached the planet, she departed from it. She rejoined the *Dauntless,* in whose control room Kinnison lined out a solid communicator beam to the Z9M9Z and to Port Admiral Haynes. He reported crisply, rapidly, everything that had transpired.

"So our best bet is for you and the Fleet to get out of here as fast as Klono will let you," he concluded. "Go straight out Rift Ninety Four, staying as far away as possible from both the spiral arm and the galaxy proper. Unlimber every spotting-screen you've got—put them to work along the line between Lyrane and the Second Galaxy. Plot all the punctures, extending the line as fast as you can. We'll join you at max and transfer to the Z9M9Z—her tank is just what the doctors ordered for the job we've got to do."

"Well, if you say so, I suppose that's the way it's got to be," Haynes grumbled. He had been growling and snorting under his breath ever since it had become evident what Kinnison's recommendation was to be. "I don't like this thing of standing by and letting zwilniks thumb their noses at us, like Prellin did on Bronseca. That once was once too damned often."

"Well, you got him, finally, you know," Kinnison reminded, quite cheerfully, "and you can have these Eich, too—sometime."

"I hope," Haynes acquiesced, something less than sweetly. "QX, then—but put out a few jets. The quicker you get out here the sooner we can get back and clean out this hoo-raw's nest."

Kinnison grinned as he cut his beam. He knew that it would be some time before the Port Admiral could hurl the metal of the Patrol against Lyrane VIII; but even he did not realize just how long a time it was to be.

What occasioned the delay was not the fact that the communicator was in operation only at intervals: so many screens were out, they were spaced so far apart, and the punctures were measured and aligned so accurately that the periods of non-operation caused little or no loss of time. Nor was it the vast distance involved; since, as has already been pointed out, the matter in the inter-galactic void is so tenuous that space-ships are capable of enormously greater velocities than any attainable in the far denser medium filling interstellar space.

No: what gave the Boskonians of Lyrane VIII their greatly length-ened reprieve was simply the direction of the line established by the communicator-beam punctures. Reasoning from analogy, the Lensmen had supposed that it would lead them into a star-cluster, fairly well away from the main body of the Second Galaxy, in either the zenith or the nadir direction. Instead of that, however, when the Patrol surveyors got close enough so that their possible error was very small, it became clear that their objective lay inside the galaxy itself.

"I don't like this line a bit, chief," Kinnison told the admiral then. "It'd smell like Limburger to have a fleet of this size and power nosing into their home territory, along what must be one of the hottest lines of communication they've got."

"Check," Port Admiral Haynes agreed. "QX so far, but it would begin to stink pretty quick now. We've got to assume that they know about spotting screens, whether they really do or not. If they do, they'll have this line trapped from stem to gudgeon, and the minute they detect us they'll cut this line out entirely. Then where'll you be?"

"Right back where I started from—that's what I'm yowling about. To make matters worse, it's credits to millos that the ape we're looking for isn't going to be anywhere near the end of this line."

"Huh? How do you figure that?" Haynes demanded.

"Logic. We're getting up now to where these zwilniks can really think. We've already assumed that they know about our beam tracers and detector nullifiers. Aren't they apt to know that we have inherently indetectable ships and almost perfectly absorptive coatings? Where does that land you?"

"Um . . . m . . . m. I see. Since they can't change the nature of the beam, they'll run it through a series of relays . . . with each leg trapped with everything they can think of . . . at the first sign of interference they'll switch, maybe halfway across the galaxy. Also, they might very well switch around once in a while, anyway, just on general principles."

"Check. That's why you'd better take the fleet back home, leaving Nadreck and me to work the rest of this line with our speedsters."

"Don't be dumb, son; you can think straighter than that." Haynes gazed quizzically at the younger man.

"What else? Where am I overlooking a bet?" Kinnison demanded.

"It is elementary tactics, young man," the admiral instructed, "to cover up any small, quiet operation with a large and noisy one. Thus, if I want to make an exploratory sortie in one sector I should always attack in force in another."

"But what would it get us?" Kinnison expostulated. "What's the advantage to be gained, to make up for the unavoidable losses?"

"Advantage? Plenty! Listen!" Haynes' bushy gray hair fairly bristled in eagerness. "We've been on the defensive long enough. They must be weak, after their losses at Tellus; and now, before they can rebuild, is the time to strike. It's good tactics, as I said, to make a diversion to cover you up, but I want to do more than that. We should start an actual, serious invasion, right now. When you can swing it, the best possible defense—even in general—is a powerful offense, and we're all set to go. We'll begin it with this fleet, and then, as soon as we're sure that they haven't got enough power to counter-invade, we'll bring over everything that's loose. We'll hit them so hard that they won't be able to worry about such a little thing as a communicator line."

"Hm . . . m. Never thought of it from that angle, but it'd be nice. We were coming over here sometime, anyway—why not now? I suppose you'll start on the edge, or in a spiral arm, just as though you were going ahead with the conquest of the whole galaxy?"

"Not 'just as though'," Haynes declared. "We *are* going through with it. Find a planet on the outer edge of a spiral arm, as nearly like Tellus as possible . . ."

"Make it nearly enough like Tellus and maybe I can use it for our headquarters on this 'coordinator' thing," Kinnison grinned.

"More truth than poetry in that, fellow. We find it and take over. Comb out the zwilniks with a fine-tooth comb. Make it the biggest, toughest base the universe ever saw—like Jarnevon, only more so. Bring in everything we've got and expand from that planet as a center, cleaning everything out as we go. We'll civilize 'em!"

And so, after considerable ultra-range communicator work, it was decided that the Galactic Patrol would forthwith assume the offensive.

Haynes assembled Grand Fleet. Then, while the two black speedsters kept unobtrusively on with the task of plotting the line, Civilization's mighty armada moved a few thousand parsecs aside and headed at normal touring blast for the nearest outcropping of the Second Galaxy.

There was nothing of stealth in this maneuver, nothing of finesse, excepting in the arrangements of the units. First, far in the van, flew the prodigious, irregular cone of scout cruisers. They were comparatively small, not heavily armed or armored, but they were ultra-fast and were provided with the most powerful detectors, spotters, and locators known. They adhered to no rigid formation, but at the will of their individual commanders, under the direct supervision of Grand Fleet Operations in the $Z9M9Z$, flashed hither and thither ceaselessly—searching, investigating, mapping, reporting.

Backing them up came the light cruisers and the cruising bombers—a new type, this latter, designed primarily to bore in to close quarters and to hurl bombs of negative matter. Third in order were the heavy defensive cruisers. These ships had been developed specifically for hunting down Boskonian commerce raiders within the galaxy. They wore practically impenetrable screen, so that they could lock to and hold even a super-dreadnought. They had never before been used in Grand Fleet formation; but since they were now equipped with tractor zones and bomb-tubes, theoretical strategy found a good use for them in this particular place.

Next came the real war-head—a solidly packed phalanx of maulers. All the ships up ahead had, although in varying degrees, freedom of motion and of action. The scouts had practically nothing else; fighting was not their business. They could fight, a little, if they had to; but they always ran away if they could, in whatever direction was most expedient at the time. The cruising bombers could either take their fighting or leave it alone, depending upon circumstances—in other words, they fought light cruisers, but ran away from big stuff, stinging as they ran. The heavy cruisers would fight anything short of a mauler, but never in formation: they always broke ranks and fought individual dog-fights, ship to ship.

But that terrific spear-head of maulers had no freedom of motion whatever. It knew only one direction—straight ahead. It would swerve aside for an inert planet, but for nothing smaller; and when it swerved it did so as a whole, not by parts. Its function was to blast through—straight through—any possible opposition, if and when that opposition should have been successful in destroying or dispersing the screens of lesser vessels preceding it. A sunbeam was the only conceivable weapon with which that stolid, power-packed mass of metal could not cope; and, the Patrolmen devoutly hoped, the zwilniks didn't have any sunbeams—yet.

A similar formation of equally capable maulers, meeting it head-on, could break it up, of course. Theoretical results and war-game solutions of this problem did not agree, either with each other or among themselves, and the thing had never been put to the trial of actual battle. Only one thing was certain—when and if that trial did come there was bound to be, as in the case of the fabled meeting of the irresistible force with the immovable object, a lot of very interesting by-products.

Flanking the maulers, streaming gracefully backward from their massed might in a parabolic cone, were arranged the heavy battleships and the super-dreadnoughts; and directly behind the bulwark of flying fortresses, tucked away inside the protecting envelope of big battle-wagons, floated the *Z9M9Z*—the brains of the whole outfit.

There were no free planets, no negaspheres of planetary anti-mass, no sunbeams. Such things were useful either in the defense of a Prime Base or for an all-out, ruthlessly destructive attack upon such a base. Those slow, cumbersome, supremely powerful weapons would come later, after the Patrol had selected the planet which they intended to hold against everything the Boskonians could muster. This present expedition had as yet no planet to defend, it sought no planet to destroy. It was the vanguard of Civilization, seeking a suitable foothold in the Second Galaxy and thoroughly well equipped to argue with any force mobile enough to bar its way.

While it has been said that there was nothing of stealth in this approach to the Second Galaxy, it must not be thought that it was unduly blatant or obvious: any carelessness or ostentation would have been very poor tactics indeed. Civilization's Grand Fleet advanced in strict formation, with every routine military precaution. Its nullifiers were full on, every blocking screen was out, every plate upon every ship was hot and was being scanned by alert and keen-eyed observers.

But every staff officer from Port Admiral Haynes down, and practically every line officer as well, knew that the enemy would locate the invading fleet long before it reached even the outer fringes of the galaxy toward which it was speeding. That stupendous tonnage of ferrous metal could not be disguised; nor could it by any possible artifice be made to simulate any normal tenant of the space which it occupied.

The gigantic flares of the heavy stuff could not be baffled, and the combined grand flare of Grand Fleet made a celestial object which would certainly attract the electronic telescopes of plenty of observatories. And the nearest such 'scopes, instruments of incredible powers of resolution, would be able to pick them out, almost ship by ship, against the relatively brilliant background of their own flares.

The Patrolman, however, did not care. This was, and was intended to be, an open, straightforward invasion; the first wave of an attack which would not cease until the Galactic Patrol had crushed Boskonia throughout the entire Second Galaxy.

Grand Fleet bored serenely on. Superbly confident in her awful might, grandly contemptuous of whatever she was to face, she stormed along; uncaring that at that very moment the foe was massing his every defensive arm to hurl her back or to blast her out of existence.

15

KLOVIA

As Haynes and the Galactic Council had already surmised, Boskonia was now entirely upon the defensive. She had made her supreme bid in the effort which had failed so barely to overcome the defenses of hard-held Tellus. It was, as has been seen, a very near thing indeed, but the zwilnik chieftains did not and could not know that. Communication through the hyper-spatial tube was impossible, no ordinary communicator beam could be driven through the Patrol's scramblers, no Boskonian observers could be stationed near enough to the scene of action to perceive or to record anything that had occurred, and no single zwilnik ship or entity survived to tell of how nearly Tellus had come to extinction.

And, in fine, it would have made no difference in the mind of Alcon of Thrale if he had known. A thing which was not a full success was a complete failure; to be almost a success meant nothing. The invasion of Tellus had failed. They had put everything they had into that gigantically climactic enterprise. They had shot the whole wad, and it had not been enough. They had, therefore, abandoned for the nonce humanity's galaxy entirely, to concentrate their every effort upon the rehabilitation of their own depleted forces and upon the design and construction of devices of hitherto unattempted capability and power.

But they simply had not had enough time to prepare properly to meet the invading Grand Fleet of Civilization. It takes time—lots of time—to build such heavy stuff as maulers and flying fortresses, and they had not been allowed to have it. They had plenty of lighter stuff, since the millions of Boskonian planets could furnish upon a few hours notice more cruisers, and even more first-line battleships, than could possibly be used efficiently, but their back-bone of brute force and fire-power was woefully weak.

Since the destruction of a solid center of maulers was, theoretically, improbable to the point of virtual impossibility, neither Boskonia nor the Galactic Patrol had built up any large reserve of such structures. Both would now build up such a reserve as rapidly as possible, of course, but half-built structures could not fight.

The zwilniks had many dirigible planets, but they were *too* big. Planets, as has been seen, are too cumbersome and unwieldly for use against a highly mobile and adequately-controlled fleet.

Conversely, humanity's Grand Fleet was up to its maximum strength and perfectly balanced. It had suffered losses in the defense of Prime Base, it is true; but those losses were of comparatively light craft, which Civilization's inhabited worlds could replace as quickly as could Boskonia's.

Hence Boskonia's fleet was at a very serious disadvantage as it formed to defy humanity just outside the rim of its galaxy. At two disadvantages, really, for Boskonia then had neither Lensmen nor a $Z9M9Z$; and Haynes, canny old master strategist that he was, worked upon them both.

Grand Fleet so far had held to one right-line course, and upon this line the zwilnik defense had been built. Now Haynes swung aside, forcing the enemy to re-form: they had to engage him, he did not have to engage them. Then, as they shifted—raggedly, as he had supposed and had hoped that they would—he swung again. Again, and again; the formation of the enemy becoming more and more hopelessly confused with each shift.

The scouts had been reporting constantly; in the seven-hundred-foot lenticular tank of the $Z9M9Z$ there was spread in exact detail the disposition of every unit of the foe. Four Rigellian Lensmen, now thoroughly trained and able to perform the task almost as routine, condensed the picture—summarized it—in Haynes' ten-foot tactical tank. And finally, so close that another swerve could not be made, and with the line of flight of his solid fighting core pointing straight through the loosely disorganized nucleus of the enemy, Haynes gave the word to engage.

The scouts, remaining free, flashed aside into their prearranged observing positions. Everything else went inert and bored ahead. The light cruisers and the cruising bombers clashed first, and a chill struck at Haynes' stout old heart as he learned that the enemy did have negative-matter bombs.

Upon that point there had been much discussion. One view was that the Boskonians would have them, since they had seen them in action and since their scientists were fully as capable as were those of Civilization. The other was that, since it had taken all the massed intellect of the Conference of Scientists to work out a method of handling and of propelling such bombs, and since the Boskonians were probably not as cooperative as were the civilized races, they could not have them.

Approximately half of the light cruisers of Grand Fleet were bombers. This was deliberate, for in the use of the new arm there were involved problems which theoretical strategy could not completely solve. Theoretically, a bomber could defeat a conventional light cruiser of equal tonnage one hundred percent of the time, *provided*—here was the rub!—that the conventional cruiser did not blast her out of the ether before she could get her bombs into the vitals of the foe. For, in order to accommodate the new equipment, something of the old had to be decreased: something of power, of armament, of primary or secondary beams, or of defensive screen. Otherwise the size and mass must be so increased that the ship would no longer be a light cruiser, but a heavy one.

And the Patrol's psychologists had had ideas, based upon facts which they had gathered from Kinnison and from Illona and from many spools of tape—ideas by virtue of which it was eminently possible that the conventional light cruisers of Civilization, with their heavier screen and more and hotter beams, could vanquish the light cruisers of the foe, even though they should turn out to be negative-matter bombers.

Hence the fifty-fifty division of types; but, since Haynes was not thoroughly sold upon either the psychologists or their ideas, the commanders of his standard light cruisers had received very explicit and definite orders. If the Boskonians should have bombs and if the high-brows' idea did not pan out, they were to turn tail and run, at maximum and without stopping to ask questions or to get additional instructions.

Haynes had not really believed that the enemy would have nega-bombs, they were so new and so atrociously difficult to handle. He wanted—but was unable—to believe implicitly in the psychologist's findings. Therefore, as soon as he saw what was happening, he abandoned his tank for a moment to seize a plate and get into full touch with the control room of one of the conventional light cruisers then going into action.

He watched it drive boldly toward a Boskonian vessel which was in the act of throwing bombs. He saw that the agile little vessel's tractor zone was out. He watched the bombs strike that zone and bounce. He watched the tractor-men go to work and he saw the psychologists' idea bear splendid fruit. For what followed was a triumph, not of brute force and striking power, but of morale and manhood. The brain-men had said, and it was now proved, that the Boskonian gunners, low-class as they were and driven to their tasks like the slaves they were, would hesitate long enough before using tractor-beams as pressors so that the Patrolmen could take their own bombs away from them!

For negative matter, it must be remembered, is the exact opposite of ordinary matter. To it a pull is, or becomes, a push; the tractor beam which pulls ordinary matter toward its projector actually pushed negative matter away.

The "boys" of the Patrol knew that fact thoroughly. They knew all about what they were doing, and why. They were there because they wanted to be, as Illona had so astoundingly found out, and they worked with their officers, not because of them. With the Patrol's gun-crews it was a race to see which crew could capture the first bomb and the most.

Aboard the Boskonian how different it was! There the dumb cattle had been told what to do, but not why. They did not know the fundamental mechanics of the bomb-tubes they operated by rote; did not know that they were essentially tractor-beam projectors. They did know, however, that tractor beams pulled things toward them; and when they were ordered to swing their ordinary tractors upon the bombs which the Patrolmen were so industriously taking away from them, they hesitated for seconds, even under the lash.

This hesitation was fatal. Haynes' gleeful gunners, staring through their special finders, were very much on their toes; seconds were enough. Their fierce-driven tractors seized the inimical bombs in mid-space, and before the Boskonians could be made to act in the only possible opposition hurled them directly backward against the ships which had issued them. Ordinary defensive screen did not affect them; repulsor screen, meteorite- and wall-shields only sucked them inward the faster.

And ordinary matter and negative matter cannot exist in contact. In the instant of touching, the two unite and disappear, giving rise to vast quantities of intensely hard radiation. One negabomb was enough to put any cruiser out of action, but here there were usually three or four at once. Sometimes as many as ten; enough almost, to consume the total mass of a ship.

A bomb struck; ate in. Through solid armor it melted. Atmosphere rushed out, to disappear en route—for air is normal matter. Along beams and trusses the hellish hyper-sphere travelled freakishly, although usually in the direction of greatest mass. It clung, greedily. Down stanchions it flowed; leaving nothing in its wake, flooding all circumambient space with lethal emanations. Into and through converters. Into pressure tanks, which blew up enthusiastically. Men's bodies it did not seem to favor— not massive enough, perhaps—but even them it did not refuse if offered. A Boskonian, gasping frantically for air which was no longer there and already half mad, went completely mad as he struck savagely at the thing and saw his hand and his arm to the shoulder vanish instantaneously, as though they had never been.

Satisfied, Haynes wrenched his attention back to his tank. Most of his light cruisers were through and in the clear; they were reporting by thousands. Losses were very small. The conventional-type cruisers had won either by using the enemies' own bombs, as he had seen them used, or by means of their heavier armor and armament. The bombers had won in almost every case; not by superior force, for in arms and equipment they were to all intents and purposes identical with their opponents, but because of their infinitely higher quality of personnel. To brief it, scarcely a handful of Boskonia's light cruisers got away.

The heavy cruisers came up, broke formation, and went doggedly to work. They were the blockers. Each took one ship—a heavy cruiser or a battleship—out of the line, and held it out. It tried to demolish it with every weapon it could swing, but even if it could not vanquish its foe, it could and did hang on until some big bruiser of a battleship could come up and administer the *coup de grace.*

And battleships and super-dreadnoughts were coming up in their thousands and their myriads. All of them, in fact, save enough to form a tight globe, packed screen to screen, around the $Z9M9Z$.

Slowly, ponderously, inert, the war-head of maulers came crawling up. The maulers and fortresses of the Boskonians were hopelessly out- numbered and were badly scattered in position. Hence this meeting of the ultra-heavies was not really a battle at all, but a slaughter. Ten or more of Haynes' gigantic structures could concentrate their entire com- bined fire-power upon any luckless one of the enemy; with what awful effect it would be superflous to enlarge upon.

When the mighty fortresses had done their work they englobed the $Z9M9Z$, enabling the guarding battleships to join their sister moppers-up; but there was very little left to do. Civilization had again triumphed; and, this time, at very little cost. Some of the pirates had escaped, of course; observers from afar might very well have had scanners and recorders upon the entire conflict; but, whatever of news was transmitted or how, Alcon of Thrale and Boskonia's other master minds would or could derive little indeed of comfort from the happenings of this important day.

"Well, that's probably that—for a while, at least, don't you think?" Haynes asked his Council of War.

It was decided that it was; that if Boskonia could not have mustered a heavier center for her defensive action here, she would be in no position to make any really important attack for months to come.

Grand Fleet, then, was re-formed; this time into a purely defensive and exploratory formation. In the center, of course, was the $Z9M9Z$. Around her was a close-packed quadruple globe of maulers. Outside of them in order, came sphere after sphere of super-dreadnoughts, of battleships, of heavy cruisers, and of light cruisers. Then, not in globe at all, but ranging far and wide, were the scouts. Into the edge of the nearest spiral arm of the Second Galaxy the stupendous formation advanced, and along it it proceeded at dead slow blast. Dead slow, to enable the questing scouts to survey thoroughly each planet of every solar system as they came to it.

And finally an Earth-like planet was found. Several approximately Tellurian worlds had been previously discovered and listed as possibilities; but this one was so perfect that the search ended then and there. Apart from the shape of the continents and the fact that there was somewhat less land-surface and a bit more salt water, it was practically identical with Tellus. As was to be expected, its people were human to the limit of classification. Entirely unexpectedly, however, the people of Klovia—which is as close as English can come to the native name—were not zwilniks. They had never heard of, nor had they ever been approached by, the Boskonians. Space-travel was to them only a theoretical possibility, as was atomic energy.

They had no planetary organization, being still divided politically into sovereign states which were all too often at war with each other. In fact, a world war had just burned itself out, a war of such savagery that only a fraction of the world's population remained alive. There had been no victor, of course. All had lost everything—the survivors of each nation, ruined as they were and without either organization or equipment, were trying desperately to rebuild some semblance of what they had once had.

Upon learning these facts the psychologists of the Patrol breathed deep sighs of relief. This kind of thing was made to order; civilizing this planet would be simplicity itself. And it was. The Klovians did not have to be overawed by a show of superior force. Before this last, horribly internecine war, Klovia had been a heavily industrialized world, and as soon as the few remaining inhabitants realized what Civilization had to offer, that no one of their neighboring competitive states was to occupy a superior position, and that full, worldwide production was to be resumed as soon as was humanly possible, their relief and joy were immeasurable.

Thus the Patrol took over without difficulty. But they were, the Lensmen knew, working against time. As soon as the zwilniks could get enough heavy stuff built they would attack, grimly determined to blast Klovia and everything upon it out of space. Even though they had known nothing about the planet previously, it was idle to hope that they were still in ignorance either of its existence or of what was in general going on there.

Haynes' first care was to have the heaviest metalry of the Galactic Patrol—loose planets, negaspheres, sunbeams, fortresses, and the like—rushed across the void to Klovia at maximum. Then, as well as putting every employable of the new world to work, at higher wages than he had ever earned before, the Patrol imported millions upon millions of men, with their women and families, from hundreds of Earth-like planets in the First Galaxy.

They did not, however, come blindly. They came knowing that Klovia was to be primarily a military base, the most supremely powerful base that had ever been built. They knew that it would bear the brunt of the most furious attacks that Boskone could possibly deliver; they knew full well that it might fall. Nevertheless, men and women, they came in their multitudes. They came with high courage and high determination, glorying in that which they were to do. People who could and did so glory were the only ones who came; which fact accounts in no small part for what Klovia is today.

People came, and worked, and stayed. Ships came, and trafficked. Trade and commerce increased tremendously. And further and further abroad, as there came into being upon that formerly almost derelict planet some seventy-odd gigantic defensive establishments, there crept out an ever-widening screen of scout-ships, with all their high-powered feelers hotly outstretched.

Meanwhile Kinnison and frigid-blooded Nadreck had worked their line, leg by tortuous leg, to Onlo and thence to Thrale. A full spool should be devoted to that working alone; but, unfortunately, as space here must be limited to the barest essentials, it can scarcely be mentioned. As Kinnison and Haynes had foreseen, that line was heavily trapped. Luckily, however, it had not been moved so radically that the searchers could not re-discover it; the zwilniks were, as Haynes had promised, very busily engaged with other and more important matters. All of those traps were deadly, and many of them were ingenious indeed—so ingenious as to test to the utmost the "cowardly" Palainian's skill and mental scope. All, however, failed. The two Lensmen held to the line in spite of the pitfalls and followed it to the end. Nadreck stayed upon or near Onlo, to work in its frightful environment against the monsters to whom he was biologically so closely allied, while the Tellurian went on to try conclusions with Alcon, the Tyrant of Thrale.

Again he had to build up an unimpeachable identity and here there were no friendly thousands to help him do it. He had to get close—*really* close—to Alcon, without antagonizing him or in any way arousing his hair-trigger suspicions. Kinnison had studied that problem for days. Not one of his previously-used artifices would work, even had he dared to repeat a procedure. Also, time was decidedly of the essence.

There was a way. It was not an easy way, but it was fast and, if it worked at all, it would work perfectly. Kinnison would not have risked it even a few months back, but now he was pretty sure that he had jets enough to swing it.

He needed a soldier of about his own size and shape—details were unimportant. The man should not be in Alcon's personal troops, but should be in a closely-allied battalion, from which promotion into that select body would be logical. He should be relatively inconspicuous, yet with a record of accomplishment, or at least of initiative, which would square up with the rapid promotions which were to come.

The details of that man-hunt are interesting, but not of any real importance here, since they did not vary in any essential from other searches which have been described at length. He found him—a lieutenant in the Royal Guard—and the ensuing mind-study was as assiduous as it was insidious. In fact, the Lensman memorized practically every memory-chain in the fellow's brain. Then the officer took his regular furlough and started for home—but he never got there.

Instead, it was Kimball Kinnison who wore the Thralian's gorgeous full-dress uniform and who greeted in exactly appropriate fashion the Thralian's acquaintances and lifelong friends. A few of these, who chanced to see the guardsman first, wondered briefly at his changed appearance or thought that he was a stranger. Very few, however, and very briefly; for the Lensman's sense of perception was tensely alert and his mind was strong. In moments, then, those chance few forgot that they had ever had the slightest doubt concerning this soldier's identity; they knew calmly and as a matter of fact that he was the Traska Gannel whom they had known so long.

Living minds presented no difficulty except for the fact that of course he could not get in touch with everyone who had ever known the real Gannel. However, he did his best. He covered plenty of ground and he got most of them—all that could really matter.

Written records, photographs, and tapes were something else again. He had called Worsel in on that problem long since, and the purely military records of the Royal Guard were QX before Gannel went on leave. Although somewhat tedious, that task had not proved particularly difficult. Upon a certain dark night a certain light-circuit had gone dead, darkening many buildings. Only one or two sentries or guards saw anything amiss, and they never afterward recalled having done so. And any record that has ever been made can be remade to order by the experts of the Secret Service of the Patrol!

And thus it was also with the earlier records. He had been born in a hospital. QX—that hospital was visited, and thereafter Gannel's baby foot-prints were actually those of infant Kinnison. He had gone to certain schools—those schools' records also were made to conform to the new facts.

Little could be done, however, about pictures. No man can possibly remember how many times he has had his picture taken, or who has the negatives, or to whom he had given photographs, or in what papers, books, or other publications his likeness has appeared.

The older pictures, Kinnison decided, did not count. Even if the likenesses were good, he looked enough like Gannel so that the boy or the callow youth might just about as well have developed into something that would pass for Kinnison in a photograph as into the man which he actually did become. Where was the dividing line? The Lensman decided—or rather, the decision was forced upon him—that it was at his graduation from the military academy.

There had been an annual, in which volume appeared an individual picture, fairly large, of each member of the graduating class. About a thousand copies of the book had been issued, and now they were scattered all over space. Since it would be idle even to think of correcting them all, he could not correct any of them. Kinnison studied that picture for a long time. He didn't like it very well. The cub was just about grown up, and this photo looked considerably more like Gannel than it did like Kinnison. However, the expression was self-conscious, the pose strained—and, after all, people hardly ever looked at old annuals. He'd have to take a chance on that. Later poses—formal portraits, that is; snap-shots could not be considered—would have to be fixed up.

Thus it came about that certain studios were raided very surreptitiously. Certain negatives were abstracted and were deftly re-touched. Prints were made therefrom, and in several dozens of places in Gannel's home town, in albums and in frames, stealthy substitutions were made.

The furlough was about to expire. Kinnison had done everything that he could do. There were holes, of course—there couldn't help but be—but they were mighty small and, if he played his cards right, they would never show up. Just to be on the safe side, however, he'd have Worsel stick around for a couple of weeks or so, to watch developments and to patch up any weak spots that might develop. The Velantian's presence upon Thrale would not create suspicion—there were lots of such folks flitting from planet to planet—and if anybody did get just a trifle suspicious of Worsel, it might be all the better.

Mentor of Arisia, however, knew many things that Kinnison of Tellus did not; he had powers of which Kinnison would never dream. Mentor knew exactly what entity stood behind Tyrant Alcon's throne; knew exactly what it could and would do; knew that this was one of the most critical instants of Civilization's long history.

Wherefore every negative of every picture that had ever been taken of Traska Gannel, and every print and reproduction made therefrom, was made to conform; nowhere, throughout the reaches of space or the vistas of time, was there any iota of evidence that the present Traska Gannel had not borne that name since infancy.

So it was done, and Lieutenant Traska Gannel of the Royal Guard went back to duty.

16

GANNEL FIGHTS A DUEL

Nadreck, the furtive Palainian, had prepared as thoroughly in his own queerly under-handed fashion as had Kinnison in his bolder one. Nadreck was cowardly, in Earthly eyes, there can be no doubt of that; as cowardly as he was lazy. To his race, however, those traits were eminently sensible; and those qualities did in fact underlie his prodigious record of accomplishment. Being so careful of his personal safety, he had lived long and would live longer: by doing everything in the easiest possible way he had conserved his resources. Why take chances with a highly valuable life? Why be so inefficient as to work hard in the performance of a task when it could always be done in some easy way?

Nadreck moved in upon Onlo, then, absolutely imperceptibly. His dark, cold, devious mind, so closely akin to those of the Onlonians, reached out, indetectably *en rapport* with theirs. He studied, dissected, analyzed and neutralized their defenses, one by one. Then, his ultra-black speedster securely hidden from their every prying mechanism and sense, although within easy working distance of the control dome itself, he snuggled down into his softly-cushioned resting place and methodically, efficiently, he went to work.

Thus, when Alcon of Thrale next visited his monstrous henchmen, Nadreck flipped a switch and every thought of the zwilniks' conference went permanently on record.

"What have you done, Kandron, about the Lensman?" the Tyrant demanded, harshly. "What have you concluded?"

"We have done very little," the chief psychologist replied, coldly. "Beyond the liquidation of a few Lensmen—with nothing whatever to indicate that any of them had any leading part in our recent reverses—our agents have accomplished nothing.

"As to conclusions, I have been unable to draw any except the highly negative one that every Boskonian psychologist who has ever summed up the situation has, in some respect or other, been seriously in error."

"And only *you* are right!" Alcon sneered. "Why?"

"I am right only in that I admit my inability to draw any valid conclusions," Kandron replied, imperturbably. "The available data are too meager, too inconclusive, and above all, too contradictory to justify any positive statements. There is a possibility that there are two Lensmen who have been and are mainly responsible for what has happened. One of these, the lesser, may be—note well that I say 'may be', not 'is'—a Tellurian or an Aldebaranian or some other definitely human being; the other and by far the more powerful one is apparently entirely unknown, except by his works."

"Star A Star," Alcon declared.

"Call him so if you like," Kandron assented, flatly. "But this Star A Star is an operator. As the supposed Director of Lensmen he is merely a figment of the imagination."

"But this information came from the Lensman Morgan!" Alcon protested. "He was questioned under the drug of truth; he was tortured and all but slain; the Overlord of Delgon consumed all his life-force except for the barest possible moiety!"

"How do you know all these things?" Kandron asked, unmoved. "Merely from the report of the Overlords and from the highly questionable testimony of one of the Eich, who was absent from the scene during all of the most important time."

"You suspect, then, that . . ." Alcon broke off, shaken visibly.

"I do," the psychologist replied, dryly. "I suspect very strongly indeed that there is working against us a mind of a power and scope but little inferior to my own. A mind able to overcome that of an Overlord; one able, at least if unsuspected and hence unopposed, to deceive even the admittedly capable minds of the Eich. I suspect that the Lensman Morgan was, if he existed at all, merely a puppet. The Eich took him too easily by far. It is therefore eminently possible that he had no physical actuality of existence . . ."

"Oh, come, now! Don't be ridiculous!" Alcon snapped. "With all Boskone there as witnesses? Why, his hand and Lens remained!"

"Improbable, perhaps, I admit—but still eminently possible," Kandron insisted. "Admit for the moment that he was actual, and that he did lose a hand—but remember also that the hand and the Lens may very well have been brought along and left there as reassurance; we cannot be sure even that the Lens matched the hand. But admitting all this, I am still of the opinion that Lensman Morgan was not otherwise tortured, that he lost none of his vital force, that he and the unknown I have already referred to returned practically unharmed to their own galaxy. And not only did they return, they must have carried with them the information which was later used by the Patrol in the destruction of Jarnevon."

"Preposterous!" Alcon snorted. "Tell me, if you can, upon what facts you have been able to base such fantastic opinions?"

"Gladly," Kandron assented. "I have been able to come to no really valid conclusions, and it may very well be that your fresh viewpoint will enable us to succeed where I alone have failed. I will therefore summarize very briefly the data which seem to me most significant. Attend closely, please:

"For many years, as you know, everything progressed smoothly. Our first set-back came when a Tellurian war-ship, manned by Tellurians and Valerians, succeeded in capturing almost intact one of the most modern and most powerful of our vessels. The Valerians may be excluded from consideration, insofar as mental ability is concerned. At least one Tellurian escaped, in one of our own, supposedly derelict, vessels. This one, whom Helmuth thought of, and reported, as 'the' Lensman, eluding all pursuers, went to Velantia; upon which planet he so wrought as to steal bodily six of our ships sent there specifically to hunt him down. In those ships he won his way back to Tellus in spite of everything Helmuth and his force could do.

"Then there were the two episodes of the Wheelmen of Aldebaran I. In the first one a Tellurian Lensman was defeated—possibly killed. In the second our base was destroyed—tracelessly. Note, however, that the base next above it in order was, so far as we know, not visited or harmed.

"There was the Boyssia affair, in which the human being Blakeslee did various unscheduled things. He was obviously under the control of some far more powerful mind; a mind which did not appear, then or ever.

"We jump then to this, our own galaxy—the sudden, inexplicable disappearance of the planet Medon.

"Back to theirs again—the disgraceful and closely-connected debacles at Shingvors and Antigan. Traceless both, but again neither was followed up to any higher headquarters.

Nadreck grinned at that, if a Palainian can be said to grin. Those matters were purely his own. He had done what he had been requested to do—thoroughly—no following up had been either necessary or desirable.

"Then Radelix." Kandron's summary went concisely on. "The female agents, Bominger, the Kalonian observers—all wiped out. Was or was not some human Lensman to blame? Everyone, from Chester Q. Forsyce down to a certain laborer upon the docks, was suspected, but nothing definite could be learned.

"The senselessly mad crew of the *27L462P*—Wynor—Grantlia. Again completely traceless. Reason obscure, and no known advantage gained, as this sequence also was dropped."

Nadreck pondered briefly over this material. He knew nothing of any such matters nor, he was pretty sure, did Kinnison. THE Lensman apparently was getting credit for something that must have been accidental or wrought by some internal enemy. QX. He listened again:

"After the affair of Bronseca, in which so many Lensman were engaged that particularization was impossible, and which again was not followed up, we jump to the Asteroid Euphrosyne, Miner's Rest, and Wild Bill Williams of Aldebaran II. If it was a coincidence that Bill Williams became William Williams and followed our line to Tressilia, it is a truly remarkable one—even though, supposedly, said Williams was so stupefied with drugs as to be incapable either of motion or perception.

"Jalte's headquarters was, apparently, missed. However, it must have been invaded—tracelessly—for it was the link between Tressilia and Jarnevon, and Jarnevon was found and was destroyed.

"Now, before we analyze the more recent events, what do you yourself deduce from the above facts?" Kandron asked.

While the tyrant was cogitating, Nadreck indulged in a minor gloat. This psychologist, by means of impeccable logic and reasoning from definitely known facts, had arrived at such erroneous conclusions! However, Nadreck had to admit, his own performances and those in which Kinnison had acted indetectably, when added to those of some person or persons unknown, did make a really impressive total.

"You may be right," Alcon admitted finally. "At least two entirely different personalities and methods of operation. Two Lensmen are necessary to satisfy the above requirements . . . and, as far as we know, sufficient. One of the necessary two is a human being, the other an unknown. Cartiff was, of course, the human Lensman. A masterly piece of work, that—but, with the cooperation of the Patrol, both logical and fairly simple. This human being is always in evidence, yet is so cleverly concealed by his very obviousness that nobody ever considers him important enough to be worthy of a close scrutiny. Or . . . perhaps . . ."

"That is better," Kandron commented. "You are beginning to see why I was so careful in saying that the known Tellurian factor 'may be', not 'is', of any real importance."

"But he *must* be!" Alcon protested. "It was a human being who tried and executed our agent; Cartiff was a human being—to name only two."

"Of course." Kandron admitted, half contemptuously. "But we have no proof whatever that any of those human beings actually did, of their own volition, any of the things for which they have been given credit. Thus, it is now almost certain that that widely advertised 'mind-ray machine' was simply a battery of spot-lights—the man operating them may very well have done nothing else. Similarly, Cartiff may have been an ordinary gangster controlled by the Lensman—we may as well call him Star A Star as anything else—or a Lensman or some other member of the Patrol acting as a dummy to distract our attention from Star A Star, who himself did the real work, all unperceived."

"Proof?" the Tyrant snapped.

"No proof—merely a probability," the Onlonian stated flatly. "We *know*, however, definitely and for a fact—visiplates and long-range communicators cannot be hypnotized—that Blakeslee was one of Helmuth's own men. Also that he was the same man, both as a loyal Boskonian of very ordinary mental talents and as an enemy having a mental power which he as Blakeslee never did and never could possess."

"I see." Alcon thought deeply. "Very cogently put. Instead of there being two Lensmen, working sometimes together and sometimes separately, you think that there is only one really important mind and that this mind at times works with or through some Tellurian?"

"But not necessarily the same Tellurian—exactly. And there is nothing to give us any indication whatever as to Star A Star's real nature or race. We cannot even deduce whether or not he is an oxygen-breather . . . and that is bad."

"Very bad," the Tyrant assented. "Star A Star, or Cartiff, or both working together, found Lonabar. They learned of the Overlords, or at least of Lyrane II . . ."

"By sheer accident, if they learned it there at all, I am certain of that," Kandron insisted. "They did not get any information from Menjo Bleeko's mind; there was none there to get."

"Accident or not, what boots it?" Alcon impatiently brushed aside the psychologist's protests. "They found Bleeko and killed him. A raid upon the cavern of the Overlords of Lyrane II followed immediately. From the reports sent by the Overlords to the Eich of Lyrane VIII we know that there were two Patrol ships involved. One, not definitely identified as Cartiff's, took no part in the real assault. The other, the super-dreadnought *Dauntless,* did that alone. She was manned by Tellurians, Valerians, and at least one Velantian. Since they went to the trouble of taking the Overlords alive, we may take it for granted that they obtained from them all the information they possessed before they destroyed them and their cavern?"

"It is at least highly probable that they did so," Kandron admitted.

"We have, then, many questions and few answers," and the Tyrant strode up and down the dimly blue-lit room. "It would be idle indeed, in view of the facts, to postulate that Lyrane II was left, as were some others, a dead end. Has Star A Star attempted Lyrane VIII? If not, why has he delayed? If so, did he succeed or fail in penetrating the defenses of the Eich? They swear that he did not, that he could not . . ."

"Of course," Kandron sneered. "But while asking questions why not ask why the Patrol chose this particular time to invade our galaxy in such force as to wipe out our Grand Fleet? To establish themselves so strongly as to make it necessary for us of the High Command to devote our entire attention to the problem of dislodging them?"

"What!" Alcon exclaimed, then sobered quickly and thought for minutes. "You think, then, that . . ." His thoughts died away.

"I do so think," Kandron thought, glumly. "It is very decidedly possible—perhaps even probable—that the Eich of Lyrane VIII were able to offer no more resistance to the penetration of Star A Star than was Jalte the Kalonian. That this massive thrust was timed to cover the insidious tracing of our lines of communication or whatever other leads the Lensman had been able to discover."

"But the traps—the alarms—the screens and zones!" Alcon exclaimed, manifestly jarred by this new and disquietingly keen thought.

"No alarm was tripped, as you know; no trap was sprung," Kandron replied, quietly. "The fact that we have not as yet been attacked here may or may not be significant. Not only is Onlo very strongly held, not only is it located in such a central position that their lines of communication would be untenable, but also . . ."

"Do you mean to admit that *you* may have been invaded and searched—tracelessly?" Alcon fairly shrieked the thought.

"Certainly," the psychologist replied, coldly. "While I do not believe that it has been done, the possibility must be conceded. What we could do, we have done; but what science can do, science can circumvent. To finish my thought, it is a virtual certainty that it is not Onlo and I who are their prime objectives, but Thrale and you. Especially you."

"You may be right. You probably *are* right; but with no data whatever upon who or what Star A Star really is, with no tenable theory as to how he could have done what actually has been done, speculation is idle."

Upon this highly unsatisfactory note the interview closed. Alcon the Tyrant went back to Thrale; and as he entered his palace grounds he passed within forty inches of his Nemesis. For Star-A-Star-Kinnison-Traska-Gannel was, as Alcon himself so clearly said, rendered invisible and imperceptible by his own obviousness.

Although obvious, Kinnison was very busy indeed. As a lieutenant of Guardsmen, the officer in charge of a platoon whose duties were primarily upon the ground, he had very little choice of action. His immediate superior, the first lieutenant of the same company, was not much better off. The captain had more authority and scope, since he commanded aerial as well as ground forces. Then, disregarding side-lines of comparative seniority, came the major, the colonel, and finally the general, who was in charge of all the regular armed forces of Thrale's capital city. Alcon's personal troops were of course a separate organization, but Kinnison was not interested in them—yet.

The major would be high enough, Kinnison decided. Big enough to have considerable authority and freedom of motion, and yet not important enough to attract undesirable attention.

The first lieutenant, a stodgy, strictly rule-of-thumb individual, did not count. He could step right over his head into the captaincy. The real Gannel had always, in true zwilnik fashion, hated his captain and had sought in devious ways to undermine him. The pseudo-Gannel despised the captain as well as hating him, and to the task of sapping he brought an ability enormously greater than any which the real Gannel had ever possessed.

Good Boskonian technique was to work upward by stealth and treachery, aided by a carefully-built-up personal following of spies and agents. Gannel had already formed such a staff; had already selected the man who, in the natural course of events, would assassinate the first lieutenant. Kinnison retained Gannel's following, but changed subtly its methods of operation. He worked almost boldly. He himself criticized the captain severely, within the hearing of two men whom he knew to belong, body and soul, to his superior.

This brought quick results. He was summoned brusquely to the captain's office; and, knowing that the company commander would not dare to have him assassinated there, he went. In that office there were a dozen people: it was evident that the captain intended this rebuke to be a warning to all upstarts.

"Lieutenant Traska Gannel, I have had my eye on you and your subversive activities for some time," the captain orated. "Now, purely as a matter of form, and in accordance with paragraph 5, section 724 of General Regulations, you may offer whatever you have of explanation before I reduce you to the ranks for insubordination."

"I have a lot to say," Kinnison replied, coolly. "I don't know what your spies have reported, but to whatever it was I would like to add that having this meeting here as you are having it proves that you are as fat in the head as you are in the belly . . ."

"Silence! Seize him, men!" the captain commanded, fiercely. He was not really fat. He had only a scant inch of equatorial bulge; but that small surplusage was a sore point indeed. "Disarm him!"

"The first man to move dies in his tracks," Kinnison countered; his coldly venemous tone holding the troopers motionless. He wore two handweapons more or less similar to DeLameters, and now his hands rested lightly upon their butts. "I cannot be disarmed until after I have been disrated, as you know very well; and that will never happen. For if you demote me I will take an appeal, as is my right, to the colonel's court; and there I will prove that you are stupid, inefficient, cowardly, and unfit generally to command. You really are, and you know it. Your discipline is lax and full of favoritism; your rewards and punishments are assessed, not by logic, but by whim, passion, and personal bias. Any court that can be named would set you down into the ranks, where you belong, and would give me your place. If this is insubordination and if you want to make something out of it, you pussy-gutted, pusillanimous, brainless tub of lard, cut in your jets!"

The maligned officer half-rose, white-knuckled hands gripping the arms of his chair, then sank back craftily. He realized now that he had blundered; he was in no position to face the rigorous investigation which Gannel's accusation would bring on. But there was a way out. This could now be made a purely personal matter, in which a duel would be *de rigueur*. And in Boskonian duelling the superior officer, not the challenged, had the choice of weapons. He was a master of the saber; he had outpointed Gannel regularly in the regimental games. Therefore he choked down his wrath and:

"These personal insults, gratuitous and false as they are, make it a matter of honor," he declared smoothly. "Meet me, then, tomorrow, half an hour before sunset, in the Place of Swords. It will be sabers."

"Accepted," Kinnison meticulously followed the ritual. "To first blood or to the death?" This question was superfluous—the stigma of the Lensman's epithets, delivered before such a large group, could not possibly be expunged by the mere letting of a little blood.

"To the death," curtly.

"So be it, Oh captain!" Kinnison saluted punctiliously, executed a snappy about-face, and marched stiffly out of the room.

QX. This was fine—strictly according to Hoyle. The captain was a swordsman, of course; but Kinnison was no slouch. He didn't think he'd have to use a thought-beam to help him. He had had five years of intensive training. Quarter-staff, night-stick, club, knife, and dagger; foil, epee, rapier, saber, broadsword, scimitar, bayonet, what-have-you—with practically any nameable weapon any Lensman had to be as good as he was with fists and feet.

The Place of Swords was in fact a circular arena, surrounded by tiers of comfortably-padded seats. It was thronged with uniforms, with civilian formal afternoon dress, and with modish gowns; for such duels as this were sporting events of the first magnitude.

To guard against such trickery as concealed armor, the contestants were almost naked. Each wore only silken trunks and a pair of low shoes, whose cross-ribbed, flexible composition soles could not be made to slip upon the corrugated surface of the cork-like material of the arena's floor.

The colonel himself, as master of ceremonies, asked the usual perfunctory questions. No, reconciliation was impossible. No, the challenged would not apologize. No, the challenger's honor could not be satisfied with anything less than mortal combat. He then took two sabers from an orderly, measuring them to be sure that they were of precisely the same length. He tested each edge for keenness, from hilt to needle point, with an expert thumb. He pounded each hilt with a heavy testing club. Lastly, still in view of the spectators, he slipped a guard over each point and put his weight upon the blades. They bent alarmingly; but neither broke and both snapped back truly into shape. No spy or agent, everyone then knew, had tampered with either one of those beautiful weapons.

Removing the point-guards, the colonel again inspected those slenderly lethal tips and handed one saber to each of the duelists. He held out a baton, horizontal and shoulder-high. Gannel and the captain crossed their blades upon it. He snapped his stick away and the duel was on.

Kinnison fought in Gannel's fashion exactly; in his characteristic crouch and with his every mannerism. He was, however, the merest trifle faster than Gannel had ever been—just enough faster so that by the exertion of everything he had of skill and finesse, he managed to make the

zwilnik's blade meet steel instead of flesh during the first long five minutes of furious engagement. The guy was good, no doubt of that. His saber
came writhing in, to disarm. Kinnison flicked his massive wrist. Steel
slithered along steel; hilt clanged against heavy basket hilt. Two mighty
right arms shot upward, straining to the limit. Breast to hard-ridged breast,
left arms pressed against bulgingly-corded backs, every taut muscle from
floor-gripping feet up to powerful shoulders thrown into the effort, the
battlers stood motionlessly *en tableau* for seconds.

The ape wasn't fat, at that, Kinnison realized then; he was as hard
as cord-wood underneath. Not fat enough, anyway, to be anybody's push-
over; although he was probably not in good enough shape to last very
long—he could probably wear him down. He wondered fleetingly, if
worst came to worst, whether he would use his mind or not. He didn't
want to . . . but he might have to. Or would he, even then—*could* he?
But he'd better snap out of it. He couldn't get anywhere with this body-
check business; the zwilnik was just about as strong as he was.

They broke, and in the breaking Kinnison learned a brand new cut.
He sensed it coming, but he could not parry or avoid it entirely; and the
crowd shrieked wildly as the captain's point slashed into Gannel's trunks
and a stream of crimson trickled down Gannel's left leg.

Stamp! Stamp! Cut, thrust, feint, slash and parry, the grim game went
on. Again, in spite of all he could do, Kinnison was pinked; this time by
a straight thrust aimed at his heart. He was falling away from it, though,
so got only half an inch or so of the point in the fleshy part of his left
shoulder. It bled spectacularly, however, and the throng yelled ragingly
for the kill. Another—he never did know exactly how he got that one—in
the calf of his right leg; and the bloodthirsty mob screamed still louder.

Then, the fine edge of the captain's terrific attack worn off, Kinnison
was able to assume the offensive. He maneuvered his foe into an awk-
ward position, swept his blade aside, and slashed viciously at the neck.
But the Thralian was able partially to cover. He ducked frantically, even
while his parrying blade was flashing up. Steel clanged, sparks flew;
but the strength of the Lensman's arm could not be entirely denied.
Instead of the whole head, however, Kinnison's razor-edged weapon
snicked off only an ear and a lock of hair.

Again the spectators shrieked frenzied approval. They did not care
whose blood was shed, so long as it *was* shed; and this duel, of two superb
swordsmen so evenly matched, was the best they had seen for years. It
was, and promised to keep on being, a splendidly gory show indeed.

Again and again the duelists engaged at their flashing top speed;
once again each drew blood before the colonel's whistle shrilled.

Time out for repairs: to have either of the contestants bleed to death, or even to the point of weakness, was no part of the code. The captain had out-pointed the lieutenant, four to two, just as he always did in the tournaments; but he now derived very little comfort from the score. He was weakening, while Gannel seemed as strong and fast as at the bout's beginning.

Surgeons gave hasty but effective treatment, new and perfect sabers replaced the nicked weapons, the ghastly thing went on. The captain tired slowly but surely; Gannel took, more and more openly and more and more savagely, the offensive.

When it was over Kinnison flipped his saber dexterously, so that its point struck deep into the softly resilient floor beside that which had once been his captain. Then, while the hilt swung back and forth in slow arcs, he faced one segment of the now satiated throng and crisply saluted the colonel.

"Sir, I trust that I have won honorably the right to be examined for fitness to become the captain of my company?" he asked, formally; and:

"You have, sir," the colonel as formally replied.

17

INTO NTH SPACE

Kinnison's wounds, being superficial, healed rapidly. He passed the examination handily. He should have; since, although it was rigorous and comprehensive, Traska Gannel himself could have passed and Kinnison, as well as knowing practically everything that the Thralian had ever learned, had his own vast store of knowledge upon which to draw. Also, if necessary, he could have read the answers from the minds of the examiners.

As a captain, the real Gannel would have been a hard and brilliant commander, noticeable even among the select group of tried and fire-polished veterans who officered the Guards. Hence Kinnison became so; in fact, considerably more so than most. He was harsh, he was relentless and inflexible; but he was absolutely fair. He did not punish a given breach of discipline with twenty lashes one time and with a mere reprimand the next; fifteen honest, scarring strokes it became for each and every time, whoever the offender. Whatever punishment a man deserved by the book he got, promptly and mercilessly; whatever reward was earned was bestowed with equal celerity, accompanied by a crisply accurate statement of the facts in each case, at the daily parade-review.

His men hated him, of course. His non-coms and lieutenants, besides hating him, kept on trying to cut him down. All, however, respected him and obeyed him without delay and without question, which was all that any Boskonian officer could expect and which was far more than most of them ever got.

Having thus consolidated his position, Kinnison went blithely to work to undermine and to supplant the major. Since Alcon, like all dictators everywhere, was in constant fear of treachery and of revolution, war-games were an almost constant form of drill. The general himself planned and various officers executed the mock attacks, by space, air, and land; the Royal Guards and Alcon's personal troops, heavily outnumbered, always constituted the defense. An elaborate system of scoring had been worked out long since, by means of which the staff officers could study in detail every weak point that could be demonstrated.

"Captain Gannel, you will have to hold passes 25, 26, and 27," the obviously worried major told Kinnison, the evening before a particularly important sham battle was to take place. The Lensman was not surprised. He himself had insinuated the idea into his superior's mind. Moreover, he already knew, from an intensive job of spying, that his major was to be in charge of the defense, and that the colonel, who was to direct the attacking forces, had decided to route his main column through Pass 27.

"Very well, sir," Kinnison acknowledged. "I wish to protest formally, however, against those orders. It is manifestly impossible, sir, to hold all three of those passes with two platoons of infantry and one squadron of speedsters. May I offer a suggestion . . ."

"You may not," the major snapped. "We have deduced that the real attack is coming from the north, and that any activity in your sector will be merely a feint. Orders are orders, captain!"

"Yes, sir," Kinnison replied, meekly, and signed for the thick sheaf of orders which stated in detail exactly what he was to do.

The next evening, after Kinnison had won the battle by disregarding every order he had been given, he was summoned to the meeting of the staff. He had expected that, too, but he was not at all certain of how it was coming out. It was in some trepidation, therefore, that he entered the lair of the Big Brass Hats.

"Har-rumph!" he was greeted by the adjutant. "You have been called . . ."

"I know why I was called," Kinnison interrupted, brusquely. "Before we go into that, however, I wish to prefer charges before the general against Major Delios of stupidity, incompetence, and inefficiency."

Astonishment resounded throughout the room in a ringing silence, broken finally by the general.

"Those are serious charges indeed, Captain Gannel; but you may state your case."

"Thank you, sir. First, stupidity: He did not perceive, at even as late a time as noon, when he took all my air away from me to meet the feint from the north, that the attack was not to follow any orthodox pattern. Second, incompetence: The orders he gave me could not possibly have stopped any serious attack through any one of the passes I was supposed to defend. Third, inefficiency: No efficient commander refuses to listen to suggestions from his officers, as he refused to listen to me last night."

"Your side, Major?" and the staff officers listened to a defense based upon blind, dumb obedience to orders.

"We will take this matter under advisement," the general announced then. "Now, Captain, what made you suspect that the colonel was coming through Pass 27?"

"I didn't," Kinnison replied, mendaciously. "To reach any one of those passes, however, he would have to come down this valley," tracing it with his forefinger upon the map. "Therefore I held my whole force back here at Hill 562, knowing that, warned by my air of his approach, I could reach any one of the passes before he could."

"Ah. Then, when your air was sent elsewhere?"

"I commandeered a flitter—my own, by the way—and sent it up so high as to be indetectable. I then ordered motorcycle scouts out, for the enemy to capture; to make the commander of any possible attacking or reconnaissance force think that I was still blind."

"Ah . . . smart work. And then?"

"As soon as my scout reported troop movements in the valley, I got my men ready to roll. When it became certain that Pass 27 was the objective, I rushed everything I had into preselected positions commanding every foot of that pass. Then, when the colonel walked into the trap, I wiped out most of his main column. However, I had a theoretical loss of three-quarters of my men in doing it," bitterly. "If I had been directing the defense I would have wiped out the colonel's entire force, ground and air both, with a loss of less than two percent."

This was strong talk. "Do you realize, Captain Gannel, that this is sheer insubordination?" the general demanded. "That you are in effect accusing me also of stupidity in planning and in ordering such an attack?"

"Not at all, sir," Kinnison replied instantly. "It was quite evident, sir, that you did it deliberately, to show all of us junior officers the importance of thought. To show us that, while unorthodox attacks may possibly be made by unskilled tacticians, any such attack is of necessity fatally weak if it be opposed by good tactics. In other words, that orthodox strategy is the only really good strategy. Was not that it, sir?"

Whether it was or not, that viewpoint gave the general an out, and he was not slow in taking advantage of it. He decided then and there, and the always subservient staff agreed with him, that Major Delios had indeed been stupid, incompetent, and inefficient; and Captain Gannel forthwith became Major Gannel.

Then the Lensman took it easy. He wangled and phenagled various and sundry promotions and replacements, until he was once more surrounded by a thoroughly subsidized personal staff and in good position to go to work upon the colonel. Then, however, instead of doing so, he violated another Boskonian precedent by having a frank talk with the man whom normally he should have been trying to displace.

"You have found out that you can't kill me, colonel," he told his superior, after making sure that the room was really shielded. "Also that I can quite possibly kill you. You know that I know more than you do—that all my life, while you other fellows were helling around, I have been working and learning—and that I can, in a fairly short time, take your job away from you without killing you. However, I don't want it."

"You don't *want* it!" The colonel stared, narrow-eyed. "What *do* you want, then?" He knew, of course, that Gannel wanted something.

"Your help," Kinnison admitted, candidly. "I want to get onto Alcon's personal staff, as adviser. With my experience and training, I figure that there's more in it for me there than here in the Guards. Here's my proposition—if I help you, by showing you how to work out your field problems and in general building you up however I can instead of tearing you down, will you use your great influence with the general and Prime Minister Fossten to have me transferred to the Household?"

"Will I? I'll say I will!" the colonel agreed, with fervor. He did not add "If I can't kill you first"—that was understood.

And Kinnison did build the colonel up. He taught him things about the military business which that staff officer had never even suspected; he sounded depths of strategy theretofore completely unknown to the zwilnik. And the more Kinnison taught him, the more eager the colonel became to get rid of him. He had been suspicious and only reluctantly cooperative at first; but as soon as he realized that he could not kill his tutor and that if the latter stayed in the Guards it would be only a matter of days—at most of weeks—until Gannel would force himself into the colonelcy by sheer force of merit, he pulled in earnest every wire he could reach.

Before the actual transfer could be effected, however, Kinnison received a call from Nadreck.

"Excuse me, please, for troubling you," the Palainian apologized, "but there has been a development in which you may perhaps be interested. This Kandron has been given orders by Alcon to traverse a hyper-spatial tube, the terminus of which will appear at coordinates 217-493-28 at hour eleven of the seventh Thralian day from the present."

"Fine business! And you want to chase him, huh?" Kinnison jumped at the conclusion. "Sure—go ahead. I'll meet you there. I'll fake up some kind of an excuse to get away from here and we'll run him ragged . . ."

"I do not," Nadreck interrupted, decisively. "If I leave my work here it will all come undone. Besides, it would be dangerous—foolhardy. Not knowing what lies at the other end of that tube, we could make no plans and could have no assurance of safety, or even of success. You should not go, either—that is unthinkable. I am reporting this matter in view of the possibility that you may think it significant enough to warrant the sending of some observer whose life is of little or no importance."

"Oh . . . uh-huh . . . I see. Thanks, Nadreck." Kinnison did not allow any trace of his real thought to go out before he broke the line. Then:

"Funny ape, Nadreck," he cogitated, as he called Haynes. "I don't get his angle at all—I simply can't figure him out . . . Haynes? Kinnison," and he reported in full.

"The *Dauntless* has all the necessary generators and equipment, and the place is far enough out so that she can make the approach without any trouble," the Lensman concluded. "We'll burn whatever is at the other end of that tube clear out of the ether. Send along as many of the old gang as you can spare. Wish we had time to get Cardynge—he'll howl like a wolf at being left out—but we've got only a week . . ."

"Cardynge is here," Haynes broke in. "He has been working out some stuff for Thorndyke on the sunbeam. He is finished now, though, and will undoubtedly want to go along."

"Fine!" and explicit arrangements for the rendezvous were made.

It was not unduly difficult for Kinnison to make his absence from duty logical, even necessary. Scouts and observers reported inexplicable interferences with certain communications lines. With thoughts of THE Lensman suffusing the minds of the higher-ups, and because of Gannel's already-demonstrated prowess and keenness, he scarcely had to signify a willingness to investigate the phenomena in order to be directed to do so.

Nor did he pick a crew of his own sycophants. Instead, he chose the five highest-ranking privates of the battalion to accompany him upon this supposedly extremely dangerous mission; apparently entirely un-aware that two of them belonged to the colonel, two to the general, and one to the captain who had taken his place.

The colonel wished Major Gannel luck—verbally—even while hop-ing fervently that THE Lensman would make cold meat of him in a hurry; and Kinnison gravely gave his well-wisher thanks as he set out. He did not, however, go near any communications lines; although his spying crew did not realize the fact. They did not realize anything; they did not know even that they became unconscious within five minutes after leaving Thrale.

They remained unconscious while the speedster in which they were was drawn into the *Dauntless'* capacious hold. In the Patrol ship's sickbay, under expert care, they remained unconscious during the entire duration of their stay on board.

The Patrol pilots picked up Kandron's flying vessel with little difficulty; and, nullifiers full out, followed it easily. When the zwilnik ship slowed down to feel for the vortex the *Dauntless* slowed also, and baffled her driving jets as she sneaked up to the very edge of electro-detector range. When the objective disappeared from three-dimensional space the point of vanishment was marked precisely, and up to that point the Patrol ship flashed in seconds.

The regular driving blasts were cut off, the special generators were cut in. Then, as the force-fields of the ship reacted against those of the Boskonian "shore" station, the Patrolmen felt again in all their gruesome power the appallingly horrible sensations of inter-dimensional acceleration. For that sensation is, literally, indescribable. A man in good training can overcome sea-sickness, air-sickness, and space-sickness. He can overcome the nausea and accustom himself to the queasily terrifying endless-fall sensation of weightlessness. He can become inured to the physical and mental ills accompanying inertialessness. No man ever has, however, been able to get used to inter-dimensional acceleration.

It is best likened to a compression; not as a whole, but atom by atom. A man feels as though he were being twisted—corkscrewed in some monstrously obscure fashion which permits him neither to move from his place nor to remain where he is. It is a painless but utterly revolting transformation, progressing in a series of waves; a re-arrangement, a writhing, crawling distortion, an incomprehensibly impossible extrusion of each ultimate particle of his substance in an unknowable, ordinarily non-existent direction.

The period of acceleration over, the *Dauntless* began to travel at uniform velocity along whatever course it was that the tube took. The men, although highly uncomfortable and uneasy, could once more move about and work. Sir Austin Cardynge in particular was actually happy and eager as he flitted from one to another of the automatic recording instruments upon his special panel. He resembled more closely than ever a lean, gray tomcat, Kinnison thought—he almost expected to see him begin to lick his whiskers and purr.

"You see, my ignorant young friend," the scientist almost did purr as one of the recording pens swung wildly across the ruled paper, "it is as I told you—the lack of exact data upon even one tiny factor of this extremely complex phenomenon is calamitous. While my notes were apparently complete and were certainly accurate, our experimental tubes did not function perfectly. The time factor was irreconcilable—completely so, in every aspect, even that of departure from and return to normal space—and it is unthinkable that time, one of the fundamental units, is or can be intrinsically variable . . ."

"You think so?" Kinnison broke in. "Look at that," pointing to the ultimate of timepieces, Cardynge's own triplex chronometer. "Number One says we've been in this tube for an hour, Number Two says a little over nine minutes, and according to Number Three we won't be starting for twenty minutes yet—it must be running backwards—let's see you comb *that* out of your whiskers!"

"Oh-h . . . ah . . . a-hum." But only momentarily was Sir Austin taken aback. "Ah, I was right all the time!" he cackled gleefully. "I thought it was practically impossible for me to commit an error or to overlook any possibilities, and I have now proved that I did not. Time, in this hyper-spatial region or condition, *is* intrinsically variable, and in major degree!"

"And what does that get you?" Kinnison asked, pointedly.

"Much, my impetuous youngster, much," Cardynge replied. "We observe, we note facts. From the observations and facts we theorize and we deduce; thus arriving very shortly at the true inwardness of time."

"You hope," the Lensman snorted, dubiously; and in his skepticism he was right and Sir Austin was wrong. For the actual nature and mechanism of time remained, and still constitute, a mystery, or at least an unsolved problem. The Arisians—perhaps—understand time; no other race does.

To some of the men, then, and to some of the clocks and other time-measuring devices, the time seemed—or actually was?—very long; to other and similar beings and mechanisms it seemed—or was—short. Short or long, however, the *Dauntless* did not reach the Boskonian end of the hyper-spatial tube.

In mid-flight there came a crunching, twisting *cloonk!* and an abrupt reversal of the inexplicably horrible inter-dimensional acceleration—a deceleration as sickeningly disturbing, both physically and mentally, as the acceleration had been.

While within the confines of the hyper-spatial tube every eye of the *Dauntless* had been blind. To every beam upon every frequency, visible or invisible, ether-borne or carried upon the infinitely faster waves of the sub-ether, the murk was impenetrable. Every plate showed the same mind-numbing blankness; a vague, eerily-shifting, quasi-solid blanket of formless, textureless grayness. No lightness or darkness, no stars or constellation or nebulae, no friendly, deep-space blackness—nothing.

Deceleration ceased; the men felt again the wonted homeliness and comfort of normal pseudo-gravity. Simultaneously the gray smear of the visiplates faded away into commonplace areas of jetty black, pierced by the brilliantly dimensionless vari-colored points of light which were the familiar stars of their own familiar space.

But were they familiar? Was that our galaxy, or anything like it? They were not. It was not. Kinnison stared into his plate, aghast.

He would not have been surprised to have emerged into three-dimensional space anywhere within the Second Galaxy. In that case, he would have seen a Milky Way; and from its shape, apparent size, and texture he could have oriented himself fairly closely in a few minutes. But the *Dauntless* was not within any lenticular galaxy—nowhere was there any sign of a Milky Way!

He would not have been really surprised to have found himself and his ship out in open inter-galactic space. In that case he would have seen a great deal of dead-black emptiness, blotched with lenticular bodies which were in fact galaxies. Orientation would then have been more difficult; but, with the aid of the Patrol charts, it could have been accomplished. But here there were no galaxies—no nebulae of any kind!

18

PRIME MINISTER FOSSTEN

Here, upon a background of a blackness so intense as to be obviously barren of nebular material, there lay a multitude of blazingly resplendent stars—and nothing except stars. A few hundred were of a visual magnitude of about minus three. Approximately the same number were of minus two or thereabouts, and so on down; but there did not seem to be a star or other celestial object in that starkly incredible sky of an apparent magnitude greater than about plus four.

"What do you make of this, Sir Austin?" Kinnison asked, quietly. "It's got me stopped like a traffic light."

The mathematician ran toward him and the Lensman stared. He had never known Cardynge to hurry—in fact, he was not really running now. He was walking, even though his legs were fairly twinkling in their rapidity of motion. As he approached Kinnison his pace gradually slowed to normal.

"Oh—time must be cock-eyed here, too," the Lensman observed. "Look over there—see how fast those fellows are moving, and how slow those others over that way are?"

"Ah, yes. Interesting—intensely interesting. Truly, a most remarkable and intriguing phenomenon," the fascinated mathematician enthused.

"But that wasn't what I meant. Swing this plate—it's on visual—

around outside, so as to get the star aspect and distribution. What do you think of it?"

"Peculiar—I might almost say unique," the scientist concluded, after his survey. "Not at all like any normal configuration or arrangement with which I am familiar. We could perhaps speculate, but would it not be preferable to secure data first? Say by approaching a solar system and conducting systematic investigations?"

"Uh-huh," and again Kinnison stared at the wispy little physicist in surprise. Here was a *man!* "You're certainly something to tie to, ace, do you know it?" he asked, admiringly. Then, as Cardynge gazed at him questioningly, uncomprehendingly:

"Skip it. Can you feel my thought, Henderson?"

"Yes."

"Shoot us across to one of those nearer stars, stop, and go inert."

"QX, chief." The pilot obeyed.

And in the instant of inerting, the visiplate into which the two men stared went black. The thousands of stars studding the sky a moment before had disappeared as though they had never been.

"Why . . . what . . . How in all the yellow hells of space can *that* happen?" Kinnison blurted.

Without a word Cardynge reached out and snapped the plate's receiver over from "visual" to "ultra," whereupon the stars reappeared as suddenly as they had vanished.

"Something's screwy somewhere!" the Lensman protested. "We *can't* have an inert velocity greater than that of light—it's impossible!"

"Few things, if any, can be said definitely to be impossible; and everything is relative, not absolute," the old scientist declared, pompously. "This space, for instance. You have not yet perceived, I see, even that you are not in the same three-dimensional space in which we have heretofore existed."

Kinnison gulped. He was going to protest about that, too, but in the face of Cardynge's unperturbed acceptance of the fact he did not quite dare to say what he had in mind.

"That is better," the old man declaimed. "Do not get excited—to do so dulls the mind. Take nothing for granted, do not jump at conclusions— to commit either of those errors will operate powerfully against success. Working hypotheses, young man, must be based upon accurately determined facts; not upon mere guesses, superstitions, or figments of personal prejudices."

"Bub—bub—but . . . QX—skip it!" Nine tenths of the *Dauntless'* crew would have gone out of control at the impact of the knowledge of what had happened; even Kinnison's powerful mind was shaken.

Cardynge, however, was—not seemed to be, but actually was—as calm and as self-contained as though he were in his own quiet study. "Explain it to me, will you please, in words of as nearly one syllable as possible?"

"Our looser thinkers have for centuries speculated upon the possibility of an entire series of different spaces existing simultaneously, side by side in a hypothetical hyper-continuum. I have never indulged in such time-wasting; but now that actual corroborative data have become available, I regard it as a highly fruitful field of investigation. Two extremely significant facts have already become apparent; the variability of time and the non-applicability of our so-called 'laws' of motion. Different spaces, different laws, it would seem."

"But when we cut our generators in that other tube we emerged into our own space," Kinnison argued. "How do you account for that?"

"I do not as yet try to account for it!" Cardynge snapped. "Two very evident possibilities should already be apparent, even to your feeble brain. One, that at the moment of release your vessel happened to be situated within a fold of our own space. Two, that the collapse of the ship's force-fields always returns it to its original space, while the collapse of those of the shore station always forces it into some other space. In the latter case, it would be reasonable to suppose that the persons or beings at the other end of the tube may have suspected that we were following Kandron, and, as soon as he landed, cut off their forces deliberately to throw us out of space. They may even have learned that persons of lesser ability, so treated, never return. Do not allow yourself to be at all impressed by any of these possibilities, however, as the truth may very well lie in something altogether different. Bear it, in mind that we have as yet very little data upon which to formulate any theories, and that the truth can be revealed only by a very careful, accurate, and thorough investigation. Please note also that I would surely have discovered and evaluated all these unknowns during the course of my as yet incomplete study of our own hyper-spatial tubes; that I am merely continuing here a research in which I have already made noteworthy progress."

Kinnison really gasped at that—the guy was certainly terrific! He called the chief pilot. "Go free, Hen, and start flitting for a planet—we've got to sit down somewhere before we can start back home. When you find one, land free. Stay free, and watch your Bergs—I don't have to tell you what will happen if they quit on us."

Then Thorndyke. "Verne? Break out some personal neutralizers. We've got a job of building to do—inertialess," and he explained to both men in flashing thoughts what had happened and what they had to do.

"You grasp the basic idea, Kinnison," Cardynge approved, "that it is necessary to construct a station apart from the vessel in which we propose to return to our normal environment. You err grievously, however, in your insistence upon the necessity of discovering a planet, satellite, asteroid, or other similar celestial body upon which to build it."

"Huh?" Kinnison demanded.

"It is eminently possible—yes, even practicable—for us to use the *Dauntless* as an anchorage for the tube and for us to return in the life-boats," Cardynge pointed out.

"What? Abandon this ship? Waste all that time rebuilding all the boats?"

"It is preferable, of course, and more expeditious, to find a planet, if possible," the scientist conceded. "However, it is plain that it is in no sense necessary. Your reasoning is fallacious, your phraseology is deplorable. I am correcting you in the admittedly faint hope of teaching you scientific accuracy of thought and of statement."

"Wow! Wottaman!" Kinnison breathed to himself, as, heroically, he "skipped it."

Somewhat to Kinnison's surprise—he had more than half expected that planets would be non-existent in that space—the pilots did find a solid world upon which to land. It was a peculiar planet indeed. It did not move right, it did not look right, it did not feel right. It was waterless, airless, desolate; a senseless jumble of jagged fragments, mostly metallic. It was neither hot nor cold—indeed, it seemed to have no temperature of its own at all. There was nothing whatever right about it, Kinnison declared.

"Oh, yes, there is!" Thorndyke contradicted. "Time is constant here, whatever its absolute rate may be, these metals are nice to work with, and some of this other stuff will make insulation. Or hadn't you thought of that? Which would be faster, cutting down an intrinsic velocity of fifteen lights to zero or building the projector out of native materials? And if you match intrinsics, what will happen when you hit our normal space again?

"Plenty, probably—uh-huh, faster to use the stuff that belongs here. Careful, though, fella!"

And care was indeed necessary; extreme care that not a particle of matter from the ship was used in the construction and that not a particle of the planet's substance by any mischance got aboard the space-ship.

The actual work was simple enough. Cardynge knew exactly what had to be done. Thorndyke knew exactly how to do it, as he had built precisely similar generators for the experimental tubes upon Tellus. He had a staff of experts; the *Dauntless* carried a machine shop and equipment second to none. Raw material was abundant, and it was an easy matter to block out an inertialess room within which the projectors and motors were built. And, after they were built, they worked.

It was not the work, then, but the strain which wore Kinnison down. The constant, wearing strain of incessant vigilance to be sure that the Bergenholms and the small units of the personal neutralizers did not falter for a single instant. He did not lose a man, but again and again there flashed into his mind the ghastly picture of one of his boys colliding with the solid metal of the planet at a relative velocity fifteen times that of light! The strain of the endless checking and rechecking to make certain that there was no exchange of material, however slight, between the ship and the planet.

Above all, the strain of knowing a thing which, apparently, no one else suspected; that Cardynge, with all his mathematical knowledge, was not going to be able to find his way back! He had never spoken of this to the scientist. He did not have to. He knew that without a knowledge of the fundamental distinguishing characteristics of our normal space—a knowledge even less to be expected than that a fish should know the fundamental equations and structure of water—they never could, save by sheerest accident, return to their own space. And as Cardynge grew more and more tensely, unsocially immersed in his utterly insoluble problem, the more and more uneasy the Gray Lensman became. But this last difficulty was resolved first, and in a totally unexpected fashion.

"Ah, Kinnison of Tellus, here you are—I have been considering your case for some twenty nine of your seconds," a deep, well-remembered voice resounded within his brain.

"Mentor!" he exclaimed, and at the sheer shock of his relief he came very near indeed to fainting. "Thank Klono and Noshabkeming you found us! How did you do it? How do we get ourselves out of here?"

"Finding you was elementary," the Arisian replied, calmly. "Since you were not in your own environment you must be elsewhere. It required but little thought to perceive what was a logical, in fact an inevitable, development. Such being the case, it needed very little additional effort to determine what had happened, and how, and why; likewise precisely where you must now be. As for departure therefrom, your mechanical preparations are both correct and adequate. I could give you the necessary information, but it is rather technically specialized and not negligible in amount; and since your brain is not of infinite capacity, it is better not to fill any part of it with mathematics for which you will have no subsequent use. Put yourself en rapport, therefore, with Sir Austin Cardynge. I will follow."

He did so, and as mind met mind there ensued a conversation whose barest essentials Kinnison could not even dimly grasp. For Cardynge, as has been said, could think in the universal language of mathematics; in the esoteric symbology which very few minds have ever been able even partially to master. The Lensman did not get it, nor any part of it; he knew only that in that to him completely meaningless gibberish the Arisian was describing to the physicist, exactly and fully, the distinguishing characteristics of a vast number of parallel and simultaneously co-existent spaces.

If that was "rather" technical stuff, the awed Lensman wondered, what would really deep stuff be like? Not that he wanted to find out! No wonder these mathematical wizards were nuts—went off the beam—he'd be pure squirrel-food if he had half that stuff in *his* skull!

But Sir Austin took to it like a cat lapping up cream or doing away with the canary. He brightened visibly; he swelled; and, when the Arisian had withdrawn from his mind, he preened himself and swaggered as he made meticulous adjustments of the delicate meters and controls which the technicians had already built.

Preparations complete, Cardynge threw in the switches and everything belonging to the *Dauntless* was rushed aboard—everything, that is, that was demonstrably uncontaminated by any particle of Nth-space matter. The spacesuits that had been worn on the planet and everything else, no matter what it was, that could not show an unquestionable bill of health were dumped. The neutralizers, worn so long and cherished so assiduously, were taken off with profound sighs of relief. The vessel was briefly, tentatively inerted. QX—no faster-than-light meteorites tore volatizingly through her mass. So far, so good.

Then the ship's generators were energized and smoothly, effortlessly the big battle-wagon took the inter-dimensional plunge. There came the expected, but nevertheless almost unendurable acceleration; the imperceptible, unloggable flight through the drably featureless grayness; the horrible deceleration. Stars flashed beautifully upon the plates.

"We made it!" Kinnison shouted in relief when he had assured himself that they had emerged into "real" space inside the Second Galaxy, only a few parsecs away from their point of departure. "By Klono's golden grin, Sir Austin, you figured it to a red whisker! And when the Society meets, Tuesday week, won't you just blast that ape Weingarde to a cinder? Hot dog!"

"Having the basic data, the solution and the application followed of necessity—automatically—uniquely," the scientist said, austerely. He was highly pleased with himself, he was tremendously flattered by the Lensman's ebullient praise; but not for anything conceivable would he have so admitted.

"Well, the first thing we'd better do is to find out what time of what day it is," Kinnison went on, as he directed a beam to the Patrol headquarters upon Klovia.

"Better ask 'em the year, too," Henderson put in, pessimistically—he had missed Illona poignantly—but it wasn't that bad.

In fact, it was not bad at all; they had been gone only a little over a week of Thralian time. This finding pleased Kinnison immensely, as he had been more than half afraid that it had been a month. He could explain a week easily enough, but anything over two weeks would have been tough to handle.

The supplies of the Thralian speedster were adjusted to fit the actual elapsed time, and Worsel and Kinnison engraved upon the minds of the five unconscious Guardsmen completely detailed—even though equally completely fictitious—memories of what they and Major Gannel had done since leaving Thrale. Their memories were not exactly alike, of course—each man had had different duties and experiences, and no two observers see precisely the same things even while watching the same event—but they were very convincing. Also, and fortunately, not even the slightest scars were left by the operations, for in these cases no memory chain had to be broken at any point.

The *Dauntless* blasted off for Klovia; the speedster started for Thrale. Kinnison's crew woke up—without having any inkling that they had ever been unconscious or that their knowledge of recent events did not jibe exactly with the actual occurrences—and resumed work.

Immediately upon landing, Kinnison turned in a full official report of the mission, giving himself neither too much nor too little credit for what had been accomplished. They had found a Patrol sneak-boat near Line Eleven. They had chased it so many parsecs, upon such-and-such a course, before forcing it to engage. They had crippled it and boarded, bringing away material, described as follows, which had been turned over to Space Intelligence. And so on. It would hold, Kinnison knew; and it would be corroborated fully by the ultra-private reports which his men would make to their real bosses.

The colonel made good; hence with due pomp and ceremony Major Traska Gannel was inducted into the Household. He was given one of the spy-ray-screened cigarette boxes in which Alcon's most trusted officers were allowed to carry their private, secret insignia. Kinnison was glad to get that—he could carry his Lens with him now, if the thing was really ray-proof, instead of leaving it buried in a can outside the city limits.

The Lensman went to his first meeting of the Advisory Cabinet with his mind set on a hair-trigger. He hadn't been around Alcon very much, but he knew that the Tyrant had a stronger mind-shield than any untreated human being had any right to have. He'd have to play this mighty close to his chest—he didn't want any zwilnik reading his mind, yet he didn't want to create suspicion by revealing the fact that he, too, had an impenetrable block.

As he approached the cabinet chamber he walked into a zone of compulsion, and practically bounced. He threw up his head; it was all he could do to keep his barriers down. It was general, he knew, not aimed specifically at him—to fight the hypnotist would be to call attention to himself as the only man able either to detect his work or to resist him; would give the whole show away. Therefore he let the thing take hold—with reservations—of his mind. He studied it. He analyzed it. Sight only, eh? QX—he'd let Alcon have superficial control, and he wouldn't put too much faith in anything he saw.

He entered the room; and, during the preliminaries, he reached out delicately, to touch imperceptibly mind after mind. All the ordinary officers were on the level; now he'd see about the prime minister. He'd heard a lot about this Fossten, but had never met him before—he'd see what the guy really had on the ball.

He did not find out, however. He did not even touch his mind, for that worthy also had an automatic block; a block as effective as Alcon's or as Kinnison's own.

Sight was unreliable; how about the sense of perception? He tried it, very daintily and gingerly, upon Alcon s feet, legs, arms, and torso. Alcon was real, and present in the flesh. Then the Premier—and he yanked his sense back, cancelled it, appalled. Perception was blocked, at exactly what his eyes told him was the fellow's skin!

That tore it—that busted it wide open. What in all nine prime iridescent hells did that mean? He didn't know of anything except a thought-screen that could stop a sense of perception. He thought intensely. Alcon's mind was bad enough. It had been treated, certainly; mind-shields like that didn't grow naturally on human or near-human beings. Maybe the Eich, or the race of super-Eich to which Kandron belonged, could give mental treatments of that kind. Fossten, though, was worse.

Alcon's boss! Probably not a man at all. It was he, it was clear, and not Alcon, who was putting out the zone of compulsion. An Eich, maybe? No, he was a warm-blooded oxygen-breather; a frigid-blooded super-big-shot would make Alcon come to him. A monster, almost certainly, though; possibly of a type Kinnison had never seen before. Working by remote control? Possibly; but not necessarily. He could be—probably was—right here, inside the dummy or figment or whatever it was that everybody thought was the Prime Minister—that was it, for all the tea in China . . .

"And what do you think, Major Gannel?" the prime minister asked, smoothly, insinuating his mind into Kinnison's as he spoke.

Kinnison, who knew that they had been discussing an invasion of the

First Galaxy, hesitated as though in thought. He *was* thinking, too, and ultra-carefully. If that ape was out to do a job of digging he'd never dig again—QX, he was just checking Gannel's real thoughts against what he was going to say.

"Since I am such a newcomer to this Council I do not feel as though my opinions should be given too much weight," Kinnison said—and thought—slowly, with the exactly correct amount of obsequiousness. "However, I have a very decided opinion upon the matter. I believe very firmly that it would be better tactics to consolidate our position here in our own galaxy first."

"You advise, then, against any immediate action against Tellus?" the prime minister asked. "Why?"

"I do, definitely. It seems to me that short-sighted, half-prepared measures, based upon careless haste, were the underlying causes of our recent reverses. Time is not an important factor—the Great Plan was worked out, not in terms of days or of years, but of centuries and millenia—and it seems to me self-evident that we should make ourselves impregnably secure, then expand slowly; seeing to it that we can hold, against everything that the Patrol can bring to bear, every planet that we take."

"Do you realize that you are criticizing the chiefs of staff who are in complete charge of military operations?" Alcon asked, venomously.

"Fully," the Lensman replied, coldly. "I ventured this opinion because I was asked specifically for it. The chiefs of staff failed, did they not? If they had succeeded, criticism would have been neither appropriate nor forthcoming. As it is, I do not believe that mere criticism of their conduct, abilities, and tactics is sufficient. They should be disciplined and demoted. New chiefs should be chosen; persons abler and more efficient than the present incumbents."

This was a bomb-shell. Dissentions waxed rife and raucous, but amidst the turmoil the Lensman received from the prime minister a flash of coldly congratulatory approval.

And as Major Traska Gannel made his way back to his quarters two things were starkly plain:

First, he would have to cut Alcon down and himself become the Tyrant of Thrale. It was unthinkable to attack or to destroy this planet. It had too many too promising leads—there were too many things that didn't make sense—above all, there were the stupendous files of information which no one mind could scan in a lifetime.

Second, if he wanted to keep on living he would have to keep his detectors shoved out to maximum—this prime minister was just about as touchy and just about as safe to play with as a hundred kilograms of dry nitrogen iodide!

19

GANNEL, TYRANT OF THRALE

Nadreck, the Palainian Lensman, had not exaggerated in saying that he could not leave his job, that his work would come undone if he did.

As has been intimated, Nadreck was cowardly and lazy and characterized otherwise by traits not usually regarded by humankind as being noble. He was, however, efficient; and he was now engaged in one of the most colossal tasks ever attempted by any one Lensman. Characteristically, he had told no one, not even Haynes or Kinnison, what it was that he was trying to do—he never talked about a job until after it was done, and his talking then was usually limited to a taped, Lensman's-sealed, tersely factual report. He was "investigating" Onlo; that was all that anybody knew.

Onlo was at that time perhaps the most heavily fortified planet in the universe. Compared to its massed might Jarnevon was weak; Tellus, except for its sunbeams and its other open-space safeguards, a joke. Onlo's defenses were all, or nearly all, planetary; Kandron's strategy, unlike Haynes', was to let any attacking force get almost down to the ground and then blast it out of existence.

Thus Onlo was in effect one tremendously armed, titanically powered fortress; not one cubic foot of its poisonous atmosphere was out of range of projectors theoretically capable of puncturing any defensive screen possible of mounting upon a mobile base.

And Nadreck, the cowardly, the self-effacing, the apologetic, had tackled Onlo—alone!

Using the technique which has already been described in connection with his highly successful raid upon the Eich stronghold of Lyrane VIII, he made his way through the Onlonian defensive screens and settled down comfortably near one of the gigantic domes. Then, as though time were of no consequence whatever, he proceeded to get acquainted with the personnel. He learned the identifying pattern of each entity and analyzed every one psychologically, mentally, intellectually, and emotionally. He tabulated his results upon the Palainian equivalent of index cards, then very carefully arranged the cards into groups.

In the same fashion he visited and took the census of dome after dome. No one knew that he had been near, apparently he had done nothing; but in each dome as he left it there had been sown seeds of discord and of strife which, at a carefully calculated future time, would yield bitter fruit indeed.

For every mind has some weakness, each intellect some trait of which it does not care to boast, each Achilles his heel. That is true even of Gray Lensmen—and the Onlonians, with their heredity and environment of Boskonianism, were in no sense material from which Lensmen could be made.

Subtly, then, and coldly and callously, Nadreck worked upon the basest passions, the most ignoble traits of that far-from-noble race. Jealousy, suspicion, fear, greed, revenge—quality by quality he grouped them, and to each group he sent series after series of horridly stimulating thoughts.

Jealousy, always rife, assumed fantastic proportions. Molehills became mountains overnight. A passing word became a studied insult. No one aired his grievances, however, for always and everywhere there was fear—fear of discipline, fear of reprisal, fear of betrayal, fear of the double cross. Each monster brooded, sullenly intense. Each became bitterly, gallingly, hatingly aware of an unwarranted and intolerable persecution. Not much of a spark would be necessary to touch off such explosive material as that!

Nadreck left the headquarters dome until the last. In one sense it was the hardest of all; in another the easiest. It was hard in that the entities there had stronger minds than those of lower station; minds better disciplined, minds more accustomed to straight thinking and to logical reasoning. It was easy, however, in that those minds were practically all at war already—fighting either to tear down the one above or to resist the attacks of those below. Every mind in it already hated, or feared, or distrusted, or was suspicious of or jealous of some other.

And while Nadreck labored thus deviously his wonders to perform,

Kinnison went ahead in his much more conventional and straightforward fashion upon Thrale. His first care, of course, was to surround himself with the usual coterie of spies and courtiers.

The selection of this group gave Kinnison many minutes of serious thought. It was natural enough that he had not been able to place any of his own men in the secret service of Alcon or the prime minister, since they both had minds of power. It would not be natural, however, for either of them not to be able to get an agent into his. For to be too good would be to invite a mental investigation which he simply could not as yet permit. He would have to play dumb enough so that his hitherto unsuspected powers of mind would remain unsuspected.

He could, however, do much. Since he knew who the spies were, he was able quite frequently to have his more trusted henchmen discover evidence against them, branding them for what they were. Assassinations were then, of course, very much in order. And even a strong suspicion, even though it could not be documented, was reason enough for a duel.

In this fashion, then, Kinnison built up his entourage and kept it reasonably free from subversive elements; and, peculiarly enough, those elements never happened to learn anything which the Lensman did not want them to know.

Building up a strong personal organization was now easy, for at last Kinnison was a real Boskonian big shot. As a major of the Household he was a power to be toadied to and fawned upon. As a personal adviser to Alcon the Tyrant he was one whose ill-will should be avoided at all costs. As a tactician who had so boldly and yet so altruistically put the skids under the chiefs of staff, thereby becoming a favorite even of the dreaded prime minister, he was marked plainly as a climber to whose coat-tails it would be wise to cling. In short, Kinnison made good in a big—it might almost be said in a stupendous—way.

With such powers at work the time of reckoning could not be delayed for long. Alcon knew that Gannel was working against him; learned very quickly, since he knew exactly the personnel of Kinnison's "private" secret service and could read at will any of their minds, that Gannel held most of the trumps. The Tyrant had tried many times to read the major's mind, but the latter, by some subterfuge or other, had always managed to elude his inquisitor without making an issue of the matter. Now, however, Alcon drove in a solid questing beam which, he was grimly determined, would produce results of one kind or another.

It did: but, unfortunately for the Thralian, they were nothing he could use. For Kinnison, instead either of allowing the Tyrant to read his whole mind or of throwing up an all-too-revealing barricade, fell back upon the sheer native power of will which made him unique in his generation. He concentrated upon an all-inclusive negation; which in effect was a rather satisfactory block and which was entirely natural.

"I don't know what you're trying to do, Alcon," he informed his superior, stiffly, "but whatever it is I do NOT like it. I think you're trying to hypnotize me. If you are, know now that you can't do it. No possible hypnotic force can overcome my definitely and positively opposed will."

"Major Gannel, you will . . ." the Tyrant began, then stopped. He was not quite ready yet to come openly to grips with this would-be usurper. Besides, it was now plain that Gannel had only an ordinary mind. He had not even suspected all the prying that had occurred previously. He had not recognized even this last powerful thrust for what it really was; he had merely felt it vaguely and had supposed that it was an attempt at hypnotism!

A few more days and he would cut him down. Hence Alcon changed his tone and went on smoothly, "It is not hypnotism, Major Gannel, but a sort of telepathy which you cannot understand. It is, however, necessary; for in the case of a man occupying such a high position as yours, it is self-evident that we can permit no secrets whatever to be withheld from us—that we can allow no mental reservations of any kind. You see the justice and the necessity of that, do you not?"

Kinnison did. He saw also that Alcon was being super-humanly forbearing. Moreover, he knew what the Tyrant was covering up so carefully—the real reason for this highly unusual tolerance.

"I suppose you're right; but I still *don't* like it," Gannel grumbled. Then, without either denying or acceding to Alcon's right of mental search, he went to his own quarters.

And there—or thereabouts—he wrought diligently at a thing which had been long in the making. He had known all along that his retinue would be useless against Alcon, hence he had built up an organization entirely separate from, and completely unknown to any member of, his visible following. Nor was this really secret outfit composed of spies or sycophants. Instead, its members were hard, able, thoroughly proven men, each one carefully selected for the ability and the desire to take the place of one of Alcon's present department heads. One at a time he put himself en rapport with them; gave them certain definite orders and instructions.

Then he put on a mechanical thought-screen. Its use could not make the prime minister any more suspicious than he already was, and it was the only way he could remain in character. This screen was, like those of Lonabar, decidedly pervious in that it had an open slit. Unlike Bleeko's, however, which had their slits set upon a fixed frequency, the open channel of this one could be varied, both in width and in wave-length, to any setting which Kinnison desired.

Thus equipped, Kinnison attended the meeting of the Council of Advisers, and to say that he disrupted the meeting is no exaggeration. The other advisers perceived nothing out of the ordinary, of course, but both Alcon and the prime minister were so perturbed that the session was cut very short indeed. The other members were dismissed summarily, with no attempt at explanation. The Tyrant was raging, furious; the premier was alertly, watchfully intent.

"I did not expect any more physical privacy than I have been granted," Kinnison grated, after listening quietly to a minute or two of Alcon's unbridled language. "This thing of being spied upon continuously, both by men and by mechanisms, while it is insulting and revolting to any real man's self-respect, can—just barely—be borne. I find it impossible however, to force myself to submit to such an ultimately degrading humiliation as the surrender of the only vestiges of privacy I have remaining; those of my mind. I will resign from the Council if you wish, I will resume my status as an officer of the line, but I cannot and will not tolerate your extinction of the last spark of my self-respect," he finished, stubbornly.

"Resign? Resume? Do you think I'll let you off *that* easily, fool?" Alcon sneered. "Don't you realize what I'm going to do to you? That, were it not for the fact that I am going to watch you die slowly and hideously, I would have you blasted where you stand?"

"I do not, no, and neither do you," Gannel answered, as quietly as surprisingly. "If you were sure of your ability, you would be doing something instead of talking about it." He saluted crisply, turned, and walked out.

Now the prime minister, as the student of this history already knows, was considerably more than he appeared upon the surface to be. His, not Alcon's, was the voice of authority, although he worked so subtly that the Tyrant himself never did realize that he was little better than a figure-head.

Therefore, as Gannel departed, the premier thought briefly but cogently. This major was smart—too smart. He was too able, he knew too much. His advancement had been just a trifle too rapid. That thought-screen was an entirely unexpected development. The mind behind it was not quite right, either—a glimpse through the slit had revealed a flash of something that might be taken to indicate that Major Gannel had an ability which ordinary Thralians did not have. This open defiance of the Tyrant of Thrale did not ring exactly true—it was not quite in character. If it had been a bluff, it was too good—much too good. If it had not been a bluff, where was his support? How could Gannel have grown so powerful without his, Fossten's, knowledge?

If Major Gannel were bona-fide, all well and good. Boskonia needed the strongest possible leaders, and if any other man showed himself superior to Alcon, Alcon should and would die. However, there was a bare possibility that . . . Was Gannel bona-fide? That point should be cleared up without delay. And Fossten, after a quizzical, searching, more than half contemptuous inspection of the furiously discomfited Tyrant, followed the rebellious, the contumaceous, the enigmatic Gannel to his rooms.

He knocked and was admitted. A preliminary and entirely meaningless conversation occurred. Then:

"Just when did you leave the Circle?" the visitor demanded, sharply.

"What do you want to know for?" Kinnison shot back. That question didn't mean a thing to him. Maybe it didn't to the big fellow, either—it could be just a catch—but he didn't intend to give any kind of an analyzable reply to any question that this ape asked him.

Nor did he, through thirty minutes of viciously skillful verbal fencing. That conversation was far from meaningless, but it was entirely unproductive of results; and it was a baffled, intensely thoughtful Fossten who at its conclusion left Gannel's quarters. From those quarters he went to the Hall of Records, where he requisitioned the major's dossier. Then to his own private laboratory, where he applied to those records every test known to the scientists of his ultra-suspicious race.

The photographs were right in every detail. The prints agreed exactly with those he himself had secured from the subject not twenty four hours since. The typing was right. The ink was right. Everything checked. And why not? Ink, paper, fiber, and film were in fact exactly what they should have been. There had been no erasures, no alterations. Everything had been aged to the precisely correct number of days. For Kinnison had known that this check-up was coming; and while the experts of the Patrol were not infallible, Mentor of Arisia was.

Even though he had found exactly what he had expected to find, the suspicions of the prime minister were intensified rather than allayed. Besides his own, there were two unreadable minds upon Thrale, where there should have been only one. He knew how Alcon's had been treated—could Gannel's possibly be a natural phenomenon? If not, who had treated it, and why?

There were three, and only three, possibilities. Another Eddorian, another member of the Innermost Circle, working against him? Probably not; this job was too important. The All-Highest would not permit it. The Arisian who had been hampering him so long? Much more likely. Star A Star? Most likely of all

Not enough data . . . but in any event, circumspection was very definitely indicated. The show-down would come at a time and a place of his own choosing, not the foe's.

He left the palace then, ostensibly to attend a function at the Military Academy. There, too, everything checked. He visited the town in which Gannel had been born—finding no irregularities whatever in the records of the birth. He went to the city in which Gannel had lived for the greater part of his life; where he assured himself that school records, club records, even photographs and negatives, all dead-centered the beam.

He studied the minds of six different persons who had known Gannel from childhood. As one they agreed that the Traska Gannel who was now Traska Gannel was in fact the real Traska Gannel, and could not by any possibility be anyone else. He examined their memory tracks minutely for scars, breaks, or other evidences of surgery; finding none. In fact, none existed, for the therapists who had performed those operations had gone back clear to the very beginnings, to the earliest memories of the Gannel child.

In spite of the fact that all the data thus far investigated were so precisely what they should have been—or because of it—the prime minister was now morally certain that Gannel was, in some fashion or other, completely spurious. Should he go further, delve into unimportant but perhaps highly revealing side issues? He should. He did so with a minute attention to detail anticipated only by Mentor of Arisia. He found nothing amiss in any particular, but he was still unsatisfied. The mind who had falsified those records so flawlessly—if they had in fact been falsified—had done a beautiful piece of work; as masterly a job as he himself could have done. He himself would have left no traces; neither, in all probability, had the unknown.

Who, then, and why? This was no ordinary plot, no part of any ordinary scheme to overthrow Alcon. It was bigger, deeper, far more sinister. Nothing so elaborate and efficient originating upon Thrale could possibly have been developed and executed without his knowledge and at least his tacit consent. It could not be Eddorian. That narrowed the field to two—the Arisian or Star A Star.

His mind flashed back, reviewing everything that had been ascribed to that mysterious Director of Lensmen. Something clicked.

BLAKESLEE!

This was much finer than the Blakeslee affair, of course; more subtle and more polished by far. It was not nearly as obvious, as blatant, but the basic similarity was nevertheless there. Could this similarity have been accidental? No—unthinkable. In this undertaking accidents could be ruled out—definitely. Whatever had been done had been done deliberately and after meticulous preparation.

But Star A Star *never* repeated . . . Therefore, this time, he *had* repeated; deliberately, to throw Alcon and his psychologists off the trail. But he, Fossten, was not to be deceived by even such clever tactics.

Gannel was, then, really Gannel, just as Blakeslee had really been Blakeslee. Blakeslee had obviously been under control. Here, however, there were two possibilities. First, Gannel might be under similar control. Second, Star A Star might have operated upon Gannel's mind so radically as to make an entirely different man of him. Either hypothesis would explain Gannel's extreme reticence in submitting to any except the most superficial mental examination. Each would account for Gannel's calm certainty that Alcon was afraid to attack him openly. Which of these hypotheses was the correct one could be determined later. It was unimportant, anyway, for in either case there was now accounted for the heretofore inexplicable power of Gannel's mind.

In either case it was not Gannel's mind at all, but that of THE Lensman, who was making Gannel act as he could not normally have acted. Somewhere hereabouts, in either case, there actually was lurking Boskonia's Nemesis; the mentality whom above all others Boskonia was raving to destroy; the one Lensman who had never been seen or heard or perceived; the feared and detested Lensman about whom nothing whatever had ever been learned.

That Lensman, whoever he might be, had at last met his match. Gannel, as Gannel, was of no importance whatever; the veriest pawn. But he who stood behind Gannel . . . Ah! . . . He, Gharlane himself, would wait and he would watch. Then, at precisely the correct instant, he would pounce!

And Kinnison, during the absence of the prime minister, worked swiftly and surely. Twelve men died, and as they ceased to live twelve others, grimly ready and thoroughly equipped for any emergency, took their places. And during that same minute of time Kinnison strode into Alcon's private sanctum.

The Tyrant hurled orders to his guards—orders which were not obeyed. He then went for his own weapons, and he was fast—but Kinnison was faster. Alcon's guns and hands disappeared and the sickened Tellurian slugged him into unconsciousness. Then, grimly, relentlessly, he took every item of interest from the Thralian's mind, killed him, and assumed forthwith the title and the full authority of the Tyrant of Thrale.

Unlike most such revolutions, this one was accomplished with very little bloodshed and with scarcely any interference with the business of the realm. Indeed, if anything, there was an improvement in almost every respect, since the new men were more thoroughly trained and were more competent than the previous officers had been. Also, they had arranged matters beforehand so that their accessions could be made with a minimum of friction.

They were as yet loyal to Kinnison and to Boskonia; and in a rather faint hope of persuading them to stay that way, without developing any queer ideas about overthrowing him, the Lensman called them into conference.

"Men, you know how you got where you are," he began, coldly. "You are loyal to me at the moment. You know that real cooperation is the only way to achieve maximum productivity, and that true cooperation cannot exist in any regime in which the department heads, individually or en masse, are trying to do away with the dictator.

"Some of you will probably be tempted very shortly to begin to work against me instead of for me and with me. I am not pleading with you, nor even asking you out of gratitude for what I have done for you, to refrain from such activities. Instead, I am telling you as a simple matter of fact that any or all of you, at the first move toward any such disloyalty, will die. In that connection, I know that all of you have been exerting every resource to discover in what manner your predecessors came so conveniently to die, and that none of you have succeeded."

One by one they admitted that they had not.

"Nor will you, ever. Be advised that I know vastly more than Alcon did, and that I am far more powerful. Alcon, while in no sense a weakling, did not know how to command obedience. I do. Alcon's sources of information were meager and untrustworthy; mine are comprehensive and reliable. Alcon very often did not know that anything was being plotted against him until the thing was well along; I shall always know of the first seditious move. Alcon blustered, threatened, and warned; he tortured; he gave some offenders a second chance before he killed. I shall do none of these things. I do not threaten, I do not warn, I do not torture. Above all, I give no snake a second chance to strike at me. I execute traitors without bluster or fanfare. For your own good, gentlemen, I advise you in all seriousness to believe that I mean precisely every word I say."

They slunk out, but Boskonian habit was too strong. Thus, within three days, three of Kinnison's newly appointed head men died. He called another cabinet meeting.

"The three new members have listened to the recording of our first meeting, hence there is no need to repeat what I said at that time," the Tyrant announced, in a voice so silkily venomous that his listeners cringed. "I will add to it merely that I will have full cooperation, and only cooperation, if I have to kill all of you and all of your successors to get it. You may go."

20

GANNEL VS. FOSSTEN

This killing made Kinnison ill; physically and mentally sick. It was ruthless, cowardly murder. It was worse than stabbing a man in the back; the poor devils didn't have even the faintest shadow of a chance. Nevertheless he did it.

When he had first invaded the stronghold of the Wheelmen of Aldebaran I, he had acted almost without thought. If there was a chance of success, Lensmen went in. When he had scouted Jarnevon he had thought but little more. True—and fortunately—he took Worsel along; but he did not stop to consider whether or not there were minds in the Patrol better fitted to cope with the problem than was his own. It was his problem, he figured, and it was up to him to solve it

Now, however, he knew bitterly that he could no longer act in that comparatively thoughtless fashion. At whatever loss of self-esteem, of personal stature, or of standing, he had to revise the Tellurian Lensmen's Code. It griped him to admit it, but Nadreck was right. It was not enough to give his life in an attempt to conquer a half-way station; he must remain alive in order to follow through to completion the job which was so uniquely his. He must *think,* assaying and evaluating every factor of his entire task. Then, without considering his own personal feelings, he must employ whatever forces and methods were best fitted to do the work at the irreducible minimum of cost and of risk.

Thus Kinnison sat unharmed upon the throne of the Tyrant of Thrale, and thus the prime minister returned to the palace to find the fact accomplished. That worthy studied with care every aspect of the situation before he sought an audience with the new potentate.

"Allow me to congratulate you, Tyrant Gannel," he said, smoothly. "I cannot say that I am surprised, since I have been watching you and your activities for some little time—with distinct approval, I may add. You have fulfilled—more than fulfilled, perhaps—my expectations. Your regime is functioning superbly; you have established in this very short time a smoothness of operation and an esprit de corps which are decidedly unusual. There are, however, certain matters about which it is possible that you are not completely informed."

"It is possible," Kinnison agreed, with the merest trace of irony. "Such as?"

"In good time. You know, do you not, who is the real authority here upon Thrale?"

"I know who was," the Tellurian corrected, with the faintest perceptible accent upon the final verb. "In part only, however, for if you had concerned yourself wholly, the late Alcon would not have made so many nor so serious mistakes."

"I thank you. You know, of course, the reason for that. I want the Tyrant of Thrale to be the strongest man of Thrale, and I may say without flattery that I believe he now is. And I would suggest that you add 'sire' when you speak to me."

"I thank you in turn. I will so address you when you call me 'Your Supremacy'—not sooner."

"We will let it pass for the moment. To come to your question, you apparently do not know that the Tyrant of Thrale, whoever he may be, opens his mind to me."

"I have suspected that such a condition has existed in the past. However, please be informed that I trust fully only those who fully trust me; and that thus far in my short life such persons have been few. You will observe that I am still respecting your privacy in that I am allowing your control of my sense of sight to continue. It is not because I trust you, but because your true appearance is to me a matter of complete indifference. For, frankly, I do not trust you at all. I will open my mind to you just exactly as wide as you will open yours to me—no wider."

"Ah . . . the bravery of ignorance. It is as I thought. You do not realize, Gannel, that I can slay you at any moment I choose, or that a very few more words of defiance from you will be enough." Fossten did not raise his voice, but his tone was instinct with menace.

"I do not, and neither do you, as I remarked to the then Tyrant Alcon in this very room not long ago. I am sure that you will understand without elaboration the connotations and implications inherent in that remark." Kinnison's voice also was low and level, freighted in its every clipped syllable with the calm assurance of power. "Would you be interested in knowing why I am so certain that you will not accept my suggestion of a mutual opening of minds?"

"Very much so."

"Because I suspect that you are, or are in league with, Star A Star of the Galactic Patrol." Even at that astounding charge Fossten gave no sign of surprise or of shock. "I have not been able as yet to obtain any evidence supporting that belief, but I tell you now that when I do so, you die. Not by power of thought, either, but in the beam of my personal ray-gun."

"Ah—you interest me strangely," and the Premier's hand strayed almost imperceptibly toward an inconspicuous button.

"Don't touch that switch!" Kinnison snapped. He did not quite see why Fossten was letting him see the maneuver, but he would bite, anyway.

"Why not, may I ask? It is merely a . . ."

"I know what it is, and I do not like thought-screens. I prefer that my mind be left free to roam."

Fossten's thoughts raced in turn. Since the Tyrant was on guard, this was inconclusive. It might—or might not—indicate that Gannel was controlled by or in communication with Star A Star.

"Do not be childish," he chided. "You know as well as I do that your accusations are absurd. However, as I reconsider the matter, the fact that neither of us trusts unreservedly the other may not after all be an insuperable obstacle to our working together for the good of Boskonia. I think now more than ever that yours is the strongest Thralian mind, and as such the logical one to wield the Tyrant's power. It would be a shame to destroy you unnecessarily, especially in view of the probability that you will come later of your own accord to see the reasonableness of that which I have suggested."

"It is possible," Kinnison admitted, "but not, I would say, probable." He thought that he knew why the lug had pulled in his horns, but he wasn't sure. "Now that we have clarified our attitudes toward each other, have decided upon an armed and suspicious truce, I see nothing to prevent us from working together in a completely harmonious mutual distrust for the good of all. The first thing to do, as I see it, is to devote our every effort to the destruction of the planet Klovia and all the Patrol forces based upon it."

"Right" If Fossten suspected that the Tyrant was somewhat less than frank he did not show it, and the conversation became strictly technical.

"We must not strike until we are completely ready," was Kinnison's first statement, and he repeated it so often thereafter during the numerous conferences with the chiefs of staff that it came almost to be a slogan.

The prime minister did not know that Kinnison's main purpose was to give the Patrol plenty of time to make Klovia utterly impregnable. Fossten could know nothing of the Patrol's sunbeam, to which even the mightiest fortress possible for man to build could offer scarcely more resistance than could the lightest, the most fragile pleasure yacht.

Hence he grew more and more puzzled, more and more at a loss week by week, as Tyrant Gannel kept on insisting upon building up the strongest, the most logically perfect fleet which all the ability of their pooled brains could devise. Once or twice he offered criticisms and suggestions which, while defensible according to one theory, would actually have weakened their striking power. These offerings Gannel rejected flatly; insisting, even to an out-and-out break with his co-administrator if necessary, upon the strongest possible armada

The Tyrant wanted, and declared that he must and would have, more and bigger of everything. More and heavier flying fortresses, more and stronger battleships and super-dreadnoughts, more and faster cruisers and scouts, more and deadlier weapons.

"We want more of everything than our operations officers can possibly handle in battle," he declared over and over; and he got them. Then:

"Now, you operations officers, learn how to handle them!" he commanded.

Even the prime minister protested at that, but it was finally accomplished. Fossten was a real thinker. So, in a smaller way, was Kinnison, and between them they worked out a system. It was crudeness and inefficiency incarnate in comparison with the Z_9M_9Z, but it was so much better than anything previously known to the Boskonians that everyone was delighted. Even the suspicious and cynical Fossten began to entertain some doubts as to the infallibility of his own judgment. Tyrant Gannel might be working under his own power, after all.

And these doubts grew apace as the Tyrant drilled his Grand Fleet. He drove the personnel unmercifully, especially the operations officers; as relentlessly as he drove himself. He simply could not be satisfied, his ardor and lust for efficiency were insatiable. His reprimands were scathingly accurate; officer after officer he demoted bitingly during ever more complicated, ever more inhumanly difficult maneuvers; until finally he had what were unquestionably his best men in those supremely important positions. Then, one day:

"QX, Kim, come ahead—we're ready," Haynes Lensed him, briefly.

For Kinnison had been in touch with the Port Admiral every day. He had learned long since that the prime minister could not detect a Lensed thought, particularly when the Lensman was wearing a thought-screen, as he did practically constantly; wherefore the strategists of the Patrol were as well informed as was Kinnison himself of every move made by the Boskonians.

Then Kinnison called Fossten, and was staring glumly at nothing when the latter entered the room.

"Well, it would seem that we're about as nearly ready as we ever will be," the Tyrant brooded, pessimistically. "Have you any suggestions, criticisms, or other contributions to offer, of however minor a nature?"

"None whatever. You have done very well indeed."

"Unnhh," Gannel grunted, without enthusiasm. "You have observed, no doubt, that I have said little if anything as to the actual method of approach?"

The prime minister had indeed noticed that peculiar over-sight, and said so. Here, undoubtedly, he thought, was the rub. Here was where Star A Star's minion would get in his dirty work.

"I have thought about it at length," Kinnison said, still in his brown study. "But I know enough to recognize and to admit my own limitations. I do know tactics and strategy, and thus far I have worked with known implements toward known objectives. That condition, however, no longer exists. The simple fact is that I do not know enough about the possibilities, the techniques and the potentialities, the advantages and the disadvantages of the hyper-spatial tube as an avenue of approach to enable me to come to a defensible decision one way or the other. I have decided, therefore, that if you have any preference in the matter I will give you full authority and let you handle the approach in any manner you please. I shall of course direct the actual battle, as in that I shall again be upon familiar ground."

The premier was flabbergasted. This was incredible. Gannel must really be working for Boskonia after all, to make such a decision as that. Still skeptical, unprepared for such a startling development as that one was, he temporized.

"The bad—the *very* bad—features of the approach via tube are two," he pondered aloud. "We have no means of knowing anything about what happens; and, since our previous such venture was a total failure, we must assume that, contrary to our plans and expectations, the enemy was not taken by surprise."

"Right," Kinnison concurred, tonelessly.

"Upon the other hand, an approach via open space, while conducive to the preservation of our two lives, would be seen from afar and would certainly be met by an appropriate formation."

"Check," came emotionlessly non-commital agreement.

"Haven't you the slightest bias, one way or the other?" Fossten demanded, incredulously.

"None whatever," the Tyrant was coldly matter-of-fact. "If I had had any such, I would have ordered the approach made in the fashion I preferred. Having none, I delegated authority to you. When I delegate authority I do so without reservations."

This was a stopper.

"Let it be open space, then," the prime minister finally decided.

"So be it." And so it was.

Each of the component flotillas of Grand Fleet made a flying trip to some nearby base, where each unit was serviced. Every item of mechanism and of equipment was checked and rechecked. Stores were replenished, and munitions—especially munitions. Then the mighty armada, the most frightfully powerful aggregation ever to fly for Boskonia—the mightiest fleet ever assembled anywhere, according to the speeches of the politicians—remade its stupendous formation and set out for Klovia. And as it flew through space, shortly before contact was made with the Patrol's Grand Fleet, the premier called Kinnison into the control room.

"Gannel, I simply can not make you out," he remarked, after studying him fixedly for five minutes. "You have offered no advice. You have not interfered with my handling of the Fleet in any way. Nevertheless, I still suspect you of treacherous intentions. I have been suspicious of you from the first . . ."

"With no grounds whatever for your suspicions," Kinnison reminded him, coldly.

"What? With all the reason possible!" Fossten declared. "Have you not steadily refused to bare your mind to me?"

"Certainly. Why not? Do we have to go over that again? Just how do you figure that I should so trust any being who refuses to reveal even his true shape to me?"

"That is for your own good. I have not wanted to tell you this, but the truth is that no human being can perceive my true self and retain his sanity."

Fossten's Eddorian mind flashed. Should he reveal this form of flesh, which was real enough, as Tellurians understood reality? Impossible. Star-A-Star-Gannel was no more Tellurian than Fossten was Thralian. He would not be satisfied with perceiving the flesh; he would bore in for the mind.

"I'll take a chance on that," Kinnison replied, skeptically. "I've seen a lot of monstrous entities in my time and I haven't conked out yet."

"There speaks the sheer folly of callow youth; the rashness of an ignorance so abysmal as to be possible only to one of your ephemeral race." The voice deepened, became more resonant. Kinnison, staring into

those inscrutable eyes which he knew did not in fact exist, thrilled fore-
bodingly; the timbre and the overtones of that voice reminded him very
disquietingly of something which he could not at the moment recall to mind.
"I forbear to discipline you, not from any doubt as to my ability to do so, as
you suppose, but because of the sure knowledge that breaking you by force
will destroy your usefulness. On the other hand, it is certain that if you
cooperate with me willingly you will be the strongest, ablest leader that
Boskonia has ever had. Think well upon these matters, Oh Tyrant."

"I will," the Lensman agreed, more seriously than he had intended.
"But just what, if anything, has led you to believe that I am not working
to the fullest and best of my ability for Boskonia?"

"Everything," Fossten summarized. "I have been able to find no flaw
in your actions, but those actions do not fit in with your unexplained and
apparently unexplainable reticence in letting me perceive for myself exactly what is in your mind. Furthermore, you have never even troubled
to deny accusations that you are in fact playing a far deeper game than
you appear upon the surface to be playing."

"That reticence I have explained over and over as an over-mastering
repugnance—call it a phobia if you like," Kinnison rejoined, wearily. "I
simply can't and won't. Since you cannot understand that, denials would
have been entirely useless. Would you believe anything that I could possibly say—that I would swear by everything I hold sacred—whether it
was that I am whole-heartedly loyal to Boskonia or that I am in fact Star
A Star himself?"

"Probably not," came the measured reply. "No, certainly not. Men—
especially men such as you, bent ruthlessly upon the acquisition of
power—are liars . . . ah, could it, by any chance, be that the reason for
your intractability is that you have the effrontery to entertain some insane
idea of supplanting ME?"

Kinnison jumped mentally. That tore it—that was a flare-lit tip-off.
This man—this thing—being—entity—whatever he really was—instead
of being just another Boskonian big shot, must be the clear quill—the
real McCoy—BOSKONE HIMSELF! The end of the job must be right
here! This was—*must* be—the real Brain for whom he had been searching
so long; here within three feet of him sat the creature with whom he had
been longing so fervently to come to grips!

"The reason is as I have said," the Tellurian stated, quietly. "I will
attempt to make no secret, however, of a fact which you must already
have deduced; that if and when it becomes apparent that you have any
authority above or beyond that of the Tyrant of Thrale I shall take it away
from you. Why not? Now that I have come so far, why should I not aspire
to sit in the highest seat of all?"

"Hrrummphhh!" the monster—Kinnison could no longer think of him as Fossten, or as the prime minister, or as anything even remotely human—snorted with such utter, such searing contempt that even the Lensman's burly spirit quailed. "As well might you attempt to pit your vaunted physical strength against the momentum of an inert planet. Now, youth, have done. The time for temporizing is past. As I have said, I desire to spare you, as I wish you to rule this part of Boskonia as my viceroy. Know, however, that you are in no sense essential, and that if you do not yield your mind fully to mine, here and now, before this coming battle is joined, you most certainly die." At the grim finality the calmly assured certainty of the pronouncement, a quick chill struck into the Gray Lensman's vitals.

This thing who called himself Fossten . . . who or what was he? What was it that he reminded him of? He thought and talked like . . . like . . . MENTOR! But it *couldn't* be an Arisian, possibly—that wouldn't make sense . . . But then, it didn't make any kind of sense, anyway, any way you looked at it . . . Whoever he was, he had plenty of jets—jets enough to lift a freighter off of the north pole of Valeria . . . and by the same token, his present line of talk didn't make sense, either—there must be some good reason why he hadn't made a real pass at him long before this, instead of arguing with him so patiently—what could it be? . . . Oh, that was it, of course . . . He needed only a few minutes more, now; he could probably stall off the final show-down that long by crawling a bit—much as it griped him to let this zwilnik think that he was licking his boots . . .

"Your forebearance is appreciated, sire." At the apparently unconscious tribute to superiority and at the fact that the hitherto completely self-possessed Tyrant got up and began to pace nervously up and down the control room, the Prime Minister's austere mien softened appreciably. "It is, however, a little strange. It is not quite in character; it does not check quite satisfactorily with the facts thus far revealed. I may, perhaps, as you say, be stupid. I may be overestimating flagrantly my own abilities. To one of my temperament, however, to surrender in such a craven fashion as you demand comes hard—extremely, almost unbearably hard. It would be easier, I think, if Your Supremacy would condescend to reveal his true identity, thereby making plainly evident and manifest that which at present must be left to unsupported words, surmise, and not too much conviction."

"But I told you, and now tell you again, that for you to look upon my real form is to lose your reason!" the creature rasped.

"What do you care whether or not I remain sane?" Kinnison shot his bolt at last, in what he hoped would be taken for a last resurgence of spirit. His time was about up. In less than one minute now the screens of scout cruisers would be in engagement, and either he or the prime minister or both would be expected to be devoting every cell of their brains to the all-important battle of giants. And in that very nick of time he would have to cripple the Bergenholms and thus inert the flagship. "Could it be that the real reason for your otherwise inexplicable forbearance is that you must know how my mind became as it now is, and that the breaking down of my barriers by mental force will destroy the knowledge which you, for your own security, must have?"

This was the blow-off. Kinnison still paced the room, but his pacings took him nearer and ever nearer to a certain control panel. Behind his thought-screen, which he could not now trust, he mustered every iota of his tremendous force of mind and of will. Only seconds now. His left hand, thrust into his breeches pocket, grasped the cigarette case within which reposed his Lens. His right arm and hand were tensely ready to draw and to fire his weapon.

"Die, then! I should have known from the sheer perfection of your work that you were what you really are—Star A Star!"

The mental blast came ahead even of the first word, but the Gray Lensman, supremely ready, was already in action. One quick thrust of his chin flicked off the thought-screen. The shielded cigarette-case flew open, his more-than-half-alive Lens blazed again upon his massive wrist. His blaster leaped out of its scabbard, flaming destruction as it came—a ravening tongue of incandescent fury which licked out of existence in the twinking of an eye the Bergenholms' control panels and the operators clustered before it. The vessel went inert—much work would have to be done before the Boskonian flagship could again fly free!

These matters required only a fraction of a second. Well indeed it was that they did not take longer, for the ever-mounting fury of the prime minister's attack soon necessitated more—much more—than an automatic block, however capable. But Kimball Kinnison, Gray Lensman, Lensman of Lensmen, had more—ever so much more—than that!

He whirled, lips thinned over tight-set teeth in a savage fighting grin. Now he'd see what this zwilnik was and what he had. No fear, no doubt of the outcome, entered his mind. He had suffered such punishment as few minds have ever endured in learning to ward off everything that Mentor, one of the mightiest intellects of this or of any other universe, could send; but through that suffering he had learned. This unknown entity was an able operator, of course, but he certainly had a thick, hard crust to think that he could rub *him* out!

So thinking, the Lensman hurled a bolt of his own, a blast of power sufficient to have slain a dozen men—and, amazedly, saw it rebound harmlessly from the premier's hard-held block.

Which of the two combatants was the more surprised it would be hard to say; each had considered his own mind impregnable and invincible. Now, as the Prime Minister perceived how astoundingly capable a foe he faced, he drove a thought toward Eddore and the All-Highest.

Blocked!

Star A Star and the Arisian, then, were not two, but one!

He ordered the officers on duty to blast their Tyrant down. In vain. For, even so early in that ultimately lethal struggle, he could not spare enough of his mind to control effectively any outsider; and in a matter of seconds there were no minds left throughout that entire room in any condition to be controlled.

For the first reverberations, the ricochets, the spent forces of the monster's attack against Kinnison's shield had wrought grievously among the mentalities of all bystanders. Those forces were deadly—deadly beyond telling—so inimical to and destructive of intelligence that even their transformation products affected tremendously the nervous systems of all within range.

Then, instants later, the spectacle of the detested and searingly feared Lens scintillating balefully upon the wrist of their own ruler was an utterly inexpressible shock. Some of the officers tried then to go for their blasters, but it was already too late; their shaking, trembling, almost paralyzed muscles could not be forced to function.

An even worse shock followed almost instantly, for the Prime Minister, under the incredibly mounting intensity of the Lensman's poignant thrusts, found it necessary to concentrate his every iota of power upon his opponent. Fossten's form of flesh dissolved, revealing to all beholders except Kinnison what their Prime Minister actually was—and he had not been very much wrong in saying that that sight would drive any human being mad. Most of the Boskonians did go mad, then and there; but they did not rush about nor scream. They could not move purposefully, but only twitched and writhed horribly as they lay grotesquely a-sprawl. They could not scream or shriek, but only mouthed and mumbled meaningless burblings.

And ever higher, ever more brilliant flamed the Lens as Kinnison threw all of this prodigious will-power, all of his tremendous, indomitable drive, through it and against the incredibly resistant thing to which he was opposed. This was the supreme, the climactic battle of his life thus far. Ether and sub-ether seethed and boiled invisibly under the frightful violence of the forces there unleashed. The men in the control room lay still; all life rived away. Now death spread throughout the confines of the vast space-ship.

Indomitably, relentlessly, the Gray Lensman held his offense upon that unimaginably high level; his Lens flooding the room with intensely coruscant polychromatic light. He did not know, then or ever, how he did it. He never did suspect that he was not alone. It seemed as though his Lens, of its own volition in this time of ultimate need, reached out into unguessable continua and drew therefrom an added, an extra something. But, however it was done, Kinnison and his Lens managed to hold; and under the appalling, the never-ceasing concentration of force the monster's defenses began gradually to weaken and go down.

Then sketchily, patchily, there was revealed to Kinnison's sight and sense of perception—a—a—a BRAIN!

There was a body, of sorts, of course—a peculiarly neckless body designed solely to support that gigantic, thin-skulled head. There were certain appendages of limbs, and such-like appurtenances and incidentalia to nourishment, locomotion, and the like; but to all intents and purposes the thing was simply and solely a brain.

Kinnison knew starkly that it was an Arisian—it looked enough like old Mentor to be his twin brother. He would have been stunned, except for the fact that he was far too intent upon victory to let any circumstance, however distracting, affect his purpose. His concentration upon the task in hand was so complete that nothing—literally nothing whatever—could sway him from it.

Step by short, hard, jerky step, Kinnison advanced. Close enough, he selected certain areas upon the sides of that enormous head and with big, hard, open hands he went viciously to work. Right, left, right, left, he slapped those bulging temples brutally, rocking monstrous head and repulsive body from side to side, pendulum-like, with every stunning blow.

His fist would have smashed that thin skull, would perhaps have buried itself deep within the soft tissues of that tremendous brain; and Kinnison did not want to kill his inexplicable opponent—yet. He had to find out first what this was all about.

He knew that he was due to black out soon as he let go, and he intended to addle the thing's senses so thoroughly that he would be completely out of action for hours—long enough to give the Lensman plenty of time in which to recover his strength.

He did so.

Kinnison did not quite faint. He did, however, have to lie down flat upon the floor; as limp, almost, as the dead men so thickly strewn about.

And thus, while the two immense Grand Fleets met in battle, Boskonia's flagship hung inert and silent in space afar; manned by fifteen hundred corpses, one unconscious Brain, and one utterly exhausted Gray Lensman.

21

THE BATTLE OF KLOVIA

Boskonia's Grand Fleet was, as has been said, enormous. It was not as large as that of the Patrol in total number of ships, since no ordinary brain nor any possible combination of such brains could have coordinated and directed the activities of so vast a number of units. Its center was, however, heavier; composed of a number and a tonnage of super-maulers which made it self-evidently irresistible.

In his training of his operations staff Kinnison had not overlooked a single bet, had not made a single move which by its falsity might have excited Premier Fossten's all-too-ready suspicions. They had handled Grand Fleet as a whole in vast, slow maneuvers; plainly the only kind possible to so tremendous a force. Kinnison and his officers had in turn harshly and thoroughly instructed the sub-fleet commanders in the various arts and maneuvers of conquering units equal to or smaller than their own.

That was all; and to the Boskonians, even to Fossten, that had been enough. That was obviously all that was possible. Not one of them realized that Tyrant Gannel very carefully avoided any suggestion that there might be any intermediate tactics, such as that of three or four hundred sub-fleets, too widely spread in space and too numerous to be handled by any ordinary mind or apparatus, to englobe and to wipe out simultaneously perhaps fifty sub-fleets whose commanders were not even in communication with each other. This technique was as yet the exclusive property of the Patrol and the $Z9M9Z$.

And in that exact operation, a closed book to the zwilniks, lay—supposedly and tactically—the Patrol's overwhelming advantage. For Haynes, through his four highly-specialized Rigellian Lensmen and thence through the two hundred Rigellian operator-computers, could perform maneuvers upon any intermediate scale he pleased. He could handle his whole vast Grand Fleet and its every component part—he supposed—as effectively, as rapidly, and almost as easily as a skilled chess player handles his pieces and his pawns. Neither Kinnison nor Haynes can be blamed, however, for the fact that their suppositions were somewhat in error; it would have taken an Arisian to deduce that this battle was not to be fought exactly as they had planned it.

Haynes had another enormous advantage in knowing the exact number, rating, disposition, course, and velocity of every main unit of the aggregation to which he was opposed. And third, he had the sunbeam, concerning which the enemy knew nothing at all and which was now in good working order.

It is needless to say that the sunbeam generators were already set to hurl that shaft of irresistible destruction along the precisely correct line, or that Haynes' Grand Fleet formation had been made with that particular weapon in mind. It was not an orthodox formation; in any ordinary space-battle it would have been sheerly suicidal. But the Port Admiral, knowing for the first time in his career every pertinent fact concerning his foe, knew exactly what he was doing.

His fleet, instead of driving ahead to meet the enemy, remained inert and practically motionless well within the limits of Klovia's solar system. His heavy stuff, instead of being massed at the center, was arranged in a vast ring. There was no center except for a concealing screen of heavy cruisers.

When the far-flung screens of scout cruisers came into engagement, then, the Patrol scouts near the central line did not fight, but sped lightly aside. So did the light and heavy cruisers and the battleships. The whole vast center of the Boskonians drove onward, unopposed, into—nothing.

Nevertheless they kept on driving. They could, without orders, do nothing else, and no orders were forthcoming from the flagship. Commanders tried to get in touch with Grand Fleet Operations, but could not; and, in failing, kept on under their original instructions. They had, they could have, no suspicion that any minion of the Patrol was back of what had happened to their top brass. The flagship had been in the safest possible position and no attack had as yet been made. They probably wondered futilely as to what kind of a mechanical breakdown could have immobilized and completely silenced their High Command, but that was—strictly—none of their business. They had had orders, very definite orders, that no matter what happened they were to go on to Klovia and to destroy it. Thus, however wondering, they kept on. They were on the line. They would hold it. They would blast out of existence anything and everything which might attempt to bar their way. They would reach Klovia and they would reduce it to its component atoms.

Unresisted, then, the Boskonian center bored ahead into nothing, until Haynes, through his Rigellians, perceived that it had come far enough. Then Klovia's brilliantly shining sun darkened almost to the point of extinction. Along the line of centers, through the space so peculiarly empty of Patrol ships, there came into being the sunbeam—a bar of quasi-solid lightning into which there had been compressed all the energy of well over four million tons *per second* of disintegrating matter.

Scouts and cruisers caught in that ravening beam flashed briefly, like sparks flying from a forge, and vanished. Battleships and super-dreadnoughts the same. Even the solid warhead of fortresses and maulers was utterly helpless. No screen has ever been designed capable of handling that hellish load; no possible or conceivable substance can withstand save momentarily the ardor of a sunbeam. For the energy liberated by the total annihilation of four million tons per second of matter is in fact as irresistible as it is incomprehensible.

The armed and armored planets did not disappear. They contained too much sheer mass for even that inconceivably powerful beam to volitalize in any small number of seconds. Their surfaces, however, melted and boiled. The controlling and powering mechanisms fused into useless pools of molten metal. Inert, then, inactive and powerless, they no longer constituted threats to Klovia's well-being.

The negaspheres also were rendered ineffective by the beam. Their anti-masses were not decreased, of course—in fact, they were probably increased a trifle by the fervor of the treatment—but, with the controlling superstructures volatilized away, they became more of a menace to the Boskonian forces than to those of Civilization. Indeed, several of the terrible things were drawn into contact with ruined planets. Then negasphere and planet consumed each other, flooding all nearby space with intensely hard and horribly lethal radiation.

The beam winked out; Klovia's sun flashed on. The sunbeam was— and is—clumsy, unwieldy, quite definitely not rapidly maneuverable. But it had done its work; now the component parts of Civilization's Grand Fleet started in to do theirs.

Since the Battle of Klovia—it was and still is called that, as though it were the only battle which that warlike planet has ever seen—has been fought over in the classrooms of practically every civilized planet of two galaxies, it would be redundant to discuss it in detail here.

It was, of course, unique. No other battle like it has ever been fought, either before or since—and let us hope that no other ever will be. It is studied by strategists, who have offered many thousands of widely variant profundities as to what Port Admiral Haynes should have done. Its profound emotional appeal, however, lies only and sheerly in its unorthodoxy. For in the technically proper space battle there is no hand-to-hand fighting, no purely personal heroism, no individual deeds of valor. It is a thing of logic and of mathematics and of science, the massing of superior fire-power against a well-chosen succession of weaker opponents. When the screens of a space-ship go down that ship is done, her personnel only memories.

But here how different! With the supposed breakdown of the lines of communication to the flagship, the sub-fleets carried on in formation. With the destruction of the entire center, however, all semblance of organization or of cooperation was lost. Every staff officer knew that no more orders would emanate from the flagship. Each knew chillingly that there could be neither escape nor succor. The captain of each vessel, thoroughly convinced that he knew vastly more than did his fleet commander, proceeded to run the war to suit himself. The outcome was fantastic, so utterly bizarre that the Z9M9Z and her trained coordinating officers were useless. Science and tactics and the million lines of communication could do nothing against a foe who insisted upon making it a ship-to-ship, yes, a man-to-man affair!

The result was the most gigantic dog-fight in the annals of military science. Ships—Civilization's perhaps as eagerly as Boskonia's—cut off their projectors, cut off their screens, the better to ram, to board, to come to grips personally with the enemy. Scout to scout, cruiser to cruiser, battleship to battleship, the insane contagion spread. Haynes and his staff men swore fulminantly, the Rigellians hurled out orders, but those orders simply could not be obeyed. The dog-fight spread until it filled a good sixth of Klovia's entire solar system.

Board and storm! Armor—DeLameters—axes! The mad blood-lust of hand-to-hand combat, the insensately horrible savagery of our pirate forbears, multiplied by millions and spread out to fill a million million cubic miles of space!

Haynes and his fellows wept unashamed as they stood by helpless, unable to avoid or to prevent the slaughter of so many splendid men, the gutting of so many magnificent ships. It was ghastly—it was appall-ing—it was WAR!

And far from this scene of turmoil and of butchery lay Boskonian's great flagship, and in her control room Kinnison began to recover. He sat up groggily. He gave his throbbing head a couple of tentative shakes. Nothing rattled. Good—he was QX, he guessed, even if he did feel as limp as nine wet dishrags. Even his Lens felt weak; its usually refulgent radiance was sluggish, wan, and dim. This had taken plenty out of them, he reflected soberly; but he was mighty lucky to be alive. But he'd better get his batteries charged. He couldn't drive a thought across the room, the shape he was in now, and he knew of only one brain in the universe capable of straightening out *this* mess.

After assuring himself that the highly inimical brain would not be able to function normally for a long time to come, the Lensman made his way to the galley. He could walk without staggering already—fine! There he fried himself a big, thick, rare steak—his never-failing remedy for all the ills to which flesh is heir—and brewed a pot of Thralian coffee; making it viciously, almost corrosively strong. And as he ate and drank his head cleared magically. Strength flowed back into him in waves. His Lens flamed into its normal splendor. He stretched prodi-giously; inhaled gratefully a few deep breaths. He was QX.

Back in the control room, after again checking up on the still qui-escent brain—he wouldn't trust this Fossten as far as he could spit—he hurled a thought to far-distant Arisia and to Mentor, its ancient sage.

"What's an Arisian doing in this Second Galaxy, working *against* the Patrol? Just what is somebody trying to pull off?" he demanded heatedly, and in a second of flashing thought reported what had happened.

"Truly, Kinnison of Tellus, my mind is not entirely capable," the deeply resonant, slow simulacrum of a voice resounded within the Lensman's brain. The Arisian never hurried; nothing whatever, appar-ently, not even such a cataclysmic upheaval as this, could fluster or excite him. "It does not seem to be in accord with the visualization of the Cosmic All which I hold at the moment that any one of my fellows is in fact either in the Second Galaxy or acting antagonistically to the Galactic Patrol. It is, however, a truism that hypotheses, theories, and visualizations must fit themselves to known or observed facts, and even your immature mind is eminently able to report truly upon actualities. But before I attempt to revise my visualization to conform to this ad-mittedly peculiar circumstance, we must be very sure indeed of our facts. Are you certain, youth, that the being whom you have beaten into unconsciousness is actually an Arisian?"

"Certainly I'm certain!" Kinnison snapped. "Why, he's enough like you to have been hatched out of half of the same egg. Take a look!" and he knew that the Arisian was studying every external and internal detail, part, and organ of the erstwhile Fossten of Thrale.

"Ah, it would appear to be an Arisian, at that, youth," Mentor finally agreed. "He appears to be old, as you said—as old, perhaps, as I am. Since I have been of the opinion that I am acquainted with every member of my race this will require some little thought—allow me therefore, please, a moment of time." The Arisian fell silent, presently to resume:

"I have it now. Many millions of years ago—so long ago that it was with some little difficulty that I recalled it to mind—when I was scarcely more than an infant, a youth but little older than myself disappeared from Arisia. It was determined then that he was aberrant—insane—and since only an unusually capable mind can predict truly the illogical workings of a diseased and disordered mind for even one year in advance, it is not surprising that in my visualization that unbalanced youth perished long ago. Nor is it surprising that I do not recognize him in the creature before you."

"Well, aren't you surprised that I could get the best of him?" Kinnison asked, naively. He had really expected that Mentor would compliment him upon his prowess, he figured that he had earned a few pats on the back; but here the old fellow was mooning about his own mind and his own philosophy, and acting as though knocking off an Arisian were something to be taken in stride. And it wasn't, by half!

"No," came the flatly definite reply. "You have a force of will, a totalizable and concentrable power, a mental and psychological drive whose capabilities you do not and cannot fully appreciate. I perceived those latent capabilities when I assembled your Lens, and developed them when I developed you. It was their presence which made it certain that you would return here for that development; they made you what you intrinsically are."

"QX, then—skip it. What shall I do with him? It's going to be a real job of work, any way you figure it, for us to keep him alive and harmless until we get him back there to Arisia."

"We do not want him here," Mentor replied without emotion. "He has no present or future place within our society. Nor, however I consider the matter, can I perceive that he has any longer a permissible or condonable place in the all-inclusive Scheme of Things. He has served his purpose. Destroy him, therefore, forthwith, before he recovers consciousness; lest much and grievous harm befall you."

"I believe you, Mentor. You said something then, if anybody ever did. Thanks," and communication ceased.

The Lensman's ray-gun flamed briefly and whatever it was that lay there became a smoking, shapeless heap.

Kinnison noticed then that a call-light was shining brightly upon a communicator panel. This thing must have taken longer than he had supposed. The battle must be over, otherwise all space would still be filled with interference through which no long-range communicator beam could have been driven. Or . . . could Boskonia have . . . no, that was unthinkable. The Patrol *must* have won. This must be Haynes, calling him . . .

It was. The frightful Battle of Klovia was over. While many of the Patrol ships had yielded, either by choice or by necessity, to the Boskonians' challenge, most of them had not. And the majority of those who did so yield, came out victorious.

While fighting in any kind of recognized formation against such myriads of independently-operating, widely-spaced individual ships was of course out of the question, Haynes and his aides had been able to work out a technique of sorts. General orders were sent out to sub-fleet commanders, who in turn relayed them to the individual captains by means of visual beams. Single vessels, then, locked to equal or inferior craft—avoiding carefully anything larger than themselves—with tractor zones and held grimly on. If they could defeat the foe, QX. If not, they hung on; until shortly one of the Patrol's maulers—who had no opposition of their own class to face—would come lumbering up. And when the dreadful primary batteries of one of *those* things cut loose that was, very conclusively, that.

Thus Boskonia's mighty fleet vanished from the skies.

The all-pervading interference was cut off and Port Admiral Haynes, not daring to use his Lens in what might be a critical instant, sat down at his board and punched a call. Time after time he punched it. Finally he shoved it in and left it in; and as he stared, minute after minute, into the coldly unresponsive plate his face grew gray and old.

Just before he decided to Lens Kinnison anyway, come what might, the plate lighted up to show the smiling, deeply space-tanned face of the one for whom he had just about given up hope.

"Thank God!" Haynes' exclamation was wholly reverent; his strained old face lost twenty years in half that many seconds. "Thank God you're safe. You did it, then?"

"I managed it, but just by the skin of my teeth—I didn't have half a jet to spare. It was Old Man Boskone himself, in person. And you?"

"Clean-up—one hundred point zero zero zero percent."

"Fine business!" Kinnison exulted. "Everything's on the exact center of the green, then—come on!"

And Civilization's Grand Fleet went.

The *Z9M9Z* flashed up to visibility, inerted, and with furious driving blasts full ablaze, matched her intrinsic velocity to that of the Boskonian flagship—the only Boskonian vessel remaining in that whole vast volume of space. Tractors and pressors were locked on and balanced. Flexible—or, more accurately, not ultimately rigid—connecting tubes were pushed out and sealed. Hundreds, yes thousands, of men—men in full Thralian uniform—strode through those tubes and into the Thralian ship. The *Z9M9Z* unhooked and a battleship took her place. Time after time the maneuver was repeated, until it seemed as though Kinnison's vessel, huge as she was, could not possibly carry the numbers of men who marched aboard.

Those men were all human or approximately so—nearly enough human, at least, to pass as Thralians under a casual inspection. More peculiarly, that army contained an astounding number of Lensmen. So many Lensmen, it is certain, had never before been gathered together into so small a space. But the fact that they were Lensmen was not apparent; their Lenses were not upon their wrists, but were high upon their arms, concealed from even the most prying eyes within the sleeves of their tunics.

Then the captured flagship, her Bergenholms again at work, the *Z9M9Z*, and the battleships which had already assumed the intrinsic velocity possessed originally by the Boskonians, spread out widely in space. Each surrounded itself with a globe of intensely vivid red light. Orders as to course and power flashed out. The word was given and spectacular fire flooded space as that vast host of ships, guided by those red beacons, matched in one prodigious and beautiful maneuver its intrinsic velocity to theirs.

Finally, all the intrinsics in exact agreement, Grand Fleet formation was remade. The term "remade" is used advisedly, since this was not to be a battle formation. For Traska Gannel had long since sent a message to his capital; a terse and truthful message which was, nevertheless, utterly misleading. It was:

"My forces have won, my enemy has been wiped out to the last man. Prepare for a two-world broadcast, to cover both Thrale and Onlo, at hour ten today of my palace time."

The formation, then, was not one of warfare, but of boasting triumph. It was the consciously proud formation of a Grand Fleet which, secure in the knowledge that it has blasted out of the ether everything which can threaten it, returns victoriously home to receive as its just due the plaudits and the acclaim of the populace.

Well in the van—alone in the van, in fact, and strutting—was the flagship. She, having originated upon Thrale and having been built specifically for a flagship, would be recognized at sight. Back of her came, in gigantic co-axial cones, the sub-fleets; arranged now not class by class of ships, but world by world of origin. One mauler, perhaps, or two; from four or five to a dozen or more battleships; an appropriate number of cruisers and of scouts; all flying along together in a tight little group.

But not all of the Patrol's armada was in that formation. It would have been very poor technique indeed to have had Boskonia's Grand Fleet come back to home ether forty percent larger than it had set out. Besides, the Z9M9Z simply could not be allowed to come within detector range of any Boskonian look-out. She was utterly unlike any other vessel ever to fly: she would not, perhaps, be recognized for what she really was, but it would be evident to the most casual observer that she was not and could not be of Thrale or Boskonia.

The Z9M9Z, then, hung back—far back—escorted and enveloped by the great number of warships which could not be made to fit into the roll-call of the Tyrant's original Grand Fleet.

The sub-fleet which was originally from Thrale could land without any trouble without arousing any suspicion. Boskonian and Patrol designs were not identical, of course; but the requirements of sound engineering dictated that externals should be essentially the same. The individual ships now bore the correct identifying symbols and insignia. The minor differences could not be perceived until after the vessels had actually landed, and that would be—for the Thralians—entirely too late.

Thralian hour ten arrived. Kinnison, after a long, minutely searching inspection of the entire room, became again in every millimeter Traska Gannel, the Tyrant of Thrale. He waved a hand. The scanner before him glowed: for a full minute he stared into it haughtily, to give his teeming millions of minions ample opportunity to gaze upon the inspiring countenance of His Supremacy the Feared.

He knew that the scanner revealed clearly every detail of the control room behind him, but everything there was QX. There wasn't a chance that some person would fail to recognize a familiar face at any post, for not a single face except his own would be visible. Not a head back of him would turn, not even a rear-quarter profile would show: it would be *lese majeste* of the most intolerable for any face, however inconspicuous, to share the lime-light with that of the Tyrant of Thrale while

His Supremacy was addressing his subjects. Serenely and assuredly enough, then, Tyrant Gannel spoke:

"MY people! As you have already been told, my forces have won the complete victory which my foresight and my leadership made inevitable. This milestone of progress is merely a repetition upon a grander scale of those which I have already accomplished upon a somewhat smaller; an extension and a continuation of the carefully considered procedure by virtue of which I shall see to it that My Plan succeeds.

"As one item in that scheduled procedure I removed the weakling Alcon, and in the stead of his rule of oppression, short-sightedness, corruption, favoritism, and greed, I substituted my beneficient regime of fair play, of mutual cooperation for the good of all.

"I have now accomplished the next major step in my program; the complete destruction of the armed forces which might be, which would be employed to hamper and to nullify the development and the fruition of My Plan.

"I shall take the next step immediately upon my return to my palace. There is no need to inform you now as to the details of what I have in mind. In broad, however, it pleases me to inform you that, having crushed all opposition, I am now able to institute and shall proceed at once to institute certain changes in policy, in administration, and in jurisdiction. I assure you that all of these changes will be for the best good of all save the enemies of society.

"I caution you therefore to cooperate fully and willingly with my officers who may shortly come among you with instructions; some of these, perhaps, of a nature not hitherto promulgated upon Thrale. Those of you who do so cooperate will live and will prosper; those who do not will die in the slowest, most hideous fashions which all the generations of Thralian torturers have been able to devise."

22

THE TAKING OF THRALE

Up to the present, Kinnison's revolution, his self-advancement into the dictatorship, had been perfectly normal; in perfect accordance with the best tenets of Boskonian etiquette. While it would be idle to contend that any of the others of the High Command really approved of it—each wanted intensely that high place for himself—none of them had been strong enough at the moment to challenge the Tyrant effectively and all of them knew that an ineffective challenge would mean certain death. Wherefore each perforce bided his time; Gannel would slip, Gannel would become lax or over-confident—and that would be the end of Gannel.

They were, however, loyal to Boskonia. They were very much in favor of the rule of the strong and the ruthless. They believed implicitly that might made right. They themselves bowed the knee to anyone strong enough to command such servility from them; in turn they commanded brutally an even more abject servility from those over whom they held in practice, if not at law, the power of life and death.

Thus Kinnison knew that he could handle his cabinet easily enough as long as he could make them believe that he was a Boskonian. There was, there could be, no real unity among them under those conditions; each would be fighting his fellows as well as working to overthrow His Supremacy the Tyrant. But they all hated the Patrol and all that it stood for with a whole-hearted fervor which no one adherent to Civilization can really appreciate. Hence at the first sign that Gannel might be in league with the Patrol they would combine forces instantly against him; automatically there would go into effect a tacit agreement to kill him first and then, later, to fight it out among themselves for the prize of the Tyrancy.

And that combined opposition would be a formidable one indeed. Those men were really able. They were as clever and as shrewd and as smart and as subtle as they were hard. They were masters of intrigue; they simply could not be fooled. And if their united word went down the line that Traska Gannel was in fact a traitor to Boskonia, an upheaval would ensue which would throw into the shade the bloodiest revolutions of all history. Everything would be destroyed.

Nor could the Lensman hurl the metal of the Patrol against Thrale in direct frontal attack. Not only was it immensely strong, but also there were those priceless records, without which it might very well be the work of generations for the Patrol to secure the information which it must, for its own security, have.

No. Kinnison, having started near the bottom and worked up, must now begin all over again at the top and work down; and he must be very, *very* sure that no alarm was given until at too late a time for the alarmed ones to do anything of harm to the Lensman's cause. He didn't know whether he had jets enough to swing the load or not—a lot depended on whether or not he could civilize those twelve devils of his— but the scheme that the psychologists had worked out was a honey and he would certainly give it the good old college try.

Thus Grand Fleet slowed down; and, with the flagship just out of range of the capital's terrific offensive weapons, it stopped. Half a dozen maulers, towing a blackly indetectable, imperceptible object, came up and stopped. The Tyrant called, from the safety of his control room, a conference of his cabinet in the council chamber.

"While I have not been gone very long in point of days," he addressed them smoothly, via plate, "and while I of course trust each and every one of you, there are certain matters which must be made clear before I land. None of you has, by any possible chance, made any effort to lay a trap for me, or anything of the kind?" There may have been a trace of irony in the speaker's voice.

They assured him, one and all, that they had not had the slightest idea of even considering such a thing.

"It is well. None of you have discovered, then, that by changing locks and combinations, and by destroying or removing certain inconspicuous but essential mechanisms of an extremely complicated nature—and perhaps substituting others—I made it quite definitely impossible for any one or all of you to render this planet inertialess. I have brought back with me a negasphere of planetary anti-mass, which no power at your disposal can effect. It is here beside me in space; please study it attentively. It should not be necessary for me to inform you that there are countless other planets from which I can rule Boskonia quite as effectively as from Thrale; or that, while I do not relish the idea of destroying my home planet and everything upon it, I would not hesitate to do so if it became a matter of choice between that action and the loss of my life and my position."

They believed the statement. That was the eminently sensible thing to do. Any one of them would have done the same; hence they knew that Gannel would do exactly what he threatened—if he could. And as they studied Gannel's abysmally black ace of trumps they knew starkly that Gannel could. For they had found out, individually, that the Tyrant had so effectively sabotaged Thrale's Bergenholms that they could not possibly be made operative until after his return. Consequently repairs had not been started—any such activity, they knew, would be a fatal mistake.

By out-guessing and out-maneuvering the members of his cabinet Gannel had once more shown his fitness to rule. They accepted that fact with a good enough grace; indeed, they admired him all the more for the ability thus shown. No one of them had given himself away by any overt moves; they could wait. Gannel would slip yet—quite possibly even before he got back into his palace. So they thought, not knowing that the Tyrant could read at will their most deeply-hidden plans; and, so thinking, each one pledged anew in unreserved terms his fealty and his loyalty.

"I thank you, gentlemen." The Tyrant did not, and the officers were pretty sure that he did not, believe a word of their protestations. "As loyal cabinet members, I will give you the honor of sitting in the front of those who welcome me home. You men and your guards will occupy the front boxes in the Royal Stand. With you and around you will be the entire palace personnel—I want no person except the usual guards inside the buildings or even within the grounds when I land. Back of these you will have arranged the Personal Troops and the Royal Guards. The remaining stands and all of the usual open grounds will be for the common people—first come, first served.

"But one word of caution. You may wear your sidearms, as usual. Bear in mind, however, that armor is neither usual nor a part of your full-dress uniform, and that any armored man or men in or near the concourse will be blasted by a needle-ray before I land. Be advised also that I myself shall be wearing full armor. Furthermore, no vessel of the fleet will land until I, personally, from my private sanctum, order them to do so."

This situation was another poser; but it, too, they had to take. There was no way out of it, and it was still perfect Boskonian generalship. The welcoming arrangements were therefore made precisely as Tyrant Gannel had directed.

The flagship settled toward ground, her under-jets blasting unusually viciously because of her tremendous load; and as she descended Kinnison glanced briefly down at the familiar terrain. There was the immense space-field, a dock-studded expanse of burned, scarred, pock-marked concrete and steel. Midway of its extreme northern end, that nearest the palace, was the berth of the flagship, Dock No. 1. An eighth of a mile straight north from the dock—the minimum distance possible because of the terrific fury of the under-jets—was the entrance to the palace grounds. At the northern end of the western side of the field, a good three-quarters of a mile from Dock No. 1 and somewhat more than that distance from the palace gates, were the Stands of Ceremony. That made the Lensman completely the master of the situation.

The flagship landed. Her madly blasting jets died out. A car of state rolled grandly up. Airlocks opened. Kinnison and his bodyguards seated themselves in the car. Helicopters appeared above the stands and above the massed crowds thronging the western approaches to the field; hovering, flitting slowly and watchfully about.

Then from the flagship there emerged an incredible number of armed and armored soldiers. One small column of these marched behind the slowly-moving car of state, but by far the greater number went directly to and through the imposing portals of the palace grounds. The people in general, gathered there to see a major spectacle, thought nothing of these circumstances—who were they to wonder at what the Tyrant of Thrale might choose to do?—but to Gannel's Council of Advisers they were extremely disquieting departures from the norm. There was, however, nothing they could do about them, away out there in the grandstand; and they knew with a stark certainty what those helicopters had orders to do in case of any uprising or commotion anywhere in the crowd.

The car rolled slowly along before the fenced-back, wildly-cheering multitudes, with blaring bands and the columns of armored spacemen marching crisply, swingingly behind it. There was nothing to indicate that those selected men were not Thralians; nothing whatever to hint that over a thousand of them were in fact Lensmen of the Galactic Patrol. And Kinnison, standing stiffly erect in his car, acknowledged gravely, with upraised right arm, the plaudits of his subjects.

The triumphal bus stopped in front of the most out-thrust, the most ornate stand, and through loud-voiced amplifiers the Tyrant invited, as a signal honor, the twelve members of his Advisory Cabinet to ride with him in state to the palace. There were exactly twelve vacant seats in the great coach. The advisers would have to leave their bodyguards and ride alone with the Tyrant: even had there been room, it was unthinkable that any one else's personal killers could ride with the Presence. This was no honor, they knew chillingly, no matter what the mob might think—it looked much more like a death-sentence. But what could they do? They glanced at their unarmored henchmen; then at the armor and the semi-portables of Gannel's own heelers; then at the 'copters now clustering thickly overhead, with the narrow snouts of needle-ray projectors very much in evidence.

They accepted.

It was in no quiet frame of mind, then, that they rode into the pretentious grounds of the palace. They felt no better when, as they entered the council chamber, they were seized and disarmed without a word having been spoken. And the world fairly dropped out from beneath them when Tyrant Gannel emerged from his armor with a Lens glowing upon his wrist.

"Yes, I am a Lensman," he gravely informed the stupefied but unshrinking Boskonians. "That is why I know that all twelve of you tried while I was gone to cut me down, in spite of everything I told you and everything you have seen me do. If it were still necessary for me to pose as Traska Gannel I would have to kill you here and now for your treachery. That phase is, however, past.

"I am one of the Lensmen whose collective activities you have ascribed to 'the' Lensman or to Star A Star. All those others who came with me into the palace are Lensmen. All those outside are either Lensmen or tried and seasoned veterans of the Galactic Patrol. The fleet surrounding this world is the Grand Fleet of that Patrol. The Boskonian force was completely destroyed—every man and every ship except your flagship—before it reached Klovia. In short, the power of Boskonia is broken forever; Civilization is to rule henceforth throughout both galaxies.

"You are the twelve strongest, the twelve ablest men of the planet, perhaps of your whole dark culture. Will you help us to rule according to the principles of Civilization that which has been the Boskonian Empire or will you die?"

The Thralians stiffened themselves rigidly against the expected blasts of death, but only one spoke. "We are fortunate at least, Lensman, in that you do not torture," he said, coldly, his lips twisted into a hard, defiant sneer.

"Good!" and the Lensman actually smiled. "I expected no less. With that solid bottom, all that is necessary is to wipe away a few of your misconceptions and misunderstandings, correct your viewpoints, and . . ."

"Do you think for a second that your therapists can fit *us* into the pattern of your Civilization?" the Boskonian spokesman demanded, bitingly.

"I don't have to think, Lanion—I know," Kinnison assured him. "Take them away, fellows, and lock them up—you know where. Everything will go ahead as scheduled."

It did.

And while the mighty vessels of war landed upon the spacefield and while the thronging Lensmen took over post after post in an ever-widening downward course, Kinnison led Worsel and Tregonsee to the cell in which the outspoken Thralian chieftain was confined.

"I do not know whether I can prevent you from operating upon me or not," Lanion of Thrale spoke harshly, "but I will try. I have seen the pitiful, distorted wrecks left after such operations and I do not like them. Furthermore, I do not believe that any possible science can eradicate from my subconscious the fixed determination to kill myself the instant you release me. Therefore you had better kill me now, Lensman, and save your time and trouble."

"You are right, and wrong," Kinnison replied, quietly. "It may very well be impossible to remove such a fixation." He knew that he could remove any such, but Lanion must not know it. Civilization needed those twelve hard, shrewd minds and he had no intention of allowing an inferiority complex to weaken their powers. "We do not, however, intend to operate, but only and simply to educate. You will not be unconscious at any time. You will be in full control of your own mind and you will know beyond peradventure that you are so in control. We shall engrave, in parallel with your own present knowledges of the culture of Boskonia, the equivalent or corresponding knowledges of Civilization."

They did so. It was not a short undertaking, nor an easy one; but it was thorough and it was finally done. Then Kinnison spoke.

"You now have completely detailed knowledge both of Boskonia and of Civilization, a combination possessed by but few intelligences indeed. You know that we did not alter, did not even touch, any track of your original mind. Being fully en rapport with us, you know that we gave you as unprejudiced a concept of Civilization as we possibly could. Also, you have assimilated completely the new knowledge."

"That is all true," Lanion conceded. "Remarkable, but true. I was, and remained throughout, myself; I checked constantly to be sure of that. I can still kill myself at any moment I choose."

"Right." Kinnison did not smile, even mentally, at the unconscious alteration of intent. "The whole proposition can now be boiled down into one clear-cut question, to which you can formulate an equally clear-cut reply. Would you, Lanion, personally, prefer to keep on as you have been, working for personal power, or would you rather team up with others to work for the good of all?"

The Thralian thought for moments, and as he pondered an expression of consternation spread over his hard-hewn face. "You mean actually—personally—apart from all consideration of your so-called altruism and your other infantile weaknesses?" he demanded, resistantly.

"Exactly," Kinnison assured him. "Which would you *rather* do? Which would you, personally, get the most good—the most fun—out of?"

The bitter conflict was plainly visible in Lanion's bronzed face; so was the direction in which it was going.

"Well . . . I'll . . . be . . . damned! You win, Lensman!" and the ex-Boskonian executive held out his hand. Those were not his words, of course; but as nearly as Tellurian English can come to it, that is the exact sense of his final decision. And the same, or approximately the same, was the decision of each of his eleven fellows, each in his turn.

Thus it was, then, that Civilization won over the twelve recruits who were so potently instrumental in the bloodless conquest of Thrale, and who were later to be of such signal service throughout the Second Galaxy. For they knew Boskonia with a sure knowledge, from top to bottom and from side to side, in every aspect and ramification; they knew precisely where and when and how to work to secure the desired ends. And they worked—*how* they worked!—but space is lacking to go into any of their labors here.

Specialists gathered, of a hundred different sorts; and when, after peace and security had been gained, they began to attack the stupendous files of the Hall of Records, Kinnison finally yielded to Haynes' insistence and moved out to the *Z9M9Z*.

"It's about time, young fellow!" the Port Admiral snapped. "I've gnawed my finger-nails off just about to the elbow and I still haven't figured out how to crack Onlo. Have you got any ideas?"

"Thrale first," Kinnison suggested. "Everything QX here, you sure?"

"Absolutely," Haynes grunted. "As strongly held at Tellus or Klovia. Primaries, helices, super-tractors, Bergenholms, sunbeam—everything. They don't need us here any longer, any more than a hen needs teeth. Grand Fleet is all set to go, but we haven't been able to work out a feasible plan of campaign. The best way would be not to use the fleet at all, but a sunbeam—but we can't move the sun and Thorndyke can't hold the beam together that far. I don't suppose we could use a negasphere?"

"I don't see how," Kinnison pondered. "Ever since we used it first they've been ready for it. I'd be inclined to wait and see what Nadreck works out. He's a wise old owl, that bird—what does he tell you?"

"Nothing. Nothing flat." Haynes' smile was grimly amused. "The fact that he is still 'investigating'—whatever that means—is all he'll say. Why don't you try him? You know him better than I do or ever will."

"It wouldn't do any harm," Kinnison agreed. "Nor good, either, probably. Funny egg, Nadreck. I'd tie fourteen of his arms into lover's knots if it'd make him give, but it wouldn't—he's really tough." Nevertheless he sent out a call, which was acknowledged instantly.

"Ah, Kinnison, greetings. I am even now on my way to Thrale and the *Directrix* to report."

"You are? Fine!" Kinnison exclaimed. "How did you come out?"

"I did not—exactly—fail, but the work was very incompletely and very poorly done," Nadreck apologized, the while the Tellurian's mind felt very strongly the Palainian equivalent of a painful blush of shame. "My report of the affair is going in under Lensman's Seal."

"But what did you *do?*" both Tellurians demanded as one.

"I scarcely know how to confess to such blundering," and Nadreck actually squirmed. "Will you not permit me to leave my shame to the spool of record?"

They would not, they informed him.

"If you must have it, then, I yield. The plan was to make all Onlonians destroy themselves. In theory it was sound and simple, but my execution was pitifully imperfect. My work was so poorly done that the commanding officer in each one of three of the domes remained alive, making it necessary for me to slay those three commanders personally, by the use of crude force. I regret exceedingly the lack of finish of this undertaking, and I apologize profoundly for it. I trust that you will not allow this information to become a matter of public knowledge," and the apologetic, mentally sweating, really humiliated Palainian broke the connection.

Haynes and Kinnison stared at each other, for moments completely at a loss for words. The Port Admiral first broke the silence.

"Hell's—jingling—bells!" he wrenched out, finally, and waved a hand at the points of light crowding so thickly his tactical tank. "A thing that the whole damned Grand Fleet couldn't do, and he does it alone, and then he *apologizes* for it as though he ought to be stood up in a corner or sent to bed without any supper!"

"Uh-huh, that's the way he is," Kinnison breathed, in awe. "What a brain! . . . what a man!"

Nadreck's black speedster arrived and a three-way conference was held. Both Haynes and Kinnison pressed him for the details of his really stupendous achievement, but he refused positively even to mention any phase of it.

"The matter is closed—finished," he declared, in a mood of anger and self-reproach which neither of the Tellurians had ever supposed that the gently scientific monster could assume. "I practically failed. It is the poorest piece of work of which I have been guilty since cubhood, and I desire and I insist that it shall not be mentioned again. If you wish to lay plans for the future, I will be very glad indeed to place at your disposal my small ability—which has now been shown to be even smaller than I had supposed—but if you insist upon discussing my fiasco, I shall forthwith go home. I will *not* discuss it. The record of it will remain permanently under Lensman's Seal. That is my last word."

And it was. Neither of the two Tellurians mentioned the subject, of course, either then or ever, but many other persons—including your historian—have done so, with no trace whatever of success. It is a shame, it is positively outrageous, that no details are available of the actual fall of Onlo. No human mind can understand why Nadreck will not release his seal, but the bitter fact of his refusal to do so has been made all too plain.

Thus, in all probability, it never will become publicly known how those monstrous Onlonians destroyed each other, nor how Nadreck penetrated the defensive screens of Onlo's embattled domes, nor in what fashions he warred upon the three surviving commanders. These matters, and many others of perhaps equal interest and value, must have been of such an epic nature that it is a cosmic crime that they cannot be recorded here; that this, one of the most important incidents of the campaign, must be mentioned merely and baldly as having happened. But, unless Nadreck relents—and he apparently never does—that is the starkly tragic fact.

Other Lensmen were called in then, and admirals and generals and other personages. It was decided to man the fortifications of Onlo immediately, from the several fleets of frigid-blooded poison-breathers which made up a certain percentage of Civilization's forces. This decision was influenced markedly by Nadreck, who said in part:

"Onlo is a beautiful planet. Its atmosphere is perfect, its climate is ideal; not only for us of Palain VII, but also for the inhabitants of many other planets such as . . ." and he mentioned some twenty names. "While I personally am not a fighter, there are some who are; and while those of a more warlike disposition man Onlo's defenses and weapons, my fellow researchers and I might very well be carrying on with the same type of work which you fire-blooded oxygen-breathers are doing elsewhere."

This eminently sensible suggestion was adopted at once. The conference broke up. The selected sub-fleets sailed. Kinnison went to see Haynes.

"Well, sir, that's it . . . I hope . . . what do you think? Am I, or am I not, due for a spot of free time ?" The Gray Lensman's face was drawn and grim.

"I wish I knew, son . . . but I don't." Eyes and voice were deeply troubled. "You ought to be . . . I hope you are . . . but you're the only judge of that, you know."

"Uh-huh . . . that is, I know how to find out . . . but I'm afraid to—afraid he'll say no. However, I'm going to see Cris first—talk it over with her. How about having a gig drop me down to the hospital?"

For he did not have to travel very far to find his fiancee. From the time of leaving Lyrane until the taking over of Thrale she had as a matter of course been chief nurse of the hospital ship *Pasteur,* and with the civilizing of that planet she had as automatically become chief nurse of the Patrol's Base Hospital there.

"Certainly, Kim—anything you want, whenever you please."

"Thanks, chief . . . Now that this fracas is finally over—if it is—I suppose you'll have to take over as president of the Galactic Council?"

"I suppose so—after we clean up Lyrane VIII, that you've been holding me away from so long—but I don't relish the thought. And you'll be Coordinator Kinnison."

"Uh-huh," gloomily. "By Klono, I hate to put my Grays away! I'm not going to do it, either, until after we're married and I'm really settled down onto the job."

"Of course not. You'll be wearing them for some time yet, I'm thinking." Haynes' tone was distinctly envious. "Getting *your* job reduced to routine will take a long, long time . . . It'll probably take years even to find out what it's really going to be."

"That's so, too," Kinnison brightened visibly. "Well, clear ether, President Haynes!" and he turned away, whistling unmelodiously—in fact, somewhat raucously—through his teeth.

23

ATTAINMENT

At Base Hospital it was midnight. The two largest of Thrale's four major moons were visible, close together in the zenith, almost at the full; shining brilliantly from a cloudless, star-besprinkled sky upon the magnificent grounds.

Fountains splashed and tinkled musically. Masses of flowering shrubs, bordering meandering walks, flooded the still air with a perfume almost cloying in its intensity. No one who has once smelled the fragrance of Thralian thorn-flower at midnight will ever forget it—it is as though the poignant sweetness of the mountain syringe has been blended harmoniously with the heavy, entrancing scent of the jasmine and the appealing pungency of the lily-of-the-valley. Statues of gleaming white stone and of glinting metal were spaced infrequently over acres and acres of springy, close-clipped turf. Trees, not over-high but massive of bole and of tremendous spread and thickness of foliage, cast shadows of impenetrable black.

"QX, Cris?" Kinnison Lensed the thought as he entered the grounds: she had known that he was coming. "Kinda late, I know, but I wanted to see you, and you don't have to punch the clock."

"Surely, Kim," and her low, infectious chuckle welled out. "What's the use of being a Red Lensman, else? This is just right—you couldn't make it any sooner and tomorrow would have been too late—much too late."

They met at the door and with arms around each other strolled wordless down a walk. Across the resilient sward they made their way and to a bench beneath one of the spreading trees.

Kinnison swept her into both arms, hers went eagerly around his neck. How long, how unutterably long it had been since they had stood thus, nurse's white crushed against Lensman's Gray!

They had no need, these Lensmen, of sight. Nor of language. Hence, since words are so pitifully inadequate, no attempt will be made to chronicle the ecstasy of that reunion. Finally, however:

"Now that we're together again I'll never let you go," the man declared aloud.

"If they separate us again it will simply break my heart," Clarissa agreed. Then, woman-like, she faced the facts and made the man face them, too. "Let's sit down, Kim, and have this out. You know as well as I do that we can't go on if . . . if we can't . . . that's all."

"I do not," Kinnison said, flatly. "We've got a right to *some* happiness, you and I. They can't keep us apart forever, sweetheart—we're going straight through with it this time."

"Uh-uh, Kim," she denied gently, shaking her spectacular head. "What would have happened if we'd have gone ahead before, leaving those horrible Thralians free to ruin Civilization?"

"But Mentor stopped us then," Kinnison argued. Deep down, he knew that if the Arisian called he would have to answer, but he argued nevertheless. "If the job wasn't done, he would have stopped us before we got this far—I think."

"You hope, you mean," the girl contradicted. "What makes you think—if you really do—that he might not wait until the ceremony has actually begun?"

"Not a thing in the universe. He might, at that," Kinnison confessed, bleakly.

"You've been afraid to ask him, haven't you?"

"But the job must be done!" he insisted, avoiding the question. "The prime minister—that Fossten—*must* have been the top; there couldn't *possibly* be anything bigger than an Arisian to be back of Boskone. It's unthinkable! They've got no military organization left—not a beam hot enough to light a cigarette or a screen that would stop a firecracker. We have all their records—everything. Why, it's just a matter of routine now for the boys to uproot them completely; system by system, planet by planet."

"Uh-huh." She eyed him shrewdly, there in the dark. "Cogent. Really pellucid. As clear as so much crystal—and twice as fragile. If you're so sure, why not call Mentor and ask him, right now? You're not afraid of just the calling part, like I am; you're afraid of what he'll say."

"I'm going to marry you before I do another lick of work of any kind, anywhere," he insisted, doggedly.

"I just love to hear you say that, even if I do know you're just popping off!" She snuggled deeper into the curve of his arm. "I feel that way too, but both of us know very well that if Mentor stops us . . . even at the altar . . ." her thought slowed, became tense, solemn. "We're Lensmen, Kim, you and I. We both know exactly what that means. We'll have to muster jets enough, some way or other, to swing the load. Let's call him now, Kim, together. I just simply can't stand this not knowing . . . I can't, Kim . . . I can't!" Tears come hard and seldom to such a woman as Clarrissa MacDougall; but they came then—and they hurt.

"QX, ace." Kinnison patted her back and her gorgeous head. "Let's go—but I tell you now that if he says 'no' I'll tell him to go out to the Rim and take a swan-dive off into inter-galactic space."

She linked her mind with his, thinking in affectionate half-reproach, "I'd like to, too, Kim, but that's pure balloon juice and you know it. You couldn't . . ." she broke off as he hurled their joint thought to Arisia the Old, going on frantically:

"You think at him, Kim, and I'll just listen. He scares me into a shrinking, quivering pulp!"

"QX, ace," he said again. Then: "Is it permissible that we do what we are about to do?" he asked crisply of Arisia's ancient sage.

"Ah, 'tis Kinnison and MacDougall; once of Tellus, henceforth of Klovia," the calmly unsurprised thought rolled in. "I was expecting you at this time. Any mind, however far from competent, could have visualized this event in its entirety. That which you contemplate is not merely permissible; it has now become necessary," and as usual, without tapering off or leave-talking, Mentor broke the line.

The two clung together rapturously then for minutes, but something was obtruding itself disquietingly upon the nurse's mind.

"But his thought was 'necessary', Kim?" she asked, rather than said. "Isn't there a sort of a sinister connotation in that, somewhere? What did he mean?"

"Nothing—exactly nothing," Kinnison assured her, comfortably. "He's got a complete picture of the macrocosmic universe in his mind—his 'Visualization of the Cosmic All', he calls it—and in it we get married now, just as I've been telling you we are going to. Since it gripes him no end to have even the tiniest thing not conform to his visualization, our marriage is NECESSARY, in capital letters. See?"

"Uh-huh . . . Oh, I'm *glad!*" she exclaimed. "That shows you how scared of him I am," and thoughts and actions became such that, although they were no doubt of much personal pleasure and satisfaction, they do not require detailed treatment here.

Clarrissa MacDougall resigned the next day, without formality or fanfare. That is, she thought that she did so then, and rather wondered at the frictionless ease with which it went through: it had simply not occurred to her that in the instant of being made an Unattached Lensman she had been freed automatically from every man-made restraint. That was one of the few lessons hard for her to learn; it was the only one which she refused consistently even to try to learn.

Nothing was said or done about the ten thousand credits which had been promised her upon the occasion of her fifteen-minutes-long separation from the Patrol following the fall of Jarnevon. She thought about it briefly, but with no real sense of loss. Some way or other, money did not seem important. Anyway, she had some—enough for a fairly nice, if limited, trousseau—in a Tellurian bank. She could undoubtedly get it through the Disbursing Office here.

She took off her Lens and stuffed it into a pocket. That wasn't so good, she reflected. It bulged, and besides, it might fall out; and anyone who touched it would die. She didn't have a bag; in fact, she had with her no civilian clothes at all. Wherefore she put it back on, pausing as she did so to admire the Manarkan star-drop flashing pale fire from the third finger of her left hand. Of Cartiff's whole stock of fine gems, this was the loveliest.

It was not far to the Disbursing Office, so she walked; window-shopping as she went. It was a peculiar sensation, this being out of harness—it felt good, though, at that—and upon arriving at the bank she found to her surprise that she was both well known and expected. An officer whom she had never seen before greeted her cordially and led her into his private office.

"We have been wondering why you didn't pick up your kit, Lensman MacDougall." He went on, briskly, "Sign here, please, and press your right thumb in this box here, after peeling off this plastic strip, so." She wrote in her boldly flowing script, and peeled, and pressed; and watched fascinatedly as her thumb-print developed itself sharply black against the bluish off-white of the Patrol's stationery. "That transfers your balance upon Tellus to the Patrol's general fund. Now sign and print this, in quadruplicate . . . Thank you. Here's your kit. When this book of slips is gone you can get another one at any bank or Patrol station anywhere. It has been a real pleasure to have met you, Lensman MacDougall; come in again whenever you happen to be upon Thrale," and he escorted her to the street as briskly as he had ushered her in.

Clarrissa felt slightly dazed. She had gone in there to get the couple of hundred credits which represented her total wealth; but instead of getting it she had meekly surrendered her savings to the Patrol and had been given—what? She leafed through the little book. One hundred blue-white slips; small things, smaller than currency bills. A little printing, two lines for description, a blank for figures, a space for signature, and a plastic-covered oblong area for thumb-print. That was all—but what an all! Any one of those slips, she knew, would be honored without hesitation or question for any amount of cash money she pleased to draw; for any object or thing she chose to buy. Anything—absolutely *anything*—from a pair of half-credit stockings up to and beyond a hundred-million-credit space-ship. ANYTHING! The thought chilled her buoyant spirit, took away her zest for shopping.

"Kim, I can't!" she wailed through her Lens. "Why didn't they give me my own money and let me spend it the way I please?"

"Hold everything, ace—I'll be with you in a sec." He wasn't—quite—but it was not long. "You can get all the money you want, you know—just give them a chit."

"I know, but all I wanted was my own money. I didn't ask for this stuff!"

"None of that, Cris—when you get to be a Lensman you've got to take what goes with it. Besides, if you spend money foolishly all the rest of your life, the Patrol knows that it will still owe you plenty for what you did on Lyrane II. Where do you want to begin?"

"Brenleer's," she decided, after she had been partially convinced. "They aren't the largest, but they give real quality at a fair price."

At the shop the two Lensmen were recognized at sight and Brenleer himself did the honors.

"Clothes," the girl said succinctly, with an all-inclusive wave of her hand. "All kinds of clothes, except white uniforms."

They were ushered into a private room and Kinnison wriggled as mannequins began to appear in various degrees of enclothement.

"This is no place for me," he declared. "I'll see you later, ace. How long—half an hour or so?"

"Half an hour?" The nurse giggled, and:

"She will be here all the rest of today, and most of the time for a week," the merchant informed him severely—and she was.

"Oh, Kim, I'm having the most *marvelous* time!" she told him excitedly, a few days later. "But it makes me feel sick to think of how much of the Patrol's money I'm spending."

"That's what *you* think."

"Huh? What do you mean?" she demanded, but he would not talk.

She found out, however, after the long-drawn-out business of selecting and matching and designing and fitting was over.

"You've only seen me in real clothes once, and that time you hardly looked at me. Besides, I got myself all prettied up in the beauty shop." She posed provocatively. "Do you like me, Kim?"

"*Like* you!" The man could scarcely speak. She had been a seven-sector call-out in faded moleskin breeches and a patched shirt. She had been a thionite dream in uniform. But now—radiantly, vibrantly beautiful, a symphony in her favorite dark green . . . "Words fail, ace. Thoughts, too. They fold up and quit. The universe's best, is all I can say . . ."

And—later—they sought out Brenleer.

"I would like to ask you to do me a tremendous favor," he said, hesitantly, without filling in any of the blanks upon the blue-white slip the girl had proffered. "If, instead of paying for these things, you would write upon this voucher the date and 'my fall outfit and much of my trousseau were made by Brenleer of Thrale . . .' " His voice expired upon a wistful note.

"Why . . . I never even thought of such a thing . . . would it be quite ethical, do you think, Kim?"

"You said that he gives value for price, so I don't see why not . . . Lots of things they never let any of us pay for . . ." Then, to Brenleer, "Never thought of that angle, of what a terrific draw she'd be . . . you're figuring on displaying that chit unobtrusively in a gold and platinum frame four feet square."

Brenleer nodded. "Something like that. This will be the most fantastically lucky break a man in my position ever had, if you approve of it."

"I don't see why not," Kinnison said again. "You might as well give him a break, Cris. What tore it was buying so much stuff here, not admitting the fact over your signature and thumb-print."

She wrote and they went out.

"You mean to tell me I'm so . . . so . . ."

"Famous? Notorious?" he helped out.

"Uh-huh. Or words to that effect." A touch of fear darkened her glorious eyes.

"All of that, and then some. I never thought of what your buying so much plunder in one store would do, but it'd have the pulling power of a planetary tractor. It's bad enough with us regulars—half the chits we issue are never cashed—but *you* are absolutely unique. The first Lady Lensman—the only Red Lensman—and *what* a Lensman! Wow! As I think it over one gets you a hundred if any chit you ever sign ever will get cashed. There have been collectors, you know, ever since Civilization began—maybe before."

"But I don't like it!" she stormed.

"That won't change the facts," he countered, philosophically. "Are you ready to flit? The *Dauntless* is hot, they tell me."

"Uh-huh, all my stuff is aboard," and soon they were en route to Klovia.

The trip was uneventful, and even before they reached that transformed planet it became evident that it was theirs from pole to pole. Their cruiser was met by a horde of space-ships of all types and sizes, which formed a turbulent and demonstrative escort of honor. The seething crowd at the space-port could scarcely be kept out of range of the dreadnought's searing landing-blasts. Half the brass bands of the world, it seemed, burst into "Our Patrol" as the Lensmen disembarked, and their ground-car and the street along which it slowly rolled were decorated lavishly with deep-blue flowers.

"Thorn-flowers!" Clarrissa choked. "Thralian thorn-flowers, Kim—how could they?"

"They grow here as well as there, and when they found out that you liked them so well they imported them by the shipload," and Kinnison himself swallowed a lump.

Their brief stay upon Klovia was a hectic one indeed. Parties and balls, informal and formal, and at least a dozen Telenews poses every day. Receptions, at which there were presented the personages and the potentates of a thousand planets; at which the uniforms and robes and gowns put the solar spectrum to shame.

And from tens of thousands of planets came Lensmen, to make or to renew acquaintance with the Galactic Coordinator and to welcome into their ranks the Lensman-bride. From Tellus, of course, they came in greatest number and enthusiasm, but other planets were not too far behind. They came from Manarka and Velantia and Chickladoria and Alsakan and Vandemar, from the worlds of Canopus and Vega and Antares, from all over the galaxy. Human, near-human, non-human, monstrous; there even appeared briefly quite large numbers of frigid-blooded Lensmen, whose fiercely-laboring refrigerators chilled the atmosphere for yards around their insulated and impervious suits. All those various beings came with a united purpose, with a common thought—to con-

gratulate Kinnison of Tellus and to wish his Lensman-mate all the luck
and all the happiness of the universe.

Kinnison was surprised at the sincerity with which they acclaimed
him; he was amazed at the genuineness and the intensity of their adop-
tion of his Clarrissa as their own. He had been afraid that some of them
would think he was throwing his weight around when he violated precedent by making her a Lensman. He had been afraid of animosity and
ill-will. He had been afraid that outraged masculine pride would set up
a sex antagonism. But if any of these things existed, the keenest use of
his every penetrant sense could not discover them.

Instead, the human Lensmen literally mobbed her as they took her
to their collective bosom. No party, wherever or for what reason held,
was complete without her. If she ever had less than ten escorts at once,
she was slighted. They ran her ragged, they danced her slippers off, they
stuffed her to repletion, they would not let her sleep, they granted her the
privacy of a gold-fish—and she loved every tumultuous second of it.

She had wanted, as she had told Haynes and Lacy so long ago, a
big wedding; but this one was already out of hand and was growing
more so by the minute. The idea of holding it in a church had been
abandoned long since; now it became clear that the biggest armory of
Klovia would not hold even half of the Lensmen, to say nothing of the
notables and dignitaries who had come so far. It would simply have to
be the Stadium.

Even that tremendous structure could not hold enough people, hence
speakers and plates were run outside, clear up to the space-field fence.
And, although neither of the principals knew it, this marriage had so
fired public interest that Universal Telenews men had already arranged
the hook-up which was to carry it to every planet of Civilization. Thus
the number of entities who saw and heard that wedding has been esti-
mated, but the figures are too fantastic to be repeated here.

But it was in no sense a circus. No ceremony ever held, in home or
in church or in cathedral, was ever more solemn. For when half a million
Lensmen concentrate upon solemnity, it prevails.

The whole vast bowl was gay with flowers—it seemed as though a
state must have been stripped of blooms to furnish so many—and ferns
and white ribbons were everywhere. There was a mighty organ, which
pealed out triumphal melody as the bridal parties marched down the
aisles, subsiding into a lilting accompaniment as the betrothal couple
ascended the white-brocaded stairway and faced the Lensman-Chaplain
in the heavily-garlanded little open-air chapel. The minister raised both

hands. The massed Patrolmen and nurses stood at attention. A profound silence fell.

"Dearly beloved . . ." The grand old service—short and simple, but utterly impressive—was soon over. Then, as Kinnison kissed his wife, half a million Lensed members were thrust upward in silent salute.

Through a double lane of glowing Lenses the wedding party made its way up to the locked and guarded gate of the space-field where lay the *Dauntless*—the super-dreadnought "yacht" in which the Kinnisons were to take a honeymoon voyage to distant Tellus. The gate opened. The couple, accompanied by the Port Admiral and the Surgeon Marshal, stepped into the car, which sped out to the battleship; and as it did so the crowd loosed its pent-up feelings in a prolonged outburst of cheering.

And as the newlyweds walked up the gangplank Kinnison turned his head and Lensed a thought to Haynes:

"You've been griping so long about Lyrane VIII, chief—I forgot to tell you—you can go mop up on it now!"

Acknowledgment

Your historian, not wishing to take credit which is not rightfully his, wishes to say here that without the fine cooperation of many persons and entities this history must have been of much less value and importance than it now is.

First, of course, there were the Lensmen. It is unfortunate that Nadreck of Palain VII could not be induced either to release his spool of the Fall of Onlo or to enlarge upon his other undertakings.

Coordinator Kinnison, Worsel of Velantia, and Tregonsee of Rigel IV, however, were splendidly cooperative, giving in personal conversations much highly useful material which is not heretofore of public record. The gracious and queenly Red Lensman also was of great assistance.

Dr. James R. Enright was both prolific and masterly in deducing that certain otherwise necessarily obscure events and sequences must have in fact occurred, and it is gratefully admitted here that the author has drawn heavily upon "Doctor Jim's" profound knowledge of the mind.

The Galactic Roamers, those intrepid spacemen, assisted no little: E. Everett Evans, their Chief Communications Officer, F. Edwin Counts, Paul Leavy, Jr., Alfred Ashley, to name only a few who aided in the selection, arrangement, and presentation of material.

Verna Trestrail, the exquisite connoisseuse, was of help, not only by virtue of her knowledge of the jewels of Lonabar, but also in her interpretations of many things concerning Illona Potter of which Illona Henderson—characteristically—will not speak.

To all these, and to many others whose help was only slightly less, the writer extends his sincere thanks.

EDWARD E. SMITH

Children
of the
Lens

To
Dan

CONTENTS

MESSAGE OF TRANSMITTAL

Subject: The Conclusion of the Boskonian War; A Report:
By: Christopher K. Kinnison, L3, of Klovia:
To: The Entity Able to Obtain and to Read It.

To you, the third-level intellect who has been guided to this imperishable container and who is able to break the Seal and to read this tape, and to your fellows, greetings:

For reasons which will become obvious, this report will not be made available for an indefinite but very long time; my present visualization of the Cosmic All does not extend to the time at which such action will become necessary. Therefore it is desirable to review briefly the most pertinent facts of the earlier phases of Civilization's climactic conflict: information which, while widely known at present, will probably in that future time exist otherwise only in the memories of my descendants.

In early Civilization law enforcement lagged behind crime because the police were limited in their spheres of action, while criminals were not. Each technological advance made that condition worse until finally, when Bergenholm so perfected the crude inertialess space-drive of Rodebush and Cleveland that commerce throughout the galaxy became an actuality, crime began to threaten Civilization's very existence.

Of course it was not then suspected that there was anything organized, coherent, or of large purpose about this crime. Centuries were to pass before my father, Kimball Kinnison of Tellus, now galactic coordinator, was to prove that Boskonia—an autocratic, dictatorial culture diametrically opposed to every ideal of Civilization—was in fact back of practically all the pernicious activities of the First Galaxy. Even he, however, has never had any inkling either of the eons-long conflict between the Arisians and the Eddorians or of the fundamental *raisin d'etre* of the Galactic Patrol—material which can never be revealed to any mind not inherently stable at the third level of stress.

Virgil Samms, then chief of the Triplanetary Service, perceived the general situation and foresaw the shape of the inevitable. He realized that unless and until his organization could secure an identifying symbol which could not be counterfeited, police work would remain relatively ineffectual. Tellurian science had done its best in the golden meteors of the Service, and its best was not good enough.

Through one Dr. Nels Bergenholm, an Arisian-activated form of human flesh, Virgil Samms became the first wearer of Arisia's Lens, and during his life he began the rigid selection of those worthy of wearing it. For centuries the Patrol grew and spread. It became widely known that the Lens was a perfect telepath, that it glowed with colored light only when worn by the individual to whose ego it was attuned, that it killed any other living being who attempted to wear it. Whatever his race or shape, any wearer of the Lens was accepted as the embodiment of Civilization.

Kimball Kinnison was the first Lensman to realize that the Lens was more than an identification and a telepath. He was thus the first Lensman to return to Arisia to take the second stage of Lensmanship— the treatment which only an exceptional brain can withstand, but which gives the second-stage Lensman any mental power which he needs and which he can both visualize and control.

Aided by Lensmen Worsel of Velantia and Tregonsee of Rigel IV— the former a winged reptile, the latter a four-legged, barrel-shaped creature with the sense of perception instead of sight—Kimball Kinnison traced and surveyed Boskone's military organization in the First Galaxy. He helped plan the attack on Grand Base, the headquarters of Helmuth, who "spoke for Boskone." By flooding the control dome of Grand Base with thionite, that deadly drug native to the peculiar planet Trenco, he made it possible for Civilization's Grand Fleet, under the command of Port Admiral Haynes, to reduce that base. He, personally, killed Helmuth in hand-to-hand combat.

He was instrumental in the almost-complete destruction of the Overlords of Delgon; those sadistic, life-eating reptiles who were the first to employ the hyper-spatial tube against humanity.

He was wounded more than once; in one of his hospitalizations becoming acquainted with Surgeon-Marshal Lacy and with Sector Chief Nurse Clarrissa MacDougall, who was later to become the widely-known "Red" Lensman and, still later, my mother.

In spite of the military defeat, however, Boskonia's real organization remained intact, and Kinnison's further search led into Lundmark's Nebula, thenceforth called the Second Galaxy. The planet Medon, being attacked by Boskonians, was rescued from the enemy and was moved across inter-galactic space to the First Galaxy. Medon made two notable contributions to Civilization: first, electrical insulation, conductors, and switches by whose means voltages and amperages theretofore undreamed-of could be handled; and later Phillips, a Posenian surgeon, was able there to complete the researches which made it possible for human bodies to grow anew lost members or organs.

Kinnison, deciding that the drug syndicate was the quickest and surest line to Boskone, became Wild Bill Williams the meteor-miner; a hard-drinking, bentlam-eating, fast-shooting space-hellion. As Williams he traced the zwilnik line upward, step by step, to the planet Jarnevon in the Second Galaxy. Upon Jarnevon lived the Eich; frigid-blooded monsters more intelligent, more merciless, more truly Boskonian even than the Overlords.

He and Worsel, second-stage Lensmen both, set out to investigate Jarnevon. He was captured, tortured, dismembered; but Worsel brought him back to Tellus with his mind and knowledge intact—the enormously important knowledge that Jarnevon was ruled by a council of nine of the Eich, a council named Boskone.

Kinnison was given a Phillips treatment, and again Clarrissa MacDougall nursed him back to health. They loved each other, but they could not marry until the Gray Lensman's job was done; until Civilization had triumphed over Boskonia.

The Galactic Patrol assembled its Grand Fleet, composed of millions of units, under the flagship *Z9M9Z*. It attacked. The planet of Jalte, Boskonia's director of the First Galaxy, was consumed by a bomb of negative matter. Jarnevon was crushed between two colliding planets; positioned inertialess, then inerted especially for that crushing. Grand Fleet returned, triumphant.

But Boskonia struck back, sending an immense fleet against Tellus through a hyper-spatial tube instead of through normal space. This method of approach was not, however, unexpected. Survey-ships and detectors were out; the scientists of the Patrol had been for months hard at work on the "sunbeam"—a device to concentrate the energy of the sun into one frightful beam. With this weapon re-enforcing the already vast powers of Grand Fleet, the invaders were wiped out.

Again Kinnison had to search for a high Boskonian; some authority higher than the Council of Boskone. Taking his personal super-dread-nought, the *Dauntless,* which carried his indetectable, non-ferrous speed-ster, he found a zwilnik trail and followed it to Dunstan's Region, an unexplored, virtually unknown, outlying spiral arm of the First Galaxy. It led to the planet Lyrane II, with its humanoid matriarchy, ruled by Helen, its queen.

There he found Illona Potter, the ex-Aldebaranian dancer; who, turning against her Boskonian masters, told him all she knew of the Boskonian planet Lonabar, where she had spent most of her life. Lonabar was unknown to the Patrol and Illona knew nothing of its location in space. She did, however, know its unique jewelry—gems also completely unknown to Civilization.

Nadreck of Palain VII, a frigid-blooded Second-Stage Lensman, with one jewel as a clue, set out to find Lonabar; while Kinnison began to investigate Boskonian activities among the matriarchs.

The Lyranians, however, were fanatically non-cooperative. They hated all males; they despised and detested all foreigners. Kinnison, with the consent and assistance of Mentor of Arisia, made Clarrissa MacDougall an Unattached Lensman and assigned to her the task of working Lyrane II.

Nadreck found and mapped Lonabar; and to build up an unimpeach-able Boskonian identity Kinnison became Cartiff the jeweler—Cartiff the jewel-thief and swindler—Cartiff the fence—Cartiff the murderer-outlaw—Cartiff the Boskonian big shot. He challenged and overthrew Menjo Bleeko, the dictator of Lonabar, and before killing him took from his mind everything he knew.

The Red Lensman secured information from which it was deduced that a cavern of Overlords existed on Lyrane II. This cavern was raided and destroyed, the Patrolmen learning that the Eich themselves had a heavily-fortified base on Lyrane VIII.

Nadreck, master psychologist, invaded that base tracelessly; learning that the Eich received orders from the Thralian solar system in the Second Galaxy and that frigid-blooded Kandron of Onlo (Thrallis IX) was second in power only to human Alcon, the Tyrant of Thrale (Thrallis II).

Kinnison went to Thrale, Nadreck to Onlo; the operations of both being covered by the Patrol's invasion of the Second Galaxy. In that invasion Boskonia's Grand Fleet was defeated and the planet Klovia was occupied and fortified.

Assuming the personality of Traska Gannel, a Thralian, Kinnison worked his way upward in Alcon's military organization. Trapped in a hyper-spatial tube, ejected into an unknown one of the infinity of parallel, co-existent, three-dimensional spaces comprising the Cosmic All, he was rescued by Mentor, working through the brain of Sir Austin Cardynge, the Tellurian mathematician.

Returning to Thrale, he fomented a revolution, in which he killed Alcon and took his place as the Tyrant of Thrale. He then discovered that his prime minister, Fossten, who concealed his true appearance by means of a zone of hypnosis, had been Alcon's superior instead of his adviser. Neither quite ready for an open break, but both supremely confident of victory when that break should come, subtle hostilities began.

Gannel and Fossten planned and launched an attack on Klovia, but just before engagement the hostilities between the two Boskonian leaders flared into an open fight for supremacy. After a terrific mental struggle, during which the entire crew of the flagship died, leaving the Boskonian fleet at the mercy of the Patrol, Kinnison won.

He did not know, of course, then or ever, either that Fossten was in fact Gharlane of Eddore or that it was Mentor of Arisia who in fact overcame Fossten. Kinnison thought, and Mentor encouraged him to believe, that Fossten was an Arisian who had been insane since youth, and that Kinnison had killed him without assistance. It is a mere formality to emphasize at this point that none of this information must ever become available to any mind below the third level; since to any entity able either to obtain or to read this report it will be obvious that such revealment would set up an inferiority complex which must inevitably destroy both the Patrol and Civilization.

With Fossten dead and with Kinnison already the despot of Thrale, it was comparatively easy for the Patrol to take over. Nadreck drove the Onlonian garrisons insane, so that all fought to the death among themselves; thus rendering Onlo's mighty armament completely useless.

Then, thinking that the Boskonian War was over—encouraged, in fact, by Mentor so to think—Kinnison married Clarrissa, established his headquarters upon Klovia, and assumed his duties as galactic coordinator.

Kimball Kinnison, while in no sense a mutant, was the penultimate product of a prodigiously long line of selective, controlled breeding. So was Clarrissa MacDougall. Just what course the science of Arisia took in making those two what they are I can deduce, but I do not as yet actually know. Nor, for the purpose of this record, does it matter. Port Admiral

Haynes and Surgeon-Marshal Lacy thought that they brought them together and promoted their romance. Let them think so—as agents, they did. Whatever the method employed, the result was that the genes of those two uniquely complementary penultimates were precisely those necessary to produce the first, and at present the only third-stage Lensmen.

I was born on Klovia, as were, three and four galactic-standard years later, my four sisters—two pairs of non-identical twins. I had little babyhood, no childhood. Fathered and mothered by Second-Stage Lensmen, accustomed from infancy to wide-open two-ways with such beings as Worsel of Velantia, Tregonsee of Rigel IV, and Nadreck of Palain VII, it would seem obvious that we did not go to school. We were not like other children of our ages; but before I realized that it was anything unusual for a baby who could scarcely walk to be computing highly perturbed asteroidal orbits as "mental arithmetic," I knew that we would have to keep our abnormalities to ourselves, insofar as the bulk of mankind and of Civilization was concerned.

I traveled much; sometimes with my father or mother or both, sometimes alone. At least once each year I went to Arisia for treatment. I took the last two years of Lensmanship, for physical reasons only, at Wentworth Hall instead of the Academy of Klovia because upon Tellus the name Kinnison is not at all uncommon, while upon Klovia the fact that "Kit" Kinnison was the son of the coordinator could not have been concealed.

I graduated, and with my formal enlensment this record properly begins.

I have recorded this material as impersonally as possible, realizing fully that my sisters and I did only the work for which we were specifically developed and trained; even as you who read this will do that for which you shall have been developed and are to be trained.

Respectfully submitted,

Christopher K. Kinnison, L3, Klovia.

1

KIM AND KIT; GRAY LENSMEN

Galactic Coordinator Kimball Kinnison finished his second cup of Tellurian coffee, got up from the breakfast table, and prowled about in black abstraction. Twenty-odd years had changed him but little. He weighed the same, or a few pounds less; although a little of his mass had shifted downward from his mighty chest and shoulders. His hair was still brown; his stern face was only faintly lined. He was mature, with a conscious maturity no young man can know.

"Since when, Kim, did you think you could get away with blocking *me* out of your mind?" Clarrissa Kinnison directed a quiet thought. The years had dealt as lightly with the Red Lensman as with the Gray. She had been gorgeous; she was now magnificent. "This room is shielded, you know, against even the girls."

"Sorry, Cris—I didn't mean it that way."

"I know," she laughed. "Automatic. But you've had that block up for two solid weeks, except when you force yourself to keep it down. That means you're 'way off the green."

"I've been thinking, incredible as it may seem."

"I know it. Let's have it, Kim."

"QX—you asked for it. Queer things have been going on; all over. Inexplicable things . . . no apparent reason."

"Such as?"

"Almost any kind of insidious deviltry you care to name. Disaffections, psychoses, mass hysterias, hallucinations; pointing toward a Civilization-wide epidemic of revolutions and uprisings for which there seems to be no basis or justification whatever."

"Why, Kim! How could there be? I haven't heard of anything like that!"

"It hasn't got around. Each solar system thinks it's a purely local condition, but it isn't. As galactic coordinator, with a broad view of the entire picture, my office would of course see such a thing before anyone else could. We saw it, and set out to nip it in the bud . . . but . . ." He shrugged his shoulders and grinned wryly.

"But what?" Clarrissa persisted.

"It didn't nip. We sent Lensmen to investigate, but none of them got to the first check-station. Then I asked our Second-Stage Lensmen—Worsel, Nadreck, and Tregonsee—to drop whatever they were doing and solve it for me. They hit it and bounced. They followed, and are still following, leads and clues galore, but they haven't got a millo's worth of results so far."

"What? You mean it's a problem *they* can't solve?"

"That they haven't, to date," he corrected, absently. "And that 'gives me furiously to think.' "

"It would," she conceded, "and it also would make you itch to join them. Think at me, it'll help you correlate. You should have gone over the data with me right at first."

"I had reasons not to, as you'll see. But I'm stumped now, so here goes. We'll have to go away back, to before we were married. First; Mentor told me, quote, only your descendants will be ready for that for which you now so dimly grope, unquote. Second; you were the only being ever able to read my thoughts without a Lens. Third; Mentor told us, when we asked him if it was QX for us to go ahead, that our marriage was *necessary,* a choice of phraseology which bothered you somewhat at the time, but which I then explained as being in accord with his visualization of the Cosmic All. Fourth; the Patrol formula is to send the man best fitted for any job to do that job, and if he can't swing it, to send the Number One graduate of the current class of Lensmen. Fifth; a Lensman has got to use everything and everybody available, no matter what or who it is. I used even you, you remember, in that Lyrane affair and others. Sixth; Sir Austin Cardynge believed to the day of his death that we were thrown out of that hyper-spatial tube, and out of space, deliberately."

"Well, go on. I don't see much, if any, connection."

"You will, if you think of those six points in connection with our present predicament. Kit graduates next month, and he'll rank number one of all Civilization, for all the tea in China."

"Of course. But after all, he's a Lensman. He'll have to be assigned some problem; why not that one?"

"You don't see yet what that problem is. I've been adding two and two together for weeks, and can't get any other answer than four. And if two and two are four, Kit has got to tackle Boskone—the *real* Boskone; the one I never did and probably never can reach."

"No, Kim—no!" she almost shrieked. "Not Kit, Kim—he's just a boy!"

Kinnison waited, wordless.

She got up, crossed the room to him. He put his arm around her in the old but ever new gesture.

"Lensman's load, Cris," he said, quietly.

"Of course," she replied then, as quietly. "It was a shock at first, coming after all these years, but . . . if it has to be, it must. But he—surely we can help him, Kim?"

"Surely." The man's arm tightened. "When he hits space I go back to work. So do Nadreck and Worsel and Tregonsee. So do you, if your kind of a job turns up. And with us to do the blocking, and with Kit to carry the ball . . ." His thought died away.

"I'll say so," she breathed. Then: "But you won't call me, I know, unless you absolutely *have* to . . . and to give up you and Kit both . . . why did we have to be Lensmen, Kim?" she protested, rebelliously. "Why couldn't we have been ground-grippers? You used to growl that thought at me before I knew what a Lens really meant . . ."

"Vell, some of us has got to be der first violiners in der orchestra," Kinnison misquoted, in an attempt at lightness. "Ve can't all push vind t'rough der trombone."

"I suppose that's true." The Red Lensman's somber air deepened. "Well, we were going to start for Tellus today, anyway, to see Kit graduate. This doesn't change that."

And in a distant room four tall, shapely, auburn-haired girls stared at each other briefly, then went en rapport; for their mother had erred greatly in saying that the breakfast room was screened against their minds. Nothing was or could be screened against them; they could think above, below, or, by sufficient effort, straight through any thought-screen known to Tellurian science. Nothing in which they were interested was safe from them, and they were interested in practically everything.

"Kay, we've got ourselves a job!" Kathryn, older by minutes than Karen, excluded pointedly the younger twins, Camilla and Constance— "Cam" and "Con."

"At last!" Karen exclaimed. "I've been wondering what we were born for, with nine-tenths of our minds so deep down that nobody except Kit even knows they're there and so heavily blocked that we can't let even each other in without a conscious effort. This is it. We'll go places now, Kat, and really do things."

"What do you mean *you'll* go places and do things?" Con demanded, indignantly. "Do you think for a second you carry screen enough to block *us* out of all the fun?"

"Certainly," Kat said, equably. "You're too young."

"We'll let you know what we're doing, though," Kay conceded, magnanimously. "You might, just conceivably, contribute an idea we could use."

"Ideas—phooey!" Con jeered. "A real idea would shatter both your skulls. You haven't any more plan than a . . ."

"Hush—shut up, everybody!" Kat commanded. "This is too new for any of us to have any worthwhile ideas on, yet. Tell you what let's do— we'll all think this over until we're aboard the *Dauntless,* halfway to Tellus; then we'll compare notes and decide what to do."

They left Klovia that afternoon. Kinnison's personal super-dreadnought, the mighty *Dauntless*—the fourth to bear that name—bored through inter-galactic space. Time passed. The four young red-heads convened.

"I've got it all worked out!" Kat burst out, enthusiastically, forestalling the other three. "There'll be four Second-Stage Lensmen at work and there are four of us. We'll circulate—percolate, you might say— around and throughout the universe. We'll pick up ideas and facts and feed 'em to our Gray Lensmen. Surreptitiously, sort of, so they'll think they got 'em themselves. I'll take dad for my partner, Kay can have . . ."

"You'll do no such thing!" A general clamor arose, Con's thought being the most insistent. "If we aren't going to work with them all, indiscriminately, we'll draw lots or throw dice to see who gets him, so there!"

"Seal it, snake-hips, please," Kat requested, sweetly. "It is trite but true to say that infants should be seen, but not heard. This is serious business . . ."

"Snake-hips! Infant!" Con interrupted, venomously. "Listen, my steatopygous and senile friend!" Constance measured perhaps a quarter of an inch less in gluteal circumference than did her oldest sister; she tipped the beam at one scant pound below her weight. "You and Kay are a year older than Cam and I, of course; a year ago your minds were stronger than ours. That condition, however, no longer exists. We too are grown up. And to put that statement to test, what can you do that I can't?"

"This." Kathryn extended a bare arm, narrowed her eyes in concentration. A Lens materialized about her wrist; not attached to it by a metallic bracelet, but a bracelet in itself, clinging sentiently to the smooth, bronzed skin. "I felt that in this work there would be a need. I learned to satisfy it. Can you match that?"

They could. In a matter of seconds the three others were similarly enlensed. They had not previously perceived the need, but at Kathryn's demonstration their acquisition of full knowledge had been virtually instantaneous.

Kat's Lens disappeared.

So did the other three. Each knew that no hint of this knowledge or of this power should ever be revealed; each knew that in any moment of stress the Lens of Civilization could be and would be hers.

"Logic, then, and by reason, not by chance." Kat changed her tactics. "I still get him. Everybody knows who works best with whom. You, Con, have tagged around after Worsel all your life. You used to ride him like a horse . . ."

"She still does," Kay snickered. "He pretty nearly split her in two a while ago in a seven-gravity pull-out, and she almost broke a toe when she kicked him for it."

"Worsel is nice," Con defended herself vigorously. "He's more human than most people, and more fun, as well as having infinitely more brains. And *you* can't talk, Kay—what anyone can see in that Nadreck, so cold-blooded that he freezes you even through armor at twenty feet— you'll get as cold and hard as he is if you don't . . ."

"And every time Cam gets within five hundred parsecs of Tregonsee she goes into the silences with him, contemplating rapidly the whichnesses of the why," Kathryn interrupted, forestalling recriminations. "So you see, by the process of elimination, dad's mine."

Since they could not all have him it was finally agreed that Kathryn's claim would be allowed and, after a great deal of discussion and argument, a tentative plan of action was developed. In due course the *Dauntless* landed at Prime Base. The Kinnisons went to Wentworth Hall, the towering, chromium-and-glass home of the Tellurian cadets of the Galactic Patrol. They watched the impressive ceremonies of graduation. Then, as the new Lensmen marched out to the magnificent cadences of "Our Patrol," the Gray Lensman, leaving his wife and daughters to their own devices, made his way to his Tellurian office.

"Lensman Christopher K. Kinnison, sir, by appointment," his secretary announced, and as Kit strode in Kinnison stood up and came to attention.

"Christopher K. Kinnison of Klovia, sir, reporting for duty." Kit saluted crisply.

The coordinator returned the salute punctiliously. Then: "At rest, Kit. I'm proud of you, mighty proud. We all are. The women want to heroize you, but I had to see you first, to clear up a few things. An explanation, an apology, and, in a sense, commiseration."

"An apology, sir?" Kit was dumbfounded. "Why, that's unthinkable . . ."

"For not graduating you in Gray. It has never been done, but that wasn't the reason. Your commandant, the board of examiners, and Port Admiral LaForge, all recommended it, agreeing that none of us is qualified to give you either orders or directions. I blocked it."

"Of course. For the son of the coordinator to be the first Lensman to graduate Unattached would smell—especially since the fewer who know of my peculiar characteristics the better. That can wait, sir."

"Not too long, son." Kinnison's smile was a trifle forced. "Here's your Release and your kit, and a request that you go to work on whatever it is that's going on. We rather think it heads up somewhere in the Second Galaxy, but that's just a guess."

"I start out from Klovia, then? Good—I can go home with you."

"That's the idea, and on the way there you can study the situation. We've made tapes of the data, with our best attempts at analysis and interpretation. The stuff's up to date, except for a thing I got this morning . . . I can't figure out whether it means anything or not, but it should be inserted . . ." Kinnison paced the room, scowling.

"Might as well tell me. I'll insert it when I scan the tape."

"QX. I don't suppose you've heard much about the unusual shipping trouble we've been having, particularly in the Second Galaxy?"

"Rumor—gossip only. I'd rather have it straight."

"It's all on the tapes, so I'll just hit the high spots. Losses are twenty-five percent above normal. A few very peculiar derelicts have been found—they seem to have been wrecked by madmen. Not only wrecked, but gutted, and every mark of identification wiped out. We can't determine even origin or destination, since the normal disappearances outnumber the abnormal ones by four to one. On the tapes this is lumped in with the other psychoses you'll learn about. But this morning they found another derelict, in which the chief pilot had scrawled 'WARE HELLHOLE IN SP' across a plate. Connection with the other derelicts, if any, obscure. If the pilot was sane when he wrote that message it means something—but nobody knows what. If he wasn't, it doesn't, any more than the dozens of obviously senseless—excuse me, I should say apparently senseless—messages on the tapes."

"Hm . . . m. Interesting. I'll bear it in mind and tape it in its place. But speaking of peculiar things, I've got one I wanted to tell you about— getting my Release was such a shock I almost forgot it. Reported it, but nobody thought it was anything important. Maybe—probably—it isn't. Tune your mind up to the top of the range—there—did you ever hear of a race that thinks on that band?"

"I never did—it's practically unreachable. Why—have you?"

"Yes and no. Only once, and that only a touch. Or, rather, a burst; as though a hard-held mind-block had exploded, or the creature had just died a violent, instantaneous death. Not enough of it to trace, and I never found any more of it."

"Any characteristics? Bursts can be quite revealing."

"A few. It was on my last break-in trip in the Second Galaxy, out beyond Thrale—about here." Kit marked the spot upon a mental chart. "Mentality very high—precisionist grade—possibly beyond social needs, as the planet was a bare desert and terrifically hot. No thought of cities. Nor of water, although both may have existed without appearing in that burst of thought. The thing's bodily structure was RTSL, to four places. No gross digestive tract—atmosphere-nourished or an energy-converter, perhaps. The sun was a blue giant. No spectral data, of course, but at a rough guess I'd say somewhere around class B5 or Ao. That's all I could get."

"That's a lot to get from one burst. It doesn't mean a thing to me right now . . . but I'll watch for a chance to fit it in somewhere."

How casually they dismissed as unimportant that cryptic burst of thought! But if they both, right then, together, had been authoritatively informed that that description fitted exactly the physical form forced upon its denizens in its summer by the accurately-described, simply hellish climatic conditions obtaining during that season on the noxious planet Ploor, the information would still not have seemed important to either of them—then.

"Anything else we ought to discuss before night?" The older Lensman went on without a break.

"Not that I know of."

"You said your Release was a shock. You've got another one coming."

"I'm braced—blast!"

"Worsel, Tregonsee, Nadreck and I are quitting our jobs and going Gray again. Our main purpose in life is going to be rallying 'round at max whenever you whistle."

"That *is* a shock, sir . . . Thanks . . . I hadn't expected—it's really overwhelming. And you said something about *commiserating* me?" Kit lifted his red-thatched head—all of Clarrissa's children had inherited her startling hair—and gray eyes stared level into eyes of gray.

"In a sense, yes. You'll understand later . . . Well, you'd better go hunt up your mother and the girls. After the clambake is over . . ."

"I'd better cut it, hadn't I?" Kit asked, eagerly. "Don't you think it'd be better for me to get started right away?"

"Not on your life!" Kinnison demurred, positively. "Do you think I want that mob of red-heads snatching me bald? You're in for a large day and evening of lionization, so take it like a man. As I was about to say, as soon as the brawl is over tonight we'll all board the *Dauntless* and do a flit for Klovia, where we'll fix you up an outfit. Until then, son . . ." Two big hands gripped.

"But I'll be seeing you around the Hall!" Kit exclaimed. "You can't . . ."

"No I can't run out on it, either," Kinnison grinned, "but we won't be in a sealed and shielded room. So, son . . . I'm proud of you."

"Right back at you, big fellow—and thanks a million." Kit strode out and, a few minutes later, the coordinator did likewise.

The "brawl," which was the gala event of the Tellurian social year, was duly enjoyed by all the Kinnisons. The *Dauntless* made an uneventful flight to Klovia. Arrangements were made. Plans, necessarily sketchy and elastic, were laid.

Two big, gray-clad Lensmen stood upon the deserted space-field between two blackly indetectable speedsters. Kinnison was massive, sure, calm with the poised calmness of maturity, experience, and power. Kit, with the broad shoulders and narrow waist of his years and training, was taut and tense, fiery, eager to come to grips with Civilization's foes.

"Remember, son," Kinnison said as the two gripped hands. "There are four of us—old-timers who've been through the mill—on call every second. If you can use any one of us or all of us don't wait—snap out a call."

"I know, dad . . . thanks. The four best. One of you may make a strike before I do. With the thousands of leads we have, and your experience and know-how, you probably will. So remember it cuts both ways. If any of you can use me any time, *you* whistle."

"QX. We'll keep in touch. Clear ether, Kit!"

"Clear ether, dad!" What a wealth of meaning there was in that low-voiced, simple exchange of the standard bon voyage!

For minutes, as his speedster flashed through space, Kinnison thought only of the boy. He knew exactly how he felt; he re-lived in memory the supremely ecstatic moments of his own first launching into space as a Gray Lensman. But Kit had the stuff—stuff which he, Kinnison could never know anything about—and he had his own job to do. Therefore, methodically, like the old campaigner he was, he set about it.

2

WORSEL AND THE OVERLORDS

Worsel the Velantian, hard and durable and long-lived as Velantians are, had in twenty Tellurian years changed scarcely at all. As the first Lensman and the only Second-Stage Lensman of his race, the twenty years had been very fully occupied indeed.

He had solved the varied technological and administrative problems incident to the welding of Velantia into the structure of Civilization. He had worked at the many tasks which, in the opinion of the Galactic Council, fitted his peculiarly individual talents. In his "spare" time he had sought out in various parts of two galaxies, and had ruthlessly slain, widely-scattered groups of the Overlords of Delgon.

Continuously, however, he had taken an intense sort of godfatherly interest in the Kinnison children, particularly in Kit and in the youngest daughter, Constance; finding in the girl a mentality surprisingly akin to his own.

When Kinnison's call came he answered it. He was now out in space; not in the *Dauntless,* but in a ship of his own, under his own command. And what a ship! The *Velan* was manned entirely by beings of his own race. It carried Velantian air, at Velantian temperature and pressure. Above all, it was built and powered for inert maneuvering at the atrocious accelerations employed by the Velantians in their daily lives; and Worsel loved it with enthusiasm and elan.

He had worked conscientiously and well with Kinnison and with other entities of Civilization. He and they had all known, however, that he could work more efficiently alone or with others of his own kind. Hence, except in emergencies, he had done so; and hence, except in similar emergencies, he would so continue to do.

Out in deep space, Worsel entwined himself, in a Velantian's idea of comfort, in an intricate series of figures-of-eight around a pair of parallel bars and relaxed in thought. There were insidious deviltries afoot, Kinnison had said. There were disaffections, psychoses, mass hysterias, and—Oh happy thought!—hallucinations. There were also certain revolutions and sundry uprisings, which might or might not be connected or associated with the disappearances of a considerable number of persons of note. In these latter, however, Worsel of Velantia was not interested. He knew without being told that Kinnison would pounce upon such blatant manifestations as those. He himself would work upon something much more to his taste.

Hallucination was Worsel's dish. He had been born among hallucinations; had been reared in an atmosphere of them. What he did not know about hallucinations could have been printed in pica on the smallest one of his scales.

Therefore, isolating one section of his multi-compartmented mind from all others and from any control over his physical self, he sensitized it to receive whatever hallucinatory influences might be abroad. Simultaneously he set two other parts of his mind to watch over the one to be victimized; to study and to analyze whatever figments of obtrusive mentality might be received and entertained.

Then, using all his naturally tremendous sensitivity and reach, all his Arisian super-training, and the full power of his Lens, he sent his mental receptors out into space. And then, although the thought is staggeringly incomprehensible to any Tellurian or near-human mind, he *relaxed.* For day after day, as the *Velan* hurtled randomly through the void, he hung blissfully slack upon his bars, most of his mind a welter of the indescribable thoughts in which it is a Velantian's joy to revel.

Suddenly, after an unknown interval of time, a thought impinged: a thought under the impact of which Worsel's long body tightened so convulsively as to pull the bars a foot out of true. Overlords! The unmistakable, the body-and-mind-paralyzing hunting call of the Overlords of Delgon!

His crew had not felt it yet, of course; nor would they feel it. If they should, they would be worse than useless in the conflict to come;

for they could not withstand that baneful influence. Worsel could. Worsel was the only Velantian who could.

"Thought-screens all!" his commanding thought snapped out. Then, even before the order could be obeyed: "As you were!"

For the impenetrably shielded chamber of his mind told him instantly that this was no ordinary Delgonian hunting call; or rather, that it was more than that. Much more.

Mixed with, superimposed upon the overwhelming compulsion which generations of Velantians had come to know so bitterly and so well, were the very things for which he had leeen searching—hallucinations! To shield his crew or, except in the subtlest possible fashion himself, simply would not do. Overlords everywhere knew that there was at least one Velantian Lensman who was mentally their master; and, while they hated this Lensman tremendously, they feared him even more. Therefore, even though a Velantian was any Overlord's choicest prey, at the first indication of an ability to disobey their commands the monsters would cease entirely to radiate; would withdraw at once every strand of their far-flung mental nets into the fastnesses of their superbly hidden and indetectably shielded cavern.

Therefore Worsel allowed the inimical influence to take over, not only the total minds of his crew, but also the unshielded portions of his own. And stealthily, so insidiously that no mind affected could discern the change, values gradually grew vague and reality began to alter.

Loyalty dimmed, and *esprit de corps*. Family ties and pride of race waned into meaninglessness. All concepts of Civilization, of the Galactic Patrol, degenerated into strengthless gossamer, into oblivion. And to replace those hitherto mighty motivations there crept in an overmastering need for, and the exact method of obtainment of, whatever it was that was each Velantian's deepest, most primal desire. Each crewman stared into an individual visiplate whose substance was to him as real and as solid as the metal of his ship had ever been; each saw upon that plate whatever it was that, consciously or unconsciously, he wanted most to see. Noble or base, lofty or low, intellectual or physical, spiritual or carnal, it made no difference to the Overlords. Whatever each victim wanted most was there.

No figment was, however, even to the Velantians, actual or tangible. It was a picture on a plate, transmitted from a well-defined point in space. There, upon that planet, was the actuality, eagerly await; toward and to that planet must the *Velan* go at maximum blast. Into that line and at that blast, then, the pilots set their vessel without orders, and each of the crew saw upon his non-existent plate that she had so been set. If she had not been, if the pilots had been able to offer any resistance, the crew would have slaughtered them out of hand. As it was, all was well.

And Worsel, watching the affected portion of his mind accept those hallucinations as truths and admiring unreservedly the consummate artistry with which the work was being done, was well content. He knew that only a hard, solidly-driven, individually probing beam could force him to reveal the fact that a portion of his mind and all of his bodily controls were being withheld; he knew that unless he made a slip no such investigation was to be expected. He would not slip.

No human or near-human mind can really understand how the mind of a Velantian works. A Tellurian can, by dint of training, learn to do two or more unrelated things simultaneously. But neither is done very well and both must be more or less routine in nature. To perform any original or difficult operation successfully he must concentrate on it, and he can concentrate upon only one thing at a time. A Velantian can and does, however, concentrate upon half-a-dozen totally unrelated things at once; and, with his multiplicity of arms, hands, and eyes, he can perform simultaneously an astonishing number of completely independent operations.

The Velantian's is, however, in no sense such a multiple personality as would exist if six or eight human heads were mounted upon one body. There is no joint tenancy about it. There is only one ego permeating all those pseudo-independent compartments; no contradictory orders are, or ordinarily can be, sent along the bundled nerves of the spinal cord. While individual in thought and in the control of certain actions, the mind-compartments are basically, fundamentally, one mind.

Worsel had progressed beyond his fellows. He was different; unique. The perception of the need of the ability to isolate certain compartments of his mind, to separate them completely from his real ego, was one of the things which had enabled him to become the only Second-Stage Lensman of his race.

L2 Worsel, then, held himself aloof and observed appreciatively everything that went on. More, he did a little hallucinating of his own. Under the Overlords' compulsion he was supposed to remain motionless, staring raptly into an imaginary visiplate at an orgiastic saturnalia of which no description will be attempted. Therefore, as far as the occupied portion of his mind and through it the Overlords were concerned, he did so. Actually, however, his body moved purposefully about, directed solely by his own grim will; moved to make ready against the time of landing.

For Worsel knew that his opponents were not fools. He knew that they reduced their risks to the irreducible minimum. He knew that the mighty *Velan,* with her prodigious weaponry, would not be permitted to be within extreme range of the cavern, if the Overlords could possibly prevent it, when that cavern's location was revealed. His was the task to see to it that she was not only within range, but was at the very portal.

The speeding space-ship approached the planet . . . went inert . . . matched the planetary intrinsic . . . landed. Her airlocks opened. Her crew rushed out headlong, sprang into the air, and arrowed away en masse. Then Worsel, Grand Master of Hallucinations, went blithely but intensely to work.

Thus, although he stayed at the *Velan's* control board instead of joining the glamored Velantians in their rush over the unfamiliar terrain, and although the huge vessel lifted lightly into the air and followed them, neither the fiend-possessed part of Worsel's mind, nor any of his fellows, nor through them any one of the many Overlords, knew that either of those two things was happening. To that part of his mind Worsel's body was, under full control, flying along upon tireless wings in the midst of the crowd; to it and to all other Velantians and hence to the Overlords the *Velan* lay motionless and deserted upon the rocks far below and behind them. They watched her diminish in the distance; they saw her vanish beyond the horizon!

This was eminently tricky work, necessitating as it did such nicety of synchronization with the Delgonians' own compulsions as to be in-detectable even to the monsters themselves. Worsel was, however, an expert; he went at the job not with any doubt as to his ability to carry it through, but only with an uncontrollably shivering physical urge to come to grips with the hereditary enemies of his race.

The flyers shot downward, and as a boulder-camouflaged entrance yawned open in the mountain's side Worsel closed up and shot out a widely enveloping zone of thought-screen. The Overlords' control vanished. The Velantians, realizing instantly what had happened, flew madly back to their ship. They jammed through the airlocks, flashed to their posts. The cavern's gates had closed by then, but the monsters had no screen fit to cope with the *Velan's* tremendous batteries. Down they went. Barriers, bastions, and a considerable portion of the mountain's face flamed away in fiery vapor or flowed away in molten streams. Through reeking atmosphere, over red-hot debris, the armored Velantians flew to the attack.

The Overlords had, however, learned. This cavern, as well as being hidden, was defended by physical, as well as mental, means. There were inner barriers of metal and of force, there were armed and armored defenders who, dominated completely by the monsters, fought with the callous fury of the robots which in effect they were. Nevertheless, against all opposition, the attackers bored relentlessly in. Heavy semi-portables blazed, hand-to-hand combat raged in the narrow confines of that noisome tunnel. In the wavering, glaring light of the contending beams and screens, through the hot and rankly stinking steam billowing away from the reeking walls, the invaders fought their way. One by one and group by group the defenders died where they stood and the Velantians drove onward over their burned and dismembered bodies.

Into the cavern at last. To the Overlords. Overlords! They who for ages had preyed upon generation after generation of helpless Velantians, torturing their bodies to the point of death and then devouring ghoulishly the life-forces which their mangled bodies could no longer retain!

Worsel and his crew threw away their DeLameters. Only when it is absolutely necessary does any Velantian use any artificial weapon against any Overlord of Delgon. He is too furious, too berserk, to do so. He is scared to the core of his being; the cold grue of a thousand fiendishly eaten ancestors has bred that fear into the innermost atoms of his chemistry. But against that fear, negating and surmounting it, is a hatred of such depth and violence as no human being has ever known; a starkly savage hatred which can be even partially assuaged only by the ultimate of violences—by rending his foe apart member by member; by actually feeling the Delgonian's life depart under gripping hands and tearing talons and constricting body and shearing tail.

It is best, then, not to go into too fine detail as to this conflict. Since there were almost a hundred of the Delgonians, since they were insensately vicious fighters when cornered, and since their physical make-up was very similar to the Velantians' own, many of Worsel's troopers died. But since the *Velan* carried over fifteen hundred and since less than half of her personnel could even get into the cavern, there were plenty of them left to operate and to fight the space-ship.

Worsel took great care that the opposing commander was not killed with his minions. The fighting over, the Velantians chained this sole survivor into one of his own racks and stretched him out into immobility. Then, restraining by main strength the terrific urge to put the machine then and there to its fullest ghastly use, Worsel cut his screen, threw a couple of turns of tail around a convenient anchorage, and faced the Boskonian almost nose to nose. Eight weirdly stalked eyes curled out as he drove a probing thought-beam against the monster's shield.

"I could use this—or this—or this," Worsel gloated. As he touched various wheels and levers the chains hummed slightly, sparks flashed, the rigid body twitched. "I am not going to, however—yet. While you are still sane I shall take your total knowledge."

Face to face, eye to eye, brain to brain, that silently and motionlessly cataclysmic battle was joined.

As has been said, Worsel had hunted down and had destroyed many Overlords. He had hunted them, however, like vermin. He had killed them with bombs and beams, with talons, teeth, and tail. He had not engaged an Overlord mind to mind for over twenty Tellurian years; not since he and Nadreck of Palain Seven had captured alive the leaders of those who had been preying upon Helen's matriarchs and warring upon Civilization from their cavern on Lyrane II. Nor had he ever dueled one mentally to the death without powerful support; Kinnison or some other Lensman had always been near by.

But Worsel would need no help. He was not shivering in eagerness now. His body was as still as the solid rock upon which most of it lay; every chamber and every faculty of his mind was concentrated upon battering down or blasting through the Overlord's stubbornly-held shields.

Brighter and brighter flamed Worsel's Lens, flooding the gloomy cave with pulsating polychromatic light. Alert for any possible trickery, guarding intently against any possibility of counterthrust, Worsel slammed in bolt after bolt of mental force. He surrounded the monster's mind with a searing, constricting field. He squeezed; relentlessly and with appalling power.

The Overlord was beaten. He, who had never before encountered a foreign mind or a vital force stronger than his own, knew that he was beaten. He knew that at long last he had met that half-fabulous Velantian Lensman with whom not one of his monstrous race could cope. He knew starkly, with the chilling, numbing terror possible only to such a being in such a position, that he was doomed to die the same hideous and long-drawn-out death he had dealt out to so many others. He did not read into the mind of the bitterly vengeful, the implacably ferocious Velantian any more mercy, any more compunction, than were actually there. He knew perfectly that there was no slightest trace of either. Knowing these things with the black certainty that was his, he quailed.

There is an old saying that the brave man dies only once, the coward a thousand times. The Overlord, during that lethal combat, died more times than it is pleasant to contemplate. Nevertheless, he fought. His mind was keen and powerful; he brought to the defense of his beleagured ego every resource of skill and of trickery and of sheer power at his command. In vain. Deeper and deeper, in spite of everything he could do, the relentless Lensman squeezed and smashed and cut and pried and bored; little by little the Overlord gave mental ground.

"This station is here . . . this staff is here . . . I am here, then . . . to wreak damage . . . all possible damage to the commerce . . . and to the personnel of . . . the Galactic Patrol . . . and Civilization in every aspect . . ." the Overlord admitted haltingly as Worsel's pressure became intolerable; but such admissions, however unwillingly made or however revealing in substance, were not enough.

Worsel wanted, and would be satisfied with nothing less than, his enemy's total knowledge. Hence he maintained his assault until, unable longer to withstand the frightful battering, the Overlord's barriers went completely down; until every convolution of his brain and every track of his mind lay open, helplessly exposed to Worsel's poignant scrutiny. Then, scarcely taking time to gloat over his victim, Worsel did scrutinize.

Period.

Hurtling through space, toward a definite objective now, Worsel studied and analyzed some of the things he had just learned. He was not surprised that this Overlord had not known any of his superior officers in things or enterprises Boskonian; that he did not consciously know that he had been obeying orders or that he had superiors. That technique, by this time, was familiar enough. The Boskonian psychologists were able operators; to attempt to unravel the unknowable complexities of their subconscious compulsions would be a sheer waste of time.

What the Overlords had been doing, however, was clear enough. That outpost had indeed been wreaking havoc with Civilization's commerce. Ship after ship had been lured from its course; had been compelled to land upon this barren planet. Some of those vessels had been destroyed; some of them had been stripped and rifled as though by pirates of old; some of them had been set upon new courses with hulls, mechanical equipment, and cargoes almost untouched. No crewman or passenger, however, escaped unscathed; even though only ten percent of them died in the Overlordish fashion Worsel knew so well.

The Overlord himself had wondered why they had not been able to kill them all. They wanted intensely enough to do so; their lust for lifeforce simply could not be sated. He knew only that *something* had limited their killing to ten percent of the bag.

Worsel grinned wolfishly at that thought, even while he was admiring the quality of the psychology able to impress such a compulsion upon such intractable minds as those. That was the work of the Boskonian higher-ups; to spread confusion wider and wider.

The other ninety percent had merely been "played with"—a procedure which, although less satisfying to the Overlords than the ultimate treatment, was not very different as far as the victims' egos were concerned. For none of them emerged from the ordeal with any memory of what had happened, or of who or what he had ever been. They were not all completely mad; some were only partially so. All had, however, been . . . altered. Changed; shockingly transformed. No two were alike. Each Overlord, it appeared, had tried with all his ultra-hellish might to excel his fellows in the manufacture of an outrageous something whose like had never before been seen on land or sea or in the depths of space.

These and many other things Worsel studied carefully. He'd head for the "Hell-Hole in Space," he decided. This planet, the Overlords he had just slain, were not the Hell-Hole; could have had nothing to do with it—wrong location.

He knew now, though, what the Hell-Hole really was. It was a cavern of Overlords—couldn't be anything else—and in himself and his crew and his mighty vessel he, the Overlord-slayer supreme of two galaxies, had everything it took to extirpate any number of Overlords. That Hell-Hole was just as good as out, as of that minute.

And just then a solid, diamond-clear thought came in.

"Worsel! Con calling. What goes on there, fellow old snake?"

3

KINNISON WRITES A SPACE-OPERA

Each of the Second-Stage Lensmen had exactly the same facts, the same data, upon which to theorize and from which to draw conclusions. Each had shared his experiences, his findings, and his deductions and inductions with all of the others. They had discussed minutely, in wide-open four-ways, every phase of the Boskonian problem. Nevertheless the approach of each to that problem and the point of attack chosen by each was individual and characteristic.

Kimbell Kinnison was by nature forthright; direct. As has been seen, he could use the approach circuitous if necessary, but he much preferred and upon every possible occasion employed the approach direct. He liked plain, unambiguous clues much better than obscure ones; the more obvious and factual the clue was, the better he liked it.

He was now, therefore, heading for Antigan IV, the scene of the latest and apparently the most outrageous of a long series of crimes of violence. He didn't know much about it; the request had come through regular channels, not via Lens, that he visit Antigan and direct the investigation of the supposed murder of the Planetary President.

As his speedster flashed through space the Gray Lensman mulled over in his mind the broad aspects of this crime-wave. It was spreading far and wide, and the wider it spread and the intenser it became the more vividly one salient fact struck out. Selectivity—distribution. The solar systems of Thrale, Velantia, Tellus, Klovia, and Palain had not been affected. Thrale, Tellus, and Klovia were full of Lensmen. Velantia, Rigel, Palain, and a good part of the time Klovia, were the working headquarters of Second-Stage Lensmen. It seemed, then, that the trouble was roughly in inverse ratio to the numbers or the abilities of the Lensmen in the neighborhood. Something, therefore, that Lensmen—particularly Second-Stage Lensmen—were bad for. That was true, of course, for all crime. Nevertheless, this seemed to be a special case.

And when he reached his destination he found out that it was. The planet was seething. Its business and its every day activities seemed to be almost paralyzed. Martial law had been declared; the streets were practically deserted except for thick-clustered groups of heavily-armed guards. What few people were abroad were furtive and sly; slinking hastily along with their fear-filled eyes trying to look in all directions at once.

"QX, Wainwright, go ahead," Kinnison directed bruskly when, alone with the escorting Patrol officers in a shielded car, he was being taken to the Capitol grounds. "There's been too much pussyfooting about the whole affair."

"Very well, sir," and Wainwright told his tale. Things had been happening for months. Little things, but disturbing. Then murders and kidnappings and unexplained disappearances had begun to increase. The police forces had been falling farther and farther behind. The usual cries of incompetence and corruption had been raised, only further to confuse the issue. Circulars—dodgers—handbills appeared all over the planet; from where nobody knew. The keenest detectives could find no clue to paper-makers, printers, or distributors. The usual inflammatory, subversive, propaganda—"Down with the Patrol!" "Give us back our freedom!" and so on—but, because of the high tension already prevailing, the stuff had been unusually effective in breaking down the morale of the citizenry as a whole.

"Then this last thing. For two solid weeks the whole world was literally plastered with the announcement that at midnight on the thirty-fourth of Dreel—you're familiar with our calendar, I think?—President Renwood would disappear. Two weeks warning—daring us to do our damndest." Wainwright got that far and stopped.

"Well, go on. He disappeared, I know. How? What did you fellows do to prevent it? Why all the secrecy?"

"If you insist I'll have to tell you, of course, but I'd rather not." Wainwright flushed uncomfortably. "You wouldn't believe it. Nobody could. I wouldn't believe it myself if I hadn't been there. I'd rather you'd wait, sir, and let the vice-president tell you, in the presence of the treasurer and the others who were on duty that night."

"Um . . . m . . . I see . . . maybe." Kinnison's mind raced. "That's why nobody would give me details? Afraid I wouldn't believe it—that I'd think they'd been . . ." He stopped "Hypnotized" would have been the next word, but that would have been jumping at conclusions. Even if true, there was no sense in airing that hypothesis—yet.

"Not afraid, sir. They *knew* you wouldn't believe it."

After entering Government Reservation they went, not to the president's private quarters, but into the Treasury and down into the sub-basement housing the most massive, the most utterly impregnable vault of the planet. There the nation's most responsible officers told Kinnison, with their entire minds as well as their tongues, what had happened.

Upon that black day business had been suspended. No visitors of any sort had been permitted to enter the Reservation. No one had been allowed to approach Renwood except old and trusted officers about whose loyalty there could be no question. Air-ships and spaceships had filled the sky. Troops, armed with semi-portables or manning fixed-mount heavy stuff, had covered the grounds. At five minutes before midnight Renwood, accompanied by four secret-service men, had entered the vault, which was thereupon locked by the treasurer. All the cabinet members saw them go in, as did the attendant corps of specially-selected guards. Nevertheless, when the treasurer opened the vault at five minutes after midnight, the five men were gone. No trace of any one of them had been found from that time on.

"And that—every word of it—is TRUE!" the assembled minds yelled as one, all unconsciously, into the mind of the Lensman.

During all this telling Kinnison had been searching mind after mind; inspecting each minutely for the tell-tale marks of mental surgery. He found none. No hypnosis. This thing had actually happened, exactly as they told it. Convinced of that fact, his eyes clouded with foreboding, he sent out his sense of perception and studied the vault itself. Millimeter by cubic millimeter he scanned the inner-most details of its massive structure—the concrete, the neocarballoy, the steel, the heat-conductors and the closely-spaced gas cells. He traced the intricate wiring of the networks of alarms. Everything was sound. Everything functioned. Nothing had been disturbed.

The sun of this system, although rather on the small side, was intensely hot; this planet, Four, was pretty far out. Well beyond Cardynge's Limit. A tube, of course . . . for all the tea in China it had to be a tube.

Kinnison sagged; the indomitable Gray Lensman showed his years and more.

"I know it happened." His voice was grim, quiet, as he spoke to the still protesting men. "I also know how it was done, but that's all."

"HOW?" they demanded, practically in one voice.

"A hyper-spatial tube," and Kinnison went on to explain, as well as he could, the functioning of a thing which was intrinsically beyond the grasp of any non-mathematical three-dimensional mind.

"But what can we or anybody else *do* about it?" the treasurer asked, numbly.

"Nothing whatever." Kinnison's voice was flat. "When it's gone, it's gone. Where does the light go when a lamp goes out? No more trace. Hundreds of millions of planets in this galaxy, as many in the Second. Millions and millions of galaxies. All that in one universe—our own universe. And there are an infinite number—too many to be expressed, let alone to be grasped—of universes, side by side, like pages in a book except thinner, in the hyper-dimension. So you can figure out for yourselves the chances of ever finding either President Renwood or the Boskonians who took him—so close to zero as to be indistinguishable from zero absolute."

The treasurer was crushed. "Do you mean to say that there's no protection at all from this thing? That they can keep on doing away with us just as they please? The nation is going mad, sir, day by day—one more such occurrence and we will be a planet of maniacs."

"Oh, no—I didn't say that." The tension lightened. "Just that we can't do anything about the president and his aides. The tube can be detected while it's in place, and anyone coming through it can be shot as soon as he can be seen. What you need is a couple of Rigellian Lensmen, or Ordoviks. I'll see to it that you get them. I don't think, with them here, they'll even try to repeat." He did not add what he knew somberly to be a fact, that the enemy would go elsewhere, to some other planet not protected by a Lensman able to perceive the intangible structure of a sphere of force.

Frustrated, the Lensman again took to space. It was terrible, this thing of having everything happening where he wasn't and when he got there having nothing left to work on. Hit-and-run—stab-in-the-back—how could a man fight something he couldn't see or sense or feel or find? But this chewing his fingernails to the elbow wasn't getting him anywhere, either; he'd have to find something that he *could* stick a tooth into. What?

All former avenues of approach were blocked; he was sure of that. The Boskonians who were now in charge of things could really think.

No underling would know anything about any one of them except at such times and places as the directors chose, and those conferences would be as nearly detection-proof as they could be made. What to do?

Easy. Catch a big operator in the act. He grinned wryly to himself. Easy to say, but not . . . however, it wasn't impossible. The Boskonians were not super-men—they didn't have any more jets than he did. Put himself in the other fellow's place—what would he do if he were a Boskonian big shot? He had had quite a lot of experience in the role. Were there any specific groups of crimes which revealed techniques similar to those which he himself would use in like case?

He, personally, preferred to work direct and to attack in force. At need, however, he had done a smooth job of boring from within. In the face of the Patrol's overwhelming superiority of armament, especially in the First Galaxy, they would have to bore from within. How? By what means? He was a Lensman; they weren't. Jet black! Or were they, perhaps? How did he know they weren't, by this time? Fossten the renegade Arisian. . . . No use kidding himself; Fossten might have known as much about the Lens as Mentor himself, and might have developed an organization that even Mentor didn't know anything about. Or Mentor might be figuring that it would be good for what ailed a certain fat-headed Gray Lensman to have to dope this out for himself. QX.

He shot a call to Vice-Coordinator Maitland, who was now in complete charge of the office which Kinnison had temporarily abandoned.

"Cliff? Kim. Just gave birth to an idea." He explained rapidly what the idea was. "Maybe nothing to it, but we'd better get up on our toes and find out. You might suggest to the boys that they check up here and there, particularly around the rough spots. If any of them find any trace anywhere of off-color, sour, or even slightly rancid Lensmanship, with or without a Lens appearing in the picture, burn a hole in space getting it to me. QX? . . . Thanks."

Viewed in this new perspective, Renwood of Antigan IV might have been neither a patriot nor a victim, but a saboteur. The tube could have been a prop, used deliberately to cap the mysterious climax. The four honest and devoted guards were the real casualties. Renwood—or whoever he was—having accomplished his object of undermining and destroying the whole planet's morale, might simply have gone elsewhere to continue his nefarious activities. It was fiendishly clever. That spectacularly theatrical finale was certainly one for the book. The whole thing, though, was very much of a piece in quality of workmanship with what he had done in becoming the Tyrant of Thrale. Farfetched? No. He had already denied in his thoughts that the Boskonian operators were super-men. Conversely, he wasn't, either. He would have to admit that they might very well be as good as he was; to deny them the ability to do anything he himself could do would be sheer stupidity.

Where did that put him? On Radelix, by Klono's golden gills! A good-sized planet. Important enough, but not too much so. People human. Comparatively little hell being raised there—yet. Very few Lensmen, and Gerrond the top. Hm . . . m. Gerrond. Not too bright, as Lensmen went, and inclined to be a bit brass-hattish. To Radelix, by all means, next.

He went to Radelix, but not in the *Dauntless* and not in gray. He was a passenger aboard a luxury liner, a writer in search of local color for another saga of the space-ways. Sybly Whyte—one of the Patrol's most carefully-established figments—had a bullet-proof past. His omnivorous interest and his uninhibited nosiness were the natural attributes of his profession—everything is grist which comes to an author's mill.

Sybly Whyte, then, prowled about Radelix. Industriously and, to some observers, pointlessly. He and his red-leather notebook were apt to be seen anywhere at any time, day or night. He visited space-ports, he climbed through freighters, he lost small sums in playing various games of so-called chance in spacemen's dives. On the other hand, he truckled assiduously to the social elite and attended all functions into which he could wangle or could force his way. He made a pest of himself in the offices of politicians, bankers, merchant princes, tycoons of business and manufacture, and all other sorts of greats.

He was stopped one day in the outer office of an industrial potentate. "Get out and stay out," a peg-legged guard told him. "The boss hasn't read any of your stuff, but I have, and neither of us wants to talk to you. Data, huh? What the hell do you need of data on atomic cats and bulldozers to write them damn space-operas of yours? Why don't you get a roustabout job on a freighter and learn something first-handed? Get yourself a space-tan instead of that imitation you got under a lamp; work some of that lard off your carcass!" Whyte was definitely fatter than Kinnison had been; and, somehow, softer; he peered owlishly through heavy lenses which, fortunately, did not interfere with his sense of perception. "Then maybe some of your tripe will be half-fit to read—beat it!"

"Yes, sir. Thank you, sir; very much, sir." Kinnison bobbed obsequiously and scurried out, writing industriously in his notebook the while. He had, however, found out what he wanted to know. The boss was nobody he wanted.

Nor was an eminent statesman whom he button-holed at a reception. "I fail to see, sir, entirely, any point in your interviewing *me*," that worthy informed him, frigidly. "I am not, I am—uh—sure, suitable material for any opus upon which you may be at work."

"Oh, you can't ever tell, sir," Kinnison said. "You see, I never know who or what is going to get into any of my stories until after I start to write it, and sometimes not even then." The statesman glared and Kinnison retreated in disorder.

To stay in character Kinnison actually wrote a novel; it was later acclaimed as one of Sybly Whyte's best.

"Qadgop the Mercotan slithered flatly around the after-bulge of the tranship. One claw dug into the meters-thick armor of pure neutronium, then another. Its terrible xmex-like snout locked on. Its zymolosely polydactile tongue crunched out, crashed down, rasped across. *Slurp! Slurp!* At each abrasive stroke the groove in the tranship's plating deepened and Qadgop leered more fiercely. Fools! Did they think that the airlessness of absolute space, the heatlessness of absolute zero, the yieldlessness of absolute neutronium, could stop QADGOP THE MERCOTAN? And the stowaway, that human wench Cynthia, cowering in helpless terror just beyond this thin and fragile wall . . ." Kinnison was taping verbosely along when his first real clue developed.

A yellow "attention" light gleamed upon his visiphone panel, a subdued chime gave notice that a message of importance was about to be broadcast to the world. Kinnison-Whyte flipped his switch and the stern face of the provost-marshal appeared upon the screen.

"Attention, please," the image spoke. "Every citizen of Radelix is urged to be on the lookout for the source of certain inflammatory and subversive literature which is beginning to appear in various cities of this planet. Our officers cannot be everywhere at once; you citizens are. It is hoped that by the aid of your vigilance this threat to our planetary peace and security can be removed before it becomes really serious; that we can avoid the imposition of martial law."

This message, while not of extreme or urgent import to most Radeligians, held for Kinnison a profound and unique meaning. He was right. He had deduced the thing one hundred percent. He knew what was going to happen next, and how; he knew that neither the law-enforcement officers of Radelix nor its massed citizenry could stop it. They could not even impede it. A force of Lensmen could stop it—but that would not get the Patrol anywhere unless they could capture or kill the beings really responsible for what was done. To alarm them would not do.

Whether or not he could do much of anything before the grand climax depended on a lot of factors. On what that climax was; who was threatened with what; whether or not the threatened one was actually a Boskonian. A great deal of investigation was indicated.

If the enemy were going to repeat, as seemed probable, the president would be the victim. If he, Kinnison, could not get the big shots lined up before the plot came to a head, he would have to let it develop right up to the point of disappearance; and for Whyte to appear at that time would be to attract undesirable attention. No—by that time he must already have been kicking around underfoot long enough to have become an unnoticeable fixture.

Wherefore he moved into quarters as close to the executive offices as he could possibly get; and in those quarters he worked openly and wordily at the bringing of the affair of Qadgop and the beautiful-but-dumb Cynthia to a satisfactory conclusion.

4

NADRECK OF PALAIN VII AT WORK

In order to understand these and subsequent events it is necessary to cut back briefly some twenty-odd years, to the momentous interview upon chill, dark Onlo between monstrous Kandron and his superior in affairs Boskonian, the unspeakable Alcon, the Tyrant of Thrale. At almost the end of that interview, when Kandron had suggested the possibility that his own base had perhaps been vulnerable to Star A Star's insidious manipulations:

"Do you mean to admit that *you* may have been invaded and searched—tracelessly?" Alcon fairly shrieked the thought.

"Certainly," Kandron replied, coldly. "While I do not believe that it has been done, the possibility must be conceded. What science can devise science can circumvent. It is not Onlo and I who are their prime objectives, you must realize, but Thrale and you. Especially you."

"You may be right. With no data whatever upon who or what Star A Star really is, with no tenable theory as to how he could have done what actually has been done, speculation is idle." Thus Alcon ended the conversation and, almost immediately, went back to Thrale.

After the Tyrant's departure Kandron continued to think, and the more he thought the more uneasy he became. It was undoubtedly true that Alcon and Thrale were the Patrol's prime objectives. But, those objectives attained, was it reasonable to suppose that he and Onlo would be spared?

It was not. Should he warn Alcon further? He should not. If the Tyrant, after all that had been said, could not see the danger he was in, he wasn't worth saving. If he preferred to stay and fight it out, that was his lookout. Kandron would take no chances with his own extremely valuable life.

Should he warn his own men? How could he? They were able and hardened fighters all; no possible warning could make them defend their fortresses and their lives any more efficiently than they were already prepared to do; nothing he could say would be of any use in preparing them for a threat whose basic nature, even, was completely unknown. Furthermore, this hypothetical invasion probably had not happened and very well might not happen at all, and to flee from an imaginary foe would not redound to his credit.

No. As a personage of large affairs, not limited to Onlo, he would be called elsewhere. He would stay elsewhere until after whatever was going to happen had happened. If nothing happened during the ensuing few weeks he would return from his official trip and all would be well.

He inspected Onlo thoroughly, he cautioned his officers repeatedly and insistently to keep alert against every conceivable emergency while he was so unavoidably absent. Then he departed, with a fleet of vessels manned by handpicked crews, to a long-prepared and hitherto secret retreat.

From that safe place he watched, through the eyes and the instruments of his skilled observers, everything that occurred. Thrale fell, and Onlo. The Patrol triumphed. Then, knowing the full measure of the disaster and accepting it with the grim passivity so characteristic of his breed, Kandron broadcast certain signals and one of his—and Alcon's—superiors got in touch with him. He reported concisely. They conferred. He was given orders which were to keep him busy for over twenty Tellurian years.

He knew now that Onlo had been invaded, tracelessly, by some feat of mentality beyond comprehension and almost beyond belief. Onlo had fallen without any of its defenders having energized a single one of their gigantic engines of war. The fall of Thrale, and the manner of that fall's accomplishment, were plain enough. Human stuff. The work, undoubtedly, of human Lensmen; perhaps the work of the human Lensman who was so frequently associated with Star A Star.

But Onlo! Kandron himself had set those snares along those intricately zig-zagged communications lines; he knew their capabilities. Kandron himself had installed Onlo's blocking and shielding screens; he knew their might. He knew, since no other path existed leading to Thrale, that those lines had been followed and those screens had been penetrated, and all without setting off a single alarm. Those things had actually happened.

Hence Kandron set his stupendous mind to the task of envisaging what the being must be, mentally, who could do them; what the mind of this Star A Star—it could have been no one else—must in actuality be.

He succeeded. He deduced Nadreck of Palain VII, practically in toto; and for the Star A Star thus envisaged he set traps throughout both galaxies. They might or might not kill him. Killing him immediately, however, was not really of the essence; that matter could wait until he could give it his personal attention. The important thing was to see to it that Star A Star could never, by any possible chance, discover a true lead to any high Boskonian.

Sneeringly, gloatingly, Kandron issued orders; then flung himself with all his zeal and ability into the task of reorganizing the shattered fragments of the Boskonian Empire into a force capable of wrecking Civilization.

Thus it is not strange that for more than twenty years Nadreck of Palain VII made very little progress indeed. Time after time he grazed the hot edge of death. Indeed, it was only by the exertion of his every iota of skill, power, and callous efficiency that he managed to survive. He struck a few telling blows for Civilization, but most of the time he was strictly on the defensive. Every clue he followed, it seemed, led subtly into a trap; every course he pursued ended, always figuratively and all too often literally, in a cul-de-sac filled with semi-portable projectors all agog to blast him out of the ether.

Year by year he became more conscious of some imperceptible, undetectable, but potent foe, an individual enemy obstructing his every move and determined to make an end of him. And year by year, as material accumulated, it became more and more certain that the inimical entity was in fact Kandron, once of Onlo.

When Kit went into space, then, and Kinnison called Nadreck into consultation, the usually reticent and unloquacious Palainian was ready to talk. He told the Gray Lensman everything he knew and everything he deduced or suspected about the ex-Onlonian chieftain.

"Kandron of Onlo!" Kinnison exploded, so violently as to sear the sub-ether through which the thought passed. "Holy Klono's gadolinium guts! And you can sit there on your spiny tokus and tell me Kandron got away from you back there? You knew it, and not only didn't do a damn thing about it yourself, but didn't even tell me or anybody else about it so we could do it? *What* a brain!"

"Certainly. Why do anything before action becomes necessary?" Nadreck was entirely unmoved by the Tellurian's passion. "My powers are admittedly small, my intellect feeble. However, even to me it was clear then and it is clear now that Kandron was then of no importance. My assignment was to reduce Onlo. I reduced it. Whether or not Kandron was there at the time did not then have and cannot now have anything to do with that task. Kandron, personally, is another, an entirely distinct problem."

Kinnison swore a blistering deep-space oath; then, by main strength, shut himself up. Nadreck wasn't human; there was no use even trying to judge him by human or near-human standards. He was fundamentally, incomprehensibly, and radically different. And it was just as well for humanity that he was. For if his hellishly able race had possessed the characteristically human abilities, in addition to their own, Civilization would of necessity have been basically Palainian instead of basically human, as it now is. "QX, ace," he growled, finally. "Skip it."

"But Kandron has been hampering my activities for years, and, now that you also have become interested in his operations, he has become a factor of which cognizance should be taken," Nadreck went imperturbably on. He could no more understand Kinnison's viewpoint than the Tellurian could understand his. "With your permission, therefore, I shall find—and slay—this Kandron."

"Go to it, little chum," Kinnison sighed, bitingly—and uselessly. "Clear ether."

While this conference was taking place, Kandron reclined in a bitterly cold, completely un-lighted room of his headquarters and indulged in a little gloating concerning the predicament in which he was keeping Nadreck of Palain VII, who was, in all probability, the once-dreaded Star A Star of the Galactic Patrol. It was true that the Lensman was still alive. He would probably, Kandron mused quite pleasurably, remain alive until he himself could find the time to attend to him in person. He was an able operator, but one presenting no real menace, now that he was known and understood. There were other things more pressing, just as there had been ever since the fall of Thrale. The revised Plan was going nicely, and as soon as he had resolved that human thing . . . The Ploorans had suggested . . . could it be possible, after all, that Nadreck of Palain was not he who had been known so long only as Star A Star? That the human factor was actually . . . ?

Through the operation of some unknowable sense Kandron knew that it was time for his aide to be at hand to report upon those human affairs. He sent out a signal and another Onlonian scuttled in.

"That unknown human element," Kandron radiated harshly. "I assume that you are not reporting that it has been resolved?"

"Sorry, Supremacy, but your assumption is correct," the creature radiated back, in no very conciliatory fashion. "The trap at Antigan IV was set particularly for him; specifically to match the man whose mentality you computed and diagrammed for us. Was it too obvious, think you, Supremacy? Or perhaps not quite obvious enough? Or, the galaxy being large, is it perhaps that he simply did not learn of it in time? In the next attempt, what degree of obviousness should I employ and what degree of repetition is desirable?

"The technique of the Antigan affair was flawless," Kandron decided. "He did not learn of it, as you suggest, or we should have caught him. He is a master workman, always concealed by his very obviousness until after he has done his work. Thus we can never, save by merest chance, catch him before the act; we must make him come to us. We must keep on trying until he does come to us. It is of no great moment, really, whether we catch him now or five years hence. This work must be done in any event—it is simply a fortunate coincidence that the necessary destruction of Civilization upon its own planets presents such a fine opportunity of trapping him.

"As to repeating the Antigan technique, we should not repeat it exactly—or, hold! It might be best to do just that. To repeat a process is, of course, the mark of an inferior mind; but if that human can be made to believe that our minds are inferior, so much the better. Keep on trying; report as instructed. Remember that he must be taken alive, so that we can take from his living brain the secrets we have not yet been able to learn. Forget, in the instant of leaving this room, everything about me and about any connection between us until I force recollection upon you. Go."

The minion went, and Kandron set out to do more of the things which he could best do. He would have liked to take Nadreck's trail himself; he could catch and he could kill that evasive entity and the task would have been a pleasant one. He would have liked to supervise the trapping of that enigmatic human Lensman who might—or might not—be that frequently and copiously damned Star A Star. That, too, would be an eminently pleasant chore. There were, however, other matters more pressing by far. If the Great Plan were to succeed, and it absolutely must and would, every Boskonian must perform his assigned duties. Nadreck and his putative accomplice were side issues. Kandron's task was to set up and to direct certain psychoses and disorders; a ghastly train of mental ills of which he possessed such supreme mastery, and which were surely and safely helping to destroy the foundation upon which Galactic Civilization rested. That part was his, and he would do it to the best of his ability. The other things, the personal and non-essential matters, could wait.

Kandron set out then, and traveled fast and far; and wherever he went there spread still further abroad the already widespread blight. A disgusting, a horrible blight with which no human physician or psychiatrist, apparently, could cope; one of, perhaps the worst of, the corrosive blights which had been eating so long at Civilization's vitals.

And L2 Nadreck, having decided to find and slay the ex-ruler of Onlo, went about it in his usual unhurried but eminently thorough fashion. He made no effort to locate him or to trace him personally. That would be bad—foolish. Worse, it would be inefficient. Worst, it would probably be impossible. No, he would find out where Kandron would be at some suitable future time, and wait for him there.

To that end Nadreck collected a vast mass of data concerning the occurrences and phenomena which the Big Four had discussed so thoroughly. He analyzed each item, sorting out those which bore the characteristic stamp of the arch-foe whom by now he had come to know so well. The internal evidence of Kandron's craftsmanship was unmistakable; and, not now to his surprise, Nadreck discerned that the number of the Onlonian's dark deeds was legion.

There was the affair of the Prime Minister of DeSilva III, who at a cabinet meeting shot and killed his sovereign and eleven chiefs of state before committing suicide. The president of Viridon; who, at his press conference, ran amuck with a scimitar snatched from a wall, hewed unsuspecting reporters to gory bits until overpowered, and then swallowed poison.

A variant of the theme, but still plainly Kandron's doing, was the interesting episode in which a Tellurian tycoon named Edmundson, while upon an ocean voyage, threw fifteen women passengers overboard, then leaped after them dressed only in a life-jacket stuffed with lead. Another out of the same whimsical mold was that of Dillway, the highly respected operations chief of Central Spaceways. That potentate called his secretaries one by one into his 60th floor office and unconcernedly tossed them, one by one, out of the window. He danced a jig on the coping before diving after them to the street.

A particularly juicy and entertaining bit, Nadreck thought, was the case of Narkor Base Hospital, in which four of the planet's most eminent surgeons decapitated every other person in the place—patients, nurses, orderlies, and all, with a fine disregard of age, sex, or condition—arranged the severed heads, each upright and each facing due north, upon the tiled floor to spell the word "Revenge," and then hacked each other to death with scalpels.

These, and a thousand or more other events of similar technique, Nadreck tabulated and subjected to statistical analysis. Scattered so widely throughout such a vast volume of space, they had created little or no general disturbance; indeed, they had scarcely been noticed by Civilization as a whole. Collected, they made a truly staggering, a revolting and appalling total. Nadreck, however, was inherently incapable of being staggered, revolted, or appalled. That repulsive summation, a thing which in its massed horror would have shaken to the core any being possessing any shred of sympathy or tenderness, was to Nadreck an interesting and not too difficult problem in psychology and mathematics.

He placed each episode in space and in time, correlating each with all of its fellows in a space-time matrix. He determined the locus of centers and derived the equations of its most probable motion. He extended it by extrapolation in accordance with that equation. Then, assuring himself that his margin of error was as small as he could make it, he set out for a planet which Kandron would most probably visit at a time far enough in the future to enable him to prepare to receive the Onlonian.

That planet, being inhabited by near-human beings, was warm, brightly sun-lit, and had an atmosphere rich in oxygen. Nadreck detested it, since his ideal of a planet was precisely the opposite. Fortunately, however, he would not have to land upon it until after Kandron's arrival—possibly not then—and the fact that his proposed quarry was, like himself, a frigid-blooded poison-breather, made the task of detection a simple one.

Nadreck set his undetectable speedster into a circular orbit around the planet, far enough out to be comfortable, and sent out course after course of delicate, extremely sensitive screen. Precision of pattern-analysis was of course needless. The probability was that all legitimate movement of personnel to and from the planet would be composed of warm-blooded oxygen-breathers; that any visitor not so classified would be Kandron. Any frigid blooded visitor had at least to be investigated, hence his analytical screens had to be capable only of differentiation between two types of beings as far apart as the galactic poles in practically every respect. Nadreck knew that no supervision would be necessary to perform such an open-and-shut separation as that; he would have nothing more to do until his electronic announcers should warn him of Kandron's approach—or until the passage of time should inform him that the Onlonian was not coming to this particular planet.

Being a mathematician, Nadreck knew that any datum secured by extrapolation is of doubtful value. He thus knew that the actual probability of Kandron's coming was less, by some indeterminable amount, than the mathematical one. Nevertheless, having done all that he could do, he waited with the monstrous, unhuman patience known only to such races as his.

Day by day, week by week, the speedster circled the planet and its big, hot sun; and as it circled, the lone voyager studied. He analyzed more data more precisely; he drew deeper and deeper upon his store of knowledge to determine what steps next to take in the event that this attempt should end, as so many previous ones had ended, in failure.

5

THE ABDUCTION OF A PRESIDENT

Kinnison the Author toiled manfully at his epic of space whenever he was under any sort of observation, and enough at other times to avert any suspicion. Indeed, he worked as much as Sybly Whyte, an advertisedly temperamental writer, had ever worked. Besides interviewing the high and the low, and taking notes everywhere, he attended authors' teas, at which he cursed his characters fluently and bitterly for their failure to cooperate with him. With short-haired women and long-haired men he bemoaned the perversity of a public which compelled them to prostitute the real genius of which each was the unique possessor. He sympathized particularly with a fat woman writer of whodunits, whose extremely unrealistic yet amazingly popular Gray Lensman hero had lived through ten full-length novels and twenty million copies.

Even though her real field was the drama, she wasn't writing the kind of detective tripe that most of these crankturners ground out, she confided to Kinnison. She had known lots of Gray Lensmen *very* intimately, and *her* stories were drawn from real life in every particular!

Thus Kinnison remained in character; and thus he was enabled to work completely unnoticed at his real job of finding out what was going on, how the Boskonians were operating to ruin Radelix as they had ruined Antigan IV.

His first care was to investigate the planet's president. That took doing, but he did it. He examined that mind line by line and channel by channel, with no results whatever. No scars, no sign of tampering. Calling in assistance, he searched the president's past. Still no soap. Everything checked. Boring from within, then, was out. His first hypothesis was wrong; this invasion and this sabotage were being done from without. How?

Those first leaflets were followed by others, each batch more vitriolic in tone than the preceding one. Apparently they came from empty stratosphere; at least, no ships were to be detected in the neighborhood after any shower of the handbills had appeared. But that was not surprising. With its inertialess drive any space-ship could have been parsecs away before the papers touched atmosphere. Or they could have been bombed in from almost any distance. Or, as Kinnison thought most reasonable, they could have been simply dumped out of the mouth of a hyper-spatial tube. In any event the method was immaterial. The results only were important; and those results, the Lensman discovered, were entirely disproportionate to the ostensible causes. The subversive literature had some effect, of course, but essentially it must be a blind. No possible tonnage of anonymous printing could cause that much sheer demoralization.

Crack pot societies of all kinds sprang up everywhere, advocating everything from absolutism to anarchy. Queer cults arose, preaching free love, the imminent end of the world, and many other departures from the norm of thought. The Author's League, of course, was affected more than any other organization of its size, because of its relatively large content of strong and intensely opinionated minds. Instead of becoming one radical group it split into a dozen.

Kinnison joined one of those "Down with Everything!" groups, not as a leader, but as a follower. Not too sheep-like a follower, but just inconspicuous enough to retain his invisibly average status; and from his place of concealment in the middle of the front row he studied the minds of each of his fellow anarchists. He watched those minds change, he found out who was doing the changing. When Kinnison's turn came he was all set for trouble. He expected to battle a powerful mentality. He would not have been overly surprised to encounter another mad Arisian, hiding behind a zone of hypnotic compulsion. He expected anything, in fact, except what he found—which was a very ordinary Radeligian therapist. The guy was a clever enough operator, of course, but he could not work against even the feeblest opposition. Hence the Gray Lensman had no trouble at all, either in learning everything the fellow knew, or, upon leaving him, in implanting within his mind the knowledge that Sybly Whyte was now exactly the type of worker desired.

The trouble was that the therapist didn't know a thing. This not entirely unexpected development posed Kinnison three questions. Did the high-ups ever communicate with such small fry, or did they just give them one set of orders and cut them loose? Should he stay in this Radeligian's mind until he found out? If he was in control of the therapist when a big shot took over, did he have jets enough to keep from being found out? Risky business; better scout around first, anyway. He'd do a flit.

He drove his black speedster a million miles. He covered Radelix like a blanket, around the equator and from pole to pole. Everywhere he found the same state of things. The planet was literally riddled with the agitators; he found so many that he was forced to a black conclusion. There could be no connection or communication between such numbers of saboteurs and any real authority. They must have been given one set of do-or-die instructions—whether they did or died was immaterial. Experimentally, Kinnison had a few of the leaders taken into custody. Nothing happened.

Martial law was finally declared, but this measure succeeded only in driving the movement underground. What the subversive societies lost in numbers they more than made up in desperation and violence. Crime raged unchecked and uncheckable, murder became an every-day commonplace, insanity waxed rife. And Kinnison, knowing now that no channel to important prey would be opened until the climax, watched grimly while the rape of the planet went on.

President Thompson and Lensman Gerrond sent message after message to Prime Base and to Klovia, imploring help. The replies to these pleas were all alike. The matter had been referred to the galactic council and to the coordinator. Everything that could be done was being done. Neither office would say anything else, except that, with the galaxy in such a disturbed condition, each planet must do its best to solve its own problems.

The thing built up toward its atrocious finale. Gerrond invited the president to a conference in a down-town hotel room, and there, eyes glancing from moment to moment at the dials of a complete little test-kit held open upon his lap:

"I have just had some startling news, Mr. Thompson," Gerrond said, abruptly. "Kinnison has been here on Radelix for weeks."

"What? Kinnison? Where is he? Why didn't he . . . ?"

"Yes, Kinnison. Kinnison of Klovia. The coordinator himself. I don't know where he is, or was. I didn't ask him." The Lensman smiled fleetingly. "One doesn't, you know. He discussed the situation with me at length. I'm still amazed . . ."

"Why doesn't he stop it, then?" the president demanded. "Or can't he stop it?"

"That's what I've got to explain to you. He won't be able to do a thing, he says, until the last minute . . ."

"Why not? I tell you, if this thing can be stopped it's *got* to be stopped, and no matter what has to be done—"

"Just a minute!" Gerrond snapped. "I know you're out of control—I don't like to see Radelix torn apart any better than you do—but you ought to know by this time that Galactic Coordinator Kimball Kinnison is in a better position to know what to do than any other man in the universe. Furthermore, his word is the last word. What he says, goes."

"Of course," Thompson apologized. "I am overwrought . . . but to see our entire world pulled down around us, our institutions, the work of centuries, destroyed, millions of lives lost . . . all needlessly . . ."

"It won't come to that; he says, if we all do our parts. And you, sir, are very much in the picture."

"I? How?"

"Are you familiar with what happened to Antigan IV?"

"Why, no. They had some trouble over there, I recall, but . . ."

"That's it. That's why this must go on. No planet cares particularly about what happens to any other planet, but Kinnison cares about them all as a whole. If this trouble is headed off now it will simply spread to other planets; if it is allowed to come to a climax there's a chance to put an end to the whole trouble, for good."

"But what has that to do with me? What can I, personally, do?"

"Much. The last act at Antigan IV, the thing that made it a planet of maniacs, was the kidnapping of Planetary President Renwood. Murdered, supposedly, since no trace of him has been found."

"Oh." The older man's hands clenched, then loosened. "I am willing . . . provided . . . is Kinnison fairly certain that my death will enable him . . ."

"It won't get that far, sir. He intends to stop it just before that. He and his associates—I don't know who they are—have been listing every enemy agent they can find, and they will all be taken care of at once. He believes that Boskone will publish in advance a definite time at which they will take you away from us. That was the way it went at Antigan."

"Even from the Patrol?"

"From the main base itself. Coordinator Kinnison is pretty sure they can do it, except for something he can bring into play only at the last moment. Incidentally, that's why we're having this meeting here, with this detector he gave me. He's afraid this base is porous."

"In that case . . . what can he . . ." The president fell silent.

"All I know is that we're to dress you in a certain suit of armor and have you in my private office a few minutes before the time they set. We and the guards leave the office at minus two minutes and walk down the corridor, just fast enough to be exactly in front of Room Twenty-four at minus one. We're to rehearse it until our timing is perfect. I don't know what will happen then, but *something* will."

Time passed; the Boskonian infiltration progressed according to plan. It appeared that Radelix was going in the same fashion in which Antigan IV had gone. Below the surface, however, there was one great difference. Every ship reaching Radelix brought at least one man who did not leave. Some of these visitors were tall and lithe, some were short and fat. Some were old, some were young. Some were pale, some were burned to the color of ancient leather by the fervent rays of space. They were alike only in the "look of eagles" in their steady, quiet eyes. Each landed and went about his ostensible business, interesting himself not at all in any of the others.

Again the Boskonians declared their contempt of the Patrol by setting the exact time at which Planetary President Thompson was to be taken. Again the appointed hour was midnight.

Lieutenant-admiral Lensman Gerrond was, as Kinnison had intimated frequently, somewhat of a brass hat. He did not, he simply could not believe that his base was as pregnable as the coordinator had assumed it to be. Kinnison, knowing that all ordinary defenses would be useless, had not even mentioned them. Gerrond, unable to believe that his hitherto invincible and invulnerable weapons and defenses were all of a sudden useless, mustered them of his own volition.

All leaves had been cancelled. Every detector, every beam, every device of defense and offense was fully manned. Every man was keyed up and alert. And Gerrond, while apprehensive that something was about to happen which wasn't in the book, was pretty sure in his stout old war-dog's soul that he and his men had stuff enough.

At two minutes before midnight the armored president and his escorts left Gerrond's office. One minute later they were passing the door of the specified room. A bomb exploded shatteringly behind them, armored men rushed yelling out of a branch corridor in their rear. Everybody stopped and turned to look. So, the hidden Kinnison assured himself, did an unseen observer in an invisible hovering, three-dimensional hyper-circle.

Kinnison threw the door open, flashed an explanatory thought at the president, yanked him into the room and into the midst of a corps of Lensmen armed with devices not usually encountered even in Patrol bases. The door snapped shut and Kinnison stood where Thompson had stood an instant before, clad in armor identical with that which the president had worn. The exchange had required less than one second.

"QX, Gerrond and you fellows!" Kinnison drove the thought. "The president is safe—I'm taking over. Double time straight ahead—hipe! Get clear—give us a chance to use our stuff!"

The unarmored men broke into a run, and as they did so the door of Room Twenty-four swung open and stayed open. Weapons erupted from other doors and from more branch corridors. The hyper-circle, which was in fact the terminus of a hyper-spatial tube, began to thicken toward visibility.

It did not, however, materialize. Only by the intensest effort of vision could it be discerned as the sheerest wisp, more tenuous than fog. The men within the ship, if ship it was, were visible only as striations in air are visible, and no more to be made out in detail. Instead of a full materialization, the only thing that was or became solid was a dead-black thing which reached purposefully outward and downward toward Kinnison, a thing combined of tongs and coarse-meshed, heavy net.

Kinnison's DeLameters flamed at maximum intensity and minimum aperture. Useless. The stuff was dureum; that unbelievably dense and ultimately refractory synthetic which, saturated with pure force, is the only known substance which can exist as an actuality both in normal space and in that pseudo-space which composes the hyper-spatial tube. The Lensman flicked on his neutralizer and shot away inertialess; but that maneuver, too, had been foreseen. The Boskonian engineers matched every move he made, within a split second after he made it; the tong-net closed.

Semi-portables flamed then—heavy stuff—but they might just as well have remained cold. Their beams could not cut the dureum linkages; they slid harmlessly *past*—not through—the wraith-like, figmental invaders at whom they were aimed. Kinnison was hauled aboard the Boskonian vessel; its structure and its furnishings and its crew becoming ever firmer and more substantial to his senses as he went from normal into pseudo space.

As the pseudo world became real, the reality of the base behind him thinned into unreality. In seconds it disappeared utterly, and Kinnison knew that to the senses of his fellow human beings he had simply vanished. This ship, though, was real enough. So were his captors.

The net opened, dumping the Lensman ignominiously to the floor. Tractor beams wrenched his blazing DeLameters out of his grasp—

whether or not hands and arms came with them was entirely his own look-out. Tractors and pressors jerked him upright, slammed him against the steel wall of the room, held him motionless against it.

Furiously he launched his ultimately lethal weapon, the Worsel-designed, Thorndyke-built, mind-controlled projector of thought-borne vibrations which decomposed the molecules without which thought and life itself could not exist. Nothing happened. He explored, finding that even his sense of perception was stopped a full foot away from every part of every one of those humanoid bodies. He settled down then and thought. A great light dawned; a shock struck sickeningly home.

No such elaborate and super-powered preparations would have been made for the capture of any civilian. Presidents were old men, physically weak and with no extraordinary powers of mind. No—this whole chain of events had been according to plan—a high Boskonian's plan. Ruining a planet was, of course, a highly desirable thing in itself, but it could not have been the main feature.

Somebody with a real brain was out after the four Second Stage Lensmen and he wasn't fooling. And if Nadreck, Worsel, Tregonsee and himself were all to disappear, the Patrol would know that it had been nudged. But jet back—which of the four other than himself would have taken that particular bait? Not one of them. Weren't they out after them, too? Sure they were—they must be. Oh, if he could only warn them—but after all, what good would it do? They had all warned each other repeatedly to watch out for traps; all four had been constantly on guard. What possible foresight could have avoided a snare set so perfectly to match every detail of a man's make-up?

But he wasn't licked yet. They had to know what he knew, how he had done what he had done, whether or not he had any superiors and who they were. Therefore they had had to take him alive, just as he had had to take various Boskonian chiefs. And they'd find out that as long as he was alive he'd be a dangerous buzz-saw to monkey with.

The captain, or whoever was in charge, would send for him; that was a foregone conclusion. He'd have to find out what he had caught; he'd have to make a report of some kind. And somebody would slip. One hundred percent vigilance was impossible, and Kinnison would be on his toes to take advantage of that slip, however slight it might be.

But the captors did not take Kinnison to the captain. Instead, accompanied by half a dozen unarmored men, that worthy came to Kinnison.

"Start talking, fellow, and talk fast," the Boskonian directed crisply in the lingua franca of deep space as the armored soldiers strode out. "I want to know who you are, what you are, what you've done, and everything about you and the Patrol. So talk—or do you want me to pull you apart with these tractors, armor and all?"

Kinnison paid no attention, but drove at the commander with his every mental force and weapon. Blocked. This ape too had a full-body, full-coverage screen.

There was a switch at the captain's hip, handy for fingertip control. If he could only move! It would be *so* easy to flip that switch! Or if he could throw something—or make one of those other fellows brush against him just right—or if the guy happened to sit down a little too close to the arm of a chair—or if there were a pet animal of any kind around—or a spider or a worm or even a gnat . . .

6

TREGONSEE, CAMILLA, AND "X"

Second-Stage Lensman Tregonsee of Rigel IV did not rush madly out into space in quest of something or anything Boskonian in response to Kinnison's call. To hurry was not Tregonsee's way. He could move fast upon occasion, but before he would move at all he had to know exactly how, where, and why he should move.

He conferred with his three fellows, he furnished them with all the data he possessed, he helped integrate the totaled facts into one composite. That composite pleased the others well enough so that they went to work, each in his own fashion, but it did not please Tregonsee. He could not visualize any coherent whole from the available parts. Therefore, while Kinnison was investigating the fall of Antigan IV, Tregonsee was sitting—or rather, standing—still and thinking. He was still standing still and thinking when Kinnison went to Radelix.

Finally he called in an assistant to help him think. He had more respect for the opinions of Camilla Kinnison than for those of any other entity, outside of Arisia, of the two galaxies. He had helped train all five of the Kinnison children, and in Cam he had found a kindred soul. Possessing a truer sense of values than any of his fellows, he alone realized that the pupils had long since passed their tutors; and it is a measure of his quality that the realization brought into Tregonsee's tranquil soul no tinge of rancor, but only wonder. What those incredible

Children of the Lens had he did not know, but he knew that they—particularly Camilla—had extraordinary gifts.

In the mind of this scarcely-grown woman he perceived depths which he could not plumb, extensions and vistas the meanings of which he could not even vaguely grasp. He did not try either to plumb the abysses or to survey the expanses; he made no slightest effort, ever, to take from any of the children anything which the child did not first offer to reveal. In his own mind he tried to classify theirs; but, realizing in the end that that task was and always would be beyond his power, he accepted the fact as calmly as he accepted the numberless others of Nature's inexplicable facts. Tregonsee came the closest of any Second-Stage Lensman to the real truth, but even he never did suspect the existence of the Eddorians.

Camilla, as quiet as her twin sister Constance was boisterous, parked her speedster in one of the capacious holds of the Rigellian's space-ship and joined him in the control room.

"You believe, I take it, that dad's logic is faulty, his deductions erronous?" the girl thought; after a casual greeting. "I'm not surprised. So do I. He jumped at conclusions. But then, he does that, you know."

"Oh, I wouldn't say that, exactly. However, it seems to me," Tregonsee replied carefully, "that he did not have sufficient basis in fact to form any definite conclusion as to whether or not Renwood of Antigan was a Boskonian operative. It is that point which I wish to discuss with you first."

Cam concentrated. "I don't see that it makes any difference, fundamentally, whether he was or not," she decided, finally. "A difference in method only, not in motivation. Interesting, perhaps, but immaterial. It is virtually certain in either case that Kandron of Onlo or some other entity is the prime force and is the one who must be destroyed."

"Of course, my dear, but that is only the first differential. How about the second, and the third? Method governs. Nadreck, concerning himself only with Kandron, tabulated and studied only the Kandronesque manifestations. He may—probably will—eliminate Kandron. It is by no means assured, however, that that step will be enough. In fact, from my preliminary study, I would risk a small wager that the larger and worse aspects would remain untouched. I would therefore suggest that we ignore, for the time being, Nadreck's findings and examine anew all the data available."

"I wouldn't bet you a millo on that." Camilla caught her lower lip between white, even teeth. "Check. The probability is that Renwood was a loyal citizen. Let us consider every possible argument for and against that assumption . . ."

They went into contact of minds so close that the separate thoughts simply could not be resolved into terms of speech. They remained that way, not for the period of a few minutes which would have exhaused any ordinary brain, but for four solid hours; and at the end of that conference they had arrived at a few tentative conclusions.

Kinnison had said that there was no possibility of tracing a hyperspatial tube after it had ceased to exist. There were millions of planets in the two galaxies. There was an indefinite, quite possibly an infinite number of co-existent parallel spaces, into any one of which the tube might have led. Knowing these things, Kinnison had decided that the probability was infinitesimally small that any successful investigation could be made along those lines.

Tregonsee and Camilla, starting with the same facts, arrived at entirely different results. There were many spaces, true, but the inhabitants of any one space belonged to that space and would not be interested in the conquest or the permanent taking over of any other. Foreign spaces, then, need not be considered. Civilization had only one significant enemy; Boskonia. Boskonia, then, captained possibly by Kandron of Onlo, was the attacker. The tube itself could not be traced and there were millions of planets, yes, but those facts were not pertinent.

Why not? Because "X," who might or might not be Kandron, was not operating from a fixed headquarters, receiving reports from subordinates who did the work. A rigid philosophical analysis, of which few other minds would have been capable, showed that "X" was doing the work himself, and was moving from solar system to solar system to do it. Those mass psychoses in which entire garrisons went mad all at once, those mass hysterias in which vast groups of civilians went reasonlessly out of control, could not have been brought about by an ordinary mind. Of all Civilization, only Nadreck of Palain VII had the requisite ability; was it reasonable to suppose that Boskonia had many such minds? No. "X" was either singular or a small integer.

Which? Could they decide the point? With some additional data, they could. Their linked minds went en rapport with Worsel, with Nadreck, with Kinnison, and with the Principal Statistician at Prime Base.

In addition to Nadreck's locus, they determined two more—one of all inimical manifestations, the other of those which Nadreck had not used in his computations. Their final exhaustive analysis showed that there were at least two, and very probably only two, prime intelligences directing those Boskonian activities. They made no attempt to identify either of them. They communicated to Nadreck their results and their conclusions.

"I am working on Kandron," the Palainian replied, flatly. "I made no assumptions as to whether or not there were other prime movers at work, since the point has no bearing. Your information is interesting, and may perhaps prove valuable, and I thank you for it—but my present assignment is to find and to kill Kandron of Onlo."

Tregonsee and Camilla, then, set out to find "X"; not any definite actual or deduced entity, but the perpetrator of certain closely related and highly characteristic phenomena, viz, mass psychoses and mass hysterias. Nor did they extrapolate. They visited the last few planets which had been affected, in the order in which the attacks occurred. They studied every phase of every situation. They worked slowly, but—they hoped and they believed—surely. Neither of them had any idea then that behind "X" lay Ploor, and beyond Ploor, Eddore.

Having examined the planet latest to be stricken, they made no effort to pick out definitely the one next to be attacked. It might be any one of ten worlds, or possibly even twelve. Hence, neglecting entirely the mathematical and logical probabilities involved, they watched them all, each taking six. Each flitted from world to world, with senses alert to perceive the first sign of subversive activity. Tregonsee was a retired magnate, spending his declining years in seeing the galaxy. Camilla was a Tellurian business girl on vacation.

Young, beautiful, innocent-looking girls who traveled alone were, then as ever, regarded as fair game by the Dons Juan of any given human world. Scarcely had Camilla registered at the Hotel Grande when a well-groomed, self-satisfied man-about-town made an approach.

"Hel-lo, beautiful! Remember me, don't you—old Tom Thomas? What say we split a bottle of fayalin, to renew old . . ." He broke off, for the red-headed eyeful's reaction was in no sense orthodox. She was not coldly unaware of his presence. She was neither coy nor angry, neither fearful nor scornful. She was only and vastly *amused*.

"You think, then, that I am human and desirable?" Her smile was devastating. "Did you ever hear of the Canthrips of Ollenole?" She had never heard of them either, before that instant, but this small implied mendacity did not bother her.

"No . . . o, I can't say that I have." The man, while very evidently taken aback by this new line of resistance, persevered. "What kind of a brush-off do you think you're trying to give me?"

"Brush-off? See me as I am, you beast, and thank whatever gods you recognize that I am not hungry, having eaten just last night." In his sight her green eyes darkened to a jetty black, the flecks of gold in them scintillated and began to emit sparks. Her hair turned into a mass of horribly clutching tentacles. Her teeth became fangs, her fingers talons, her strong, splendidly-proportioned body a monstrosity out of hell's grisliest depths.

After a moment she allowed the frightful picture to fade back into her charming self, keeping the Romeo from fainting by the power of her will.

"Call the manager if you like. He has been watching and has seen nothing except that you are pale and sweating. I, a friend of yours, have been giving you some bad news, perhaps. Tell your stupid police all about me, if you wish to spend the next few weeks in a padded cell. I'll see you again in a day or two, I hope: I'll be hungry again by that time." She walked away, serenely confident that the fellow would never willingly come within sight of her again.

She had not damaged his ego permanently—he was not a neurotic type—but she had given him a jolt that he'd never forget. Camilla Kinnison nor any of her sisters had anything to fear from any male or males infesting any planet or roaming any depths of space.

The expected and awaited trouble developed. Tregonsee and Camilla landed and began their hunt. The League for Planetary Purity, it appeared, was the primary focal point; hence the two attended a meeting of that crusading body. That was a mistake; Tregonsee should have stayed out in deep space, concealed behind a solid thought-screen.

For Camilla was an unknown. Furthermore, her mind was inherently stable at the third level of stress; no lesser mind could penetrate her screens or, having failed to do so, could recognize the fact of failure. Tregonsee, however, was known throughout all civilized space. He was not wearing his Lens, of course, but his very shape made him suspect. Worse, he could not hide from any mind as powerful as that of "X" the fact that his mind was very decidedly not that of a retired Rigellian gentleman.

Thus Camilla had known that the procedure was a mistake. She intimated as much, but she could not sway the unswerving Tregonsee from his determined course without revealing things which must forever remain hidden from him. She acquiesced, therefore, but she knew what to expect.

Hence, when the invading intelligence blanketed the assemblage lightly, only to be withdrawn instantly upon detecting the emanations of a mind of real power, Cam had a bare moment of time in which to act. She synchronized with the intruding thought, began to analyze it and to trace it back to its source. She did not have time enough to succeed fully in either endeavor, but she did get a line. When the foreign influence vanished she shot a message to Tregonsee and they sped away.

Hurtling through space along the established line, Tregonsee's mind was a turmoil of thought; thoughts as plain as print to Camilla. She flushed uncomfortably—she could of course blush at will.

"I'm not half the super-woman you're picturing," she said. That was true enough; no one this side of Arisia could have been. "You're so famous, you know, and I'm not—while he was examining you I had a fraction of a second to work in. You didn't."

"That may be true." Although Tregonsee had no eyes, the girl knew that he was staring at her; scanning, but not intruding. She lowered her barriers so far that he thought they were completely down. "You have, however, extraordinary and completely inexplicable powers . . . but, being the daughter of Kimball and Clarrissa Kinnison . . ."

"That's it, I think." She paused, then, in a burst of girlish confidence, went on: "I've got something, I really do think, but I don't know what it is or what to do with it. Maybe in fifty years or so I will."

This also was close enough to the truth, and it did serve to restore to Tregonsee his wonted poise. "Be that as it may, I will take your advice next time, if you will offer it."

"Try and stop me—I love to give advice." She laughed unaffectedly. "It might not be any better next time."

Then, further to quiet the shrewd Rigellian's suspicions, she strode over to the control panel and checked the course. Having done so, she fanned out detectors, centering upon that course, to the fullest range of their power. She swaggered a little when she speared with a CRX tracer a distant vessel in a highly satisfactory location. That act would cut her down to size in Tregonsee's mind.

"You think, then, that 'X' is in that ship?" he asked quietly.

"Probably not." She could not afford to act too dumb—she could fool a Second Stage Lensman a little, but nobody could fool one much. "It may, however, give us a lead."

"It is practically certain that 'X' is not in that vessel." Tregonsee thought. "In fact, it may be a trap. We must, however, make the customary arrangements to take it into custody."

Cam nodded and the Rigellian communications officers energized their long-range beams. Far ahead of the fleeing vessel, centering upon its line of flight, fast cruisers of the Galactic Patrol began to form a gigantic cup. Hours passed, and—a not unexpected circumstance— Tregonsee's super-dreadnought gained rapidly upon the supposed Boskonian.

The quarry did not swerve or dodge. Straight into the mouth of the cup it sped. Tractors and pressors reached out, locked on, and were neither repulsed nor cut. The strange ship did not go inert, did not put out a single course of screen, did not fire a beam. She did not reply to signals. Spy-rays combed her from needle nose to driving jets, searching every compartment. There was no sign of life aboard.

Spots of pink appeared upon Camilla's deliciously smooth cheeks, her eyes flashed. "We've been had, Uncle Trig—*how* we've been had!" she exclaimed, and her chagrin was not all assumed. She had not quite anticipated such a complete fiasco as this.

"Score one for 'X'," Tregonsee said. He not only seemed to be, but actually was, calm and unmoved. "We will now go back and pick up where we left off."

They did not discuss the thing at all, nor did they wonder how "X" escaped them. After the fact, they both knew. There had been at least two vessels; at least one of them had been inherently indetectable and screened against thought. In one of these latter "X" had taken a course at some indeterminable angle to the one which they had followed.

"X" was now at a safe distance.

"X" was nobody's fool.

7

KATHRYN ON GUARD

Kathryn Kinnison, trim and taut in black glamorette, strolled into the breakfast nook humming a lilting song. Pausing before a full-length mirror, she adjusted her cocky little black toque at an even more piquant angle over her left eye. She made a couple of passes at her riot of curls and gazed at her reflected self in high approval as, putting both hands upon her smoothly rounded hips, she—"wriggled" is the only possible term for it—in sheer joy of being alive.

"Kathryn . . ." Clarissa Kinnison chided gently. "Don't be exhibitionistic, dear." Except in times of stress the Kinnison women used spoken language, "to keep in practice," as they said.

"Why not? It's fun." The tall girl bent over and kissed her mother upon the lobe of an ear. "You're sweet, mums, you know that? You're the most *precious* thing—Ha! Bacon and eggs? Goody!"

The older woman watched half-enviously as her eldest daughter ate with the care-free abandon of one completely unconcerned about either digestion or figure. She had no more understood her children, ever, than a hen can understand the brood of ducklings she has so unwittingly hatched out, and that comparison was more strikingly apt than Clarissa Kinnison ever would know. She now knew, more than a little ruefully, that she never would understand them.

She had not protested openly at the rigor of the regime to which her son Christopher had been subjected from birth. That, she knew, was necessary. It was inconceivable that Kit should not be a Lensman, and for a man to become a Lensman he had to be given everything he could possibly take. She was deeply glad, however, that her four other babies had been girls. Her daughters were *not* going to be Lensmen. She, who had known so long and so heavily the weight of Lensman's Load, would see to that. Herself a womanly, feminine woman, she had fought with every resource at her command to make her girl babies grow up into replicas of herself. She had failed.

They simply would not play with dolls, nor play house with other little girls. Instead, they insisted upon "intruding," as she considered it, upon Lensmen; preferably upon Second-Stage Lensmen, if any one of the four chanced to be anywhere within reach. Instead of with toys, they played with atomic engines and flitters; and, later, with speedsters and space-ships. Instead of primers, they read galactic encyclopedias. One of them might be at home, as now, or all of them; or none. She never did know what to expect.

But they were in no sense disloyal. They loved their mother with a depth of affection which no other mother, anywhere, has ever known. They tried their best to keep her from worrying about them. They kept in touch with her wherever they went—which might be at whim to Tellus or to Thrale or to Alsakan or to any unplumbed cranny of inter-galactic space—and they informed her, apparently without reservation, as to everything they did. They loved their father and their brother and each other and themselves with the same whole-hearted fervor they bestowed upon her. They behaved always in exemplary fashion. None of them had ever shown or felt the slightest interest in any one of numerous boys and men; and this trait, if the truth is to be told, Clarissa could understand least of all.

No. The only thing basically wrong with them was the fact, made abundantly clear since they first toddled, that they should not be and could not be subjected to any jot or tittle of any form of control, however applied.

Kathryn finished eating finally and gave her mother a bright, quick grin. "Sorry, mums, you'll just have to give us up as hard cases, I guess." Her fine eyes, so like Clarissa's except in color, clouded as she went on: "I *am* sorry, mother, really, that we can't be what you so want us to be. We've tried *so* hard, but we just can't. It's something here, and here." She tapped one temple and prodded her midsection with a pink fore-finger. "Call it fatalism or anything you please, but I think we're slated to do a job of some kind, some day, even though none of us has any idea of what it's going to be."

Clarissa paled. "I've been thinking just that for years, dear . . . I've been afraid to say it, or even to think it . . . You are Kim's children, and mine . . . If there ever was a perfect, a predestined marriage, it is ours . . . And Mentor said that our marriage was necessary . . ." She paused, and in that instant she almost perceived the truth. She was closer to it than she had ever been before or ever would be again. But that truth was far too vast for her mind to grasp. She went on: "But I'd do it over again, Kathryn, knowing everything I know now. 'Vast rewards,' you know . . ."

"Of course you would," Kat interrupted. "Any girl would be a fool not to. The minute I meet a man like dad I'm going to marry him, if I have to scratch Kay's eyes out and snatch Cam and Con bald-headed to get him. But speaking of dad, just what do you think of l'affaire Radelix?"

Gone every trace of levity, both women stood up. Gold-flecked tawny eyes stared deeply into gold-flecked eyes of dark and velvety green.

"I don't know." Clarrissa spoke slowly, meaningfully. "Do you?"

"No. I wish I did." Kathryn's was not the voice of a girl, but that of an avenging angel. "As Kit says, I'd give four front teeth and my right leg to the knee joint to know who or what is back of that, but I don't. I feel very much in the mood to do a flit out that way."

"Do you?" Clarrissa paused. "I'm glad. I'd go myself, in spite of everything he says, except that I couldn't do anything . . . If that *should* be the job you were talking about . . . Oh, do anything you can, dear; *anything* to make sure he comes back to me!"

"Of course, mums." Kathryn broke away almost by force from her mother's emotion. "I don't think it is; at least, I haven't got any cosmic hunch to that effect. And don't worry; it puts wrinkles in the girlish complexion. I'll do just a little look-see, stick around long enough to find out what's what, and let you know all about it. 'Bye."

At high velocity Kathryn drove her indetectable speedster to Radelix, and around and upon that planet she conducted invisible investigations. She learned a part of the true state of affairs, she deduced more of it, but she could not see, even dimly, the picture as a whole. This part, though, was clear enough.

A third-level operator, she did not have to be at the one apparent mouth of a hyper-spatial tube in order to enter it; she knew that while communication was impossible either through such a tube from space to space or from the interior of the tube to either space, the quality of the tube was not the barrier. The interface was. Wherefore, knowing what to expect first and working diligently to solve the whole problem, she waited.

She watched Kinninson's abduction. There was nothing she could do about that. She could not interfere then without setting up repercussions which might very well shatter the entire structure of the Galactic Patrol. When the Boskonian ship had disappeared, however, she tapped the tube and followed it. Almost nose to tail she pressed it, tensely alert to do some helpful deed which could be ascribed to accident or to luck. For she knew starkly that Kinnison's present captors would not slip and that his every ability had been discounted in advance.

Thus she was ready, when Kinnison's attention concentrated on the switch controlling the Boskonian captain's thought-screen generator. There were no pets or spiders or worms, or even gnats, but the captain could sit down. Around his screen, then, she drove a solid beam of thought, on a channel which neither the pirate nor the Lensman knew existed. She took over in a trice the fellow's entire mind. He sat down, as Kinnison had so earnestly willed him to do, the merest fraction of an inch too close to the chair's arm. The switch-handle flipped over and Kathryn snatched her mind away. She was sure that her father would think that bit of luck purely fortuitous. She was equally sure that the situation was safe, for a time at least, in Kinnison's highly capable hands. She slowed down, allowed the distance between the two vessels to increase. But she kept within range, for one or two more accidents might have to happen.

In the instant of the flicking of the switch the captain's mind became Kinnison's. He was going to issue orders, to take the ship over in an orderly way, but his first contact with the subjugated mind made him change his plans. Instead of uttering orders, the captain leaped out of the chair toward the beam-controllers.

And not an instant too soon. Others had seen what had happened, had heard that tell-tale click. All had been warned against that and many other contingencies. As the captain leaped one of his fellows drew a bullet-projector and calmly shot him through the head.

The shock of that bullet, the death of the mind in his own mind's grasp, jarred the Gray Lensman to the core. It was almost the same as though he himself had been killed. Nevertheless, by sheer force of will he held on, by sheer power of will he made that dead body take those last three steps and forced those dead hands to cut the master circuit of the beams which were holding him helpless.

Free, he leaped forward; but not alone. The others leaped, too, and for the same controls. Kinnison got there first—just barely first—and as he came he swung his armored fist.

What a dureum-inlaid glove, driven by all the brawn of Kimball Kinnison's mighty right arm and powerful torso backed by all the momentum of body- and armor-mass, will do to a human head met in direct central impact is nothing to detail here. Simply, that head splashed. Pivoting nimbly, considering his encumbering armor, he swung a terrific leg. His steel boot sank calf-deep into the abdomen of the foe next in line. Two more utterly irresistible blows disposed of two more of the Boskonians; the last two turned and, frantically, ran. But the Lensman by that time had the juice back on; and when a man has been smashed against a bulkhead by the full power of a D2P pressor, all that remains to be done must be accomplished with a scraper and a sponge.

Kinnison picked up his DeLameters, reconnected them, and took stock. So far, so good. But there were other men aboard this heap—how many, he'd better find out—and at least some of them wore dureum-inlaid armor as capable as his own.

And in her speedster, concluding that this wasn't going to be so bad, after all, Kathryn glowed with pride in her father's prowess. She was no shrinking violet, this Third-Stage Lensman; she held no ruth whatever for Civilization's foes. She herself would have driven that beam as mercilessly as had the Gray Lensman. She could have told Kinnison what next to do; could even have inserted the knowledge stealthily into his mind; but, heroically, she refrained. She'd let him handle this in his own fashion as long as he possibly could.

The Gray Lensman sent his sense of perception abroad. Twenty more of them—the ship wasn't very big. Ten aft, armored. Six forward, also armored. Four, unarmored, in the control-room. That control-room was pure poison; he'd go aft first. He searched around . . . surely they'd have dureum space-axes? Oh, yes, there they were. He hefted them, selected one of the right weight and balance. He strode down the companionway to the wardroom. He flung the door open and stepped inside.

His first care was to blast the communicator panels with his DeLameters. That would delay the mustering of reinforcements. The control room couldn't guess, at least for a time, that one man was setting out to capture their ship single-handed. His second, ignoring the beams of handweapons splashing refulgently from his screens, was to weld the steel door to the jamb. Then, sheathing his projectors, he swung up his axe and went grimly to work. He thought fleetingly of how nice it would be to have vanBuskirk, that dean of all axe-men, at his back; but he wasn't too old or too fat to swing a pretty mean axe himself. And, fortunately, these Boskonians, here in their quarters, didn't have axes. They were heavy, clumsy, and for emergency use only; they were not a part of the regular uniform, as with Valerians.

The first foe swung up his DeLameter involuntarily as Kinnison's axe swept down. When the curved blade, driven as viciously as the Lensman's strength could drive it, struck the ray-gun it did not even pause. Through it it sliced, the severed halves falling to the floor.

The dureum inlay of the glove held, and glove and axe smashed together against the helmet. The Boskonian went down with a crash; but, beyond a broken arm or some such trifle, he wasn't hurt much. And no armor that a man had to carry around could be made of solid dureum.

Hence, Kinnison reversed his weapon and swung again, aiming carefully at a point between the inlay strips. The axe's wicked beak tore through steel and skull and brain, stopping only with the sharply ringing impact of dureum shaft against dureum stripping.

They were coming at him now, not only with DeLameters, but with whatever of steel bars and spanners and bludgeons they could find. QX— his armor could take oodles of that. They might dent it, but they couldn't possibly get through. Planting one boot solidly on his victim's helmet, he wrenched his axe out through flesh and bone and metal—no fear of breakage; not even a Valerian's full savage strength could break the helve of a space-axe—and struck again. And struck—and struck.

He fought his way to the door—two of the survivors were trying to unseal it and get away. They failed; and, in failing, died. A couple of the remaining enemies shrieked and ran in blind panic, and tried to hide; the others battled desperately on. But whether they ran or fought there was only one possible end, if the Patrolman were to survive. No enemy must or could be left alive behind him, to bring to bear upon his back some semi-portable weapon with whose energies his armor's screens could not cope.

When the grisly business was over Kinnison, panting, rested briefly. This was the first real brawl he had been in for twenty years; and for a veteran—a white-collar man, a coordinator to boot—he hadn't done so bad, he thought. It was damned hard work and, while he was maybe a hair short of wind, he hadn't weakened a particle. To here, QX.

And lovely Kathryn, far enough back but not too far and reading imperceptibly his every thought, agreed with him enthusiastically. She did not have a father complex, but in common with her sisters she knew exactly what her father was. With equal exactitude she knew what other men were. Knowing them, and knowing however imperfectly herself, each of the Kinnison girls knew that it would be a physical and psychological impossibility for her to become even mildly interested in any man not at least her father's equal. They each had dreamed of a man who would be her own equal, physically and mentally, but it had not yet occurred to any of them that one such man already existed.

Kinnison cut the door away and again sent out his sense of perception. With it fanning out ahead of him he retraced his previous path. The apes in the control room had done something; he didn't know just what. Two of them were tinkering with a communicator panel; probably the one to the ward-room. They probably thought the trouble was at their end. Or did they? Why hadn't they reconnoitered? He dismissed that problem as being of no pressing importance. The other two were doing something at another panel. What? He couldn't make head or tail of it—damn those full-coverage screens! And Nadreck's fancy drill, even if he had had one along, wouldn't work unless the screen were absolutely steady. Well, it didn't make much, if any, difference. They had called the men back from up forward, and here they came. He'd rather meet them in the corridor than in an open room, anyway, he could handle them a lot easier . . .

But tensely watching Kathryn gnawed her lip. Should she tell him, or control him, or not? No. She wouldn't—she couldn't—yet. Dad could figure out that pilot-room trap without her help . . . and she herself, with all her power of brain, could not visualize with any degree of clarity the menace which was—which *must* be—at the tube's end or even now rushing along it to meet that Boskonian ship . . .

Kinnison met the oncoming six and vanquished them. By no means as easily as he had conquered the others, since they had been warned and since they also now bore space-axes, but just as finally. Kinnison did not consider it remarkable that he escaped practically unscratched—his armor was battered and dinged up, cut and torn, but he had only a couple of superficial wounds. He had met the enemy where they could come at him only one at a time; he was still the master of any weapon known to space warfare; it had been at no time evident that any outside influence was interfering with the normally rapid functioning of the Boskonians' minds.

He was full of confidence, full of fight, and far from spent when he faced about to consider what he should do about that control-room. There was plenty of stuff in there . . . tougher stuff than he had met up with so far . . .

Kathryn in her speedster gritted her teeth and clenched her hands into hard fists. This was bad—very, *very* bad—and it was going to get worse. Closing up fast, she uttered a bitter and exceedingly unladylike expletive.

Couldn't he *see*—couldn't the damn dumb darling *sense*—that he was apt to run out of time almost any minute now?

She fairly writhed in an agony of indecision; and indecision, in a Third-Stage Lensman, is a rare phenomenon indeed. She wanted intensely to take over, but if she did, was there any way this side of Palain's purple hells for her to cover up her tracks?

There was none . . . yet.

8

BLACK LENSMEN

But Kinnison's mind, while slower than his daughter's and much less able, was sure. The four Boskonians in the control room were screened against his every mental force and it was idle even to hope for another such lucky break as he had just had. They were armored by this time and they had both machine rifles and semi-portable projectors. They were entrenched; evidently intending to fight a delaying and defensive battle, knowing that if they could hold him off until the tube had been traversed, the Lensman would not have a chance. Armed with all they could use of the most powerful mobile weapons aboard and being four to one, they undoubtedly thought they could win easily enough.

Kinnison thought otherwise. Since he could not use his mind against them he would use whatever he could find, and this ship, having come upon such a mission, would be carrying plenty of weapons—and those four men certainly hadn't had time to tamper with them all. He might even find some negative-matter bombs.

Setting up a spy-ray block, he proceeded to rummage. They couldn't see him, and if any one of them had a sense of perception and cut his screen for even a fraction of a second to use it the battle would end right then. And if they decided to rush him, so much the better. They remained, however, forted up, as he had thought they would, and he rummaged in peace. Various death-dealing implements, invitingly set up, he ignored after one cursory glance into their interiors. He knew weapons—these had been fixed. He went on to the armory.

He did not find any negabombs, but he found plenty of untouched weapons like those now emplaced in the control room. The rifles were beauties; high-caliber, water-cooled things, each with a heavy dureum shield-plate and a single-ply screen. Each had a beam, too, but machine-rifle beams weren't so hot. Conversely, the semi-portables had lots of screen, but very little dureum. Kinnison lugged one rifle and two semi-portables, by easy stages, into the room next to the control room; so placing them that the control panels would be well out of the line of fire.

What gave Kinnison his chance was the fact that the enemies' weapons were set to cover the door. Apparently they had not considered the possibility that the Lensman would attempt to flank them by blasting through an inch and a half of high-alloy steel. Kinnison did not know whether he could do it fast enough to mow them down from the side before they could reset their magnetic clamps, or not; but he'd give it the good old college try. It was bound to be a mighty near thing, and the Lensman grinned wolfishly behind the guard-plates of his helmet as he arranged his weapons to save every possible fractional second of time.

Aiming one at a spot some three feet above the floor, the other a little lower, Kinnison cut in the full power of his semis and left them on. He energized the rifle's beam—every little bit helped—set the defensive screens at "full," and crouched down into the saddle behind the dureum shield. He had checked the feeds long since: he had plenty of rounds.

Two large spots and a small one smoked briefly, grew red. They turned bright red, then yellow, merged into one blinding spot. Metal melted, sluggishly at first, then thinly, then flaring, blowing out in raging corruscations of sparks as the fiercely-driven beams ate in. Through!

The first small opening appeared directly in line between the muzzle of Kinnison's rifle and one of the guns of the enemy, and in the moment of its appearance the Patrolman's weapon began its stuttering, shattering roar. The Boskonians had seen the hot spot upon the wall, had known instantly what it meant, and were working frantically to swing their gun-mounts around so as to interpose their dureum shields and to bring their own rifles to bear. They had almost succeeded. Kinnison caught just the bulge of one suit of armor in his sights, but that was enough. The kinetic energy of the stream of metal tore him out of the saddle; he was literally riddled while still in air. Two savage bursts took care of the semi-portables and their operators—as has been intimated, the shields of the semis were not designed to withstand the type of artillery Kinnison was using.

That made it cannon to cannon, one to one; and the Lensman knew that those two identical rifles could hammer at each others' defenses for an hour without doing any serious damage. He had, however, one big advantage. Being closer to the bulkhead he could depress his line of fire more than could the Boskonian. He did so, aiming at the clamps, which were not built to take very much of that sort of punishment. One front clamp let go, then the other, and the Lensman knew what to do about the rear pair, which he could not reach. He directed his fire against the upper edge of the dureum plate. Under the awful thrust of that terrific storm of steel the useless front clamps lifted from the floor. The gun mount, restrained from sliding by the unbreakable grip of the rear clamps, reared up. Over it went, straight backward, exposing the gunner to the full blast of Kinnison's fire. That, definitely, was that.

Kathryn heaved a sigh of relief: as far as she could "see," the tube was still empty. "That's my pop!" she applauded inaudibly to herself. "Now," she breathed, "if the darling has just got jets enough to figure out that something may be coming at him down this tube—and sense enough to run back home before it can catch him!"

Kinnison had no suspicion that any danger to himself might lie within the tube. He had no desire, however, to land alone in an enemy ship in the exact center of an enemy base, and no intention whatever of doing so. Moreover, he had once come altogether too close to permanent immolation in a foreign space because of the discontinuance of a hyperspatial tube while he was in it, and once was once too many. Also, he had just got done leading with his chin, and once of that, too, was once too many. Therefore his sole thought was to get back into his own space as fast as he could get there, so as soon as the opposition was silenced he hurried into the control room and reversed the vessel's drive.

Behind him, Kathryn flipped her speedster end for end and led the retreat. She left the tube before—"before" is an extremely loose and inaccurate word in this connection, but it conveys the idea better than any other ordinary term—she got back to Base. She caused an officer to broadcast an "evacuation" warning, then hung poised, watching intently. She knew that Kinnison could not leave the tube except at its terminus, hence would have to materialize inside the building itself. She had heard of what happened when two dense, hard solids attempted to occupy the same three-dimensional space at the same time; but to view that occurrence was not her purpose in lingering. She did not actually know whether there was anything in the tube or not; but she did know that if there were, and if it or they should follow her father out into normal space, even she would have need of every jet she could muster.

Kinnison, maneuvering his Boskonian cruiser to a halt just at the barest perceptible threshold of normal space, in the intermediate zone in which nothing except dureum was solid in either space or pseudo-space, had already given a great deal of thought to the problem of dis-embarkation. The ship was small, as space-ships go, but even so it was a lot bigger than any corridor of any ordinary structure. Those corridor walls and floors were thick and contained a lot of steel; the ship's walls were solid alloy. He had never seen metal materialize within metal and, frankly, he didn't want to be around, even inside G-P armor, when it happened. Also, there were a lot of explosives aboard, and atomic power plants, and the chance of touching off a loose atomic vortex within a few feet of himself was not one to be taken lightly.

He had already rigged a line to a master switch. Power off, with the ship's dureum catwalk as close to the floor of the corridor as the dimen-sions of the tube permitted, he reversed the controls and poised himself for a running headlong dive. He could not feel Radeligian gravitation, of course, but he was pretty sure that he could jump far enough to get through the interface. He took a short run, jerked the line, and hurled himself through the spaceship's immaterial wall. The ship disappeared.

Going through that interface was more of a shock than the Lensman had anticipated. Even taken very slowly, as it customarily is, inter-dimensional acceleration brings malaise to which no one has ever become accustomed, and taking it so rapidly fairly turned Kinnison inside out. He was going to land with the rolling impact which con-stitutes perfect technique in such armored maneuvering. As it was, he never did know how he landed, except that he made a boiler-shop racket and brought up against the far wall of the corridor with a cli-mactic clang. Beyond the addition of a few more bruises and contusions to his already abundant collection, however, he was not hurt.

As soon as he could collect himself he leaped to his feet and rapped out orders. "Tractors—pressors—shears! Heavy stuff, to anchor, not to clamp! Hipe!" He knew what he was up against now, and if they'd only come back he'd yank them out of that blank tube so fast it'd break every blank blank one of their blank blank blank necks!

And Kathryn, still watching intently, smiled. Her dad was a pretty smart old duck, but he wasn't using his noggin now—he was cockeyed as Trenco's ether in even thinking they *might* come back. If anything at all erupted from that hyper-circle it would be something against which everything he was mustering would be precisely as effective as so much thin air. And she *still* had no concrete idea of what she so feared. It wouldn't be essentially physical, she was pretty sure. It would almost have to be mental. But who or what could possibly put it across? And how? And above all, what could she do about it if they did?

Eyes narrowed, brow furrowed in concentration, she thought as she had never thought before; and the harder she thought the more clouded the picture became. For the first time in her triumphant life she felt small—weak—impotent. It was in that hour that Kathryn Kinnison really grew up.

The tube vanished; she heaved a tremendous sigh of relief. They, whoever they were, having failed to bring Kinnison to them—this time— were not coming after him—this time. Not an important enough game to play to the end? No, that wasn't it. Maybe they weren't ready. But the next . . .

Mentor the Arisian had told her bluntly, the last time she had seen him, to come to him again when she realized that she didn't know quite everything. Deep down, she had not expected that day ever to come. Now, however, it had. This escape—if it had been an escape—had taught her much.

"Mother!" She shot a call to distant Klovia. "I'm on Radelix. Everything's on the green. Dad has just knocked a flock of Boskonians into an outside loop and come through QX. I've got to do a little flit, though, before I come home. 'Bye."

Kinnison stood intermittent guard over the base for four days after the hyper-spatial tube had disappeared before he gave up; before he did any very serious thinking about what he should do next.

Could he and should he keep on as Sybly Whyte? He could and he should, he decided. He hadn't been gone long enough for Whyte's absence to have been noticed; nothing whatever connected Whyte with Kinnison. If he really knew what he was doing a more specific alias might be better; but as long as he was merely smelling around, Whyte's was the best identity to use. He could go aywhere, do anything, ask anything of anybody, and all with a perfectly good excuse.

And as Sybly Whyte, then, for days that stretched into weeks, he roamed—finding, as he had feared, nothing whatever. It seemed as though all Boskonian activity of the type in which he was most interested had ceased with his return from the hyper-spatial tube. Just what that meant he did not know. It was unthinkable that they had given up on him: much more probable they were hatching something new. And the frustration of inaction and the trying to figure out what was coming next was driving him not-so-slowly nuts.

Then, striking through the doldrums, came a call from Maitland.

"Kim? You told me to Lens you immediately about any off-color work. Don't know whether this is or not. The guy may be—probably is—crazy. Conklin, who reported him, couldn't decide. Neither can I, from Conklin's report. Do you want to send somebody special, take over yourself, or what?"

"I'll take over," Kinnison decided instantly. If neither Conklin nor Maitland, Gray Lensmen both, could decide, there was no point in sending anyone else. "Where and who?"

"Planet, Meneas II, not too far from where you are now. City, Meneateles; 116-3-29, 45-22-17. Place, Jack's Haven, a meteor-miner's hangout at the corner of Gold and Sapphire Streets. Person, a man called 'Eddie.' "

"Thanks, I'll check." Maitland did not send, and Kinnison did not want, any additional information. Both knew that since the coordinator was going to investigate this thing himself, he should get his facts, and particularly his impressions, at first and unprejudiced hand.

To Meneas II, then, and to Jack's Haven, Sybly Whyte went, notebook very much in evidence. An ordinary enough space-dive Jack's turned out to be—higher-toned than that Radeligian space-dock saloon of Bominger's; much less flamboyant than notorious Miners' Rest on far Euphrosyne.

"I wish to interview a person named Eddie," he announced, as he bought a bottle of wine. "I have been informed that he has had deepspace adventures worthy of incorporation into one of my novels."

"Eddie? Haw!" The barkeeper laughed raucously. "That spacelouse? Somebody's been kidding you, mister. He's nothing but a brokendown meteor-miner—you know what a space-louse is, don't you?—that we let clean cuspidors and do such-like odd jobs for his keep. We don't throw him out, like we do the others, because he's kind of funny in one way. Every hour or so he throws a fit, and that amuses people."

Whyte's eager-beaver attitude did not change; his face reflected nothing of what Kinnison thought of this callous speech. For Kinnison did know exactly what a space-louse was. More, he knew what turned a man into one. Ex-meteor miner himself, he knew what the awesome depths of space, the ever-present dangers, the privations, the solitude, the frustrations, did to any mind not adequately integrated. He knew that only the strong survived; that the many weak succumbed. From sickening memory he knew just what pitiful wrecks those many became. Nevertheless, and despite the fact that the information was not necessary:

"Where is this Eddie now?"

"That's him, over there in the corner. By the way he's acting, he'll have another fit pretty quick now."

The shambling travesty of a man accepted avidly the invitation to table and downed at a gulp the proffered drink. Then, as though the mild potion had been a trigger, his wracked body tensed and his features began to writhe.

"Cateagles!" he screamed; eyes rolling, breath coming in hard, frantic gasps. "Gangs of cateagles! Thousands! They're clawing me to bits! And the Lensman! He's sicking them on! *Ow!!* YOW!!!" He burst into unintelligible screams and threw himself to the floor. There, rolling convulsively over and over, he tried the impossible feat of covering simultaneously with his two claw-like hands his eyes, ears, nose, mouth, and throat.

Ignoring the crowding spectators, Kinnison invaded the helpless mind before him. He winced mentally as he scanned the whole atrocious enormity of what was there. Then, while Whyte busily scribbled notes, he shot a thought to distant Klovia.

"Cliff! I'm here in Jack's Haven, and I've got Eddie's data. What did you and Conklin make of it? You agree, of course, that the Lensman is the crux."

"Definitely. Everything else is hop-happy space-drift. The fact that there are not—there *can't* be—many such Lensman as Eddie imagined, makes him space-drift, too, in our opinion. We called you in on the millionth chance—sorry we sent you out on a false alarm, but you said we had to be sure."

"You needn't be sorry." Kinnison's thought was the grimmest Clifford Maitland had ever felt. "Eddie isn't an ordinary space-louse. You see, I know one thing that you and Conklin don't. You noticed the woman? Very faint, decidedly in the background?"

"Now that you mention her—yes. Too far in the background and too faint to be a key. Most every spaceman has a woman—or a lot of different ones—more or less on his mind all the time, you know. Immaterial, I'd say."

"So would I, maybe, except for the fact that she isn't a woman at all, but a Lyranian . . ."

"A LYRANIAN!" Maitland interrupted. Kinnison could feel the racing of his assistant's thoughts. "That complicates things . . . But how in Palain's purple hells, Kim, could Eddie ever have got to Lyrane—and if he did, how did he get away alive?"

"I don't know, Cliff." Kinnison's mind, too, was working fast. "But you haven't got all the dope yet. To cinch things, I know her personally—she's that airport manager who tried her damndest to kill me all the time I was on Lyrane II."

"Hm ... m ... m." Maitland tried to digest that undigestible bit. Tried, and failed. "That would seem to make the Lensman real, too, then—real enough, at least, to investigate—much as I hate to think of the possibility of a Lensman going that far off the beam." Maitland's convictions died hard. "You'll handle this yourself, then?"

"Check. At least, I'll help. There may be people better qualified than I am. I'll get them at it. Thanks, Cliff—clear ether."

He lined a thought to his wife; and after a short, warmly intimate contact, he told her the story.

"So you see, beautiful," he concluded, "Your wish is coming true. I couldn't keep you out of this if I wanted to. So check with the girls, put on your Lens, shed your clothes, and go to work."

"I'll do that." Clarrissa laughed and her soaring spirit flooded his mind. "Thanks, my dear."

Then and only then did Kimball Kinnison, master therapist, pay any further attention to that which lay contorted upon the floor. But when Whyte folded up his notebook and left the place, the derelict was resting quietly; and in a space of time long enough so that the putative writer of space-opera would not be connected with the cure, those fits would end. Moreover, Eddie would return, whole, to the void: he would become what he had never before been—a successful meteor-miner.

Lensmen pay their debts; even to spiders and to worms.

9

AN ARISIAN EDUCATION

Her adventure in the hyper-spatial tube had taught Kathryn Kinnison much. Realizing her inadequacy and knowing what to do about it, she drove her speedster at high velocity to Arisia. Unlike the Second-Stage Lensmen, she did not even slow down as she approached the planet's barrier; but, as one sure of her welcome, merely threw out ahead of her an identifying thought.

"Ah, daughter Kathryn, again you are in time." Was there, or was there not, a trace of emotion—of welcome, even of affection?—in that usually utterly emotionless thought? "Land as usual."

She neutralized her controls as she felt the mighty beams of the landing-engine take hold of her little ship. During previous visits she had questioned nothing—this time she was questioning *everything*. Was she landing, or not? Directing her every force inwardly, she probed her own mind to its profoundest depths. Definitely, she was her own mistress throughout—*no* conceivable mind could take *hers* over so tracelessly. As definitely, then, she was actually landing.

She landed. The ground upon which she stepped was real. So was the automatic flyer—neither plane nor helicopter—which whisked her from the spaceport to her familiar destination, an unpretentious residence in the grounds of the immense hospital. The graveled walk, the flowering shrubs, and the indescribably sweet and pungent perfume were real; as were the tiny pain and the drop of blood which resulted when a needle-sharp thorn pierced her incautious finger.

Through automatically-opening doors she made her way into the familiar, comfortable, book-lined room which was Mentor's study. And there, at his big desk, unchanged, sat Mentor. A lot like her father, but older—much older. About ninety, she had always thought, even though he didn't look over sixty. This time, however, she drove a probe—and got the shock of her life. Her thought was stopped—cold—not by superior mental force, which she could have taken unmoved, but by a seemingly ordinary thought-screen, and her fast-disintegrating morale began visibly to crack.

"Is all this—are you—real, or not?" she burst out, finally. "If it isn't, I'll go mad!"

"That which you have tested—and I—are real, for the moment and as you understand reality. Your mind in its present state of advancement cannot be deceived concerning such elementary matters."

"But it all wasn't, before? Or don't you want to answer that?"

"Since the knowledge will affect your growth, I will answer. It was not. This is the first time that your speedster has landed physically upon Arisia."

The girl shrank, appalled. "You told me to come back when I found out that I didn't know it all," she finally forced herself to say. "I learned that in the tube; but I didn't realize until just now that I don't know *anything*. Is there any use, Mentor, in going on with me?" she concluded, bitterly.

"Much," he assured her. "Your development has been eminently satisfactory, and your present mental condition is both necessary and sufficient."

"Well, I'll be a spr . . ." Kathryn bit off the expletive and frowned. "What were you doing to me before, then, when I thought I got everything?"

"Power of mind," he informed her. "Sheer power, and penetration, and control. Depth, and speed, and all the other factors with which you are already familiar."

"But what is left? I know there is—lots of it—but I can't imagine what."

"Scope," Mentor replied, gravely. "Each of those qualities and characteristics must be expanded to encompass the full sphere of thought. Neither words nor thoughts can give any adequate concept of what it means; a practically wide-open two-way will be necessary. This cannot be accomplished, daughter, in the adolescent confines of your present mind; therefore enter fully into mine."

She did so: and after less than a minute of that awful contact slumped, inert and boneless, to the floor.

The Arisian, unchanged, unmoved, unmoving, gazed at her until finally she began to stir.

"That . . . father Mentor, that was . . ." she blinked, shook her head savagely, fought her way back to full consciousness. "That was a shock."

"It was," he agreed. "More so than you realize. Of all the entities of your Civilization, your brother and now you are the only ones it would not kill instantly. You now know what the word 'scope' means, and are ready for your last treatment, in the course of which I shall take your mind as far along the road of knowledge as mine is capable of going."

"But that would mean . . . you're implying . . . But my mind *can't* be superior to yours, Mentor! Nothing could be, *possibly*—it's sheerly, starkly unthinkable!"

"But true, daughter, nevertheless. While you are recovering your strength from that which was but the beginning of your education, I will explain certain matters previously obscure. You have long known, of course, that you five children are not like any others. You have always known many things without having learned them. You think upon all possible bands of thought. Your senses of perception, of sight, of hearing, of touch, are so perfectly merged into one sense that you perceive at will any possible manifestation upon any possible plane or dimension of vibration. Also, although this may not have occurred to you as extraordinary, since it is not obvious, you differ physically from your fellows in some important respects. You have never experienced the slightest symptom of physical illness; not even a headache or a decayed tooth. You do not really require sleep. Vaccinations and inoculations do not 'take.' No pathogenic organism, however virulent; no poison, however potent . . ."

"Stop, Mentor!" Kathryn gasped, turning white. "I can't take it— you really mean, then, that we aren't human at all?"

"Before going into that I should give you something of background. Our Arisian visualizations foretold the rise and fall of galactic civilizations long before any such civilizations came into being. That of Atlantis, for instance. I was personally concerned in that, and could not stop its fall." Mentor *was* showing emotion now; his thought was bleak and bitter.

"Not that I expected to stop it," he resumed. "It had been known for many cycles of time that the final abatement of the opposing force would necessitate the development of a race superior to ours in every respect.

"Blood lines were selected in each of the four strongest races of this that you know as the First Galaxy. Breeding programs were set up, to eliminate as many as possible of their weaknesses and to concentrate all of their strengths. From your knowledge of genetics you realize the magnitude of the task; you know that it would take much time uselessly to go into the details of its acomplishment. Your father and your mother were the penultimates of long—*very* long—lines of mating; their reproductive cells were such that in their fusion practically every gene carrying any trait of weakness was rejected. Conversely, you carry the genes of every trait of strength ever known to any member of your human race. Therefore, while in outward seeming you are human, in every factor of importance you are not; you are even less human than am I myself."

"And just how human is that?" Kathryn flared, and again her most penetrant probe of force flattened out against the Arisian's screen.

"Later, daughter, not now. That knowledge will come at the end of your education, not at its beginning."

"I was afraid so." She stared at the Arisian, her eyes wide and hopeless; brimming, in spite of her efforts at control, with tears. "You're a monster, and I am . . . or am going to be—a worse one. A monster, . . . and I'll have to live a million years . . . alone . . . why? *Why,* Mentor, did you have to do this to me?"

"Calm yourself, daughter. The shock, while severe, will pass. You have lost nothing, have gained much."

"Gained? Bah!" The girl's thought was loaded with bitterness and scorn. "I've lost my parents—I'll still be a girl long after they have died. I've lost every possibility of ever really living. I want love—and a husband—and children—and I can't have any of them, ever. Even without this, I've never seen a man I wanted, and now I can't ever love anybody. I don't *want* to live a million years, Mentor—especially alone!" The thought was a veritable wail of despair.

"The time has come to stop this muddy, childish thinking." Mentor's thought, however, was only mildly reproving. "Such a reaction is only natural, but your conclusions are entirely erroneous. One single clear thought will show you that you have no present psychic, intellectual, emotional, or physical need of a complement."

"That's true . . ." wonderingly. "But other girls of my age . . ."

"Exactly," came Mentor's dry rejoinder. "Thinking of yourself as an adult of *Homo Sapiens,* you were judging yourself by false standards. As a matter of fact, you are an adolescent, not an adult. In due time you will come to love a man, and he you, with a fervor and depth which you at present cannot even dimly understand."

"But that still leaves my parents," Kathryn felt much better. "I can apparently age, of course, as easily as I can put on a hat . . . but I really do love them, you know, and it will simply break mother's heart to have all her daughters turn out to be—as she thinks—spinsters."

"On that point, too, you may rest at ease. I am taking care of that. Kimball and Clarrissa both know, without knowing how they know it, that your life cycle is tremendously longer than theirs. They both know that they will not live to see their grandchildren. Be assured, daughter, that before they pass from this cycle of existence into the next—about which I know nothing—they shall know that all is to be supremely well with their line; even though, to Civilization at large, it shall apparently end with you Five."

"End with us? What do you mean?"

"You have a destiny, the nature of which your mind is not yet qualified to receive. In due time the knowledge shall be yours. Suffice it now to say that the next forty or fifty years will be but a fleeting hour in the span of life which is to be yours. But time, at the moment, presses. You are now fully recovered and we must get on with this, your last period of study with me, at the end of which you will be able to bear the fullest, closest impact of my mind as easily as you have heretofore borne full contact with your sisters'. Let us proceed with the work."

They did so. Kathryn took and survived those shattering treatments, one after another; emerging finally with a mind whose power and scope can no more be explained to any mind below the third level than can the general theory of relativity be explained to a chimpanzee.

"It was forced, not natural, yes," the Arisian said, gravely, as the girl was about to leave. "You are many millions of your years ahead of your natural time. You realize, however, the necessity of that forcing. You also realize that I can give you no more formal instruction. I will be with you or on call at all times; I will be of aid in crises; but in larger matters your further development is in your own hands."

Kathryn shivered. "I realize that, and it scares me clear through . . . especially this coming conflict, at which you hint so vaguely. I wish you'd tell me at least *something* about it, so I can get ready for it!"

"Daughter, I can't." For the first time in Kathryn's experience, Mentor the Arisian was unsure. "It is certain that we have been on time; but since the Eddorians have minds of power little if any inferior to our own, there are many details which we cannot derive with certainty, and to advise you wrongly would be to do you irreparable harm. All I can say is that sufficient warning will be given by your learning, with no specific effort on your part and from some source other than myself, that there does in fact exist a planet named 'Ploor'—a name which to you is now only a meaningless symbol. Go now, daughter Kathryn, and work."

Kathryn went; knowing that the Arisian had said all that he would say. In truth, he had told her vastly more than she had expected him to divulge; and it chilled her to the marrow to think that she, who had always looked up to the Arisians as demi-gods of sorts, would from now on be expected to act as their equal—in some ways, perhaps, as their superior! As her speedster tore through space toward distant Klovia she wrestled with herself, trying to shake her new self down into a personality as well integrated as her old one had been. She had not quite succeeded when she felt a thought.

"Help! I am in difficulty with this, my ship. Will any entity receiving my call and possessing the tools of a mechanic please come to my assistance? Or, lacking such tools, possessing a vessel of power sufficient to tow mine to the place where I must immediately go?"

Kathryn was startled out of her introspective trance. That thought was on a terrifically high band; one so high that she knew of no race using it, so high that an ordinary human mind could not possibly have either sent or received it. Its phraseology, while peculiar, was utterly precise in definition—the mind behind it was certainly of precisionist grade. She acknowledged upon the stranger's wave, and sent out a locator. Good—he wasn't far away. She flashed toward the derelict, matched intrinsics at a safe distance, and began scanning, only to encounter a spy-ray block around the whole vessel! To her it was porous enough—but if the creature thought that his screen was tight, let him keep on thinking so. It was his move.

"Well, what are you waiting for?" The thought fairly snapped. "Come close, so that I may bring you in."

"Not yet," Kathryn snapped back. "Cut your block so that I can see what you are like. I carry equipment for many environments, but I must know what yours is and equip for it before I can come aboard. You will note that my screens are down."

"Of course. Excuse me—I supposed that you were one of our own"—there came the thought of an unspellable and unpronounceable name—"since none of the lower orders can receive our thoughts direct. Can you equip yourself to come aboard with your tools?"

"Yes." The stranger's light was fierce stuff; ninety-eight percent of its energy being beyond the visible. His lamps were beam-held atomics, nothing less: but there was very little gamma and few neutrons. She could handle it easily enough, she decided, as she finished donning her heat-armor and a helmet of practically opaque, diamond-hard plastic.

As she was wafted gently across the intervening space upon a pencil of force, Kathryn took her first good look at the precisionist himself—or herself. She—it—looked something like a Dhilian, she thought at first. There was a squat, powerful, elephantine body with its four stocky legs; the tremendous double shoulders and enormous arms; the domed, almost immobile head. But there the resemblance ended. There was only one head—the thinking head, and that one had no eyes and was not covered with bone. There was no feeding head—the thing could neither eat nor breathe. There was no trunk. And what a skin!

It was worse than a hide, really—worse even than a Martian's. The girl had never seen anything like it. It was incredibly thick, dry, pliable; filled minutely with cells of a liquid-gaseous something which she knew to be a more perfect insulator even than the fibres of the tegument itself.

"R-T-S-L-Q-P." She classified the creature readily enough to six places, then stopped and wrinkled her forehead. "Seventh place—that incredible skin—what? S? R? T? It would have to be R . . .

"You have the requisite tools, I perceive," the creature greeted Kathryn as she entered the central compartment of the strange speedster, no larger than her own. "I can tell you what to do, if . . ."

"I know what to do." She unbolted the cover, worked deftly with wrenches and cable and splicer and torch, and in ten minutes was done. "It doesn't make sense that a person of your obvious intelligence, manifestly knowing enough to make such minor repairs yourself, would go so far from home, alone in such a small ship, without any tools. Burnouts and shorts are apt to happen any time, you know."

"Not in vessels of the . . ." Again Kathryn felt that unpronounceable symbol. She also felt the stranger stiffen in offended dignity. "We of the higher orders, you should know, do not perform labor. We think. We direct. Others work, and do their work well, or suffer accordingly. This is the first time in nine full four-cycle periods that such a thing has happened, and it will be the last. The punishment which I shall mete out to the guilty mechanic will ensure that. I shall, at end, have his life."

"Oh, come, now!" Kathryn protested. "Surely it's no life-and-death mat . . ."

"Silence!" came curt command. "It is intolerable that one of the lower orders should attempt to . . ."

"Silence yourself!" At the fierce power of the riposte the creature winced, physically and mentally. "I did this bit of dirty work for you because you apparently couldn't do it for yourself. I did not object to the matter-of-course way you accepted it, because some races are made that way and can't help it. But if you insist on keeping yourself placed five rungs above me on any ladder you can think of, I'll stop being a lady—or even a good Girl Scout—and start doing things about it, and I'll start at any signal you care to call. Get ready, and say when!"

The stranger, taken fully aback, threw out a lightning tentacle of thought; a feeler which was stopped cold a full foot from the girl's radiant armor. This was a human female—or was it? It was not. No human being had ever had, or ever would have, a mind like that. Therefore:

"I have made a grave error," the thing apologized handsomely, "in thinking that you are not at least my equal. Will you grant me pardon, please?"

"Certainly—if you don't repeat it. But I still don't like the idea of your torturing a mechanic for a thing . . ." She thought intensely, lip caught between white teeth. "Perhaps there's a way. Where are you going, and when do you want to get there?"

"To my home planet," pointing out mentally its location in the galaxy. "I must be there in two hundred G-P hours."

"I see." Kathryn nodded her head. "You can—if you promise not to harm him. And I can tell whether you really mean it or not."

"As I promise, so I do. But in case I do not promise?"

"In that case you'll get there in about a hundred thousand G-P years, frozen stiff. For I shall fuse your Bergenholm down into a lump; then, after welding your ports to the shell, I'll mount a thought-screen generator outside, powered for seven hundred years. Promise, or that. Which?"

"I promise not to harm the mechanic in any way." He surrendered stiffly, and made no protest at Kathryn's entrance into his mind to make sure that the promise would be kept.

Flushed by her easy conquest of a mind she would previously have been unable to touch, and engrossed in the problem of setting her own tremendously enlarged mind to rights, why should it have occurred to the girl that there was anything worthy of investigation concealed in the depths of that chance-met stranger's mentality?

Returning to her own speedster, she shed her armor and shot away; and it was just as well for her peace of mind that she was not aware of the tight-beamed thought even then speeding from the flitter so far behind her to dread and distant Ploor.

". . . but it was very definitely not a human female. I could not touch it. It may very well have been one of the accursed Arisians themselves. But since I did nothing to arouse its suspicions, I got rid of it easily enough. Spread the warning!"

10

CONSTANCE OUT-WORSELS WORSEL

While Kathryn Kinnison was working with her father in the hyper-spatial tube and with Mentor of Arisia, and while Camilla and Tregonsee were sleuthing the inscrutable "X," Constance was also at work. Although she lay flat on her back, not moving a muscle, she was working as she had never worked before. Long since she had put her indetectable speedster into the control of a director-by-chance. Now, knowing nothing and caring less of where she and her vessel might be or might go, physically completely relaxed, she drove her "sensories" out to the full limit of their prodigious range and held them there for hour after hour. Worsel-like, she was not consciously listening for any particular thing; she was merely increasing her already incredibly vast store of knowledge. One hundred percent receptive, attached to and concerned with only the brain of her physical body, her mind sped at large: sampling, testing, analyzing, cataloguing every item with which its most tenuous fringe came in contact. Through thousands of solar systems that mind went; millions upon millions of entities either did or did not contribute something worthwhile.

Suddenly there came something that jarred her into physical movement: a burst of thought upon a band so high that it was practically always vacant. She shook herself, got up, lighted an Alsakanite cigarette, and made herself a pot of coffee.

"This is important, I think," she mused. "I'd better get to work on it while it's fresh."

She sent out a thought tuned to Worsel, and was surprised when it went unanswered. She investigated: finding that the Velantian's screens were full up and held hard—he was fighting Overlords so savagely that he had not felt her thought. Should she take a hand in this brawl? She should not, she decided, and grinned fleetingly. Her erstwhile tutor would need no help in that comparatively minor chore. She'd wait until he wasn't quite so busy.

"Worsel! Con calling. What goes on there, fellow old snake?" She finally launched her thought.

"As though you didn't know!" Worsel sent back. "Been quite a while since I saw you—how about coming aboard?"

"Coming at max," and she did.

Before entering the *Velan*, however, she put on a gravity damper, set at 980 centimeters. Strong, tough, and supple as she was she did not relish the thought of the atrocious accelerations used and enjoyed by Velantians everywhere.

"What did you make of that burst of thought?" she asked by way of greeting. "Or were you having so much fun you missed it?"

"What burst?" Then, after Constance had explained, "I was busy; but *not* having fun."

"Somebody who didn't know you might believe that," the girl derided. "This thought was important, I think—much more so than dilly-dallying with Overlords, as you were doing. It was 'way up—on this band here." She illustrated.

"So?" Worsel came as near to whistling as one of his inarticulate race could come. "What are they like?"

"VWZY, to four places." Con concentrated. "Multilegged. Not exactly carapaceous, but pretty nearly. Spiny, too, I believe. The world was cold, dismal, barren; but not frigid, but he—it—didn't seem exactly like an oxygen-breather—more like what a warm-blooded Palainian would perhaps look like, if you can imagine such a thing. Mentality very high—precisionist grade—no thought of cities as such. The sun was a typical yellow dwarf. Does any of this ring a bell in your mind?"

"No." Worsel thought intensely for minutes. So did Constance. Neither had any idea—then—that the girl was describing the form assumed in their autumn by the dread inhabitants of the planet Ploor!

"This may indeed be important," Worsel broke the mental silence. "Shall we explore together?"

"We shall." They tuned to the desired band. "Give it plenty of shove, too—Go!"

Out and out and out the twinned receptors sped; to encounter a tenuous, weak, and utterly cryptic vibration. One touch—the merest possible contact—and it disappeared. It vanished before even Con's almost-instantaneous reactions could get more than a hint of directional alignment; and neither of the observers could read any part of it.

Both of these developments were starkly incredible, and Worsel's long body tightened convulsively, rock-hard, in the violence of the mental force now driving his exploring mind. Finding nothing, he finally relaxed.

"Any Lensmen, anywhere, can read and understand any thought, however garbled or scrambled, or however expressed," he thought at Constance. "Also, I have always been able to get an exact line on anything I could perceive, but all I know about this one is that it seemed to come mostly from somewhere over that way. Did you do any better?"

"Not much, if any." If the thing was surprising to Worsel, it was sheerly astounding to his companion. She, knowing the measure of her power, thought to herself—not to the Velantian—"Girl, file *this* one carefully away in the big black book!"

Slight as were the directional leads, the *Velan* tore along the indicated line at maximum blast. Day after day she sped, a wide-flung mental net out far ahead and out farther still on all sides. They did not find what they sought, but they did find—something.

"What is it?" Worsel demanded of the quivering telepath who had made the report.

"I don't know, sir. Not on that ultra-band, but well below it . . . there. Not an Overlord, certainly, but something perhaps equally unfriendly."

"An Eich!" Both Worsel and Con exclaimed the thought, and the girl went on, "It was practically certain that we couldn't get them all on Jarnevon, of course, but none have been reported before . . . where are they, anyway? Get me a chart, somebody . . . It's Novena IX . . . QX—tune up your heavy artillery, Worsel—it'd be nice if we could take the head man alive, but that's a little too much luck to expect."

The Velantian, even though he had issued instantaneously the order to drive at full blast toward the indicated planet, was momentarily at a loss. Kinnison's daughter entertained no doubts as to the outcome of the encounter she was proposing—but she had never seen an Eich close up. He had. So had her father. Kinnison had come out a very poor second in that affair, and Worsel knew that he could have done no better, if as well. However, that had been upon Jarnevon, actually inside one of its strongest citadels, and neither he nor Kinnison had been prepared.

"What's the plan, Worsel?" Con demanded, vibrantly. "How're you figuring on taking 'em?"

"Depends on how strong they are. If it's a long-established base, we'll simply have to report it to LaForge and go on about our business. If, as seems more probable because it hasn't been reported before, it's a new establishment—or possibly only a grounded space-ship so far—we'll go to work on them ourselves. We'll soon be close enough to find out."

"QX," and a fleeting grin passed over Con's vivacious face. For a long time she had been working with Mentor the Arisian, specifically to develop the ability to "out-Worsel Worsel," and now was the best time she ever would have to put her hard schooling to test.

Hence, Master of Hallucination though he was, the Velantian had no hint of realization when his Klovian companion, working through a channel which he did not even know existed, took control of every compartment of his mind. Nor did the crew, in particular or en masse, suspect anything amiss when she performed the infinitely easier task of taking over theirs. Nor did the unlucky Eich, when the flying *Velan* had approached their planet closely enough to make it clear that their establishment was indeed a new one, being built around the nucleus of a Boskonian battleship. Except for their commanding officer they died then and there—and Con was to regret bitterly, later, that she had made this engagement such a one-girl affair.

The grounded battleship was a formidable fortress indeed. Under the fierce impact of its offensive beams the Velantians saw their very wall-shields flame violet. In return they saw their mighty secondary beams stopped cold by the Boskonian's inner screens, and had to bring into play the inconceivable energies of their primaries before the enemy's space-ship-fortress could be knocked out. And this much of the battle was real. Instrument- and recorder-tapes could be and were being doctored to fit; but spent primary shells could not be simulated. Nor was it thinkable that this super-dreadnaught and its incipient base should be allowed to survive.

Hence, after the dreadful primaries had quieted the Eich's main batteries and had reduced the ground-works to flaming pools of lava, needle-beamers went to work on every minor and secondary control board. Then, the great vessel definitely helpless as a fighting unit, Worsel and his hard-bitten crew thought that they went—thought-screened, full-armored, armed with semi-portables and DeLameters—joyously into the hand-to-hand combat which each craved. Worsel and two of his strongest henchmen attacked the armed and armored Boskonian captain. After a satisfyingly terrific struggle, in the course of which all three of the Velantians—and some others—were appropriately burned and wounded, they overpowered him and carried him bodily into the control room of the *Velan*. This part of the episode, too, was real; as was the complete melting down of the Boskonian vessel which occurred while the transfer was being made.

Then, while Con was engaged in the exceedingly delicate task of withdrawing her mind from Worsel's without leaving any detectable trace that she had ever been in it, there happened the completely unexpected; the one thing for which she was utterly unprepared. The mind of the captive captain was wrenched from her control as palpably as a loosely-held stick is snatched from a physical hand; and at the same time there was hurled against her impenetrable barriers an attack which could not possibly have stemmed from any Eichian mind!

If her mind had been free, she could have coped with the situation, but it was not. She *had* to hold Worsel—she knew with cold certainty what would ensue if she did not. The crew? They could be blocked out temporarily—unlike the Velantian Lensman, no one of them could even suspect that he had been in a stasis unless it were long enough to be noticeable upon such timepieces as clocks. The procedure, however, occupied a millisecond or so of precious time; and a considerably longer interval was required to withdraw with the required tracelessness from Worsel's mind. Thus, before she could do anything except protect herself and the Velantian from that surprisingly powerful invading intelligence, all trace of it disappeared and all that remained of their captive was a dead body.

Worsel and Constance stared at each other, wordless, for seconds. The Velantian had a completely and accurately detailed memory of everything that had happened up to that instant, the only matter not quite clear being the fact that their hard-won captive was dead; the girl's mind was racing to fabricate a bullet-proof explanation of that startling fact. Worsel saved her the trouble.

"It is of course true," he thought at her finally, "that any mind of sufficient power can destroy by force of will alone the entity of flesh in which it resides. I never thought about this matter before in connection with the Eich, but no detail of the experience your father and I had with them on Jarnevon would support any contention that they do not have minds of the requisite power . . . and today's battle, being purely physical, would not throw any light on the subject. . . . I wonder if a thing like that could be stopped? That is, if we had been on time . . . ?"

"That's it, I think." Con put on her most disarming, most engaging grin in preparation for the most outrageous series of lies of her long career. "And I don't think it can be stopped—at least I couldn't stop him. You see, I got into him a fraction of a second before you did, and in that instant, just like that." In spite of the fact that Worsel could not hear, she snapped her finger ringingly, "Faster even than that, he was gone. I didn't think of it until you brought it up, but you're right as can be—he killed himself to keep us from finding out whatever he knew."

Worsel stared at her with six eyes now instead of one, gimlet probes which glanced imperceptibly off her shield. He was not consciously trying to break down her barriers—to his fullest perception they were already down; no barriers were there. He was not consciously trying to integrate or reintegrate any detail or phase of the episode just past—no iota of falsity had appeared at any point or instant. Nevertheless, deep down within those extra reaches that made Worsel of Velantia what he was, a vague disquiet refused to down. It was too . . . too . . . Worsel's consciousness could not supply the adjective.

Had it been too easy? Very decidedly it had not. His utterly wornout, battered and wounded crew refuted that thought. So did his own body, slashed and burned, as well as did the litter of shells and the heaps of smoking slag which had once been an enemy stronghold.

Also, even though he had not theretofore thought that he and his crew possessed enough force to do what had just been done, it was starkly unthinkable that anyone, even an Arisian, could have helped him do anything without his knowledge. Particularly how could this girl, daughter of Kimball Kinnison although she was, possibly have stuff enough to play unperceived the part of guardian angel to him, Worsel of Velantia?

Least able of all the five Second-Stage Lensmen to appreciate what the Children of the Lens really were, he did not, then or ever, have any inkling of the real truth. But Constance, far behind her cheerfully innocent mask, shivered as she read exactly his disturbed and disturbing thoughts. For, conversely, an unresolved enigma would affect him more than it would any of his fellow L2's. He would work on it until he did resolve it, one way or another. This thing had to be settled, *now.* And there was a way—a good way.

"But I *did* help you, you big lug!" she stormed, stamping her booted foot in emphasis. "I was in there every second, slugging away with everything I had. Didn't you even feel me, you dope?" She allowed a thought to become evident; widened her eyes in startled incredulity. "You *didn't!*" she accused, hotly. "You were reveling so repulsively in the thrill of body-to-body fighting, just like you were back there in that cavern of Overlords, that you couldn't have felt a thought if it was driven into you with a D2P pressor! Of *course* I helped you, you wigglesome clunker! If I hadn't been in there pitching, dulling their edges here and there at critical moments, you'd've had a hell of a time getting them at all! I'm going to flit right now, and I hope I *never* see you again as long as I live!"

This vicious counter-attack, completely mendacious though it was, fitted the facts so exactly that Worsel's inchoate doubts vanished. Moreover, he was even less well equipped than are human men to cope with the peculiarly feminine weapons Constance was using so effectively. Wherefore the Velantian capitulated, almost abjectly, and the girl allowed herself to be coaxed down from her high horse and to become her usual sunny and impish self.

But when the *Velan* was once more on course and she had retired to her cabin, it was not to sleep. Instead, she thought. Was this intellect of the same race as the one whose burst of thought she had caught such a short time before, or not? She could not decide—not enough data. The first thought had been unconscious and quite revealing; this one simply a lethal weapon, driven with a power the memory of which made her gasp again. They could, however, be the same: the mind with which she had been en rapport could very well be capable of generating the force she had felt. If they were the same, they were something that should be studied, intensively and at once; and she herself had kicked away her only chance to make that study. She had better tell somebody about this, even if it meant confessing her own bird-brained part, and get some competent advice. Who?

Kit? No. Not because he would smack her down—she *ought* to be smacked down!—but because his brain wasn't enough better than her own to do any good. In fact, it wasn't a bit better than hers.

Mentor? At the very thought she shuddered, mentally and physically. She would call him in, fast enough, regardless of consequences to herself, if it would do any good, but it wouldn't. She was starkly certain of that. He wouldn't smack her down, like Kit would, but he wouldn't help her, either. He'd just sit there and sneer at her while she stewed, hotter and hotter, in her own juice . . .

"In a childish, perverted, and grossly exaggerated way, daughter Constance, you are right," the Arisian's thought rolled sonorously into her astounded mind. "You got yourself into this: get yourself out. One promising fact, however, I perceive—although seldom and late, you at last begin really to think."

In that hour Constance Kinnison grew up.

11

NADRECK TRAPS A TRAPPER

Any human or near human Lensman would have been appalled by the sheer loneliness of Nadreck's long vigil. Almost any one of them would have cursed, fluently and bitterly, when the time came at which he was forced to concede that the being for whom he lay in wait was not going to visit that particular planet.

But utterly unhuman Nadreck was not lonely. In fact, there was no word in the vocabulary of his race even remotely resembling the term in definition, connotation, or implication. From his galaxy-wide study he had a dim, imperfect idea of what such an emotion or feeling might be, but he could not begin to understand it. Nor was he in the least disturbed by the fact that Kandron did not appear. Instead, he held his orbit until the minute arrived at which the mathematical probability became point nine nine nine that his proposed quarry was not going to appear. Then, as matter-of-factly as though he had merely taken half an hour out for lunch, he abandoned his position and set out upon the course so carefully planned for exactly this event.

The search for further clues was long and uneventful; but monstrously, unhumanly patient Nadreck stuck to it until he found one. True, it was so slight as to be practically non-existent—a mere fragment of a whisper of zwilnik instruction—but it bore Kandron's unmistakable imprint. The Palainian had expected no more. Kandron would not slip.

Momentary leakages from faulty machines would have to occur from time to time, but Kandron's machines would not be at fault either often or long at a time.

Nadreck, however, had been ready. Course after course of the most delicate spotting screen ever devised had been out for weeks. So had tracers, radiation absorbers, and every other insidious locating device known to the science of the age. The standard detectors remained blank, of course—no more so than his own conveyance would that of the Onlonian be detectable by any ordinary instruments. And as the Palainian speedster shot away along the most probable course, some fifty delicate instruments in its bow began stabbing that entire region of space with a pattern of needles of force through which a Terrestrial barrel could not have floated untouched.

Thus the Boskonian craft—an inherently indetectable speedster—was located; and in that instant was speared by three modified CRX tracers. Nadreck then went inert and began to plot the other speedster's course. He soon learned that that course was unpredictable; that the vessel was being operated statistically, completely at random. This too, then, was a trap.

This knowledge disturbed Nadreck no more than had any more-or-less similar event of the previous twenty-odd years. He had realized fully that the leakage could as well have been deliberate as accidental. He had at no time underestimated Kandron's ability; the future alone would reveal whether or not Kandron would at any time underestimate his. He would follow through—there might be a way in which this particular trap could be used against its setter.

Leg after leg of meaningless course Nadreck followed, until there came about that which the Palainian knew would happen in time—the speedster held a straight course for more parsecs than six-sigma limits of probability could ascribe to pure randomness. Nadreck knew what that meant. The speedster was returning to its base for servicing, which was precisely the event for which he had been awaiting. It was the base he wanted, not the speedster; and that base would never, under any conceivable conditions, emit any detectable quantity of traceable radiation. To its base, then, Nadreck followed the little space-ship, and to say that he was on the alert as he approached that base is a gross understatement indeed. He expected to set off at least one, and probably many blasts of force. That would almost certainly be necessary in order to secure sufficient information concerning the enemy's defensive screens. It was necessary—but when those blasts arrived Nadreck was elsewhere, calmly analyzing the data secured by his instruments during the brief contact which had triggered the Boskonian projectors into action.

So light, so fleeting, and so unorthodox had been Nadreck's touch that the personnel of the now doomed base could not have known with any certainty that any visitor had actually been there. If there had been, the logical supposition would have been that he and his vessel had been resolved into their component atoms. Nevertheless Nadreck waited—as has been shown, he was good at waiting—until the burst of extra vigilance set up by the occurrence would have subsided into ordinary watchfulness. Then he began to act.

At first this action was in ultra-slow motion. One millimeter per hour his drill advanced. Drill was synchronized precisely with screen, and so guarded as to give an alarm at a level of interference far below that necessary to energize any probable detector at the generators of the screen being attacked.

Through defense after defense Nadreck made his cautious, indetectable way into the dome. It was a small base, as such things go; manned, as expected, by escapees from Onlo. Scum, too, for the most part; creatures of even baser and more violent passions than those upon whom he had worked in Kandron's Onlonian stronghold. To keep those intractable entities in line during their brutally long tours of duty, a psychological therapist had been given authority second only to that of the base commander. That knowledge, and the fact that there was only one populated dome, made the Palainian come as close to grinning as one of his unsmiling race can.

The psychologist wore a multiplex thought-screen, of course, as did everyone else; but that did not bother Nadreck. Kinnison had opened such screens many times; not only by means of his own hands, but also at various times by the use of a dog's jaws, a spider's legs and mandibles, and even a worm's sinuous body. Wherefore, through the agency of a quasi-fourth-dimensional life form literally indescribable to three-dimensional man, Nadreck's ego was soon comfortably ensconced in the mind of the Onlonian.

That entity knew in detail every weakness of each of his personnel. It was his duty to watch those weaknesses, to keep them down, to condition each of his wards in such fashion that friction and strife would be minimized. Now, however, he proceeded to do exactly the opposite. One hated another. That hate became a searing obsession, requiring the concentration of every effort upon ways and means of destroying its objects. One feared another. That fear ate in, searing as it went, destroying every normality of outlook and of reason. Many were jealous of their superiors. This emotion, requiring as it does nothing except its own substance upon which to feed, became a fantastically-spreading, caustically corrosive blight.

To name each ugly, noisome passion or trait resident in that dome is to call the complete roster of the vile; and calmly, mercilessly, unmovedly, ultra-efficiently, Nadreck manipulated them all. As though he were playing a Satanic organ he touched a nerve here, a synapse there, a channel somewhere else, bringing the whole group, with the lone exception of the commander, simultaneously to the point of explosion. Nor was any sign of this perfect work evident externally; for everyone there, having lived so long under the iron code of Boskonia, knew exactly the consequences of any infraction of that code.

The moment came when passion overmastered sense. One of the monsters stumbled, jostling another. That nudge became, in its recipient's seething mind, a lethal attack by his bitterest enemy. A forbidden projector flamed viciously: the offended one was sating his lust so insensately that he scarcely noticed the bolt that in turn rived away his own life. Detonated by this incident, the personnel of the base exploded as one. Blasters raved briefly; knives and swords bit and slashed; improvised bludgeons crashed against pre-selected targets; hard-taloned appendages gouged and tore. And Nadreck, who had long since withdrawn from the mind of the psychologist, timed with a stop-watch the duration of the whole grisly affair, from the instant of the first stumble to the death of the last Onlonian outside the commander's locked and armored sanctum. Ninety-eight and three-tenths seconds. Good—a nice job.

The commander, as soon as it was safe to do so, rushed out of his guarded room to investigate. Amazed, disgruntled, dismayed by the to him completely inexplicable phenomenon he had just witnessed, he fell an easy prey to the Palainian Lensman. Nadreck invaded his mind and explored it, channel by channel; finding—not entirely unexpectedly—that this Number One knew nothing whatever of interest.

Nadreck did not destroy the base. Instead, after setting up a small instrument in the commander's private office, he took that unfortunate wight aboard his speedster and drove off into space. He immobilized his captive, not by loading him with manacles, but by deftly severing a few essential nerve trunks. Then he really studied the Onlonian's mind—line by line, this time; almost cell by cell. A master—almost certainly Kandron himself—had operated here. There was not the slightest trace of tampering; no leads to or indications of what the activating stimulus would have to be; all that the fellow now knew was that it was his job to hold his base inviolate against any and every form of intrusion and to keep that speedster flitting around all over space on a director-by-chance as much as possible of the time, leaking slightly a certain signal now and then.

Even under this microscopic re-examination, he knew nothing whatever of Kandron; nothing of Onlo or of Thrale; nothing of any Boskonian organization, activity, or thing; and Nadreck, although baffled still, remained undisturbed. This trap, he thought, could almost certainly be used against the trapper. Until a certain call came through his relay in the base, he would investigate the planets of this system.

During the investigation a thought impinged upon his Lens from Karen Kinnison, one of the very few warm-blooded beings for whom he had any real liking or respect.

"Busy, Nadreck?" she asked, as casually as though she had just left him.

"In large, yes. In detail and at the moment, no. Is there any small problem in which I can be of assistance?"

"Not small—big. I just got the funniest distress call I ever heard or heard of. On a high band—way, 'way up—there. Do you know of any race that thinks on that band?"

"I do not believe so." He thought for a moment. "Definitely, no."

"Neither do I. It wasn't broadcast, either, but was directed at any member of a special race or tribe—very special. Classification, straight Z's to ten or twelve places, she—or it—seemed to be trying to specify."

"A frigid race of extreme type, adapted to an environment having a temperature of approximately one degree absolute."

"Yes. Like you, only more so." Kay paused, trying to put into intelligible thought a picture inherently incapable of reception or recognition by her as yet strictly three-dimensional intelligence. "Something like the Eich, too, but not much. Their visible aspect was obscure, fluid . . . amorphous . . . Indefinite? . . . skip it—I couldn't really perceive it, let alone describe it. I wish you had caught that thought."

"I wish so, too—it is very interesting. But tell me—if the thought was directed, not broadcast, how could you have received it?"

"That's the funniest part of the whole thing." Nadreck could feel the girl frown in concentration. "It came at me from all sides at once—never felt anything like it. Naturally I started feeling around for the source—particularly since it was a distress signal—but before I could get even a general direction of the origin it . . . it . . . well, it didn't really disappear or really weaken, but something happened to it. I couldn't read it any more—and *that* really did throw me for a loss." She paused, then went on. "It didn't so much go away as go *down,* some way or other. Then it vanished completely, without really going any-where. I'm not making myself clear—I simply can't—but have I given you enough leads so that you can make any sense at all out of any part of it?"

"I'm very sorry to say that I can not."

Nor could he, ever, for excellent reasons. That girl had a mind whose power, scope, depth, and rage she herself did not, could not even dimly understand; a mind to be fully comprehended only by an adult of her own third level. That mind had in fact received in toto a purely fourth-dimensional thought. If Nadreck had received it, he would have under-stood it and recognized it for what it was only because of his advanced Arisian training—no other Palainian could have done so—and it would have been sheerly unthinkable to him that any warm-blooded and there-fore strictly three-dimensional entity could by any possibility receive such a thought; or, having received it, could understand any part of it. Nevertheless, if he had really concentrated the full powers of his mind upon the girl's attempted description, he might very well have recognized in it the clearest possible three-dimensional delineation of such a thought; and from that point he could have gone on to a full understand-ing of the Children of the Lens.

However, he did not so concentrate. It was constitutionally impos-sible for him to devote real mental effort to any matter not immediately pertaining to the particular task in hand. Therefore neither he nor Karen Kinnison were to know until much later that she had been en rapport with one of Civilization's bitterest, most implacable foes; that she had seen with clairvoyant and telepathic accuracy the intrinsically three-dimensionally-indescribable form assumed in their winter by the horrid, the monstrous inhabitants of that viciously hostile world, the unspeakable planet Ploor!

"I was afraid you couldn't." Kay's thought came clear. "That makes it all the more important—important enough for you to drop whatever you're doing and join me in getting to the bottom of it, if you could be made to see it, which of course you can't."

"I am about to take Kandron, and nothing in the Universe can be as important as that," Nadreck stated quietly, as a simple matter of fact "You have observed this that lies here?"

"Yes." Karen, en rapport with Nadreck, was of course cognizant of the captive, but it had not occurred to her to mention this monster. When dealing with Nadreck she, against all the tenets of her sex, exhibited as little curiosity as did the coldly emotionless Lensman himself. "Since you bid so obviously for the question, why are you keeping it alive—or rather, not dead?"

"Because he is my sure link to Kandron." If Nadreck of Palain ever was known to gloat, it was then. "He is Kandron's creature, placed by Kandron personally as an agency of my destruction. Kandron's brain alone holds the key compulsion which will restore his memories. At some future time—perhaps a second from now, perhaps a cycle of years—Kandron will use that key to learn how his minion fares. Kandron's thought will energize my re-transmitter in the dome; the compulsion will be forwarded to this still-living brain. The brain, however, will be in my speedster, not in that undamaged fortress. You now understand why I cannot stray far from this being's base; you should see that you should join me instead of me joining you."

"No; not definite enough," Karen countered decisively, "I can't see myself passing up a thing like this for the opportunity of spending the next ten years floating around in an orbit, doing nothing. However, I check you to a certain extent—when and if anything really happens, shoot me a thought and I'll rally 'round."

The linkage broke without formal adieus. Nadreck went his way. Karen went hers. She did not, however, go far along the way she had had in mind. She was still precisely nowhere in her quest when she felt a thought, of a type that only her brother or an Arisian could send. It was Kit.

"Hi, Kay!" A warm, brotherly contact. "How'r'ya doing, sis—are you growing up?"

"Of *course* I'm grown up! What a question!"

"Don't get stiff, Kay, there's method in this. Got to be sure." All trace of levity gone, he probed her unmercifully. "Not too bad, at that, for a kid. As dad would express it, if he could feel you this way, you're twenty-nine numbers Brinnell harder than a diamond drill. Plenty of jets for this job, and by the time the real one comes, you'll probably be ready."

"Cut the rigmarole, Kit!" she snapped, and hurled a vicious bolt of her own. If Kit did not counter it as easily as he had handled her earlier efforts, he did not reveal the fact. "What job? What d'you think you're talking about? I'm on a job now that I wouldn't drop for Nadreck, and I don't think I'll drop it for you."

"You'll have to." Kit's thought was grim. "Mother is going to have to go to work on Lyrane II. The probability is pretty bad that there is or will be something there that she can't handle. Remote control is out, or I'd do it myself, but I can't work on Lyrane II in person. Here's the

586 CHRONICLES OF THE LENSMEN, VOLUME 2

whole picture—look it over. You can see, sis, that you're elected, so hop to it."

"I won't!" she stormed. "I can't—I'm too busy. How about asking Con, or Kat, or Cam?"

"They don't fit the picture," he explained patiently—for him. "In this case hardness is indicated, as you can see for yourself."

"Hardness, phooey!" she jeered. "To handle Ladora of Lyrane? She thinks she's a hard-boiled egg, I know, but . . ."

"Listen, you bird-brained knot-head!" Kit cut in, venomously. "You're fogging the issue deliberately—stop it! I spread you the whole picture—you know as well as I do that while there's nothing definite as yet, the thing needs covering and you're the one to cover it. But no—just because I'm the one to suggest to or ask anything of you, you've always got to go into that damned mulish act of yours . . ."

"Be silent, children, and attend!" Both flushed violently as Mentor came between them. "Some of the weaker thinkers here are beginning to despair of you, but my visualization of your development is still clear. To mold such characters as yours sufficiently, and yet not much, is a delicate task indeed; but one which must and shall be done. Christopher, come to me at once, in person. Karen, I would suggest that you go to Lyrane and do there whatever you find necessary to do."

"I won't—I've *still* got this job here to do!" Karen defied even the ancient Arisian sage.

"That, daughter, can and should wait. I tell you solemnly, as a fact, that if you do not go to Lyrane you will never get the faintest clue to that which you now seek."

12

KALONIA BECOMES OF INTEREST

Christopher Kinnison drove toward Arisia, seething. Why couldn't those damned sisters of his have sense to match their brains—or why couldn't he have had some brothers? Especially—right now—Kay. If she had the sense of a Zabriskan fontema she'd know that this job was *important* and would snap into it, instead of wild-goose-chasing all over space. If he were Mentor he'd straighten her out. He had decided to straighten her out once himself, and he grinned wryly to himself at the memory of what had happened. What Mentor had done to him, before he even got started, was really rugged. What he would like to do, next time he got within reach of her, was to shake her until her teeth rattled.

Or would he? Uh-uh. By no stretch of the imagination could he picture himself hurting any one of them. They were swell kids—in fact, the finest people he had ever known. He had rough-housed and wrestled with them plenty of times, of course—he liked it, and so did they. He could handle any one of them—he surveyed without his usual complacence his two-hundred-plus pounds of meat, bone, and gristle—he ought to be able to, since he outweighed them by fifty or sixty pounds; but it wasn't easy. Worse than Valerians—just like taking on a combination of boa constrictor and cateagle—and when Kat and Con ganged up on him that time they mauled him to a pulp in nothing flat.

But jet back! Weight wasn't it, except maybe among themselves.

He had never met a Valerian yet whose shoulders he couldn't pin flat to the mat in a hundred seconds, and the smallest of them outweighed him two to one. Conversely, although he had never thought of it before, what his sisters had taken from him, without even a bruise, would have broken any ordinary women up into masses of compound fractures. They were—they must be—made of different stuff.

His thoughts took a new tack. The kids were special in another way, too, he had noticed lately, without paying it any particular attention. It might tie in. They didn't *feel* like other girls. After dancing with one of them, other girls felt like robots made out of putty. Their flesh *was* different. It was firmer, finer, infinitely more responsive. Each individual cell seemed to be endowed with a flashing, sparkling life; a life which, interlinking with that of one of his own cells, made their bodies as intimately one as were their perfectly synchronized minds.

But what did all this have to do with their lack of sense? QX, they were nice people. QX, he couldn't beat their brains out, either physically or mentally. But damn it all, there ought to be *some* way of driving some ordinary common sense through their fine-grained, thick, hard, tough skulls!

Thus it was that Kit approached Arisia in a decidedly mixed frame of mind. He shot through the barrier without slowing down and without notification. Inerting his ship, he fought her into an orbit around the planet. The shape of the orbit was immaterial, as long as its every inch was inside Arisia's innermost screen. For young Kinnison knew precisely what those screens were and exactly what they were for. He knew that distance of itself meant nothing—Mentor could give anyone either basic or advanced treatments just as well from a distance of a thousand million parsecs as at hand to hand. The reason for the screens and for the personal visits was the existence of the Eddorians, who had minds probably as capable as the Arisians' own. And throughout all the infinite reaches of the macro-cosmic Universe, only within these highly special screens was there *certainty* of privacy from the spying senses of the ultimate foe.

"The time has come, Christopher, for the last treatment I am able to give you," Mentor announced without preamble, as soon as Kit had checked his orbit.

"Oh—so soon? I thought you were pulling me in to pin my ears back for fighting with Kay—the dim-wit!"

"That, while a minor matter, is worthy of passing mention, since it is illustrative of the difficulties inherent in the project of developing, without over-controlling, such minds as yours. En route here, you made a masterly summation of the situation, with one outstanding omission."

"Huh? What omission? I covered it like a blanket!"

"You assumed throughout, and still assume, as you always do in dealing with your sisters, that you are unassailably right; that your conclusion is the only tenable one; that they are always wrong."

"But damn it, they *are!* That's why you sent Kay to Lyrane!"

"In these conflicts with your sisters, you have been right in approximately half of the cases," Mentor informed him.

"But how about their fights with each other?"

"Do you know of any such?"

"Why . . . uh . . . can't say that I do." Kit's surprise was plain. "But since they fight with me so much, they must . . ."

"That does not follow, and for a very good reason. We may as well discuss that reason now, as it is a necessary part of the education which you are about to receive. You already know that your sisters are very different, each from the other. Know now, youth, that each was specifically developed to be so completely different that there is no possible point which could be made an issue between any two of them."

"Ungh . . . um . . ." It took some time for Kit to digest that news. "Then where do I come in that they *all* fight with me at the drop of a hat?"

"That, too, while regrettable, is inevitable. Each of your sisters, as you may have suspected, is to play a tremendous part in that which is to come. The Lensmen, we of Arisia, all will contribute, but upon you Children of the Lens—especially upon the girls—will fall the greater share of the load. Your individual task will be that of coordinating the whole; a duty which no Arisian is or ever can be qualified to perform. You will have to direct the efforts of your sisters; re-enforcing every heavily-attacked point with your own incomparable force and drive; keeping them smoothly in mesh and in place. As a side issue, you will also have to coordinate the feebler efforts of us of Arisia, the Lensmen, the Patrol, and whatever other minor forces we may be able to employ."

"Holy—Klono's—claws!" Kit was gasping like a fish. "Just where, Mentor, do you figure I'm going to pick up the jets to swing *that* load? And as to coordinating the kids—that's out. I'd make just one suggestion to any one of them and she'd forget all about the battle and tear into me—no, I'll take that back. The stickier the going, the closer they rally 'round."

"Right. It will always be so. Now, youth, that you have these facts, explain these matters to me, as a sort of preliminary exercise."

"I think I see." Kit thought intensely. "The kids don't fight with each other because they don't overlap. They fight with me because my central field overlaps them all. They have no occasion to fight with anybody else, nor have I, because with anybody else our viewpoint is always right and the other fellow knows it—except for Palainians and such, who think along different lines than we do. Thus, Kay never fights with Nadreck. When he goes off the beam, she simply ignores him and goes on about her business. But with them and me . . . we'll have to learn to arbitrate, or something, I suppose . . ." his thought trailed off.

"Manifestations of adolescence; with adulthood, now coming fast, they will pass. Let us get on with the work."

"But wait a minute!" Kit protested. "About this coordinator thing. I can't do it. I'm too much of a kid—I won't be ready for a job like that for a thousand years!"

"You must be ready," Mentor's thought was inexorable. "And, when the time comes, you shall be. Now, youth, come fully into my mind."

There is no use repeating in detail the progress of an Arisian super-education, especially since the most accurate possible description of the most important of those details would be intrinsically meaningless. When, finally, Kit was ready to leave Arisia, he looked much older and more mature than before; he felt immensely older than he looked. The concluding conversation of that visit, however, is worth recording.

"You now know, Christopher," Mentor mused, "What you children are and how you came to be. You are the accomplishment of long lifetimes of work. It is with profound satisfaction that I now perceive clearly that those lifetimes have not been spent in vain."

"Yours, you mean." Kit was embarrassed, but one point still bothered him. "Dad met and married mother, yes, but how about the others? Tregonsee, Worsel, and Nadreck? They and the corresponding females— don't take that literally for Nadreck, of course—were also penultimates, of lines as long as ours. You Arisians decided that the human stock was best, so none of the other Second-Stage Lensmen ever met their complements. Not that it could make any difference to them, of course, but I should think that three of your fellow students wouldn't feel so good."

"Ah, youth, I am very glad indeed that you mention the point." The Arisian's thought was positively gleeful. "You have at no time, then, detected anything peculiar about this that you know as Mentor of Arisia?"

"Why, of course not. How could I? Or, rather, why should I?"

"Any lapse on our part, however slight, from practically perfect synchronization would have revealed to such a mentality as yours that I whom you know as Mentor am not an individual, but four. While we each worked as individuals upon all of the experimental lines, whenever we dealt with any one of the penultimates or ultimates we did so as a fusion. This was necessary, not only for your fullest possible development, but also to be sure that each of us had complete data upon every minute facet of the truth. While it was in no sense important to the work itself to keep you in ignorance of Mentor's plurality, the fact that we could keep you ignorant of it, particularly now that you have become adult, showed that our work was being done in a really workmanlike fashion."

Kit whistled; a long, low whistle which was tribute enough to those who knew what it meant. He knew what he meant, but there were not enough words or thoughts to express it.

"But you're going to keep on being Mentor, aren't you?" he asked.

"I am. The real task, as you know, lies ahead."

"QX. You say I'm adult. I'm not. You imply that I'm more than several notches above you in qualifications. I could laugh myself silly about that one, if it wasn't so serious. Why, any one of you Arisians has forgotten more than I know, and could tie me up into bow-knots!"

"There are elements of truth in your thought. That you can now be called adult, however, does not mean that you have attained your full power; only that you are able to use effectively the powers you have and are able to acquire other and larger powers."

"But what *are* those powers?" Kit demanded. "You've hinted on that same theme a thousand times, and I don't know what you mean any better than I did before!"

"You must develop your own powers." Mentor's thought was as final as Fate. "Your mind is potentially far abler than mine. You will in time come to know my mind in full; I never will be able to know yours. For the lesser, but full mind to attempt to instruct in methodology the greater, although emptier one, is to set that greater mind in an undersized mold and thus to do it irreparable harm. You have the abilities and the powers. You will have to develop them yourself, by the perfection of techniques concerning which I can give you no instructions whatever."

"But surely you can give me some kind of a hint!" Kit pleaded. "I'm just a kid, I tell you—I don't even know how or where to begin!"

Under Kit's startled mental gaze, Mentor split suddenly into four parts, laced together by a pattern of thoughts so intricate and so rapid as to be unrecognizable. The parts fused and again Mentor spoke.

"I can point the way in only the broadest, most general terms. It has been decided, however, that I can give you one hint—or, more properly, one illustration. The surest test of knowledge known to us is the visualization of the Cosmic All. All science is, as you know, one. The true key to power lies in the knowledge of the underlying reasons for the succession of events. If it is pure causation—that is, if any given state of things follows as an inevitable consequence because of the state existing an infinitesimal instant before—then the entire course of the macro-cosmic universe was set for the duration of all eternity in the instant of its coming into being. This well-known concept, the stumbling-block upon which many early thinkers came to grief, we now know to be false. On the other hand, if pure randomness were to govern, natural laws as we know them could not exist. Thus neither pure causation nor pure randomness alone can govern the succession of events.

"The truth, then, must lie somewhere in between. In the macro-cosmos, causation prevails; in the micro-, randomness; both in accord with the mathematical laws of probability. It is in the region between them—the intermediate zone, or the interface, so to speak—that the greatest problems lie. The test of validity of any theory, as you know, is the accuracy of the predictions which are made possible by its use, and our greatest thinkers have shown that the completeness and fidelity of any visualization of the Cosmic All are linear functions of the clarity of definition of the components of that interface. Full knowledge of that indeterminate zone would mean infinite power and a statistically perfect visualization. None of these things, however, will ever be realized; for the acquirement of that full knowledge would require infinite time.

"That is all I can tell you. It will, properly studied, be enough. I have built within you a solid foundation; yours alone is the task of erecting upon that foundation a structure strong enough to withstand the forces which will be thrown against it.

"It is perhaps natural, in view of what you have recently gone through, that you should regard the problem of the Eddorians as one of insuperable difficulty. Actually, however, it is not, as you will perceive when you have spent a few weeks in re-integrating yourself. You must not, you shall not, and in my clear visualization you do not, fail."

Communication ceased. Kit made his way groggily to his control board, went free, and lined out for Klovia. For a guy whose education was supposed to be complete, he felt remarkably like a total loss with no insurance. He had asked for advice and had got—what? A dissertation on philosophy, mathematics, and physics—good enough stuff, probably, if he could see what Mentor was driving at, but not of much immediate use. He did have a brainful of new stuff, though—didn't know yet what half of it was—he'd better be getting it licked into shape. He'd "sleep" on it.

He did so, and as he lay quiescent in his bunk the tiny pieces of an incredibly complex jigsaw puzzle began to click into place. The ordinary zwilniks—all the small fry fitted in well enough. The Overlords of Delgon. The Kalonians . . . hm . . . he'd better check with dad on that angle.

The Eich—under control. Kandron of Onlo, ditto. "X" was in safe hands; Cam had already been alerted to watch her step. Some planet named Ploor—what in all the purple hells of Palain had Mentor meant by that crack? Anyway, that piece didn't fit anywhere—yet. That left Eddore— and at the thought a series of cold waves raced up and down the young Lensman's spine. Nevertheless, Eddore was his oyster—his, and nobody else's. Mentor had made that plain enough. Everything the Arisians had done for umpteen skillions of years had been aimed at the Eddorians. They had picked him out to emcee the show—and how could a man coordinate an attack against something he knew nothing about? And the only way to get acquainted with Eddore and its denizens was to go there. Should he call in the kids? He should not. Each of them had her hands full of her own job; that of developing her own full self. He had his; and the more he studied the question, the clearer it became that the first number on the program of his self-development was—would *have* to be—a single-handed expedition against the key planet of Civilization's top-ranking foes.

He sprang out of his bunk, changed his vessel's course, and lined out a thought to his father.

"Dad? Kit. Been flitting around out Arisia way, and picked up an idea I want to pass along to you. It's about Kalonians. What do you know about them?"

"They're blue . . ."

"I don't mean that."

"I know you don't. There were Helmuth, Jalte, Prellin, Crowninshield . . . all I can think of at the moment. Big operators, son, and smart hombres, if I do say so myself as shouldn't; but they're all ancient history . . . hold it! Maybe I know of a modern one, too—Eddie's Lensman. The only part of that picture that was sharp was the Lens, since Eddie was never analytically interested in any of the hundreds of types of people he met, but there was something about that Lensman . . . I'll bring him back and focus him as sharply as I can . . . there." Both men studied the blurred statue posed in the Gray Lensman's mind. "Wouldn't you say he could be a Kalonian?"

"Check. I wouldn't want to say much more than that. But about that Lens—did you really examine it? It *is* sharp—under the circumstances, of course, it would be."

"Certainly! Wrong in every respect—rhythm, chroma, context, and aura. Definitely not Arisian; therefore Boskonian. That's the point— that's what I was afraid of, you know."

"Double check. And that point ties in tight with the one that made me call you just now, that everybody, including you and me, seems to have missed. I've been searching my memory for five hours—you know what my memory is like—and I have heard of exactly two other Kalonians. They were big operators, too. I have never heard of the planet itself. To me it is a startling fact that the sum total of my information on Kalonia, reliable or otherwise, is that it produced seven big-shot zwilniks; six of them before I was born. Period."

Kit felt his father's jaw drop.

"No, I don't remember of hearing anything about the planet, either," the older man finally replied. "But I'll bet I can get you all the information you want in fifteen minutes."

"Credits to millos it'll be a lot nearer fifteen days. You can find it sometime, though, if anybody can—that's why I'm taking it up with you. While I don't want to seem to be giving a Gray Lensman orders"—that jocular introduction had come to be a sort of ritual in the Kinnison family—"I would very diffidently suggest that there might be some connection between that completely unnoticed planet and some of the things we don't know about Boskonia."

"Diffident! You?" The Gray Lensman laughed deeply. "Like a hydride bomb! I'll start a search of Kalonia right away. As to your credits-to-millos-fifteen-days thing, I'd be ashamed to take your money. You don't know our librarians or our system. Ten millos, even money, that we get operational data in less than five G-P days from right now. Want it?"

"I'll say so. I'll wear that cento on my tunic as a medal of victory over the Gray Lensman. I *do* know the size of these here two galaxies!"

"QX—it's a bet. I'll Lens you when we get the dope. In the meantime, Kit, remember that you're my favorite son."

"Well, you're not so bad, yourself. Any time I want mother to divorce you so as to change fathers for me I'll suggest it to her." What a terrific, what a tremendous meaning was heterodyned upon that seemingly light exchange! "Clear ether, dad!"

"Clear ether, son!"

13

CLARRISSA TAKES HER L-2 WORK

Thousands of years were to pass before Christopher Kinnison could develop the ability to visualize, from the contemplation of one fact or artifact, the entire Universe to which it belonged. He could not even plan in detail his one-man invasion of Eddore until he could integrate all available data concerning the planet Kalonia into his visualization of the Boskonian Empire. One unknown, Ploor, blurred his picture badly enough; two such completely unknown factors made visualization, even in broad, impossible.

Anyway, he decided, he had one more job to do before he tackled the key planet of the enemy; and now, while he was waiting for the dope on Kalonia, would be the best time to do it. Wherefore he sent out a thought to his mother.

"Hi, First Lady of the Universe! 'Tis thy first-born who wouldst fain converse with thee. Art pressly engaged in matters of moment or import?"

"Art not, Kit." Clarrissa's characteristic chuckle was as infectious, as full of the joy of life, as ever. "Not that it would make any difference— but methinks I detect an undertone of seriosity beneath thy persiflage. Spill it."

"Let's make it a rendezvous, instead," he suggested. "We're fairly close, I think—closer than we've been for a long time. Where are you, exactly?"

"Oh! Can we? Wonderful!" She marked her location and velocity in his mind. She made no effort to conceal her joy at the idea of a personal meeting. She never had tried and she never would try to make him put first matters other than first. She had not expected to see him again, physically, until this war was over. But if she could . . . !

"QX. Hold your course and speed; I'll be seeing you in eighty-three minutes. In the meantime, it'll be just as well if we don't communicate, even by Lens . . ."

"Why, son?"

"Nothing definite—just a hunch, is all. 'Bye, gorgeous!"

The two speedsters approached each other—inerted—matched intrinsics—went free—flashed into contact—sped away together upon Clarrissa's original course.

"Hi, mums!" Kit spoke into a visiphone. "I should of course come to you, but it might be better if you come in here—I've got some special rigs set up here that I don't want to leave. QX?" He snapped on one of the special rigs as he spoke—a device which he himself had built and installed; the generator of the most efficient thought-screen then known.

"Why, of course!" She came, and was swept off her feet in the exuberance of her tall son's embrace; a greeting which she returned with equal fervor.

"It's nice, mother, seeing you again." Words, or thoughts even, were *so* inadequate! Kit's voice was a trifle rough; his eyes were not completely dry.

"Uh-huh. It *is* nice," she agreed, snuggling her spectacular head even more firmly into the curve of his shoulder. "Mental contact is better than nothing, of course, but *this* is perfect!"

"Just as much a menace to navigation as ever, aren't you?" He held her at arms' length and shook his head in mock disapproval. "Do you think it's quite right for one woman to have so much of everything when all the others have so little of anything?"

"Honestly, I don't." She and Kit had always been exceptionally close; now her love for and her pride in this splendid creature, her son and her first-born, simply would not be denied. "You're joking, I know, but that strikes too deep for comfort. I wake up in the night to wonder why, of all the women in existence, I should be so lucky, especially in my husband and children . . . QX, skip it." Kit was shying away—she should have known better than to try in words even to skirt the profound depths of sentiment which both she and he knew so well were there.

"Get back onto the beam, gorgeous, you know what I meant. Look at yourself in the mirror some day—or do you, perchance?"

"Once in a while—maybe twice." She giggled unaffectedly. "You don't think all this charm and glamor comes without effort, do you? But maybe you'd better get back onto the beam yourself—you didn't come all these parsecs out of your way to say pretty things to your mother—even though I admit they've built up my ego no end."

"On target, dead center." Kit had been grinning, but he sobered quickly. "I wanted to talk to you about Lyrane and the job you're figuring on doing out there."

"Why?" she demanded. "Do you know anything about it?"

"Unfortunately, I don't." Kit's black frown of concentration reminded her forcibly of his father's characteristic scowl. "Guesses—suspicions— theories—not even good hunches. But I thought . . . I wondered . . ." He paused, embarrassed as a schoolboy, then went on with a rush: "Would you mind it too much if I went into something pretty personal?"

"You know I wouldn't, son." In contrast to Kit's usual clarity and precision of thought, the question was highly ambiguous, but Clarrissa covered both angles. "I can conceive of no subject, event, action, or thing, in either my life or yours, too intimate or too personal to discuss with you in full. Can you?"

"No, I can't—but this is different. As a woman, you're tops—the finest and best that ever lived." This statement, made with all the matter-of-factness of stating that a triangle had three corners, thrilled Clarrissa through and through. "As a Gray Lensman you're over the rest of them like a cirrus cloud. But you should rate full Second Stage, and . . . well, you may run up against something too hot to handle, some day, and I . . . that is, you . . ."

"You mean that I don't measure up?" she asked, quietly. "I know very well I don't, and admitting an evident fact should not hurt my feelings a bit. Don't interrupt, please," as Kit began to protest. "In fact, it is sheerest effrontery—it has always bothered me terribly, Kit—to be classed as a Lensman at all, considering what splendid men they all are and what each one of them had to go through to earn his Lens, to say nothing of a Release. You know as well as I do that I've never done a single thing to earn or to deserve it. It was handed to me on a silver platter. I'm not worthy of it, Kit, and all the real Lensmen know I'm not. They must know it, Kit—they *must* feel that way!"

"Did you ever express yourself in exactly that way before, to anybody? You didn't, I know." Kit stopped sweating; this was going to be easier than he had feared.

"I couldn't, Kit, it was too deep; but as I said, I can talk *anything* over with you."

"QX. We can settle that fast enough if you'll answer just one question. Do you honestly believe that you would have been given the Lens if you were not absolutely worthy of it? Perfectly—in every minute particular?"

"Why, I never thought of it that way . . . probably not . . . no, certainly not." Clarrissa's somber mien lightened markedly. "But I still don't see how or why . . ."

"Clear enough," Kit interrupted. "You were born with what the rest of them had to work so hard for—with stuff that no other woman, anywhere, ever had."

"Except the girls, of course," Clarrissa corrected, half absently.

"Except the kids," he concurred. It could do no harm to agree with his mother's statement of a self-evident fact. "You can take it from me, as one who *knows* that the other Lensmen know you've got plenty of jets. They know very well that the Arisians wouldn't make a Lens for anybody who hasn't got what it takes. And so, very neatly, we've stripped ship for the action I came over here to see you about. It isn't a case of you not measuring up, because you do, in every respect. It's simply that you're short a few jets that you ought by rights to have. You really are a Second-Stage Lensman—you know that, mums—but you never went to Arisia for your L2 work. I hate to see you blast off without full equipment into what may prove to be a big-time job; especially when you're so eminently able to take it. Mentor could give you the works in a few hours. Why don't you flit for Arisia right now, or let me take you there?"

"No—NO!" Clarrissa backed away, shaking her head emphatically. "Never! I couldn't, Kit, ever—not *possibly!*"

"Why not?" Kit was amazed. "Why, mother, you're actually shaking!"

"I know I am—I can't help it. That's why. He's the only thing in the entire Universe that I'm really afraid of. I can talk *about* him without quite getting goose-bumps all over me, but the mere thought of actually being with him simply scares me into shivering, quivering fits—no less."

"I see . . . it might very well work that way, at that. Does dad know it?"

"Yes—or, that is, he knows I'm afraid of him, but he doesn't know it the way you do—it simply doesn't register in true color. Kim can't conceive of me being either a coward or a cry-baby. And I don't want him to, either, Kit, so please don't tell him, ever."

"I won't—he'd fry me to a cinder in my own grease if I did. Frankly, I can't see any part of your self-portrait, either. As a matter of cold fact, you are so obviously neither a coward nor a cry-baby . . . well, that's about the silliest crack you ever made. What you've really got, mums, is a fixation, and if it can't be removed . . ."

"It can't," she declared flatly. "I've tried that, now and then, ever since before you were born. Whatever it is, it's a permanent installation and it's really deep. I've known all along that Kim didn't give me the whole business—he couldn't—and I've tried again and again to make myself go to Arisia, or at least to call Mentor about it, but I can't do it, Kit—I simply *can't!*"

"I understand." Kit nodded. He did understand, now. What she felt was not, in essence and at bottom, fear at all. It was worse than fear, and deeper. It was true revulsion; the basic, fundamental, sub-conscious, sex-based reaction of an intensely vital human female against a mental monstrosity who had not had a sexual thought for countless thousands of her years. She could neither analyze nor understand her feeling; but it was as immutable, as ineradicable, and as old as the surging tide of life itself.

"But there's another way, just as good—probably better, as far as you're concerned. You aren't afraid of me, are you?"

"What a *question!* Of course I'm not . . . why, do you mean *you* . . ." Her expressive eyes widened. "You children—especially you—are far beyond us . . . as of course you should be . . . but *can* you, Kit? Really?"

Kit keyed a part of his mind to an ultra-high level. "I know the techniques, Mentor, but the first question is, should I do it?"

"You should, youth. The time has come when it is necessary."

"Second—I've never done anything like this before, and she's my own mother. If I make one slip I'll never forgive myself. Will you stand by and see that I don't slip? And stand guard?"

"I will stand by and stand guard."

"I really can, mums." Kit answered her question with no perceptible pause. "That is, if you're willing to put everything you've got into it. Just letting me into your mind isn't enough. You'll have to sweat blood—you'll think you've been run through a hammer-mill and spread out on a Delgonian torture screen to dry."

"Don't worry about that, Kit." All the passionate intensity of Clarrissa's being was in her vibrant voice. "If you just knew how utterly I've been longing for it—I'll work; and whatever you give me I can take."

"I'm sure of that. And, not to work under false pretenses, I'd better tell you how I know. Mentor showed me what to do and told me to do it."

"Mentor!"

"Mentor," Kit agreed. "He knew that it was a psychological impossibility for you to work with him, and that you could and would work with me. So he appointed me a committee of one." Clarrissa was reacting to this news as it was inevitable that she should react; and to give her time to steady down he went on:

"Mentor also knew, and so do you and I, that even though you are afraid of him, you know what he is and what he means to Civilization. I had to tell you this so you'd know, without any tinge of doubt, that I'm not a half-baked kid setting out to do a man's job of work."

"Jet back, Kit! I may have thought a lot of different things about you at times, but 'half-baked' was never one of them. That's your own thinking, not mine."

"I wouldn't wonder." Kit grinned wryly. "My ego could stand some stiffening right now. This isn't going to be funny. You're too fine a woman, and I think too much of you, to enjoy the prospect of mauling you around so unmercifully."

"Why, Kit!" Her mood was changing fast. Her old-time, impish smile came back in force. "You aren't weakening, surely? Shall I hold your hand?"

"Uh-huh—cold feet," he admitted. "It might be a smart idea, at that, holding hands. Physical linkage. Well, I'm as ready as I ever will be, I guess—whenever you are, say so. And you'd better sit down before you fall down."

"QX, Kit—come in."

Kit came; and at the first terrific surge of his mind within hers the Red Lensman caught her breath, stiffened in every muscle, and all but screamed in agony. Kit's fingers needed their strength as her hands clutched his and closed in a veritable spasm. She had thought that she knew what to expect; but the reality was different—much different. She had suffered before. On Lyrane II, although she had never told anyone of it, she had been burned and wounded and beaten. She had borne five children. This was as though every poignant experience of her past had been rolled into one, raised to the nth power, and stabbed relentlessly into the deepest, tenderest, most sensitive centers of her being.

And Kit, boring in and in and in, knew exactly what to do; and, now that he had started, he proceeded unflinchingly and with exact precision to do what had to be done. He opened up her mind as she had never dreamed it possible for a mind to open. He separated the tiny, jammed compartments, each completely from every other. He showed her how to make room for this tremendous expansion and watched her do it, against the shrieking protests of every cell and fiber of her body and of her brain. He drilled new channels everywhere, establishing an inconceivably complex system of communication lines of infinite conductivity. He knew just what he was doing to her, since the same thing had been done to him so recently, but he kept on relentlessly until the job was done. Completely done.

Then, working together, they sorted and labeled and classified and catalogued. They checked and double checked. Finally she knew, and Kit knew that she knew, every hitherto unplumbed recess of her mind and

every individual cell of her brain. Every iota of every quality and characteristic, every scrap of knowledge she had ever acquired or ever would
acquire, would be at her command instantaneously and effortlessly. Then,
and only then, did Kit withdraw his mind from hers.

"Did you say that I was short just a *few* jets, Kit?" She got up groggily
and mopped her face; upon which her few freckles stood out surprisingly
dark upon a background of white. "I'm a wreck—I'd better go and . . ."

"As you were for just a sec—I'll break out a bottle of fayalin. This
rates a celebration of sorts, don't you think?"

"Very much so." As she sipped the pungently aromatic red liquid her
color began to come back. "No wonder I felt as though I were missing
something all these years. Thanks, Kit. I really appreciate it. You're a . . ."

"Seal it, mums." He picked her up and squeezed her, hard. He
scarcely noticed her sweat-streaked face and disheveled hair, but she did.

"Good Heavens, Kit, I'm a perfect *hag!*" she exclaimed. "I've *got*
to go and put on a new face!"

"QX. I don't feel quite so fresh, myself. What I need, though, is a
good, thick steak. Join me?"

"Uh-uh. How can you even think of *eating,* at a time like this?"

"Same way you can think of war-paint and feathers, I suppose. Different people, different reactions. QX, I'll be in there and see you in
fifteen or twenty minutes. Flit!"

She left, and Kit heaved an almost explosive sigh of relief. Mighty
good thing she hadn't asked too many questions—if she had become
really curious, he would have had a horrible time keeping her away from
the fact that that kind of work never had been done and never would be
done outside of solid Arisian screen. He ate, cleaned up, ran a comb
through his hair, and, when his mother was ready, crossed over into her
speedster.

"Whee—whee-yu!" Kit whistled descriptively. *"What* a seven-sector
call-out! Just who do you think you're going to knock out of the ether on
Lyrane Two?"

"Nobody at all." Clarrissa laughed. "This is all for you, son—and
maybe a little bit for me, too."

"I'm stunned. You're a blinding flash and a deafening report. But
I've got to do a flit, gorgeous. So clear . . ."

"Wait a minute—you *can't* go yet! I've got questions to ask you
about these new networks and things. How do I handle them?"

"Sorry—you've got to develop your own techniques. You know that
already."

"In a way. I thought maybe, though, I could wheedle you into helping me a little. I should have known better—but tell me, all Lensmen don't have minds like this, do they?"

"I'll say they don't. They're all like yours was before, but not as good. Except the other L2's, of course—dad, Worsel, Tregonsee, and Nadreck. Theirs are more or less like yours is now; but you've got a lot of stuff they haven't."

"Huh?" she demanded. "Such as?"

" 'Way down—there." He showed her. "You worked all that stuff yourself. I only showed you how, without getting in too close."

"Why? Oh, I see—you would. Life force. I would have lots of that, of course." She did not blush, but Kit did.

"Life force" was a pitifully inadequate term indeed for that which Civilization's only Lensman-mother had in such measure, but they both knew what it was. Kit ducked.

"You can always tell all about a Lensman by looking at his Lens; it's the wiring diagram of his total mind. You've studied dad's of course."

"Yes. Three times as big as the ordinary ones—or mine—and much finer and brighter. But *mine* isn't, Kit?"

"It *wasn't,* you mean. Look at it now."

She opened a drawer, reached in, and stared; her eyes and mouth becoming three round O's of astonishment. She had never seen that Lens before, or anything like it. It was three times as big as hers, seven times as fine and as intricate, and ten times as bright.

"Why, this isn't mine!" she gasped. "But it *must* be . . ."

"Sneeze, beautiful," Kit advised. "Cobwebs. You aren't thinking a lick. Your mind changed, so your Lens had to. See?"

"Of course—I wasn't thinking; that's a fact. Let me look at *your* Lens, Kit—you never seem to wear it—I haven't seen it since you graduated."

"Sure. Why not?" He reached into a pocket. "I take after you, that way; neither of us gets any kick out of throwing his weight around."

His Lens flamed upon his wrist. It was larger in diameter than Clarissa's, and thicker. Its texture was finer; its colors were brighter, harsher, and seemed, somehow, *solider.* Both studied both Lenses for a moment, then Kit seized his mother's hand, brought their wrists together, and stared.

"That's it," he breathed. "That's it . . . That's IT, just as sure as Klono has got teeth and claws."

"What's it? What do you see?" she demanded.

"I see how and why I got the way I am—and if the kids had Lenses theirs would be the same. Remember dad's? Look at your dominants—notice that every one of them is duplicated in mine. Blank them out of mine, and see what you've got left—pure Kimball Kinnison, with just enough extras thrown in to make me an individual instead of a carbon copy. Hm . . . hm . . . credits to millos this is what comes of having Lensmen on both sides of the family. No wonder we're freaks! Don't know whether I'm in favor of it or not—I don't think they should produce any more Lady Lensmen, do you? Maybe that's why they never did."

"Don't try to be funny," she reproved; but her dimples were again in evidence. "If it would result in more people like you and your sisters, I'd be very much in favor of it; but, some way or other, I doubt it. I know you're squirming to go, so I won't hold you any longer. What you just found out about Lenses is fascinating. For the rest of it . . . well . . . thanks, son, and clear ether."

"Clear ether, mother. This is the worst part of being together, leaving so quick. I'll see you again, though, soon and often. It you get stuck, yell, and one of the kids or I—or all of us—will be with you in a split second."

He gave her a quick, hard hug; kissed her enthusiastically, and left. He did not tell her, and she never did find out, that his "discovery" of one of the secrets of the Lens was made to keep her from asking questions which he could not answer.

The Red Lensman was afraid that she would not have time to put her new mind in order before reaching Lyrane II; but, being naturally a good housekeeper, she did. More, so rapidly and easily did her mind now work, she had time to review and to analyze every phase of her previous activities upon that planet and to lay out in broad her first lines of action. She wouldn't put on the screws at first, she decided. She would let them think that she didn't have any more jets than before. Helen was nice, but a good many of the others, especially that airport manager, were simply quadruply-distilled vixens. She'd take it easy at first, but she'd be very sure that she didn't get into any such jams as last time.

She coasted down through Lyrane's stratosphere and poised high above the city she remembered so well.

"Helen of Lyrane!" she sent out a sharp, clear thought. "That is not your name, I know, but we did not learn any other . . ."

She broke off, every nerve taut. Was that, or was it not, Helen's thought; cut off, wiped out by a guardian block before it could take shape?

"Who are you stranger, and what do you want?" the thought came, almost instantly, from a person seated at the desk which had been Helen's.

Clarissa glanced at the sender and thought that she recognized the face. Her new channels functioned instantaneously; she remembered every detail.

"Lensman Clarissa, formerly of Sol III. Unattached. I remember you, Ladora, although you were only a child when I was here. Do you remember me?"

"Yes, I repeat, what do you want?" The memory did not decrease Ladora's hostility.

"I would like to speak to the former Elder Person, if I may."

"You may not. It is no longer with us. Leave at once, or we will shoot you down."

"Think again, Ladora." Clarrissa held her tone even and calm. "Surely your memory is not so short that you have forgotten the *Dauntless* and its capabilities."

"I remember. You may take up with me whatever it is that you wish to discuss with my predecessor."

"You are familiar with the Boskonian invasion of years ago. It is suspected that they are planning new and galaxy-wide outrages, and that this planet is in some way involved. I have come here to investigate the situation."

"We will conduct our own investigations," Ladora declared, curtly. "We insist that you and all other foreigners stay away from this planet."

"*You* investigate a galactic condition?" In spite of herself, Clarrissa almost let the connotations of that question become perceptible. "If you give me permission I will land alone. If you do not, I shall call the *Dauntless* and we will land in force. Take your choice."

"Land alone, then, if you must land." Ladora yielded seethingly. "Land at City Airport."

"Under those guns? No, thanks; I am neither invulnerable nor immortal. I land where I please."

She landed. During her previous visit she had had a hard enough time getting any help from these pig-headed matriarchs, but this time she encountered a non-cooperation so utterly fanatical that it put her completely at a loss. None of them tried to harm her in any way; but not one of them would have anything to do with her. Every thought, even the friendliest, was stopped by a full-coverage block; no acknowledgment, even, was ever made.

"I can crack those blocks easily enough, if I want to," she declared, one bad evening, to her mirror, "and if they keep this up very much longer, by Klono's emerald-filled gizzard, I will!

14

KINNISON-THYRON, DRUG RUN-
NER

When Kimball Kinnison received his son's call he was in Ultra Prime, the Patrol's stupendous Klovian base, about to enter his ship. He stopped for a moment; practically in mid-stride. While nothing was to be read in his expression or in his eyes, the lieutenant to whom he had been talking had been an interested, if completely uninformed, witness to many such Lensed conferences and knew that they were usually important. He was therefore not surprised when the Lensman turned around and headed for an exit.

"Put her back, please. I won't be going out for a while, after all," Kinnison explained, briefly. "Don't know exactly how long."

A fast flitter took him to the hundred story pile of stainless steel and glass which was the coordinator's office. He strode along a corridor, through an unmarked door.

"Hi, Phyllis—the boss in?"

"Why, Coordinator Kinnison! Yes, sir . . . no, I mean . . ." His startled secretary touched a button and a door opened; the door of his private office.

"Hi, Kim—back so soon?" Vice-Coordinator Maitland also showed surprise as he got up from the massive desk and shook hands cordially. "Good! Taking over?"

"Emphatically no. Hardly started yet. Just dropped in to use your plate, if you've got a free high-power wave. QX?"

"Certainly. If not, you can free one fast enough."

"Communications." Kinnison touched a stud. "Will you please get me Thrale? Library One; Principal Librarian Nadine Ernley. Plate to plate."

This request was surprising enough to the informed. Since the coordinator practically never dealt personally with anyone except Lensmen, and usually Unattached Lensmen at that, it was a rare event indeed for him to use any ordinary channels of communication. And as the linkage was completed, subdued murmurs and sundry squeals gave evidence of the intense excitement at the other end of the line.

"Mrs. Ernley will be on in one moment, sir." The operator's business was done. Her crisp, clear-cut voice ceased, but the background noise increased markedly.

"Sh . . . sh . . . sh! It's the Gray Lensman, himself!" Everywhere upon Klovia, Tellus, and Thrale, and in many localities of many other planets, the words "Gray Lensman," without surname, had only one meaning.

"Not the *Gray Lensman!*"

"It can't be!"

"It *is,* really—I know him—I actually *met* him once!"

"Let *me* look—just a peek!"

"Sh . . . sh! He'll *hear* you!"

"Switch on the vision. If we've got a moment, let's get acquainted," Kinnison suggested, and upon his plate there burst into view a bevy of excitedly embarrassed blondes, brunettes, and redheads. "Hi, Madge! Sorry I don't know the rest of you, but I'll make it a point to meet you all—before long, I think. Don't go away." The head of the library was coming on the run. "You're all in on this. Hi, Nadine! Long time no see. Remember that bunch of squirrel food you rounded up for me?"

"I remember, sir." What a question! As though Nadine Ernley, nee Hostetter, could ever forget her share in that famous meeting of the fifty-three greatest scientific minds of all Civilization! "I'm sorry that I was out in the stacks when you called."

"QX—we all have to work sometime, I suppose. What I'm calling about is that I've got a mighty big job for you and those smart girls of yours. Something like that other one, only a lot more so. I want all the information you can dig up about a planet named Kalonia, just as fast as you can possibly get it. What makes it extra tough is that I have never even heard of the planet itself and don't know of anyone who has. There may be a million other names for it, on a million other planets, but we don't know any of them. Here's all I know." He summarized; concluding: "If you can get it for me in less than four point nine five G-P days from now I'll bring you, Nadine, a Manarkan star-drop; and you can have each of your girls go down to Brenleer's and pick out a wristwatch, or whatever else she likes, and I'll have it engraved to her 'In appreciation, Kimball Kinnison.' This job is important—my son Kit bet me ten millos that we can't do it that fast."

"Ten *millos!*" Four or five of the girls gasped as one.

"Fact," he assured them, gravely. "So whenever you get the dope, tell Communications—no, you listen while I tell them myself. Communications, all along the line, come in!" They came. "I expect one of these librarians to call me, plate to plate, within the next few days. When she does, no matter what time of day or night it is, and no matter what I or anyone else happen to be doing, that call will have the right-of-way over any other business in the universe. Cut!" The plates went dead, and in Library One:

"But he was joking, surely!"

"Ten *millos*—and a star-drop—why, there aren't more than a dozen of them on all Thrale!"

"Wristwatches—or something—from the Gray Lensman!"

"Be quiet, everybody!" Madge exclaimed, "I see now. That's the way Nadine got *her* watch, that she always brags about so insufferably and that makes everybody's eyes turn green. But I don't understand that silly ten-millo bet . . . do you, Nadine?"

"I think so. He does the nicest things—things that nobody else would think of. You've all seen Red Lensman's Chit, in Brenleer's." This was a statement, not a question. They all had, with what emotions they all knew. "How would you like to have that one-cento piece, in a thousand-credit frame, here in our main hall, with the legend 'won from Christopher Kinnison for Kimball Kinnison by . . .' and our names? He's got something like that in mind, I'm sure."

The ensuing clamor indicated that they liked the idea.

"He knew we would; and he knew that doing it this way would make us dig like we never dug before. He'll give us the watches and things anyway, of course, but we won't get that one-cento piece unless we win it. So let's get to work. Take everything out of the machines, finished or not. Madge, you might start by interviewing Lanion and the other—no, I'd better do that myself, since you are more familiar with the encyclopedia than I am. Run the whole English block, starting with K, and follow up any leads, however slight, that you can find. Betty, you can analyze for synonyms, starting with the Thralian equivalent of Kalonia and spreading out to the other Boskonian planets. Put half a dozen techs on it, with transformers. Frances, you can study Prellin and Bronseca. Joan, Leona, Edna—Jalte, Helmuth, and Crowninshield. Beth, as our best linguist, you can do us the most good by sensitizing a tech to the sound of Kalonia in each of all the languages you know or that the rest of us can find, and running and re-running all the transcripts we have of Boskonian meetings. How many of us are left? Not enough . . . we'll have to spread ourselves thin on this list of Boskonian planets . . ."

Thus Principal Librarian Ernley organized a search beside which the proverbial one of finding a needle in a haystack would have been as simple as locating a football in a bushel basket. And she and her girls worked. *How* they worked! And thus, in four days and three hours, Kinnison's crash-priority person-to-person call came through. Kalonia was no longer a planet of mystery.

"Fine work, girls! Put it on a tape and I'll pick it up."

He then left Klovia—precipitately. Since Kit was not within rendezvous distance, he instructed his son—after giving him the high points of what he had learned—to forward one one-cento piece to Brenleer of Thrale, personal delivery. He told Brenleer what to do with it upon arrival. He landed. He bestowed the star-drop; one of Cartiff's collection of fine gems. He met the girls, and gave each one her self-chosen reward. He departed.

Out in open space, he ran the tape, and sat still, scowling blackly. It was no wonder that Kalonia had remained unknown to Civilization for over twenty years. There was a lot of information on that tape—and all of it stunk—but it had been assembled, one unimportant bit at a time, from the more than eight hundred million cards of Thrale's Boskonian Archives; and all the really significant items had been found on vocal transcriptions which had never before been played.

Civilization in general had assumed that Thrale had housed the top echelons of the Boskonian Empire, and that the continuing inimical activity had been due solely to momentum. Kinnison and his friends had had their doubts, but they had not been able to find any iota of evidence that any higher authority had ever issued any orders to Thrale. The Gray Lensman now knew, however, that Thrale had never been the top. Nor was Kalonia. The information on this tape, by its paucity, its brevity, its incidental and casual nature, made that fact startlingly clear. Thrale and Kalonia were not in the same ladder. Neither gave the other any orders—in fact, they had surprisingly little to do with each other. While Thrale formerly directed the activities of a half-million or so planets— and Kalonia apparently still did much the same—their fields of action had not overlapped at any point.

His conquest of Thrale, hailed so widely as such a triumph, had got him precisely nowhere in the solution of the real problem. It might be possible for him to conquer Kalonia in a similar fashion, but what would it get him? Nothing. There would be no more leads upward from Kalonia than there had been from Thrale. How in all of Noshabkeming's variegated and iridescent hells was he going to work this out?

A complete analysis revealed only one possible method of procedure. In one of the transcriptions—made twenty-one years ago and unsealed for the first time by Beth, the librarian-linguist—one of the speakers had mentioned casually that the new Kalonian Lensmen seemed to be doing a good job, and a couple of the others had agreed with him. That was all. It might, however, be enough; since it made it highly probable that Eddie's Lensman was in fact a Kalonian, and since even a Black Lensman would certainly know where he got his Lens. At the thought of trying to visit the Boskonian equivalent of Arisia he flinched, but only momentarily. Invasion, or even physical approach, would of course be impossible; but any planet, even Arisia itself, could be destroyed. If it could be found, that planet would be destroyed. He had to find it—that was probably what Mentor had been wanting him to do all the time! But how?

In his various previous enterprises against Boskonia he had been a gentleman of leisure, a dock-walloper, a meteor miner, and many other things. None of his already established aliases would fit on Kalonia; and besides, it was very poor technique to repeat himself, especially at this high level of opposition. To warrant appearance on Kalonia at all, he would have to be an operator of some kind—not too small, but not big enough so that an adequate background could not be synthesized in not too long a time. A zwilnik—an actual drug-runner with a really worth-while cargo—would be the best bet.

His course of action decided, the Gray Lensman started making calls. He first called Kit, with whom he held a long conversation. He called the captain of his battleship-yacht, the *Dauntless*, and gave him many and explicit orders. He called Vice-Coordinator Maitland, and various other Unattached Lensmen who had plenty of weight in Narcotics, Public Relations, Criminal Investigation, Navigation, Homicide, and many other apparently totally unrelated establishments of the Galactic Patrol. Finally, after ten solid hours of mind-racking labor, he ate a tremendous meal and told Clarrissa—he called her last of all—that he was going to go to bed and sleep for one whole G-P week.

Thus it was that the name of Bradlow Thyron began to obtrude itself above the threshold of Galactic consciousness. For seven or eight years that name had been below the middle of the Patrol's long, black list of the wanted; now it was well up toward the top. That notorious zwilnik and his villainous crew had been chased from one side of the First Galaxy to the other. For a few months it had been supposed that they had been blown out of the ether. Now, however, it was known definitely that he was operating in the Second Galaxy, and he and every one of his cutthroat gang—fiends who had blasted thousands of lives with noxious wares— were wanted for piracy, drug-mongering, and first-degree murder. From the Patrol's standpoint, the hunting was very poor. G-P planetographers have charted only a small percentage of the planets of the Second Galaxy; and only a few of those are peopled by the adherents of Civilization.

Therefore it required some time, but finally there came the message for which Kinnison was so impatiently waiting. A Boskonian pretty-big-shot and drug-master named Harkleroy, on the planet Phlestyn II, city, Nelto, coordinates so-and-so, fitted his specifications to a "T"; a middle-sized operator neither too close to nor too far away from Kalonia. And Kinnison, having long since learned the lingua franca of the region from a local meteor-miner, was ready to act.

First, he made sure that the mighty *Dauntless* would be where he wanted her when he needed her. Then, seated at his speedster's communicator, he put through regular channels a call to the Boskonian.

"Harkleroy? I've got a proposition you'll be interested in. Where and when do you want to see me?"

"What makes you think I want to see you at all?" a voice snarled, and the plate showed a gross, vicious face. "Who are you, scum?"

"Who I am is nobody's business—and if you don't clamp a baffle on that damn mouth of yours I'll come down there and shove a glop-skinner's glove so far down your throat you can sit on it."

At the first defiant word the zwilnik began visibly to swell; but in a matter of seconds he recognized Bradlow Thyron, and Kinnison knew that he did. That pirate could, and would be expected to, talk back to anybody.

"I didn't recognize you at first." Harkleroy almost apologized. "We might do some business, at that. What have you got?"

"Cocaine, heroin, bentlam, hashish, nitrolabe—most anything a warm-blooded oxygen-breather would want. The prize, though, is two kilograms of clear-quill thionite."

"Thionite—two kilograms!" The Phlestan's eyes gleamed. "Where and how did you get it?"

"I asked the Lensman on Trenco to make it for me, special, and he did."

"So you won't talk, huh?" Kinnison could see Harkleroy's brain work. Thyron could be made to talk, later. "We can maybe do business at that. Come down here right away."

"I'll do that, but listen!" and the Lensman's eyes burned into the zwilnik's. "I know what you're figuring on, and I'm telling you right now not to try it if you want to keep on living. You know this ain't the first planet I ever landed on, and if you've got a brain you know that a lot of smarter guys than you are have tried monkey business on me—and I'm still here. So watch your step!"

The Lensman landed, and made his way to Harkleroy's inner office in what seemed to be an ordinary enough, if somewhat over-size, suit of light space-armor. But it was no more ordinary than it was light. It was a power-house, built of dureum a quarter of an inch thick. Kinnison was not walking in it; he was merely the engineer of a battery of two-thousand-horsepower motors. Unaided, he could not have lifted one leg of that armor off the ground.

As he had expected, everyone he encountered wore a thought-screen; nor was he surprised at being halted by a blaring loud-speaker in the hall, since the zwilnik's search-beams were being stopped four feet away from his armor.

"Halt! Cut your screens or we'll blast you where you stand!"

"Yeah? Act your age, Harkleroy. I told you I had something up my sleeve besides my arm, and I meant it. Either I come as I am or I flit somewhere else, to do business with somebody who wants this stuff bad enough to act like half a man. 'Smatter—afraid you ain't got blasters enough in there to handle me?"

This taunt bit deep, and the visitor was allowed to proceed. As he entered the private office, however, he saw that Harkleroy's hand was poised near a switch, whose closing would signal a score or more of concealed gunners to burn him down. They supposed that the stuff was either on his person or in his speedster just outside. Time was short.

"I abase myself—that's the formula you insist on, ain't it?" Kinnison sneered, without bending his head a millimeter.

Harkleroy's finger touched the stud.

"*Dauntless!* Come down!" Kinnison snapped out the order.

Hand, stud, and a part of the desk disappeared in the flare of Kinnison's beam. Wall-ports opened; projectors and machine rifles erupted vibratory and solid destruction. Kinnison leaped toward the desk; the attack slowing down and stopping as he neared and seized the Boskonian. One fierce, short blast reduced the thought-screen generator to blobs of fused metal. Harkleroy screamed to his gunners to resume fire, but before bullet or beam took the zwilnik's life, Kinnison learned what he most wanted to know.

The ape did know something about Black Lensmen. He didn't know where the Lenses came from, but he did know how the men were chosen. More, he knew a Lensman personally—one Melasnikov, who had his office in Cadsil, on Kalonia III itself.

Kinnison turned and ran—the alarm had been given and they were bringing up stuff too heavy for even his armor to handle. But the *Dauntless* was landing already; smashing to rubble five city blocks in the process. She settled; and as the dureum-clad Gray Lensman began to fight his way out of Harkleroy's fortress, Major Peter vanBuskirk and a full battalion of Valerians, armed with space-axes and semi-portables, began to hew and to blast their way in.

15

THYRON FOLLOWS A LEAD

Inch by inch, foot by foot, Kinnison fought his way back along the corpse-littered corridor. Under the ravening force of the attackers' beams his defensive screens flared into pyrotechnic splendor, but they did not go down. Fierce-driven metallic slugs spanged and whanged against the unyielding dureum of his armor; but that, too, held. Dureum is incredibly massive, unbelievably tough, unimaginably hard—against these qualities and against the thousands of horsepower driving that veritable tank and energizing its screens the zwilniks might just as well have been shining flashlights at him and throwing confetti. His immediate opponents could not touch him, but the Boskonians were bringing up reserves that he didn't like a little bit; mobile projectors with whose energies even those screens could not cope.

He had, however, one great advantage over his enemies. He had the sense of perception; they did not. He could see them, but they could not see him. All he had to do was to keep at least one opaque wall between them until he was securely behind the mobile screens, powered by the stupendous generators of the *Dauntless,* which vanBuskirk and his Valerians were so earnestly urging toward him. If a door was handy in the moment of need, he used it. If not, he went through a wall.

The Valerians were fighting furiously and were coming fast. Those two words, when applied to members of that race, mean something starkly incredible to anyone who has never seen Valerians in action. They average something less than seven feet in height; something over four hundred pounds in weight; and are muscled, boned, and sinewed against a normal gravitational force of almost three times that of Earth. VanBuskirk's weakest warrior could do, in full armor, a standing high jump of fourteen feet against one Tellurian gravity; he could handle himself and the thirty-pound monstrosity which was his space-axe with a blinding speed and a devastating efficiency literally appalling to contemplate. They are the deadliest hand-to-hand fighters ever known; and, unbelievable as it may seem to any really highly advanced intelligence, they did and still do fairly revel in that form of combat.

The Valerian tide reached the battling Gray Lensman; closed around him.

"Hi . . . you little . . . Tellurian . . . wart!" Major Peter vanBuskirk boomed this friendly thought, a yell of pure joy, in cadence with the blows of his utterly irresistible weapon. His rhythm broke—his frightful axe was stuck. Not even dureum-inlaid armor could bar the inward course of those furiously-driven beaks; but sometimes it made it fairly difficult to get them out. The giant pulled, twisted put one red-splashed boot on the battered breastplate—bent his mighty back—heaved viciously. The weapon came free with a snap that would have broken any ordinary man's arms, but the Valerian's thought rolled smoothly on: "Ain't we got fun?"

"Ho, Bus, you big Valerian baboon!" Kinnison thought back in kind. "Thought maybe we'd need you and your gang—thanks a million. But back now, and fast!"

Although the Valerians did not like to retreat, after even a successful operation, they knew how to do it. Hence in a matter of minutes all the survivors—and the losses had been surprisingly small—were back inside the *Dauntless*.

"You picked up my speedster, Frank." It was a statement, not a question, directed at the young Lensman sitting at the "big board."

"Of course, sir. They're massing fast, but without any hostile demonstration, as you said they would." He nodded unconcernedly at a plate, which showed the sky dotted with warlike shapes.

"No maulers?"

"None detectable as yet, sir."

"QX. Original orders stand. At detection of one mauler, execute Operation Able. Tell everybody that while the announcement of Operation Able will put me out of control instantly and automatically, until such announcement I will give instructions. What they'll be like I haven't the foggiest notion. It depends on what his nibs upstairs decides to do—it's his move next."

As though the last phrase were a cue, a burst of noise rattled from the speaker—of which only the words "Bradlow Thyron" were intelligible to the un-Lensed members of the crew. That name, however, explained why they were not being attacked—yet. Kalonia had heard much of that intransigent and obdurate pirate and of the fabulous prowess of his ship; and Kinnison was pretty sure that they were much more interested in his ship than in him.

"I can't understand you!" The Gray Lensman barked, in the polyglot language he had so lately learned. "Talk pidgin!"

"Very well. I see that you are indeed Bradlow Thyron, as we were informed. What do you mean by this outrageous attack? Surrender! Disarm your men, take off their armor, and march them out of your vessel, or we will blast you as you lie there—Vice-Admiral Mendonai speaking!"

"I abase myself." Kinnison-Thyron did not sneer—exactly—and he did incline his stubborn head perhaps the sixteenth part of an inch; but he made no move to comply with the orders so summarily issued. Instead:

"What the hell kind of planet is this, anyway?" he demanded, hotly. "I come here to see this louse Harkleroy because a friend of mine tells me he's a big shot and interested enough in my line so we can do a lot of business. I give the lug fair warning, too—tell him plain I've been around plenty and if he tries to give me the works I'll rub him out like a pencil mark. So what happens? In spite of what I just tell him he tries dirty work and I knock hell out of him, which he certainly has got coming to him. Then you and your flock of little tin boats come barging in like I'd busted a law or something. Who do you think you are, anyway? What license you got to stick your beak into private business?"

"Ah, I had not heard that version." Vision came on; the face upon the plate was typically Kalonian—blue, cold, cruel, and keen. "Harkleroy was warned, you say? Definitely?"

"Plenty definitely. Ask any of the zwilniks in that private office of his. They're mostly alive and they all must of heard it."

The plate fogged, the speaker again gave out gibberish. The Lensman knew, however, that the commander of the forces above them was indeed questioning the dead zwilnik's guards. They knew that Kinnison's story was being corroborated in full.

"You interest me." The Boskonian's language again became intelligible to the group at large. "We will forget Harkleroy—stupidity brings its own reward and the property damage is of no present concern. From what I have been able to learn of you, you have never belonged to that so-called Civilization. I know for a fact that you are not, and never have been, one of us. How have you been able to survive? And why do you work alone?"

" 'How' is easy enough—by keeping one jump ahead of the other guy, like I did with your pal here, and by being smart enough to have good engineers put into my ship everything that any other one ever had and everything they could dream up besides. As to 'why,' that's simple, too. I don't trust nobody. If nobody knows what I'm going to do, nobody's going to stick a knife into me when I ain't looking—see? So far, it's paid off big. I'm still around and still healthy. Them that trusted other guys ain't."

"I see. Crude, but graphic. The more I study you, the more convinced I become that you make a worthwhile addition to our force . . ."

"No deal, Mendonai," Kinnison interrupted, shaking his unkempt head positively. "I never yet took no orders from no damn boss, and I ain't going to."

"You misunderstand me, Thyron." The zwilnik was queerly patient and much too forbearing. Kinnison's insulting omission of his title should have touched him off like a rocket. "I was not thinking of you in any minor capacity, but as an ally. An entirely independent ally, working with us in certain mutually advantageous undertakings."

"Such as?" Kinnison allowed himself to betray his first sign of interest. "You may be talking sense now, brother, but what's in it for me? Believe me, there's got to be plenty."

"There will be plenty. With the ability you have already shown, and with our vast resources back of you, you will take more every week than you have been taking in a year."

"Yeah? People like you just love to do things like that for people like me. What do *you* figure on getting out of it?" Kinnison wondered, and Lensed a sharp thought to his junior at the board.

"On your toes, Frank. He's stalling for something, and I'm betting it's maulers."

"None detectable yet, sir."

"We stand to gain, of course," the pirate admitted, smoothly. "For instance, there are certain features of your vessel which might—just possibly, you will observe, and speaking only to mention an example—be of interest to our naval designers. Also, we have heard that you have an unusually hot battery of primary beams. You might tell me about some of those things now; or at least re-focus your plate so that I can see something besides your not unattractive face."

"I might not, too. What I've got here is my own business, and stays mine."

"Is that what we are to expect from you in the way of cooperation?" The commander's voice was still low and level, but now bore a chill of deadly menace.

"Cooperation, hell!" The cutthroat chief was unimpressed. "I'll maybe tell you a thing or two—eat out of your dish—after I get good and sold on your proposition, whatever it is, but not one damn second sooner!"

The commander glared. "I weary of this. You probably are not worth the trouble, after all. I might as well blast you out now as later. You know that I can, of course, as well as I do."

"Do I?" Kinnison did sneer, this time. "Act your age, pal. As I told that fool Harkleroy, this ain't the first planet I ever sat down on, and it won't be the last. And don't call no maulers," as the Boskonian officer's hand moved almost imperceptibly toward a row of buttons. "If you do, *I* start blasting as soon as we spot one on our plates, and they're full out right now."

"*You* would start blasting?" The zwilnik's surprise was plain, but the hand stopped its motion.

"Yeah—me. Them heaps you got up there don't bother me a bit, but maulers I can't handle, and I ain't afraid to tell you so because you probably know it already. I can't stop you from calling 'em, if you want to, but bend both ears to this—I can out-run 'em and I'll guarantee that you personally won't be alive to see me run. Why? Because your ship will be the first one I'll whiff on the way out. And if the rest of your junkers stick around long enough to try to stop me I'll whiff twenty-five or thirty more before your maulers get close enough so I'll have to do a flit. Now, if your brains are made out of the same kind of thick, blue mud as Harkleroy's, start something!"

This was an impasse. Kinnison knew what he wanted the other to do, but he could not give him a suggestion, or even a hint, without tipping his hand. The officer, quite evidently, was in a quandary. He did not want to open fire upon this tremendous, this fabulous ship. Even if he could destroy it, such a course would be unthinkable—unless, indeed, the very act of destruction would brand as false rumor the tales of invincibility and invulnerability which had heralded its coming, and thus would operate in his favor at the court-martial so sure to be called. He was very much afraid, however, that those rumors were not false—a

view which was supported very strongly both by Thyron's undisguised
contempt for the Boskonian warships threatening him and by his equally
frank declaration of his intention to avoid engagement with any craft of
really superior force. Finally, however, the Boskonian perceived one
thing that did not quite fit.

"If you are as good as you claim to be, why aren't you blasting
right now?" he asked, skeptically.

"Because I don't *want* to, that's why. Use your head, pal." This was
better. Mendonai had shifted the conversation into a line upon which
the Lensman could do a bit of steering. "I had to leave the First Galaxy
because it got too hot for me, and I got no connections at all, yet, here
in the Second. You folks need certain kinds of stuff that I've got, and I
need other kinds, that you've got. So we could do a nice business, if
you wanted to. Like I told you, that's why I come to see Harkleroy. I'd
like to do business with some of you people, but I just got bit pretty
bad, and I've got to have some kind of solid guarantee that you mean
business, and no monkey business, before I take a chance again. See?"

"I see. The idea is good, but the execution may prove difficult. I
could give you my word, which I assure you has never been broken."

"Don't make me laugh," Kinnison snorted. "Would you take
mine?"

"The case is different. I would not. Your point, however, is well
taken. How about the protection of a high court of law? I will bring you
a unalterable writ from any court you say."

"Uh-uh," the Gray Lensman dissented. "There never was no court
yet that didn't take orders from the big shots who keep the fat cats fat,
and lawyers are the crookedest damn crooks in the universe. You'll have
to do better than that, pal."

"Well, then, how about a Lensman? You know about Lensmen, don't
you?"

"A Lensman!" Kinnison gasped. He shook his head violently. "Are
you completely nuts, or do you think I am? I *do* know Lensmen, cully—a
Lensman chased me from Alsakan to Vandemar once, and if I hadn't
had a dose of hell's own luck he'd of got me. Lensmen chased me out
of the First Galaxy—why the hell else do you think I'm here? Use your
brain, mister; use you brain!"

"You're thinking of Civilization's Lensmen; particularly of Gray
Lensmen." Mendonai was enjoying Thyron's passion. "Ours are different—entirely different. They have as much power, or more, but don't
use it the same way. They work with us right along. In fact, they've been
bumping Gray Lensmen off right and left lately."

"You mean he could open up, for instance, your mind and mine, so we could see the other guy wasn't figuring on running in no stacked decks? And he'd sort of referee this business we got on the fire? Do you know one yourself, personally?"

"He could, and would, do all that. Yes, I know one personally. His name is Melasnikov, and his office is on Three, just a short flit from here. He may not be there at the moment, but he'll come in if I call. How about it—shall I call him now?"

"Don't work up a sweat. Sounds like it might work, if we can figure the approach. I don't suppose you and him would come out to me in space?"

"Hardly. You wouldn't expect us to, would you?"

"It wouldn't be very bright of you to. And since I want to do business, I guess I got to meet you part way. How'd this be? You pull your ships out of range. My ship takes station right over your Lensman's office. I go down in my speedster, like I did here, and go inside to meet him and you. I wear my armor—and when I say it's real armor I ain't just snapping my choppers, neither."

"I can see only one slight flaw." The Boskonian was really trying to work out a mutually satisfactory solution. "The Lensman will open our minds to you in proof, however, that we will have no intention of bringing up our maulers or other heavy stuff while we're in conference."

"Right then you'll find out you hadn't better, too." Kinnison grinned wolfishly.

"What do you mean?" Mendonai demanded.

"I've got enough super-atomic bombs aboard to blow this planet to hellangone and the boys'll drop 'em all the second you make a queer move. I've got to take a little chance to start doing business, but it's a damn small one, 'cause if I go you go too, pal. You and your Lensman and your fleet and everything alive on your whole damn planet. And your bosses still won't get any dope on what makes this ship of mine tick the way she does. So I'm betting you won't make that kind of a swap."

"I certainly would not." Hard as he was, Mendonai was shaken. "Your suggested method of procedure is satisfactory."

"QX. Are you ready to flit?"

"We are ready."

"Call your Lensman, then, and lead the way. Boys, take her up-stairs!"

16

RED LENSMAN IN GRAY

Karen Kinnison was worried. She, who had always been so sure of herself, had for weeks been conscious of a gradually increasing—what was it, anyway? Not exactly a loss of control . . . a *change* . . . a something that manifested itself in increasingly numerous fits of senseless—sheerly idiotic—stubbornness. And always and only it was directed at—all the people in the universe!—her brother. She got along with her sisters perfectly; their tiny tiffs barely rippled the surface of any of their minds. But any time her path of action crossed Kit's, it seemed, the profoundest depths of her being flared into opposition like exploding duodec. Worse than senseless and idiotic, it was inexplicable, for the feeling which the Five had for each other was much deeper than that felt by ordinary brothers and sisters.

She didn't want to fight with Kit. She *liked* the guy! She liked to feel his mind en rapport with hers, just as she liked to dance with him; their bodies as completely in accord as were their minds. No change of step or motion, however suddenly conceived and executed or however bizarre, had ever succeeded in taking the other by surprise or in marring by a millimeter the effortless precision of their performance. She could do things with Kit that would tie any other man into knots and break half his bones. All other men were lumps. Kit was so far ahead of any other man in existence that there was simply no comparison. If she were Kit she would give her a going-over that would . . . or could even he . . .

At the thought she turned cold inside. He could not. Even Kit, with all his tremendous power, would hit that solid wall and bounce. Well, there was one—not a man, but an entity—who could. He might kill her, but even that would be better than to allow the continued growth within her mind of this monstrosity which she could neither control nor understand. Where was she, and where was Lyrane, and where was Arisia? Good—not too far off line. She would stop off at Arisia en route.

She did so, and made her way to Mentor's quiet office on the hospital grounds. She told her story.

"Fighting with Kit was bad enough," she concluded, "but when I start defying *you*, Mentor, it's high time that something was done about it. Why didn't Kit ever knock me into a logarithmic spiral? Why didn't you work me over? You called Kit in, with the distinct implication that he needed more education—why didn't you pull me in here, too, and pound some sense into me?"

"Concerning you, Christopher had definite instructions, which he obeyed. I did not touch you for the same reason that I did not order you to come to me; neither course would have been of any use. Your mind, daughter Karen, is unique. One of its prime characteristics—the one, in fact, which is to make you an all-important player in the drama which is to come—is a yieldlessness very nearly absolute. Your mind might, just conceivably, be broken; but it cannot be coerced by any imaginable external force, however applied. Thus it was inevitable from the first that nothing could be done about the untoward manifestations of this characteristic until you yourself should recognize the fact that your development was not complete. It would be idle for me to say that during adolescence you have not been more than a trifle trying. I was not speaking idly when I said that the development of you Five has been a tremendous task. It is with equal seriousness, however, that I now tell you that the reward is commensurate with the magnitude of the undertaking. It is impossible to express the satisfaction I feel—the fulfillment, the completion, the justification—as you children come, one by one, each in his proper time, for final instruction."

"Oh—you mean, then, that there's nothing really the matter with me?" Hard as she was, Karen trembled as her awful tension eased. "That I was *supposed* to act that way? And I can tell Kit, right away?"

"No need. Your brother has known that it was a passing phase; he shall know very shortly that it has passed. It is not that you were 'supposed' to act as you acted. You could not help it. Nor could your brother, nor I. From now on, however, you shall be completely the mistress of your own mind. Come fully, daughter Karen, into mine."

She did so, and in a matter of time her "formal education" was complete.

"There is one thing that I don't quite understand . . ." she began, just before she boarded her speedster.

"Consider it, and I am sure that you will," Mentor assured her. "Explain it, whatever it is, to me."

"QX—I'll try. It's about Fossten and dad." Karen cogitated. "Fossten was, of course, Gharlane—your making dad believe him to be an insane Arisian was a masterpiece. I see, of course, how you did that— principally by making Fossten's 'real' shape exactly like the one he saw of you on Arisia. But his physical actions as Fossten . . ."

"Go on, daughter. I am sure that your visualization will be sound."

"While acting as Fossten he had to act as a Thralian would have acted," she decided with a rush. "He was watched everywhere he went, and knew it. To display his real power would have been disastrous. Just like you Arisians, they have to follow the pattern to avoid setting up an inferiority complex that would ruin everything for them. Gharlane's actions as Fossten, then, were constrained. Just as they were when he was Gray Roger, so long ago—except that then he did make a point of unhuman longevity, deliberately to put a insoluble problem up to First Lensman Samms and his men. Just as you—you *must* have . . . you *did* coach Virgil Samms, Mentor, and some of you Arisians *were* there, as men!"

"We were. We lived and wrought as men and seemed to die as men."

"But you weren't Virgil Samms, please!" Karen almost begged. "Not that it would break me if you were, but I'd much rather you hadn't been."

"No, none of us was Samms," Mentor assured her. "Nor Cleveland, nor Rodebush, nor Costigan, nor even Clio Marsden. We worked with— 'coached,' as you express it—those persons and others from time to time in certain small matters, but we were at no time integral with any of them. One of us was, however, Nels Bergenholm. The full inertialess space-drive became necessary at that time, and it would have been poor technique to have had either Rodebush or Cleveland develop so suddenly the ability to perfect the device as Bergenholm did perfect it."

"QX. Bergenholm isn't important—he was just an inventor. To get back to the subject of Fossten: when he was there on the flagship with dad, and in position to throw his full weight around, it was too late—you

Arisians were on the job. You'll have to take it from there, though; I'm out beyond my depth."

"Because you lack data. In those last minutes Gharlane knew that Kimball Kinnison was neither alone nor unprotected. He called for help, but help did not come. He was isolated; no one of his fellows received his call. Nor could he escape from the form of flesh he was then energizing. I myself saw to that." Karen had never before felt the Arisia display emotion, but his thought was grim and cold. "From that form, which your father never did perceive, Gharlane of Eddore passed into the next plane of existence."

Karen shivered. "It served him right . . . That clears everything up, I think. But are you *sure,* Mentor"—wistfully—"that you can't, or rather shouldn't, teach me any more than you have? It's . . . I feel . . . well, 'incompetent' is putting it very mildly indeed."

"To a mind of such power and scope as yours, in its present state of development, such a feeling is inevitable. Nor can anyone except yourself do anything about it. Cold comfort, perhaps, but it is the stark truth that from now on your development is your own task. Yours alone. As I have already told Christopher and Kathryn, and will very shortly tell Camilla and Constance, you have had your last Arisian treatment. I will be on call to any of you at any instant of any day, to aid you or to guide you or to reinforce you at need; but of formal instruction there can be no more."

Karen left Arisia and drove for Lyrane, her thoughts in a turmoil. The time was too short by far; she deliberately cut her vessel's speed and took a long detour so that the vast and chaotic library of her mind could be reduced to some semblance of order before she landed.

She reached Lyrane II, and there, again to all outward seeming a happy, carefree girl, she hugged her mother rapturously.

"You're the most *wonderful* thing, mums!" Karen exclaimed. "It's simply marvelous, seeing you again in the flesh . . ."

"Now why bring *that* up?" Clarrissa had—just barely—become accustomed to working undraped, in the Lyranian fashion.

"I didn't mean it that way at all, and you know I didn't," Kay snickered. "Shame on you—fishing for compliments, and at your age, too!" Ignoring the older woman's attempt at protest she went on: "All kidding aside, mums, you're a mighty smart-looking hunk of woman. I approve of you exceedingly much. In fact, we're a keen pair and I like both of us. I've got one advantage over you, of course, in that I never did care whether I had any clothes on or not. How are you doing?"

"Not so well—of course, though, I haven't been here very long."

Forgetting her undressedness, Clarrissa frowned. "I haven't found Helen, and I haven't found out yet why she retired. I can't quite decide whether to put pressure on now, or wait a while longer. Ladora, the new Elder Person, is . . . that is, I don't know . . . Oh, here she comes now. I'm glad—I want you to meet her."

If Ladora was glad to see Karen, however, she did not show it. Instead, for an inappreciable instant of time which was nevertheless sufficient for the acquirement of much information, each studied the other. Like Helen, the former queen, Ladora was tall, beautifully proportioned, flawless of skin and feature, hard and fine. But so, and in most respects even more so, to Ladora's astonishment and quickly-mounting wrath, was this pink-tanned stranger. Practically instantaneously, therefore, the Lyranian hurled a vicious mental bolt; only to get the surprise of her life.

She hadn't found out yet what this strange near-person, Clarrissa of Sol III, had in the way of equipment, but from the meek way she acted, it couldn't be much. So Clarrissa's offspring, younger and less experienced, would be easy enough prey.

But Ladora's bolt, the heaviest she could send, did not pierce even the outermost fringes of her intended victim's defenses, and so vicious was the almost simultaneous counter-thrust that it went through the Lyranian's hard-held block in nothing flat. Inside her brain it wrought such hellishly poignant punishment that the matriarch, forgetting everything, tried only and madly to scream. She could not. She could not move a muscle of her face or of her body. She could not even fall. And the one brief glimpse she had into the stranger's mind showed it to be such a blaze of incandescent fury that she, who had never feared in the slightest any living creature, knew now in full measure what fear was.

"I'd like to give that alleged brain of yours a good going over, just for fun." Karen forced her emotion to subside to a mere seething rage, and Ladora watched her do it. "But since this whole stinking planet is my mother's dish, not mine, she'd blast me to a cinder—she's done it before—if I dip in." She cooled still more—visibly. "At that, I don't suppose you're too bad an egg, in your own poisonous way—you just don't know any better. So maybe I'd better warn you, you poor fool, since you haven't got sense enough to see it, that you're playing with an atomic vortex when you push her around like you've been doing. Just a very little more of it and she'll get mad, like I did a second ago except more so, and you'll wish to Klono you'd never been born. She won't make a sign until she blows her top, but I'm telling you she's as much harder and tougher than I am as she is older, and what she does to people she gets mad at I wouldn't want to watch happen again, even to a snake. She'll pick you up, curl you into a circle, pull off your arms, shove your feet down your throat, and roll you across that field there like a hoop. After that I don't know what she'll do—depends on how much pressure she develops before she goes off. One thing, though; she's always sorry afterwards. Why, she even attends the funerals, sometimes, and insists on paying all the expenses!"

With which outrageous thought she kissed Clarrissa an enthusiastic goodbye. "Told you I couldn't stay a minute—got to do a flit—'see a man about a dog,' you know—came a million parsecs to squeeze you, mums, but it was worth it—clear ether!"

She was gone, and it was a dewy-eyed and rapt mother, not a Lensman, who turned to the still completely disorganized Lyranian. Clarrissa had perceived nothing whatever of what had happened; Karen had very carefully seen to that.

"My daughter," Clarrissa mused, as much to herself as to Ladora. "One of four. The four dearest, finest, sweetest girls that ever lived. I often wonder how a woman of my limitations, of my faults, could possibly have borne such children."

And Ladora of Lyrane, humorless and literal as all Lyranians are, took those thoughts at their face value and correlated their every connotation and implication with what she herself had perceived in that "dear, sweet" daughter's mind; with what that daughter had done and had said. The nature and quality of this hellish near-person's "limitations" and "faults" became eminently clear; and as she perceived what she thought was the truth, the Lyranian literally cringed.

"As you know, I have been in doubt as to whether or not to support you actively, as you wish," Ladora offered, as the two walked across the field, toward the line of ground-cars. "On the one hand, the certainty that the safety, and perhaps the very existence, of my race will be at hazard. On the other, the possibility that you are right in saying that the situation will continue to deteriorate if we do nothing. The decision has not been an easy one to make." Ladora was no longer aloof. She was just plain scared. She had been talking against time, and hoping that the help for which she had long since called would arrive in time. "I have touched only the outer surface of your mind. Will you allow me, without offense, to test its inner quality before deciding definitely?" In the instant of asking, Ladora sent out a full-driven probe.

"I will not." Ladora's beam struck a barrier which seemed to her exactly like Karen's. None of her race had developed anything like it. She had never seen . . . yes, she had, too—years ago, when she was a child, that time in the assembly hall—that utterly hated male, Kinnison of Tellus! Tellus—Sol III! Clarrissa of Sol III, then, wasn't a near-person at all, but a *female*—Kinnison's kind of female—and a creature who was physically a person, but mentally that inconceivable monstrosity, a *female,* might be anything and might do *anything!* Ladora temporized.

"Excuse me; I did not mean to intrude against your will," she apologized, smoothly enough. "Since your attitude makes it extremely difficult for me to cooperate with you, I can make no promises as yet. What is it that you wish to know first?"

"I wish to interview your predecessor, the person we called Helen." Strangely refreshed, in a sense galvanized by the brief personal visit with her dynamic daughter, it was no longer Mrs. Kimball Kinnison who faced the Lyranian queen. Instead, it was the Red Lensman; a full-powered Second-Stage Lensman who had finally decided that, since appeals to reason, logic, and common sense had no perceptible effect upon this stiff-necked near-woman, the time had come to bear down. "Furthermore, I intend to interview her now, and not at some such indefinite future time as your whim may see fit to allow."

Ladora sent out a final desperate call for help and mustered her every force against the interloper. Fast and strong as her mind was, however, the Red Lensman's was faster and stronger. The Lyranian's defensive structure was wrecked in the instant of its building, the frantically struggling mind was taken over in toto. Help arrived—uselessly; since although Clarrissa's newly enlarged mind had not been put to warlike use, it was brilliantly keen and ultimately sure. Nor, in time of stress, did the softer side of her nature operate to stay mind or hand. While carrying Lensman's Load she contained no more of ruth for Civilization's foes than did abysmally frigid Nadreck himself.

Head thrown back, taut and tense, gold-flecked tawny eyes flashing, she stood there for a moment and took on her shield everything those belligerent persons could send. More, she returned it in kind, plus; and under those withering blasts of force more than one of her attackers died. Then, still holding her block, she and her unwilling captive raced across the field toward the line of peculiar little fabric-and-wire machines that were still the last word in Lyranian air-transport.

Clarrissa knew that the Lyranians had no modern offensive or defensive weapons. They did, however, have some fairly good artillery at the airport; and she hoped fervently as she ran that she could put out jets enough to spoil aim and fuzing—luckily, they hadn't developed proximity fuzes yet!—of whatever ack-ack they could bring to bear on her crate during the few minutes she would have to use it. Fortunately, there was no artillery at the small, unimportant airport on which her speedster lay.

"Here we are. We'll take this tripe—it's the fastest thing here!"

Clarrissa could operate the triplane, of course—any knowledge or ability that Ladora had ever had was now and permanently the Lensman's. She started the queer engines; and as the powerful little plane screamed into the air, hanging from its props, she devoted what of her mind she could spare to the problem of anti-aircraft fire. She could not handle all the gun-crews; but she could and did control the most important members of most of them. Thus, nearly all the shells either went wide or exploded too soon. Since she knew every point of aim of the few guns with whose operations she could not interfere, she avoided their missiles by not being at any one of those points at the predetermined instant of functioning.

Thus plane and passengers escaped unscratched; and in a matter of minutes arrived at their destination. The Lyranians there had been alerted, of course; but they were few in number and they had not been informed that it would take physical force, not mental, to keep that red-headed pseudo-person from boarding her outlandish ship of space.

In a few more minutes, then, Clarrissa and her captive were high in the stratosphere. Clarrissa sat Ladora down—hard—in a seat and fastened the safety straps.

"Stay in that seat and keep your thoughts to yourself," she directed, curtly. "If you don't, you'll never again either move or think in this life." She opened a sliding door, put on a couple of wisps of Manarkan glamorette, reached for a dress, and paused. Eyes glowing, she gazed hungrily at a suit of plain gray leather; a costume which she had not as yet so much as tried on. Should she wear it, or not?

She could work efficiently—at service maximum, really—in ordinary clothes. Ditto, although she didn't like to, unclothed. In Gray, though, she could hit absolute max if she had to. Nor had there ever been any question of right involved; the only barrier had been her own hyper-sensitivity.

For over twenty years she herself had been the only one to deny her right. What license, she was wont to ask, did an imitation or synthetic or amateur or "Red" Lensman have to wear the garb which meant so much to so many? Over those years, however, it had become increasingly widely known that hers was one of the five finest and most powerful minds in the entire Gray Legion; and when Coordinator Kinnison recalled her to active duty in Unattached status, that Legion passed by unanimous vote a resolution asking her to join them in Gray. Psychics all, they knew that nothing less would suffice; that if there was any trace of resentment or of antagonism or of feelings that she did not intrinsically belong, she would never don the uniform which every adherent of Civilization so revered and for which, deep down, she had always so intensely longed. The Legion had sent her these Grays. Kit had convinced her that she did actually deserve them.

She really should wear them. She would.

She put them on, thrilling to the core as she did so, and made the quick little gesture she had seen Kim make so many times. Gray Seal. No one, however accustomed, has ever donned or ever will don unmoved the plain gray leather of the Unattached Lensman of the Galactic Patrol.

Hands on hips, she studied herself minutely and approvingly, both in the mirror and by means of her vastly more efficient sense of perception. She wriggled a little, and giggled inwardly as she remembered deploring as "exhibitionistic" this same conduct in her oldest daughter.

The Grays fitted her perfectly. A bit revealing, perhaps, but her figure was still good—very good, as a matter of fact. Not a speck of dirt or tarnish. Her DeLameters were fully charged. Her tremendous Lens flamed brilliantly upon her wrist. She looked—and felt—ready. She could hit absolute max in a fraction of a micro-second. If she had to get really tough, she would. She sent out a call.

"Helen of Lyrane! I know they've got you around here somewhere, and if any of your guards try to screen out *this* thought I'll burn their brains out. Clarissa of Sol III calling. Come in, Helen!"

"Clarissa!" This time there was no interference. A world of welcome was in every nuance of the thought. "Where are you?"

"High up, at . . ." Clarissa gave her position. "I'm in my speedster, so can get to anywhere on the planet in minutes. More important, where are you? And why?"

"In jail, in my own apartment." Queens should have palaces, but Lyrane's ruler did not. Everything was strictly utilitarian. "The tower on the corner, remember? On the top floor? 'Why' is too long to go into now—I'd better tell you as much as possible of what you should know, while there's still time."

"Time? Are you in danger?"

"Yes. Ladora would have killed me long ago if it had dared. My following grows less daily, the Boskonians stronger. The guards have already summoned help. They are coming now, to take me."

"That's what *they* think!" Clarissa had already reached the scene. She had exactly the velocity she wanted. She slanted downward in a screaming dive. "Can you tell whether they're limbering up any ack-ack around there?"

"I don't believe so—I don't feel any such thoughts."

"QX. Get away from the window." If they hadn't started already they never would; the Red Lensman was deadly sure of that.

She came within range—her range—of the guns. She was in time. Several gunners were running toward their stations. None of them arrived. The speedster leveled off and stuck its hard, sharp nose into and almost through the indicated room; reinforced concrete, steel bars, and glass showering abroad as it did so. The port snapped open. As Helen leaped in, Clarrissa practically threw Ladora out.

"Bring Ladora back!" Helen demanded. "I shall have its life!"

"Nix!" Clarrissa snapped. "I know everything she does. We've other fish to fry, my dear."

The massive door clanged shut. The speedster darted forward, straight through the solid concrete wall. Clarrissa's vessel, solidly built of beryllium alloys, had been designed to take brutal punishment. She took it.

Out in open space, Clarrissa went free, leaving the artificial gravity at normal. Helen stood up, took Clarrissa's hand, and shook it gravely and strongly; a gesture at which the Red Lensman almost choked.

Helen of Lyrane had changed even less than had the Earth-woman. She was still six feet tall; erect, taut, springy, and poised. She didn't weigh a pound more than the one-eighty she had scaled twenty-odd years ago. Her vivid auburn hair showed not one strand of gray. Her eyes were as clear and as proud; her skin almost as fine and firm.

"You are, then, alone?" In spite of her control, Helen's thought showed relief.

"Yes. My hus . . . Kimball Kinnison is very busy elsewhere." Clarrissa understood perfectly. Helen, after twenty years of thinking things over, really liked her; but she still simply couldn't stand a male, not even Kim; any more than Clarrissa could ever adapt herself to the Lyranian habit of using the neuter pronoun "it" when referring to one of themselves. She couldn't. Anybody who ever got one glimpse of Helen would simply have to think of her as *she!* But enough of this wool-gathering— which had taken perhaps one millisecond of time.

"There's nothing to keep us from working together perfectly," Clarrissa's thought flashed on. "Ladora didn't know much, and you do. So tell me all about things, so we can decide where to begin!"

17

NADRECK VS. KANDRON

When Kandron called his minion in that small and nameless base to learn whether or not he had succeeded in trapping the Palainian Lensman, Nadreck's relay station functioned so perfectly, and Nadreck was so completely in charge of his captive's mind, that the caller could feel nothing out of the ordinary. Ultra-suspicious though Kandron was, there was nothing whatever to indicate that anything had changed at that base since he had last called its commander. That individual's subconscious mind reacted properly to the key stimulus. The conscious mind took over, remembered, and answered properly a series of trick questions.

These things occurred because the minion was still alive. His ego, the pattern and matrix of his personality, was still in existence and had not been changed. What Kandron did not and could not suspect was that that ego was no longer in control of mind, brain, or body; that it was utterly unable, of its own volition, either to think any iota of independent thought or to stimulate any single physical cell. The Onlonian's ego was present—just barely present—but that was all. It was Nadreck who, using that ego as a guide and, in a sense, as a helplessly impotent transformer, received the call. Nadreck made those exactly correct replies. Nadreck was now ready to render a detailed and fully documented—and completely mendacious—report upon his own destruction!

Nadreck's special tracers were already out, determining line and intensity. Strippers and analyzers were busily at work on the fringes of the beam, dissecting out, isolating, and identifying each of the many scraps of extraneous thought accompanying the main beam. These side-thoughts, in fact, were Nadreck's prime concern. The Second-Stage Lensman had learned that no being—except possibly an Arisian—could narrow a beam of thought down to one single, pure sequence. Of the four, however, only Nadreck recognized in those side-bands a rich field; only he had designed and developed mechanisms with which to work that field.

The stronger and clearer the mind, the fewer and less complete were the extraneous fragments of thought; but Nadreck knew that even Kandron's brain would carry quite a few such non-germane accompaniments, and from each of those bits he could reconstruct an entire sequence as accurately as a competent paleontologist reconstructs a prehistoric animal from one fossilized piece of bone.

Thus Nadreck was completely ready when the harshly domineering Kandron asked his first real question.

"I do not suppose that you have succeeded in killing the Lensman?"

"Yes, Your Supremacy, I have." Nadreck could feel Kandron's start of surprise; could perceive without his instruments Kandron's fleeting thoughts of the hundreds of unsuccessful previous attempts upon his life. It was clear that the Onlonian was not at all credulous.

"Report in detail!" Kandron ordered.

Nadreck did so, adhering rigidly to the truth up to the moment in which his probes of force had touched off the Boskonian alarms. Then:

"Spy-ray photographs taken at the instant of alarm show an indetectable speedster, with one, and only one occupant, as Your Supremacy anticipated. A careful study of all the pictures taken of that occupant shows: first, that he was definitely alive at that time, and was neither a projection nor an artificial mechanism; and second, that his physical measurements agree in every particular with the specifications furnished by Your Supremacy as being those of Nadreck of Palain VII.

"Since Your Supremacy personally computed and supervised the placement of those projectors," Nadreck went smoothly on, "you know that the possibility is vanishingly small that any material thing, free or inert, could have escaped destruction. As a check, I took seven hundred twenty-nine samples of the circumambient space, statistically at random, for analysis. After appropriate allowances for the exactly-observed elapsed times of sampling, diffusion of droplets and molecular and atomic aggregates, temperatures, pressures, and all other factors known or assumed to be operating, I determined that there had been present in the center of action of our beams a mass of approximately four thousand six hundred seventy eight point zero one metric tons. This value, Your Supremacy will note, is in close agreement with the most efficient mass of an indetectable speedster designed for long distance work."

That figure was in fact closer than close. It was an almost exact statement of the actual mass of Nadreck's ship.

"Exact composition?" Kandron demanded.

Nadreck recited a rapid-fire string of elements and figures. They, too, were correct within the experimental error of a very good analyst. The base commander had not known them, but it was well within the bounds of possibility that the insidious Kandron would. He did. He was now practically certain that his ablest and bitterest enemy had been destroyed at last, but there were still a few lingering shreds of doubt.

"Let me look over your work," Kandron directed.

"Yes, Your Supremacy." Nadreck the Thorough was ready for even that extreme test. Through the eyes of the ultimately enslaved monstrosity Kandron checked and rechecked Nadreck's pictures, Nadreck's charts and diagrams, Nadreck's more than four hundred pages of mathematical, physical, and chemical notes and determinations; all without finding a single flaw.

In the end Kandron was ready to believe that Nadreck had in fact ceased to exist. However, he himself had not done the work. There was no corpse. If he himself had killed the Palainian, if he himself had actually felt the Lensman's life depart in the grasp of his own tentacles; then, and only then, would he have *known* that Nadreck was dead. As it was, even though the work had been done in exact accordance with his own instructions, there remained an infinitesimal uncertainty. Wherefore:

"Shift your field of operations to cover X-174, Y-240, Z-16. Do not relax your vigilance in the slightest because of what has happened." He considered briefly the idea of allowing the underling to call him, in case anything happened, but decided against it. "Are the men standing up?"

"Yes, Your Supremacy, they are in very good shape indeed."

And so on. "Yes, Your Supremacy, the psychologist is doing a very fine job. Yes, Your Supremacy . . . yes . . . yes . . . yes . . ."

Very shortly after the characteristically Kandronesque ending of that interview, Nadreck had learned everything he needed to know. He knew where Kandron was and what he was doing. He knew much of what Kandron had done during the preceding twenty years; and, since he himself figured prominently in many of those sequences, they constituted invaluable checks upon the validity of his other reconstructions. He knew the construction, the armament, and the various ingenious mechanisms, including the locks, of Kandron's vessel; he knew more than any other outsider had ever known of Kandron's private life. He knew where Kandron was going next, and what he was going to do there. He knew in broad what Kandron intended to do during the coming century.

Thus well informed, Nadreck set his speedster into a course toward the planet of Civilization which was Kandron's next objective. He did not hurry; it was no part of his plan to interfere in any way in the horrible program of planet-wide madness and slaughter which Kandron had in mind. It simply did not occur to him to try to save the planet as well as to kill the Onlonian; Nadreck, being Nadreck, took without doubt or question the safest and surest course.

Nadreck knew that Kandron would set his vessel into an orbit around the planet, and that he would take a small boat—a flitter—for the one personal visit necessary to establish his lines of communication and control. Vessel and flitter would be alike indetectable, of course; but Nadreck found the one easily enough and knew when the other left its mother-ship. Then, using his lightest, stealthiest spy-rays, the Palainian set about the exceedingly delicate business of boarding the Boskonian craft.

That undertaking could be made a story in its own right, for Kandron did not leave his ship unguarded. However, merely by thinking about his own safety, Kandron had all unwittingly given away the keys to his supposedly impregnable fortress. While Kandron was wondering whether or not the Lensman was really dead, and especially after he had been convinced that he most probably was, the Onlonian's thoughts had touched fleetingly upon a multitude of closely-related subjects. Would it be safe to abandon some of the more onerous precautions he had always taken, and which had served him so well for so many years? And as he thought of them, each one of his safeguards flashed at least partially into view; and for Nadreck, any significant part was as good as the whole. Kandron's protective devices, therefore, did not protect. Projectors, designed to flame out against intruders, remained cold. Ports opened; and as Nadreck touched sundry buttons various invisible beams whose breaking would have produced unpleasant results, ceased to exist. In short, Nadreck knew all the answers. If he had not been coldly certain that his information was complete, he would not have acted at all.

After entry, his first care was to send out spotting devices which would give warning in case Kandron should return unexpectedly soon. Then, working in the service-spaces behind instrument-boards and panels, in junction boxes, and in various other out-of-the-way places, he cut into lead after lead, ran wire after wire, and installed item after item of apparatus and equipment upon which he had been at work for weeks. He finished his work undisturbed. He checked and rechecked the circuits, making absolutely certain that every major one of the vessel's controlling leads ran to or through at least one of the things he had just installed. With painstaking nicety he obliterated every visible sign of his visit. He departed as carefully as he had come; restoring to full efficiency as he went each one of Kandron's burglar-alarms.

Kandron returned, entered his ship as usual, stored his flitter, and extended a tentacular member toward the row of switches on his panel.

"Don't touch anything, Kandron," he was advised by a thought as cold and as deadly as any one of his own; and upon the Onlonian equivalent of a visiplate there appeared the one likeness which he least expected and least desired to perceive.

"Nadreck of Palain VII—Star A Star—THE Lensman!" The Onlonian was physically and emotionally incapable of gasping, but the idea is appropriate. "You have, then, wired and mined this ship."

There was a subdued clicking of relays. The Bergenholm came up to speed, the speedster spun about and darted away under a couple of kilodynes of drive.

"I am Nadreck of Palain VII, yes. One of the group of Lensmen whose collective activities you have ascribed to Star A Star and *the* Lensman. Your ship is, as you have deduced, mined. The only reason you did not die as you entered it is that I wish to be really certain, and not merely statistically so, that it is Kandron of Onlo, not someone else, who dies."

"That unutterable fool!" Kandron quivered in helpless rage. "Oh, that I had taken the time and killed you myself!"

"If you had done your own work, the techniques I used here could not have been employed, and you might have been in no danger at the present moment," Nadreck admitted, equally enough. "My powers are small, my intellect feeble, and what might have been has no present bearing. I am inclined, however, to question the validity of your conclusions, due to the known fact that you have been directing a campaign against me for over twenty years without success; whereas I have succeeded against you in less than half a year. . . . My analysis is now complete. You may now touch any control you please. By the way, you do not deny that you are Kandron of Onlo, do you?"

Neither of those monstrous beings mentioned or even thought of mercy. In neither of their languages was there any word for or concept of such a thing.

"That would be idle. You know my pattern as well as I know yours. . . . I cannot understand how you got through that . . ."

"It is not necessary that you should. Do you wish to close one of those switches or shall I?"

Kandron had been thinking for minutes, studying every aspect of his predicament. Knowing Nadreck, he knew just how desperate the situation was. There was, however, one very small chance—just one. The way he had come was clear. That was the *only* clear way. Wherefore, to gain an extra instant of time, he reached out toward a switch; but even while he was reaching he put every ounce of his tremendous strength into a leap which hurled him across the room toward his flitter.

No luck. One of Nadreck's minor tentacles was already curled around a switch, tensed and ready. Kandron was still in air when a relay snapped shut and four canisters of duodec detonated as one. Duodecaplylatomate, that frightful detonant whose violence is exceeded only by that of nuclear disintegration!

There was an appalling flash of viciously white light, which expanded in milliseconds into an enormous globe of incandescent gas. Cooling and darkening as it expanded rapidly into the near-vacuum of interplanetary space, the gases and vapors soon became invisible. Through and throughout the entire volume of volatilization Nadreck drove analyzers and detectors, until he knew positively that no particle of material substance larger in diameter than five microns remained of either Kandron or his space-ship. He then called the Gray Lensman.

"Kinnison? Nadreck of Palain VII calling, to report that my assignment has been completed. I have destroyed Kandron of Onlo."

"Good! Fine business, ace! What kind of a picture did you get? He must have known something about the higher eschelons—or did he? Was he just another dead end?"

"I did not go into that."

"Huh? Why not?" Kinnison demanded, exasperation in every line of his thought.

"Because it was not included in the project," Nadreck explained, patiently. "You already know that one must concentrate in order to work efficiently. To secure the requisite minimum of information it was necessary to steer his thoughts into one, and only one, set of channels. There were some foreign side-bands, of course, and it may be that some of them touched upon this new subject which you have now, too late, introduced . . . no, there were no such."

"Damnation!" Kinnison exploded; then by main strength shut himself up. "QX, ace; skip it. But listen, my spiny and murderous friend. Get this—engrave it in big type right on the top-side inside of your thick skull—what we want is INFORMATION, not mere liquidation. Next time you get hold of such a big shot as Kandron must have been, don't kill him until either: first, you get some leads as to who or what the real head of the outfit is; or, second, you make sure that he doesn't know. Then kill him all you want to, but FIND OUT WHAT HE KNOWS FIRST. Have I made myself clear this time?"

"You have, and as coordinator your instructions should and will govern. I point out, however, that the introduction of a multiplicity of objectives into a problem not only destroys its unity, but also increases markedly both the time necessary for, and the actual personal danger involved in, its solution."

"So what?" Kinnison countered, as evenly as he could. "That way, we may be able to get the answer some day. Your way, we never will. But the thing's done—there's no use yapping and yowling about it now. Have you any ideas as to what you should do next?"

"No. Whatever you wish, that I shall try to do."

"I'll check with the others." He did so, receiving no helpful ideas until he consulted his wife.

"Hi, Kim, my dear!" came Clarrissa's buoyant thought; and, after a brief but intense greeting: "Glad you called. Nothing definite enough yet to report to you officially, but there are indications that Lyrane IX may be an important . . ."

"Nine?" Kinnison interrupted. "Not Eight again?"

"Nine," she confirmed. "A new item. So I may be doing a flit over there one of these days."

"Uh-uh," he denied. "Lyrane Nine would be none of your business. Stay away from it."

"Says who?" she demanded. "We went into this once before, Kim, about you telling me what I could and couldn't do."

"Yeah, and I came out second best." Kinnison grinned. "But now, as coordinator, I make suggestions to even Second-Stage Lensmen, and they follow them—or else. I therefore suggest officially that you stay away from Lyrane IX on the grounds that since it is colder than a Palainian's heart, it is definitely not your problem, but Nadreck's. And I'm adding this—if you don't behave yourself I'll come over there and administer appropriate physical suasion."

"Come on over—that'd be fun!" Clarrissa giggled, then sobered quickly. "But seriously, you win, I guess—this time. You'll keep me informed?"

"I'll do that. Clear ether, Cris!" and he turned back to the Palainian.

". . . so you see this is your problem. Go to it, little chum."

"I go, Kinnison."

18

CAMILLA KINNISON, DETECTOR

For hours Camilla and Tregonsee wrestled separately and fruitlessly with the problem of the elusive "X." Then, after she had studied the Rigellian's mind in a fashion which he could neither detect nor employ, Camilla broke the mental silence.

"Uncle Trig, my conclusions frighten me. Can you conceive of the possibility that it was contact with *my* mind, not yours, that made 'X' run away?"

"That is the only tenable conclusion. I know the power of my own mind, but I have never been able to guess at the capabilities of yours. I fear that I, at least, underestimated our opponent."

"I know I did, and I was terribly wrong. I shouldn't have tried to fool you, either, even a little bit. There are some things about me that I just *can't* show to most people, but you are different—you're *such* a wonderful person!"

"Thanks, Camilla, for your trust." Understandingly, he did not go on to say that he would keep on being worthy of it. "I accept the fact that you five, being children of two Second-Stage Lensmen, are basically beyond my comprehension. There are indications that you do not as yet thoroughly understand yourself. You have, however, decided upon a course of action."

"Oh—I'm *so* relieved! Yes, I have. But before we go into that, I haven't been able to solve the problem of 'X'. More, I have proved that I cannot solve it without more data. Therefore, you can't either. Check?"

"I had not reached that conclusion, but I accept your statement as truth."

"One of those uncommon powers of mine, to which you referred a while ago, is a wide range of perception, from large masses down to extremely tiny components. Another, or perhaps a part of the same one, is that, after resolving and analyzing these fine details, I can build up a logical and coherent whole by processes of interpolation and extrapolation."

"I can believe that such things would be possible to such a mind as yours must be. Go on."

"Well, that is how I know that I underestimated Mr. 'X.' Whoever or whatever he is, I am completely unable to resolve the structure of his thought. I gave you all I got of it. Look at it again, please—hard. What can you make of it now?"

"It is exactly the same as it was before; a fragment of a simple and plain introductory thought to an audience. That is all."

"That's all I can see, too, and that's what surprises me so." The hitherto imperturbable and serene Camilla got up and began to pace the floor. "That thought is apparently absolutely solid; and since that is a definitely impossible condition, the truth is that its structure is so fine that I cannot resolve it into its component units. This shows that I am not nearly as competent as I thought I was. When you and dad and the others reached that point, you each went to Arisia. I've decided to do the same thing."

"That decision seems eminently sound."

"Thanks, Uncle Trig—that was what I hoped you'd say. I've never been there, you know, and the idea scared me a little. Clear ether!"

There is no need to go into detail as to Camilla's bout with Mentor. Her mind, like Karen's, had had to mature of itself before any treatment could be really effective; but, once mature, she took as much in one session as Kathryn had taken in all her many. She had not suggested that the Rigellian accompany her to Arisia; they both knew that he had already received all he could take. Upon her return she greeted him casually as though she had been gone only a matter of hours.

"What Mentor did to me, Uncle Trig, shouldn't have been done to a Delgonian catlat. It doesn't show too much, though, I hope—does it?"

"Not at all." He scanned her narrowly, both physically and mentally. "I can perceive no change in gross. In fine, however, you have changed. You have developed."

"Yes, more than I would have believed possible. I can't do much with my present very poor transcription of that thought, since the all-important fine detail is missing. We'll have to intercept another one. I'll get it *all*, this time."

"But you did something with this one, I am sure. There must have been some developable features—a sort of latent-image effect?"

"A little. Practically infinitesimal compared to what was really there. Physically, his classification to four places is TUUV; quite a bit like the Nevians, you notice. His home planet is big, and practically covered with liquid. No real cities, just groups of half-submerged, temporary structures. Mentality very high, but we knew that already. Normally, he thinks upon a very short wave, so short that he was then working at the very bottom of his range. His sun is a fairly hot main-sequence star, of spectral class somewhere around F, and it's probably more or less variable, because there was quite a distinct implication of change. But that's normal enough, isn't it?"

Within the limits imposed by the amount and kind of data available, Camilla's observations and analyses had been perfect, her reconstruction flawless. She did not then have any idea, however, that "X" was in fact a spring-form Plooran. More, she did not even know that such a planet as Ploor existed, except for Mentor's one mention of it.

"Of course. Peoples of planets of variable suns think that such suns are the only kind fit to have planets. You cannot reconstruct the nature of the change?"

"No. Worse, I can't find even a hint of where his planet is in space—but then, I probably couldn't, anyway, even with a whole, fresh thought to study."

"Probably not. 'Rigel Four' would be an utterly meaningless thought to anyone ignorant of Rigel; and, except when making a conscious effort, as in directing strangers, I never think of its location in terms of galactic coordinates. I suppose that the location of a home planet is always taken for granted. That would seem to leave us just about where we were before in our search for 'X,' except for your implied ability to intercept another of his thoughts, almost at will. Explain, please."

"Not *my* ability—ours." Camilla smiled, confidently. "I couldn't do it alone, neither could you, but between us it won't be too difficult. You, with your utterly calm, utterly unshakable certainty, can drive a thought to any corner of the universe. You can fix and hold it steady on any indicated atom. I can't do that, or anything like it, but with my present ability to detect and to analyze I'm not afraid of missing 'X' if we can come within parsecs of him. So my idea is a sort of piggy-back hunting trip; you to take me for a ride, mentally, very much as Worsel takes Con, physically. That would work, don't you think?"

"Perfectly, I am sure." The stolid Rigellian was immensely pleased. "Link your mind with mine, then, and we will set out. If you have no better plan of action mapped out, I would suggest starting at the point where we lost him and working outward, covering an expanding sphere."

"You know best. I'll stick to you wherever you go."

Tregonsee launched his thought; a thought which, at a velocity not to be measured even in multiples of that of light, generated the surface of a continuously enlarging sphere of space. And with that thought, a very part of it, sped Camilla's incomprehensibly delicate, instantaneously reactive detector web. The Rigellian, with his unhuman perseverance, would have surveyed total space had it been necessary; and the now adult Camilla would have stayed with him. However, the patient pair did not have to comb all of space. In a matter of hours the girl's almost infinitely tenuous detector touched, with infinitesimal power and for an inappreciable instant of time, the exact thought-structure to which it had been so carefully attuned.

"Halt!" she flashed, and Tregonsee's mighty super-dreadnaught shot away along the indicated line at maximum blast.

"You are not now thinking at him, of course, but how sure are you that he did not feel your detector?" Tregonsee asked.

"Positive," the girl replied. "I couldn't even feel it myself until after a million-fold amplification. It was just a web, you know, not nearly solid enough for an analyzer or a recorder. I didn't touch his mind at all. However, when we get close enough to work efficiently, which will be in about five days, we will have to touch him. Assuming that he is as sensitive as we are, he will feel us; hence we will have to work fast and according to some definite plan. What are your ideas as to technique?"

"I may offer a suggestion or two, later, but I resign leadership to you. You already have made plans, have you not?"

"Only a framework; we'll have to work out the details together. Since we agree that it was my mind that he did not like, you will have to make the first contact."

"Of course. But since the action of thought is so nearly instantaneous, are you sure that you will be able to protect yourself in case he overcomes me at that first contact?" If the Rigellian gave any thought at all to his own fate in such a case, no trace of it was evident.

"My screens are good. I am fairly certain that I could protect both of us, but it might slow me down a trifle; and even an instant's delay might keep me from getting the information we want. It would be better, I think, to call Kit in. Or, better yet, Kay. She can stop a super-atomic bomb. With Kay covering us, we will both be free to work."

Again they went into a union of minds; considering, weighing, analyzing, rejecting, and—a few times—accepting. And finally, well within the five-day time limit, they had drawn up a completely detailed plan of action.

How uselessly that time was spent! For that action, instead of progressing according to their carefully worked-out plan, was ended almost in the instant of its beginning.

According to plan, Tregonsee tuned his mind to "X's" pattern as soon as they had come within working range. He reached out as delicately as he could, and his best was very fine work indeed. He might just as well have struck with all his power, for at first touch of the fringe, extremely light and entirely innocuous though it was, the stranger's barriers flared into being and there came back instantly a mental bolt of such vicious intensity that it would have gone through Tregonsee's hardest-held block as though no barrier had been there. But that bolt did not strike Tregonsee's shield. Instead, it struck Karen Kinnison's, which has already been described.

It did not exactly bounce, nor did it cling, nor did it linger, even for a microsecond, to do battle as expected. It simply vanished; as though that minute interval of time had been sufficient for the enemy to have recovered from the shock of encountering a completely unexpected resistance, to have analyzed the texture of the shield, to have deduced from that analysis the full capabilities of its owner and operator, to have decided that he did not care to have any dealings with the entity so deduced, and finally, as he no doubt supposed, to have begun to retreat in good order.

His retreat, however, was not in good order. He did not escape, this time. This time, as she had declared that she would be, Camilla was ready for anything—literally anything. Everything she had—and she had plenty—was on the trips; tense, taut, and poised. Knowing that Karen, the Ultimate of Defense, was on guard, she was wholly free to hurl her every force on the instant. Scarcely had the leading element of her probe touched the stranger's screens, however, when those screens, "X" himself, his vessel and any others that might have been accompanying it, and everything tangible in nearby space, all disappeared at once in the inconceivably violent, the ultimately cataclysmic detonation of a super-atomic bomb.

It may not, perhaps, be generally known that the "completely liberating" or "super-atomic" bomb liberates one hundred percent of the component energy of its total mass in approximately sixty nine hundredths of one microsecond. Its violence and destructiveness thus differ, both in degree and in kind, from those of the earlier type, which liberated only the energy of nuclear fission, very much as the radiation of S-Doradus differs from that of Earth's moon. Its mass attains, and holds for an appreciable length of time, a temperature to be measured only in millions of Centigrade degrees; which fact accounts in large part for its utterly incredible vehemence.

Nothing inert in its entire sphere of primary action can even begin to move out of the way before being reduced to its sub-atomic constituents and thus contributing in some measure to the cataclysm. Nothing is or becomes visible until the secondary stage begins; until the frightful globe has expanded to a diameter of thousands of yards and by this expansion has cooled down to a point at which some of its radiation lies in the visible violet. And as for lethal radiation—there are radiations and they are lethal.

The conflict with "X" had occupied approximately two milliseconds of actual time. The expansion had been progressing for a second or two when Karen lowered her shield.

"Well, that finishes that," she commented. "I'd better get back on the job. Did you find out what you want to know, Cam, or not?"

"I got a little in the moment before the explosion. Not much." Camilla was deep in study. "It's going to be quite a job of reconstruction. One thing of interest to you, though, is that this 'X' had quit sabotage temporarily and was on his way to Lyrane IX, where he had some important . . ."

"Nine?" Karen asked sharply. "Not Eight? I've been watching Eight, you know—I haven't even thought of Nine."

"Nine, definitely. The thought was clear. You might give it a scan once in a while. How is mother doing?"

"She's doing a grand job, and that Helen is quite an operator, too. I'm not doing much—just a touch here and there—I'll see what I can see on Nine. I'm not the scanner or detector you are, though, you know—maybe you'd better come over here too. Suppose?"

"I think so—don't you, Uncle Trig?" Tregonsee did. "We can do some exploring as we come, but since I have no definite patterns for web work, we may not be able to do much until we get close. Clear ether, Kay!"

"The fine structure is there, and I can resolve it and analyze it," Camilla informed Tregonsee, after a few hours of intense concentration.

"There are quite a few clear extraneous sequences, instead of the blurred latent images we had before, but there's still no indication of the location of his home planet. I can see his physical classification to ten places instead of four, more detail as to the sun's variation, the seasons, their habits, and so on. Things that seem mostly to be of very little importance, as far as we're concerned. I learned one fact, though, that is new and important. According to my reconstruction, his business on Lyrane IX was the induction of Boskonian Lensmen—*Black* Lensmen, Tregonsee, just as father suspected!"

"In that case, he must have been the Boskonian counterpart of an Arisian, and hence one of the highest echelon. I am very glad indeed that you and Karen relieved me of the necessity of trying to handle him myself . . . your father will be very glad to know that we have at last and in fact reached the top . . ."

Camilla was paying attention to the Rigellian's cogitations with only a fraction of her mind; most of it being engaged in a private conversation with her brother.

". . . so you see, Kit, he was under a sub-conscious compulsion. He *had* to destroy himself, his ship, and everything in it, in the very instant of attack by any mind definitely superior to his own. Therefore he couldn't have been an Eddorian, possibly, but merely another intermediate, and I haven't been of much help."

"Sure you have, Cam! You got a lot of information, and some mighty good leads to Lyrane IX and what goes on there. I'm on my way to Eddore now; and by working down from there and up from Lyrane IX we can't go wrong. Clear ether, sis!"

19

THE HELL-HOLE IN SPACE

Constance Kinnison did not waste much time in idle recriminations, even at herself. Realizing at last that she was still not fully competent, and being able to define exactly what she lacked, she went to Arisia for final treatment. She took that treatment and emerged from it, as her brother and sisters had emerged, a completely integrated personality.

She had something of everything the others had, of course, as did they all; but her dominants, the characteristics which had operated to make Worsel her favorite Second-Stage Lensman, were much like those of the Velantian. Her mind, like his, was quick and facile, yet of extraordinary power and range. She did not have much of her father's flat, driving urge or of his indomitable will to do; she was the least able of all the Five to exert long-sustained extreme effort. Her top, however, was vastly higher than theirs. Her armament was almost entirely offensive: she was far and away the deadliest fighter of them all. She only of them all had more than a trace of pure killer instinct; and when roused to full fighting pitch her mental bolts were weapons of as starkly incomprehensible an effectiveness as the sphere of primary action of a super-atomic bomb.

As soon as Constance had left the *Velan,* remarking that she was going to Arisia to take her medicine, Worsel called a staff meeting to discuss in detail the matter of the "Hell-Hole in Space."

That conference was neither long nor heated; it was unanimously agreed that the phenomenon was—*must* be—simply another undiscovered cavern of Overlords.

In view of the fact that Worsel and his crew had been hunting down and killing Overlords for more than twenty years, the only logical course of action was for them to deal similarly with one more, perhaps the only remaining large group of their hereditary foes. Nor did any doubt of their ability to do so enter any one of the Velantians' minds.

How wrong they were!

They did not have to search for the "Hell-Hole." Long since, to stop its dreadful toll, a spherical cordon of robot guard-ships had been posted to warn all traffic away from the outer fringes of its influence. Since they merely warned against, but could not physically prohibit, entry into the dangerous space, Worsel did not pay any attention to the guard-ships or to their signals as the *Velan* went through the warning web. His plans were, he thought, well laid. His ship was free. Its speed, by Velantian standards, was very low. Each member of his crew wore a full-coverage thought-screen; a similar and vastly more powerful screen would surround the whole vessel if one of Worsel's minor members were either to tighten or to relax its grip upon a spring-mounted control. Worsel was, he thought, ready for anything.

But the "Hell-Hole in Space" was not a cavern of Overlords. No sun, no planet, nothing material existed within that spherical volume of space. But *something* was there. Slow as was the *Velan*'s pace, it was still too fast by far; for in a matter of seconds, through the supposedly impervious thought-screens, there came an attack of utterly malignant ferocity; an assault which tore at Worsel's mind in a fashion he had never imagined possible; a poignant, rending, unbearably crescendo force whose violence seemed to double with every mile of distance.

The *Velan*'s all-encompassing screen snapped on—uselessly. Its tremendous power was as unopposed as were the lesser powers of the personal shields; that highly inimical thought was coming past, not through, the barriers. An Arisian, or one of the Children of the Lens, would have been able to perceive and to block that band; no one of lesser mental stature could.

Strong and fast as Worsel was, mentally and physically, he acted just barely in time. All his resistance and all his strength had to be called into play to maintain his mind's control over his body; to enable him to spin his ship end for end and to kick her drive up to maximum blast. To his surprise, his agony decreased with distance as rapidly as it had built up; disappearing entirely as the *Velan* reached the web she had crossed such a short time before.

Groggy, sick, and shaken, hanging slackly from his bars, the Valantian Lensman was roused to action by the mental and physical frenzy of his crew. Ten of them had died in the Hell-Hole; six more were torn to bits before their commander could muster enough force to stop their insane rioting. Then Master Therapist Worsel went to work; and one by one he brought the survivors back. They remembered; but he made those memories bearable.

He then called Kinnison. ". . . but there didn't seem to be anything personal about it, as one would expect from an Overlord," he concluded his brief report. "It did not concentrate on us, reach for us, or follow us as we left. Its intensity seemed to vary only with distance—perhaps inversely as distance squared; it might very well have been radiated from a center. While it is nothing like anything I ever felt before, I still think it must be an Overlord—maybe a sort of second-stage Overlord, just as you and I are Second-Stage Lensmen. He's too strong for me now, just as they used to be too strong for us before we met you. By the same reasoning, however, I'm pretty sure that if you can come over here, you and I together could figure out a way of taking him. How about it?"

"Mighty interesting, and I'd like to, but I'm right in the middle of a job," Kinnison replied, and went on to explain rapidly what he, as Bradlow Thyron, had done and what he still had to do. "As soon as I can get away I'll come over. In the meantime, chum, keep away from there. Do a flit—find something else to keep you amused until I can join you."

Worsel set out, and after a few days—or weeks? Idle time means practically nothing to a Velantian—a sharply-Lensed thought drove in.

"Help! A Lensman calling help! Line this thought and come fast . . ." The message ended as sharply as it had begun; in a flare of agony which, Worsel knew, meant that that Lensman, whoever he was, had died.

Since the thought, although broadcast, had come in strong and clear, Worsel knew that its sender had been close by. While the time had been very short indeed, he had bean able to get a line of sorts. Into that line he whirled the *Velan's* sharp prow and along it she hurtled at the literally inconceivable pace of her maximum drive. As the Gray Lensman had often remarked, the Velantian super-dreadnought had more legs than a centipede, and now she was using them all. In minutes, then, the scene of battle grew large upon her plates.

The Patrol ship, hopelessly outclassed, could last only minutes longer. Her screens were down; her very wall-shield was dead. Red pockmarks sprang into being along her sides as the Boskonian needle-beamers wiped out her few remaining controls. Then, as the helplessly raging Worsel looked on, his brain seething with unutterable Velantian profanity, the enemy prepared to board; a course of action which, Worsel could see, was changed abruptly by the fact—and perhaps as well by the terrific velocity—of his own unswerving approach. The conquered Patrol cruiser disappeared in a blaze of detonating duodec; the conqueror devoted his every jet to the task of running away; strewing his path as he did so with sundry items of solid and explosive destruction. Such things, however, whether inert or free, were old and simple stuff to the *Velan*'s war-wise crew. Their spotters and detectors were full out, as was also a fore-fan of annihilating and disintegrating beams.

Thus none of the Boskonian's missiles touched the *Velan,* nor, with all his speed, could he escape. Few indeed were the ships of space able to step it, parsec for parsec, with Worsel's mighty craft, and this luckless pirate vessel was not one of them. Up and up the *Velan* rushed; second by second the intervening distance lessened. Tractors shot out, locked on, and pulled briefly with all the force of their stupendous generators.

Briefly, but long enough. As Worsel had anticipated, that savage yank had, in the fraction of a second required for the Boskonian commander to recognize and to cut the tractors, been enough to bring the two inertialess warcraft almost screen to screen.

"Primaries! Blast!" Worsel hurled the thought even before his tractors snapped. He was in no mood for a long-drawn-out engagement. He *might* be able to win with his secondaries, his needles, his tremendously powerful short-range stuff, and his other ordinary offensive weapons; but he was taking no chances.

One! Two! Three! The three courses of Boskonian defensive screen scarcely winked as each, locally overloaded, flared through the visible into the black and went down.

Crash! The stubborn fabric of the wall-shield offered little more resistance before it, too, went down, exposing the bare metal of the Boskonian hull—and, as is well known, any conceivable material substance simply vanishes at the touch of such fields of force as those.

Driving projectors carved away and main batteries silenced, Worsel's needle-beamers proceeded systematically to riddle every control panel and every lifeboat, to make of the immense space-rover a completely helpless hulk.

"Hold!" An observer flashed the thought. "Number Eight slip is empty—Number Eight lifeboat got away!"

"Damnation!" Worsel, at the head of his armed and armored storming party, as furiously eager as they to come to grips with the enemy, paused briefly. "Trace it—or can you?"

"I did. My tracers can hold it for fifteen minutes, perhaps twenty. No longer than twenty."

Worsel thought intensely. Which had first call, ship or lifeboat? The ship, he decided. Its resources were vastly greater; most of its personnel were probably unharmed. Given any time at all, they might be able to jury-rig a primary, and that would be bad—very bad. Besides, there were more people here; and even if, as was distinctly possible, the Boskonian captain had abandoned his vessel and his crew in an attempt to save his own life, there was plenty of time.

"Hold that lifeboat," he instructed the observer. "Ten minutes is all we need here."

And it was. The Boskonians—barrel-bodied, blocky-limbed monstrosities resembling human beings about as much as they did the Velantians—wore armor, possessed hand-weapons of power, and fought viciously. They had even managed to rig a few semi-portable projectors, but none of these was allowed a single blast. Spy-ray observers were alert, and needle-beam operators; hence the fighting was all at hand to hand, with hand-weapons only. For, while the Velantians to a man lusted to kill, they had had it drilled into them for twenty years that the search for information came first; the pleasure of killing, second.

Worsel himself went straight for the Boskonian officer in command. That wight had a couple of guards with him, but they did not matter— needle-ray men took care of them. He also had a pair of heavy blasters, which he held steadily on the Velantian. Worsel paused momentarily; then, finding his screens adequate, he slammed the control-room door shut with a flick of his tail and launched himself, straight and level at his foe, with an acceleration of ten gravities. The Boskonian tried to dodge but could not. The frightful impact did not kill him, but it hurt him, badly. Worsel, on the other had, was scarcely jarred. Hard, tough, and durable, Velantians are accustomed from birth to knockings-about which would pulverize human bones.

Worsel batted the Boskonian's guns away with two terrific blows of an armored paw, noting as he did so that violent contact with a steel wall didn't do their interior mechanisms a bit of good. Then, after cutting off both his enemy's screens and his own, he batted the Boskonian's helmet; at first experimentally, then with all his power. Unfortunately, however, it held. So did the thought-screen, and there were no external controls. That armor, damn it, was good stuff!

Leaping to the ceiling, he blasted his whole mass straight down upon the breastplate, striking it so hard this time that he hurt his head. Still no use. He wedged himself between two heavy braces, flipped a loop of tail around the Boskonian's feet, and heaved. The armored form flew across the room, struck the heavy steel wall, bounced, and dropped. The bulges of the armor were flattened by the force of the collision, the wall was dented—but the thought-screen still held!

Worsel was running out of time, fast. He couldn't treat the thing very much rougher without killing him, if he wasn't dead already. He couldn't take him aboard; he *had* to cut that screen here and now! He could see how the armor was put together; but, armored as he was, he could not take it apart. And, since the whole ship was empty of air, he could not open his own.

Or could he? He could. He could breathe space long enough to do what had to be done. He cut off his air, loosened a plate enough to release four or five hands, and, paying no attention to his laboring lungs, set furiously to work. He tore open the Boskonians armor, snapped off his thought-screen. The creature wasn't quite dead yet—good! He didn't know a damn thing, though, nor did any member of his crew . . . but . . . a ground-gripper—a big shot—had got away. Who, or what, was he?

"Tell me!" Worsel demanded, with the full power of mind and Lens, even while he was exploring with all his skill and speed. "TELL ME!"

But the Boskonian was dying fast. The ungentle treatment, and now the lack of air, were taking toll. His patterns were disintegrating by the second, faster and faster. Meaningless blurs, which, under Worsel's vicious probing, condensed into something which seemed to be a Lens.

A Lensman? Impossible—starkly unthinkable! But jet back—hadn't Kim intimated a while back that there might be such things as Black Lensmen?

But Worsel himself wasn't feeling so good. He was only half conscious. Red, black, and purple spots were dancing in front of every one of his eyes. He sealed his suit, turned on his air, gasped, and staggered. Two of the nearest Velantians, both of whom had been en rapport with him throughout, came running to his aid; arriving just as he recovered full control.

"Back to the *Velan,* everybody!" he ordered. "No time for any more fun—we've got to get that lifeboat!" Then, as soon as he had been obeyed: "Bomb that hulk . . . Good! Flit!"

Overtaking the lifeboat did not take long. Spearing it with a tractor and yanking it alongside required only seconds. For all his haste, Worsel found in it only something that looked as though it once might have been a Delgonian Lensman. It had blown itself apart. Because of its reptilian tenacity of life, however, it was not quite dead: its Lens still showed an occasional flicker of light and its disintegrating mind was not yet entirely devoid of patterns. Worsel studied that mind until all trace of life had vanished. Then he called Kinnison.

". . . so you see I guessed wrong. The Lens was too dim to read, but he must have been a Black Lensman. The only readable thought in his mind was an extremely fuzzy one of the planet Lyrane Nine. I hate to have hashed the job up so; especially since I had one chance in two of guessing right."

"Well, no use squawking now . . ." Kinnison paused in thought. "Besides, he could have done it anyway, and would have. You haven't done too badly, at that. You found a Black Lensman who isn't a Kalonian, and you've got confirmation of Boskonian interest in Lyrane Nine. What more do you want? Stick around fairly close to the Hell-Hole, Slim, and as soon as I can make it, I'll join you there."

20

KINNISON AND
THE BLACK LENSMAN

Boys, take her upstairs," Kinnison-Thyron ordered, and the tremendous raider—actually the *Dauntless* in disguise—floated serenely upward to a station immediately astern of Mendonai's flagship. All three courses of multi-ply defensive screen were out, as were full-coverage spy-ray blocks and thought-screens.

As the fleet blasted in tight formation for Kalonia III, Boskonian experts tested the *Dauntless'* defenses thoroughly, and found them bottle-tight. No intrusion was possible. The only open channel was to Thyron's plate, which was so villainously fogged that nothing could be seen except Thyron's face. Convinced at last of that fact, Mendonai sat back and seethed quietly; his pervasive Kalonian blueness pointing up his grim and vicious mood.

He had never, in all his life, been insulted so outrageously. Was there anything—*anything!*—he could do about it? There was not. Thyron, personally, he could not touch—yet—and the fact that the outlaw had so brazenly and so nonchalantly placed his vessel in the exact center of the Boskonian fleet made it pellucidly clear to any Boskonian mind that he had nothing whatever to fear from that fleet.

Wherefore the Kalonian seethed, and his minions stepped ever more softly and followed with ever-increasing punctilio the rigid Boskonian code. For the grapevine carries news swiftly; by this time the whole fleet knew that His Nibs had been taking a God-awful kicking around, and the first guy who gave him an excuse to blow his stack would be lucky if he only got skinned alive.

As the fleet spread out for inert maneuvering above the Kalonian atmosphere, Kinnison turned again to the young Lensman.

"One last word, Frank. I'm sure everything's covered—a lot of smart people worked on this problem. Nevertheless, something may happen, so I'll send you the data as fast as I get it. Remember what I told you before—if I get the dope we need, I'm expendable and it'll be your job to get it back to Base. No heroics. Is that clear?"

"Yes, sir." The young Lensman gulped. "I hope, though, that it doesn't . . ."

"So do I," Kinnison grinned as he climbed into his highly special dureum armor, "and the chances are a million to one that it won't. That's why I'm going down there."

In their respective speedsters Kinnison and Mendonai made the long drop to ground, and side by side they went into the office of Black Lensman Melasnikov. That worthy, too, wore heavy armor; but he did not have a mechanical thought-screen. With his terrific power of mind, he did not need one. Thyron, of course, did; a fact of which Melasnikov became instantly aware.

"Release your screen," he directed, bruskly.

"Not yet, pal—don't be so hasty," Thyron advised. "Some things about this here hook-up don't exactly click. We got a little talking to do before I open up."

"No talk, worm. Talk, especially your talk, is meaningless. From you I want, and will have, the truth, and not talk. CUT THOSE SCREENS!"

And lovely Kathryn, in her speedster not too far away, straightened up and sent out a call.

"Kit—Kay—Cam—Con . . . are you free?" They were, for the moment. "Stand by, please, all of you. I'm pretty sure something is going to happen. Dad can handle this Melasnikov easily enough, if none of the higher-ups step in, but they probably will. Their Lensmen are probably important enough to rate protection. Check?"

"Check."

"So, as soon as dad begins to get the best of the argument, the protector will step in," Kathryn continued, "and whether I can handle him alone or not depends on how high a higher-up they send in. So I'd like to have you all stand by for a minute or two, just in case."

How different was Kathryn's attitude now than it had been in the hyper-spatial tube! And how well for Civilization that it was!

"Hold it, kids, I've got a thought," Kit suggested. "We've never done any teamwork since we learned how to handle heavy stuff, and we'll have to get in some practice sometime. What say we link up on this?"

"Oh, yes!" "Let's do!" "Take over, Kit!" Three approvals came as one, and:

"QX, Kit," came Kathryn's less enthusiastic concurrence, a moment later. Naturally enough, she would rather do it alone if she could; but she had to admit that her brother's plan was the better.

Kit laid out the matrix and the four girls came in. There was a brief moment of snuggling and fitting; then each of the Five caught his breath in awe. This was new—brand new. Each had thought himself complete and full; each had supposed that much practice and at least some give-and-take would be necessary before they could work efficiently as a group. But this! This was the supposedly ultimately unattainable—perfection itself! This was UNITY: full; round; complete. No practice was or ever would be necessary. Not one micro-micro-second of doubt or of uncertainty would or ever could exist. This was the UNIT, a thing for which there are no words in any written or spoken language, a thing theretofore undreamed-of save as a purely theoretical concept in an unthinkably ancient, four-ply Arisian brain.

"U-m-n-g-n-k." Kit swallowed a lump as big as his fist. "This, kids, is really . . ."

"Ah, children, you have done it." Mentor's thought rolled smoothly in. "You now understand why I could not attempt to describe the Unit to any one of you. This is the culminating moment of my life—of our lives, we may now say. For the first time in more years than you can understand, we are at last sure that our lives have not been lived in vain. But attend—that for which you are waiting will soon be here."

"What is it?" "Who?" "Tell us how to . . ."

"We cannot." Four separate Arisians smiled as one; a wash of ineffable blessing and benediction suffused the Five. "We who made the Unit possible are almost completely ignorant of the details of its higher functions. But that it will need no help from our lesser minds is certain; it is the most powerful and the most nearly perfect creation this universe has ever seen."

The Arisian vanished; and, even before Kimball Kinnison had released his screen, a cryptic, utterly untraceable and all-pervasive foreign thought came in.

To aid the Black Lensman? To study this disturbing new element? Or merely to observe? Or what? The only certainty was that that thought was coldly, clearly, and highly inimical to all Civilization.

Again everything happened at once. Karen's impenetrable block flared into being—not instantly, but instantaneously. Constance assembled and hurled, in the same lack of time, a mental bolt of whose size and power she had never been capable. Camilla, the detector-scanner, synchronized with the attacking thought and steered. And Kathryn and Kit, with all the force, all the will, and all the drive of human heredity, got behind it and pushed.

Nor was this, any of it, conscious individual effort. The children of the Lens were not now five, but one. This was the Unit at work; doing its first job. It is literally impossible to describe what happened; but each of the Five knew that one would-be Protector, wherever he had been in space or whenever in time, would never think again. Seconds passed. The Unit held tense, awaiting the riposte. No riposte came.

"Fine work, kids!" Kit broke the linkage and each girl felt hard, brotherly pats on her back. "That's all there is to this one, I guess—must have been only one guard on duty. You're good eggs, and I like you— *How* we can operate now!"

"But it was too easy, Kit!" Kathryn protested. "Too easy by far for it to have been an Eddorian. We aren't that good. Why, I could have handled him alone . . . I think," she added hastily, as she realized that she, although an essential part of the Unit, had as yet no real understanding of what that Unit really was.

"You *hope,* you mean!" Constance jeered. "If that bolt was as big and as hot as I'm afraid it was, anything it hit would have looked easy. Why didn't you slow us down, Kit? You're supposed to be the Big Brain, you know. As it was, we haven't the faintest idea of what happened. Who was he, anyway?"

"Didn't have time," Kit grinned. "Everything got out of hand. All of us were sort of inebriated by the exuberance of our own enthusiasm, I guess. Now that we know what our speed is, though, we can slow down next time—if we want to. As for your last question, Con, you're asking the wrong guy. Was it Eddorian, Cam, or not?"

"What difference does it make?" Karen asked.

"On the practical side, none. For the completion of the picture, maybe a lot. Come in, Cam."

"It was not an Eddorian," Camilla decided. "It was not of Arisian, or even near-Arisian, grade. Sorry to say it, Kit, but it was another member of that high-thinking race you've already got down on Page One of your little black book."

"I thought it might be. The missing link between Kalonia and Eddore. Credits to millos it's that dopey planet Ploor Mentor was yowling about. Oh, DAMN!"

"Why the capital damn?" asked Constance, brightly. "Let's link up and let the Unit find it and knock hell out of it. That'd be fun."

"Act your age, baby," Kit advised. "Ploor is taboo—you know that as well as I do. Mentor told us all not to try to investigate it—that we'd learn of it in time, so we probably will. I told him a while back I was going to hunt it up myself, and he told me if I did he'd tie both my legs around my neck in a lovers' knot, or words to that effect. Sometimes I'd like to half-brain the old buzzard, but everything he has said so far has dead-centered the beam. We'll just have to take it, and try to like it."

Kinnison was eminently willing to cut his thought-screen, since he could not work through it to do what had to be done here. Nor was he over-confident. He knew that he could handle the Black Lensman—*any* Black Lensman—but he also knew enough of mental phenomena in general and of Lensmanship in particular to realize that Melasnikov might very well have within call reserves about whom he, Kinnison, could know nothing. He knew that he had lied outrageously to young Frank in regard to the odds applicable to this enterprise; that instead of a million to one, the actuality was one to one, or even less.

Nevertheless, he was well content. He had neither lied nor exaggerated in saying that he himself was expendable. That was why Frank and the *Dauntless* were upstairs now. Getting the dope and getting it back to Base were what mattered. Nothing else did.

He was coldly certain that he could get all the information that Melasnikov had, once he had engaged the Kalonian Lensman mind to mind. No Boskonian power or thing, he was convinced, could treat him rough enough or kill him fast enough to keep him from doing that. And he could and would shoot the stuff along to Frank as fast as he got it. And he stood an even—almost even, anyway—chance of getting away afterward. If he could, QX. If he couldn't . . . well that would have to be QX, too.

Kinnison flipped his switch and there ensued a conflict of wills that made the sub-ether boil. The Kalonian was one of the strongest, hardest, and ablest individuals of his hellishly capable race; and the fact that he believed implicity in his own complete invulnerability operated to double and to quadruple his naturally tremendous strength.

On the other hand, Kimball Kinnison was a Second-Stage Lensman of the Galactic Patrol.

Back and back, then, inch by inch and foot by foot, the Black Lensman's defensive zone was forced; back to and down into his own mind. And there, appallingly enough, Kinnison found almost nothing of value.

No knowledge of the higher reaches of the Boskonian organization; no hint that any real organization of Black Lensmen existed; only the peculiarly disturbing fact that he had picked up his Lens on Lyrane IX. And "picked up" was literal. He had not seen, nor heard, nor had any dealings of any kind with anyone while he was there.

Since both armored figures stood motionless, no sign of the tremendous actuality of their mental battle was evident. Thus the Boskonians were not surprised to hear their Black Lensman speak.

"Very well, Thyron, you have passed this preliminary examination. I know all that I now need to know. I will accompany you to your vessel, to complete my investigation there. Lead the way."

Kinnison did so, and as the speedster came to rest inside the *Dauntless* the Black Lensman addressed Vice-Admiral Mendonai via plate.

"I am taking Bradlow Thyron and his ship to the space-yards on Four, where a really comprehensive study of it can be made. Return to and complete your original assignment."

"I abase myself, Your Supremacy, but . . . but I . . . I *discovered* that ship!" Mendonai protested.

"Granted," the Black Lensman sneered. "You will be given full credit in my report for what you have done. The fact of discovery, however, does not excuse your present conduct. Go—and consider yourself fortunate that, because of that service, I forbear from disciplining you for your intolerable insubordination."

"I abase myself, Your Supremacy. I go." He really did abase himself, this time, and the fleet disappeared.

Then, the mighty *Dauntless* safely away from Kalonia and on her course to rendezvous with the *Velan,* Kinnison again went over his captive's mind; line by line and almost cell by cell. It was still the same. It was still Lyrane IX and it still didn't make any kind of sense. Since Boskonians were certainly not supermen, and hence could not possibly have developed their own Lenses, it followed that they must have obtained them from the Boskonian counterpart of Arisia. Hence, Lyrane IX must be IT—a conclusion which was certainly fallacious. Ridiculous—preposterous—utterly untenable: Lyrane IX never had been, was not, and never would be the home of any Boskonian super-race. Nevertheless, it was a definite fact that Melasnikov had got his Lens there. Also, if he had ever had any special training, such as any Lensman must have had, he didn't have any memory of it. Nor did he carry any scars of surgery. What a hash! How could *anybody* make any sense out of such a mess as that?

Ever-watchful Kathryn, eyes narrowed now in concentration, could have told him, but she did not. Her visualization was beginning to clear up. Lyrane was out. So was Ploor. The Lenses originated on Eddore; that was certain. The fact that their training was subconscious weakened the Black Lensman in precisely the characteristics requisite for ultimate strength—although probably neither the Eddorians nor the Ploorans, with their warped, Boskonian sense of values, realized it. The Black Lensmen would never constitute a serious problem. QX.

Kinnison, having attended to the unpleasant but necessary job of resolving Melasnikov into his component atoms, turned to his Lensman-aide.

"Hold everything, Frank, until I get back. This won't take long."

Nor did it, although the outcome was not at all what the Gray Lensman had expected.

Kinnison and Worsel, in an inert speedster, crossed the Hell-Hole's barrier web at a speed of only miles per hour, and then slowed down. The ship was backing in on her brakes, with everything set to hurl her forward under full free drive should either Lensman flick a finger. Kinnison could feel nothing, even though, being en rapport with Worsel, he knew that his friend was soon suffering intensely.

"Let's flit," the Gray Lensman suggested, and threw on the drive. "I probed my limit, and couldn't touch or feel a thing. Had enough, didn't you?"

"More than enough—I couldn't have taken much more."

Each boarded his ship; and as the *Dauntless* and the *Velan* tore through space toward far Lyrane, Kinnison paced his room, scowling in black abstraction. Nor would a mind-reader have found his thoughts either cogent or informative.

"Lyrane Nine . . . *Lyrane* Nine . . . Lyrane *Nine* . . . LYRANE NINE . . . and something I can't feel or sense or perceive that kills anybody and everybody else . . . KLONO'S tungsten TEETH and CURVING CARBALLOY CLAWS!!!"

21

THE RED LENSMAN ON LYRANE

Helen's story was short and bitter. Human or near-human Boskonians came to Lyrane II and spread insidious propaganda all over the planet. Lyranian matriarchy should abandon its policy of isolationism. Matriarchs were the highest type of life. Matriarchy was the most perfect of all existing forms of government—why keep on confining it to one small planet, when it should by rights be ruling the entire galaxy? The way things were, there was only one Elder Person; all other Lyranians, even though better qualified than the then incumbent, were nothing . . . and so on. Whereas, if things were as they should be, each individual Lyranian person could be and would be the Elder Person of a planet at least, and perhaps of an entire solar system . . . and so on. And the visitors, who, they insisted, were no more males than the Lyranian persons were females, would teach them. They would be amazed at how easily, under Boskonian guidance, this program could be put into effect.

Helen fought the intruders with everything she had. She despised the males of her own race; she detested those of all others. Believing hers to be the only existing matriarchal race, especially since neither Kinnison nor the Boskonians seemed to know of any other, she was sure that any prolonged contact with other cultures would result, not in the triumph of matriarchy, but in its fall. She not only voiced these beliefs as she held them—violently—but also acted upon them in the same fashion.

Because of the ingrained matriarchially conservative habit of Lyranian thought, particularly among the older persons, Helen found it comparatively easy to stamp out the visible manifestations; and, being in no sense a sophisticate, she thought the whole matter settled. Instead, she merely drove the movement underground, where it grew tremendously. The young, of course, rebellious as always against the hide-bound, mossbacked, and reactionary older generation, joined the subterranean New Deal in droves. Nor was the older generation solid. In fact, it was riddled by the defection of many thousands who could not expect to attain any outstanding place in the world as it was and who believed that the Boskonians' glittering forecasts would come true.

Disaffection spread, then, rapidly and unobserved; culminating in the carefully-planned uprising which made Helen an ex-queen and put her under restraint to await a farcical trial and death.

"I see." Clarrissa caught her lower lip between her teeth. "Very unfunny. . . . You didn't mention or think of any of your persons as ringleaders . . . peculiar that you couldn't catch them, with your telepathy . . . no, natural enough, at that . . . but there's one I want very much to get hold of. Don't know whether she was really a leader, or not, but she was mixed up in some way with a Boskonian Lensman. I never did know her name. She was the wom—the person who managed your airport here when Kim and I were . . ."

"Cleonie? Why, I never thought . . . but it might have, at that . . . yes, as I look back . . ."

"Yes, hindsight *is* a lot more accurate than foresight," the Red Lensman grinned. "I've noticed that myself, lots of times."

"It *did!* It *was* a leader!" Helen declared, furiously. "I shall have its life, too, the damned, jealous cat—the blood-sucking, back-biting *louse!*"

"She's all of that, in more ways than you know," Clarrissa agreed, grimly, and spread in the Lyranian's mind the story of Eddie the derelict. "So you see that Cleonie has got to be our starting-point. Have you any idea of where we can find her?"

"I haven't seen or heard anything of Cleonie lately." Helen paused in thought. "If, though, as I am now almost certain, it was one of the prime movers behind this brainless brat Ladora, it wouldn't dare leave the planet for very long at a time. As to how to find it, I don't quite know . . . Anybody would be apt to shoot me on sight . . . would you dare fly this funny plane of yours down close to a few of our cities?"

"Certainly. I don't know of anything around here that my screens and fields can't stop. Why?"

"Because I know of several places where Cleonie might be, and if I can get fairly close to them, I can find it in spite of anything it can do to hide itself from me. But I don't want to get you into too much trouble, and I don't want to get killed myself, either, now that you have rescued me—at least, until after I have killed Cleonie and Ladora."

"QX. What are you waiting for? Which way, Helen?"

"Back to the city first, for several reasons. Cleonie probably is not there, but we must make sure. Also, I want my guns . . ."

"Guns? No. DeLameters are better. I have several spares." In one fleeting mental contact Clarrissa taught the Lyranian all there was to know about DeLameters. And that feat impressed Helen even more than did the nature and power of the weapon.

"What a mind!" she exclaimed. "You didn't have any such equipment as that, the last time I saw you. Or were you—no, you weren't hiding it."

"You're right; I have developed considerably since then. But about guns—what do you want of one?"

"To kill that nitwit Ladora on sight, and that snake Cleonie, too, as soon as you get done with it."

"But why guns? Why not the mental force you always used?"

"Except by surprise, I couldn't," Helen admitted, frankly. "All adult persons are of practically equal mental strength. But speaking of strength, I marvel that a craft as small as this should be able to ward off the attack of one of those tremendous Boskonian ships of space . . ."

"But she *can't!* What made you think she could?"

"Your own statement—or were you thinking of purely Lyranian dangers, not realizing that Ladora of course called Cleonie as soon as you showed your teeth, and that Cleonie as surely called the Lensman or some other Boskonian? And that they must have ships of war not too far away?"

"Heavens, no! It never occurred to me!"

Clarrissa thought briefly. It wouldn't do any good to call Kim. Both the *Dauntless* and the *Velan* were coming as fast as they could, but it would be a day or so yet before they arrived. Besides, he would tell her to lay off, which was exactly what she was not going to do. She turned her thought back to the matriarch.

"Two of our best ships are coming, and I hope they get here first. In the meantime, we'll just have to work fast and keep our detectors full out. Anyway, Cleonie won't know that I'm looking for her—I haven't even mentioned her to anyone except you."

"No?" pessimistically. "Cleonie knows that *I* am looking for it, and since it knows by now that I am with you, it would think that both of us were hunting it even if we weren't. But we are nearly close enough now; I must concentrate. Fly around quite low over the city, please."

"QX. I'll tune in with you too. 'Two heads,' you know." Clarrissa learned Cleonie's pattern, tuned to it, and combed the city while Helen was getting ready.

"She isn't here, unless she's behind one of those thought-screens," the Red Lensman remarked. "Can you tell?"

"Thought-screens! The Boskonians had a few of them, but none of us ever did. How can you find them? Where are they?"

"One there—two over there. They stick out like big black spots on a white screen. Can't you see them? I supposed your scanners were the same as mine, but apparently they aren't. Take a quick peek at them with the spy—you work it like so. If they've got spy-ray blocks up, too, we'll have to go down there and blast."

"Politicians only," Helen reported, after a moment's manipulation of the suddenly familiar instrument. "They need killing, of course, on general principles, but perhaps we shouldn't take time for that now. The next place to look is a few degrees east of north of here."

Cleonie was not, however, in that city. Nor in the next, nor the next. But the speedster's detector screens remained blank and the two allies, so much alike physically, so different mentally, continued their hunt. There was opposition, of course—all that the planet afforded—but Clarrissa's second-stage mind took care of the few items of offense which her speedster's defenses could not handle.

Finally two things happened almost at once. Clarrissa found Cleonie, and Helen saw a dim and fuzzy white spot upon the lower left-hand corner of the detector plate.

"Can't be ours," the Red Lensman decided instantly. "Almost exactly the wrong direction. Boskonians. Ten minutes—twelve at most—before we have to flit. Time enough—I hope—if we work fast."

She shot downward, going inert and matching intrinsics at a lack of altitude which would have been suicidal for any ordinary pilot. She rammed her beryllium-bronze torpedo through the first-floor wall of a forbidding, almost windowless building—its many stories of massive construction, she knew, would help no end against the heavy stuff so sure to come. Then, while every hitherto-hidden offensive arm of the Boskone-coached Lyranians converged, screaming through the air and crashing and clanking along the city's streets, Clarrissa probed and probed and probed. Cleonie had locked herself into a veritable dungeon cell in the deepest sub-basement of the structure. She was wearing a thought-screen, too, but she had been releasing it, for an instant at a time, to see what was going on. One of those instants was enough—that screen would never work again. She had been prepared to kill herself at need; but her full-charged weapons emptied themselves futilely against a massive lock and she threw her vial of poison across the corridor and into an empty cell.

So far, so good; but how to get her out of there? Physical approach was out of the question. There must be somebody around, somewhere, with keys, or hack-saws, or sledgehammers, or something. Ha—oxyacetylene torches! Very much against their wills, two Lyranian mechanics trundled a dolly along a corridor, into an elevator. The elevator went down four levels; the artisans began to burn away a barrier of thick steel bars.

By this time the whole building was rocking to the detonation of high explosive. Much more of that kind of stuff and she would be trapped by the sheer mass of the rubble. She was handling six jackass-stubborn people already and that Boskonian warship was coming fast; she did not quite know whether she was going to get away with this or not.

But somehow, from the unplumbed and unplumbable depths which made her what she so uniquely was, the Red Lensman drew more and ever more power. Kinnison, who had once made heavy going of handling two-and-a-fraction Lensmen, guessed, but never did learn from her, what his beloved wife really did that day.

Even Helen, only a few feet away, could not understand what was happening. Left parsecs behind long since, the Lyranian could not help in any particular, but could only stand and wonder. She knew that this queerly powerful Lens-bearing Earth-person—white-faced, sweating, strung to the very snapping-point as she sat motionless at her board—was exerting some terrible, some tremendous force. She knew that the heaviest of the circling bombers sheered away and crashed. She knew that certain mobile projectors, a few blocks away, did not come any closer. She knew that Cleonie, against every iota of her mulish Lyranian will, was coming toward the speedster. She knew that many persons, who wished intensely to bar Cleonie's progress or to shoot her down, were physically unable to act. She had no faint idea, however, of how such work could possibly be done.

Cleonie came aboard and Clarrissa snapped out of her trance. The speedster nudged and blasted its way out of the wrecked stronghold, then tore a hole through protesting air into open space. Clarrissa shook her head, wiped her face, studied a tiny dot in the corner of the plate opposite the one now showing clearly the Boskonian warship, and set her controls.

"We'll make it—I think," she announced. "Even though we're indetectable, they of course know our line, and they're so much faster that they'll be able to find us on their visuals before long. On the other hand, they must be detecting our ships now, and my guess is that they won't dare follow us long enough to do us any harm. Keep an eye on things, Helen, while I find out what Cleonie really knows. And while I think of it, what's your real name? It isn't polite to keep on calling you by a name that you never even heard of until you met us."

"Helen," the Lyranian made surprising answer. "I liked it, so I adopted it—officially."

"Oh . . . That's a compliment, really, to both Kim and me. Thanks." The Red Lensman then turned her attention to her captive, and as mind fitted itself precisely to mind her eyes began to gleam in gratified delight. Cleonie was a real find; this seemingly unimportant Lyranian knew a lot—an immense lot—about things that no adherent of the Patrol had ever heard before. And she, Clarrissa Kinnison, would be the first of all the Gray Lensmen to learn of them! Therefore, taking her time now, she allowed every detail of the queer but fascinating picture-story-history to imprint itself upon her mind.

And Karen and Camilla, together in Tregonsee's ship, glanced at each other and exchanged flashing thoughts. Should they interfere? They hadn't had to so far, but it began to look as though they might have to, now—it would wreck their mother's mind, if she could understand. She probably could not understand it, any more than Cleonie could—but even if she could, she had so much more inherent stability, even than dad, that she might be able to take it, at that. Nor would she ever leak, even to dad—and he, bless his tremendous boots, was not the type to pry. Maybe, though, just to be on the safe side, it would be better to screen the stuff, and to edit it a little if necessary. The two girls synchronized their minds all imperceptibly with their mother's and Cleonie's, and "listened."

The time was in the unthinkably distant past; the location was unthinkably remote in space. A huge planet circled slowly about a cooling sun. Its atmosphere was not air; its liquid was not water. Both were noxious; composed in large part of compounds known to man only in his chemical laboratories.

Yet life was there; a race which was even then ancient. Not sexual, this race. Not androgynous, nor hermaphroditic, but absolutely sexless. Except for the many who died by physical or mental violence, its members lived endlessly: after hundreds of thousands of years each being, having reached his capacity to live and to learn, divided into two individuals; each of which, although possessing in toto the parent's memories, knowledges, skills, and powers, had also a renewed and increased capacity.

And, since life was, there had been competition. Competition for power. Knowledge was desirable only insofar as it contributed to power. Power for the individual—the group—the city. Wars raged—*what* wars!—and internecine strifes which lasted while planets came into being, grew old, and died. And finally, to the survivors, there came peace. Since they could not kill each other, they combined their powers and hurled them outward—together they would dominate and rule solar systems—regions—the Galaxy itself—the entire macrocosmic universe! More and more they used their minds, to bring across gulfs of space and to enslave other races, to labor under their direction. By nature and by choice they were bound to their own planet; few indeed were the planets upon which their race could possibly live. Thus, then, they lived and ruled by proxy, through echelon after echelon of underlings, an ever-increasing number of worlds.

Although they had long since learned that their asexuality was practically unique, that sexual life dominated the universe, this knowledge served only to stiffen their determination not only to rule the universe, but also to change its way of life to conform with their own. They were still seeking a better proxy race; the more nearly asexual a race, the better. The Kalonians, whose women had only one function in life—the production of men—approached that ideal.

Now these creatures had learned of the matriarchs of Lyrane. That they were physically females meant nothing; to the Eddorians one sex was just as good—or as bad—as any other. The Lyranians were strong; not tainted by the weaknesses which seemed to characterize all races believing in even near-equality of the sexes. Lyranian science had been trying for centuries to do away with the necessity for males; in a few more generations, with some help, that goal could be achieved and the perfect proxy race would have been developed.

This story was not obtained in any such straightforward fashion as it is presented here. It was dim, murky, confused. Cleonie never had understood it. Clarrissa understood it somewhat better: that unnamed and as yet unknown race was the highest of Boskone, and the place of the Kalonians in the Boskonian scheme was at long last clear.

"I am giving you this story," the Kalonian Lensman told Cleonie coldly, "not of my own free will but because I must. I hate you as much as you hate me. What I would like to do to you, you may imagine. Nevertheless, so that your race may have its chance, I am to take you on a trip and, if possible, make a Lensman out of you. Come with me." And, urged by her jealousy of Helen, her seething ambition, and probably, if the truth were to be known, by an Eddorian mind, Cleonie went.

There is no need to dwell at length upon the horrors, the atrocities, of that trip; of which the matter of Eddie the meteor-miner was only a very minor episode. It will suffice to say that Cleonie was very good Boskonian material; that she learned fast and passed all tests successfully.

"That's all," the Black Lensman informed her then, "and I'm glad to see the last of you. You'll get a message when to hop over to Nine and pick up your Lens. Flit—and I hope the first Gray Lensman you meet rams his Lens down your throat and turns you inside out."

"The same to you, brother, and soon," Cleonie sneered. "Or, better, when my race supplants yours as Proxies of Power, I shall give myself the pleasure of doing just that to you."

"Clarrissa! Clarrissa! Pay attention, please!" The Red Lensman came to herself with a start—Helen had been thinking at her, with increasing power, for seconds. The *Velan's* image filled half the plate.

In minutes, then, Clarrissa and her party were in Kinnison's private quarters in the *Dauntless*. There had been warm mental greetings; physical demonstrations would come later. Worsel broke in.

"Excuse it, Kim, but seconds count. Better we split, don't you think? You find out what the score around here is, from Clarrissa, and take steps, and I'll chase that damn Boskonian. He's flitting—fast."

"QX, Slim," and the *Velan* disappeared.

"You remember Helen, of course, Kim." Kinnison bent his head, flipping a quick grin at his wife, who had spoken aloud. The Lyranian, trying to unbend, half-offered her hand, but when he did not take it she withdrew it as enthusiastically as she had twenty years before. "And this is Cleonie, the . . . the wench I've been telling you about. You knew her before."

"Yeah. She hasn't changed much, either—still as unbarbered a mess as ever. If you've got what you want, Cris, we'd better . . ."

"Kimball Kinnison, I demand Cleonie's life!" came Helen's vibrant thought. She had snatched one of Clarrissa's DeLameters and was swinging it into line when she was caught and held as though in a vise.

"Sorry, Toots." The Gray Lensman's thought was more than a little grim. "Nice little girls don't play so rough. 'Scuse me, Cris, for dipping into your dish. Take over."

"Do you really mean that, Kim?"

"Yes. It's your meat—slice it as thick or as thin as you please."

"Even to letting her go?"

"Check. What else could you do? In a lifeboat—I'll even show the jade how to run it."

"Oh . . . Kim . . ."

"Quartermaster! Kinnison. Please check Number Twelve lifeboat and break it out. I am loaning it to Cleonie of Lyrane II."

22

KIT INVADES EDDORE; AND—

Kit had decided long since that it was his job to scout the planet Eddore. His alone. He had told several people that he was en route there, and in a sense he had been, but he was not hurrying. Once he started *that* job, he would have to see it through with absolutely undisturbed attention, and there had been altogether too many other things popping up. Now, however, his visualization showed a couple of weeks of free time, and that would be enough. He wasn't sure whether he was grown-up enough yet to do a man's job of work or not, and Mentor wouldn't tell him. This was the best way to find out. If so, QX. If not, he would back off, wait, and try again later.

The kids had wanted to go along, of course.

"Come on, Kit, don't be a pig!" Constance started what developed into the last violent argument of their long lives. "Let's gang up on it—think what a grand work-out that would be for the Unit!"

"Uh-uh, Con. Sorry, but it isn't in the cards, any more than it was the last time we discussed it," he began, reasonably enough.

"We didn't agree to it then," Kay cut in, stormily, "and I for one am not going to agree to it now. You don't have to do it today. In fact, later on would be better. Anyway, Kit, I'm telling you right now that if you go in, we all go, as individuals if not as the Unit."

"Act your age, Kay," he advised. "Get conscious. This is one of the two places in the universe that can't be worked from a distance, and by the time you could get here I'll have the job done. So what difference does it make whether you agree or not? I'm going in now and I'm going in alone. Pick *that* one out of your pearly teeth!"

That stopped Karen, cold—they all knew that even she would not endanger the enterprise by staging a useless demonstration against Eddore's defensive screens—but there were other arguments. Later, he was to come to see that his sisters had some right upon their side, but he could not see it then. None of their ideas would hold air, he declared, and his temper wore thinner and thinner.

"No, Cam—NO! You know as well as I do that we can't all be spared at once, either now or at any time in the near-enough future. Kay's full of pickles, and you all know it. Right now is the best time I'll ever have . . ."

"Seal it, Kat—you can't be that dumb! Taking the Unit in would blow things wide open. There isn't a chance that I can get in, even alone, without touching *something* off. I, alone, won't be giving too much away, but the Unit would be a flare-lit tip-off and all hell would be out for noon. Or are you actually nit-witted enough to think, all Arisia to the contrary, that we're ready for the grand show-down? . . .

"Hold it, all of you! Pipe down!" he snorted, finally. "Have I got to bash in your skulls to make you understand that I can't coordinate an attack against something without even the foggiest idea of what it is? Use your brains, kids—*please* use your brains!"

He finally won them over, even Karen; and while his speedster covered the last leg of the flight he completed his analysis.

He had all the information he could get—in fact, all that was available—and it was pitifully meager and confusingly contradictory in detail. He knew the Arisians, each of them, personally; and had studied, jointly and severally, the Arisian visualizations of the ultimate foe. He knew the Lyranian impression of the Plooran version of the story of Eddore . . . Ploor! Merely a name. A symbol which Mentor had always kept rigorously apart from any Boskonian actuality . . . Ploor *must* be the missing link between Kalonia and Eddore . . . and he knew practically everything about it except the two really important facts—whether or not it really was that link, and where, within eleven thousand million parsecs, it was in space!

He and his sisters had done their best. So had many librarians; who had found, not at all to his surprise, that no scrap of information or conjecture concerning Eddore or the Eddorians was to be found in any library, however comprehensive or exclusive.

Thus he had guesses, hypotheses, theories, and visualizations galore; but none of them agreed and not one of them was convincing. He had no real facts whatever. Mentor had informed him, equably enough, that such a state of affairs was inevitable because of the known power of the Eddorian mind. That state, however, did not make Kit Kinnison any too happy as he approached dread and dreaded Eddore. He was in altogether too much of a dither as to what, actually, to expect.

As he neared the boundary of the star-cluster within which Eddore lay, he cut his velocity to a crawl. An outer screen, he knew, surrounded the whole cluster. How many intermediate protective layers existed, where they were, or what they were like, nobody knew. That information was only a small part of what he had to have.

His far-flung detector web, at practically zero power, touched the barrier without giving alarm and stopped. His speedster stopped. Everything stopped.

Christopher Kinnison, the matrix and the key element of the Unit, had tools and equipment about which even Mentor of Arisia knew nothing in detail; about which, it was hoped and believed, the Eddorians were completely in ignorance. He reached deep into the storehouse-toolbox of his mind, arranged his selections in order, and went to work.

He built up his detector web, one infinitesimal increment at a time, until he could just perceive the structure of the barrier. He made no attempt to analyze it, knowing that any fabric or structure solid enough to perform such an operation would certainly touch off an alarm. Analysis could come later, after he had found out whether the generator of this outer screen was a machine or a living brain.

He felt his way along the barrier; slowly—carefully. He completely outlined one section, studying the fashion in which the joints were made and how it must be supported and operated. With the utmost nicety of which he was capable he synchronized a probe with the almost impossibly complex structure of the thing and slid it along a feeder-beam into the generator station. A mechanism—they didn't waste live Eddorians, then, any more than the Arisians did, on outer defenses. QX.

A precisely-tuned blanket surrounded his speedster—a blanket which merged imperceptibly into, and in effect became an integral part of, the barrier itself. The blanket thinned over half of the speedster. The speedster crept forward. The barrier—unchanged, unaffected—was *behind* the speedster. Man and vessel were through!

Kit breathed deeply in relief and rested. This didn't prove much, of course. Nadreck had done practically the same thing in getting Kandron—except that the Palainian would never be able to analyze or to synthesize such screens as these. The real test would come later; but this had been mighty good practice.

The real test came with the fifth, the innermost screen. The others, while of ever-increasing sensitivity, complexity, and power, were all generated mechanically, and hence posed problems differing only in degree, and not in kind, from that of the first. The fifth problem, however, involving a living and highly capable brain, differed in both degree and kind from the others. The Eddorian would be sensitive to form and to shape, as well as to interference. Bulges were out, unless he could do something about the Eddorian—and the speedster couldn't go through a screen without making a bulge.

Furthermore, this zone had visual and electromagnetic detectors, so spaced as not to let a microbe through. There were fortresses, maulers, battleships, and their attendant lesser craft. There were projectors, and mines, and automatic torpedoes with super-atomic warheads, and other such things. Were these things completely dependent upon the Eddorian guardian, or not?

They were not. The officers—Kalonians for the most part—would go into action at the guardian's signal, of course; but they could at need act without instructions. A nice set-up—a mighty hard nut to crack! He would have to use zones of compulsion. Nothing else would do.

Picking out the biggest fortress in the neighborhood, with its correspondingly large field of coverage, he insinuated his mind into that of one observing officer after another. When he left, a few minutes later, he knew that none of those officers would initiate any action in response to the alarms which he would so soon set off. They were alive, fully conscious, alert; and would have resented bitterly any suggestion that they were not completely normal in every respect. Nevertheless, whatever colors the lights flashed, whatever pictures the plates revealed, whatever noises blared from the speakers, in their consciousnesses would be only blankness and silence. Nor would recorder tapes reveal later what had occurred. An instrument cannot register fluctuations when its movable member is controlled by a couple of steady fingers.

Then the Eddorian. To take over his whole mind was, Kit knew, beyond his present power. A partial zone, though, could be set up—and young Kinnison's mind had been developed specifically to perform the theretofore impossible. Thus the guardian, without suspecting it, suffered an attack of partial blindness which lasted for the fraction of a second necessary for the speedster to flash through the screen. And there was no recorder to worry about. Eddorians, never sleeping and never relaxing their vigilance, had no doubt whatever of their own capabilities and needed no checks upon their own performances.

Christopher Kinnison, Child of the Lens, was inside Eddore's innermost defensive sphere. For countless cycles of time the Arisians had been working toward and looking forward to the chain of events of which this was the first link. Nor would he have much time here: he would have known that even if Mentor had not so stressed the point. As long as he did nothing he was safe; but as soon as he started sniffing around he would be open to detection and some Eddorian would climb his frame in mighty short order. Then blast and lock on—he might get something, or a lot, or nothing at all. Then—win, lose, or draw—he had to get away. Strictly under his own power, against an unknown number of the most powerful and the most ruthless entities ever to live. The Arisian couldn't get in here to help him, and neither could the kids. Nobody could. It was strictly and solely up to him.

For more than a moment his spirit failed. The odds against him were far too long. The load was too heavy; he didn't have half enough jets to swing it. Just how did a guy as smart as Mentor figure it that he, a dumb, green kid, stood a Zabriskan fontema's chance against all Eddore?

He was scared; scared to the core of his being; scared as he never had been before and never would be again. His mouth felt dry, his tongue cottony. His fingers shook, even as he doubled them into fists to steady them. To the very end of his long life he remembered the fabric and the texture of that fear; remembered how it made him decide to turn back, before it was too late to retrace his way as unobserved as he had come.

Well, why not? Who would care, and what matter? The Arisians? Nuts! It was all their fault, sending him in half-ready. His parents? They wouldn't know what the score was, and wouldn't care. They'd be on his side, no matter what happened. The kids? . . . The *kids!* . . . Oh-oh—THE KIDS!

They'd tried to talk him out of coming in alone. They'd fought like wildcats to make him take them along. He'd smacked 'em down. Now, if he sneaked back with his tail between his legs, how'd they take it? What'd they do? What would they *think?* Then, later, after he had loused everything up and let the Arisians and the Patrol and all Civilization get knocked out—then what? The kids would know exactly how and why it had happened. He couldn't defend himself, even if he tried, and he wouldn't try. Did he have any idea how much sheer, vitriolic, corrosive contempt those four red-headed sisters of his could generate? Or, even if they didn't—or as a follow-up—their condescending, sisterly pity would be a thousand million times worse. And what would he think of himself? No soap. It was out. Definitely. The Eddorians could kill him only once. QX.

He drove straight downward, noting as he did so that his senses were clear, his hands steady, his tongue normally moist. He was still scared, but he was no longer paralyzed.

Low enough, he let his every perceptive sense roam abroad—and he came instantly too busy to worry about anything. There was an immense amount of new stuff here—if he could only be granted time enough to get it all!

He wasn't. In a second or so, it seemed, his interference was detected and an Eddorian came in to investigate. Kit threw everything he had, and in the brief moment before the completely surprised denizen died, the young Klovian learned more of the real truth of Eddore and of the whole Boskonian Empire than all the Arisians had ever found out. In that one flash of ultimately intimate fusion, he *knew* Eddorian history, practically in toto. He knew the enemies' culture; he knew how they behaved, and why. He knew their ideals and their ideologies. He knew a great deal about their organization; their systems of offense and of defense. He knew their strengths and, more important, their weaknesses. He knew exactly how, if Civilization were to triumph at all, its victory must be achieved.

This seems—or rather, it is—incredible. It is, however, simple truth. Under such stresses as those, an Eddorian mind can yield, and the mind of such a one as Christopher Kinnison can absorb, an incredible amount of knowledge in an incredibly brief interval of time.

Kit, already seated at his controls, cut in his every course of thought-screen. They would help a little in what was coming, but not much—no mechanical screen then known to Civilization could block third-level thought. He kicked in full drive toward the one small area in which he and his speedster would not encounter either beams or bombs—the fortress whose observers would not perceive that anything was amiss. He did not fear physical pursuit, since his speedster was the fastest thing in space.

For a second or so it was not so bad. Another Eddorian came in, suspicious and on guard. Kit blasted him down—learning still more in the process—but he could not prevent him from radiating a frantic and highly revealing call for help. And although the Eddorians could scarcely realize that such an astonishing thing as physical invasion had actually happened, that fact neither slowed them down nor made their anger less violent.

When Kit flashed past his friendly fortress he was taking about all he could handle, and more and more Eddorians were piling on. At the fourth screen it was worse; at the third he reached what he was sure was his absolute ceiling. Nevertheless, from some hitherto unsuspected profundity of his being, he managed to draw enough reserve force to endure that hellish punishment for a little while longer.

Hang on, Kit, hang on! Only two more screens to go. Maybe only one. Maybe less. Living Eddorian brains, and not mechanical generators, are now handling all the screens, of course; but if the Arisians' visualization is worth a tinker's damn, they must have that first screen knocked down by this time and must be working on the second. Hang on, Kit, and keep on slugging!

And grimly; doggedly; toward the end sheerly desperately: Christopher Kinnison, eldest Child of the Lens, hung on and slugged.

23

—ESCAPES WITH HIS LIFE

If the historian has succeeded in his attempt to describe the characters and abilities concerned, it is not necessary to enlarge upon what Kit went through in escaping Eddore. If he has not succeeded, enlargement would be useless. Therefore it is enough to say that the young Lensman, by dint of calling up and putting out everything he had, hung on long enough and slugged his way through.

Arisia had acted precisely on time. The Eddorian guardians had scarcely taken over the first screen when it was overwhelmed by a tremendous wave of Arisian thought. It is to be remembered, however, that this was not the first time that the massed might of Arisia had been thrown against Eddore's defenses, and the Eddorians had learned much, during the intervening years, from their exhaustive analyses of the offensive and defensive techniques of the Arisians. Thus the Arisian drive was practically stopped at the second zone of defense as Kit approached it. The screen was wavering, shifting; yielding stubbornly wherever it must and springing back into place whenever it could.

Under a tremendous concentration of Arisian force the screen weakened in a limited area directly ahead of the hurtling speedster. A few beams lashed out aimlessly, uselessly—if the Eddorians could not hold their main screens proof against the power of the Arisian attack, how could they protect such minor things as gunners' minds? The little ship flashed through the weakened barrier and into the center of a sphere of impenetrable, impermeable Arisian thought.

At the shock of the sudden ending of his terrific battle—the instantaneous transition from supreme to zero effort—Kit fainted in his control chair. He lay slumped, inert, in a stupor which changed gradually into a deep and natural sleep. And as the sleeping man in his inertialess speedster traversed space at full touring blast, that peculiar sphere of force still enveloped and still protected him.

Kit finally began to come to. His first foggy thought was that he was hungry—then, wide awake and remembering, he grabbed his levers.

"Rest quietly, youth, and eat your fill," a grave, resonant pseudo-voice assured him. "Everything is exactly as it should be."

"Hi, Ment . . . well, well, if it isn't my old chum Eukonidor! Hi, young fellow! What's the good word? And what's the big idea of letting—or making—me sleep for a week when there's work to do?"

"Your part of the work, at least for the immediate present, is done; and, let me say, very well done."

"Thanks . . . but . . ." Kit broke off, flushing darkly.

"Do not reproach yourself, youth, nor us. Consider, please, and recite, the manufacture of a fine tool of ultimate quality."

"The correct alloy. Hot working—perhaps cold, too. Forging—heating—quenching—drawing . . ."

"Enough, youth. Think you that the steel, if sentient, would enjoy those treatments? While you did not enjoy them, you are able to appreciate their necessity. You are now a finished tool, forged and tempered."

"Oh . . . you may have something there, at that. But as to ultimate quality, don't make me laugh." There was no nuance of merriment in Kit's thought. "You can't square that with cowardice."

"Nor is there need. The term ultimate was used advisedly, and still stands. It does not mean or imply, however, a state of perfection, since that condition is unattainable. I am not advising you to try to forget; nor am I attempting to force forgetfulness upon you, since your mind cannot now be coerced by any force at my command. Be assured that nothing that occurred should irk you; for the simple truth is, that although stressed as no other mind has ever before been stressed, you did not yield. Instead, you secured and retained information which we of Arisia have never been able to obtain; information which will in fact be the means of preserving your Civilization."

"I can't believe . . . that is, it doesn't seem . . ." Kit, knowing that he was thinking muddily and foolishly, paused and pulled himself together. Overwhelming, almost paralyzing as that information was, it must be true. It *was* true!

"Yes, youth, it is the truth. While we of Arisia have at various times made ambiguous statements, to lead certain Lensmen and others to arrive at erroneous conclusions, you know that we do not lie."

"Yes, I know that." Kit plumbed the Arisian's mind. "It sort of knocks me out of my orbit—that's an awfully big bite to swallow at one gulp, you know."

"It is. That is one reason I am here, to convince you of the truth, which you would not otherwise believe fully. Also to see to it that your rest, without which you might have taken hurt, was not disturbed; as well as to make sure that you were not permanently damaged by the Eddorians."

"I wasn't . . . at least, I don't think so . . . was I?"

"You were not."

"Good. I was wondering . . . Mentor will be tied up for a while, of course, so I'll ask you. . . . They must have got a sort of pattern of me, in spite of all I could do, and they'll be camping on my trail from now on. So I suppose I'll have to keep a solid block up all the time?"

"They will not, Christopher, and you need not. Guided by those whom you know as Mentor, I myself am to see to that. But time presses—I must rejoin my fellows."

"One more question first. You've been trying to sell me a bill of goods I'd certainly like to buy. But damn it, Eukonidor, the kids will know that I showed a streak of yellow a meter wide. What will *they think?*"

"Is *that* all?" Eukonidor's thought was almost a laugh. "They will make that eminently plain in a moment."

The Arisian's presence vanished, as did his sphere of force, and four clamoring thoughts came jamming in.

"Oh, Kit, we're *so* glad!" "We *tried* to help, but they wouldn't let us!" "They smacked us down!" *"Honestly,* Kit!" *"Oh,* if we'd *only* been in there, too!"

"Hold it, everybody! Jet back!" This was Con, Kit knew, but an entirely new Con. "Scan him, Cam, as you never scanned anything before. If they burned out even one cell of his mind I'm going to hunt Mentor up right now and kick his cursed teeth out one by one!"

"And listen, Kit!" This was an equally strange Kathryn; blazing with fury and yet suffusing his mind with a more than sisterly tenderness, a surpassing richness. "If we'd had the faintest idea of what they were doing to you, all the Arisians and all the Eddorians and all the devils in all the hells of the macrocosmic Universe couldn't have kept us away. You *must* believe that, Kit—or can you, quite?"

"Of course, sis—you don't have to prove an axiom. Seal it, all of you. You're swell people—absolute tops. But I . . . you . . . that is . . ." He broke off and marshaled his thoughts.

He knew that they knew, in every minute particular, everything that had occurred. Yet to a girl they thought he was wonderful; their common thought was that they should have been in there, too: taking what he took; giving what he gave!

"What I don't get is that you're trying to blame yourselves for what happened to me, when you were on the dead center of the beam all the time. You *couldn't* have been in there, kids; it would have blown the whole works higher than up. You knew that then, and you know it even better now. You also know that I flew the yellow flag. Didn't that even *register?*"

"Oh, *that!*" Practically identical thoughts of complete dismissal came in unison, and Karen followed through:

"Since you knew exactly what to expect, we marvel that you ever managed to go in at all—no one else could have, possibly. Or, once in, and seeing what was really there, that you didn't flit right out again. Believe me, brother of mine, you qualify!"

Kit choked. This was too much; but it made him feel good all over. These kids . . . the universe's best . . .

As he thought, a partial block came unconsciously into being. For not one of those gorgeous, those utterly splendid creatures suspected, even now, that which he so surely knew—that each one of them was very shortly to be wrought and tempered as he himself had been. And, worse, he would have to stand aside and watch them, one by one, walk into it. Was there anything he could do to ward off, or even to soften, what was coming to them? There was not. With his present power, he could step in, of course—at what awful cost to Civilization only he, Christopher Kinnison, of all Civilization, really knew. No. That was out. Definitely. He could come in afterward to ease their hurts, as each had come to him, but that was all . . . and there was a difference. They hadn't known about it in advance. It was tough . . .

Could he do *anything?*

He could not.

And on clammy, noisome Eddore, the Arisian attackers having been beaten off and normality restored, a meeting of the Highest Command was held. No two of those entities were alike in form; some were changing from one horrible shape into another; all were starkly, indescribably monstrous. All were concentrating upon the problem which had been so suddenly thrust upon them; each of them thought at and with each of the others. To do justice to the complexity or the cogency of that maze of intertwined thoughts is impossible; the best that can be done is to pick out a high point here and there.

"This explains the Star A Star whom the Ploorans and the Kalonians so fear."

"And the failure of our operator on Thrale, and its fall."

"Also our recent quite serious reverses."

"Those stupid—those utterly brainless underlings!"

"We should have been called in at the start!"

"Could you analyze, or even perceive, its pattern save in small part?"

"No."

"Nor could I; an astounding and highly revealing circumstance."

"An Arisian; or, rather, an Arisian development, certainly. No other entity of Civilization could possibly do what was done here. Nor could any Arisian as we know them."

"They have developed something very recently which we had not visualized . . ."

"Kinnison's son? Bah! Think they to deceive us by the old device of energizing a form of ordinary flesh?"

"Kinnison—his son—Nadreck—Worsel—Tregonsee—what matters it?"

"Or, as we now know, the completely imaginary Star A Star."

"We must revise our thinking," an authoritatively composite mind decided. "We must revise our theory and our plan. It may be possible that this new development will necessitate immediate, instead of later, action. If we had had a competent race of proxies, none of this would have happened, as we would have been kept informed. To correct a situation which may become grave, as well as to acquire fullest and latest information, we must attend the conference which is now being held on Ploor."

They did so. With no perceptible lapse of time or mode of transit, the Eddorian mind was in an assembly room upon that now flooded world. Resembling Nevians as much as any other race with which man is familiar, the now amphibious Ploorans lolled upon padded benches and argued heatedly. They were discussing, upon a lower level, much of the same material which the Eddorians had been considering so shortly before.

Star A Star. Kinnison had been captured easily enough, but had, almost immediately, escaped from an escape-proof trap. Another trap was set, but would it take him? Would it hold him if it did? Kinnison was—*must* be—Star A Star. No, he could not be, there had been too many unrelated and simultaneous occurrences. Kinnison, Nadreck, Clarrissa, Worsel, Tregonsee, even Kinnison's young son, had all shown intermittent flashes of inexplicable power. Kinnison most of all. It was a fact worthy of note that the beginning of the long series of Boskonian set-backs coincided with Kinnison's appearance among the Lensmen.

The situation was bad. Not irreparable, by any means, but grave. The fault lay with the Eich, and perhaps with Kandron of Onlo. Such stupidity! Such incompetence! Those lower-echelon operators should have had brains enough to have reported the matter to Ploor before the situation got completely out of hand. But they didn't; hence this mess. None of them, however, expressed a thought that the present situation was already one with which they themselves could not cope; nor suggested that it be referred to Eddore before it should become too hot for even the Masters to handle.

"Fools! Imbeciles! We, the Masters, although through no foresight or design of yours, are already here. Know now that you have been and still are yourselves guilty of the same conduct which you are so violently condemning in others." Neither Eddorians nor Ploorans realized that that deficiency was inherent in the Boskonian Scheme of Things, or that it stemmed from the organization's very top. "Sheer stupidity! Gross overconfidence! Those are the reasons for our recent reverses!"

"But, Masters," a Plooran argued, "now that we have taken over, we are winning steadily. Civilization is rapidly going to pieces. In a few more years we will have smashed it flat."

"That is precisely what they wish you to think. They have been and are playing for time. Your bungling and mismanagement have already given them sufficient time to develop an object or an entity able to penetrate our screens; so that Eddore suffered the disgrace of an actual physical invasion. It was brief, to be sure, and unsuccessful, but it was an invasion, none the less—the first in our long history."

"But, Masters . . ."

"Silence! We are not here to indulge in recriminations, but to determine facts. Since you do not know Eddore's location in space, it is a certainty that you did not, either wittingly or otherwise, furnish that information. That in turn makes it clear who, basically, the invader was . . ."

"Star A Star?" A wave of questions swept the group.

"One name serves as well as another for what is almost certainly an Arisian entity or device. It is enough for you to know that it is something with which your massed minds would be completely unable to deal. To the best of your knowledge, have you been invaded, either physically or mentally?"

"We have not, Masters; and it is unbelievable that . . ."

"Is it so?" The Masters sneered. "Neither our screens nor our Eddorian guardsmen gave any alarm. We learned of the Arisian's presence only when he attempted to probe our very minds, at Eddore's very surface. Are your screens and minds, then, so much better than ours?"

"We erred, Masters. We abase ourselves. What do you wish us to do?"

"That is better. You will be informed, as soon as certain details have been worked out. Although nothing is established by the fact that you know of no occurrences here on Ploor, the probability is that you are still unknown and unsuspected. Nevertheless, one of us is now taking over control of the trap which you set for Kinnison, in the belief that he is Star A Star."

"Belief, Masters? It is certain that he is Star A Star!"

"In essence, yes. In exactness, no. Kinnison is, in all probability, merely a puppet through whom an Arisian works at times. If *you* take Kinnison in that trap, however, the entity you call Star A Star will assuredly kill you all."

"But, Masters . . ."

"Again, fools, silence!" The thought dripped vitriol. "Remember how easily Kinnison escaped from you? It was the supremely clever move of not following through and destroying you then that obscured the truth. You are completely powerless against the one you call Star A Star. Against any lesser force, however—and the probability is great that only such forces, if any, will be sent against you—you should be able to win. Are you ready?"

"We are ready, Masters." At last the Ploorans were upon familiar ground. "Since ordinary weapons will be useless against us, they will not attempt to use them; especially since they have developed three extraordinary and supposedly irresistible weapons of attack. First; projectiles composed of negative matter, particularly those of planetary anti-mass. Second; loose planets, driven inertialess, but inerted at the point at which their intrinsic velocities render collision unavoidable. Third, and worst; the sunbeam. These gave us some trouble, particularly the last, but the problems were solved and if any one of the three, or all of them, are used against us, disaster for the Galactic Patrol is assured.

"Nor did we stop there. Our psychologists, working with our engineers, after having analyzed exhaustively the capabilities of the so-called

Second-Stage Lensmen, developed counter-measures against every super-weapon which they will be able to develop during the next century."

"Such as?" The Masters were unimpressed.

"The most probable one is an extension of the sunbeam principle, to operate from a distant sun; or, preferably, a nova. We are now installing fields and grids by the use of which we, not the Patrol, will direct that beam."

"Interesting—if true. Spread in our minds the details of all that you have foreseen and the fashions in which you have safeguarded yourselves."

It was a long operation, even at the speed of thought. At the end the Eddorians were unconvinced, skeptical, and pessimistic.

"We can visualize several other things which the forces of Civilization may be able to develop well within the century," the Master mind said, coldly. "We will assemble data concerning a few of them for your study. In the meantime, hold yourselves in readiness to act, as we shall issue final orders very shortly."

"Yes, Masters," and the Eddorians went back to their home planet as effortlessly as they had left it. There they concluded their conference.

". . . It is clear that Kinnison will enter that trap. He cannot do otherwise. Kinnison's protector, whoever or whatever he or it may be, may or may not enter it with him. It may or may not be taken with him. Whether or not the new Arisian figment is taken, Kimball Kinnison must die. He is the very keystone of the Galactic Patrol. At his death, as we will advertise it to have come about, the Patrol will fall apart. The Arisians, themselves unknown to the rank and file, will be forced to try to rebuild it around another puppet; but neither his son nor any other man will ever be able to take Kinnison's place in the esteem of the hero-worshipping, undisciplined mob which is Civilization. Hence the importance of your project. You, personally, will supervise the operation of the trap. You, personally, will kill him."

"With one exception, I agree with everything said. I am not at all certain that death is the answer. One way or another, however, I shall deal effectively with Kinnison."

"Deal with? We said kill!"

"I heard you. I still say that mere death may not be adequate. I shall consider the matter at length, and shall submit in due course my conclusions and recommendations, for your consideration and approval."

Although none of the Eddorians knew it, their pessimism in regard to the ability of the Ploorans to defend their planet against the assaults of Second-Stage Lensmen was even then being justified. Kimball Kinnison, after pacing the floor for hours, called his son.

"Kit, I've been working on a thing for months, and I don't know whether I've got a workable solution at last, or not. It may depend entirely on you. Before I go into it, though, when we find Boskonia's top planet we've got to blow it out of the ether, and nothing we've used before will work. Check?"

"Check, on both." Kit thought soberly for minutes. "Also, it should be faster than anything we have."

"My thought exactly. I've got something, I think, but nobody except old Cardynge and Mentor of Arisia . . ."

"Hold it, dad, while I do a bit of spying and put out some coverage . . . QX, go ahead."

"Nobody except those two knew anything about the mathematics involved. Even Sir Austin knew only enough to be able to understand Mentor's directions—he didn't do any of the deep stuff himself. Nobody in the present Conference of Scientists could even begin to handle it. It's that foreign space, you know, that we called the Nth Space, where that hyper-spatial tube dumped us that time. You've been doing a lot of work with some of the Arisians on that sort of stuff—suppose you could get them to help you compute a tube to take a ship there and back?"

"Hm . . . m. Let me think a second. Yes, I can. When do you need it?"

"Today—or even yesterday."

"Too fast. It'll take a couple of days, but it'll be ready for you long before you can get your ship ready and get your gang and the stuff for your gadget aboard her."

"That won't take so long, son. Same ship we rode before. She's still in commission, you know—*Space Laboratory Twelve,* her name is now. Special generators, tools, instruments, everything. We'll be ready in two days."

They were, and Kit smiled as he greeted Lieutenant-Admiral LaVerne Thorndyke, Principal Technician, and the other surviving members of his father's original crew.

"*What* a tonnage of brass!" Kit said to Kim, later. "Heaviest load I ever saw on one ship. One sure thing, though, they earned it. You must have been able to pick *men,* too, in those days."

"What d'ya mean, 'those days,' you disrespectful young ape? I can still pick *men,* son!" Kim grinned back at Kit, but sobered quickly. "There's more to this than meets the eye. They went through the strain once, and know what it means. They can take it, and just about all of them will come back. With a crew of kids, twenty percent would be a high estimate."

As soon as the vessel was outside the system, Kit got another surprise. Even though those men were studded with brass and were, by a boy's standard, *old,* they were not passengers. In their old *Dauntless* and well away from port, they gleefully threw off their full-dress regalia. Each donned the uniform of his status of twenty-odd years back and went to work. The members of the regular crew, young as all regular space crewmen are, did not know at first whether they liked the idea of working watch-and-watch with so much braid or not; but they soon found out that they did. Those men were men.

It is an iron-clad rule of space, however, that operating pilots must be young. Master Pilot Henry Henderson cursed that ruling sulphurously, even while he watched with a proud, if somewhat jaundiced eye, the smooth performance of Henry Junior at his own old board.

They approached their destination—cut the jets—felt for the vortex—found it—cut in the special generators. Then, as the fields of the ship reacted against those of the tube, every man aboard felt a malaise to which no being has ever become accustomed. Most men become immune rather quickly to seasickness, to airsickness, and even to spacesickness. Inter-dimensional acceleration, however, is something else. It is different—just how different cannot be explained to anyone who has never experienced it.

The almost unbearable acceleration ceased. They were in the tube. Every plate showed blank; everywhere there was the same drab and featureless gray. There was neither light nor darkness; there was simply and indescribably—nothing whatever, not even empty space.

Kit threw a switch. There was wrenching, twisting, shock, followed by a deceleration exactly as sickening as the acceleration had been. It ceased. They were in that enigmatic Nth space which each of the older men remembered so well; in which so many of their "natural laws" did not hold. Time still raced, stopped, or ran backward, seemingly at whim; inert bodies had intrinsic velocities far above that of light—and so on. Each of those men, about to be marooned of his own choice in this utterly hostile environment, drew a deep breath and squared his shoulders as he prepared to disembark.

"That's computation, Kit!" Kinnison applauded, after one glance into a plate. "That's the same planet we worked on before, right there. All our machines and stuff, untouched. If you'd figured it any closer it'd have been a collision course. Are you dead sure, Kit, that everything's QX?"

"Dead sure, Dad."

"QX. Well, fellows, I'd like to stay here with you, and so would Kit, but we've got chores to do. I don't have to tell you to be careful, but I'm going to, anyway. BE CAREFUL! And as soon as you get done, come back home just as fast as Klono will let you. Clear ether, fellows!"

"Clear ether, Kim!"

Lensman father and Lensman son boarded their speedster and left. They traversed the tube and emerged into normal space. All without a word.

"Kit," the older man ground out, finally. "This gives me the colly wobblies, no less. Suppose some of them—or all of them—get killed out there? Is it worth it? I know it's my own idea, but will we need it badly enough to take such a chance?"

"We will, dad. Mentor says so."

And that was that.

24

THE CONFERENCE SOLVES
A PROBLEM

Kit wanted to get back to normal space as soon as possible, in order to help his sisters pull themselves together, just as they had helped him. Think as he would, he had not been able to find any flaw in any one of them; but he knew that Mentor would; and he stood aside and watched while Mentor did.

Kinnison had to get back because he had a lot of business, all of it pressing. Finally, however, he took time to call a conference of all the Second Stage Lensmen and his children; a conference which, bizarrely enough, was to be held in person and not via Lens.

"Not strictly necessary, of course," the Gray Lensman half-apologized to his son as their speedsters approached the *Dauntless*. "I still think it was a good idea, though, especially since we were all so close to Lyrane anyway."

"So do I. It's been mighty long since we were all together."

They boarded. Clarrissa met Kinnison head-on just inside the portal. The girls hung back a bit, with a trace, almost, of diffidence; even while Kit was attempting the physically impossible feat of embracing all four of them at once.

By common consent the Five used only their eyes. Nothing showed.

Nevertheless, the girls blushed vividly and Kit's face twisted into a dry, wry grin.

"It was good for what ailed us, though, at that—I guess." Kit did not seem at all positive. "Mentor, the lug, told me no less than six times that I had arrived—or at least made statements which I interpreted as meaning that. And Eukonidor told me I was a 'finished tool,' whatever that means. Personally, I think they were sitting back and wondering how long it was going to take us to realize that we never could be half as good as we used to think we were. Suppose?"

"Something like that, probably. We've shivered more than once, wondering whether we're finished products *yet* or not."

"We've learned—I hope." Karen, hard as she was, did shiver, physically. "If we aren't, it'll be . . . *p-s-s-t*—dad's starting the meeting!"

". . . so settle down, all of you, and we'll get going."

What a group! Tregonsee of Rigel IV—stolid, solid, blocky, immobile; looking as little as possible like one of the profoundest thinkers Civilization had ever produced—did not move. Worsel, the ultra-sensitive yet utterly implacable Velantian, curled out three or four eyes and looked on languidly while Constance kicked a few coils of his tail into a comfortable chaise lounge, reclined unconcernedly in the seat thus made, and lighted an Alsakanite cigarette. Clarrissa Kinnison, radiant in her Grays and looking scarcely older than her daughters, sat beside Kathryn, each with an arm around the other. Karen and Camilla, neither of whom could ordinarily be described by the adjective "cuddlesome," were on a davenport with Kit, snuggling as close to him as they could get. And in the farthest corner the heavily-armored, heavily-insulated space-suit which contained Nadreck of Palain VII chilled the atmosphere for yards around.

"QX?" Kinnison began. "We'll take Nadreck first, since he isn't any too happy here, and let him flit—he'll keep in touch from outside after he leaves. Report, please, Nadreck."

"I have explored Lyrane IX *thoroughly*." Nadreck made the statement and paused. When he used such a thought at all, it meant much. When he emphasized it, which no one there had ever before known him to do, it meant that he had examined the planet practically atom by atom. "There was no life of the level of intelligence in which we are interested to be found on, beneath, or above its surface. I could find no evidence that such life has ever been there, either as permanent dwellers or as occasional visitors."

"When Nadreck settles anything as definitely as that, it stays settled," Kinnison remarked as soon as the Palainian had left. "I'll report next. You all know what I did about Kalonia, and so on. The only significant fact that I've been able to find—the only lead to the Boskonian higher-ups—is that Black Lensman Melasnikov got his Lens on Lyrane IX. There were no traces of mental surgery. I can see two, and only two, alternatives. Either there was mental surgery which I could not detect, or there were visitors to Lyrane IX who left no traces of their visits. More reports may enable us to decide. Worsel?"

The other Second-Stage Lensmen reported in turn. Each had uncovered leads to Lyrane IX, but Worsel and Tregonsee, who had also studied that planet with care, agreed with Nadreck that there was nothing to be found there.

"Kit?" Kinnison asked then. "How about you and the girls?"

"We believe that Lyrane IX was visited by beings having sufficient power of mind to leave no traces whatever as to who they were or where they came from. We also believe that there was no surgery, but an infinitely finer kind of work—an indetectable subconscious compulsion— done on the minds of the Black Lensmen and others who came into physical contact with the Boskonians. These opinions are based upon experiences which we five have had and upon deductions we have made. If we are right, Lyrane is actually, as well as apparently, a dead end and should be abandoned. Furthermore, we believe that the Black Lensmen have not been and cannot become important."

The coordinator was surprised, but after Kit and his sisters had detailed their findings and their deductions, he turned to the Rigellian.

"What next, then, Tregonsee?"

"After Lyrane IX, it seems to me that the two most promising subjects are those entities who think upon such a high band, and the phenomenon which has been called 'The Hell-Hole in Space.' Of the two, I preferred the first until Camilla's researches showed that the available data could not be reconciled with the postulate that the life-forms of her reconstruction were identical with those reported to you as coordinator. This data, however, was scanty and casual. While we are here, therefore, I suggest that we review this matter much more carefully, in the hope that additional information will enable us to come to a definite conclusion, one way or the other. Since it was her research, Camilla will lead."

"First, a question," Camilla began. "Imagine a sun so variable that it periodically covers practically the entire possible range. It has a planet whose atmosphere, liquid, and distance are such that its surface temperature varies from approximately two hundred degrees Centigrade in mid-summer to about five degrees absolute in midwinter. In the spring its surface is almost completely submerged. There are terrible winds and storms in the spring, summer, and fall; but the fall storms are the worst.

Has anyone here ever heard of such a planet having an intelligent life-form able to maintain a continuing existence through such varied environments by radical changes in its physical body?" A silence ensued, which Nadreck finally broke.

"I know of two such planets. Near Palain there is an extremely variable sun, two of whose planets support life. All of the higher life-forms, the highest of which are quite intelligent, undergo regular and radical changes, not only of form, but of organization."

"Thanks, Nadreck. That will perhaps make my story believable. From the thoughts of one of the entities in question, I reconstructed such a solar system. More, that entity himself belonged to just such a race. It was *such* a nice reconstruction," Camilla went on, plaintively, "and it fitted all those other life-forms so beautifully, especially Kat's 'four-cycle periods.' And to prove it, Kat—put up your block, now—you never told anybody the classification of your pet to more than seven places, did you, or even thought about it?"

"No." Kathryn's mind, since the moment of warning, had been unreadable.

"Take the seven, RTSL and so on. The next three were S-T-R. Check?"

"Check."

"But that makes it *solid,* sis!" Kit exclaimed.

"That's what I thought, for a minute—that we had Boskone at last. However, when Tregonsee and I first felt 'X,' long before you met yours, Kat, his classification was TUUV. That would fit in well enough as a spring form, with Kat's as the summer form. What ruins it, though, is that when he killed himself, just a little while ago and long after a summer form could possibly exist—to say nothing of a spring form—his classification was *still* TUUV. To ten places it was TUUVWYXXWT."

"Well, go on," Kinnison suggested. "What do you make of it?"

"The obvious explanation is that one or all of those entities were planted or primed—not specifically for us, probably, since we are relatively unknown, but for any competent observer. If so, they don't mean a thing." Camilla was not now overestimating her own powers or underestimating those of Boskonia. "There are a few other things, less obvious, leading to the same conclusion. Tregonsee is not ready to believe any of them, however, and neither am I. Assuming that our data was not biased, we must also account for the fact that the locations in space were . . ."

"Just a minute, Cam, before you leave the classifications," Constance interrupted. "I'm guarded—what was my friend's, to ten places?"

"VWZYTXSYZY," Camilla replied, unhesitatingly.

"Right; and I don't believe it was planted, either, so there . . ."

"Let me in a second!" Kit demanded. "I didn't know you were on that band at all. I got that RTSL thing even before I graduated . . ."

"Huh? What RTSL?" Cam broke in, sharply.

"My fault," Kinnison put in then. "Skipped my mind entirely, when she asked me for the dope. None of us thought any of this stuff important until just now, you know. Tell her, Kit."

Kit repeated his story, concluding:

"Beyond four places was pretty dim, but Q P arms and legs— Dhilian, eh?—would fit, and so would an R-type hide. Both Kat's and mine, then, could very well have been summer forms, one of their years apart. The thing I felt was on its own planet, and it *died* there, and credits to millos the thought I got wasn't primed. And the location . . ."

"Brake down, Kit," Camilla instructed. "Let's settle this thing of timing first. I've got a theory, but I want some ideas from the rest of you."

"Maybe something like this?" Clarrissa asked, after a few minutes of silence. "In many forms which metamorphose completely the change depends on temperature. No change takes place as long as the temperature stays constant. Your TUUV could have been flitting around in a space-ship at constant temperature. Could this apply here, Cam, do you think?"

"Could it?" Kinnison exclaimed. "That's it, Cris, for all the tea in China!"

"That was my theory," Camilla said, still dubiously, "but there is no proof that it applies. Nadreck, do you know whether or not it applies to your neighbors?"

"Unfortunately, I do not; but I can find out—by experiment if necessary."

"It might be a good idea," Kinnison suggested. "Go on, Cam."

"Assuming its truth, there is still left the problem of location, which Kit has just made infinitely worse than it was before. Con's and mine were so indefinite that they might possibly have been reconciled with any precisely-known coordinates; but yours, Kit, is almost as definite as Kat's, and cannot possibly be made to agree with it. After all, you know, there are many planets peopled by races similar to ten places. And if there are four different races, none of them can be the one we want."

"I don't believe it," Kit argued. "Not that thing on that peculiar band. I'm sure enough of my dope so that I want to cross-question Kat on hers. QX, Kat?"

"Surely, Kit. Any questions you like."

"Those minds both had plenty of jets—how do you know he wasn't lying to you? Did you drive in to see? Are you sure even that you saw his real shape?"

"Certainly I'm sure of his shape!" Kathryn snapped. "If there had been any zones of compulsion around, I would have known it and got suspicious right then."

"Maybe, and maybe not," Kit disagreed. "That might depend, you know, on how good the guy was who was putting out the zone."

"Nuts!" Kathryn snorted, inelegantly. "But as to his telling the truth about his home planet . . . um . . . I'm not sure of that, no. I didn't check his channels. I was thinking about other things then." The Five knew that she had just left Mentor. "But why should he want to lie about a thing like that—he would have, though, at that. Good Boskonian technique."

"Sure. In your official capacity of coordinator, dad, what do you think?"

"The probability is that all those four forms of life belong on one planet. Your location must be wrong, Kat—he gave you the wrong galaxy, even. Too close to Trenco, too—Tregonsee and I both know that region like a book and no such variable is anywhere near there. We've got to find out all about that planet—and fast. Worsel, will you please get the charts of Kit's region? Kit, will you check with the planetographers of Klovia as to the variable stars anywhere near where you want them, and how many planets they've got? I'll call Tellus."

The charts were studied, and in due time the reports of the planetographers were received. The Klovia scientists reported that there were four long-period variables in the designated volume of space, gave the spatial coordinates and catalogue numbers of each, and all available data concerning their planets. The Tellurians reported only three, in considerably less detail; but they had named each sun and each planet.

"Which one did they leave out?" Kinnison wondered audibly as he fitted the two transparencies together. "This one they call Artonon, no planets. Dunlie, two planets, Abab and Dunster. Descriptions, and so on. Rontieff, one planet that they don't know anything about except the name they have given it. Silly-sounding names—suppose they assemble them by grabbing letters at random?—Ploor . . ."

PLOOR! At last! Only their instantaneous speed of reaction enabled the Five to conceal from the linkage the shrieked thought of what Ploor really meant. After a flashing exchange of thought, Kit smoothly took charge of the conference.

"The planet Ploor should be investigated first, I think," he resumed communication with the group as though his attention had not wavered. "It is the planet nearest the most probable point of origin of that thought-burst. Also, the period of the variable and the planet's distance seem to fit our observations and deductions better than any of the others. Any arguments?"

No arguments. They all agreed. Kinnison, however, demanded action; direct and fast.

"We'll investigate it!" he exclaimed. "With the *Dauntless,* the Z_9M_9Z, and Grand Fleet; and with our very special knick-knack as an ace up our sleeve!"

"Just a minute, dad!" Kit protested. "If, as some of this material seems to indicate, the Ploorans actually are the top echelon of Boskonia, even that array may not be enough."

"You may be right—probably are. What, then? What do you say, Tregonsee?"

"Fleet action, yes," the Rigellian agreed. "Also, as you implied, but did not clearly state, independent but correlated action by us five Second-Stage Lensmen, with our various skills. I would suggest, however, that your children be put first—very definitely first—in command."

"We object—we haven't got jets enough to . . ."

"Overruled!" Kinnison did not have to think to make that decision. He knew. "Any other objections? . . . Approved. I'll call Cliff Maitland right now, then, and get things going."

That call, however, was never sent; for at that moment the mind of Mentor of Arisia flooded the group.

"Children, attend! This intrusion is necessary because a matter has come up which will permit of no delay. Boskonia is now launching the attack which has been in preparation for over twenty years. Arisia is to be the first point of attack. Kinnison, Tregonsee, Worsel, and Nadreck will take immediate steps to assemble the Grand Fleet of the Galactic Patrol in defense. I will confer at length with the younger Kinnisons.

"The Eddorians, as you know," Mentor went on to the Children of the Lens, "believe primarily in the efficacy of physical, material force. While they possess minds of real power, they use them principally as tools in the development of more and ever more efficient mechanical devices. We of Arisia, on the other hand, believe in the superiority of the mind. A fully competent mind would have no need of material devices, since it could control all material substance directly. While we have made some progress toward that end, and you will make more in the cycles to come, Civilization is, and for some time will be, dependent upon physical things. Hence the Galactic Patrol and its Grand Fleet.

"The Eddorians have succeeded finally in inventing a mechanical generator able to block our most penetrant thoughts. They believe implicitly that their vessels, so protected, will be able to destroy our planet. They may believe that the destruction of our planet would so weaken us that would be able to destroy us. It is assumed that you children have deduced that neither we nor the Eddorians can be slain by physical force?"

"Yes—the clincher being that no suggestion was made about giving Eddore a planet from Nth space."

"We Arisians, as you know, have been aiding Nature in the development of minds much abler than our own. While your minds have not yet attained their full powers, you will be able to use the Patrol and its resources to defend Arisia and to destroy the Boskonia fleet. That we cannot do it ourselves is implicit in what I have said."

"But that means . . . this is the big show, then, that you have been hinting at so long?"

"Far from it. An important engagement, of course, but only preliminary to the real test, which will come when we invade Eddore. Do you agree with us that if Arisia were to be destroyed now, it would be difficult to repair the damage done to the morale of the Galactic Patrol?"

"Difficult? It would be impossible!"

"Not necessarily. We have considered the matter at length, however, and have decided that a Boskonian success at this time would not be for the good of Civilization."

"I'll say it wouldn't—that's a masterpiece of understatement if there ever was one! Also, a successful defense of Arisia would be about the best thing that the Patrol could possibly do for itself."

"Exactly so. Go then, children, and work to that end."

"But how, Mentor—*how?*"

"Again I tell you that I do not know. You have powers—individually, collectively, and as the Unit—about which I know little or nothing. *Use them!*"

25

THE DEFENSE OF ARISIA

The "Big Noise"—socially the *Directrix,* technically the *Z9M9Z*—floated through space at the center of a hollow sphere of maulers packed almost screen to screen. She was the Brain. She had been built around the seventeen million cubic feet of unobstructed space which comprised her "tank"—the three-dimensional chart in which vari-colored lights, stationary and moving, represented the positions and motions of solar systems, ships, loose planets, negaspheres, and all other objects and items in which Grand Fleet Operations was, or might become, interested. Completely encircling the tank's more than two thousand feet of circumference was the Rigellian-manned, multi-million-plug board; a crew and a board capable of handling efficiently more than a million combat units.

In the "reducer," the comparatively tiny ten-foot tank set into an alcove, there were condensed the continuously-changing major features of the main chart, so that one man could comprehend and direct the broad strategy of the engagement.

Instead of Port Admiral Haynes, who had conned that reducer and issued general orders during the only previous experience of the *Z9M9Z* in serious warfare, Kimball Kinnison was now in supreme command. Instead of Kinnison and Worsel, who had formerly handled the big tank and the board, there were Clarrissa, Worsel, Tregonsee, and the Children of the Lens. There also, in a built-in, thoroughly competent refrigerator, was Nadreck. Port Admiral Raoul LaForge and Vice-Coordinator Clifford Maitland were just coming aboard.

Might he need anybody else, Kinnison wondered. Couldn't think of anybody—he had just about the whole top echelon of Civilization. Cliff and Laf weren't L2's, of course, but they were mighty good men . . . besides, he *liked* them! Too bad the fourth officer of their class couldn't be there, too . . . gallant Wiedel Holmberg, killed in action . . . at that, three out of four was a high average—mighty high . . .

"Hi, Cliff—Hi, Laf" "Hi, Kim!"

The three old friends shook hands cordially, then the two newcomers stared for minutes into the maze of lights flashing and winking in the tremendous space-chart.

"Glad I don't have to try to make sense out of that," LaForge commented, finally. "Looks a lot different in battle harness than on practice cruises. You want me on that forward wall there, you said?"

"Yes. You can see it plainer down in the reducer. The white star is Arisia. The yellows, all marked, are suns and other fixed points, such as the markers along the arbitrary rim of the galaxy, running from there to there. Reds will be Boskonians when they get close enough to show. Greens are ours. Up in the big tank everything is identified, but down here there's no room for details—each green light marks the location of a whole operating fleet. That block of green circles, there, is your command. It's about eighty parsecs deep and covers everything within two hours—say a hundred and fifty parsecs—of the line between Arisia and the Second Galaxy. Pretty loose now, of course, but you can tighten it up and shift it as you please as soon as some reds show up. You'll have a Rigellian talker—here he is now—when you want anything done, think at him and he'll give it to the right panel on the board. QX?"

"I think so. I'll practice a bit."

"Now you, Cliff. These green crosses, halfway between the forward wall and Arisia, are yours. You won't have quite as much depth as Laf, but a wider coverage. The green tetrahedrons are mine. They blanket Arisia, you notice, and fill the space out to the second wall."

"Do you think you and I will have anything to do?" Maitland asked, waving a hand at LaForge's tremendous barrier.

"I wish I could hope not, but I can't. They're going to throw everything they've got at us."

For weeks Grand Fleet drilled, maneuvered, and practiced. All space within ten parsecs of Arisia was divided into cubes, each of which was given a reference number. Fleets were so placed that any point in that space could be reached by at least one fleet in thirty seconds or less of elapsed time.

Drill went on until, finally, it happened. Constance, on guard at the moment, perceived the slight "curdling" of space which presages the appearance of the terminus of a hyper-spatial tube and gave the alarm. Kit, the girls, and all the Arisians responded instantly—all knew that this was to be a thing which not even the Five could handle unaided.

Not one, or a hundred, or a thousand, but at least two hundred thousand of those tubes erupted, practically at once. Kit could alert and instruct ten Rigellian operators every second, and so could each of his sisters; but since every tube within striking distance of Arisia had to be guarded or plugged within thirty seconds of its appearance, it is seen that the Arisians did practically all of the spotting and placing during those first literally incredible two or three minutes.

If the Boskonians could have emerged from a tube's terminus in the moment of its appearance, it is quite probable that nothing could have saved Arisia. As it was, however, the enemy required seconds, or sometimes even whole minutes, to traverse their tubes, which gave the defenders much valuable time.

Upon arriving at the tube's end, the fleet laced itself, by means of tractors and pressors, into a rigid although inertialess structure. Then, if there was time, and because the theory was that the pirates would probably send a negasphere through first, with an intrinsic velocity aimed at Arisia, a suitably-equipped loose planet was tossed into "this end" of the tube. Since they might send a loose or an armed planet through first, however, the fleet admiral usually threw a negasphere in, too.

What happened when planet met negasphere, in the unknown medium which makes up the "interior" of a hyper-spatial tube, is not surely known. Several highly abstruse mathematical treatises and many volumes of rather gruesome fiction have been written upon the subject—none of which, however, has any bearing here.

If the Patrol fleet did not get there first, the succession of events was different; the degree of difference depending upon how much time the enemy had had. If, as sometimes happened, a fleet was coming through it was met by a super-atomic bombs and by the concentrated fire of every primary projector that the englobing task force could bring to bear; with consequences upon which it is neither necessary or desirable to dwell. If a planet had emerged, it was met by a negasphere . . .

Have you ever seen a negasphere strike a planet?

The negasphere is built of negative matter. This material—or, rather, anti-material—is in every respect the exact opposite of the everyday matter of normal space. Instead of electrons, it has positrons. To it a push, however violent, is a pull; a pull is a push. When negative matter strikes positive, then, there is no collision in the usual sense of the word. One electron and one positron neutralize each other and disappear; giving rise to two quanta of extremely hard radiation.

Thus, when the spherical hyper-plane which was the aspect of the negasphere tended to occupy the same three-dimensional space in which the loose planet already was, there was no actual collision. Instead, the materials of both simply vanished, along the surface of what should have been a contact, in a gigantically crescendo burst of pure, raw energy. The atoms and the molecules of the planet's substance disappeared; the physically incomprehensible texture of the negasphere's anti-mass changed into that of normal space. And all circumambient space was flooded with inconceivably lethal radiation; so intensely lethal that any being not adequately shielded from it died before he had time to realize that he was being burned.

Gravitation, of course, was unaffected; and the rapid disappearance of the planet's mass set up unbalanced forces of tremendous magnitude. The hot, dense, pseudo-liquid magma tended to erupt as the sphere of nothingness devoured so rapidly the planet's substance, but not a particle of it could move. Instead, it vanished. Mountains fell, crashingly. Oceans poured. Earth-cracks appeared; miles wide, tens of miles deep, hundreds of miles long. The world heaved . . . shuddered . . . disintegrated . . . vanished.

The shock attack upon Arisia itself, which in the Eddorian mind had been mathematically certain to succeed, was over in approximately six minutes. Kinnison, Maitland, and LaForge, fuming at their stations, had done nothing at all. The Boskonians had probably thrown everything they could; the probability was vanishingly small that that particular attack was to be or could be resumed. Nevertheless a host of Kinnison's task forces remained on guard and a detail of Arisians still scanned all nearby space.

"What shall I do next, Kit?" Camilla asked. "Help Connie crack that screen?"

Kit glanced at his youngest sister, who was stretched out flat, every muscle rigidly tense in an extremity of effort.

"No," he decided. "If she can't crack it alone, all four of us couldn't help her much. Besides, I don't believe she can break it. It's a mechanical, you know, powered by atomic-motored generators. My guess is that it'll have to be *solved*, not cracked, and the solution will take time. When she comes down off that peak, Kay, you might tell her so, and both of you start solving it. The rest of us have another job. The Boskonian moppers-up are coming in force, and there isn't a chance that either we or the Arisians can derive the counter-formula of that screen in less than a week. Therefore the rest of this battle will have to be fought out on conventional lines. We can do the most good, I think, by spotting the Boskonians into the big tank—our scouts aren't locating five percent of them—for the L2's to pass on to dad and the rest of the top brass so they can run this battle the way it ought to be run. You'll do the spotting, Cam, of course; Kat and I will do the pushing. And if you thought that Tregonsee took you for a ride . . . ! It'll work, don't you think?"

"Of *course* it'll work!"

Thus, apparently as though by magic, red lights winked into being throughout a third of the volume of the immense tank; and the three master strategists, informed of what was being done, heaved tremendous sighs of relief. They now had real control. They knew, not only the positions of their own task forces, but also, and exactly, the position of *every* task-force of the enemy. More, by merely forming in his mind the desire for the information, any one of the three could know, with no appreciable lapse of time, the exact composition and the exact strength of any individual fleet, flotilla, or squadron!

Kit and his two sisters stood close-grouped, motionless; heads bent and almost touching, arms interlocked. Kinnison perceived with surprise that Lenses, as big and as bright as Kit's own, flamed upon his daughters' wrists; a surprise which changed to awe as the very air around those three red-bronze-auburn heads began to thicken, to pulsate, and to glow with that indefinable, indescribable polychromatic effulgence so uniquely characteristic of the Lens of the Galactic Patrol. But there was work to do, and Kinnison did it.

Since the Z9M9Z was now working as not even the most optimistic of her planners and designers had dared to hope, the war could now be fought strategically; that is, with the object of doing the enemy as much harm as possible with the irreducible minimum of risk. It was not sporting. It was not clubby. There was nothing whatever of chivalry. There was no thought whatever of giving the enemy a break. It was massacre—it was murder—it was war.

It was not ship to ship. No, nor fleet to fleet. Instead, ten or twenty Patrol task-forces, under sure pilotage, dashed out to englobe at extreme range one fleet of the Boskonians. Then, before the opposing admiral could assemble a picture of what was going on, his entire command became the center of impact of hundreds or even thousands of super-atomic bombs, as well as the focus of an immensely greater number of scarcely less ravaging primary beams. Not a ship nor a scout nor a lifeboat of the englobed fleet escaped, ever. In fact, few indeed were the blobs, or even droplets, of hard alloy or of dureum which remained merely liquefied or which, later, were able to condense.

Fleet by fleet the Boskonians were blown out of the ether; one by one the red lights in the tank and in the reducer winked out. And finally the slaughter was done.

Kit and his two now Lensless sisters unlaced themselves. Karen and Constance came up for air, announcing that they knew how to work the problem Kit had handed them, but that it would take time. Clarrissa, white and shaken by what she had driven herself to do, looked and felt sick. So did Kinnison; nor had either of the other two commanders derived any pleasure from the engagement. Tregonsee deplored it. Of all the Lensed personnel, only Worsel had enjoyed himself. He liked to kill enemies, at close range or far, and he could not understand or sympathize with squeamishness. Nadreck, of course, had neither liked nor disliked any part of the whole affair; to him his part had been merely another task, to be performed with the smallest outlay of physical and mental effort consistent with good workmanship.

"What next?" Kinnison asked then, of the group at large. "I say the Ploorans. They're not like these poor devils were—they probably sent them in. *They've* got it coming!"

"They certainly have!"

"Ploor!"

"By all means Ploor!"

"But how about Arisia here?" Maitland asked.

"Under control," Kinnison replied. "We'll leave a heavy guard and a spare tank—the Arisians will do the rest."

As soon as the tremendous fleet had shaken itself down into the course for Ploor, all seven of the Kinnisons retired to a small dining room and ate a festive meal. They drank after-dinner coffee. Most of them smoked. They discussed, for a long time and not very quietly, the matter of the Hell-Hole in Space. Finally:

"I know it's a trap, as well as you do." Kinnison got up from the table, rammed his hands into his breeches pockets, and paced the floor. It's got T-R-A-P painted all over it, in bill-poster letters seventeen meters high. So what? Since I'm the only one who can, I've got to go in, if it's still there after we knock Ploor off. And it'll still be there, for all the tea in China. All the Ploorans aren't on Ploor."

Four young Kinnisons flashed thoughts at Kathryn, who frowned and bit her lip. She had hit that hole with everything she had, and simply bounced. She had been able to block the radiation, of course, but such solid barriers had been necessary that she had blinded herself by her own screens. That it was Eddorian there could be no doubt . . . warned by her own activities in the other tube—Plooran of course—and dad would be worth taking in more way than one . . .

"I can't say that I'm any keener about going in than any of you are about having me do it," the big Lensman went on, "but unless some of you can figure out a reason for my *not* going in that isn't fuller of holes than a sponge, I'm going to tackle it just as soon after we blow Ploor apart as I can possibly get there."

And Kathryn, his self-appointed guardian, knew that nothing could stop him. Nor did anyone there, even Clarrissa, try to stop him. Lensmen all, they knew that he had to go in.

To the Five, the situation was not too serious. Kinnison would come through unhurt. The Eddorians could take him, of course. But whether or not they could do anything to him after they got him would depend on what the Kinnison kids would be doing in the meantime—and that would be plenty. They couldn't delay his entry into the tube very much without making a smell, but they could and would hurry Arisia up. And even if, as seemed probable, he was already in the tube when Arisia was ready for the big push, a lot could be done at the other end. Those amoeboid monstrosities would be fighting for their own precious lives, this time, not for the lives of slaves; and the Five promised each other grimly that the Eddorians would have too much else to worry about to waste any time on Kimball Kinnison.

Clarrissa Kinnison, however, fought the hardest and bitterest battle of her life. She loved Kim with a depth and a fervor which very few women, anywhere, have ever been able to feel. She knew with a sick, cold certainty, knew with every fibre of her being and with every cell of her brain, that if he went into that trap he would die in it. Nevertheless, she would have to let him go in. More, and worse, she would have to send him in—to his death—with a smile. She could not ask him not to go in. She could not even suggest again that there was any possibility that he need not go in. He had to go in. He *had* to . . .

And if Lensman's Load was heavy on him, on her it was almost unbearable. His part was vastly the easier. He would only have to die; she would have to live. She would have to keep on living—without Kim—living a lifetime of deaths, one after another. And she would have to hold her block and smile, not only with her face, but with her whole mind. She could be scared, of course, apprehensive, as he himself was; she could wish with all her strength for his safe return: but if he suspected the thousandth part of what she really felt it would break his heart. Nor would it do a bit of good. However broken-hearted at her rebellion against the inflexible Code of the Lens, he would still go in. Being Kimball Kinnison, he could not do anything else.

As soon as she could, Clarissa went to a distant room and turned on a full-coverage block. She lay down, buried her face in the pillow, clenched her fists, and fought.

Was there any way—any *possible* way—that she could die instead? None. It was not that simple.

She would have to let him go . . .

With a SMILE . . .

Not gladly, but proudly and willingly . . . for the good of the Patrol . . .

DAMN THE PATROL!!

Clarissa Kinnison gritted her teeth and writhed.

She would simply *have* to let him go into that ghastly trap—go to his absolutely sure and certain death—without showing one white feather, either to her husband or to her children. Her husband, her Kim, would have to die . . . and she—would—*have*—to—*live* . . .

She got up, smiled experimentally, and snapped off the block. Then, actually smiling and apparently confident, she strolled down the corridor.

Such is Lensman's Load.

26

THE BATTLE OF PLOOR

Twenty-odd years before, when the then *Dauntless* and her crew were thrown out of a hyper-spatial tube and into that highly enigmatic Nth space, LaVerne Thorndyke had been Chief Technician. Mentor of Arisia found them, and put into the mind of Sir Austin Cardynge, mathematician extraordinary, the knowledge of how to find the way back to normal space. Thorndyke, working under nerve-shattering difficulties, had been in charge of building the machines which were to enable the vessel to return to her home space. He built them. She returned.

He was now again in charge, and every man of his present crew had been a member of his former one. He did not command the spaceship or her regular crew, of course, but they did not count. Not one of those kids would be allowed to set foot on the fantastically dangerous planet to which the inertialess *Space Laboratory Twelve* was anchored.

Older, leaner, grayer, he was now, even more than then, Civilization's Past Master of Mechanism. If anything could be built, "Thorny" Thorndyke could build it. If it couldn't be built, he could build something just as good.

He lined his crew up for inspection; men who, although many of them had as much rank and had had as many years of as much authority as their present boss, had been working for days to forget as completely as possible their executive positions and responsibilities. Each man wore not one, but three, personal neutralizers; one inside and two outside of his space-suit. Thorndyke, walking down the line, applied his test-kit to each individual neutralizer. He then tested his own. QX—all were at max.

"Fellows," he said then, "You all remember what it was like last time. This is going to be the same, except more so and for a longer time. How we did it before without any casualties I'll never know. If we can do it again it'll be a major miracle, no less. Before, all we had to do was to build a couple of small generators and some controls out of stuff native to the planet, and we didn't find that any too easy a job. This time, for a starter, we've got to build a Bergenholm big enough to free the whole planet; after which we install the Bergs, tube-generators, atomic blasts, and other stuff we brought along.

"But that native Berg is going to be a Class A Prime headache, and until we get it running it's going to be hell on wheels. The only way we can get away with it is to check and re-check every thing and every step. Check, check, double-check; then go back and double-check again.

"Remember that the fundamental characteristics of this Nth space are such that inert matter can travel faster than light; and remember, every second of the time, that our intrinsic velocity is something like fifteen lights relative to anything solid in this space. I want every one of you to picture himself going inert accidentally. You might take a tangent course or higher—but you might not, too. And it wouldn't only kill the one who did it. It wouldn't only spoil our record. It could very easily kill us all and make a crater full of boiling metal out of our whole installation. So BE CAREFUL! Also bear in mind that one piece, however small, of this planet's material, accidentally brought aboard, might wreck the *Dauntless*. Any questions?"

"If the fundamental characteristic—constants—of this space are so different, how do you know that the stuff will work here?"

"Well, the stuff we built here before worked. The Arisians told Kit Kinnison that two of the fundamentals, mass and length, are about normal. Time is a lot different, so that we can't compute power-to-mass ratios and so on, but we'll have enough power, anyway, to get any speed we can use."

"I see. We miss the really fancy stuff?"

"Yes. Well, the quicker we get started the quicker we'll get done. Let's go."

The planet was airless, waterless, desolate; a chaotic jumble of huge and jagged fragments of various metals in a non-metallic continuous phase. It was as though some playful child-giant of space had poured dipperfuls of silver, of iron, of copper, and of other granulated pure metals into a tank of something else—and then, tired of play, had thrown the whole mess away!

Neither the metals nor the non-metallic substances were either hot or cold. They had no apparent temperature, to thermometers or to the "feelers" of the suits. The machines which these men had built so long before had not changed in any particular. They still functioned perfectly; no spot of rust or corrosion or erosion marred any part. This, at least, was good news.

Inertialess machines, extravagantly equipped with devices to keep them inertialess, were taken "ashore"; nor were any of these ever to be returned to the ship. Kinnison had ordered and reiterated that no unnecessary chances were to be taken of getting any particle of Nth-space stuff aboard *Space Laboratory Twelve,* and none were taken.

Since men cannot work indefinitely in space-suits, each man had periodically to be relieved; but each such relief amounted almost to an operation. Before he left the planet his suit was scrubbed, rinsed, and dried. In the vessel's airlock it was air-blasted again before the outer port was closed. He unshelled in the lock and left his suit there—everything which had come into contact with Nth-space matter either would be left on the planet's surface or would be jettisoned before the vessel was again inerted. Unnecessary precautions? Perhaps—but Thorndyke and his crew returned unharmed to normal space in undamaged ships.

Finally the Bergenholm was done; by dint of what improvisation, substitutions and artifice only "Thorny" Thorndyke ever knew; at what strain and cost was evidenced by the gaunt bodies and haggard faces of his overworked and underslept crew. To those experts and particularly to Thorndyke, the thing was not a good job. It was not quiet, nor smooth. It was not in balance, statically, dynamically, or electrically. The Chief Technician, to whom a meter-jump of one and a half thousandths had always been a matter of grave concern, swore feelingly in all the planetary languages he knew when he saw what those meters were doing.

He scowled morosely. There might have been poorer machines built sometime, somewhere, he supposed—but damned if he had ever seen any!

But the improvised Berg ran, and kept on running. The planet became inertialess and remained that way. For hours, then, Thorndyke climbed over and around and through the Brobdingnagian fabrication, testing and checking the operation of every part. Finally he climbed down and reported to his waiting crew.

"QX, fellows, a nice job. A hell of a good job, in fact, considering— even though we all know that it isn't what any of us would call a good machine. Part of that meter-jump, of course, is due to the fact that nothing about the heap is true or balanced, but most of it must be due to this cockeyed ether. Anyway, none of it is due to the usual causes—loose bars and faulty insulation. So my best guess is that she'll keep on doing her stuff while we do ours. One sure thing, she isn't going to fall apart, even under that ungodly knocking; and I don't *think* she'll shake herself off of the planet."

After Thorndyke's somewhat less than enthusiastic approval of his brain-child, the adventurers into that fantastic region attacked the second phase of their project. The planetary Bergenholm was landed and set up. Its meters jumped, too, but the engineers were no longer worried about that. *That* machine would run indefinitely. Pits were dug. Atomic blasts and other engines were installed; as were many exceedingly complex instruments and mechanisms. A few tons of foreign matter on the planet's surface would now make no difference; but there was no relaxation of the extreme precautions against the transfer of any matter whatever from the planet to the space-ship.

When the job was done, but before the clean-up, Thorndyke called his crew into conference.

"Fellows, I know just what a God-awful shellacking you've been taking. We all feel as though we'd been on a Delgonian ciambake. Nevertheless, I've got to tell you something. Kinnison said that if we could get this one fixed up without too much trouble, it'd be a mighty good idea to have two of them. What do you say? Did we have too much trouble?"

He got exactly the reaction he had expected.

"Lead us to it!"

"Pick out the one you want!"

"Trouble? Hell, no! If this scrap-heap we built held together this long, she'll run for years. We can tow her on a tractor-pressor combo, match intrinsics with clamp-on drivers, and mount her anywhere!"

Another metal-studded, barren, lifeless world was therefore found and prepared; and no real argument arose until Thorndyke broached the matter of selecting the two men who were to stay with him and Henderson in the two lifeboats which were to remain for a time near the two loose planets after *Space Laboratory Twelve* had returned to normal space. Everybody wanted to stay. Each one *was* going to stay, too, by all the gods of space, if he had to pull rank to do it!

"Hold it!" Thorndyke commanded. "We'll do the same as we did before, then, by drawing lots. Quartermaster Allerdyce . . ."

"Not by a damn sight!" Uhlenhuth, formerly Atomic Technician 1/c, objected vigorously, and was supported by several others. "He's too clever with his fingers—look what he did to the original draw! We're not squawking about that one, you understand—a little fixing was QX back there—but *this* one's got to be on the level."

"Now that you mention it, I do remember hearing about the laws of chance being jimmied a bit." Thorndyke grinned broadly. "So you hold the pot yourself, Uhly, and Hank and I will each pull out one name."

So it was. Henderson drew Uhlenhuth, to that burly admiral's loud delight, and Thorndyke drew Nelson, the erstwhile chief communications officer. The two lifeboats disembarked, each near one of the newly "loosened" planets. Two men would stay on or near each of those planets, to be sure that all the machinery functioned perfectly. They would stay there until the atomic blasts went into action and it became clear that the Arisians would need no help in navigating those tremendous globes through Nth space to the points at which two hyper-spatial tubes were soon to appear.

Long before the advance scouts of Grand Fleet were within surveying distance of Ploor, Kit and his sisters had spread a completely detailed chart of its defenses in the tactical tank. A white star represented Ploor's sun; a white sphere the planet itself; white Ryerson string-lights marked a portion of the planetary orbit. Points of white light, practically all of which were connected to the white sphere by red string-lights, marked the directions of neighboring stars and the existence of sunbeams, installed and ready. Pink globes were loose planets; purple ones negaspheres; red points of light were, as before, Boskonian task-force fleets. Blues were mobile fortresses; bands of canary yellow and amber luminescence showed the locations and emplacements of sunbeam grids and deflectors.

Layer after layer of pinks, purples, and blues almost hid the brilliant white sphere from sight. More layers of the same colors, not quite as dense, surrounded the entire solar system. Yellow and amber bands were everywhere.

Kinnison studied the thing briefly, whistling unmelodiously through his teeth. The picture was familiar enough, since it duplicated in practically every respect the chart of the neighborhood of the Patrol's own Ultra Prime, around Klovia. Those defenses simply could not be cracked by any concentration possible of any mobile devices theretofore employed in war.

"Just about what we expected," Kinnison thought to the group at large. "Some new stuff, but not much. What I want to know, Kit and the rest of you, is there anything there that looks as though it was supposed to handle our new baby? Don't see anything, myself."

"There is not." Kit stated, definitely. "We looked. There couldn't be, anyway. It can't be handled. Looking backwards at it, they may be able to reconstruct how it was done, but in advance? No. Even Mentor couldn't—he had to call in a fellow who has studied ultra-high mathematics for Klono-only-knows-how-many-millions of years to compute the resultant vectors."

Kit's use of the word "they," which of course meant Ploorans to everyone except his sisters, concealed his knowledge of the fact that the Eddorians had taken over the defense of Ploor. Eddorians were handling those screens. Eddorians were directing and correlating those far-flung task forces, with a precision which Kinnison soon noticed.

"Much smoother work than I ever saw them do before," he commented. "Suppose they have developed a Z_9M_9Z?"

"Could be. They copied everything else you invented, why not that?" Again the highly ambiguous "they." "No sign of it around Arisia, though—but maybe they didn't think they'd need it there."

"Or, more likely, they didn't want to risk it so far from home. We can tell better after the mopping-up starts—if the widget performs as per specs . . . but if your dope is right, this is about close enough. You might tip the boys off, and I'll call Mentor." Kinnison could not reach Nth space, but it was no secret that Kit could.

The terminus of one of the Patrol's hyper-spatial tubes erupted into space close to Ploor. That such phenomena were expected was evident—a Boskonian fleet moved promptly and smoothly to englobe it. But this was an Arisian tube; computed, installed, and handled by Arisians. It would be in existence only three seconds; and anything the fleet could do, even if it got there in nothing flat, would make no difference.

To the observers in the Z_9M_9Z those three seconds stretched endlessly. What would happen when that utterly foreign planet, with its absolutely impossible intrinsic velocity of over fifteen times that of light, erupted into normal space and went inert? Nobody, not even the Arisian, knew.

Everybody there had seen pictures of what happened when the insignificant mass of a space-ship, traveled at only a hundredth of the velocity of light, collided with a planetoid. That was bad enough. This projectile, however, had a mass of about eight times ten to the twenty-first power—an eight followed by twenty-one zeroes—metric tons; would tend to travel fifteen hundred times as fast; and kinetic energy equals mass times velocity squared.

There seemed to be a theoretical possibility, since the mass would instantaneously become some higher order of infinity, that all the matter in normal space would coalesce with it in zero time; but Mentor had assured Kit that operators would come into effect to prevent such an occurrence, and that untoward events would be limited to a radius of ten or fifteen parsecs. Mentor could solve the problem in detail; but since the solution would require some two hundred Klovian years and the event was due to occur in two weeks . . .

"How about the big computer at Ultra Prime?" Kinnison had asked, innocently. "You know how fast that works."

"Roughly two thousand years—if it could take that kind of math, which it can't," Kit had replied, and the subject had been dropped.

Finally it happened. What happened? Even after the fact none of the observers knew; nor did any except the L3's ever find out. The fuses of all the recorder and analyzer circuits blew at once. Needles jumped instantly to maximum and wrapped themselves around their stops. Charts and ultra-photographic films showed only straight or curved lines running from the origin to and through the limits in zero time. Ploor and everything around it disappeared in an utterly indescribable and completely incomprehensible blast of pure, wild, raw, uncontrolled and uncontrollable energy. The infinitesimal fraction of that energy which was visible, heterodyned upon the ultra as it was and screened as it was, blazed so savagely upon the plates that it seared the eyes.

And if the events caused by the planet aimed at Ploor were indescribable, what can be said of those initiated by the one directed against Ploor's sun?

When the heat generated in the interior of a sun becomes greater than its effective surface is able to radiate, that surface expands. If the expansion is not fast enough, a more or less insignificant amount of the sun's material explodes, thus enlarging by force the radiant surface to whatever extent is necessary to restore equilibrium. Thus come into being the ordinary novae; suns which may for a few days or for a few weeks radiate energy at a rate a few hundreds of thousands of times greater than normal. Since ordinary novae can be produced at will by the collision of a planet with a sun, the scientists of the Patrol had long since completed their studies of all the phenomena involved.

The mechanisms of super-novae, however, remained obscure. No adequate instrumentation had been developed to study conclusively the occasional super-nova which occurred naturally. No super-nova had ever been produced artificially—with all its resources of mass, atomic energy, cosmic energy, and sunbeams, Civilization could neither assemble nor concentrate enough power.

At the impact of the second loose planet, accompanied by the excess energy of its impossible and unattainable intrinsic velocity, Ploor's sun became a super-nova. How deeply the intruding thing penetrated, how much of the sun's mass exploded, never was and perhaps never will be determined. The violence of the explosion was such, however, that Klovian astronomers reported—a few years later—that it was radiating energy at the rate of some five hundred and fifty million suns.

Thus no attempt will be made to describe what happened when the planet from Nth space struck the Boskonians' sun. It was indescribability cubed.

27

KINNISON TRAPPED

The Boskonian fleets defending Ploor were not all destroyed, of course. The vessels were inertialess. None of the phenomena accompanying the coming into being of the super-nova were propagated at a velocity above that of light; a speed which to any spaceship is scarcely a crawl.

The survivors were, however, disorganized. They had lost their morale when Ploor was wiped out in such a spectacularly nerve-shattering fashion. Also, they had lost practically all of their high command; for the bosses, instead of riding the ether as did the Patrol commanders, remained in their supposedly secure headquarters and directed matters from afar. Mentor and his fellows had removed from this plane of existence the Eddorians who had been present in the flesh on Ploor. The Arisians had cut all communication between Eddore and the remnants of the Boskonian defensive force.

Grand Fleet, then, moved in for the kill; and for a time the action near Arisia was repeated. Following definite flight-and-course orders from the Z_9M_9Z, ten or more Patrol fleets would make short hops. At the end of those assigned courses they would discover that they had englobed a task-force of the enemy. Bomb and beam!

Over and over—flit, bomb, and beam!

One Boskonian high officer, however, had both the time and the authority to act. A full thousand fleets massed together, their heaviest units outward, packed together screen to screen in a close-order globe of defense.

"According to Haynes, that was good strategy in the old days," Kinnison commented, "but it's no good against loose planets and negaspheres."

Six loose planets were so placed and so released that their inert masses would crash together at the center of the Boskonian globe; then, a few minutes later, ten negaspheres of high anti-mass were similarly launched. After those sixteen missiles had done their work and the resultant had attained an equilibrium of sorts, there was very little mopping-up to do.

The Boskonian observers were competent. The Boskonian commanders now knew that they had no chance whatever of success; that to stay was to be annihilated; that the only possibility of life lay in flight. Therefore each remaining Boskonian vice-admiral, after perhaps a moment of consultation with a few others, ordered his fleet to drive at maximum blast for his home planet.

"No use chasing them individually, is there, Kit?" Kinnison asked, when it became clear in the tank that the real battle was over; that all resistance had ended. "They can't do anything, and this kind of killing makes me sick at the stomach. Besides, I've got something else to do."

"No. Me, too. So have I." Kit agreed with his father in full.

As soon as the last Boskonian fleet was beyond detector range Grand Fleet broke up, its component fleets setting out for their respective worlds.

"The Hell-Hole is still there, Kit," the Gray Lensman said soberly. "If Ploor was the top—I'm beginning to think there *is* no top—it leads either to an automatic mechanism set up by the Ploorans or to Ploorans who are still alive somewhere. If Ploor wasn't the top, this seems to be the only lead we have. In either case I've got to take it. Check?"

"Well, I . . ." Kit tried to duck, but couldn't. "Yes, dad, I'm afraid it's check."

Two big hands met and gripped: and Kinnison went to take leave of his wife.

There is no need to go into detail as to what those two said or did. He knew that he was going into danger; that he might not return. That is, he knew empirically or academically, as a non-germane sort of fact, that he might die. He did not, however, really believe so. No man really believes, ever, that any given event will kill him.

Kinnison expected to be captured, imprisoned, questioned, tortured. He could understand all of those things, and he did not like any one of them. That he was more than a trifle afraid and that he hated to leave her now more than he ever had before were both natural enough—he had nothing whatever to hide from her.

She, on the other hand, knew starkly that he would never come back. She knew that he would die in that trap. She knew that she would have to live a lifetime of emptiness, alone. Hence she had much to conceal from him. She must be just as scared and as apprehensive as he was, but no more; just as anxious for their continued happiness as he was, but no more; just as intensely loving, but no more and in exactly the same sense. Here lay the test. She must kiss him goodbye as though he were going into mere danger. She *must not* give way to the almost irresistible urge to act in accordance with what she so starkly, chillingly knew to be the truth, that she would never . . . *never* . . . NEVER kiss her Kim again!

She succeeded. It is a measure of the Red Lensman's quality that she did not weaken, even when her husband approached the boundary of the Hell-Hole and sent what she knew would be his last message.

"Here it is—about a second now. Don't worry—I'll be back shortly. Clear ether, Cris!"

"Of *course* you will, dear. Clear ether, Kim!"

His speedster did not mount any special generators, nor were any needed. He and his ship were sucked into that trap as though it had been a maelstrom.

He felt again the commingled agonies of inter-dimensional acceleration. He perceived again the formless, textureless, spaceless void of blankly gray nothingness which was the three-dimensionally-impossible substance of the tube. A moment later, he felt a new and different acceleration—he was speeding up *inside the tube!* Then, very shortly, he felt nothing at all. Startled, he tried to jump up to investigate, and discovered that he could not move. Even by the utmost exertion of his will he could not stir a finger or an eyelid. He was completely immobilized. Nor could he feel. His body was as devoid of sensation as though it belonged to somebody else. Worse, for his heart was not beating. He was not breathing. He could not see. It was as though his every nerve, motor and sensory, voluntary and involuntary, had been separately anaesthetized. He could still think, but that was all. His sense of perception still worked.

He wondered whether he was still accelerating or not, and tried to find out. He could not. He could not determine whether he was moving or stationary. There were no reference points. Every infinitesimal volume of that enigmatic grayness was like each and every other.

Mathematically, perhaps, he was not moving at all; since he was in a continuum in which mass, length and time, and hence inertia and inertialessness, velocity and acceleration, are meaningless terms.

He was outside of space and beyond time. Effectively, however, he was moving; moving with an acceleration which nothing material had ever before approached. He and his vessel were being driven along that tube by every watt of power generable by one entire Eddorian atomic power plant. His velocity, long since unthinkable, became incalculable.

All things end: even Eddorian atomic power was not infinite. At the very peak of power and pace, then, all the force, all the momentum, all the kinetic energy of the speedster's mass and velocity were concentrated in and applied to Kinnison's physical body. He sensed something, and tried to flinch, but could not. In a fleeting instant of what he thought was time he went *past,* not through, his clothing and his Lens; *past,* not through, his armor; and *past,* not through, the hard beryllium-alloy structure of his vessel. He even went past but not through the N-dimensional interface of the hyper-spatial tube.

This, although Kinnison did not know it, was the Eddorian's climactic effort. He had taken his prisoner as far as he could possibly reach: then, assembling and concentrating all available power, he had given him a catapultic shove into the absolutely unknown and utterly unknowable. The Eddorian did not know any vector of the Lensman's naked flight; he did not care where he went. He did not know and could not compute or even guess at his victim's probable destination.

In what his spacehound's time sense told him was one second, Kinnison passed exactly two hundred million foreign spaces. He did not know how he knew the precise number, but he did. Hence, in the Patrol's measured cadence, he began to count groups of spaces of one hundred million each. After a few days, his velocity decreased to such a value that he could count groups of single millions. Then thousands—hundreds—tens—until finally he could perceive the salient features of each space before it was blotted out by the next.

How could this be? He wondered, but not foggily; his mind was as clear and as strong as it had ever been. Spaces were coexistent, not spread out like this. In the fourth dimension they were flat together, like pages in a book, except thinner. This was all wrong. It was impossible. Since it could not happen, it was not happening. He had not been and could not be drugged. Therefore some Plooran must have him in a zone of compulsion. *What* a zone! *What* an operator the ape must be!

It was, however, real—all of it. What Kinnison did not know, then or ever, was that he was actually outside the boundaries of space; actually beyond the confines of time. He was going past, not through, those spaces and those times.

He was now in each space long enough to study it in some detail. He was an immense distance above this one; at such a distance that he could perceive many globular super-universes; each of which in turn was composed of billions of lenticular galaxies.

Another one. Closer now. Galaxies only; the familiar random masses whose apparent lack of symmetrical grouping is due to the limitations of Civilization's observers. He was still going too fast to stop.

In the next space Kinnison found himself within the limits of a solar system and tried with all the force of his mind to get in touch with some intelligent entity upon one—any one—of its planets. Before he could succeed, that system vanished and he was dropping, from a height of a few thousand kilometers, toward the surface of a warm and verdant world, so much like Tellus that he thought for an instant he must have circumnavigated total space. The aspect, the ice-caps, the cloud-effects, were identical. The oceans, however, while similar, were different; as were the continents. The mountains were larger and rougher and harder.

He was falling much too fast. A free fall from infinity wouldn't give him *this* much speed!

This whole affair was, as he had decided once before, absolutely impossible. It was simply preposterous to believe that a naked man, especially one without blood-circulation or breath, could still be alive after spending as many weeks in open space as he had just spent. He *knew* that he was alive. Therefore none of this was happening; even though, as surely as he knew that he was alive, he knew that he was falling.

"Jet back, Lensman!" he thought viciously to himself; tried to shout it aloud.

For this could be deadly stuff, if he let himself believe it. If he believed that he was falling from any such height he would die in the instant of landing. He would not actually crash; his body would not move from wherever it was that it was. Nevertheless the shock of that wholly imaginary crash would kill him just as dead and just as instantaneously as though all his flesh had been actually smashed into a crimson smear upon one of the neighboring mountain's huge, flat rocks.

"Pretty close, my bright young Plooran friend, but you didn't quite ring the bell," he thought savagely, trying with all the power of his mind to break through the zone of compulsion. "So I'm telling you something right now. If you want to kill me you'll have to do it physically, and you haven't got jets enough to swing the load. You might as well cut your zone, because this kind of stuff has been pulled on me by experts, and it hasn't worked yet."

He was apparently falling, feet downward, toward an open, grassy mountain meadow, surrounded by forests, through which meandered a small stream. He was so close now that he could perceive the individual blades of grass in the meadow and the small fishes in the stream; and he was still apparently at terminal velocity.

Without his years of spacehound's training in inertialess maneuvering, he might have died even before he landed, but speed as speed did not affect him at all. He was used to instantaneous stops from light-speeds. The only thing that worried him was the matter of inertia. Was he inert or free?

He declared to himself that he was free. Or, rather, that he had been, was, and would continue to be motionless. It was physically, mathematically, intrinsically impossible that any of this stuff had actually occurred. It was all compulsion, pure and simple, and he—Kimball Kinnison, Gray Lensman—would not let it get him down. He clenched his mental teeth upon that belief and held it doggedly. One bare foot struck the tip of a blade of grass and his entire body came to a shockless halt. He grinned in relief—this was what he had wanted, but had not quite dared wholly to expect. There followed immediately, however, other events which he had not expected at all.

His halt was less than momentary; in the instant of its accomplishment he began to fall normally the remaining eight or ten inches to the ground. Automatically he sprung his space-trained knees, to take the otherwise disconcerting jar; automatically his left hand snapped up to the place where his controls should have been. *Legs and arms worked!*

He could see with his eyes. He could feel with his skin. He was drawing a breath, the first time he had breathed since leaving normal space. Nor was it an unduly deep breath—he felt no lack of oxygen. His heart was beating as normally as though it had never missed a beat. He was not unusually hungry or thirsty. But all that stuff could wait—where was that damned Plooran?

Kinnison had landed in complete readiness for strife. There were no rocks or clubs handy, but he had his fists, feet, and teeth; and they would do until he could find or make something better. But there was nothing to fight. Drive his sense of perception as he would, he could find nothing larger or more intelligent than a deer.

The farther this thing went along the less sense it made. A compulsion, to be any good at all, ought to be logical and coherent. It should fit into every corner and cranny of the subject's experience and knowledge. This one didn't fit anything or anywhere. It didn't even come close. Yet technically, it was a marvelous job. He couldn't detect a trace of it. This grass looked and felt real. The pebbles hurt his tender feet enough to make him wince as he walked to the water's edge. He drank deeply. The water, real or not, was cold, clear, and eminently satisfying.

"Listen, you misguided ape!" he thought probingly. "You might as well open up now as later whatever you've got in mind. If this performance is supposed to be non-fiction, it's a flat bust. If it's supposed to be science-fiction, it isn't much better. If it's space-opera, even, you're violating all the fundamentals. I've written better stuff—Qadgop and Cynthia were a lot more convincing." He waited a moment, then went on:

"Who ever heard of the intrepid hero of a space-opera as big as this one started out to be getting stranded on a completely Earth-like planet and then have nothing happen? No action at all? How about a couple of indescribable monsters of superhuman strength and agility, for me to tear apart with my steel-thewed fingers?"

He glanced around expectantly. No monsters appeared.

"Well, then, how about a damsel for me to rescue from a fate worse than death? Better make it two of them—safety in numbers, you know—a blonde and a brunette. No red-heads."

He waited again.

"QX, sport, no women. Suits me perfectly. But I hope you haven't forgotten about the tasty viands. I can eat fish if I have to, but if you want to keep your hero happy let's see you lay down here, on a platter, a one-kilogram steak, three centimeters thick, medium rare, fried in Tellurian butter and smothered in Venerian superla mushrooms."

No steak appeared, and the Gray Lensman recalled and studied intensively every detail of what had apparently happened. It *still* could not have occurred. He could not have imagined it. It could not have been compulsion or hypnosis. None of it made any kind of sense.

As a matter of plain fact, however, Kinnison's first and most positive conclusion was wrong. His memories were factual records of actual events and things. He would eat well during his stay upon that nameless planet, but he would have to procure his own food. Nothing would attack him, or even annoy him. For the Eddorian's *binding*—this is perhaps as good a word for it as any, since "geas" implies a curse—was such that the Gray Lensman could return to space and time only under such conditions and to such an environment as would not do him any iota of physical harm. He must continue alive and in good health for at least fifty more of his years.

And Clarrissa Kinnison, tense and strained, waited in her room for the instant of her husband's death. They two were one, with a oneness no other man and woman had ever known. If one died, from any cause whatever, the other would feel it.

She waited. Five minutes—ten—fifteen—half an hour—an hour. She began to relax. Her fists unclenched, her shallow breathing grew deeper.

Two hours. Kim was *still alive!* A wave of happy, bouyant relief swept through her; her eyes flashed and sparkled. If they hadn't been able to kill him in two hours they never could. Her Kim had plenty of jets.

Even the top minds of Boskonia could not kill her Kim!

28

THE BATTLE OF EDDORE

The Arisians and the Children of the Lens had known that Eddore must be attacked as soon as possible after the fall of Ploor. They were fairly certain that the interspatial use of planets as projectiles was new; but they were completely certain that the Eddorians would be able to deduce in a short time the principles and the concepts, the fundamental equations, and the essential operators involved in the process. They would find Nth space or one like it in one day; certainly not more than two. Their slaves would duplicate the weapon in approximately three weeks. Shortly thereafter both Ultra Prime and Prime Base, both Klovia and Tellus, would be blown out of the ether. So would Arisia—perhaps Arisia would go first. The Eddorians would probably not be able to aim such planets as accurately as the Arisians had, but they would keep on trying and they would learn fast.

This weapon was the sheer ultimate in destructiveness. No defense against it was possible. There was no theory which applied to it or which could be stretched to cover it. Even the Arisian Masters of Mathematics had not as yet been able to invent symbologies and techniques to handle the quantities and magnitudes involved when those interloping masses of foreign matter struck normal space.

Thus Kit did not have to follow up his announced intention of making the Arisians hurry. They did not hurry, of course, but they did not lose or waste a minute. Each Arisian, from the youngest watchman up to the oldest philosopher, tuned a part of his mind to Mentor, another part to some one of the millions of Lensmen upon his list, and flashed a message.

"Lensmen, attend—keep your mind sensitized to this, the pattern of Mentor of Arisia, who will speak to you as soon as all have been alerted."

That message went throughout the First Galaxy, throughout inter-galactic space, and throughout what part of the Second Galaxy had felt the touch of Civilization. It went to Alsakan and Vandemar and Klovia, to Thrale and Tellus and Rigel IV, to Mars and Velantia and Palain VII, to Medon and Venus and Centralia. It went to flitters, battleships, and loose planets. It went to asteroids and moonlets, to planets large and small. It went to newly graduated Lensmen and to Lensmen long since retired; to Lensmen at work and at play. It went to every First-Stage Lensman of the Galactic Patrol.

Wherever the message went, turmoil followed. Lensmen everywhere flashed questions at other Lensmen.

"What do you make of it, Fred?"

"Did you get the same thing I did?"

"*Mentor!* Grinning Noshabkeming, what's up?"

"Damfino. Must be big, though, for Mentor to be handling it."

"*Big!* It's immense! Who ever heard of Arisia stepping in before?"

"*Big!* Colossal! Mentor never talked twice to anybody except the L2's before, did he?"

Millions of Lensed questions flooded every base and every office of the Patrol. Nobody, not even the vice-coordinator, knew a thing.

"You might as well stop sending in questions as to what this is all about, because none of us knows any more about it than you do," Mait-land finally sent out a general message. "Apparently everybody with a Lens is getting the same thought, no more and no less. All I can say is that it must be a Class A Prime emergency, and everyone who is not actually tied up in a life and death matter will please drop everything and stand by."

Mentor wanted, and had to have, high tension. He got it. Tension mounted higher and higher as eventless hours passed and as, for the first time in history, Patrol business slowed down almost to a stop.

And in a small cruiser, manned by four red-headed girls and one red-headed youth, tension was also building up. The problem of the mechanical screens had long since been solved. Atomic powered counter-generators were in place, ready at the touch of a button to neutralize the mechanically-generated screens of the enemy and thus to make the engagement a mind-to-mind combat They were as close to Eddore's star-cluster as they could be without giving alarm. They had had nothing to do for hours except wait. They were probably keyed up higher than any other five Lensmen in all of space.

Kit, son of his father, was pacing the floor, chain-smoking. Constance was alternately getting up and sitting down—up—down—up. She, too, was smoking; or, rather, she was lighting cigarettes and throwing them away. Kathryn was sitting, stiffly still, manufacturing Lenses which, starting at her wrists, raced up both bare arms to her shoulders and disappeared. Karen was meticulously sticking holes in a piece of blank paper with a pin, making an intricate and meaningless design. Only Camilla made any pretense of calmness, and it was as transparent as glass. She was pretending to read a novel; but instead of absorbing its full content at the rate of one glance per page, she had read half of it word by word and still had no idea of what the story was about.

"Are you ready, children?" Mentor's thought came in at last.

"Ready!" Without knowing how they got there, the Five found themselves standing in the middle of the room, packed tight.

"Oh, Kit, I'm shaking like a torso-tosser!" Constance wailed. "I just *know* I'm going to louse up this whole damn war!"

"QX, baby, we're all in the same fix. Can't you hear my teeth chatter? Doesn't mean a thing. Good teams—champions—all feel the same way before a big game starts . . . and this is the biggest game ever . . . steady down, kids. We'll be QX as soon as the whistle blows—I hope . . ."

"*P-s-s-t!*" Kathryn hissed. "Listen!"

"Lensmen of the Galactic Patrol!" Mentor's resonant pseudo-voice filled all space. "I, Mentor of Arisia, am calling upon you because of a crisis in which no lesser force can be of use. You have been informed upon the matter of Ploor. It is true that Ploor has been destroyed; that the Ploorans, physically, are no more. You of the Lens, however, already know dimly that the physical is not the all. Know now that there is a residuum of non-material malignancy against which all the physical weapons of all the universes would be completely impotent. That evil effluvium, intrinsically vicious, is implacably opposed to every basic concept and idea of your Patrol. It has been on the move ever since the destruction of the planet Ploor. Unaided, we of Arisia are not strong enough to handle it, but the massed and directed force of your collective mind will be able to destroy it completely. If you wish me to do so, I will supervise the work of so directing your mental force as to encompass the complete destruction of this menace, which I tell you most solemnly is the last weapon of power with which Boskonia will be able to threaten Civilization. Lensmen of the Galactic Patrol, met as one for the first time in Civilization's long history, what is your wish?"

A tremendous wave of thought, expressed in millions of variant phraseologies, made the wish of the Lensmen very clear indeed. They did not know how such a thing could be done, but they were supremely eager to have Mentor of Arisia lead them against the Boskonians, whoever and wherever they might be.

"Your verdict is unanimous, as I had hoped and believed that it would be. It is well. The part of each of you will be simple, but not easy. You will all of you, individually, think of two things, and of only of two. First, of your love for and your pride in and your loyalty to your Patrol. Second, of the clear fact that Civilization must and shall triumph over Boskonia. Think these thoughts, each of you with all the strength that in him lies.

"You need not consciously direct those thoughts. Being attuned to my pattern, the force will flow at my direction. As it passes from you, you will replenish it, each according to his strength. You will find it the hardest labor you have ever performed, but it will be of permanent harm to none and it will not be of long duration. Are you ready?"

"WE ARE READY!" The crescendo roar of thought bulged the galaxy to its poles.

"Children—strike!"

The generators flared into action—the mechanical screens collapsed—the Unit struck. The outermost mental screen went down. The Unit struck again, almost instantly. Down went the second. The third. The fourth.

It was that flawless Unit, not Camilla, who detected and analyzed and precisely located the Eddorian guardsman handling each of those far-flung screens. It was the Unit, not Kathryn and Kit, who drilled the pilot hole through each Eddorian's hard-held block and enlarged it into a working orifice. It was the Unit, not Karen, whose impenetrable shield held stubbornly every circular mil of advantage gained in making such ingress. It was the Unit, not Constance, who assembled and drove home the blasts of mental force in which the Eddorians died. No time whatever was lost in consultation or decision. Action was not only instantaneous, but simultaneous with perception. The Children of the Lens were not now five, but one. The UNIT.

"Come in, Mentor!" Kit snapped then. "All you Arisians and all the Lensmen. Nothing specialized—just a general slam at the whole screen. This fifth screen is the works—they've got twenty minds on it instead of one, and they're top-notchers. Best strategy now is for us five to lay off for a second or two and show 'em what we've got in the line of defense, while the rest of you fellows give 'em hell!"

Arisia and the massed Lensmen struck; a tidal wave of such tremendous weight and power that under its impact the fifth screen sagged flat against the planet's surface. Any one Lensman's power was small, of course, in comparison with that of any Eddorian; but every available Lensman of the Galactic Patrol was giving, each according to his strength, and the output of one Lensman, multiplied by the countless millions which was the number of Lensmen then at work, made itself tellingly felt.

Countless? Yes. Only Mentor ever knew how many minds contributed to that stupendous flood of force. Bear in mind that in the First Galaxy alone there are over one hundred thousand million suns: that each sun has, on the average, something over one and thirty seven hundredths planets inhabited by intelligent life: that about one-half of these planets then adhered to Civilization; and that Tellus, an average planet, graduates approximately one hundred Lensmen every year.

"So far, Kit, so good," Constance panted. Although she was no longer trembling, she was still highly excited. "But I don't know how many more shots like that I've—we've—got left in the locker."

"You're doing fine, Connie," Camilla soothed.

"Sure you are, baby. You've got plenty of jets," Kit agreed. Except in moments of supreme stress these personal, individual exchanges of by-thoughts did not interfere with the smooth functioning of the Unit. "Fine work, all of you, kids. I thought we'd get over the shakes as soon as . . ."

"Watch it!" Camilla snapped. "Here comes the shock wave. Brace yourself, Kay. Hold us together, Kit!"

The wave came. Everything that the Eddorians could send. The Unit's barrier did not waver. After a full second of it—a time comparable to days of saturation atomic bombing in ordinary warfare—Karen, who had been standing stiff and still, began to relax.

"This is too, *too* easy," she declared. "Who's helping me? I can't feel anything, but I simply *know* I haven't got this much stuff. You, Cam—or is it all of you?" Not one of the Five was as yet thoroughly familiar with the operating characteristics of the Unit.

"All of us, more or less, but mostly Kit," Camilla decided after a moment's thought. "He's as solid as an inert planet."

"Not me," Kit denied, vigorously. "Must be you other kids. Feels to me like Kat, mostly. All I'm doing is just sort of leaning up against you a little—just in case. I haven't done a thing so far."

"Oh, no? Sure not!" Kathryn giggled, an infectious chuckle inherited or copied directly from her mother. "We know it, Kit. You wouldn't think of doing anything, even if you could. Just the same, we're mighty glad you're here, chum!"

"QX, kids, seal the chatter. We've had time to learn that they can't crack us, and so have they, so let's get to work."

Since the Unit was now under continuous attack, its technique would have to be entirely different from that used previously. Its barrier must vanish for an infinitesimal period of time, during which it must simultaneously detect and blast. Or, rather, the blast would have to be directed in mid-flight, while the Unit's own block was open. Nor could that block be open for more than the barest fractional milli-microsecond before or after the passage of the bolt. It is flight, while the Unit's own block was open. Nor could that of the Unit very much as the steady pressure of burning propellant powder compares with the disruptive force of detonating duodec: even so it would have wrought much damage to the minds of the Five had any of it been allowed to reach them.

Also, like parachute-jumping, this technique could not be practiced. Since the timing had to be so nearly absolute, the first two shots missed their targets completely; but the Unit learned fast. Eddorian after Eddorian died.

"Help, All-Highest, help!" a high Eddorian appealed, finally.

"What is it?" His Ultimate Supremacy, knowing that only utter desperation could be back of such intrusion, accepted the call.

"It is this new Arisia entity . . ."

"It is not an entity, fool, but a fusion," came curt reprimand. "We decided that point long ago."

"An entity, I say!" In his urgency the operator committed the unpardonable by omitting the titles of address. "No possible fusion can attain such perfection of timing, of synchronization. Our best fusions have attempted to match it, and have failed. Its screens are impenetrable. Its thrusts cannot be blocked. My message is this: solve for us, and quickly, the problem of this entity. If you do not or cannot do so, we perish all of us, even to you of the Innermost Circle."

"Think you so?" The thought was a sneer. "If your fusions cannot match those of the Arisians you should die, and the loss will be small."

The fifth screen went down. Eddore lay bare to the Arisian mind. There were inner defenses, of course, but Kit knew every one; their strengths and their weaknesses. He had long since spread in Mentor's mind an exact and completely detailed chart: they had long since drawn up a completely detailed plan of campaign. Nevertheless, Kit could not keep from advising Mentor:

"Pick off any who may try to get away. Start on Area B and work up. Be sure, though, to lay off of Area K or you'll get your beard singed off."

"The plan is being followed, youth," Mentor assured him. "Children, you have done very well indeed. Rest now, and recuperate your powers against that which is yet to come."

"QX. Unlace yourselves, kids. Loosen up. Relax. I'll break out a few beakers of fayalin, and all of us—you especially, Con—had better stoke up with candy bars."

"*Eat!* Why, I *couldn't . . .*" but at her brother's insistence she took an experimental bite. "But say, I *am* hungry, at that!"

"Of course you are. You've been putting out a lot of stuff, and there's more and worse coming. Now rest, all of you."

They rested. Somewhat to their surprise, they could rest; even Constance. But the respite was short. Area K, the headquarters and the citadel of His Ultimate Supremacy and the Innermost Circle of the Boskonian Empire, contained all that remained of Eddorian life.

But this, Kit knew, was the crux. This was what had stopped the Arisians cold; had held them off for all these millions upon millions of years. Everything up to now the Arisians could have done themselves; but even the totalized and integrated mind of Arisia would hit Area K and bounce.

To handle Area K two things were necessary: the Unit and the utterly inconceivable massed might of the Lensmen.

Knowing better even than Mentor what the situation was, Kit felt again a twinge of panic, but managed to throw it off.

"No tight linkage yet, kids," Kit the Organizer went smoothly to work. "Individual effort—a flash of fusion, perhaps, now and then, if any of us call for it, but no Unit until I give the word. Then give it everything you've got. Cam, analyze that screen and set us up a pattern for it—you'll find it'll take some doing. See whether it's absolutely homogeneous—hunt for weak spots, if any. Con, narrow down to the sharpest needle you can possibly make and start pecking. Not too hard—don't tire yourself—just to get acquainted with the texture of the thing and keep them awake. Kay, take over our guard so Eukonidor can join the other Arisians. Kat, come along with me—you'll have to help with the Arisians until I call you into the Unit.

"You Arisians, except Mentor, blanket this dome. Thinner than that—solider, harder . . . there. A trifle off-balance yet—give me just a little more, here on this side. QX—hold it right there! SQUEEZE! Kat, watch 'em. Hold them right there and in balance until you're sure the Eddorians aren't going to be able to put any bulges up through the blanket.

"Now, Mentor, you and the Lensmen. Tell them to give us, for the next five seconds, absolutely everything they can deliver. When they're at absolute peak, hit us with the whole charge. Dead center. Don't pull your punch. We'll be ready.

"Con, get ready to stick the needle right there—they'll think it's just another peck, I hope—and slug as you never slugged before. Kay, get ready to drop that screen and stiffen the needle—when that beam hits us it'll be NO pat on the back. The rest of us will brace you both and keep the shock from killing us all. Here it comes . . . make Unit! . . . GO!"

The Unit struck. Its needle of pure force drove against the Eddorians' supposedly absolutely impenetrable shield. The Unit's thrust was, of itself, like nothing ever before known. The Lensmen's pile-driver blow—the integrated sum total of the top effort of every Lensman of the entire Galactic Patrol—was of itself irresistible. Something had to give way.

For an instant it seemed as though nothing were happening or ever would happen. Strong young arms laced the straining Five into a group as motionless and as sculpturesque as statuary, while between their bodies and around them there came into being a gigantic Lens: a Lens whose splendor filled the entire room with radiance.

Under that awful concentration of force something *had* to give way. The Unit held. The Arisians held. The Lensmen held. The needle, superlatively braced, neither bent nor broke. Therefore the Eddorians' screen was punctured; and in the instant of its puncturing it disappeared as does a bubble when it breaks.

There was no mopping up to do. Such was the torrent of force cascading into the stronghold that within a microsecond after its shield went down all life within it was snuffed out.

The Boskonian War was over.

29

THE POWER OF LOVE

Did you kids come through QX?" The frightful combat over, the dreadful tension a thing of the past, Kit's first thought was for his sisters.

They were unharmed. None of the Five had suffered anything except mental exhaustion. Recuperation was rapid.

"Better we hunt that tube up and get dad out of it, don't you think?" Kit suggested.

"Have you got a story arranged that will hold water?" Camilla asked.

"Everything except for a few minor details, which we can put in later."

Smoothly the four girls linked their minds with their brother's; effortlessly the Unit's thought surveyed all nearby space. No hyper-spatial tube, nor any trace of one, was there. Tuned to Kinnison's pattern, the Unit then scanned not only normal space and the then present time, but also millions upon millions of other spaces and past and future times; all without finding the Gray Lensman.

Again and again the Unit reached out, farther and farther; out to the extreme limit of even its extraordinary range. Every space and every time was empty. The Children of the Lens broke their linkage and stared at each other, aghast.

They knew starkly what it must mean, but that conclusion was unthinkable. Kinnison—their dad—the hub of the universe—the unshakable, immutable Rock of Civilization—he *couldn't* be dead. They simply could not accept the logical explanation as the true one.

And while they pondered, shaken, a call from their Red Lensman mother came in.

"You are together? Good! I've been *so* worried about Kim going into that trap. I've been trying to get in touch with him, but I can't reach him. You children, with your greater power . . ."

She broke off as the dread import of the Five's surface thoughts became clear to her. At first she, too, was shaken, but she rallied magnificently.

"Nonsense!" she snapped; not in denial of an unwelcome fact, but in sure knowledge that the supposition was not and could not be a fact. "Kimball Kinnison is *alive*. He's lost, I know—I last heard from him just before he went into that tube—but he did *not* die! If he had, I would most certainly have felt it. So don't be idiots, children, please. Think—*really* think! I'm going to do something—somehow—but what? Mentor? I've never called him and I'm terribly afraid he might not do anything. I could go there and make him do something, but that would take so long—what shall I do? What *can* I do?"

"Mentor, by all means," Kit decided. "He'll do something—he'll *have* to. However, there's no need of you going to Arisia in person." Now that the Eddorians had ceased to exist, inter-galactic space presented no barrier to Arisian thought, but Kit did not go into that. "Link your mind with ours." She did so.

"Mentor of Arisia!" the clear-cut thought flashed out. "Kimball Kinnison of Klovia is not present in this, his normal space and time; nor in any other continuum we can reach. We need help."

"Ah; 'tis Lensman Clarissa and the Five." Imperturbably, Mentor's mind joined theirs on the instant. "I have given the matter no attention, nor have I scanned my visualization of the Cosmic All. It may therefore be that Kimball Kinnison has passed on from his plane of exist . . ."

"He has NOT! It is stark idiocy even to consider such a possibility!" the Red Lensman interrupted violently, so violently that her thought had the impact of a physical blow. Mentor and the Five alike could see her eyes flash and sparkle; could hear her voice crackle as she spoke aloud, the better to drive home her passionate conviction. "Kim is ALIVE! I told the children so and now I tell you so. No matter where or when he might be, in whatever possible extra-dimensional nook or cranny of the entire macro-cosmic universe or in any possible period of time between plus and minus eternity, he *couldn't* die—he could not *possibly* die—

without my knowing it. So find him, please—*please* find him, Mentor—or, if you can't or won't, just give me the littlest, *tiniest* hint as to how to go about it and I'll find him myself!"

The Five were appalled. Especially Kit, who knew, as the others did not, just how much afraid of Mentor his mother had always been. To direct such thoughts to any Arisian was unthinkable; but Mentor's only reaction was one of pleased interest.

"There is much of truth, daughter, in your thought," he replied, slowly. "Human love, in its highest manifestation, can be a mighty, a really tremendous thing. The force, the power, the capability of such a love as yours is a sector of the truth which has not been fully examined. Allow me, please, a moment in which to consider the various aspects of this matter."

It took more than a moment. It took more than the twenty-nine seconds which the Arisian had needed to solve an earlier and supposedly similar Kinnison problem. In fact, a full half hour elapsed before Mentor resumed communication; and then he did so, not to the group as a whole, but only to the Five; using an ultra-frequency to which the Red Lensman's mind could not be attuned.

"I have not been able to reach him. Since you could not do so I knew that the problem would not be simple, but I have found that it is difficult indeed. As I have intimated previously, my visualization is not entirely clear upon any matter touching the Eddorians directly, since their minds were of great power. On the other hand, their visualizations of us were probably even more hazy. Therefore none of our analyses of each other were or could be much better than approximations.

"It is certain, however, that you were correct in assuming that it was the Ploorans who set up the hyper-spatial tube as a trap for your father. The fact that the lower and middle operating echelons of Boskonia could not kill him established in the Ploorans' minds the necessity of taking him alive. That fact gave us no concern, for you, Kathryn, were on guard. Moreover, even if she alone should slip, it was manifestly impossible for them to accomplish anything against the combined powers of you Five. However, at some undetermined point in time the Eddorians took over, as is shown by the fact that you are all at a loss: it being scarcely necessary to point out to you that the Ploorans could neither transport your father to any location which you could not reach nor pose any problem, including his death, which you could not solve. It is thus certain that it was one or more of the Eddorians who either killed Kinnison or sent him where he was sent. It is also certain that, after the easy fashion in which he escaped from the Ploorans after they had captured him and had him all but in their hands, the Eddorians did not care to have the Ploorans come to grips with Kimball Kinnison; fearing, and rightly, that instead of gaining information, they would lose everything."

"Did they know I was in that tube?" Kathryn asked. "Did they deduce us, or did they think that dad was a super-man?"

"That is one of the many points which are obscure. But it made no difference, before or after the event, to them or to us, as you should perceive."

"Of course. They knew that there was at least one third-level mind at work in the field. They must have deduced that it was Arisian work. Whether it was dad himself or whether it was coming to his aid at need would make no difference. They knew very well that he was the keystone of Civilization, and that to do away with him would be the shrewdest move they could make. Therefore we still do not understand why they didn't kill him outright and be done with it—if they didn't."

"In exactness, neither do I . . . that point is the least clear of all. Nor is it at all certain that he still lives. It is sheerest folly to assume that the Eddorians either thought or acted illogically, even occasionally. Therefore, if Kinnison is not dead, whatever was done was calculated to be even more final than death itself. This premise, if adopted, forces the conclusion that they considered the possibility of our knowing enough about the next cycle of existence to be able to reach him there."

Kit frowned. "You still harp on the possibility of his death. Does not your visualization cover that?"

"Not since the Eddorians took control. I have not consciously emphasized the probability of your father's death; I have merely considered it—in the case of two mutually exclusive events, neither of which can be shown to have happened, both must be studied with care. Assume for the moment that your mother's theory is the truth, that your father is still alive. In that case, what was done and how it was done are eminently clear."

"Clear? Not to us!" the Five chorused.

"While they did not know at all exactly the power of our minds, they could establish limits beyond which neither they nor we could go. Being mechanically inclined, it is reasonable to assume that they had at their disposal sufficient energy to transport Kinnison to some point well beyond those limits. They would have given control to a director-by-chance, so that his ultimate destination would be unknown and unknowable. He would of course land safely . . ."

"How? How could they, possibly . . . ?"

"In time that knowledge will be yours. Not now. Whether or not the hypothesis just stated is true, the fact confronting us is that Kimball Kinnison is not now in any region which I am at present able to scan."

Gloom descended palpably upon the Five.

"I am not saying or implying that the problem is insoluble. Since Eddorian minds were involved, however, you already realize that its solution will require the evaluation of many millions of factors and will consume a not inconsiderable number of your years . . ."

"You mean lifetimes!" an impetuous young thought broke in. "Why, long before that . . ."

"Contain yourself, daughter Constance," Mentor reproved, gently. "I realize quite fully all the connotations and implications involved. I was about to say that it may prove desirable to assist your mother in the application of powers which may very well transcend in some respects those of either Arisia or Eddore." He widened the band of thought to include the Red Lensman and went on as though he were just emerging from contemplation:

"Children, it appears that the solution of this problem by ordinary processes will require more time than can conveniently be spared. Moreover, it affords a priceless and perhaps a unique opportunity of increasing our store of knowledge. Be informed, however, that the probability is great that in this project you, Clarrissa, will lose your life."

"Better not, mother. When Mentor says anything like that, it means suicide. We don't want to lose you, too." Kit pleaded, and the four girls added their pleas to his.

Clarrissa knew that suicide was against the Code—but she also knew that, as long as it wasn't quite suicide, Lensmen went in.

"Exactly how great?" she demanded, vibrantly. "It isn't certain—it can't be!"

"No, daughter, it is not certain."

"QX, then, I'm going in. Nothing can stop me."

"Very well. Tighten your linkage, Clarrissa, with me. Yours will be the task of sending your thought to your husband, wherever and whenever in total space and in total time he may be. If it can be done, you can do it. You alone of all the entities in existence can do it. I can neither help you nor guide you in your quest; but by virtue of your relationship to him whom we are seeking, your oneness with him, you will require neither help nor guidance. My part will be to follow you and to construct the means of his return; but the real labor is and must be yours alone. Take a moment, therefore, to prepare yourself against the effort, for it will not be small. Gather your resources, daughter; assemble all your forces and your every power."

They watched Clarrissa, in her distant room, throw herself prone upon her bed. She closed her eyes, buried her nose in the counterpane, and gripped a side-rail fiercely in each hand.

"Can't we help, too?" The Five implored, as one.

"I do not know." Mentor's thought was as passionless as the voice of Fate. "I know of no force at your disposal which can affect in any way that which is to happen. Since I do not know the full measure of your powers, however, it would be well for you to accompany us, keeping yourselves alert to take instant advantage of any opportunity to be of aid. Are you ready, daughter Clarrissa?"

"I am ready," and the Red Lensman launched her thought.

Clarrissa Kinnison did not know, then or ever; did not have even the faintest inkling of what she did or of how she did it. Nor, tied to her by bonds of heritage, love, and sympathy though they were and of immense powers of mind though they were, did any of the Five succeed, until after centuries had passed, in elucidating the many complex phenomena involved. And Mentor, the ancient Arisian sage, never did understand.

All that any of them knew was that an infinitely loving and intensely suffering woman, stretched rigidly upon a bed, hurled out through space and time a passionately questing thought: a thought behind which she put everything she had.

Clarrissa Kinnison, Red Lensman, had much—and every iota of that impressive sum total ached for, yearned for, and insistently *demanded* her Kim—her one and only Kim. Kim her husband; Kim the father of her children; Kim her lover; Kim her other half; Kim her all in all for so many perfect years.

"Kim! KIM! Wherever you are, Kim, or whenever, listen! Listen and answer! Hear me—you *must* hear me calling—I need you, Kim, from the bottom of my soul . . . Kim! *My Kim!* KIM!!"

Through countless spaces and through untellable times that poignant thought sped; driven by a woman's fears, a woman's hopes, a woman's all-surpassing love; urged ever onward and ever outward by the irresistible force of a magnificent woman's frankly bared soul.

Outward . . . farther . . . farther out . . . farther . . .

Clarrissa's body went limp upon her bed. Her heart slowed; her breathing almost stopped. Kit probed quickly, finding that those secret cells into which he had scarcely dared to glance were empty and bare.

Even the Red Lensman's tremendous reserves of vital force were exhausted.

"Mother, come back!"

"Come back to us!"

"Please, *please,* mums, come back!"

"Know you, children, your mother so little?"

They knew her. She would not come back alone. Regardless of any danger to herself, regardless of life itself, she would not come back until she had found her Kim.

"But *do* something, Mentor—DO SOMETHING!"

"Do what? Nothing can be done. It was simply a question of which was the greater; the volume of the required hyper-sphere or her remarkable store of vitality . . ."

"Shut up!" Kit blazed. "We'll do *something!* Come on, kids, and we'll try . . ."

"The Unit!" Kathryn shrieked. "Link up, quick! Cam, make mother's pattern—hurry it!! Now, Unit, grab it—make her one of us, a six-ply Unit—*make* her come in, and snap it up! There! Now, Kit, drive us . . . DRIVE US!"

Kit drove. As the surging life-force of the Unit pushed a measure of vitality back into Clarrissa's inert body, she gained a little strength and did not grow weaker. The children, however, did; and Mentor, who had been entirely unmoved by the woman's imminent death, became highly concerned.

"Children, return!" He first ordered, then entreated. "You are throwing away not only your lives, but also long lifetimes of intensive labor and study!"

They paid no attention. No more than their mother would those children abandon such a mission unaccomplished. Seven Kinnisons would come back or none.

The four-ply Arisian pondered; and brightened. Now that a theretofore impossible linkage had been made, the outlook changed. The odds shifted. The Unit's delicacy of web, its driving force, had not been enough; or rather, it would have taken too long. Adding the Red Lensman's affinity for her husband, however . . . Yes, definitely, the Unit should now succeed.

It did. Before any of the Five weakened to the danger point the Unit, again five-fold, snapped back. Clarrissa's life-force, which had tried so valiantly to fill all of space and all of time, was flowing back into her. A tight, hard, impossibly writhing and twisting multi-dimensional beam ran, it seemed, to infinity and vanished.

"A right scholarly bit of work, children," Mentor approved. "I have arranged the means of his return."

"Thanks, children. Thanks, Mentor." Instead of fainting, Clarrissa sprang from her bed and stood erect. Flushed and panting, eyes flamingly alight, she was more intensely vital than any of her children had ever seen her. Reaction might—would—come later, but she was now all buoyantly vibrant woman. "Where will he come into our space, and when?"

"In your room before you. Now."

Kinnison materialized; and as the Red Lensman and the Gray went hungrily into each other's arms, Mentor and the Five turned their attention toward the future.

"First, the hyper-spatial tube which was called the 'Hell-Hole in Space,' " Kit began. "We must establish as fact in the minds of all Civilization that the Ploorans were actually at the top of Boskone. The story as we have arranged it is that Ploor was the top, and—which happens to be the truth—that it was destroyed through the efforts of the Second-Stage Lensmen. The 'Hell-Hole' is to be explained as being operated by the Plooran 'residuum' which every Lensman knows all about and which he will never forget. The problem of dad's whereabouts was different from the previous one in degree only, not in kind. To all except us, there never were any Eddorians. Any objections? Will that version hold?"

The consensus was that the story was sound and tight.

"The time has come, then," Karen thought, "to go into the very important matter of our reason for being and our purpose in life. You have intimated repeatedly that you Arisians are resigning your Guardianship of Civilization and that we are to take over; and I have just perceived the terribly shocking fact that you four are now alone, that all the other Arisians have already gone. We're not ready, Mentor; you know we're not—this scares me through and through."

"You are ready, children, for everything that will have to be done. You have not come to your full maturity and power, of course; that stage will come only with time. It is best for you, however, that we leave you now. Your race is potentially vastly stronger and abler than ours. We reached some time ago the highest point attainable to us: we could no longer adapt ourselves to the ever-increasing complexity of life. You, a young new race amply equipped for any emergency within reckonable time, will be able to do so. In capability and in equipment you begin where we leave off."

"But we know—you've taught us—scarcely anything!" Constance protested.

"I have taught you exactly enough. That I do not know exactly what changes to anticipate is implicit in the fact that our race is out of date. Further Arisian teaching would tend to set you in the out-dated Arisian mold and thereby defeat our every purpose. As I have informed you repeatedly, we ourselves do not know what extra qualities you possess. Hence I am in no sense competent to instruct you in the natures or in the uses of them. It is certain, however, that you have those extra qualities. It is equally certain that you possess the abilities to develop them to the full. I have set your feet on the sure way to the full development of those abilities."

"But that will take much time, sir," Kit thought, "and if you leave us now we won't have it."

"You will have time enough and to spare."

"Oh—then we won't have to do it right away?" Constance broke in. "Good!"

"We're all glad of that," Camilla added. "We're too full of our own lives, too eager for experiences, to enjoy the prospect of living such lives as you Arisians have lived. I am right in assuming, am I not, that our own development will in time force us into the same or a similar existence?"

"Your muddy thinking has again distorted the truth," Mentor reproved her. "There will be no force involved. You will gain everything, lose nothing. You have no conception of the depth and breadth of the vistas now just beginning to open to you. Your lives will be immeasurably fuller, higher, greater than any heretofore known to this universe. As your capabilities increase, you will find that you will no longer care for the society of entities less able than your own kind."

"But I don't *want* to live forever!" Constance wailed.

"More muddy thinking." Mentor's thought was—for him—somewhat testy. "Perhaps, in the present instance, barely excusable. You know that you are not immortal. You should know that an infinity of time is necessary for the acquirement of infinite knowledge; and that your span of life will be just as short, in comparison with your capacity to live and to learn, as that of *Homo Sapiens*. When the time comes you will want to—you will need to—change your manner of living."

"Tell us when?" Kat suggested. "It would be nice to know, so we could get ready."

"I could tell you, since in that my visualization is clear, but I will not. Fifty years—a hundred—a thousand—what matters it? Live your lives to the fullest, year by year, developing your every obvious, latent, and nascent capability; calmly assured that long before any need for your services shall arise, you shall have established yourselves upon some planet of your choice and shall be in every respect ready for whatever may come to pass."

"You are—you must be—right," Kit conceded. "In view of what has just happened, however, and the chaotic condition of both galaxies, it seems a poor time to vacate all Guardianship."

"All inimical activity is now completely disorganized. Kinnison and the Patrol can handle it easily enough. The real conflict is finished. Think nothing of a few years of vacancy. The Lensmakers, as you know, are fully automatic, requiring neither maintenance nor attention; what little time you may wish to devote to the special training of selected Lensmen can be taken at odd moments from your serious work of developing yourselves for Guardianship."

"We still feel incompetent," the Five insisted. "Are you sure that you have given us all the instruction we need?"

"I am sure. I perceive doubt in your minds as to my own competence, based upon the fact that in this supreme emergency my visualization was faulty and my actions almost too late. Observe, however, that my visualization was clear upon every essential factor and that we were not actually too late. The truth is that our timing was precisely right—no lesser stress could possibly have prepared you as you are now prepared.

"I am about to go. The time may come when your descendants will realize, as we did, their inadequacy for continued Guardianship. Their visualizations, as did ours, may become imperfect and incomplete. If so, they will then know that the time will have come for them to develop, from the highest race then existing, new and more competent Guardians. Then they, as my fellows have done and as I am about to do, will of their own accord pass on. But that is for the remote future. As to you children, doubtful now and hesitant as is only natural, you may believe implicitly what I now tell you is the truth, that even though we Arisians are no longer here, all shall be well; with us, with you, and with all Civilization."

The deeply resonant pseudo-voice ceased; the Kinnisons knew that Mentor, the last of the Arisians, was gone.

Epilogue

TO YOU WHO HAVE SCANNED THIS REPORT, FURTHER GREETINGS:

Since I who compiled it am only a youth, a Guardian only by title, and hence unable to visualize even approximately either the time of nor the necessity for the opening of this flask of force, I have no idea as to the bodily shape or the mental attainments of you, the entity to whom it has now been made available.

You already know that Civilization is again threatened seriously. You probably know something of the basic nature of that threat. While studying this tape you have become informed that the situation is sufficiently grave to have made it again necessary to force certain selected minds prematurely into the third level of Lensmanship.

You have already learned that in ancient time Civilization after Civilization fell before it could rise much above the level of barbarism. You know that we and the previous race of Guardians saw to it that this, OUR Civilization, has not yet fallen. Know, now that the task of your race, so soon to replace us, will be to see to it that it does not fall.

One of us will become en rapport with you as soon as you have assimilated the facts, the connotations, and the implications of this material. Prepare your mind for contact.

Christopher K. Kinnison